HARLAN COBEN
Three Great Novels

Harlan Coben is the author of fifteen international bestsellers. He was the first ever author to win all three major US crime awards, and established a best-selling series of crime novels starring his powerful creation, Myron Bolitar, before turning to stand-alone books. His breakthrough novel, *Tell No One*, has recently been adapted into an award-winning, highly successful feature film. Harlan lives in New Jersey with his family.

Harlan Coben
Three Great Novels

Just One Look 9/09
The Innocent
Promise Me

Just One Look Copyright © Harlan Coben 2004
The Innocent Copyright © Harlan Coben 2005
Promise Me Copyright © Harlan Coben 2006

First published in Great Britain in 2008 by Orion Books,
an imprint of The Orion Publishing Group Ltd
Orion House, 5 Upper Saint Martin's Lane
London WC2H 9EA

An Hachette Livre UK Company

1 3 5 7 9 10 8 6 4 2

A CIP catalogue record for this book is
available from the British Library.

ISBN (Trade Paperback) 978 1 4091 0027 0

Printed and bound in the UK by
CPI Mackays Chatham ME5 8TD

The Orion Publishing Group's policy is to use papers that are
natural, renewable and recyclable products and made from wood
grown in sustainable forests. The logging and manufacturing
processes are expected to conform to the environmental
regulations of the country of origin.

www.orionbooks.co.uk

Contents

Just One Look

This book is for Jack Armstrong,
because he's one of the good guys

'Babe, give me your best memory,
But it don't equal pale ink.'

Scott Duncan sat across from the killer.

The windowless room of thundercloud gray was awkward and still, stuck in that lull when the music first starts and neither stranger is sure how to begin the dance. Scott tried a noncommittal nod. The killer, decked out in prison-issue orange, simply stared. Scott folded his hands and put them on the metal table. The killer – his file said he was Monte Scanlon, but there was no way that was his real name – might have done likewise had his hands not been cuffed.

Why, Scott wondered yet again, am I here?

His specialty was prosecuting corrupt politicians – something of a vigorous cottage industry in his home state of New Jersey – but three hours ago, Monte Scanlon, a mass executioner by any standards, had finally broken his silence to make a demand.

That demand?

A private meeting with Assistant U.S. Attorney Scott Duncan.

This was strange for a large variety of reasons, but here were two: one, a killer should not be in a position to make demands; two, Scott had never met or even heard of Monte Scanlon.

Scott broke the silence. 'You asked to see me?'

'Yes.'

Scott nodded, waited for him to say more. He didn't. 'So what can I do for you?'

Monte Scanlon maintained the stare. 'Do you know why I'm here?"

Scott glanced around the room. Besides Scanlon and himself, four people were present. Linda Morgan, the United States attorney, leaned against the back wall trying to give off the ease of Sinatra against a lamppost. Standing behind the prisoner were two beefy, nearly identical prison guards with tree-stump arms and chests like antique armoires. Scott had met the two cocky agents before, had seen them go about their task with the sereneness of yoga instructors. But today, with this well-shackled prisoner, even these guys were on edge. Scanlon's lawyer, a ferret reeking of checkout-counter cologne, rounded out the group. All eyes were on Scott.

'You killed people,' Scott answered. 'Lots of them.'

'I was what is commonly called a hit man. I was' – Scanlon paused – 'an assassin for hire.'

'On cases that don't involve me.'

'True.'

Scott's morning had started off normal enough. He'd been drafting a subpoena on a waste-disposal executive who was paying off a small-town mayor.

Routine matter. Everyday graft in the Garden State of New Jersey. That had been, what, an hour, an hour and a half ago? Now he sat across the bolted-down table from a man who had murdered – according to Linda Morgan's rough estimate – one hundred people.

'So why did you ask for me?'

Scanlon looked like an aging playboy who might have squired a Gabor sister in the fifties. He was small, wizened even. His graying hair was slicked back, his teeth cigarette-yellow, his skin leathery from midday sun and too many long nights in too many dark clubs. No one in the room knew his real name. When captured, his passport read Monte Scanlon, an Argentinean national, age fifty-one. The age seemed about right, but that would be about it. His fingerprints had not popped up in the NCIC computer banks. Facial recognition software had come up with a big goose egg.

'We need to speak alone.'

'This is not my case,' Scott said again. 'There's a U.S. attorney assigned to you.'

'This has nothing to do with her.'

'And it does with me?'

Scanlon leaned forward. 'What I'm about to tell you,' he said, 'will change your entire life.'

Part of Scott wanted to wiggle his fingers in Scanlon's face and say, 'Ooooo.' He was used to the captured criminal mindset – their serpentine maneuverings, their quest for an edge, their search for a way out, their overblown sense of importance. Linda Morgan, perhaps sensing his thoughts, shot a warning glare across his bow. Monte Scanlon, she'd told him, had worked for various connected families for the better part of thirty years. RICO hungered for his cooperation in a starving-man-near-a-buffet way. Since his capture, Scanlon had refused to talk. Until this morning.

So here Scott was.

'Your boss,' Scanlon said, gesturing with his chin at Linda Morgan, 'she hopes for my cooperation.'

'You're going to get the needle,' Morgan responded, still trying to give off the scent of nonchalance. 'Nothing you say or do will change that.'

Scanlon smiled. 'Please. You fear losing what I have to say much greater than I fear death.'

'Right. Another tough guy who doesn't fear death.' She peeled herself off the wall. 'Know what, Monte? The tough guys are always the ones who soil their pants when we strap them to the gurney.'

Again Scott fought off the desire to wiggle his fingers, this time at his boss. Scanlon kept smiling. His eyes never left Scott's. Scott didn't like what he saw. They were, as one would expect, black and shiny and cruel. But – and Scott might have been imagining things – maybe he saw something else there. Something beyond the standard vacancy. There seemed to be a pleading in the eyes; Scott couldn't turn away from them. There was regret there maybe.

Remorse even.

Scott looked up at Linda and nodded. She frowned, but Scanlon had called her bluff. She touched one of the beefy guards on the shoulder and gestured for them to leave. Rising from his seat, Scanlon's lawyer spoke for the first time. 'Anything he says is off the record.'

'Stay with them,' Scanlon ordered. 'I want you to make sure that they don't listen in.'

The lawyer picked up his briefcase and followed Linda Morgan to the door. Soon Scott and Scanlon were alone. In the movies, killers are omnipotent. In real life, they are not. They don't escape from handcuffs in the middle of a high-security federal penitentiary. The Beef Brothers, Scott knew, would be behind the one-way glass. The intercom, per Scanlon's instructions, would be off. But they'd all be watching.

Scott shrugged a well? at him.

'I am not your typical assassin for hire.'

'Uh huh.'

'I have rules.'

Scott waited.

'For example, I only kill men.'

'Wow,' Scott said. 'You're a prince.'

Scanlon ignored the sarcasm. 'That is my first rule. I kill only men. No women.'

'Right. Tell me, does rule two have anything to do with not putting out until the third date?'

'You think I'm a monster?'

Scott shrugged as if the answer was obvious.

'You don't respect my rules?'

'What rules? You kill people. You make up these so-called rules because you need the illusion of being human.'

Scanlon seemed to consider that. 'Perhaps,' he allowed, 'but the men I've killed were scum. I was hired by scum to kill scum. I am no more than a weapon.'

'A weapon?' Scott repeated.

'Yes.'

'A weapon doesn't care who it kills, Monte. Men, women, grannies, little kids. A weapon doesn't differentiate.'

Scanlon smiled. 'Touché.'

Scott rubbed his palms on his pant legs. 'You didn't call me here for an ethics class. What do you want?'

'You're divorced, aren't you, Scott?'

He said nothing.

'No children, amicable split, still friendly with the ex.'

'What do you want?'

'To explain.'

'To explain what?'

He lowered his eyes but only for a moment. 'What I did to you.'

'I don't even know you.'

'But I know you. I've known you for a long time.'

Scott let the silence in. He glanced at the mirror. Linda Morgan would be behind the glass, wondering what they were talking about. She wanted information. He wondered if they had the room bugged. Probably. Either way, it would pay to keep Scanlon talking.

'You are Scott Duncan. Thirty-nine years old. You graduated from Columbia Law School. You could be making a great deal more money in private practice, but that bores you. You've been with the U.S. attorney's office six months. Your mother and father moved to Miami last year. You had a sister, but she died in college.'

Scott shifted in his seat. Scanlon studied him.

'You finished?'

'Do you know how my business operates?'

Change of subject. Scott waited a beat. Scanlon was playing a head game, trying to keep him off balance or some such nonsense. Scott was not about to fall for it. Nothing he had 'revealed' about Scott's family was surprising. A person could pick up most of that info with a few well-placed keystrokes and phone calls.

'Why don't you tell me,' Scott said.

'Let's pretend,' Scanlon began, 'that you wanted someone dead.'

'Okay.'

'You would contact a friend, who knows a friend, who knows a friend, who can reach me.'

'And only that last friend would know you?'

'Something like that. I had only one go-between man, but I was careful even with him. We never met face to face. We used code names. The payments always went to offshore accounts. I would open a new account for every, shall we say, transaction, and I closed it as soon as the transaction was completed. You still with me?'

'It's not that complicated,' Scott said.

'No, I guess not. But you see, nowadays we communicate by e-mail. I'll set up a temporary e-mail account with Hotmail or Yahoo! or whatever, with fake names. Nothing that can be traced back. But even if it could, even if you could find out who sent it, where would it lead you? All e-mails were sent and read at libraries or public places. We were totally covered.'

Scott was about to mention that this total coverage had eventually landed Scanlon's ass in jail, but he decided to save it. 'What does this have to do with me?'

'I'm getting to that.' Scott could see that Scanlon was warming up to his own tale. 'In the old days – when I say old days, I mean, eight, ten years ago – we did it mostly with pay phones. I'd never see the name written. The guy would just tell me over the phone.'

Scanlon stopped and made sure that he had Scott's full attention. His tone softened a bit, became less matter-of-fact. 'That's the key, Scott. It was by phone. I'd only hear the name on the phone, not see it.'

He looked at Scott expectantly. Scott had no idea what he was trying to say, so he went, 'Uh huh.'

'Do you understand why I'm stressing that it was done by phone?'

'No.'

'Because a person like me, a person with rules, could make a mistake with the phone.'

Scott thought about that. 'I still don't get it.'

'I never kill women. That was rule number one.'

'So you said.'

'So if you wanted to put a hit on someone named Billy Smith, I'd figure Billy was a man. You know, with a y. I'd never think Billy would be a woman. With an ie at the end. You understand?'

Scott went very still. Scanlon saw it. He dropped the smile. His voice was very soft.

'We talked before about your sister, didn't we, Scott?'

10

Scott did not respond.

'Her name was Geri, am I right?'

Silence.

'You see the problem, Scott? Geri is one of those names. If you heard it on the phone, you'd assume it would be with a J in the front and a y at the end. So fifteen years ago, I got a phone call. From that go-between man I told you about?'

Scott shook his head.

'I was given an address. I was told exactly what time "Jerry"'?– Scanlon made quote marks with his fingers – 'would be home.'

Scott's own voice seemed to come from very far away. 'It was ruled an accident.'

'Most arsons are, if you know what you're doing.'

'I don't believe you.'

But Scott looked at the eyes again and felt his world teeter. The images flooded in: Geri's contagious smile, the unruly hair, the braces, the way she stuck her tongue out at him during family gatherings. He remembered her first real boyfriend (a dork named Brad), her not getting a date to the junior prom, the gung-ho speech she made when she ran for student council treasurer, her first rock band (they were awful), her college acceptance letter.

Scott felt his eyes well up. 'She was only twenty-one.'

No response.

'Why?'

'I don't get into the whys, Scott. I'm just a hired hand – '

'No, not that.' Scott looked up. 'Why are you telling me this now?'

Scanlon studied his reflection in the mirror. His voice was very quiet. 'Maybe you were right.'

'Right about what?'

'What you said before.' He turned back toward Scott. 'Maybe after all is said and done, I need the illusion of being human.'

three months later

1

There are sudden rips. There are tears in your life, deep knife wounds that slash through your flesh. Your life is one thing, then it is shredded into another. It comes apart as though gutted in a belly slit. And then there are those moments when your life simply unravels. A loose thread pulled. A seam gives way. The change is slow at first, nearly imperceptible.

For Grace Lawson, the unraveling began at the Photomat.

She was about to enter the photo developing shop when she heard a somewhat familiar voice. 'Why don't you get a digital camera, Grace?'

Grace turned toward the woman. 'I'm not good with that techno stuff.'

'Oh, come now. Digital technology is a snap.' The woman raised her hand and actually snapped, just in case Grace didn't know what the word meant. 'And digital cameras are sooo much more convenient than conventional cameras. You just erase the photos you don't want. Like computer files. For our Christmas card? Barry, well, he must have taken a zillion pictures of the kids, you know, snapping away because Blake blinked or Kyle was looking the wrong way, whatever, but when you shoot that many, well, like Barry says, you're going to get one that's pretty decent, am I right?'

Grace nodded. She was trying to unearth the woman's name, but it wouldn't surface. The woman's daughter – Blake, was it? – was in Grace's son's class in first grade. Or maybe it was last year in kindergarten. Hard to keep track. Grace kept the smile frozen to her face. The woman was nice enough, but she blended in with the others. Grace wondered, not for the first time, if she was blending in too, if her once great individuality had joined the unpleasant swirl of suburban uniformity.

The thought was not a comforting one.

The woman kept describing the wonders of the digital age. Grace's frozen smile began to ache. She glanced at her watch, hoping Tech Mom would pick up the hint. Two-forty-five. Almost time to pick up Max at school. Emma had swim team practice, but another mom was driving the carpool today. A car*pool* to the *pool*, as the too-jolly mother had reminded Grace with a little tee-hee. Yeah, funny stuff.

'We have to get together,' the woman said, winding down. 'With Jack and Barry. I think they'd get along.'

'Definitely.'

Grace took advantage of the pause to wave good-bye, pull open the door, and disappear inside the Photomat. The glass door closed with a snap, ringing a little bell. The chemical smell, not unlike model glue, hit her first. She wondered about the long-term effects of working in such an environment and decided the short-term ones were annoying enough.

The kid working – Grace's use of the term *working* being overly generous here – behind the counter had a white fuzz pellet under his chin, hair dyed a color that'd intimidate Crayola, and enough piercings to double as a wind instrument. One of those wrap-around-low headphones snaked around the back of his neck. The music was so loud that Grace could feel it in her chest. He had tattoos, lots of them. One read STONE. Another read KILLJOY. Grace thought that a third should read SLACKER.

'Excuse me?'

He did not look up.

'Excuse me?' she said a little louder.

Still nothing.

'Yah, like, dude?'

That got his attention. He snarled up, narrowed his eyes, offended by the interruption. He removed the headphones but grudgingly. 'Stub.'

'Pardon me?'

'Stub.'

Ah. Grace handed him the receipt. Fuzz Pellet then asked her for her name. This reminded Grace of those damn customer service phones that ask you to dial in your home phone, and then as soon as you get a real live person, they ask you for the same phone number. Like the first request was just for practice.

Fuzz Pellet – Grace was warming up to this nickname – flipped through a file of photo packets before extracting one. He ripped off the tag and told her an exorbitant price. She handed him a Val-Pak coupon, one dug out of her purse in an excavation that rivaled the search for the Dead Sea Scrolls, and watched the price drop to something closer to reasonable.

He handed her the packet of photographs. Grace thanked him, but he already had the music plugged back into his cerebrum. She waved in his direction. 'I come not for the pictures,' Grace said, 'but for the sparkling repartee.'

Fuzz Pellet yawned and picked up his magazine. The latest issue of *Modern Slacker*.

Grace hit the sidewalk. The weather was brisk. Autumn had shoved summer aside with a patented gust. The leaves hadn't really started turning yet, but the air had that apple-cider quality to it. The shop windows had started up with the Halloween decorations. Emma, her third grader, had convinced Jack to buy an eight-foot blowup Homer-Simpson-as-Frankenstein balloon. It looked, she had to admit, terrific. Her children liked *The Simpsons*, which meant that maybe, despite their best efforts, she and Jack were raising them right.

Grace wanted to slit open the envelope now. There was always an excitement with a newly developed roll of film, an opening-a-gift expectation, a hurry-to-the-mailbox-even-though-it's-always-bills rush that digital photography, for all its conveniences, could never duplicate. But there wasn't time before school let out.

As her Saab climbed up Heights Road, she took a small detour so that she could pass the town's lookout. From here, the skyline of Manhattan, especially at night, lay spread out like diamonds on black velvet. The longing tugged at her. She loved New York City. Until four years ago, that wonderful island had been their home. They'd had a loft on Charles Street down in the Village. Jack worked on the medical research for a large pharmaceutical company. She painted in her home studio while scoffing at her suburban counterparts and their SUVs and corduroy pants and toddler-referenced dialogues. Now she was one of them.

Grace parked behind the school with the other mothers. She turned the engine off, picked up the Photomat envelope, and ripped it open. The roll was from last week's annual trip to Chester for apple picking. Jack had snapped away. He liked being the family photographer. He considered it paternal manly work, taking the photos, as if this was a sacrifice a father was supposed to make for his family.

The first image was of Emma, their eight-year-old daughter, and Max, their six-year-old son, on the hayride, shoulders hunched, their cheeks reddened by wind. Grace stopped and stared for a moment. Feelings of, yes, maternal warmth, both primitive and evolutionary, rocked her back. That was the thing with kids. It was the little things that got to you. She'd remembered that it had been cold that day. The orchard, she knew, would be too crowded. She had not wanted to go. Now, looking at this photograph, she wondered about the idiocy of her priorities.

The other mothers were gathering by the school fence, making small talk and planning play-dates. It was, of course, the modern era, post-feminist America, and yet, of the roughly eighty parents waiting for their charges, only two were male. One, she knew, was a father who'd been laid off for more than a year. You could see it in his eyes, his slow shuffle, the missed spots when he shaved. The other guy was a stay-at-home journalist who always seemed a little too anxious to chat up the moms. Lonely maybe. Or something else.

Someone knocked on the car window. Grace looked up. Cora Lindley, her best friend in town, signaled for her to unlock the door. Grace did. Cora slid into the passenger seat next to her.

'So how did the date go last night?' Grace asked.

'Poorly.'

'Sorry.'

'Fifth-date syndrome.'

Cora was a divorcee, a little too sexy for the nervous, ever-protective 'ladies who lunch.' Clad in a low-cut, leopard-print blouse with spandex pants and pink pumps, Cora most assuredly did not fit in with the stream of khakis and loose sweaters. The other mothers eyed her with suspicion. Adult suburbia can be a lot like high school.

'What's fifth-date syndrome?' Grace asked.

'You're not dating much, are you?'

'Well, no,' Grace said. 'The husband and two kids have really cramped my style.'

'Pity. See – and don't ask me why – but on the fifth date, the guys always raise the subject ... how should I word this delicately?... of a ménage à trois.'

'Please tell me you're joking.'

'I joke with you not. Fifth date. At the latest. The guy asks me, on a purely theoretical basis, what my opinion is on ménage à trois. Like it's peace in the Middle East.'

'What do you say?'

'That I usually enjoy them, especially when the two men start French-kissing.'

Grace laughed and they both got out of the car. Grace's bad leg ached. After more than a decade, she shouldn't be self-conscious about it anymore, but Grace still hated for people to see the limp. She stayed by the car and watched Cora walk away. When the bell rang, the kids burst out as if they'd been fired from a cannon. Like every other parent, Grace only had eyes for her own. The rest of the pack, uncharitable as this might sound, was scenery.

Max emerged in the second exodus. When Grace saw her son – one sneaker lace untied, his Yu-Gi-Oh! backpack looking four sizes too big, his New York Rangers knit hat tilted to the side like a tourist's beret – the warmth rushed over anew. Max made his way down the stairs, adjusting the backpack up his shoulders. She smiled. Max spotted her and smiled back.

He hopped in the back of the Saab. Grace strapped him into the booster seat and asked him how his day was. Max answered that he didn't know. She asked him what he did in school that day. Max answered that he didn't know. Did he learn math, English, science, arts and crafts? Answer: Shrug and dunno. Grace nodded. A classic case of the epidemic known as Elementary-School Alzheimer's. Were the kids drugged to forget or sworn to secrecy? One of life's mysteries.

It was not until after she got home and gave Max his Go-GURT snack – think yogurt in a toothpaste-like squeeze tube – that Grace had the chance to take a look at the rest of the photographs.

The message light on the answering machine was blinking. One message. She checked the Caller ID and saw that the number was blocked. She pressed play and was surprised. The voice belonged to an old ... friend, she guessed. Acquaintance was too casual. Father-figure was probably more accurate, but only in the most bizarre sense.

'Hi, Grace. It's Carl Vespa.'

He did not have to say his name. It had been years, but she'd always know the voice.

'Could you give me a call when you have the chance? I need to talk to you about something.'

The message beeped again. Grace did not move, but she felt an old fluttering in her belly. Vespa. Carl Vespa had called. This could not be good. Carl Vespa, for all his kindnesses to her, was not one for idle chitchat. She debated calling him back and decided for the time being against it.

Grace moved into the spare bedroom that had become her make≠shift studio. When she was painting well – when she was, like any artist or athlete, 'in the zone' – she saw the world as if preparing to put it on canvas. She would look at the streets, the trees, the people and imagine the type of brush she would use, the stroke, the mix of colors, the differing lights and casts of shadows. Her work should reflect what she wanted, not reality. That was how she looked at art. We all see the world through our own prism, of course. The best art tweaked reality to show the artist's world, what she saw or, more precisely, what she wanted others to see. It was not always a more beautiful reality. It was often more provocative, uglier maybe, more gripping and magnetic. Grace wanted a reaction. You might enjoy a beautiful setting sun – but Grace wanted you immersed in her sunset, afraid to turn away from it, afraid not to.

Grace had spent the extra dollar and ordered a second set of prints. Her fingers dipped into the envelope and plucked out the photographs. The first two were the ones of Emma and Max on the hayride. Next came Max with his arm stretched up to pick a Gala apple. There was the compulsory blurry shot of flesh, the one where Jack's hand had slipped too close to the lens. She smiled and shook her head. Her big doofus. There were several more shots of Grace and the children with a variety of apples, trees, baskets. Her eyes grew moist, the way they always did when she looked at photographs of her children.

Grace's own parents had died young. Her mother was killed when a semi crossed the divide on Route 46 in Totowa. Grace, an only child, was eleven at the time. The police did not come to the door like in the movies. Her father had learned what happened from a phone call. Grace still remembered the way her father, wearing blue slacks and a gray sweater-vest, had answered the phone with his customary musical hello, how his face had drained of color, how he suddenly collapsed to the floor, his sobs first strangled and then silent, as if he could not gather enough air to express his anguish.

Grace's father raised her until his heart, weakened from a childhood bout with rheumatic fever, gave out during Grace's freshman year of college. An uncle out in Los Angeles volunteered to take her in, but Grace was of age by now. She decided to stay east and make her own way.

The deaths of her parents had been devastating, of course, but they had also given Grace's life a strange sense of urgency. There is a left-behind poignancy for the living. Those deaths added amplification to the mundane. She wanted to jam in the memories, get her fill of the life moments and – morbid as it sounds – make sure her kids had plenty to remember her by when she too was no more.

It was at that moment – thinking about her own parents, thinking about how much older Emma and Max looked now than in last year's apple-picking photo shoot – when she stumbled across the bizarre photograph.

Grace frowned.

The picture was near the middle of the pack. Closer to the back maybe. It was the same size, fitting neatly in with the others, though the backing sheet was somewhat flimsier. Cheaper stock, she thought. Like a high-end office-supply photocopy maybe.

Grace checked the next picture. No duplicate this time. That was strange. Only one copy of this photograph. She thought about that. The picture must have fallen in somehow, mixed up with another roll.

Because this photograph did not belong to her.

It was a mistake. That was the obvious explanation. Think for a moment about the quality workmanship of, say, Fuzz Pellet. He was more than capable of screwing up, right? Of putting the wrong photograph in the middle of her pack?

That was probably what was going on here.

Someone else's photograph had gotten mixed in with hers.

Or maybe ...

The photograph had an old look about it – not that it was black-and-white or antique sepia. Nothing like that. The print was in color, but the hues seemed ... off somehow – saturated, sun-faded, lacking the vibrancy one would expect in this day and age. The people in it too. Their clothes, their hair, their makeup – all dated. From fifteen, maybe twenty years ago.

Grace put it down on the table to take a closer look.

The images in the photograph were all slightly blurred. There were four people – no, wait, one more in the corner – five people in the photograph. There were two men and three women, all in their late teens, early twenties maybe – at least, the ones she could see clearly enough appeared to be around that age.

College students, Grace thought.

They had the jeans, the sweatshirts, the unkempt hair, that attitude, the casual stance of budding independence. The picture looked as if it'd been snapped when the subjects were not quite ready, in mid-gather. Some of the heads were turned so you only saw a profile. One dark-haired girl, on the very right edge of the photo, you could only see the back of her head, really, and a denim jacket. Next to her there was another girl, this one with flaming-red hair and eyes spaced wide apart.

Near the middle, one girl, a blonde, had – God, what the hell was that about? – her face had a giant X across it. Like someone had crossed her out.

How had this picture ...?

As Grace kept staring, she felt a small ping in the center of her chest. The three women – she didn't recognize them. The two men looked somewhat alike, same size, same hair, same attitude. The guy on the far left too was not someone she knew.

She was sure, however, that she recognized the other man. Or boy. He wasn't really old enough to call a man. Old enough to join the army? Sure. Old enough to be called a man? He was standing in the middle, next to the blonde with the X through her face ...

But it couldn't be. His head was in mid-turn for one thing. That adolescent-thin beard covered too much of his face ...

Was it her husband?

Grace bent closer. It was, at best, a profile shot. She hadn't known Jack when he was this young. They had met thirteen years ago on a beach in the Côte d'Azur on southern France. After more than a year of surgery and physical therapy, Grace was still not all the way back. The headaches and memory loss remained. She had the limp – still had it now – but with all the publicity and attention from that tragic night still suffocating her, Grace had just wanted to get away for a while. She matriculated at the University of Paris, studying art in earnest. It was while on break, lying in the sun on the Côte d'Azur, that she met Jack for the first time.

Was she sure it was Jack?

He looked different here, no doubt about it. His hair was a lot longer. He had this beard, though he was still too young and baby-faced for it to come in full. He wore glasses. But there was something in the way he stood, the tilt of his head, the expression.

This was her husband.

She quickly sifted through the rest of the roll. There were more hayrides, more apples, more arms raised in mid-pick. She saw one that she'd taken of Jack, the one time he'd let her have the camera, control freak that he was. He was reaching so high, his shirt had moved up enough to show his belly. Emma had told him that it was eeuw, gross. That, of course, made Jack pull up the shirt more. Grace had laughed. 'Work it, baby!' she'd said, snapping the next photo. Jack, much to Emma's ultimate mortification, obliged and undulated.

'Mom?'

She turned. 'What's up, Max?'

'Can I have a granola bar?'

'Let's grab one for the car,' she said, rising. 'We need to take a ride.'

Fuzz Pellet was not at the Photomat.

Max checked out the various themed picture frames – 'Happy Birthday,' 'We Love You, Mom,' that kind of thing. The man behind the counter, resplendent in a polyester tie, pocket protector, and short-sleeve dress shirt flimsy enough to see the V-neck tee beneath it, wore a name tag that informed one and all that he, Bruce, was an assistant manager.

'May I help you?'

'I'm looking for the young man who was here a couple of hours ago,' Grace said.

'Josh is gone for the day. Something I can do for you?'

'I picked up a roll of film a little before three o'clock . . .'

'Yes?'

Grace had no idea how to put this. 'There was a photo in there that shouldn't have been.'

'I'm not sure I understand.'

'One of the pictures. I didn't take it.'

He gestured toward Max. 'I see you have young children.'

'Excuse me?'

Assistant Manager Bruce pushed his glasses up off the end of his nose. 'I was just pointing out that you have young children. Or at least, one young child.'

'What does that have to do with anything?'

'Sometimes a child picks up the camera. When the parent isn't looking. They snap a picture or two. Then they put the camera back.'

'No, it's not that. This picture had nothing to do with us.'

'I see. Well, I'm sorry for the inconvenience. Did you get all the photos you took?'

'I think so.'

'None were missing?'

'I really didn't check that closely, but I think we got them all.'

He opened a drawer. 'Here. This is a coupon. Your next roll will be developed for free. Three by fives. If you want the four by sixes, there is a small surcharge.'

Grace ignored his outstretched hand. 'The sign on the door says you develop all the pictures on site.'

'That's right.' He petted the large machine behind him. 'Old Betsy here does the job for us.'

'So my roll would have been developed here?'

'Of course.'

Grace handed him the Photomat envelope. 'Could you tell me who developed this roll?'

'I'm sure it was just an honest error.'

'I'm not saying it wasn't. I just want to know who developed my roll.'

He took a look at the envelope. 'May I ask why you want to know?'

'Was it Josh?'

'Yes, but –'

'Why did he leave?'

'Pardon me?'

'I picked up the photos a little before three o'clock. You close at six. It's nearly five now.'

'So?'

'It seems strange that a shift would end between three and six for a store that closes at six.'

Assistant Manager Bruce straightened up a bit. 'Josh had a family emergency.'

'What kind of emergency?'

'Look, Miss ...' – he checked the envelope – 'Lawson, I'm sorry for the error and inconvenience. I'm sure a photograph from another set fell into your packet. I can't recall it happening before, but none of us are perfect. Oh, wait.'

'What?'

'May I see the photograph in question please?'

Grace was afraid he'd want to keep it. 'I didn't bring it,' she lied.

'What was it a picture of?'

'A group of people.'

He nodded. 'I see. And were these people naked?'

'What? No. Why would you ask that?'

'You seem upset. I assumed that the photograph was in some way offensive.'

'No, nothing like that. I just need to speak to Josh. Could you tell me his last name or give me a home phone number?'

'Out of the question. But he'll be in tomorrow first thing. You can talk to him then.'

Grace chose not to protest. She thanked the man and left. Might be better anyway, she thought. By driving here she had merely reacted. Check that. She had probably overreacted.

Jack would be home in a few hours. She would ask him about it then.

Grace had homebound carpool duties for the swim practice. Four girls, ages eight and nine, all delightfully energetic, piled two into the backseat and two into the 'way, way' back of the minivan. There was a swirl of giggles, of 'Hello, Ms. Lawson,' wet hair, the gentle perfume of both YMCA chlorine and bubble gum, the sound of backpacks being shucked off, of seat belts fastening. No child sat in the front – new safety rules – but despite the chauffeur feel, or maybe because of it, Grace liked doing carpool. It was time spent seeing her child interact with her friends. Children spoke freely during carpool; the driving adult might as well have been in another time zone. A parent could learn much. You could find out who was cool, who was not, who was in, who was out, what teacher was totally rad, what teacher was most assuredly not. You could, if you listened closely enough, decipher where on the pecking order your child was currently perched.

It was also entertaining as all get-out.

Jack was working late again, so when they got home, Grace quickly made Max and Emma dinner – veggie chicken nuggets (purportedly healthier and, once dipped in ketchup, the kids can never tell the difference), Tater Tots, and Jolly Green Giant frozen corn. Grace peeled two oranges for dessert. Emma did her homework – too big a load for an eight-year-old, Grace thought. When she had a free second, Grace headed down the hallway and flipped on the computer.

Grace might not be into digital photography, but she understood the necessity and even advantages of computer graphics and the World Wide Web. There was a site that featured her work, how to buy it, how to commission a portrait. At first, this had hit her as too much like shilling, but as Farley, her agent, reminded her, Michelangelo painted for money and on commission. So did Da Vinci and Raphael and pretty much every great artist the world has ever known. Who was she to be above it?

Grace scanned in her three favorite apple-picking photos for safekeeping and then, more on a whim than anything else, she decided to scan in the strange photograph too. That done, she started bathing the children. Emma went first. She was just getting out of the tub when Grace heard his keys jangle in the back door.

'Hey,' Jack called up in a whisper. 'Any hot love monkeys up there waiting for their stud muffin?'

'Children,' she said. 'Children are still awake.'

'Oh.'

'Care to join us?'

Jack bounded up the stairs, taking them two at a time. The house shook from the onslaught. He was a big man, six-two, two-ten. She loved the substance of him sleeping beside her, the rise and fall of his chest, the manly smell of him, the soft hairs on his body, the way his arm snaked around her during the night, the feeling of not only intimacy but safety. He made her feel small and protected, and maybe it was un-PC, but she liked that.

Emma said, 'Hi, Daddy.'

'Hey, Kitten, how was school?'

'Good.'

'Still have a crush on that Tony boy?'

'Eeuw!'

Satisfied with the reaction, Jack kissed Grace on the cheek. Max came out of his room, stark naked.

'Ready for your bath, mah man?' Jack asked.

'Ready,' Max said.

They high-fived. Jack scooped Max up in a sea of giggles. Grace helped Emma get in her pajamas. Laughter spilled from the bath. Jack was singing a rhyming song with Max where some girl named Jenny Jenkins couldn't decide what color to wear. Jack would start off with the color and Max filled in the rhyme line. Right now they were singing that Jenny Jenkins couldn't wear 'yellow' because she'd look like a 'fellow.' Then they both cracked up anew. They did pretty much the same rhymes every night. And they laughed their asses off over them every night.

Jack toweled Max off, got him into his pajamas, and put him to bed. He read two chapters of *Charlie and the Chocolate Factory*. Max listened to every word, totally riveted. Emma was old enough to read by herself. She lay in her bed, devouring the latest tale of the Baudelaire orphans from Lemony Snicket. Grace sat with her and sketched for half an hour. This was her favorite time of the day – working in silence in the same room as her eldest child.

When Jack finished, Max begged for just one more page. Jack stayed firm. It was getting late, he said. Max grudgingly acquiesced. They talked for another moment or two about Charlie's impending visit to Willy Wonka's factory. Grace listened in.

Roald Dahl, both her men agreed, totally rocked.

Jack turned down the lights – they had a dimmer switch because Max didn't like complete darkness – and then he entered into Emma's room. He bent down to give Emma a kiss good night. Emma, a total Daddy's Girl, reached up, grabbed his neck, and wouldn't let him go. Jack melted at Emma's nightly technique for both showing affection and stalling going to sleep.

'Anything new for the journal?' Jack asked.

Emma nodded. Her backpack was next to her bed. She dug through it and produced her school journal. She turned the pages and handed it to her father.

'We're doing poetry,' Emma said. 'I started one today.'

'Cool. Want to read it?'

Emma's face was aglow. So was Jack's. She cleared her throat and began:

'Basketball, basketball,
Why are you so round?
So perfectly bumpy,
So amazingly brown.
Tennis ball, tennis ball,
Why are you so fizzy,
When you're hit with a racket,
Do you feel kind of dizzy?'

Grace watched the scene from the doorway. Jack's hours had gotten bad lately. Most of the time Grace didn't mind. Quiet moments were becoming scarce. She needed the solace. Loneliness, the precursor to boredom, is conducive to the creative process. That was what artistic meditation was all about – boring yourself to the point where inspiration must emerge if only to preserve your sanity. A writer friend once explained that the best cure for writer's block was to read a phone book. Bore yourself enough and the Muse will be obligated to push through the most slog-filled of arteries.

When Emma was done, Jack fell back and said, 'Whoa.'

Emma made the face she made when she was proud of herself but didn't want to show it. She tucked her lips over and back under her teeth.

'That was the most brilliant poem I've ever heard ever ever,' Jack said.

Emma gave a head-down shrug. 'It's only the first two verses.'

'That was the most brilliant first two verses I've ever heard ever ever.'

'I'm going to write a hockey one tomorrow.'

'Speaking of which ...'

Emma sat up. 'What?'

Jack smiled. 'I got tickets for the Rangers at the Garden on Saturday.'

Emma, part of the 'jock' group as opposed to the group who worshipped the latest boy band, gave a yippee and reached up for another hug. Jack rolled his eyes and accepted it. They discussed the team's recent performance and set odds on their chances of beating the Minnesota Wild. A few minutes later, Jack disentangled himself. He told his daughter that he loved her. She told him that she loved him too. Jack started for the door.

'Gotta grab something to eat,' he whispered to Grace.

'There's leftover chicken in the fridge.'

'Why don't you slip into something more comfortable?'

'Hope springs eternal.'

Jack arched an eyebrow. 'Still afraid you're not enough woman for me?'

'Oh, that reminds me.'

'What?'

'Something about Cora's date last night.'

'Hot?'

'I'll be down in a second.'

He arched the other eyebrow and hustled downstairs with a whistle. Grace waited until she heard Emma's breathing deepen before following. She turned off the light and watched for a moment. This was Jack's bit. He paced the corridors at night, unable to sleep, guarding them in their beds. There were nights she'd wake up and find the spot next to her empty. Jack would be standing in one of their doorways, his eyes glassy. She'd approach and he'd say, 'You love them so much ...' He didn't need to say more. He didn't even have need to say that.

Jack didn't hear her approach, and for some reason, a reason Grace wouldn't want to articulate, she tried to stay quiet. Jack stood stiffly, his back to her, his head down. This was unusual. Jack was usually hyper, constant motion. Like Max, Jack could not stay still. He fidgeted. His leg shook whenever he sat. He was high energy.

But right now he was staring down at the kitchen counter – more specifically, at the strange photograph – still as a stone.

'Jack?'

He startled upright. 'What the hell is this?'

His hair, she noticed, was a shade longer than it should be. 'Why don't you tell me?'

He didn't say anything.

'That's you, right? With the beard?'

'What? No.'

She looked at him. He blinked and looked away.

'I picked up this roll of film today,' she said. 'At the Photomat.'

He said nothing. She stepped closer.

'That photograph was in the middle of the pack.'

'Wait.' He looked up sharply. 'It was in with our roll of film?'

'Yes.'

'Which roll?'

'The one we took at the apple orchard.'

'That doesn't make any sense.'

She shrugged. 'Who are the other people in the photo?'

'How should I know?'

'The blonde standing next to you,' Grace said. 'With the X through her. Who is she?'

Jack's cell phone rang. He snapped it up like a gunfighter on a draw. He mumbled a hello, listened, put his hand over the mouthpiece, and said, 'It's Dan.' His research partner at Pentocol Pharmaceuticals. He lowered his head and headed into the den.

Grace headed upstairs. She started getting ready for bed. What had started as a gentle nagging was growing stronger, more persistent. She flashed back to their years living in France. He would never talk about his past. He had a wealthy family and a trust fund, she knew – and he wanted nothing to do with either. There was a sister, a lawyer out in Los Angeles or San Diego. His father was still alive but

25

very old. Grace had wanted to know more, but Jack refused to elaborate, and sensing something foreboding, she had not pushed him.

They fell in love. She painted. He worked in a vineyard in Saint-Emilion in Bordeaux. They lived in Saint-Emilion until Grace had gotten pregnant with Emma. Something called her home then – a yearning, corny as it might sound, to raise her children in the land of the free and the home of the brave. Jack wanted to stay, but Grace had insisted. Now Grace wondered why.

Half an hour passed. Grace slipped under the covers and waited. Ten minutes later, she heard a car engine start up. Grace looked out the window.

Jack's minivan was pulling out.

He liked to shop at night, she knew – hit the grocery store when it wasn't crowded. So going out like this was not unusual for him. Except, of course, he hadn't called up to tell her he was going or to ask if they needed anything in particular.

Grace tried his cell phone but the voice mail picked up. She sat back and waited. Nothing. She tried to read. The words swam by in a meaningless haze. Two hours later, Grace tried Jack's cell phone again. Still voice mail. She checked on the children. They slept soundly, appropriately oblivious.

When she could stand it no longer Grace headed downstairs. She looked through the packet of film.

The strange photograph was gone.

2

Most people check out the online personals to find a date. Eric Wu found victims.

He had seven different accounts using seven different made-up personas – some male and some female. He tried to stay in e-mail contact with an average of six 'potential dates' per account. Three of the accounts were on standard any-age straight personals. Two were for singles over the age of fifty. One was for gay men. The final site hooked up lesbians looking for serious commitment.

At any one time Wu would be conducting online flirtations with as many as forty or even fifty of the forlorn. He would slowly get to know them. Most were cautious, but that was okay. Eric Wu was a patient man. Eventually they would give him enough tidbits to find out if he should pursue the relationship or cut them loose.

He only dealt with women at first. The theory was that they would be the easiest victims. But Eric Wu, who received no sexual gratification from his work, realized that he was leaving untapped an entire market that would be less likely to worry about online safety. A man does not, for example, fear rape. He does not fear stalkers. A man is less cautious, and that makes him more vulnerable.

Wu was seeking singles with few ties. If they had children, they were no good to him. If they had family living close by, they were no good to him. If they had roommates, important jobs, too many close friends, well, ditto. Wu wanted them lonely, yes, but also secluded and shut off from the many ties and bonds that connect the rest of us to something greater than the individual. Right now, he also required one with geographical proximity to the Lawson household.

He found such a victim in Freddy Sykes.

Freddy Sykes worked for a storefront tax-filing company in Waldwick, New Jersey. He was forty-eight years old. His parents were both deceased. He had no siblings. According to his online flirtations at BiMen.com, Freddy had taken care of his mother and never had the time for a relationship. When she passed away two years ago, Freddy inherited the house in Ho-Ho-Kus, a scant three miles from the Lawson residence. His online photograph, a headshot, hinted that Freddy was probably on the plump side. His hair was shoe-polish black, thin, styled in a classic comb-over. His smile seemed forced, unnatural, as if he were wincing before a blow.

Freddy had spent the past three weeks flirting online with one Al Singer, a fifty-six-year-old retired Exxon executive who'd been married twenty-two years before admitting that he was interested in 'experimenting.' The Al Singer persona still loved his wife, but she didn't understand his need to be with both men and women. Al was interested in European travel, fine dining, and watching sports on TV. For his Singer persona, Wu used a photograph he'd grabbed off a YMCA online catalogue. His Al Singer looked athletic but not too handsome. Someone too attractive might raise Freddy's suspicion. Wu wanted him to buy the fantasy. That was the key thing.

Freddy Sykes's neighbors were mostly young families who paid him no attention. His house looked like every other on the block. Wu watched now as Sykes's garage door opened electronically. The garage was attached. You could enter and exit your car without being seen. That was excellent.

Wu waited ten minutes and then rang his doorbell.

'Who is it?'

'Delivery for Mr. Sykes.'

'From whom?'

Freddy Sykes had not opened the door. That was strange. Men usually did. Again that was part of their vulnerability, part of the reason that they were easier prey than their female counterparts. Overconfidence. Wu spotted the peephole. Sykes would no doubt be peering at the twenty-six-year-old Korean man with baggy pants and a squat, compact build. He might notice Wu's earring and bemoan how today's youth mutilated their bodies. Or maybe the build and earring would turn Sykes on. Who knew?

'From Topfit Chocolate,' Wu said.

'No, I mean, who sent them?'

Wu pretended to read the note again. 'A Mr. Singer.'

That did it. The deadbolt slid open. Wu glanced about him. No one. Freddy Sykes opened the door with a smile. Wu did not hesitate. His fingers formed a spear and then darted for Sykes's throat like a bird going for food. Freddy went down. Wu moved with a speed that defied his bulk. He slid inside and closed the door behind him.

Freddy Sykes lay on his back, his hands wrapped around his own neck. He was trying to scream, but all he could make were small squawking noises. Wu bent down and flipped him onto his stomach. Freddy struggled. Wu pulled up his victim's shirt. Freddy kicked at him. Wu's expert fingers traced up his spine until he found the right spot between the fourth and fifth vertebrae. Freddy kicked some more. Using his index finger and thumb like bayonets, Wu dug into the bone, nearly breaking skin.

Freddy stiffened.

Wu applied a bit more pressure, forcing the facet joints to sublux. Still burrowing deeper between the two vertebrae, he took hold and plucked. Something in Freddy's spine snapped like a guitar string.

The kicking stopped.

All movement stopped.

But Freddy Sykes was alive. That was good. That was what Wu wanted. He used to kill them right away, but now he knew better. Alive, Freddy could call his boss and tell him that he was taking time off. Alive, he could offer up his PIN if Wu wanted money from the ATM. Alive, he could answer messages in case someone did indeed call.

And alive, Wu would not have to worry about the smell.

Wu jammed a gag in Freddy's mouth and left him naked in the bathtub. The pressure on the spine had made the facet joints jump out of position. This dislocation of the vertebrae would contuse rather than completely sever the spinal column. Wu tested the results of his handiwork. Freddy could not move his legs at all. His deltoids might work, but the hands and lower arms would not function. Most important, he could still breathe on his own.

For all practical purposes, Freddy Sykes was paralyzed.

Keeping Sykes in the tub would make it easier to rinse off any mess. Freddy's eyes were open a little too widely. Wu had seen this look before: somewhere past terror but not yet death, a hollowness that fell in that awful cusp between the two.

There was obviously no need to tie Freddy up.

Wu sat in the dark and waited for night to fall. He closed his eyes and let his mind drift back. There were prisons in Rangoon where they studied spinal fractures during hangings. They learned where to place the knot, where to apply force, what effects different placement would have. In North Korea, in the political prison Wu had called home from the age of thirteen to eighteen, they had taken the experiments one step further. Enemies of the state were killed creatively. Wu had done many with his bare hands. He had hardened his hands by punching boulders. He had studied the anatomy of the human body in a way most medical students would envy. He had practiced on human beings, perfecting his techniques.

The exact spot between the fourth and fifth vertebrae. That was key. Any higher and you could paralyze them completely. That would lead to death fairly quickly. Forget their arms and legs – their internal organs would stop working. Any lower and you would only get the legs. The arms would still work. If the pressure applied was too great, you'd snap the entire spinal column. It was all about precision. Having the right touch. Practice.

Wu turned on Freddy's computer. He wanted to keep up with the other singles on his list because he never knew when he would need a new place to live. When he was finished, Wu allowed himself to sleep. Three hours later he awoke and looked in on Freddy. His eyes were glassier now, staring straight up, blinking without focus.

When his contact called Wu's cell phone, it was nearly 10 P.M.

'Are you settled in?' the contact asked.

'Yes.'

'We have a situation.'

Wu waited.

'We need to move things up a bit. Is that a problem?'

'No.'

'He needs to be taken now.'

'You have a place?'

Wu listened, memorizing the location.

'Any questions?'

'No,' Wu said.

'Eric?'

Wu waited.

'Thanks, man.'

Wu hung up. He found the car keys and took off in Freddy's Honda.

3

Grace couldn't call the police yet. She couldn't sleep either.

The computer was still on. Their screen saver was a family photo taken last year at Disney World. The four of them posed with Goofy at Epcot Center. Jack was wearing mouse ears. His grin was ear to ear. Hers was more reserved. She'd felt silly, which just encouraged Jack. She touched the mouse – the other mouse, the computer mouse – and her family disappeared.

Grace clicked the new icon and the strange photograph of the five college-aged kids appeared. The image came up with Adobe Photoshop. For several minutes Grace just stared at the young faces, searching for – she didn't know – a clue maybe. Nothing came to her. She cropped each face, blowing them up into something approaching four inches by four inches. Any bigger and the already-blurred image became undecipherable. The good paper was in the color inkjet, so she hit the print button. She grabbed a pair of scissors and went to work.

Soon she had five separate headshots, one for each person in the picture. She studied them again, this time taking extra care with the young blonde next to Jack. She was pretty with that girl-next-door complexion and long flaxen hair. The young woman's eyes were on Jack, and the look was more than casual. Grace felt a pang of, what, jealousy? How bizarre. Who was this woman? Obviously an old girlfriend – one Jack had never mentioned. But so what? Grace had a past. So did Jack. Why would the look in that photograph bother her?

So what now?

She would have to wait for Jack. When he came home, she would demand answers.

But answers about what?

Back up here a second. What was really going on? An old photograph, probably of Jack, had popped up in her packet of pictures. It was weird, sure. It was even a little creepy, what with the blonde crossed out like that. And Jack had stayed out late before without calling. So really, what was the big deal here? Something in the photo had probably upset him. He turned off his phone and was probably in a bar. Or at Dan's house. This whole thing was probably just a bizarre joke.

Yeah, Grace, sure. A joke. Like the one about the carpool to the pool.

Sitting alone, the room dark except for the glow from the computer monitor, Grace tried a few more ways to rationalize away what was going on. She stopped when she realized that this was only scaring her more.

Grace clicked onto the face of the young woman, the one who stared at her husband with longing, zooming in for a better view. She stared at the face, really stared, and a tingle of dread began to travel across her scalp. Grace did not move.

She just kept looking at the woman's face. She didn't know the wheres or whens or hows, but she now realized something with thudding certainty.

Grace had seen this young woman before.

4

Rocky Conwell took up post by the Lawson residence.

He tried to get comfortable in his 1989 Toyota Celica, but that was impossible. Rocky was too big for this piece-of-crap car. He pulled harder on that damned seat lever, nearly ripping it out, but the seat would go back no farther. It would have to do. He settled in and let his eyes start to close.

Man, was Rocky tired. He was working two jobs. The first, his steady gig to impress his parole officer, was a ten-hour shift on the Budweiser assembly line in Newark. The second, sitting in this damn car and staring at a house, was strictly off the books.

Rocky jerked up when he heard a noise. He picked up his binoculars. Damn, someone had started up the minivan. He focused in. Jack Lawson was on the move. He lowered the binoculars, shifted into drive, and prepared to follow.

Rocky needed two jobs because he needed cash in a big, bad way. Lorraine, his ex, was making overtures about a possible reconciliation. But she was still skittish about it. Cash, Rocky knew, could tip the balance in his favor. He loved Lorraine. He wanted her back in a big, bad way. He owed her some good times, didn't he? And if that meant he had to work his butt off, well, he'd been the one to screw up. It was a price he was willing to pay.

It hadn't always been like this for Rocky Conwell. He'd been an All-State defensive end at Westfield High. Penn State – Joe Paterno himself – had recruited him and transformed him into a hard-hitting inside linebacker. Six-four, two-sixty, and blessed with a naturally aggressive nature, Rocky had been a standout for four years. He'd been All Big-Ten for two years. The St. Louis Rams drafted him in the seventh round.

For a while, it was like God Himself had perfectly planned out his life from the get-go. His real name was Rocky, his parents naming him that when his mother went into labor as they watched the movie *Rocky* in the summer of 1976. You gonna have a name like Rocky, you better be big and strong. You better be ready to rumble. Here he was, a pro football draft pick itching to get to camp. He and Lorraine – a knockout who could not only stop traffic but make it go backward – hooked up during his junior year. They fell for each other pretty hard. Life was good.

Until, well, it wasn't.

Rocky was a great college player, but there is a big difference between Division IA and the pros. At the Rams rookie camp, they loved his hustle. They loved his work ethic. They loved the way he would sacrifice his body to make a play. But they didn't love his speed – and in today's game, what with the emphasis on passing and coverage, Rocky was simply not good enough. Or so they said. Rocky would not surrender. He started taking more steroids. He got bigger but still not big enough for the front line. He managed to hang around one season playing special teams for the Rams. The next year he was cut.

The dream wouldn't die. Rocky wouldn't let it. He pumped iron nonstop. He began 'roiding big time. He had always taken some kind of anabolic supplement. Every athlete does. But desperation had made him less cautious. He didn't worry about cycling or overdoing it. He just wanted mass. His mood darkened from either the drugs or the disappointment – or more likely, the potent blend of the two.

To make ends meet, Rocky took up work with the Ultimate Fighting Federation. You may remember their octagon grudge matches. For a while, they were all the rage on pay-per-view – real, bloody, no-holds-barred brawls. Rocky was good at it. He was big and strong and a natural fighter. He had great endurance and knew how to wear down an opponent.

Eventually the violence in the ring got to be too much for people's sensibilities. States began to outlaw ultimate fighting. Some of the guys started battling in Japan where it was still legal – Rocky guessed that they had different sensibilities over there – but he didn't go. Rocky still believed that the NFL was within his grasp. He just had to work harder. Get a little bigger, a little stronger, a little faster.

Jack Lawson's minivan pulled onto Route 17. Rocky's instructions were clear. Follow Lawson. Write down where he went, who he talked to, every detail of his trip, but do not – repeat not – engage him. He was to observe. Nothing more.

Right, easy cash.

Two years ago, Rocky got into a bar fight. It was typical stuff. Some guy stared at Lorraine too long. Rocky had asked him what he was looking at, and the guy responded, 'Not much.' You know the drill. Except Rocky was juiced up from the 'roids. He pulverized the guy – put him in traction – and got nailed on an assault beef. He spent three months in jail and was now on probation. That had been the final straw for Lorraine. She called him a loser and moved out.

So now he was trying to make it up to her.

Rocky had quit the junk. Dreams die hard, but he now realized that the NFL was not going to be. But Rocky had talents. He could be a good coach. He knew how to motivate. A friend of his had an in at his old alma mater, Westfield High. If Rocky could get his record cleared, he'd be made varsity defensive coordinator. Lorraine could get a job there as a guidance counselor. They'd be on their way.

They just needed a little set-up cash.

Rocky kept the Celica a decent distance back of the minivan. He was not too worried about being spotted. Jack Lawson was an amateur. He wouldn't be looking for a tail. That was what his boss had told him.

Lawson crossed the New York border and took the thruway north. The time was ten P.M. Rocky wondered if he should call it in, but no, not yet. There was nothing here to report. The man was taking a ride. Rocky was following him. That was his job.

Rocky felt his calf start cramping. Man, he wished this piece of junk had more legroom.

Half an hour later Lawson pulled off by the Woodbury Commons, one of those massive outdoor malls where all the stores were purportedly 'outlets' for their more expensive counterparts. The Commons was closed. The minivan pulled down a quiet stretch of road on the side. Rocky hung back. If he followed now, he'd be spotted for sure.

Rocky found a position on the right, shifted into park, turned off his headlights, and picked up his binoculars.

Jack Lawson stopped the minivan, and Rocky watched him step out. There was another car not too far away. Must be Lawson's girlfriend. Strange place for a romantic rendezvous, but there you go. Jack looked both ways and then headed toward the wooded area. Damn. Rocky would have to follow on foot.

He put down the binoculars and slid out. He was still seventy, eighty yards away from Lawson. Rocky didn't want to get any closer. He squatted down and peered through the binoculars again. Lawson stopped walking. He turned around and ...

What's this?

Rocky swung the binoculars to the right. A man was standing to Lawson's left. Rocky took a closer look. The man wore fatigues. He was short and squat, built like a perfect square. Looked like he worked out, Rocky thought. The guy – he looked Chinese or something – stood perfectly still, stonelike.

At least for a few seconds.

Gently, almost like a lover's touch, the Chinese guy reached up and put his hand on Lawson's shoulder. For a fleeting moment Rocky thought that maybe he had stumbled across a gay tryst. But that wasn't it. That wasn't it at all.

Jack Lawson dropped to the ground like a puppet with his strings cut.

Rocky stifled a gasp. The Chinese guy looked down at the crumpled form. He bent down and picked Lawson up by ... hell, it looked like the neck. Like you'd pick up a puppy or something. By the scruff of his neck.

Oh damn, Rocky thought. I better call this in.

Without breaking a sweat, the Chinese guy started carrying Lawson toward his car. With one hand. Like the guy was a briefcase or something. Rocky reached for his cell phone.

Crap, he'd left it in the car.

Okay, think, Rocky. The car the Chinese guy was driving. It was a Honda Accord. New Jersey plates. Rocky tried to memorize the number. He watched while the Chinese guy opened the trunk. He dumped Lawson in as if he were a load of laundry.

Oh man, now what?

Rocky's orders were firm. Do not engage. How many times had he heard that? Whatever you do, just observe. Do not engage.

He didn't know what to do.

Should he just follow?

Uh-uh, no way. Jack Lawson was in the trunk. Look, Rocky did not know the man. He didn't know why he was supposed to follow him. He'd figured that they'd been hired to follow Lawson for the usual reason – his wife suspected him of having an affair. That was one thing. Follow and prove infidelity. But this ...?

Lawson had been assaulted. For crying out loud, he'd been locked in the trunk by this muscle-headed Jackie Chan. Could Rocky just sit back and let that happen?

No.

Whatever Rocky had done, whatever he had become, he was not about to let

34

that stand. Suppose he lost the Chinese guy? Suppose there wasn't enough air in the trunk? Suppose Lawson had been seriously injured already and was dying?

Rocky had to do something.

Should he call the police?

The Chinese guy slammed the trunk closed. He started for the front seat.

Too late to call anyone. He had to make his move now.

Rocky remained six-four, two-sixty, and rock solid. He was a professional fighter. Not a show boxer. Not a phony, staged wrestler. A real fighter. He didn't have a gun, but he knew how to take care of himself.

Rocky started running toward the car.

'Hey!' he shouted. 'Hey, you! Stop right there!'

The Chinese guy – as he got closer, Rocky could see he was more like a kid – looked up. His expression did not change. He just stared as Rocky ran toward him. He did not move. He did not try to get in the car and drive away. He waited patiently.

'Hey!'

The Chinese kid stayed still.

Rocky stopped a yard in front of him. Their eyes met. Rocky did not like what he saw. He had played football against some true headcases. He'd fought pain-happy crazies in the Ultimate Fighting ring. He had stared into the eyes of pure psychos – guys who got off on hurting people. This was not like this. This was like staring into the eyes of ... something not alive. A rock maybe. An inanimate object of some kind. There was no fear, no mercy, no reason.

'May I help you?' the Chinese kid said.

'I saw ... Let that man out of the trunk.'

The kid nodded. 'Of course.'

The kid glanced toward the trunk. So did Rocky. And that was when Eric Wu struck.

Rocky never saw the blow. Wu ducked down, twisted his hips for power, and smashed his fist into Rocky's kidney. Rocky had taken shots before. He had been punched in the kidney by men twice this size. But nothing had ever hit him like this. The blow landed like a sledgehammer.

Rocky gasped but stayed on his feet. Wu moved in and jabbed something hard into Rocky's liver. It felt like a barbecue skewer. The pain exploded through him.

Rocky's mouth opened, but the scream wouldn't come out. He fell to the ground. Wu dropped down next to him. The last thing Rocky saw – the last thing he would ever see – was Eric Wu's face, calm and serene, as he placed his hands under Rocky's rib cage.

Lorraine, Rocky thought. And then nothing more.

5

Grace caught herself mid-scream. She jerked upright. The light was still on in the hallway. A silhouette stood in her doorway. But it wasn't Jack.

She awoke, still gasping. A dream. She knew that. On some elusive level, she had known that midway through. She'd had this dream before, plenty of times, though not in a long time. Must be the upcoming anniversary, she thought.

She tried to settle back. It wouldn't happen. The dream always started and ended the same. The variations occurred in the middle.

In the dream Grace was back at the old Boston Garden. The stage was directly in front of her. There was a steel blockade, short, maybe waist-high, like something you might use to lock your bike. She leaned against it.

The loudspeaker played 'Pale Ink,' but that was impossible because the concert hadn't even started yet. 'Pale Ink' was the big hit from the Jimmy X Band, the best-selling single of the year. You still hear it on the radio all the time. It would be played live, not on some waiting-time recording. But if this dream was like some movie, 'Pale Ink' was, if you will, the soundtrack.

Was Todd Woodcroft, her boyfriend at the time, standing next to her? She sometimes imagined holding his hand – though they were never the hand-holding kind of couple – and then, when it went wrong, the stomach-dropping feel of his hand slipping away from hers. In reality, Todd was probably right next to her. In the dream, only sometimes. This time, no, he was not there. Todd had escaped that night unscathed. She never blamed him for what happened to her. There was nothing he could have done. Todd had never even visited her in the hospital. She didn't blame him for that either. Theirs was a college romance already on the skids, not a soul-mate situation. Who needed a scene at this stage of the game? Who'd want to break up with a girl in the hospital? Better for both, she thought, to let it just sort of drift away.

In the dream, Grace knows that tragedy is about to strike, but she does nothing about it. Her dream self does not call out a warning or try to make for the exit. She often wondered why, but wasn't that how dreams worked? You are powerless even with foreknowledge, a slave to some advanced hardwiring in your subconscious. Or perhaps the answer is simpler: There was no time. In the dream, the tragedy begins in seconds. In reality, according to witnesses, Grace and the others had stood in front of that stage for more than four hours.

The crowd's mood had slid from excited to antsy to restless before stopping at hostile. Jimmy X, real name James Xavier Farmington, the gorgeous rocker with the glorious hair, was supposed to take the stage at 8:30 P.M., though no one really expected him before nine. Now it was closing in on midnight. At first the crowd had been chanting Jimmy's name. Now a chorus of boos had started up. Sixteen thousand people, including those, like Grace, who had been lucky enough to get standing seats in the pit, rose as one, demanding their performance. Ten minutes passed before the loudspeaker finally offered up some feedback. The crowd, having reverted to their earlier state of fevered excitement, went wild.

But the voice that came over the loudspeaker did not introduce the band. In a straight monotone, it announced that tonight's performance had been delayed again for at least an hour. No explanation. For a moment nobody moved. Silence filled the arena.

This was where the dream began, during that lull before the devastation. Grace was there again. How old was she? She had been twenty-one, but in the dream she seemed to be older. It was a different, parallel Grace, one who was married to Jack and mother to Emma and Max and yet was still at that concert during her senior year of college. Again that was how it worked in dreams, a dual reality, your parallel self overlapping with your actual one.

Was all this, these dream moments, coming from her subconscious or from what she had read about the tragedy after the fact? Grace did not know. It was, she'd long surmised, probably a combination of both. Dreams open up memories, don't they? When she was awake, she couldn't recall that night at all – or for that matter, the few days before. The last thing she remembered was studying for a political science final she'd taken five days earlier. That was normal, the doctors assured, with her type of head trauma. But the subconscious was a strange terrain. Perhaps the dreams were actual memories. Perhaps imagination. Most likely, as with most dreams or even memories, both.

Either way, be it from memory or press reports, it was at this very moment when someone fired a shot. Then another. And another.

This was before the days of metal detector sweeps when you entered an arena. Anyone could carry in a gun. For a while, there had been much debate over the origins of those shots. Conspiracy nuts still argued over the point, as if the arena had a grassy knoll in the upper tier. Either way, the young crowd, already in a frenzy, snapped. They screamed. They broke. They rushed for exits.

They rushed toward the stage.

Grace was in the wrong spot. Her waist was crushed against the top of the steel girder. It dug into her belly. She could not pry herself free. The crowd cried out and surged as one. The boy next to her – she would later learn that he was nineteen years old and named Ryan Vespa – didn't get his hands up in time. He smacked the girder at a bad angle.

Grace saw – again was it just in the dream or in reality too? – the blood shoot from Ryan Vespa's mouth. The girder finally gave way. It tilted over. She fell to the floor. Grace tried to get her footing, tried to stand, but the current of screaming humans drove her back down.

This part, she knew, was real. This part, being buried under a mass of people, haunted more than just her dreams.

The stampede continued. People stomped on her. Trampled her arms and legs. Tripped and fell, slamming down on her like stone tablets. The weight grew. Crushing her. Dozens of desperate, struggling, slithering bodies rushed over her.

Screams filled the air. Grace was underneath it now. Buried. There was no light anymore. Too many bodies on top of her. It was impossible to move. Impossible to breathe. She was suffocating. Like someone had buried her in concrete. Like she was being dragged underwater.

There was too much weight on her. It felt as if a giant hand was pressing down on her head, squashing her skull like it was a Styrofoam cup.

There was no escape.

And that, mercifully, was when the dream ended. Grace woke up, still gulping for air.

In reality, Grace had woken up four days later and remembered almost nothing. At first she thought it was the morning of her political science final. The doctors took their time explaining the situation. She had been seriously injured. She had, for one, a skull fracture. That, the doctors surmised, explained the headaches and memory loss. This was not a case of amnesia or repressed memory or even anything psychological. The brain was damaged, which is not infrequent with this kind of severe head trauma and loss of consciousness. Losing hours, even days, was not unusual. Grace also shattered her femur, her tibia, and three ribs. Her knee had split in two. Her hip had been ripped out of its joint.

Through a haze of painkillers, she eventually learned that she had been 'lucky.' Eighteen people, ranging in age from fourteen to twenty-six, had been killed in the stampede that the media dubbed the Boston Massacre.

The silhouette in the doorway said, 'Mom?'

It was Emma. 'Hi, sweetheart.'

'You were screaming.'

'I'm okay. Even moms have bad dreams sometimes.'

Emma stayed in the shadows. 'Where's Daddy?'

Grace checked the bedside clock. It was nearly 4:45 A.M. How long had she been asleep? No more than ten, fifteen minutes. 'He'll be home soon.'

Emma did not move.

'You okay?' Grace asked.

'Can I sleep with you?'

Plenty of bad dreams tonight, Grace thought. She pulled back the blanket. 'Sure, honey.'

Emma crawled onto Jack's side of the bed. Grace threw the blanket back over her and held tight. She kept her eyes on the bedside clock. At exactly 7 A.M. – she watched the digital clock switch from 6:59 A.M. – she let panic in.

Jack had never done anything like this before. If it had been a normal night, if he had come up and told her that he was going grocery shopping, if he had made some clumsy double entendre before leaving, something about melons or bananas, something funny and stupid like that, she'd have been on the phone with the police already.

But last night had not been normal. There had been that photograph. There had been his reaction. And there had been no kiss good-bye.

Emma stirred beside her. Max entered in mid-eye rub a few minutes later. Jack was usually the one who made breakfast. He was more the early riser. Grace managed to whip up the morning meal – Cap'n Crunch with sliced banana – and deflected their questions about their father's absence. While they were busy wolfing down breakfast, she slid into the den and tried Jack's office, but nobody picked up the line. Still too early.

She threw on a pair of Jack's Adidas sweats and walked them to the bus stop.

Emma used to hug her before she boarded, but she was too old for that. She hurried aboard, before Grace could mumble something idiotically parental about Emma being too old for hugs but not too old to visit Mom when she was scared at night. Max still gave her a hug but it was quick and with a serious lack of enthusiasm. They both stepped inside, the bus door swooshing to a close as though swallowing them whole.

Grace blocked the sun with her hand and, as always, watched the bus until it turned down Bryden Road. Even now, even after all this time, she still longed to hop in her car and follow just to be sure that that seemingly fragile box of yellow tin made it safely to school.

What had happened to Jack?

She started back toward the house, but then, thinking better of it, she sprinted toward her car and took off. Grace caught up to the bus on Heights Road and followed it the rest of the way to Willard School. She shifted into park and watched the children disembark. When Emma and Max appeared, weighed down by their backpacks, she felt the familiar flutter. She sat and waited until they both headed up the path, up the stairs, and disappeared through the school doors.

And then, for the first time in a long time, Grace cried.

Grace expected cops in plainclothes. And she expected two of them. That was how it always worked on television. One would be the gruff veteran. The other would be young and handsome. So much for TV. The town police had sent one officer in the regulation stop-you-for-speeding uniform and matching car.

He had introduced himself as Officer Daley. He was indeed young, very young, with a smattering of acne on his shiny baby face. He was gym muscular. His short sleeves worked like tourniquets on his bloated biceps. Officer Daley spoke with annoying patience, a suburban-cop monotone, as if addressing a class of first graders on bike safety.

He had arrived ten minutes after her call on the non-emergency police line. Normally, the dispatcher told her, they would ask her to come in and fill out a report on her own. But it just so happened that Officer Daley was in the area, so he'd be able to swing by. Lucky her.

Daley took a letter-size sheet of paper and placed it out on the coffee table. He clicked his pen and started asking questions.

'The missing person's name?'

'John Lawson. But he goes by Jack.'

He started down the list.

'Address and phone number?'

She gave them.

'Place of birth?'

'Los Angeles, California.'

He asked his height, weight, eye and hair color, sex (yes, he actually asked). He asked if Jack had any scars, marks, or tattoos. He asked for a possible destination.

'I don't know,' Grace said. 'That's why I called you.'

Officer Daley nodded. 'I assume that your husband is over the age of emancipation?'

'Pardon?'

'He is over eighteen years old.'

39

'Yes.'

'That makes this harder.'

'Why?'

'We got new regulations on filling out a missing person report. It was just updated a couple weeks back.'

'I'm not sure I understand.'

He gave a theatrical sigh. 'See, in order to put someone in the computer, he needs to meet the criteria.' Daley pulled out another sheet of paper. 'Is your husband disabled?'

'No.'

'Endangered?'

'What do you mean?'

Daley read from the sheet. '"A person of age who is missing and in the company of another person under circumstances indicating that his/her physical safety is in danger."'

'I don't know. I told you. He left here last night ...'

'Then that would be a no,' Daley said. He scanned down the sheet. 'Number three. Involuntary. Like a kidnapping or abduction.'

'I don't know.'

'Right. Number four. Catastrophe victim. Like in a fire or airplane crash.'

'No.'

'And the last category. Is he a juvenile? Well, we covered that already.' He put the sheet down. 'That's it. You can't put the person into the system unless he fits in one of those categories.'

'So if someone goes missing like this, you do nothing?'

'I wouldn't put it that way, ma'am.'

'How would you put it?'

'We have no evidence that there was any foul play. If we receive any, we will immediately upgrade the investigation.'

'So for now you do nothing?'

Daley put down the pen. He leaned forward, his forearms on his thighs. His breathing was heavy. 'May I speak frankly, Mrs. Lawson?'

'Please.'

'Most of these cases – no, more than that, I'd say ninety-nine out of a hundred – the husband is just running around. There are marital problems. There is a mistress. The husband doesn't want to be found.'

'That's not the case here.'

He nodded. 'And in ninety-nine out of a hundred cases, that's what we hear from the wife.'

The patronizing tone was starting to piss her off. Grace hadn't felt comfortable confiding in this youth. She'd held back, as if she feared telling the entire truth would be a betrayal. Plus, when you really thought about it, how would it sound?

Well, see, I found this weird photo from the Photomat in the middle of my pack from Apple Orchard, in Chester, right, and my husband said it wasn't him and really, it's hard to tell because the picture is old and then Jack left the house ...

'Mrs. Lawson?'

'Yes.'

'Do you understand what I'm telling you?'

'I think so. That I'm hysterical. My husband ran off. I'm trying to use the police to drag him back. That sound about right?'

He remained unruffled. 'You have to understand. We can't fully investigate until we have some evidence that a crime has been committed. Those are the rules set up by the NCIC.' He pointed to the sheet of paper again and said in his gravest tone: 'That's the National Crime Information Center.'

She almost rolled her eyes.

'Even if we find your husband, we wouldn't tell you where he was. This is a free country. He is of age. We can't force him to come back.'

'I'm aware of that.'

'We could make a few calls, maybe make a few discreet inquiries.'

'Great.'

'I'll need the vehicle make and license plate number.'

'It's a Ford Windstar.'

'Color?'

'Dark blue.'

'Year?'

She didn't remember.

'License plate?'

'It begins with an M.'

Officer Daley looked up. Grace felt like a moron.

'I have a copy of the registration upstairs,' she said. 'I can check.'

'Do you use E-ZPass at tollbooths?'

'Yes.'

Officer Daley nodded and wrote that down. Grace headed upstairs and found the file. She made a copy with her scanner and gave it to Officer Daley. He wrote something down. He asked a few questions. She stuck with the facts: Jack had come home from work, helped put the children to bed, gone out, probably for groceries ... and that was it.

After about five minutes, Daley seemed satisfied. He smiled and told her not to worry. She stared at him.

'We'll check back with you in a few hours. If we hear nothing by then, let's talk some more.'

He left. Grace tried Jack's office again. Still no answer. She checked the clock. It was nearly 10 A.M. The Photomat would be opening now. Good.

She had some questions for Josh the Fuzz Pellet.

6

Charlaine Swain slipped on her new online lingerie purchase – a Regal Lace baby-doll with matching G-string – and pulled up her bedroom shade.

Something was wrong.

The day was Tuesday. The time was 10:30 A.M. Charlaine's children were at school. Her husband Mike would be at his desk in the city, the phone wedged between shoulder and ear, his fingers busy rolling and unrolling his shirtsleeves, his collar tighter by the day but his ego too proud to admit the need for a bigger size.

Her neighbor, the scuzzy creepazoid named Freddy Sykes, should be home by now.

Charlaine glanced toward the mirror. She didn't do that often. There was no need to remind herself that she was over forty. The image that stared back was still shapely, she guessed, helped no doubt by the babydoll's underwired support – but what had once been considered buxom and curvaceous had weakened and loosened. Oh, Charlaine worked out. There was yoga class – yoga being this year's Tae Bo or Step – three mornings a week. She stayed fit, battling against the obvious and unbeatable, holding tight even as it slipped away.

What had happened to her?

Forget the physical for a second. The young Charlaine Swain had been a bundle of energy. She had zest for life. She was ambitious and a go-getter. Everyone said it. There was always a spark with Charlaine, a crackle in the air, and somewhere, somehow, life – just plain living – had extinguished it.

Were the children to blame? Was it Mike? There was a time when he couldn't get enough of her, when an outfit like this would make his eyes widen and his mouth water. Now when she strutted by, he would barely look up.

When had that started?

She couldn't put her finger on it. She knew the process had been gradual, the change so slow as to be almost indiscernible, until, alas, it was a *fait accompli*. It hadn't all been his fault. She knew that. Her drive had waned, especially during the years of pregnancies, postnatal nursing, the ensuing exhaustion of infants. That was natural, she supposed. Everyone went through that. Still she wished that she had made more of an effort before the temporary changes hardened into something apathetic and enduring.

The memories, however, were still there. Mike used to romance her. He used to surprise her. He used to lust after her. He used to – and yes, this might sound crude – jump her bones. Now what he wanted was efficiency, something mechanical and precise – the dark, a grunt, a release, sleep.

When they talked, it was about the kids – the class schedules, the pickups, the homework, the dentist appointments, the Little League games, the Biddy

Basketball program, the play-dates. But that wasn't just Mike's fault either. When Charlaine had coffee with the women in the neighborhood – the Mommy and Me meetings at Starbucks – the conversations were so cloying, so boring, so stuffed with all things children, that she wanted to scream.

Charlaine Swain was being smothered.

Her mother – the idle queen of the country-club lunch – told her that this was life, that Charlaine had everything a woman could want, that her expectations were simply unrealistic. The saddest part was, Charlaine feared that her mother was right.

She checked her makeup. She applied more lipstick and rouge and then sat back and appraised herself. Yep, she looked like a whore. She grabbed a Percodan, the mommy equivalent of the lunchtime cocktail, and swallowed it. Then she took a closer look in the mirror, squinting even.

Was the old Charlaine still there somewhere?

There was this woman who lived two blocks down, a nice mother of two like Charlaine. Two months ago, this nice mother of two walked up to the Glen Rock train tracks and committed suicide by stepping in front of the 11:10 A.M. Bergen line heading south. Horrible story. Everyone talked about it for weeks. How could this woman, this nice mother of two, just abandon her children like that? How could she be so selfish? And yet, as Charlaine tsk-tsked with her fellow suburbanites, she felt a small pang of jealousy. For this nice mother, it was over. There had to be relief in that.

Where was Freddy?

Charlaine actually looked forward to this, her Tuesdays at ten, and perhaps that was the saddest thing of all. Her initial reaction to Freddy's peeping had been revulsion and rage. When and how had that slid into acceptance and even, God forgive her, arousal? No, she thought. It wasn't arousal. It was ... something. That was all. It was a spark. It was something to feel.

She waited for his shade to come up.

It didn't.

Strange. Come to think of it, Freddy Sykes never pulled down his shades. Their properties backed up to each other's, so that only they could see in each other's window. Freddy never pulled down the shade in the back. Why would he?

Her eyes roamed toward the other windows. All the shades were pulled down. Curious. The curtains in what she assumed was the den – she had never, of course, stepped foot in his house – were drawn closed.

Was Freddy traveling? Had he perhaps gone away?

Charlaine Swain caught her reflection in the window and felt a fresh wave of shame. She grabbed a robe – her husband's ratty terrycloth – and slipped into it. She wondered if Mike was having an affair, if another woman had drained that once insatiable sex drive, or was he just not interested in her? She wondered which was worse.

Where was Freddy?

And how degrading, how truly scraping-the-bottom pitiful it was, that this meant so much to her. She stared at the house.

There was movement.

It was slight. A shadow had crossed the side of a shade. But movement nonetheless. Maybe, just maybe, Freddy was truly peeping again, upping, if you

43

will, his excitement level. That could be it, right? Most peepers got off on the stealth, *I Spy* aspects of the act. Maybe he simply didn't want her to see him. Maybe he was watching her right now, surreptitiously.

Could that be it?

She loosened the robe and let it slide down her shoulders. The terrycloth reeked of man sweat and the aging remnants of cologne she'd bought Mike, what, eight, nine years ago. Charlaine felt the tears sting her eyes. But she didn't turn away.

Something else suddenly appeared between the window shades. Something ... blue?

She squinted. What was it?

The binoculars. Where were they? Mike kept a box of crap like that in his closet. She found it, dug through the many power cords and adapters, and unearthed the Leicas. She remembered when they bought them. They were on a cruise in the Caribbean. The stop was one of the Virgin Islands – she didn't remember which one – and the purchase had been spontaneous. That was why she remembered it, the buying of the binoculars, because of the spontaneity of such a mundane act.

Charlaine put the binoculars up to her eyes. They were auto-focus, so there was nothing to adjust. It took her a moment or two to find the space between the window and the shade. But the blue spot was there. She saw the flicker and her eyes closed. She should have known.

The television. Freddy had turned on the television.

He was home.

Charlaine stood without moving. She didn't know how she felt anymore. The numb was back. Her son Clay liked to play a song from the *Shrek* movie about a guy forming an L with his fingers on his forehead. Loser. That was Freddy Sykes. And now Freddy, this scuzzy creepazoid, this Loser with a finger-capital L, would rather watch television than her lingerie-clad body.

Something was still strange.

All those shades pulled down. Why? She had lived next to the Sykes house for eight years. Even when Freddy's mother was alive, the shades were never pulled down, the curtains never closed. Charlaine took another look through her binoculars.

The television flicked off.

She stopped, waiting for something to happen. Freddy had lost track of the time, she thought. The shade would open now. They would begin their perverted ritual.

But that's not what happened.

Charlaine heard the slight whir and knew immediately what it was. Freddy's electric garage door had been activated.

She moved closer to the window. There was the sound of a car starting up, and then Freddy's hunk-of-junk Honda pulled out. Sunlight reflected off the windshield. The glare made her squint. She blocked it by cupping her hand above her eyes.

The car moved and the glare cleared. She could now see who was driving.

It wasn't Freddy.

Something, something base and primitive, commanded Charlaine to duck out of sight. She did. She dropped down and crawled for the robe. She pressed the terrycloth against herself. The smell – that combination of Mike and stale cologne – now seemed oddly comforting.

Charlaine moved toward the side of the window. She pressed her back against the wall and peaked out.

The Honda Accord had stopped. The driver – the Asian man behind the wheel – was staring at her window.

Charlaine quickly flattened herself back against the wall. She stayed still, holding her breath. She stayed that way until she heard the car start moving again. And then, just to be on the safe side, she stayed down another ten minutes.

When she looked again, the car was gone.

The house next door was still.

7

At exactly 10:15 A.M., Grace arrived at the Photomat.

Josh the Fuzz Pellet was not there. As a matter of fact, nobody was there. The sign in the store window, probably left from the night before, read closed.

She checked the printed hours. Opens at 10 A.M. She waited. At ten-twenty, the first customer, a harried woman in her mid-thirties, spotted the CLOSED sign, read the hours, tried the door. She sighed in high drama. Grace gave her a commiserating shrug. The woman huffed off. Grace waited.

When the store had still not opened at 10:30 A.M., Grace knew that it was bad. She decided to try Jack's office again. His line kept going into voice mail – eerie hearing Jack's too-formal recorded voice – so she tried Dan's line this time. The two men had, after all, spoken last night. Maybe Dan could offer a clue.

She dialed his work number.

'Hello?'

'Hi, Dan, it's Grace.'

'Hey!' he said with a tad too much enthusiasm. 'I was just about to call you.'

'Oh?'

'Where's Jack?'

'I don't know.'

He hesitated. 'When you say you don't know –'

'You called him last night, right?'

'Yes.'

'What did you two talk about?'

'We're supposed to be making a presentation this afternoon. On the Phenomytol studies.'

'Anything else?'

'What do you mean, anything else? Like what?'

'Like what else did you talk about?'

'Nothing. I wanted to ask him about a PowerPoint slide. Why? What's going on, Grace?'

'He went out after that.'

'Right, so?'

'I haven't seen him since.'

'Wait, when you say you haven't seen him ...?'

'I mean, he hasn't come home, he hasn't called, I have no idea where he is.'

'Jesus, did you call the police?'

'Yes.'

'And?'

'And nothing.'

46

'My God. Look, let me get out of here. I'll be right over.'

'No,' she said. 'I'm fine.'

'You sure?'

'Positive. I have some things to do,' she said lamely. She moved the phone to the other ear, unsure how to put this. 'Has Jack been okay?'

'You mean, at work?'

'I mean anywhere.'

'Yeah, sure, he's Jack. You know.'

'You haven't noticed any change?'

'We've both been stressed about these drug trials, if that's what you mean. But nothing unusual. Grace, are you sure I shouldn't come up?'

There was a beep on her phone. Call Waiting. 'I need to go, Dan. That's the other line.'

'Probably Jack. Call me if you need anything.'

She clicked him off and checked the Caller ID. Not Jack. At least, not his cell. The number was blocked.

'Hello?'

'Ms. Lawson, this is Officer Daley. Has there been any word from your husband?'

'No.'

'We tried you at home.'

'Right, I'm out.'

There was a pause. 'Where are you?'

'In town.'

'Where in town?'

'I'm at the Photomat store.'

A longer pause. 'I don't mean to sound judgmental, but isn't that a strange place to be when you're concerned about your husband?'

'Officer Daley?'

'Yes?'

'There's this new invention. It's called the cell phone. In fact, you're calling me on it right now.'

'I didn't mean to –'

'Have you learned anything about my husband?'

'That's why I'm calling, actually. My captain is in now. He'd like to do a follow-up interview.'

'A follow-up?'

'Yes.'

'Is that standard?'

'Sure.' He sounded like it was anything but.

'Have you found something?'

'No, I mean, nothing to be alarmed about.'

'What does that mean?'

'Captain Perlmutter and I just need more information, Mrs. Lawson.'

Another Photomat customer, a recently streaked quasi-blonde about Grace's own age, approached the empty store. She cupped her hands around her eyes and peered inside. She too frowned and scoffed away.

'You're both at the station now?' Grace asked.

47

'Yes.'

'I'll be there in three minutes.'

Captain Perlmutter asked, 'How long have you and your husband lived in town?'

They were jammed into an office more fitting for the school custodian than the police captain of a town. The Kasselton cops had moved their station house to the former town library, a building with history and tradition but very little comfort. Captain Stu Perlmutter sat behind his desk. He leaned back at the first question, hands resting on a tidy paunch. Officer Daley leaned against the door frame, trying to look comfortable.

Grace said, 'Four years.'

'Like it here?'

'Well enough.'

'Great.' Perlmutter smiled at her, a teacher approving of the answer. 'And you have kids, right?'

'Yes.'

'How old?'

'Eight and six.'

'Eight and six,' he repeated with a wistful smile. 'Man, those are great ages. Not babies, and not teens yet.'

Grace decided to wait him out.

'Mrs. Lawson, has your husband ever disappeared before?'

'No.'

'Are there any problems with the marriage?'

'None.'

Perlmutter gave her a skeptical look. He didn't wink, but he came close. 'Everything is perfect, eh?'

Grace said nothing.

'How did you and your husband meet?'

'Pardon?'

'I asked –'

'What does that have to do with anything?'

'I'm just trying to get a feel here.'

'A feel for what? Have you found something or not?'

'Please.' Perlmutter tried on what he must have believed was a disarming smile. 'I just need to get some stuff down. For background, okay? Where did you and Jack Lawson meet?'

'In France.'

He wrote it down. 'You're an artist, aren't you, Mrs. Lawson?'

'Yes.'

'So you were overseas studying your art?'

'Captain Perlmutter?'

'Yes.'

'No offense, but this line of questioning is bizarre.'

Perlmutter glanced at Daley. He shrugged to signal that he meant no harm. 'Maybe you're right.'

'Have you learned something or not?'

48

'I believe Officer Daley explained to you that your husband is of age, that we really aren't obligated to tell you anything?'

'He did.'

'Right, well, we don't think he's met up with foul play, if that's your concern.'

'What makes you say that?'

'No evidence of such.'

'Meaning,' she said, 'that you haven't found bloodstains or anything like that?'

'That's correct. But more than that' – Perlmutter looked over at Daley again – 'we did find something that, well, we probably shouldn't share with you.'

Grace adjusted herself in the seat. She tried very hard to meet his eye, but he wouldn't face her. 'I'd very much appreciate knowing what you found.'

'It's not much,' Perlmutter said.

She waited.

'Officer Daley called your husband's office. He's not there, of course. I'm sure you know that already. He also didn't call in sick. So we decided to investigate a little more. Unofficially, you understand.'

'Right.'

'You were helpful enough to give us your car's E-ZPass number. We ran it through the computer. What time did you say your husband went out last night?'

'Around ten o'clock.'

'And you thought that maybe he went to the grocery store?'

'I didn't know. He didn't tell me.'

'He just upped and left?'

'Right.'

'And you never asked him where he was going?'

'I was upstairs. I heard the car start up.'

'Okay, here's what I need to know.' Perlmutter let go of the paunch. His chair creaked as he leaned forward. 'You called him on the cell phone. Pretty much right away. Is that correct?'

'Yes.'

'Well, see, that's the problem. Why didn't he answer you? I mean, if he wanted to talk to you?'

Grace saw where he was going with this.

'Do you think your husband – what? – got in an accident right away? Or maybe someone grabbed him within minutes of leaving your house?'

Grace hadn't really thought about that. 'I don't know.'

'Do you ever drive up the New York Thruway?'

The change of subject threw her. 'Not often, but sure, I've taken it.'

'Ever go to Woodbury Commons?'

'The outlet mall?'

'Yes.'

'I've been, yes.'

'How long do you figure it takes to get there?'

'Half an hour. Is that where he went?'

'I doubt it, not at that hour. The stores are all closed. But he used his E-ZPass at the tollbooth on that exit at precisely 10:26 P.M. It leads to Route 17, and heck, that's how I go to the Poconos. Give or take ten minutes either way, that would fit a scenario where your husband left your house and drove straight in that direction. From there, well, who knows where he went? It's fifteen miles to Interstate 84. From there you can go straight to California if you'd like.'

She sat there.

'So add it up, Mrs. Lawson. Your husband leaves the house. You call him immediately. He doesn't answer. Within a half hour or so, we know he's driving in New York. If someone had attacked him or if he got in an accident, well, there's no way he could have been snatched and then his E-ZPass used up there in that short a time frame. Do you understand what I'm telling you?'

Grace met his eye. 'That I'm a hysterical bimbo whose husband ran out on her.'

'That's not what I'm saying at all. It's just ... Well, we really can't investigate any further at this point. Unless ...' He leaned a little closer. 'Mrs. Lawson, is there anything else you can think of that could help us here?'

Grace tried not to squirm. She glanced behind her. Officer Daley had not moved. She had a copy of the strange photograph in her purse. She thought about Fuzz Pellet Josh and the store not opening. It was time to tell them. In hindsight she should have told Daley about it when she first showed up.

'I'm not sure it's relevant,' she began, reaching into her purse. She pulled out a copy of the photograph and passed it to Perlmutter. Perlmutter took out a pair of reading glasses, cleaned them with his shirttail, and pushed them into place. Daley walked around and bent down over the captain's shoulder. She told them about finding the photograph mixed in with her others. The two officers stared at her as if she'd taken out a razor and started shaving her head.

When Grace was done, Captain Perlmutter pointed to the picture and said, 'And you're sure that's your husband?'

'I think so.'

'But you're not sure?'

'I'm pretty sure.'

He nodded in that way people do when they think you're a lunatic. 'And the other people in the photo? The young lady somebody crossed out?'

'I don't know them.'

'But your husband. He said it wasn't him, right?'

'Right.'

'So if it isn't him, well, this is irrelevant. And if it is him' – Perlmutter took off the glasses – 'he lied to you. Isn't that correct, Mrs. Lawson?'

Her cell phone rang. Grace grabbed it fast and checked the number.

It was Jack.

For a moment she went very still. Grace wanted to excuse herself, but Perlmutter and Daley were both looking at her. Asking for privacy was not really an option here. She hit the answer button and brought the phone to her ear.

'Jack?'

'Hey.'

The sound of his voice should have filled her with relief. It didn't.

Jack said, 'I tried you at home. Where are you?'

'Where am I?'

'Listen, I can't talk long. I'm sorry about running out on you like that.'

His tone was aiming for casual, but it wasn't hitting the mark.

'I need a few days,' he said.

'What are you talking about?'

'Where are you, Grace?'

'I'm at the police station.'

'You called the police?'

Her eyes met Perlmutter's. He wiggled his fingers, as if to say, *Give me the phone, little lady. I'll handle it.*

'Look, Grace, just give me a few days. I ...' Jack stopped. And then he said something that made the dread grow tenfold. 'I need some space.'

'Space,' she repeated.

'Yes. A little space. That's all. Please tell the police that I apologize. I have to go now. Okay? I'll be back soon.'

'Jack?'

He didn't reply.

'I love you,' Grace said.

But the phone was dead.

8

Space. Jack said he needed space. And that was all wrong.

Never mind that 'needing space' was one of those lame, cloying, namby-pamby, New Age we-are-the-world terms that was worse than meaningless – 'needing space' – a terrible euphemism for 'I'm soooo outta here.' That would have been a clue perhaps, but this went much deeper.

Grace was home now. She had mumbled an apology to Perlmutter and Daley. Both men looked at her with pity and told her that it was all part of the job. They said that they were sorry. Grace offered up a solemn nod and headed for the door.

She had learned something crucial from the phone call.

Jack was in trouble.

She had not been overreacting. His disappearance had nothing to do with running away from her or fear of commitment. It was no accident. It had not been expected or planned. She had picked up the photograph from the store. Jack had seen it and run out.

And now he was in serious danger.

She could never explain this to the police. First off, they wouldn't believe her. They would claim that she was either delusional or naïve to the point of a learning disability. Maybe not to her face. Maybe they would humor her, which would be both a tremendous irritant and waste of time. They'd been convinced that Jack was on the run before the call. Her explanation would not change their minds.

And maybe that was best.

Grace was trying to read between the lines here. Jack had been concerned about police involvement. That was obvious. When she said that she was at the police station, the regret in his voice was real. That was no act.

Space.

That was the main clue. If he had just told her that he was leaving for a few days, blowing off steam, running off with a stripper he'd met at the Satin Dolls, okay, she might not believe him, but it would be in the realm of possibility. But Jack hadn't done that. He had been specific about his reasons for disappearing. He even repeated himself.

Jack needed space.

Marital codes. All couples have them. Most were pretty stupid. For example, there was a scene in the Billy Crystal movie *Mr. Saturday Night* when the comic Crystal played – Grace couldn't remember the name, barely remembered the movie – pointed at an old man with a terrible toupee and said, 'Is that a toupee? I, for one, was fooled.' So now, whenever she and Jack saw a man with a possible toupee, one would turn to the other and say, 'I for one?' and the spouse would either agree or disagree. Grace and Jack started using 'I for one' for other vanity enhancements too – nose jobs, breast implants, whatever.

The origin of 'Need space' was a bit more risqué.

Despite her current predicament, Grace's cheeks couldn't help but flush from the memory. Sex had always been very good with Jack, but in any long-term relationship, there are ebbs and flows. This was two years ago, during a time of, uh, great flow. A stage of more corporeal creativity, if you will. Public creativity, to be more specific.

There had been the quick nooky in the changing room at one of those upscale hair salons. There had been under-the-coat manipulation in a private balcony at a lush Broadway musical. But it was midway through a particularly daring encounter in a British-style red phone booth located, in of all places, a quiet street in Allendale, New Jersey, when Jack suddenly panted, 'I need space.'

Grace had looked up at him. 'Excuse me?'

'I mean, literally. Back up! The phone receiver is pressing into my neck!'

They'd both laughed. Grace closed her eyes now, a faint smile on her lips. 'Need space' had thus joined the ranks of their private marital language. Jack would not use that phrase haphazardly. He was sending her a message, warning her, letting her know that he was saying something he didn't mean.

Okay, so what did he mean then?

Jack couldn't speak freely for one thing. Someone was listening. Who? Was someone with him – or was he afraid because she was with the cops? She hoped the latter, that he was alone and simply didn't want police involvement.

But when she considered all the facts, that possibility seemed unlikely.

If Jack had been free to talk, why hadn't he called her back? He'd have to realize that she'd be out of the police station by now. If he were okay, if he was alone, Jack would have called again, just to let her know what was going on. He hadn't done that.

Conclusion: Jack was with somebody and in serious trouble.

Did he want her to react or sit tight? In the same way she knew Jack – in the same way she knew that he'd been sending her a signal – Jack would know that Grace's reaction would not be to go quietly into that good night. That was not her personality. Jack understood that. She would try to find him.

He had probably counted on that.

Of course, this was all no more than conjecture. She knew her husband well – or maybe she didn't? – so her conjectures were more than mere fancy. But how much more? Maybe she was just justifying her decision to take action.

Didn't matter. Either way, she was involved.

Grace thought about what she'd already learned. Jack had taken the Windstar up the New York Thruway. Who did they know up there? Why would he have gone that way so late at night?

She had no idea.

Hold up.

Roll it back to the start: Jack comes home. Jack sees the photograph. That was what set it off. The photograph. He sees it on the kitchen counter. She starts asking him about it. He gets a call from Dan. And then he goes into his study ...

Stop. His study.

Grace hurried down the hall. *Study* was a rather ornate word for this converted screened-in porch. The plaster was cracking in spots. There was always a draft in

53

the winter and a stifling lack of anything approaching air in the summer. There were photographs of the kids in cheap frames and two of her paintings in expensive ones. The study felt strangely impersonal to her. Nothing in here told you about the past of the room's main occupant – no mementos, no softball signed by friends, no photo of a golf foursome taking to the links. Other than some pharmaceutical freebies – pens, pads, a paperclip holder – there were no clues as to who Jack really was other than a husband, father, and researcher.

But maybe that was all there was.

Grace felt weird, snooping. There had been strength, she thought, in respecting one another's privacy. They each had a room closed off to the other. Grace had always been okay with that. She'd even convinced herself it was healthy. Now she wondered about looking away. She wondered if it'd derived from a desire to give Jack privacy – needing space?! – or because she feared poking a beehive.

His computer was up and online. Jack's default page was the 'official' Grace Lawson Web site. Grace stared at the chair for a moment, the ergonomic gray from the local Staples store, imagining Jack there, turning on the computer every morning, having her face greet him. The site's home page had a glam shot of Grace along with several examples of her work. Farley, her agent, had recently insisted that she include the photograph in all sales material because, as he put it, 'You a babe.' She reluctantly acquiesced. Looks had always been used by the arts to promote the work. On stage and in movies, well, the importance of looks was obvious. Even writers, with their glossy touched-up portraits, the smoldering dark eyes of the next literati wunderkind, marketed appearances. But Grace's world – painting – had been fairly immune to this pressure, ignoring the creator's physical beauty, perhaps because the form itself was all about the physical.

But not anymore.

An artist appreciates the importance of the aesthetical, of course. Aesthetics do more than alter perception. They altered reality. Prime example: If Grace had been fat or homely, the TV crews would not have been monitoring her vital signs after she'd been pulled from the Boston Massacre. If she'd been physically unappealing, she would have never been adopted as the 'people's survivor,' the innocent, the 'Crushed Angel,' as one tabloid headline dubbed her. The media always broadcasted her image while giving medical updates. The press – nay, the country – demanded constant updates on her condition. The families of victims visited her room, spent time with her, searched her face for ghostly wisps of their own lost children.

Would they have done the same had she been unattractive?

Grace didn't want to speculate. But as one too-honest art critic had told her: 'We have little interest in a painting that has little aesthetic appeal – why should it be different with a human being?'

Even before the Boston Massacre Grace had wanted to be an artist. But something – something elusive and impossible to explain – had been missing. The whole experience had helped take her artistic sensibilities to the next level. Yes, she knew how pretentious that sounded. She had disdained that art-school clatter: You have to suffer for your art; you need tragedy to give your work texture. It had always rung hollow before, but now she understood that there was indeed something to it.

Without her conscious viewpoint changing, her work developed that vague intangible. There was more emotion, more life, more ... swirl. Her work was darker, angrier, more vivid. People often wondered if she'd ever painted any scenes from that horrible day. The simple answer was only one portrait – a young face so full of hope that you knew it would soon be crushed – but the truer answer was that the Boston Massacre shaded and colored everything she touched.

Grace sat down at Jack's desk. The phone was to her right. She reached for it, deciding to try the simplest thing first: Hit redial on Jack's phone.

The phone – a new Panasonic model she'd picked up at Radio Shack – had an LCD screen so she could see the redialed number come up. The 212 area code. New York City. She waited. On the third ring a woman answered and said, 'Burton and Crimstein, law office.'

Grace wasn't sure how to proceed.

'Hello?'

'This is Grace Lawson calling.'

'How may I transfer your call?'

Good question. 'How many attorneys work at the firm?'

'I really couldn't say. Would you like me to connect you with one?'

'Yes, please.'

There was a pause. The voice had a shade of that trying-to-be-helpful impatience now. 'Is there one in particular?'

Grace checked the Caller ID. There were too many numbers. She saw that now. Usually long distance calls had eleven numbers. But here there were fifteen, including an asterisk. She mulled that over. If Jack had made the call, it would have been late last night. The receptionists would not have been on duty. Jack probably hit the asterisk button and plugged in an extension.

'Ma'am?'

'Extension four-six-three,' she said, reading off the screen.

'I'll connect you.'

The phone rang three times.

'Sandra Koval's line.'

'Ms. Koval please.'

'May I ask who is calling?'

'My name is Grace Lawson.'

'And what is this in reference to?'

'My husband, Jack.'

'Please hold.'

Grace gripped the phone. Thirty seconds later, the voice came back on.

'I'm sorry. Ms. Koval is in a meeting.'

'It's urgent.'

'I'm sorry –'

'I just need a second of her time. Tell her it's very important.'

The sigh was intentionally audible. 'Please hold.'

The hold music was a Muzak version of Nirvana's 'Smells Like Teen Spirit.' It was strangely calming.

'Can I help you?' The voice was all clipped professionalism.

'Ms. Koval?'

'Yes?'

'My name is Grace Lawson.'

'What do you want?'

'My husband Jack Lawson called your office yesterday.'

She did not reply.

'He's missing.'

'Pardon?'

'My husband is missing.'

'I'm sorry to hear that, but I don't see –'

'Do you know where he is, Ms. Koval?'

'Why on earth would I know?'

'He made a phone call last night. Before he disappeared.'

'So?'

'I hit the redial button. This number came up.'

'Ms. Lawson, this firm employs more than two hundred attorneys. He could have been calling any of them.'

'No. Your extension is here, on the redial display. He called you.'

No reply.

'Ms. Koval?'

'I'm here.'

'Why did my husband call you?'

'I have nothing more to say to you.'

'Do you know where he is?'

'Ms. Lawson, are you familiar with attorney-client privilege?'

'Of course.'

More silence.

'Are you saying my husband called you for legal advice?'

'I cannot discuss the situation with you. Good-bye.'

9

It didn't take Grace long to put it together.

The Internet could be a wonderful tool when used properly. Grace had Googled the words 'Sandra Koval,' for Web hits, for newsgroups, for images. She checked the Burton and Crimstein Web site. There were bios of all their lawyers. Sandra Koval had graduated from Northwestern. She had gotten her law degree at UCLA. Based on the years of graduation, Sandra Koval would be forty-two or so. She was married, according to the site, to one Harold Koval. They had three children.

They lived in Los Angeles.

That had been the giveaway.

Grace had done a little more research, some the old-fashioned way: with a telephone. The pieces started to come together. The problem was, the picture made no sense.

The drive into Manhattan had taken less than an hour. Burton and Crimstein's reception desk was on the fifth floor. The receptionist/security guard gave her a closed-mouth smile. 'Yes?'

'Grace Lawson to see Sandra Koval.'

The receptionist made a call, speaking in a voice below a whisper. A moment later, she said, 'Ms. Koval will be right out.'

That was something of surprise. Grace had been prepared to launch threats or accept a long wait. She knew what Koval looked like – there had been a photograph of her on the Burton and Crimstein Web site – so she'd even accepted the fact that she might have to confront her as she left.

In the end Grace had decided to take the chance and drive into Manhattan without calling first. Not only did she feel she'd need the element of surprise, but she very much wanted to confront Sandra Koval face to face. Call it necessity. Call it curiosity. Grace had to see this woman for herself.

It was still early enough. Emma had a play-date after school. Max attended an 'enrichment program' today. She wouldn't need to pick either of them up for several hours yet.

The reception area of Burton and Crimstein was part old-world attorney – rich mahogany, lush carpeting, tapestry-clad seating, the décor that foreshadows the billing – and part Sardi's celebrity wall. Photographs, mostly of Hester Crimstein, the famed TV attorney, adorned the walls. Crimstein had a show on Court TV cleverly dubbed *Crimstein on Crime*. The photos included Ms. Crimstein with a bevy of actors, politicos, clients, and, well, combinations of all three.

Grace was studying a photograph of Hester Crimstein standing alongside an attractive olive-skinned woman when a voice behind her said, 'That's Esperanza Diaz. A professional wrestler falsely accused of murder.'

Grace turned. 'Little Pocahontas,' she said.

'Excuse me?'

Grace pointed at the photograph. 'Her wrestling name. It was Little Pocahontas.'

'How do you know that?'

Grace shrugged. 'I'm a swarm of useless facts.'

For a moment Grace openly stared at Sandra Koval. Koval cleared her throat and made a big production of looking at her watch. 'I don't have much time. Please come this way.'

Neither woman spoke as they headed down the corridor and into a conference room. There was a long table, maybe twenty chairs, one of those gray speaker-phones in the middle that looks suspiciously like a dropped octopus. There was a variety of soft drinks and bottled water on a counter in the corner.

Sandra Koval kept her distance. She crossed her arms and made a gesture that said, *Well?*

'I did some research on you,' Grace said.

'Care to sit?'

'No.'

'Mind if I do?'

'Suit yourself.'

'How about a drink?'

'No.'

Sandra Koval poured herself a Diet Coke. She was what you'd call a handsome woman rather than pretty or beautiful. Her hair was going a gray that worked for her. Her figure was slim, her lips full. She had one of those lick-the-world pos-tures that let your adversaries know that you were comfortable with yourself and more than ready to do battle.

'Why aren't we in your office?' Grace asked.

'You don't care for this room?'

'It's a tad large.'

Sandra Koval shrugged.

'You don't have an office here, do you?'

'You tell me.'

'When I called, the woman answered "Sandra Koval's line".'

'Uh huh.'

'Line, she said. Line. Not office.'

'And that's supposed to mean something?'

'On its own, no,' Grace said. 'But I looked up the law firm on the Web. You live in Los Angeles. Near the Burton and Crimstein West Coast office.'

'True enough.'

'That's your home base. You're visiting here. Why?'

'A criminal case,' she said. 'An innocent man wrongly accused.'

'Aren't they all?'

'No,' Sandra Koval said slowly. 'Not all.'

Grace moved closer to her. 'You're not Jack's lawyer,' she said. 'You're his sister.'

Sandra Koval stared at her drink.

'I called your law school. They confirmed what I suspected. Sandra Koval was the married name. The woman who graduated was named Sandra Lawson. I double-checked it through LawMar Securities. Your grandfather's firm. Sandra Koval is listed as a member of the board.'

She smiled without humor. 'My, aren't we the little Sherlock.'

'So where is he?' Grace asked.

'How long have you two been married?'

'Ten years.'

'And in all that time, how many times has Jack talked about me?'

'Pretty much never.'

Sandra Koval spread her hands. 'Precisely. So why would I know where he is?'

'Because he called you.'

'So you say.'

'I hit the redial button.'

'Right, you told me that on the phone.'

'Are you saying he didn't call you?'

'When did this call purportedly take place?'

'Purportedly?'

Sandra Koval shrugged. 'Always the lawyer.'

'Last night. Around ten o'clock.'

'Well, there's your answer then. I wasn't here.'

'Where were you?'

'At my hotel.'

'But Jack called your line.'

'If he did, nobody would have answered. Not at that hour. It would have gone into voice mail.'

'You checked the messages today?'

'Of course. And no, none from Jack.'

Grace tried to digest that. 'When was the last time you spoke to Jack?'

'A long time ago.'

'How long?'

Her gaze flicked away. 'We haven't spoken since he went overseas.'

'That was fifteen years ago.'

Sandra Koval took another sip.

'How would he still know your phone number?' Grace asked.

She didn't reply.

'Sandra?'

'You live at 221 North End Ave in Kasselton. You have two phone lines, one the phone, one the fax.' Sandra repeated the two numbers from memory.

The two women looked at each other. 'But you've never called?'

Her voice was soft. 'Never.'

The speakerphone squawked. 'Sandra?'

'Yes.'

'Hester wants to see you in her office.'

'On my way.' Sandra Koval broke the eye contact. 'I have to go now.'

'Why would Jack try to call you?'

'I don't know.'

'He's in trouble.'

'So you say.'

'He's disappeared.'

'Not for the first time, Grace.'

The room felt smaller now. 'What happened between you and Jack?'

'It's not my place to say.'

'The hell it isn't.'

Sandra shifted in her seat. 'You said he disappeared?'

'Yes.'

'And Jack hasn't called?'

'Actually, he has.'

That puzzled her. 'And when he called, what did he say?'

'That he needed space. But he didn't mean it. It was code.'

Sandra made a face. Grace took out the photograph and placed it on the table. The air rushed out of the room. Sandra Koval looked down and Grace could see her body jolt.

'What the hell is this?'

'Funny,' Grace said.

'What?'

'Those are the exact words Jack used when he saw it.'

Sandra was still staring at the picture.

'That's him, right? In the middle with the beard?' Grace asked.

'I don't know.'

'Sure you do. Who's the blonde next to him?'

Grace dropped the blowup of the young woman onto the table. Sandra Koval looked up. 'Where did you get these?'

'The Photomat.' Grace quickly explained. Sandra Koval's face clouded over. She wasn't buying it. 'Is it Jack, yes or no?'

'I really can't say. I've never seen him with a beard.'

'Why would he call you immediately after seeing this picture?'

'I don't know, Grace.'

'You're lying.'

Sandra Koval pushed herself to a stand. 'I have a meeting.'

'What happened to Jack?'

'What makes you so sure he didn't just run away?'

'We're married. We have two kids. You, Sandra, have a niece and nephew.'

'And I had a brother,' she countered. 'Maybe neither one of us knows him that well.'

'Do you love him?'

Sandra stood there, shoulders slumped. 'Leave it alone, Grace.'

'I can't.'

Shaking her head, Sandra turned toward the door.

'I'm going to find him,' Grace said.

'Don't count on it.'

And then she was gone.

10

Okay, Charlaine thought, mind your own business.

She drew the curtains and changed back into her jeans and sweater. She put the babydoll back in the bottom of her drawer, taking her time, folding it very carefully for some reason. As if Freddy would notice if it was wrinkled. Right.

She took a bottle of seltzer water and mixed in a little of her son's fruit punch Twister. Charlaine sat on a stool at the marble kitchen block. She stared at the glass. Her finger traced loops in the condensation. She glanced at the Sub-Zero refrigerator, the new 690 model with the stainless steel front. There was nothing on it – no kid pictures, no family photographs, no finger smears, not even magnets. When they had the old yellow Westinghouse, the front had been blanketed with that stuff. There had been vitality and color. The remodeled kitchen, the one she had wanted so much, was sterile, lifeless.

Who was the Asian man driving Freddy's car?

Not that she kept tabs on him, but Freddy had very few visitors. She could, in fact, recall none. That didn't mean he didn't have any, of course. She did not spend her entire day watching his house. Still a neighborhood has a routine of its own. A vibe, if you will. A neighborhood is an entity, a body, and you can feel when something is out of place.

The ice in her drink was melting. Charlaine had not yet taken a sip. There was food shopping to be done. Mike's shirts would be ready at the cleaner. She was having lunch with her friend Myrna at Baumgart's on Franklin Avenue. Clay had karate with Master Kim after school.

She mentally ran through the rest of her to-do list and tried to come up with an order. Mindless stuff. Would there be time before lunch to do the food shopping and get back to the house? Probably not. The frozen goods would melt in the car. That errand would have to wait.

She stopped. To hell with this.

Freddy should be at work now.

That was how it'd always worked. Their perverted little dance lasted from around ten to ten-thirty. By ten-forty-five, Charlaine always heard that garage door open. She'd watch his Honda Accord pull out. Freddy worked, she knew, for H&R Block. It was in the same strip mall as the Blockbuster where she rented the DVDs. His desk was near the window. She avoided walking past it, but some days, when she parked, she would look over and see Freddy staring out the window, pencil resting against his lips, lost.

Charlaine found the yellow pages and looked up the number. A man identifying himself as a supervisor said that Mr. Sykes was not in but was expected at any moment. She pretended to be put out. 'He told me he'd be in by now.

Doesn't he normally get in at eleven?'

The supervisor admitted that he did.

'So where is he? I really need those figures.'

The supervisor apologized and assured her that Mr. Sykes would call the moment he arrived at his desk. She hung up.

Now what?

Something still felt very wrong here.

But so what? Who was Freddy Sykes to her anyway? Nothing. In a way, less than nothing. He was a reminder of her failures. He was a symptom of how pathetic she had become. She owed him nothing. More than that, imagine, just imagine, if poking around got her caught. Imagine if somehow the truth came out.

Charlaine looked over at Freddy's place. The truth coming out. Somehow that no longer bothered her all that much. She grabbed her coat and headed toward Freddy's house.

11

Eric Wu had seen the lingerie-clad woman in the window.

The previous night had been a long one for Wu. He had not anticipated any interference, and while the large man – his wallet said his name was Rocky Conwell – had presented no threat, Wu now had to get rid of a body and another car. That meant an extra trip back up to Central Valley, New York.

First things first. He packed Rocky Conwell into the trunk of his Toyota Celica. He moved Jack Lawson, whom he had originally jammed into the Honda Accord's trunk, to the back of the Ford Windstar. Once the bodies were out of sight, Wu changed license plates, got rid of the E-ZPass, and drove the Ford Windstar back to Ho-Ho-Kus. He parked the minivan in Freddy Sykes's garage. There was still enough time to catch a bus back up to Central Valley. Wu searched Conwell's car. Satisfied that it was cleared out, he took it to the Park-n-Ride on Route 17. He found a remote spot near the fence. A car being left there for days, even weeks, was not unusual. The smell would eventually bring attention, but that would not be anytime soon.

The Park-n-Ride was only three miles from Sykes's house in Ho-Ho-Kus. Wu walked. Early the next morning, he rose and caught the bus back to Central Valley. He picked up Sykes's Honda Accord. On the way back, he took a brief detour past the Lawson residence.

A patrol car was in the driveway.

Wu considered that. It did not cause him great concern, but perhaps he should nip any police involvement in the bud. He knew just how.

Wu drove back to Freddy's residence and turned on the television. Wu liked daytime TV. He enjoyed watching shows like *Springer* and *Ricki Lake*. Most people poo-pooed them. Wu did not. Only a truly great society, a free one, could allow such nonsense to air. But more than that, stupidity made Wu happy. People were sheep. The weaker they are, the stronger you are. What could be more comforting or entertaining?

During a commercial – the theme of the show, according to a graphic on the bottom: 'Mommy Won't Let Me Get a Nipple Ring!' – Wu rose. It was time to take care of the potential police problem.

Wu didn't need to touch Jack Lawson. All he had to say was one sentence: 'I know that you have two children.'

Lawson cooperated. He made the call to his wife's cell phone and told her he needed space.

At ten-forty-five – with Wu watching a mother and daughter wrestle across a stage while a crowd chanted 'Jerry!' – a call came in from a prison acquaintance.

'All okay?'

Wu said yes.

He pulled the Honda Accord out of the garage. As he did, he noticed the woman who lived next door standing in the window. She was wearing lingerie. Wu might not have thought much about the scene – a woman still in her unmentionables after ten in the morning – but something about the way she suddenly ducked away...

That might have been a natural reaction. You parade around in lingerie, forgetting to pull down your shade, and then you spot a stranger. Many people, perhaps most people, would move away or cover up. So it could be nothing.

But the woman had moved very fast, as if in a panic. More than that, she had not moved when the car first pulled out – only when she'd spotted Wu. If she had been afraid of being seen, wouldn't she have pulled the shade or ducked down when she first heard or saw the car?

Wu pondered that. He had, in fact, been pondering it all day.

He picked up his cell phone and hit the button to dial the last incoming number. A voice said, 'Problem?'

'I don't think so.' Wu turned the car around and started back toward the Sykes house. 'But I may be late.'

12

Grace didn't want to make the phone call.

She was still in New York City. There was a law against using a cell phone while driving unless it was hands-free, though that had nothing to do with her hesitation. With one hand on the steering wheel, she felt around on the floor of the car. She located the ear attachment, managed to untangle the cord, and jammed the earpiece deep into the canal.

This was supposed to be safer than using a handheld?

She turned on the cell phone. Though Grace hadn't called the number in years, she still had it programmed into the cell. For emergencies, she supposed. Like this one.

The phone was answered on the first ring.

'Yes?'

No name. No hello. No company greeting.

'This is Grace Lawson.'

'Hold.'

The wait was not long. First Grace heard the static and then, 'Grace?'

'Hello, Mr. Vespa.'

'Please call me Carl.'

'Carl, right.'

'You got my message?' he asked.

'Yes.' She did not tell Carl Vespa that it had nothing to do with why she was calling now. There was feedback on the line. 'Where are you?' she asked.

'My jet. We're about an hour outside of Stewart.'

Stewart was an air force base and airport about an hour and a half from her house.

Silence.

'Is something wrong, Grace?'

'You said to call if I ever needed anything.'

'And now, fifteen years later, you do?'

'I think so.'

'Good. And your timing couldn't be better. There's something I want to show you.'

'What's that?'

'Listen, are you home?'

'I'll be there soon.'

'I'll pick you up in two, two and a half, hours. We can talk then, okay? Do you have someone to watch the kids?'

'I should be able to find someone.'

'If you can't, I'll leave my assistant at your house. See you then.'

Carl Vespa hung up. Grace kept driving. She wondered what he wanted from her now. She wondered about the wisdom of calling him in the first place. She hit the first number on her speed-dial again – Jack's cell phone – but there was still no answer.

Grace had another idea. She called her friend of the no-ménage, Cora. 'Didn't you used to date a guy who worked in e-mail spam?' Grace asked. 'Yep,' Cora said. 'Obsessive creep named – get this – Gus. Hard to get rid of. I had to use my own version of a bunker buster on him.'

'What did you do?'

'I told Gus he had a small wee-wee.'

'Ouch.'

'Like I said, the bunker buster. Works every time, but there's often, uh, collateral damage.'

'I might need his help.'

'How?'

Grace was not sure how to put this. She decided to concentrate on the blonde with the X across her face, the one she was sure she'd seen before. 'I found this photograph ...,' she began.

'Right.'

'And there's this woman in it. She's probably late teens, early twenties.'

'Uh-huh.'

'It's an old picture. I'd say fifteen, twenty years old. Anyway, I need to find out who the girl is. I was thinking maybe I could send it out via spam mail. It could ask if anyone can identify the girl for a research project, something like that. I know most people erase those e-mails, but if a few looked, I don't know, maybe I could get a response.'

'Long shot.'

'Yeah, I know.'

'And wow, talk about creeps coming out of the woodwork. Imagine the replies.'

'Got a better idea?'

'Not really, no. It could work, I guess. By the way, you notice I'm not asking you why you need to find the identity of a woman in a picture from fifteen, twenty years ago?'

'I do.'

'I just wanted it noted for the record.'

'So noted. It's a long story.'

'You need someone to tell?'

'I might. I might also need someone to watch the kids for a few hours.'

'I'm available and alone.' Pause. 'Sheesh, I have to stop saying that.'

'Where's Vickie?' Vickie was Cora's daughter.

'She's spending the night at the McMansion with my ex and his horse-faced wife. Or as I prefer to put it, she's spending the night in the bunker with Adolf and Eva.'

Grace managed a smile.

'My car is in the shop,' Cora said. 'Can you pick me up on the way?'

'I'll be there right after I grab Max.'

Grace swung by the Montessori Enrichment program and grabbed her son. Max had that near-tears thing going on, having lost several of his Yu-Gi-Oh! cards to a classmate in some dumb game. Grace tried to humor him, but he wasn't in the mood. She gave up. She helped him get his jacket on. His hat was missing. So was one of his gloves. Another mother smiled and whistled while bundling up her little bundle in color-coordinated knit (hand-knit, no doubt) hat, scarf, and yes, matching gloves. She looked over at Grace and faked a sympathetic smile. Grace did not know this woman, but she disliked her intensely.

Being a mother, Grace thought, was a lot like being an artist – you are always insecure, you always feel like a phony, you know that everybody else is better at it than you. The mothers who doted obsessively on their offspring, the ones who performed their numbing tasks with that Stepford-ready smile and supernatural patience – you know, those mothers who always, *always,* have the right supplies for the ideal after-school craft ... Grace suspected that these women were profoundly disturbed.

Cora was waiting in the driveway of her bubble-gum-pink house. Everybody on the block hated the color. For a while, one neighbor, a prissy thing properly named Missy, had started up a petition demanding that Cora repaint it. Grace had seen Prissy Missy passing around the petition at a first-grade soccer game. Grace had asked to see it, ripped it up, and walked away.

The color was hardly to Grace's taste, but memo to the Missys of the world: Get over yourselves.

Cora teetered toward them in her stiletto heels. She was dressed slightly more demurely – a sweatshirt over the leotard – but it really didn't matter. Some women oozed sex, even if dressed in a burlap sack. Cora was one of them. When she moved, new curves were formed even as old ones disappeared. Every line from her husky voice, no matter how innocuous, came out as a double entendre. Every tilt of the head was a come-on.

Cora slid in and looked back at Max. 'Hey, handsome.'

Max grunted and didn't look up.

'Just like my ex.' Cora spun back around. 'You got that photo?'

'I do.'

'I called Gus. He'll do it.'

'Did you promise anything in return?'

'Remember what I said about fifth-date syndrome? Well, are you free Saturday night?'

Grace looked at her.

'Kidding.'

'I knew that.'

'Good. Anyway, Gus said to scan the photo and e-mail it to him. He can set up an anonymous e-mail address for you to receive replies. No one will know who you are. We'll keep the text to a minimum, just say that a journalist is doing a story and needs to know the origin of the photograph. That sound okay?'

'Yeah, thanks.'

They arrived at the house. Max stomped upstairs and then shouted down, 'Can I watch *SpongeBob*?'

Grace acquiesced. Like every parent, Grace had strict rules about no TV during the day. Like every parent, she knew that rules were made to be broken. Cora headed straight for the cupboard and made coffee. Grace thought about which photograph to send and decided to use a blowup of the right side, the blonde with the X on her face and the redhead on her left. She left Jack's image – again, assuming that *was* Jack – out. She didn't yet want him involved. She decided that having two people increased chances of getting an identity hit and made the solicitation look less like the work of a crazed stalker.

Cora looked at the original photograph. 'May I make an observation?'

'Yes.'

'This is pretty weird.'

'The guy over here' – Grace pointed – 'the one with the beard. Who does that look like to you?'

Cora squinted. 'I guess it could be Jack.'

'Could be or is?'

'You tell me.'

'Jack's missing.'

'Come again?'

She told Cora the story. Cora listened, tapping a too-long fingernail painted up in Chanel's Rouge Noir, a color not unlike blood, on the tabletop. When Grace finished, Cora said, 'You know, of course, that I have a low opinion of men.'

'I know.'

'I believe that, for the most part, they are two floors below dog turd.'

'I know that too.'

'So the obvious answer is that, yes, this is a picture of Jack. That, yes, this little blondie, the one gazing up at him like he's the messiah, is an old flame. That yes, Jack and Mary Magdalene here are having an affair. That someone, maybe her current husband, wanted you to find out about it, so he sent you that picture. That everything came to a head when Jack realized that you were onto him.'

'And that's why he ran away?'

'Correct.'

'That doesn't add up, Cora.'

'You have a better theory?'

'I'm working on it.'

'Good,' Cora said, 'because I don't buy it either. I'm just talking. The rule is thus: Men are scum. Jack, however, has always hit me as the exception that proves the rule.'

'I love you, you know.'

Cora nodded. 'Everybody does.'

Grace heard a sound and glanced out the window. A stretch limousine of glistening black slid up the driveway with the smoothness of a Motown background singer. The chauffeur, a rat-faced man with the build of a whippet, hurried to open the car's back door.

Carl Vespa had arrived.

Despite his rumored vocation, Carl Vespa did not dress in Sopranos-style velour or shiny, sealant-coated suits. He preferred khakis, Joseph Abboud sports coats, and loafers *sans* socks. He was mid-sixties but looked a solid decade younger. His hair was tickling-the-shoulders long, the color a distinguished shade of blond-gone-to-gray. His face was tanned and had the sort

68

of waxy smoothness that suggests Botox. His teeth were aggressively capped, as if the front cuspids had taken growth hormones.

He nodded an order at the whippetlike driver and approached the house on his own. Grace opened the door to greet him. Carl Vespa gave her the toothy dazzler. She smiled back, glad to see him. He greeted her with a kiss on the cheek. No words were exchanged. They didn't need them. He held both her hands and looked at her. She could see his eyes start to well up.

Max moved to his mother's right. Vespa let go and took a step back.

'Max,' Grace began, 'this is Mr. Vespa.'

'Hello, Max.'

'That your car?' Max asked.

'Yes.'

Max looked at the car, then at Vespa. 'Got a TV inside?'

'It does.'

'Whoa.'

Cora cleared her throat.

'Oh, and this is my friend, Cora.'

'Charmed,' Vespa said.

Cora looked at the car, then at Vespa. 'You single?'

'I am.'

'Whoa.'

Grace repeated the baby-sitting instructions for the sixth time. Cora pretended to listen. Grace gave her twenty dollars to order pizza and that cheesy bread Max had become enamored with of late. A classmate's mom would bring Emma home in an hour.

Grace and Vespa headed toward the limousine. The rat-faced driver had the door opened and at the ready. Vespa said, 'This is Cram,' gesturing to the driver. When Cram shook her hand, Grace had to bite back a scream.

'A pleasure,' Cram said. His smile brought on visions of a Discovery Channel documentary on sea predators. She slid in first and Carl Vespa followed.

There were Waterford glasses and a matching decanter half-filled with a liquid that appeared both caramel and luxurious. There was, as noted, a television set. Above her seat was a DVD player, multiple CD player, climate controls, and enough buttons to confuse an airline pilot. The whole thing – the crystal, the decanter, the electronics – was overstated, but maybe that was what you wanted in a stretch limousine.

'Where are we going?' Grace asked.

'It's a little hard to explain.' They were sitting next to each other, both facing forward. 'I'd rather just show it to you, if that's okay.'

Carl Vespa had been the first lost parent to loom over her hospital bed. When Grace first came out of the coma, his was the first face she saw. She had no idea who he was, where she was, what day it was. More than a week was gone from her memory banks. Carl Vespa ended up sitting in her hospital room for days on end, sleeping in the chair next to her. He made sure that plenty of flowers surrounded her. He made sure that she had a good view, soothing music, enough pain medication, private nursing. He made sure that once Grace was able to eat, the hospital staff didn't give her the standard slop.

He never asked her for details of that night because, in truth, she really could not provide any. Over the next few months they talked for countless hours. He told her stories, mostly about his failures as a father. He had used his connections to get into her hospital room that first night. He had paid off security – interestingly enough, the security firm at the hospital was actually controlled by organized crime – and then he had simply sat with her.

Eventually other parents followed his lead. It was weird. They wanted to be around her. That was all. They found comfort in it. Their child had died in Grace's presence and it was as if maybe a small part of their souls, their forever-lost son or daughter, somehow still lived inside of her. It made no sense and yet Grace thought that maybe she understood.

These heartbroken parents came to talk about their dead children, and Grace listened. She figured that she owed them at least that much. She knew that these relationships were probably unhealthy, but there was no way she could turn them away. The truth was, Grace had no family of her own. She'd thrived, for a little while at least, on the attention. They needed a child; she needed a parent. It wasn't that simple – this malaise of cross-projection – but Grace wasn't sure she could explain it any better.

The limo headed south on the Garden State Parkway now. Cram flipped on the radio. Classical music, a violin concerto from the sound of it, came through the speakers.

Vespa said, 'You know, of course, that the anniversary is coming up.'

'I do,' she said, though she had done her best to ignore it all. Fifteen years. Fifteen years since that awful night at the Boston Garden. The papers had run all the expected 'Where Are They Now?' commemorative pieces. The parents and survivors all handled it differently. Most participated because they felt it was one way to keep the memory of what happened alive. There had been heart-wrenching articles on the Garrisons and the Reeds and the Weiders. The security guard, Gordon MacKenzie, who was credited with saving many by forcing open locked emergency exits, now worked as a police captain in Brookline, a Boston suburb. Even Carl Vespa had allowed a picture of him and his wife, Sharon, sitting in their yard, both still looking as if someone had just hollowed out their insides.

Grace had gone the other way. With her art career in full swing, she did not want even the appearance of capitalizing on the tragedy. She had been injured, that was all, and to make more of it than that reminded her of those washed-up actors who come out of the woodwork to shed crocodile tears when a hated costar suddenly dies. She wanted no part of it. The attention should be given to the dead and those they left behind.

'He's up for parole again,' Vespa said. 'Wade Larue, I mean.'

She knew, of course.

The stampede that night had been blamed on Wade Larue, currently a resident of Walden Prison outside Albany, New York. He was the one who fired the shots creating the panic. The defense's claim was interesting. They argued that Wade Larue didn't do it – forget the gun residue found on his hands, the gun belonging to him, the bullet match to the gun, the witnesses who saw him fire – but if he *did* do it, he was too stoned to remember. Oh, and if neither of those rationales floated your boat, Wade Larue couldn't have known that firing a gun would cause the death of eighteen people and the injury of dozens more.

The case proved to be controversial. The prosecutors went for eighteen counts of murder, but the jury didn't see it that way. Larue's lawyer ended up cutting a deal for eighteen counts of manslaughter. Nobody really worried too much about sentencing. Carl Vespa's only son had died that night. Remember what happened when Gotti's son was killed in a car accident? The man driving the car, a family man, has never been heard from again. A similar fate, most agreed, would befall Wade Larue, except this time, the general public would probably applaud the outcome.

For a while, Larue was kept isolated in Walden Prison. Grace didn't follow the story closely, but the parents – parents like Carl Vespa – still called and wrote all the time. They needed to see her every once in a while. As a survivor, she had become a vessel of some sort, carrying the dead. Putting aside the physical recuperation, this emotional pressure – this awesome, impossible responsibility – was a big part of the reason for Grace's going overseas.

Eventually Larue had been put in general population. Rumor had it he was beaten and abused by his fellow inmates, but for whatever reason, he lived. Carl Vespa had decided to forgo the hit. Maybe it was a sign of mercy. Or maybe it was just the opposite. Grace didn't know.

Vespa said, 'He finally stopped claiming total innocence. Did you hear that? He admits he fired his gun, but that he just freaked out when the lights went out.'

Which made sense. For her part, Grace had seen Wade Larue only once. She had been called to testify, though her testimony had nothing to do with guilt and innocence – she had almost no memory of the stampede, never mind who fired the gun – and everything to do with inflaming the passion of the jury. But Grace didn't need revenge. To her Wade Larue was stoned out of his mind, a souped-up punk more worthy of pity than hate.

'Do you think he'll get out?' she asked.

'He has a new lawyer. She's damn good.'

'And if she gets him released?'

Vespa smiled. 'Don't believe everything you read about me.' Then he added, 'Besides, Wade Larue isn't the only one to blame for that night.'

'What do you mean?'

He opened his mouth and then fell silent. Then: 'It's like I said. I'd rather show you.'

Something about his tone told her to change subjects. 'You said you were single,' Grace said.

'Pardon?'

'You told my friend you were single.'

He waved his finger. No ring. 'Sharon and I divorced two years ago.'

'I'm sorry to hear that.'

'It hasn't been right for a long time.' He shrugged, looking off. 'How is your family?'

'Okay.'

'I sense some hesitation.'

She may have shrugged.

'On the phone, you said you needed my help.'

'I think so.'

'So what's wrong?'

'My husband ...' She stopped. 'I think my husband is in trouble.'

She told him the story. His eyes stayed straight ahead, avoiding her gaze. He nodded every once in a while, but the nods seemed strangely out of context. His expression didn't change, which was strange. Carl Vespa was usually more animated. After she stopped talking, he didn't say anything for a long time.

'This photograph,' Vespa said. 'Do you have it with you?'

'Yes.' She handed it to him. His hand, she noticed, had a small quake. Vespa stared at the picture for a very long time.

'Can I keep this?' he asked.

'I have copies.'

Vespa's eyes were still on the images. 'Do you mind if I ask you a few personal questions?' he asked.

'I guess not.'

'Do you love your husband?'

'Very much.'

'Does he love you?'

'Yes.'

Carl Vespa had only met Jack once. He had sent a wedding gift when they got married. He sent gifts on Emma's and Max's birthdays too. Grace wrote him thank-you notes and gave the gifts to charity. She didn't mind being connected to him, she guessed, but she didn't want her children ... what was the phrase? ... tainted by the association.

'You two met in Paris, right?'

'Southern France, actually. Why?'

'And how did you meet again?'

'What's the difference?'

He hesitated a second too long. 'I guess I'm trying to learn how well you know your husband.'

'We've been married ten years.'

'I understand that.' He shifted in his seat. 'You were there on vacation when you met?'

'I don't know if I'd call it a vacation exactly.'

'You were studying. You were painting.'

'Yes.'

'And, well, mostly you were running away.'

She said nothing.

'And Jack?' Vespa continued. 'Why was he there?'

'Same reason, I guess.'

'He was running away?'

'Yes.'

'From what?'

'I don't know.'

'May I state the obvious then?'

She waited.

'Whatever he was running from' – Vespa gestured toward the photograph – 'it caught up to him.'

The thought had occurred to Grace too. 'That was a long time ago.'

'So was the Boston Massacre. Your running away. Did it make it go away?'

In the rearview mirror she saw Cram glance at her, waiting for an answer. She kept still.

'Nothing stays in the past, Grace. You know that.'

'I love my husband.'

He nodded.

'Will you help me?'

'You know I will.'

The car veered off the Garden State Parkway. Up ahead, Grace saw an enormous bland structure with a cross on it. It looked like an airplane hangar. A neon sign stated that tickets were still available for the 'Concerts with the Lord.' A band called Rapture would be playing. Cram pulled the limo into a parking lot big enough to declare statehood.

'What are we doing here?'

'Finding God,' Carl Vespa said. 'Or maybe His opposite. Let's go inside, I want to show you something.'

13

This was nuts, Charlaine thought.

Her feet moved steadily toward Freddy Sykes's yard without thought or emotion. It had crossed her mind that she could be raising the danger stakes out of desperation, hungry as she was for any kind of drama in her life. But okay, again, so what? Really, when she thought about it, what was the worst that could happen? Suppose Mike did find out. Would he leave her? Would that be so bad?

Did she want to get caught?

Oh, enough with the amateur self-analysis. It wouldn't hurt to knock on Freddy's door, pretend to be neighborly. Two years ago, Mike had put up a four-foot-high stockade fence in the backyard. He had wanted one higher, but the town ordinance wouldn't allow it unless you owned a swimming pool.

Charlaine opened the gate separating her backyard from Freddy's. Odd. This was a first. She had never opened the gate before.

As she got closer to Freddy's back door, she realized how weathered his house was. The paint was peeling. The garden was overgrown. Weeds sprouted up through the cracks in the walk. There were patches of dead grass everywhere. She turned and glanced at her own house. She had never seen it from this angle. It too looked tired.

She was at Freddy's back door.

Okay, now what?

Knock on it, stupid.

She did. She started with a soft rap. No answer. She pounded louder. Nothing. She pressed her ear against the door. Like that would do any good. Like she'd hear a muffled cry or something.

There was no sound.

The shades were still down, but there were wedges that the shades couldn't quite cover. She put an eye up to an opening and peered in. The living room had a lime-green couch so worn it looked like it was melting. There was a vinyl recliner of maroon in the corner. The television looked new. The wall had old paintings of clowns. The piano was loaded with old black-and-white photographs. There was one of a wedding. Freddy's parents, Charlaine figured. There was another of the groom looking painfully handsome in an army uniform. There was one more photograph of the same man holding a baby, a smile spread across his face. Then the man – the soldier, the groom – was gone. The rest of the photographs were of either Freddy alone or with his mother.

The room was immaculate – no, preserved. Stuck in a time warp, unused, untouched. There was a collection of small figurines on a side table. More photographs too. A life, Charlaine thought. Freddy Sykes had a life. It was a strange thought, but there you have it.

Charlaine circled toward the garage. There was one window in the back. A flimsy curtain of pretend lace hung across it. She stood on her tiptoes. Her fingers gripped the window ledge. The wood was so old it almost broke away. Peeling paint flaked off like dandruff.

She looked into the garage.

There was another car.

Not a car actually. A minivan. A Ford Windstar. When you live in a town like this, you know all the models.

Freddy Sykes did not own a Ford Windstar.

Maybe his young Asian guest did. That would make sense, right?

She was not convinced.

So what next?

Charlaine stared down at the ground and wondered. She had been wondering since she first decided to approach the house. She had known before leaving the safety of her own kitchen that there would be no answer to her knocks. She also knew that peeking in the windows – peeping on the peeper? – would do no good.

The rock.

It was there, in what had once been a vegetable garden. She had seen Freddy use it once. It wasn't a real rock. It was one of those hide-a-keys. They were so common now that criminals probably looked for them before checking under the mat.

Charlaine bent down, picked up the rock, and turned it over. All she had to do was slide the little panel back and take the key out. She did so. The key rested in her palm, glistening in the sunlight.

Here was the line. The no-going-back line.

She moved toward the back door.

14

Still wearing the sea-predator smile, Cram opened the door and Grace stepped out of the limousine. Carl Vespa slid out on his own. The huge neon sign listed a church affiliation that Grace had never heard of. The motto, according to several signs around the edifice, seemed to indicate that this was 'God's House.' If that were true, God could use a more creative architect. The structure held all the splendor and warmth of a highway mega-store.

The interior was even worse – tacky enough to make Graceland look under-stated. The wall-to-wall carpeting was a shiny shade of red usually reserved for a mall girl's lipstick. The wallpaper was darker, more blood-colored, a velvet affair adorned with hundreds of stars and crosses. The effect made Grace dizzy. The main chapel or house of worship – or, most suitably, arena – held pews rather than seats. They looked uncomfortable, but then again wasn't standing encour-aged? The cynical side of Grace suspected that the reason all religious services had you sporadically stand had nothing to do with devotion and everything to do with keeping congregants from falling asleep.

As soon as she entered the arena, Grace felt a flutter in her heart.

The altar, done up in the green and gold of a cheerleader's uniform, was being wheeled offstage. Grace looked for preachers with bad toupees, but none were to be found. The band – Grace assumed this was Rapture – was setting up. Carl Vespa stopped in front of her, his eyes on the stage.

'Is this your church?' she asked him.

A small smile came to his lips. 'No.'

'Is it safe to assume that you're not a fan of, uh, Rapture?'

Vespa didn't answer the question. 'Let's move down closer to the stage.'

Cram took the lead. There were security guards, but they swept aside as if Cram were toxic.

'What's going on here?' Grace asked.

Vespa kept moving down the steps. When they reached what a theater would call the orchestra – what do you call the good seats in a church? – she looked up and got a whole new feel for the size of the place. It was a huge theater-in-the-round. The stage was in the center, surrounded on all sides. Grace felt the constriction in her throat.

Dress it up in a religious cloak, but there was no mistake.

This felt like a rock concert.

Vespa took her hand. 'It'll be okay.'

But it wouldn't be. She knew that. She had not been to a concert or sporting event in any 'arena venue' in fifteen years. She used to love going to concerts. She remembered seeing Bruce Springsteen and the E Street Band at Asbury Park

Convention Center during her high school days. What was strange to her, what she had realized even back then, was that the line between rock concert and intense religious service was not all that thick. There was a moment when Bruce played 'Meeting Across the River' followed by 'Jungleland' – two of Grace's favorites – when she was on her feet, her eyes closed, sheen of sweat on her face, when she was simply gone, lost, shaking with bliss, the same bliss she'd witness on TV when a televangelist got the crowd on its feet, hands raised and shaking.

She loved that feeling. And she knew that she never wanted to experience it again.

Grace pulled her hand away from Carl Vespa's. He nodded as if he understood. 'Come on,' he said gently. Grace limped behind him. The limp, it seemed to her, was getting more pronounced. Her leg throbbed. Psychological. She knew that. Tight spaces did not terrify her; huge auditoriums, especially jammed with people, did. The place was fairly empty now, thank He Who Lives Here, but her imagination entered the fray and provided the absent commotion.

Shrill feedback from the amplifier made her pull up. Someone was doing a sound test.

'What's this all about?' she asked Vespa.

His face was set. He veered to the left. Grace followed. There was a scoreboard-type sign above the stage announcing that Rapture was in the middle of a three-week gig and that they, Rapture, were: 'What God Has on His MP3.'

The band came onstage now for sound check. They gathered at center stage, had a brief discussion, and then started playing. Grace was surprised. They sounded pretty good. The lyrics were syrupy, full of stuff about skies and spread wings and ascensions and being lifted up. Eminem told a potential girlfriend to 'sit your drunk ass on that f***ing runway, ho.' These lyrics, in their own way, were equally jarring.

The lead singer was female. She had platinum blond hair, cut with bangs, and sang with her eyes cast toward the heavens. She looked about fourteen years old. A guitarist stood to her right. He was more heavy-metal rock, what with the medusa-black locks and a tattoo of a giant cross on his right bicep. He played hard, slashing at the strings as if they had pissed him off.

When there was a lull, Carl Vespa said, 'The song was written by Doug Bondy and Madison Seelinger.'

She shrugged.

'Doug Bondy wrote the music. Madison Seelinger – that's the singer up there – wrote the lyrics.'

'And I care because?'

'Doug Bondy is playing the drums.'

They moved to the side of the stage for a better look. The music started again. They stood by a speaker. Grace's ears took the pounding, but under normal conditions, she would actually have been enjoying the sound. Doug Bondy, the drummer, was pretty much hidden by the array of cymbals and snares surrounding him. She moved a little more to the side. She could see him better now. He was banging the skins, as they say, his eyes closed, his face at peace. He looked older than the other members of the band. He had a crewcut. His face was clean-shaven. He wore those black Elvis Costello glasses.

Grace felt that flutter in her chest expand. 'I want to go home,' she said.

'It's him, isn't it?'

'I want to go home.'

The drummer was still smacking the skins, lost in the music, when he turned and saw her. Their eyes met. And she knew. So did he.

It was Jimmy X.

She didn't wait. She started limping toward the exit. The music chased her down.

'Grace?'

It was Vespa. She ignored him. She pushed through the emergency exit door. The air felt cool in her lungs. She sucked it down, tried to let the dizziness fade. Cram was outside now, as if he knew that she'd take this exit. He smiled at her.

Carl Vespa came up behind her. 'It's him, right?'

'And what if it is?'

'What if ...' Vespa repeated, surprised. 'He's not innocent here. He's as much to blame –'

'I want to go home.'

Vespa stopped short as if she'd slapped him.

Calling him had been a mistake. She knew that now. She had lived. She had recovered. Sure, there was the limp. There was some pain. There was the occasional nightmare. But she was okay. She had gotten over it. They, the parents, never would. She saw it that first day – the shatter in their eyes – and while progress had been made, lives had been lived, pieces had been picked up, the shatter had never left. She looked now at Carl Vespa – at the eyes – and saw it all over again.

'Please,' she said to him. 'I just want to go home.'

15

Wu spotted the empty hide-a-key.

The rock was on the path by the back door, turned over like a dying crab. The cover had been slid open. Wu could see the key was gone. He remembered the first time he had approached a house that had been violated. He was six years old. The hut – it was one room, no plumbing – had been his own. The Kim government had not bothered with the niceties of keys. They had knocked the door down and dragged his mother away. Wu found her two days later. They had hung her from a tree. No one was allowed to cut her down, under penalty of death. A day later the birds found her.

His mother had been wrongly accused of being a traitor to the Great Leader, but guilt or innocence was irrelevant. An example was made of her anyway. This is what happens to those who defy us. Check that: This is what happens to anyone we *think may be* defying us.

No one took in the six-year-old Eric. No orphanage picked him up. He did not become a ward of the state. Eric Wu ran away. He slept in the woods. He ate out of garbage cans. He survived. At thirteen, he was arrested for stealing and thrown in jail. The chief guard, a man more crooked than anyone he housed, saw Wu's potential. And so it began.

Wu stared down at the empty hide-a-key.

Someone was in the house.

He glanced at the house next door. His best guess would be that it was the woman who lived there. She liked to watch out the window. She would know where Freddy Sykes hid a key.

He considered his options. There were two.

One, he could simply leave.

Jack Lawson was in the trunk. Wu had a vehicle. He could take off, steal another car, begin his journey, set up residence elsewhere.

Problem: Wu's fingerprints were inside the house, along with the severely wounded, perhaps dead, Freddy Sykes. The lingerie-clad woman, if it was the woman, would be able to identify him too. Wu was fresh out of prison and on parole. The DA had suspected him of terrible crimes, but they could not prove them. So they cut a deal in exchange for his testimony. Wu had spent time in a maximum security penitentiary in Walden, New York. Next to what he had experienced in his homeland, the prison might as well have been a Four Seasons.

But that didn't mean he wanted to go back.

No, option one was no good. So that left option two.

Wu silently opened the door and slid inside.

Back in the limousine, Grace and Carl Vespa fell into silence.

Grace kept flashing back to the last time she'd seen Jimmy X's face – fifteen years ago in her hospital. He'd been forced to visit, a photo op arranged by his promoter, but he couldn't even look at her, never mind speak. He just stood by her bed, flowers clutched in his hand, his head down like a little boy's waiting for the teacher to scold him. She never said a word. Eventually he handed her the flowers and walked out.

Jimmy X quit the business and ran off. Rumor had it he moved to a private island near Fiji. Now, fifteen years later, here he was in New Jersey, playing drums for a Christian rock band.

When they pulled onto her street, Vespa said, 'It hasn't gotten any better, you know.'

Grace looked out the window. 'Jimmy X didn't fire the gun.'

'I know that.'

'So what do you want from him?'

'He's never said he's sorry.'

'And that would be enough?'

He thought about that, and then said, 'There was a boy who survived. David Reed. You remember him?'

'Yes.'

'He was standing next to Ryan. They were body to body. But when the crush began, this Reed kid somehow got lifted up on someone's shoulder. He got on the stage.'

'I know.'

'You remember what his parents said?'

She did but she said nothing.

'Jesus lifted up their son. It was God's will.' Vespa's voice had not changed, but Grace could feel the hidden rage like a blast furnace. 'You see, Mr. and Mrs. Reed prayed and God responded. It was a miracle, they said. God looked out for their son, that's what they kept repeating. As if God didn't have the desire or inclination to save mine.'

They fell into silence. Grace wanted to tell him that many good people died that day, many people with good parents who prayed, that God does not discriminate. But Vespa knew all that. It would not comfort.

By the time they pulled into the driveway, night was falling. Grace could see the silhouettes of Cora and the kids in the kitchen window. Vespa said, 'I want to help you find your husband.'

'I'm not even sure what you can do.'

'You'd be surprised,' he said. 'You have my number. No matter what you need, call me. No matter what time it is, I don't care. I'll be there.'

Cram opened the door. Vespa walked her to the door.

'I'll be in touch,' he said.

'Thank you.'

'I'm also going to assign Cram here to watch your house.'

She looked at Cram. Cram sort of smiled back.

'That won't be necessary.'

'Humor me,' he said.

'No, really, I don't want that. Please.'

Vespa thought about it. 'If you change your mind ...?'

'I'll let you know.'

He turned to leave then. She watched him walk back to the car and wondered about the wisdom of making deals with the devil. Cram opened the door. The limo seemed to swallow Vespa whole. Cram nodded at her. Grace did not move. She considered herself pretty good at reading people, but Carl Vespa had changed her view. She never saw or even sensed a hint of evil in him. Yet she knew it was there.

Evil – real evil – was like that.

Cora put on boiling water for the Ronzoni penne. She threw a jar of Prego into a saucepan and then leaned close to Grace's ear.

'I'm going to check the e-mail to see if we got any replies,' Cora whispered.

Grace nodded. She was helping Emma do her homework and trying like hell to care. Her daughter was dressed in a Jason Kidd Nets basketball jersey. She called herself Bob. She wanted to be a jock. Grace didn't know how she felt about it, but she guessed it was better than buying *Teen Beat* magazine and lusting after nonthreatening boy bands.

Mrs. Lamb, Emma's young-but-quickly-aging teacher, had the kids working on the multiplication tables. They were doing the sixes. Grace tested Emma. At six times seven, Emma paused for a long time.

'You should know it by heart,' Grace said.

'Why? I can figure it out.'

'That's not the point. You learn it by heart so you can build off that when you start multiplying numbers with multiple digits.'

'Mrs. Lamb didn't say to memorize them.'

'You should.'

'But Mrs. Lamb –'

'Six times seven.'

And so it went.

Max had to find an item to put in the 'Secret Box.' You put something in the box – in this case, a hockey puck – and you made up three clues so that your fellow kindergartners could guess what it was. Clue one: The item is black. Clue two: It's used in a sport. Clue three: Ice. Fair enough.

Cora came back from the computer shaking her head. Nothing yet. She grabbed a bottle of Lindemans, a decent-yet-cheap Chardonnay from Australia, and popped the cork. Grace put the kids to bed.

'Where's Daddy?' Max asked.

Emma echoed the sentiment. 'I wrote the hockey verse for my poem.'

Grace said something vague about Jack having to work. The kids looked wary.

'I'd love to hear the poem,' Grace said.

Grudgingly Emma produced her journal.

'Hockey stick, hockey stick,
Do you love to score?

81

When you are used to shoot,
Do you feel like you want more?'

Emma looked up. Grace said, 'Wow' and clapped, but she was simply not as good at the enthusiasm game as Jack. She kissed them both good night and headed back downstairs. The wine bottle was open. She and Cora began to drink. She missed Jack. He'd been gone less than twenty-four hours – he'd been gone longer on business trips plenty of times – and yet the house seemed to sag somehow. Something felt lost, irretrievably so. The missing of him had already become a physical ache.

Grace and Cora drank some more. Grace thought about her children. She thought about a life, a whole life, without Jack. We do anything to shield our children from pain. Losing Jack would, no doubt, crush Grace. But that was okay. She could take it. Her pain, however, would be nothing next to what it would do to the two children upstairs who, she knew, lay awake, sensing something was amiss.

Grace looked at the photographs lining the walls.

Cora moved next to her. 'He's a good man.'

'Yeah.'

'You okay?'

'Too much wine,' Grace said.

'Not enough, you ask me. Where did Mr. Mobster take you?'

'To see a Christian rock band.'

'Quite the first date.'

'It's a long story.'

'I'm all ears.'

But Grace shook her head. She didn't want to think about Jimmy X. An idea came to her. She mulled it over, let it settle.

'What?' Cora said.

'Maybe Jack made more than one call.'

'You mean, besides the call to his sister?'

'Yes.'

Cora nodded. 'Have you set up an online account?'

'We have AOL.'

'No, I mean for your phone bill.'

'Not yet.'

'No time like the present then.' Cora stood up. There was a teeter to her step now. The wine was making them both warm. 'Who do you use for long distance?'

'Cascade.'

They were back by Jack's computer. Cora sat at the desk, cracked her knuckles, and went to work. She brought up Cascade's Web site. Grace gave her the necessary information – address, social security number, credit card. They came up with a password. Cascade sent an e-mail to Jack's account verifying that he'd just signed up for online billing.

'We're in,' Cora said.

'I don't get it.'

'An online billing account. I just set it up. You can now view and pay your phone bill over the Internet.'

Grace looked over Cora's shoulder. 'That's last month's bill.'

'Yep.'

'But it won't have the calls from last night.'

'Hmm. Let me e-mail a request. We can also call Cascade and ask.'

'They're not open twenty-four-seven. Part of the discount service.' Grace leaned closer to the monitor. 'Let me see if he called his sister before last night.'

Her eyes skimmed down the list. Nothing. No unfamiliar numbers either. She no longer felt weird doing this, spying on the husband she loved and trusted, which of course felt weird in and of itself.

'Who pays the bills?' Cora asked.

'Jack does most of them.'

'The phone bill comes to the house?'

'Yes.'

'You look at it?'

'Sure.'

Cora nodded. 'Jack has a cell phone, right?'

'Right.'

'What about that bill?'

'What about it?'

'Do you look at it?'

'No, it's his.'

Cora smiled.

'What?'

'When my ex was cheating on me, he used the cell because I never looked at those bills.'

'Jack isn't cheating.'

'But he may be keeping secrets, right?'

'Could be,' Grace allowed. 'Okay, yeah, probably.'

'So where would he keep the phone bills for his mobile?'

Grace checked the file cabinet. He saved the bills from Cascade. She checked under the Vs for Verizon Wireless. Nothing. 'They're not here.'

Cora rubbed her hands together. 'Ooo, suspicious.' She was into it now. 'So let's do that voodoo that they do that we do.'

'And what exactly do we do?'

'Let's say Jack is keeping something from you. He would probably destroy the bills the minute he gets them, right?'

Grace shook her head. 'This is so bizarre.'

'But am I right?'

'Yeah, okay, if Jack is keeping secrets from me –'

'Everyone has secrets, Grace. C'mon, you know that. Are you telling me that this all comes as a total surprise?'

This truth would normally have made Grace pause, but there was no time for such indulgences. 'Okay, so let's say Jack did destroy the cell phone bills – how are we going to get them?'

'Same way I just did. We set up another online account, this time under Verizon Wireless.' Cora started typing.

'Cora?'

'Yep.'

'Can I ask you something?'

'Shoot.'

'How do you know how to do all this?'

'Practical experience.' She stopped typing and looked back at Grace. 'How do you think I found out about Adolf and Eva?'

'You spied on them?'

'Yup. I bought a book called *Spying for Dodos* or something like that. It's all in there. I wanted to make sure I had all the facts before I confronted his sorry ass.'

'What did he say when you showed it to him?'

'That he was sorry. That he'd never do it again. That he'd give up Ivana of the Implant and never see her again.'

Grace watched her friend type. 'You really love him, don't you?'

'More than life itself.' Still typing, Cora added, 'How about opening another bottle of wine?'

'Only if we're not driving tonight.'

'You want me to sleep here?'

'We shouldn't drive, Cora.'

'Okay, deal.'

Grace stood and felt her head reel from the drink. She headed back into the kitchen. Cora often drank too much, but tonight Grace was happy to join her. She opened another bottle of the Lindemans. The wine was warm so she put an ice cube in both. Gauche, but they liked it cold.

When Grace got back into the office, the printer was whirring. She handed Cora a glass and sat. Grace stared at the wine. She started shaking her head.

'What?' Cora said.

'I finally met Jack's sister.'

'So?'

'I mean, think about it. Sandra Koval. I didn't even know her name before now.'

'You never asked Jack about her?'

'Not really.'

'Why not?'

Grace took a sip. 'I can't really explain it.'

'Try.'

She looked up and wondered how to put it. 'I thought it was healthy. You know, keeping parts of yourself private. I was running away from something. He never pushed me on it.'

'So you never pushed him either?'

'It was more than that.'

'What?'

Grace thought about it. 'I never bought into that "we have no secrets" stuff. Jack had a wealthy family and he wanted no part of it. There had been a falling out. I knew that much.'

'Wealthy from what?'

'What do you mean?'

'What business are they in?'

'Some kind of securities firm. Jack's grandfather started it. They have trust funds and options and voting shares, stuff like that. Nothing Onassis-like, but enough, I guess. Jack won't have anything to do with it. He won't vote. He won't touch the money. He set it up so the trust skips a generation.'

'So Emma and Max will get it?'

'Yep.'

'How do you feel about that?'

Grace shrugged. 'You know what I'm realizing?'

'I'm all ears.'

'The reason I never pushed Jack? It had nothing to do with respecting privacy.'

'Then what?'

'I loved him. I loved him more than any man I'd ever met ...'

'I feel a "but" coming here.'

Grace felt the tears press against her eyes. 'But it all felt so fragile. Does that make sense? When I was with him – this is going to sound so stupid – but when I was with Jack, it was the first time I was happy since, I don't know, since my father died.'

'You've had a lot of pain in your life,' Cora said.

Grace did not reply.

'You were scared it would go away. You didn't want to open yourself up to more.'

'So I chose ignorance?'

'Hey, ignorance is supposed to be bliss, right?'

'You buy that?'

Cora shrugged. 'If I never checked up on Adolf, he probably would have had his fling and gotten over it. Maybe I'd be living with the man I love.'

'You could still take him back.'

'Nope.'

'Why not?'

Cora thought about it. 'I need the ignorance, I guess.' She picked up her glass and took a long sip.

The printer finished whirring. Grace picked up the sheets and started examining them. Most of the phone numbers she knew. Point of fact, she knew almost all of them.

But one immediately jumped out at her.

'Where's six-oh-three area code?' Grace asked.

'Beats me. Which call?'

Grace showed her on the monitor. Cora moved the cursor over it.

'What are you doing?' Grace asked.

'You click the number, they tell you who called.'

'For real?'

'Man, what century do you live in? They have talkies now.'

'So all you have to do is click the link?'

'And it'll tell all. Unless the number is unlisted.'

Cora clicked the left mouse button. A box appeared saying:

NO RECORD OF THAT NUMBER.

'There you go. Unlisted.'

Grace checked her watch. 'It's only nine-thirty,' she said. 'Not too late to call.'

'Under the missing-husband rule, no, not too late at all.'

85

Grace picked up the phone and inputted the number. A piercing feedback, not unlike the one at the Rapture concert, slapped her eardrum. Then: 'The number you have called' – the robotic voice stated the number – 'has been disconnected. No further information is available.'

Grace frowned.

'What?'

'When was the last time Jack called it?'

Cora checked. 'Three weeks ago. He talked for eighteen minutes.'

'It's disconnected.'

'Hmm, six-oh-three area code,' Cora said, moving to another Web site. She typed in '603 area code' and hit the enter button. The answer came right up. 'It's in New Hampshire. Hold on, let's Google it.'

'Google what? New Hampshire?'

'The phone number.'

'What will that do?'

'Your number is unlisted, right?'

'Right.'

'Hold on, let me show you something. This doesn't work every time, but watch.' Cora typed Grace's phone number into the search engine. 'What it will do is search the entire Web for those numbers in a row. Not just phone directories. That won't do it because, like you said, your number is unlisted. But ...'

Cora hit return. There was one search hit. The site was for an art prize offered at Brandeis University, her alma mater. Cora clicked the link. Grace's name and number came up. 'You were judging some painting award?'

Grace nodded. 'They were giving out an art scholarship.'

'Yep, there you are. Your name, address, and phone number with other judges. You must have given it to them.'

Grace shook her head.

'Throw away your eight-tracks and welcome to the Information Age,' Cora said. 'And now that I know your name, I can do a million different searches. Your gallery Web page will come up. Where you went to college. Whatever. Now let's try with this six-oh-three number....'

Cora's fingers flew again. She hit return. 'Hold on. We got something.' She squinted at the screen. 'Bob Dodd.'

'Bob?'

'Yes. Not Robert. Bob.' Cora looked back at Grace. 'Is the name familiar?'

'No.'

'The address is a PO box in Fitzwilliam, New Hampshire. You ever been?'

'No.'

'How about Jack?'

'I don't think so. I mean, he went to college in Vermont, so he might have visited New Hampshire, but we've never been there together.'

There was a sound from upstairs. Max cried out in his sleep.

'Go,' Cora said. 'I'll see what I can dig up on our friend Mr. Dodd.'

As Grace headed up toward her son's bedroom, another pang struck deep in her chest: Jack was the house's night sentinel. He handled nightmares and nocturnal requests for water. He was the one who held the kid's foreheads at 3 A.M. when they woke up to, er, throw up. During the day, Grace took care of the sniffles, the taking of the temperatures, the heating of chicken soup, the forcing down of Robitussin. The night shift was Jack's.

Max was sobbing when she reached his room. His cries were soft now, more a whimper, and somehow that was more pitiful than the loudest of screams. Grace wrapped her arms around him. His little body was shaking. She rocked back and forth and gently shushed him. She whispered that Mommy was here, that everything was okay, that he was safe.

It took Max a while to settle. Grace brought him to the bathroom. Even though Max was barely six, he peed like a man – that is to say, he missed the bowl entirely. He swayed, falling back asleep as he stood. When he finished, she helped him pull up his *Finding Nemo* pajamas. She tucked him back in and asked if he wanted to tell her about his dream. He shook his head and fell back asleep.

Grace watched his little chest rise and fall. He looked very much like his father.

After a while she headed back downstairs. There was no sound. Cora was no longer clacking the keyboard. Grace entered the office. The chair was empty. Cora stood in the corner. She gripped the wineglass.

'Cora?'

'I know why Bob Dodd's phone was disconnected.'

There was a tightness in Cora's voice, one Grace had never heard. She waited for her friend to continue, but she seemed to be shrinking into the corner.

'What happened?' Grace asked.

Cora downed a quick sip. 'According to an article in the *New Hampshire Post*, Bob Dodd is dead. He was murdered two weeks ago.'

16

Eric Wu stepped inside the Sykes house.

The house was dark. Wu had left all the lights out. The intruder – whoever had taken the key out of the rock – had not turned them on. Wu wondered about that.

He had assumed the intruder was the nosey woman in the lingerie. Would she be smart enough to know not to turn the lights on?

He stopped. More than that: If you have the forethought not to turn on the lights, wouldn't you have the forethought not to leave the hide-a-key in plain sight?

Something did not add up.

Wu lowered himself and moved behind the recliner. He stopped and listened. Nothing. If someone was in the house, he would hear them move. He waited some more.

Still nothing.

Wu mulled it over. Could the intruder have come and gone?

He doubted it. A person who would take the risk of entering with a hidden key would look around. They would probably find Freddy Sykes in the upstairs bathroom. They would call for help. Or if they left, if they found nothing amiss, they would have put the key back in the rock. None of that had happened.

What then was the most logical conclusion?

The intruder was still in the house. Not moving. Hiding.

Wu trod gently. There were three exits. He made sure all the doors were locked. Two doors had bolt locks. He carefully slid them into place. He took the dining room chairs and placed them in front of all three exits. He wanted something, anything, to block or at least slow down an easy escape.

Trap his adversary.

The stairway was carpeted. That made it easier to pad up in silence. Wu wanted to check the bathroom, to see if Freddy Sykes was still in the tub. He thought again about the hide-a-key in plain sight. Nothing about this setup made sense. The more he thought about it, the slower his step.

Wu tried to think it through. Start from the beginning: A person who knows where Sykes keeps a hide-a-key opens the door. He or she comes inside. Now what? If he finds Sykes, panic would ensue. He would call the police. If he doesn't find Sykes, well, he leaves. He puts the key back in the rock and puts the rock away.

But neither one of those things had happened.

So again, what could Wu conclude?

The only other possibility that came to mind – unless he was missing something – was that the intruder had indeed found Sykes, just as Wu entered the house. There had been no time to call for help. There had only been time to hide.

But that scenario had problems too. Wouldn't the intruder have turned on a light? Perhaps she had. Perhaps she had turned on the light, but then she saw Wu approach. She might have turned off the lights and hidden where she was.

In the bathroom with Sykes.

Wu was in the master bedroom now. He could see the crack under the bathroom door. The light was still off. Do not underestimate your foe, he reminded himself. He had made mistakes recently. Too many of them. First, Rocky Conwell. Wu had been sloppy enough to allow him to follow. That had been mistake one. Second, Wu had been spotted by the woman next door. Sloppy.

And now this.

It was tough to look at yourself critically, but Wu tried to step away and do just that. He was not infallible. Only fools believe that. Perhaps his time in prison had rusted him somehow. Didn't matter. Wu needed to focus now. He needed to concentrate.

There were more photographs in Sykes's bedroom. This had been Freddy's mother's room for fifty years. Wu knew that from his online encounters. Sykes's father had died during the Korean War. Sykes had been an infant. The mother had never gotten over it. People react differently to the death of a loved one. Mrs. Sykes had decided to dwell with her ghost instead of the living. She spent the rest of her life in this same bedroom – in the same bed even – that she'd shared with her soldier husband. She slept on her side, Freddy said. She never let anyone, not even when young Freddy had a nightmare, touch the side of the bed where her beloved had once lain.

Wu's hand was on the doorknob now.

The bathroom, he knew, was small. He tried to picture an angle someone might use to attack. There really was none. Wu had a gun in his duffel bag. He wondered if he should take it out. If the intruder was armed, then it could be a problem.

Overconfident? Maybe. But Wu didn't think he'd need a weapon.

He turned the knob and pushed hard.

Freddy Sykes was still in the tub. The gag was in his mouth. His eyes were closed. Wu wondered if Freddy was dead. Probably. No one else was here. There was no place to hide. Nobody had come to Freddy's rescue.

Wu moved toward the window. He looked out at the house now, at the house next door.

The woman – the one who'd been in the lingerie – was there.

In her house. Standing by the window.

She stared back at him.

That was when Wu heard the car door slam. There was no siren, but now, as he turned toward the driveway, he could see the red cruiser lights.

The police were here.

Charlaine Swain was not crazy.

She watched movies. She read books. Lots of them. Escapism, she had thought. Entertainment. A way to numb the boredom every day. But maybe these movies and books were oddly educational. How many times had she shouted at the plucky heroine – the oh-so-guileless, witch-skinny, raven-haired beauty – not to go into that damned house?

Too many. So now, when it had been her turn ... uh-uh, no way. Charlaine Swain was not about to make that mistake.

She had stood in front of Freddy's back door staring at that hide-a-key. She couldn't go inside per her movie and book training, but she couldn't just leave it alone either. Something was wrong. A man was in trouble. You can't just walk away from that.

So she came up with an idea.

It was simple really. She took the key out of the rock. It was in her pocket now. She left the hide-a-key in plain view, not because she wanted the Asian guy to see it, but because that would be her excuse for calling the police.

The moment the Asian guy entered Freddy's house, she dialed 911. 'Someone is in the neighbor's house,' she told them. The clincher: The hide-a-key was strewn on the walkway.

Now the police were here.

One cruiser had made the turn onto her block. The siren was silent. The car was not speeding bat-out-of-hell style, just moving at a clip solidly above the speed limit. Charlaine risked a look back at Freddy's house.

The Asian man was watching her.

17

Grace stared at the headline. 'He was murdered?'

Cora nodded.

'How?'

'Bob Dodd was shot in the head in front of his wife. Gangland style, they called it, whatever that means.'

'They catch who did it?'

'Nope.'

'When?'

'When was he murdered?'

'Yeah, when?'

'Four days after Jack called him.'

Cora moved back toward the computer. Grace considered the date.

'It couldn't have been Jack.'

'Uh huh.'

'It would be impossible. Jack hasn't traveled out of the state in more than a month.'

'You say so.'

'What's that supposed to mean?'

'Nothing, Grace. I'm on your side, okay? I don't think Jack killed anybody either, but c'mon, let's get a grip here.'

'Meaning?'

'Meaning stop with the "hasn't traveled out of state" nonsense. New Hampshire is hardly California. You can drive up in four hours. You can fly up in one.'

Grace rubbed her eyes.

'Something else,' Cora went on. 'I know why he's listed as Bob, not Robert.'

'Why?'

'He's a reporter. That's his byline. Bob Dodd. Google listed one hundred and twenty-six hits on his name over the past three years for the *New Hampshire Post*. The obituary called him – where's the line? – "a hard-nosed investigative reporter, famous for his controversial exposés"– like the New Hampshire mob rubbed him out to keep him quiet.'

'And you don't think that's the case?'

'Who knows? But skimming through his articles, I'd say Bob Dodd was more like an "On Your Side" reporter, you know – he finds dishwasher repairmen scamming old ladies, wedding photographers who bail out with the deposit, that sorta thing.'

'He could have pissed someone off.'

Cora's tone was flat. 'Yup, could have. And, what, you think it's a coincidence – Jack calling the guy before he died?'

'No, there's no coincidence here.' Grace tried to process what she was hearing. 'Hold up.'

'What?'

'That photograph. There were five people in it. Two women, three men. This is a long shot ...'

Cora was already typing. 'But maybe Bob Dodd is one of them?'

'There are image search engines, right?'

'Already there.'

Her fingers flew, her cursor pointed, her mouse slid. There were two pages, a total of twelve picture hits for Bob Dodd. The first page featured a hunter with the same name living out in Wisconsin. On the second page – the eleventh hit – they found a table photograph taken at a charity function in Bristol, New Hampshire.

Bob Dodd, a reporter for the *New Hampshire Post*, was the first face on the left.

They didn't need to study it closely. Bob Dodd was African-American. Everyone in the mystery photograph was white.

Grace frowned. 'There still has to be a connection.'

'Let me see if I can dig up a bio on him. Maybe they went to college together or something.'

There was a gentle rapping at the front door. Grace and Cora looked at each other. 'Late,' Cora said.

The knocking came again, still soft. There was a doorbell. Whoever was there had chosen not to use it. Must know she had kids. Grace rose and Cora followed. At the door she flicked on the outside light and peered out the window on the side of the door. She should have been more surprised, but Grace guessed that maybe she was beyond that.

'Who's that?' Cora asked.

'The man who changed my life,' Grace said softly.

She opened the door. Jimmy X stood on the stoop looking down.

Wu had to smile.

That woman. As soon as he saw those siren lights, he put it together. Her ingenuity was both admirable and grating.

No time for that.

What to do ...?

Jack Lawson was tied up in the trunk. Wu realized now that he should have fled the moment he saw that hide-a-key. Another mistake. How many more could he afford?

Minimize the damage. That was the key here. There was no way to prevent it all – the damage, that is. He would be hurt here. It would cost him. His fingerprints were in the house. The woman next door had probably already given the police a description. Sykes, alive or dead, would be found. There was nothing he could do about that either.

Conclusion: If he was caught, he would go to jail for a very long time.

The police cruiser pulled into the driveway.

Wu snapped into survival mode. He hurried downstairs. Through the window he saw the cruiser glide to a stop. It was dark out now, but the street was well lit. A tall black man in full uniform came out. He put on his police cap. His gun remained in his holster.

That was good.

The black police officer was barely on the walk when Wu opened the front door and smiled widely. 'Something I can do for you, Officer?'

He did not draw his weapon. Wu had counted on that. This was a family neighborhood in the great American expanse known as the suburbs. A Ho-Ho-Kus police officer probably responds to several hundred possible burglaries during his career. Most, if not all, were false alarms.

'We got a call about a possible break-in,' the officer said.

Wu frowned, feigning confusion. He took a step outside but kept his distance. Not yet, he thought. Be nonthreatening. Wu's moves were intentionally laconic, setting a slow pace. 'Wait, I know. I forgot my key. Someone probably saw me going in through the back.'

'You live here, Mr ...?'

'Chang,' Wu said. 'Yes, I do. Oh, but it's not my house, if that's what you mean. It belongs to my partner, Frederick Sykes.'

Now Wu risked another step.

'I see,' the officer said. 'And Mr. Sykes is ...?'

'Upstairs.'

'May I see him please?'

'Sure, come on in.' Wu turned his back to the officer and yelled up the stairs. 'Freddy? Freddy, throw something on. The police are here.'

Wu did not have to turn around. He knew the tall black man was moving up behind him. He was only five yards away now. Wu stepped back into the house. He held the door open and gave the officer what he thought was an effeminate smile. The officer – his name tag read Richardson – moved toward the door.

When he was only a yard away, Wu uncoiled.

Office Richardson had hesitated, perhaps sensing something, but it was too late. The blow, aimed for the center of his gut, was a palm strike. Richardson folded in half like a deck chair. Wu moved closer. He wanted to disable. He did not want to kill.

An injured policeman produces heat. A dead policeman raises the temperature tenfold.

The cop was doubled over. Wu hit him behind the legs. Richardson dropped to his knees. Wu used a pressure point technique. He dug the knuckles of his index fingers into both sides of Richardson's head, up and into the ear cavity under the cartilage, an area known as Triple Warmer 17. You need to get the right angle. Go full strength and you could kill someone. You needed precision here.

Richardson's eyes went white. Wu released the hold. Richardson dropped like a marionette with its strings cut.

The knockout would not last long. Wu took the handcuffs from the man's belt and cuffed his wrist to the stairwell. He ripped the radio from his shoulder.

Wu considered the woman next door. She'd be watching.

She would surely call the police again. He wondered about that, but there was no time. If he tried to attack, she would see him and lock the door. It would take too long. His best bet was to use time and surprise here. He hurried to the garage and got into Jack Lawson's minivan. He checked the cargo area in the back.

Jack Lawson was there.

Wu moved to the driver's seat now. He had a plan.

Charlaine had a bad feeling the moment she saw the policeman step out of the car.

For one thing, he was alone. She had assumed that there would be two of them, partners, again from TV – *Starsky and Hutch*, *Adam-12*, Briscoe and Green. She realized now that she had made a mistake. Her call had been too casual. She should have claimed to see something menacing, something frightening, so that they would have arrived more wary and prepared. Instead she had simply come across as a nosey neighbor, a dotty woman who had nothing better to do but call the cops for any little thing.

The policeman's body language too was all wrong. He sauntered toward the door, slack and casual, not a care in the world. Charlaine couldn't see the front door from where she was, only the driveway. When the officer disappeared from view, Charlaine felt her stomach drop.

She considered shouting out a warning. The problem was – and this might sound strange – the new Pella windows they had installed last year. They opened vertically, with a hand crank. By the time she slid open both locks and cranked the handle, well, the officer would already be out of sight. And really, what could she yell? What kind of warning? What in the end did she really know?

So she waited.

Mike was in the house. He was downstairs in the den, watching the Yankees on the YES Network. The divided night. They never watched TV together anymore. The way he flipped the remote was maddening. They liked different shows. But really, she didn't think that was it. She could watch anything. Still Mike took the den; she had the bedroom. They both watched alone, in the dark. Again she didn't know when that had started. The children weren't home tonight – Mike's brother had taken them to the movies – but when they were, they stayed in their own rooms. Charlaine tried to limit the Web surf time, but it was impossible. In her youth, friends talked on the phone for hours. Now they instant-messaged and lord-knew-what over the Internet.

This was what her family became – four separate entities in the dark, interacting with one another only when necessary.

She saw the light go on in the Sykes garage. Through the window, the one covered with flimsy lace, Charlaine could see a shadow. Movement. In the garage. Why? There would be no need for the police officer to be in there. She reached for the phone and dialed 911, even as she began to head for the stairs.

'I called you a little while ago,' she told the 911 operator.

'Yes?'

'About a break-in at my neighbor's house.'

'An officer is responding.'

'Yeah, I know that. I saw him pull up.'

Silence. She felt like a dope.

'I think something might have happened.'

'What did you see?'

'I think he may have been attacked. Your officer. Please send someone quickly.'

She hung up. The more she'd explain, the stupider it would sound.

The familiar churning noise started up. Charlaine knew what it was. Freddy's electric garage door. The man had done something to the cop. He was going to escape.

And that was when Charlaine decided to do something truly stupid.

She thought back to those wicked-witch-thin heroines, the ones with the mind-scooped stupidity, and wondered if any of them, even the most brain dead, had ever done something so colossally stupid. She doubted it. She knew that when she looked back on the choice she was about to make – assuming she survived it – she would laugh and maybe, just maybe, have a little more respect for the protagonists who enter dark homes in just their bra and panties.

Here was the thing: The Asian guy was about to escape. He had hurt Freddy. He had hurt a cop; she was sure of it. By the time the cops responded, he would be gone. They wouldn't find him. It would be too late.

And if he got away, then what?

He had seen her. She knew that. At the window. He had probably already figured out that she was the one who called the police. Freddy could be dead. So too the cop. Who was the only witness left?

Charlaine.

He would come back for her, wouldn't he? And even if he didn't, even he decided to let her be, well, at best, she would live in fear. She'd be jumpy in the night. She'd look for him in crowds during the days. Maybe he would simply want revenge. Maybe he would go after Mike or the kids ...

She could not let that happen. She had to stop him now.

How?

Wanting to prevent his escape was all fine and good, but let's stay real here. What could she do? They didn't own a gun. She couldn't just run outside and jump on his back and try to claw his eyes. No, she had to be cleverer than that.

She had to follow him.

On the surface it sounded ridiculous, but add it up. If he got away, the result would be fear. Pure, unadulterated, probably unending terror until he was captured, which might be never. Charlaine had seen the man's face. She had seen his eyes. She couldn't live with that.

Following him – running a tail, as they say on TV – made sense, when you considered the alternatives. She would follow him in her car. She would keep her distance. She would have the cell phone. She would be able to tell the police where he was. The plan did not involve following him long, just until the police could take over. Right now, if she didn't act, she knew what would happen: The police would arrive; the Asian man would be gone.

There was no alternative.

The more she thought about it, the less nutsy it sounded. She'd be in a moving car. She'd stay comfortably behind him. She'd be on her cell phone with a 911 operator.

Wasn't that safer than letting him go?

She ran downstairs.

'Charlaine?'

It was Mike. He stood there, in the kitchen, standing over the sink eating peanut-butter crackers. She stopped for a second. His eyes probed her face in a way only he could, in a way only he ever had. She was taken back to her days at

95

Vanderbilt, when they first fell in love. The way he looked at her then, the way he looked at her now. He was skinnier back then and so handsome. But the look, the eyes, they were the same.

'What's wrong?' he asked.

'I need' – she stopped, caught her breath – 'I need to go somewhere.'

His eyes. Probing. She remembered the first time she ever saw him, that sunny day at Centennial Park in Nashville. How far had they come? Mike still saw. He still saw her in a way that no one else ever had. For a moment Charlaine could not move. She thought that she might cry. Mike dropped the crackers into the sink and started toward her.

'I'll drive,' Mike said.

18

Grace and the famous rocker known as Jimmy X were alone in the den-cum-playroom. Max's Game Boy was lying on its back. The battery case had broken, so now the two double As were held in place by Scotch tape. The game cartridge, lying next to it as if it'd been spit out, was called Super Mario Five, which, according to Grace's less than sophisticated eye, appeared to be exactly the same as Super Mario One through Four.

Cora had left them alone and returned to her role as cybersleuth. Jimmy had still not spoken. He sat with his forearms against his thighs, his head hanging, reminding Grace of the first time she'd seen him, in her hospital room not long after she regained consciousness.

He wanted her to talk first. She could see that. But she had nothing to say to him.

'I'm sorry to stop by so late,' he said.

'I thought you had a gig tonight.'

'Already over.'

'Early,' she said.

'The concerts usually end by nine. It's how the promoters like it.'

'How did you know where I lived?'

Jimmy shrugged. 'I guess I've always known.'

'What's that supposed to mean?'

He didn't answer and she didn't push it. For several seconds the room was dead silent.

'I'm not sure how to begin,' Jimmy said. Then, after a brief pause, he added, 'You still limp.'

'Good opening,' she said.

He tried to smile.

'Yes, I limp.'

'From ...?'

'Yes.'

'I'm sorry.'

'I got off easy.'

The shadow crossed his face. His head, the one he'd finally worked up the nerve to lift, dropped back down as if it had learned its lesson.

Jimmy still had the cheekbones. The famed blond locks were gone, from either genetics or a razor's edge, she couldn't tell which. He was older, of course. His youth was over and she wondered if that was true for her too.

'I lost everything that night,' he began. Then he stopped and shook his head. 'That didn't come out right. I'm not here for pity.'

She said nothing.

'Do you remember when I came to see you at the hospital?'

She nodded.

'I'd read every newspaper story. Every magazine story. I watched all the news reports. I can tell you about every kid that died that night. Every one of them. I know their faces. I close my eyes, I still see them.'

'Jimmy?'

He looked up again.

'You shouldn't be telling me this. Those kids had families.'

'I know that.'

'I'm not the one to give you absolution.'

'You think that's what I came here for?'

Grace did not reply.

'It's just ...' He shook his head. 'I don't know why I came, okay? I saw you tonight. At the church. And I could see you knew who I was.' He tilted his head. 'How did you find me anyway?'

'I didn't.'

'The man you were with?'

'Carl Vespa.'

'Oh Christ.' He closed his eyes. 'Father of Ryan.'

'Yes.'

'He brought you?'

'Yes.'

'What does he want?'

Grace thought about that. 'I don't think he knows.'

Now it was Jimmy's turn to stay silent.

'He thinks he wants an apology.'

'Thinks?'

'What he really wants is his son back.'

The air felt heavy. She shifted in her chair. Jimmy's face had no color.

'I tried, you know. To apologize, I mean. He's right about that. I owe them that. At the very least. And I'm not talking about that stupid photo op with you at the hospital. My manager wanted that. I was so stoned I just went along. I could barely stand.' He stared at her. He had those same intense eyes that had made him an instant MTV darling. 'Do you remember Tommy Garrison?'

She did. He had died in the stampede. His parents were Ed and Selma.

'His picture touched me. I mean, they all did, you know. These lives, they were all just starting out ...' He stopped again, took a deep breath, tried again. 'But Tommy, he looked like my kid brother. I couldn't get him out of my head. So I went to his house. I wanted to apologize to his parents ...' He stopped.

'What happened?'

'I got there. We sat at their kitchen table. I remember I put my elbows on it and the whole thing teetered. They had this linoleum floor, half coming up. The wallpaper, this awful yellow flowered stuff, was peeling off the walls. Tommy was their only child. I looked at their lives, at their empty faces ... I couldn't bear it.'

She said nothing.

'That was when I ran.'

'Jimmy?'

He looked at her.

'Where have you been?'

'Lot of places.'

'Why?'

'Why what?'

'Why did you just give it all up?'

He shrugged. 'There wasn't all that much, really. The music business, well, I won't go into it, but let's just say I hadn't received much money yet. I was new. It takes a while to get serious money. I didn't care. I just wanted out.'

'So where do you go?'

'I started in Alaska. Worked gutting fish, if you can believe that. Did that for about a year. Then I started traveling, played with a couple of small bar bands. In Seattle I found a group of old hippies. They used to do IDs for members of the Weather Underground, that kinda thing. They got me new papers. The closest I came back here, I played with a cover band in an Atlantic City casino for a while. At the Tropicana. I dyed my hair. I stuck to the drums. Nobody recognized me, or if they did, they didn't much care.'

'Were you happy?'

'You want the truth? No. I wanted to come back. I wanted to make amends and move on. But the longer I was gone, the harder it was, the more I longed for it. The whole thing was a vicious circle. And then I met Madison.'

'The lead singer of Rapture?'

'Yeah. Madison. Can you believe that name? It's huge now. You remember that movie *Splash*, the one with Tom Hanks and what's-her-name?'

'Daryl Hannah,' Grace said automatically.

'Right, the blond mermaid. Remember that scene where Tom Hanks is trying to come up with a name for her and he says all kinds of stuff like Jennifer or Stephanie and they're walking past Madison Avenue and he just mentions the street name and she wants it to be her name and that's a big laugh in the movie, right, a woman named Madison. Now it's a top-ten name.'

Grace let it go.

'Anyway, she's from a farm town in Minnesota. She ran away to the Big Apple when she was fifteen, ended up strung out and homeless in Atlantic City. She landed at a homeless shelter for runaway teens. She found Jesus, you know the deal, trading one addiction for another, and started singing. She has a voice like a Janis Joplin angel.'

'Does she know who you are?'

'No. You know how Shania has Mutt Lange in the background? That's what I wanted. I like working with her. I like the music, but I wanted to stay out of the spotlight. At least that's what I tell myself. Madison is painfully shy. She won't perform unless I'm onstage with her. She'll get over that, but for now I figured drums are a pretty good disguise.'

He shrugged, tried a smile. There was still a hint of the old knock-'em-back charisma. 'Guess I was wrong about that.'

They were silent for a moment.

'I still don't understand,' Grace said.

He looked at her.

'I said before I'm not the one to give you absolution. I meant that. But the truth is, you didn't fire a gun that night.'

Jimmy stayed still.

'The Who. When they had that stampede in Cincinnati, they got over it. And the Stones, when that Hell's Angel killed a guy at their concert. They're still playing. I can see wanting out for a little while, a year or two ...'

Jimmy looked to the right. 'I should leave.'

He stood.

'Going to disappear again?' she asked.

He hesitated and then reached into his pocket. He pulled out a card and handed it to her. There were ten digits on it and nothing more. 'I don't have a home address or anything, just this mobile phone.'

He turned and started for the door. Grace did not follow. Under normal circumstances, she might have pushed him, but in the end, his visit was an aside, a not very important one in the scheme of things. Her past had a curious pull, that was all. Especially now.

'Take care of yourself, Grace.'

'You too, Jimmy.'

She sat in the den, feeling the exhaustion begin to weigh on her shoulders, and wondered where Jack was right now.

Mike did indeed drive. The Asian man had nearly a minute head start, but what was good about their twisty development of cul-de-sacs, tract houses, nicely wooded lots – this wondrous serpentine sprawl of suburbia – was that there was only one true entrance and exit road.

In this stretch of Ho-Ho-Kus, all roads led to Hollywood Avenue.

Charlaine filled Mike in as quickly as possible. She told him most of it, about how she'd looked out the window and spotted the man and grown suspicious. Mike listened without interrupting. There were holes the size of a heartache in her story. She left out why she had been looking out the window in the first place, for example. Mike must have seen the holes, but right now he was letting it go.

Charlaine studied his profile and traveled back to the first time they met. She had been a freshman at Vanderbilt University. There was a park in Nashville, not far from campus, with a replica of the Parthenon, the one in Athens. Originally built in 1897 for the Centennial Expo, the structure was thought to be the most realistic replica of the famed site atop the Acropolis anywhere in the world. If you wanted to know what the actual Parthenon looked like in its heyday, well, people would travel to Nashville, Tennessee.

She was sitting there on a warm fall day, just eighteen years old, staring at the edifice, imagining what it must have been like in Ancient Greece, when a voice said, 'It doesn't work, does it?'

She turned. Mike had his hands in his pocket. He looked so damned handsome. 'Excuse me?'

He took a step closer, a half smile on his lips, moving with a confidence that drew her. Mike gestured with his head toward the enormous structure. 'It's an exact replica, right? You look at it, and this is what they saw, great philosophers like Plato and Socrates, and all I can think is' – he stopped, shrugged – 'is that all there is?'

She smiled at him. She saw his eyes widen and knew that the smile had landed hard. 'It leaves nothing to the imagination,' she said.

Mike tilted his head. 'What do you mean?'

'You see the ruins of the real Parthenon and you try to imagine what it would have looked like. But the reality, which this is, can never live up to what your mind conjures up.'

Mike nodded slowly, considering.

'You don't agree?' she asked.

'I had another theory,' Mike said.

'I'd like to hear it.'

He moved closer and bent down on his haunches. 'There are no ghosts.'

Now she did the head tilt.

'You need the history. You need the people in their sandals walking through it. You need the years, the blood, the deaths, the sweat from, what, four hundred years B.C. Socrates never prayed in there. Plato didn't argue by its door. Replicas never have the ghosts. They're bodies without souls.'

The young Charlaine smiled again. 'You use this line on all the girls?'

'It's new, actually. I'm trying it out. Any good?'

She lifted her hand, palm down, and turned it back and forth. 'Eh.'

Charlaine had been with no other man since that day. For years they returned to the fake Parthenon on their anniversary. This had been the first year they hadn't gone back.

'There he is,' Mike said.

The Ford Windstar was traveling west on Hollywood Avenue toward Route 17. Charlaine was back on the phone with a 911 operator. The operator was finally taking her seriously.

'We lost radio contact with our officer at the scene,' she said.

'He's heading onto Route 17 south at the Hollywood Avenue entrance,' Charlaine said. 'He's driving a Ford Windstar.'

'License plate?'

'I can't see it.'

'We have officers responding to both scenes. You can drop your pursuit now.'

She lowered the phone. 'Mike?'

'It's okay,' he said.

She sat back and thought about her own house, about ghosts, about bodies without souls.

Eric Wu was not easily surprised.

Seeing the woman from the house and this man he assumed was her husband following him – that definitely registered as something he would not have predicted. He wondered how to handle it.

The woman.

She had set him up. She was following him. She had called the police. They had sent an officer. He knew then that she would call again.

What Wu had counted on, however, was putting enough distance between himself and the Sykes household before the police responded to her call. When it comes to tracking down vehicles the police are far from omnipotent. Think about the Washington sniper a few years back. They had hundreds of officers. They had roadblocks. For an embarrassingly long time they couldn't locate two amateurs.

If Wu could get enough miles ahead, he would be safe.

But now there was a problem.

That woman again.

That woman and her husband were following him. They would be able to tell the police where he was going, what road he was on, what direction he was heading. He would not be able to put the distance between him and the authorities.

Conclusion: Wu had to stop them.

He spotted the sign for the Paramus Park Mall and took the jug-handle back over the highway. The woman and her husband followed. It was late at night. The stores were closed. The lot was empty. Wu pulled into it. The woman and her husband kept their distance.

That was okay.

Because it was time to call their bluff.

Wu had a gun, a Walther PPK. He didn't like using it. Not that he was squeamish. Wu simply preferred his hands. He was decent with a gun; he was expert with his hands. He had perfect control with them. They were a part of him. With a gun you are forced to trust the mechanics, an outside source. Wu did not like that.

But he understood the need.

He stopped the car. He made sure the gun was loaded. His car door was unlocked. He pulled the handle, stepped out of the vehicle, and aimed his weapon.

Mike said, 'What the hell is he doing?'

Charlaine watched the Ford Windstar enter the mall lot. There were no other cars. The lot was well lit, bathed in a shopping-center fluorescent glow. She could see Sears up ahead, the Office Depot, Sports Authority.

The Ford Windstar drifted to a stop.

'Keep back,' she said.

'We're in a locked car,' Mike said. 'What can he do?'

The Asian man moved with fluidity and grace, and yet there was also deliberation, as if each movement had been carefully planned in advanced. It was a strange combination, the way he moved, almost inhuman. But right now the man stood next to his car, his entire body still. His arm swept forward, only the arm, the rest of him so undisturbed by the motion that you might think it was an optical illusion.

And then their windshield exploded.

The noise was sudden and deafening. Charlaine screamed. Something splashed on her face, something wet and syrupy. There was a coppery smell in the air now. Instinctively Charlaine ducked. The glass from the windshield rained down on her head. Something slumped against her, pushing her down.

It was Mike.

She screamed again. The scream mixed with the sound of another bullet being fired. She had to move, had to get out, had to get them out of here. Mike was not moving. She shoved him off her and risked raising her head.

Another shot whistled past her.

She had no idea where it landed. Her head was back down. There was a screaming in her ears. A few seconds passed. Charlaine finally risked a glance.

The man was walking toward her.

What now?

102

Escape. Flee. That was the only thought that came through.

How?

She shifted the car into reverse. Mike's foot was still on the brake. She dropped low. Her hand stretched out and took hold of his slack ankle. She slid his foot off the brake. Still wedged into the foot area Charlaine managed to jam her palm on the accelerator. She pushed down with everything she had. The car jerked back. She could not move. She had no idea where she was going.

But they were moving.

She kept her palm pressed down to the floor. The car jolted over something, a curb maybe. The bounce banged her head against the steering column. Using her shoulder blades, she tried to keep the wheel steady. Her left hand still pressed down on the accelerator. They hit another bump. She held on. The road was smoother now. But just for a moment. Charlaine heard the honking of horns, the screech of tires and brakes, and the awful whir of cars spinning out of control.

There was an impact, a terrible jarring, and then, a few seconds later, darkness.

19

The color in Officer Daley's face had ebbed away.

Perlmutter sat up. 'What is it?'

Daley stared at the sheet of paper in his hand as if he feared it might flee. 'Something doesn't make sense here, Cap.'

When Captain Perlmutter had started working as a cop, he hated the night shift. The quiet and solitude got to him. He had grown up in a big family, one of seven kids, and he liked that life. He and his wife Marion planned on having a big family. He had the whole thing figured out – the barbecues, the weekends coaching one kid or the other, the school conferences, the family movies on Friday night, the summer nights on the front porch – the life he'd experienced growing up in Brooklyn, but with a suburban, bigger-house twist.

His grandmother used to spew Yiddish quotes all the time. Stu Perlmutter's personal favorite had been this: 'Man plans and God laughs.' Marion, the only woman he had ever loved, died of a sudden embolism when she was thirty-one. She'd been in the kitchen, making Sammy – that was their son, their only child – a sandwich when the embolism hit. She was dead before she landed on the linoleum.

Perlmutter's life pretty much ended that day. He did what he could to raise Sammy, but the truth was, his heart was never really in it. He loved the boy and enjoyed his job, but he had lived for Marion. This precinct, his work, had become his solace. Home, being with Sammy, reminded him of Marion and all they'd never have. Here, alone, he could almost forget.

All of that was a long time ago. Sammy was in college now. He had turned into a good man, despite his father's inattentiveness. There was something to be said for that, but Perlmutter did not know what.

Perlmutter signaled for Daley to sit down. 'So what's up?'

'That woman. Grace Lawson.'

'Ah,' Perlmutter said.

'Ah?'

'I was just thinking about her too.'

'Something about her case bothering you, Captain?'

'Yep.'

'I thought it was just me.'

Perlmutter tipped his chair back. 'Do you know who she is?'

'Ms. Lawson?'

'Yup.'

'She's an artist.'

'More than that. You notice the limp?'

'Yes.'

'Her married name is Grace Lawson. But once upon a time, her name – her maiden name, I guess – was Grace Sharpe.'

Daley looked at him blankly.

'You ever hear of the Boston Massacre?'

'Wait, you mean that rock concert riot?'

'More a stampede, but yeah. Lot of people died.'

'She was there?'

Perlmutter nodded. 'Badly injured too. In a coma for a while. Press gave her the full fifteen minutes and then some.'

'How long ago was that?'

'What, fifteen, sixteen years ago maybe.'

'But you remember?'

'It was big news. And I was a big fan of the Jimmy X Band.'

Daley looked surprised. 'You?'

'Hey, I wasn't always an old fart.'

'Heard their CD. It was pretty damn good. Radio still plays "Pale Ink" all the time.'

'One of the best songs ever.'

Marion had liked the Jimmy X Band. Perlmutter remembered her constantly blasting 'Pale Ink' on an old Walkman, her eyes closed, her lips moving as she silently sang along. He blinked the image away.

'So what happened to them?'

'The massacre destroyed the band. They broke up. Jimmy X – I don't remember his real name anymore – was the front man and wrote all the songs. He just up and quit.' Perlmutter pointed to the piece of paper in Daley's hand. 'So what's that?'

'That's what I wanted to talk to you about.'

'Something to do with the Lawson case?'

'I don't know.' Then: 'Yeah, maybe.'

Perlmutter put his hands behind his head. 'Start talking.'

'DiBartola got a call early tonight,' Daley said. 'Another missing husband case.'

'Similarities to Lawson?'

'No. I mean, not at first. This guy wasn't even her husband anymore. An ex. And he isn't exactly squeaky clean.'

'He's got a record?'

'Did time for assault.'

'Name?'

'Rocky Conwell.'

'Rocky? For real?'

'Yep, that's what it says on his birth certificate.'

'Parents.' Perlmutter made a face. 'Wait, why does that name ring a bell?'

'He played a little pro ball.'

Perlmutter searched the memory banks, shrugged. 'So what's the deal?'

'Okay, like I said, this case looks even more cut-and-dry than Lawson. Ex-husband who was supposed to take his wife out shopping this morning. I mean, it's nothing. It's less than nothing. But DiBartola sees the wife – her name is Lorraine – well, she's a royal babe. So you know DiBartola.'

'A pig,' Permutter said with a nod. 'Ranked in the top ten by both the AP and UPI.'

105

'Right, so he figures, what the hell, humor her, right? She's separated, so you never know. Maybe something would swing his way.'

'Very professional.' Perlmutter frowned. 'Go on.'

'This is where it gets weird.' Daley licked his lips. 'DiBartola, he does the simple thing. He runs the E-ZPass.'

'Like you.'

'*Exactly* like me.'

'What do you mean?'

'He gets a hit.' Daley took another step into the room. 'Rocky Conwell crossed the tollbooth off Exit 16 on the New York Thruway. At exactly ten-twenty-six last night.'

Perlmutter looked at him.

'Yeah, I know. Exact same time and place as Jack Lawson.'

Perlmutter scanned the report. 'You're sure about this? DiBartola didn't accidentally run the same number we did or something?'

'Checked it twice. There's no mistake. Conwell and Lawson crossed the toll at the exact same time. They had to be together.'

Perlmutter mulled it over and shook his head. 'No.'

Daley looked confused. 'You think it's a coincidence?'

'Two separate cars, crossing the toll at the same time? Not likely.'

'So how do you figure it?'

'I'm not sure,' Perlmutter said. 'Let's say they, I don't know, ran away together. Or Conwell kidnapped Lawson. Or hell, Lawson kidnapped Conwell. Whatever. They'd be in the same car. There would be only one E-ZPass hit, not two.'

'Right, okay.'

'But they were in two separate cars. That's what's throwing me. Both men in separate cars cross the toll at the same time. And now both men are missing.'

'Except Lawson called his wife,' Daley added. 'He needed space, remember?'

They both thought about it.

Daley said, 'You want me to call Ms. Lawson? See if she knows this Conwell guy?'

Perlmutter plucked on his bottom lip and thought about it. 'Not yet. Besides it's late. She's got kids.'

'So what should we do?'

'A little more investigating. Let's talk to Rocky Conwell's ex-wife first. See if we dig up a connection between Conwell and Lawson. Put his car out there, see if we get a hit.'

The phone rang. Daley was working the switchboard as well. He picked it up, listened, and then turned to Perlmutter.

'Who was that?'

'Phil over at the Ho-Ho-Kus station.'

'Something wrong?'

'They think an officer might be down. They want our help.'

20

Beatrice Smith was a fifty-three-year-old widow.

Eric Wu was back in the Ford Windstar. He took Ridgewood Avenue to the Garden State Parkway north. He headed east on Interstate 287 toward the Tappan Zee Bridge. He exited at Armonk in New York. He was on side roads now. He knew exactly where he was going. He had made mistakes, yes, but the basics were still with him.

One of those basics: Have a backup residence lined up.

Beatrice Smith's husband had been a popular cardiologist, even serving a term as town mayor. They'd had lots of friends, but they were all 'couple' friends. When Maury – that was her husband's name – died of a sudden heart attack, the friends stayed around for a month or two and then faded away. Her only child, a son, and a doctor like his father, lived in San Diego with his wife and three children. She kept the house, the same house she had shared with Maury, but it was big and lonely. She was thinking about selling it and moving into Manhattan, but the prices were just too steep right now. And she was afraid. Armonk was all she knew. Would it be jumping from the frying pan into the fire?

She had confided all of this online to the fictional Kurt McFaddon, a widower from Philadelphia who was considering relocating to New York City. Wu pulled onto her street and slowed. The surroundings were quiet and woodsy and very private. It was late. A fake delivery would not work at this hour. There would be no time or even need for subtlety. Wu would not be able to keep this host alive.

There could be nothing to connect Beatrice Smith to Freddy Sykes.

In short, Beatrice Smith could not be found. Not ever.

Wu parked the car, put on his gloves – no fingerprints this time – and approached the house.

21

At 5 a.m., Grace threw on a bathrobe – Jack's robe – and headed downstairs. She always wore Jack's clothes. He'd kindly request lingerie, but she preferred his pajama tops. 'Well?' she'd ask, modeling the top. 'Not bad,' he'd reply, 'but why not try wearing just the bottoms instead. Now that would be a look.' She shook her head at the memory and reached the computer room.

The first thing Grace did was check the e-mail address they were using to receive replies from their spam of the photograph. What she saw surprised her.

They were no replies.

Not one.

How could that be? It was conceivable, she guessed, that nobody recognized the women in the photograph. She'd been prepared for that possibility. But by now they had sent out hundreds of thousands of e-mails to people. Even with spam blocks and all that, *someone* should have responded with at the very least an expletive, some crackpot with time on his hands, someone fed up with the overflow of spam who'd need to vent.

Someone.

But she had not received even one reply.

What should she make of that?

The house was quiet. Emma and Max were still asleep. So too was Cora. Cora was snoring, stretched out on her back, her mouth open.

Switch gears, Grace thought.

She knew that Bob Dodd, the murdered reporter, was now her best, perhaps only, lead, and let's face it, it was a pretty flimsy one. She had no phone contact for him, no next of kin, not even a street address. Still, Dodd had been a reporter for a fairly major newspaper, the *New Hampshire Post*. She decided that was the best place to start.

Newspapers don't really close – at least, that was what Grace figured. Someone has to be manning the *Post* desk in case a big story broke. It also figured that the reporter stuck working at 5 A.M. might be bored and more apt to talk to her. So she picked up the phone.

Grace was not sure how to approach this. She considered various angles, pretending, for example, to be a reporter doing a story, asking for collegial assistance, but she wasn't sure she'd be able to talk the talk.

In the end she decided to try to keep as close to the truth as possible.

She pressed *67 to block the Caller ID. The newspaper had a toll-free line. Grace didn't use it. You can't block Caller ID from toll-free numbers. She had learned that somewhere and stockpiled it in the back brain closet, the same closet where she stored information about Daryl Hannah being in *Splash* and

Esperanza Diaz being the wrestler dubbed Little Pocahontas, the same closet that helped make Grace, in Jack's words, 'Mistress of the Useless Factoid.'

The first two calls to the *New Hampshire Post* went nowhere. The guy at the news desk simply could not be bothered. He hadn't really known Bob Dodd and barely listened to her pitch. Grace waited twenty minutes and tried again. This time she got routed to Metro, where a woman who sounded very young informed Grace that she had just started at the paper, that this was her first job ever, that she didn't know Bob Dodd, but gee, wasn't it awful what happened to him?

Grace checked the e-mails again. Still nothing.

'Mommy!'

It was Max.

'Mommy, come quick!'

Grace hurried up the stairs.

'What is it, honey?'

Max sat in his bed and pointed to his foot. 'My toe is growing too fast.'

'Your toe?'

'Look.'

She moved next to him and sat down.

'See?'

'See what, honey?'

'My second toe,' he began. 'It's bigger than my big toe. It's growing too fast.'

Grace smiled. 'That's normal, honey.'

'Huh?'

'Lots of people have a second toe that's longer than their big one. Your daddy has that.'

'No way.'

'Yup, way. His second toe is longer than the big one on the end.'

That seemed to appease him. Grace felt another pang. 'You want to watch *The Wiggles*?' she asked him.

'That's a baby show.'

'Let's see what's on *Playhouse Disney*, okay?'

Rolie Polie Olie was on, and Max settled into the couch to watch. He liked to use the cushions as blankets, making a total mess of the place. Grace was beyond caring. She tried the *New Hampshire Post* again. This time she asked for features.

The man who answered had a voice like old tires on a gravel road. 'What's up?'

'Good morning,' Grace said, too cheerfully, smiling into the phone like a dim-wit.

The man made a noise which, loosely translated, said: *Get on with it.*

'I'm trying to get some information on Bob Dodd.'

'Who is this?'

'I'd rather not say.'

'You're kidding, right? Look, sweetheart, I'm going to hang up now –'

'Wait a second. I can't go into details, but if it turns into a major scoop –'

'Major scoop? Did you just say major scoop?'

'Yes.'

The man started cackling. 'And what, you think I'm like Pavlov's dog or something. Say major scoop and I'll salivate.'

'I just need to know about Bob Dodd.'

'Why?'

'Because my husband is missing and I think it might have something to do with his murder.'

That made him pause. 'You're kidding me, right?'

'No,' Grace said. 'Look, I just need to find someone who knew Bob Dodd.'

The voice was softer now. 'I knew him.'

'Did you know him well?'

'Well enough. What do you want?'

'Do you know what he was working on?'

'Look, lady, do you have information on Bob's murder? Because if you do, forget the major scoop crap and tell the police.'

'Nothing like that.'

'Then what?'

'I was going through some old phone bills. My husband talked to Bob Dodd not long before he was murdered.'

'And your husband is?'

'I'm not going to tell you that. It's probably just a coincidence.'

'But you said your husband is missing?'

'Yes.'

'And you're concerned enough to be following up on this old phone call?'

'I've got nothing else,' Grace said.

There was a pause. 'You're going to have to do better than that,' the man said.

'I don't think I can.'

Silence.

'Ah, what's the harm? I don't know anything. Bob didn't confide in me.'

'Who would he confide in?'

'You can try his wife.'

Grace almost slapped herself in the head. How could she not have thought of something so obvious? Man, she was in over her head here. 'Do you know how I can locate her?'

'Not sure. I only met her, what, once, maybe twice.'

'What's her name?'

'Jillian. That's with a J, I think.'

'Jillian Dodd?'

'I guess.'

She wrote it down.

'There's another person you might try. Bob's father, Robert Senior. He must be in his eighties, but I think they were pretty close.'

'Do you have an address for him?'

'Yeah, he's in some nursing home in Connecticut. We shipped Bob's stuff there.'

'Stuff?'

'Cleaned out his desk myself. Put the stuff in a cardboard box for him.'

Grace frowned. 'And you sent it to his father's nursing home?'

'Yup.'

'Why not to Jillian, the wife?'

There was a brief pause. 'Don't know actually. I think she freaked after the murder. She was there, you know. Hold on a second, let me find the number of the nursing home. You can ask yourself.'

Charlaine wanted to sit next to the hospital bed.

You always see that in movies and on TV – doting wives sitting bedside, holding the hand of their beloved – but in this room there was no chair made for that. The one chair in the room was too low to the ground, the sort of thing that opened up into a sleeper, and yes, that might come in handy later, but now, right now, Charlaine just wanted to sit and hold her husband's hand.

She stood instead. Every once in a while she sat on the bed's edge, but she feared that might disturb Mike. So she'd stand again. And maybe that was good. Maybe that felt a little like penance.

The door behind her opened. Her back was to it. She did not bother turning around. A man's voice, one she hadn't heard before, said, 'How are you feeling?'

'I'm fine.'

'You were lucky.'

She nodded. 'I feel like I won the lottery.'

Charlaine reached up and touched the bandage on her forehead. A few stitches and possible slight concussion. That was all she had suffered during the accident. Scrapes, bruises, a few stitches.

'How is your husband?'

She did not bother replying. The bullet had hit Mike in the neck. He still had not regained consciousness, though the doctors had informed her that they believed 'the worst was over,' whatever that meant.

'Mr. Sykes is going to live,' the man behind her said. 'Because of you. He owes you his life. A few more hours in that tub ...'

The man – she assumed that he was yet another police officer – let his voice drift off. She finally turned and faced him. Yep, a cop. In uniform nonetheless. The patch on his arm said he was from the Kasselton Police Department.

'I already talked to the Ho-Ho-Kus detectives,' she said.

'I know that.'

'I really don't know any more, Officer ...?'

'Perlmutter,' he said. 'Captain Stuart Perlmutter.'

She turned back toward the bed. Mike had his shirt off. His belly rose and fell as if it were being inflated at a gas station. He was overweight, Mike, and the act of breathing, just breathing, seemed to put undue stress on him. He should have taken better care of his health. She should have insisted on it.

'Who's with your kids?' Perlmutter asked.

'Mike's brother and sister-in-law.'

'Anything I can get you?'

'No.'

Charlaine changed her grip on Mike's hand.

'I was going over your statement.'

She did not reply.

'Do you mind if I ask you a few follow-up questions?'

'I'm not sure I understand,' Charlaine said.

'Pardon?'

'I live in Ho-Ho-Kus. What does Kasselton have to do with it?'

'I'm just helping out.'

She nodded, though she had no idea why. 'I see.'

'According to your statement, you were looking out your bedroom window when you saw the hide-a-key on Mr. Sykes's back path. Is that correct?'

'Yes.'

'And that's why you called the police?'

'Yes.'

'Do you know Mr. Sykes?'

She shrugged, keeping her eyes on that rising and falling stomach. 'To say hello.'

'You mean like a neighbor?'

'Yes.'

'When was the last time you talked to him?'

'I didn't. I mean, I never really talked to him.'

'Just the neighborly hellos.'

She nodded.

'And the last time you did that?'

'Waved hello?'

'Yes.'

'I don't know. A week ago maybe.'

'I'm a little confused, Mrs. Swain, so maybe you can help me out here. You saw a hide-a-key on the path and just decided to call the police –'

'I also saw movement.'

'Pardon?'

'Movement. I saw something move in the house.'

'Like someone was inside?'

'Yes.'

'How did you know it wasn't Mr. Sykes?'

She turned around. 'I didn't. But I also saw the hide-a-key.'

'Lying there. In plain sight.'

'Yes.'

'I see. And you put two and two together?'

'Right.'

Perlmutter nodded as if suddenly understanding. 'And if Mr. Sykes had been the one to use the hide-a-key, he wouldn't have just tossed it onto the path. Was that your thinking?'

Charlaine said nothing.

'Because, see, that's what's weird to me, Mrs. Swain. This guy who broke into the house and assaulted Mr. Sykes. Why would he have left the hide-a-key out in plain sight like that? Wouldn't he have hidden it or taken it inside with him?'

Silence.

'And there's something else. Mr. Sykes sustained his injuries at least twenty-four hours before we found him. Do you think the hide-a-key was out on that path the whole time?'

'I wouldn't know.'

'No, I guess you wouldn't. It's not like you stare at his backyard or anything.'

She just looked at him.

'Why did you and your husband follow him, the guy who broke into the Sykes place, I mean?'

'I told the other officer –'

'You were trying to help out, so we wouldn't lose him.'

'I was also afraid.'

'Of what?'

'That he'd know I called the police.'

'Why would you worry about that?'

'I was watching from the window. When the police arrived. He turned and looked out and saw me.'

'And you thought, what, he'd go after you?'

'I don't know. I was scared, that's all.'

Perlmutter did that over-nod bit again. 'I guess that fits. I mean some of the pieces, well, you have to force them down, but that's normal. Most cases don't make perfect sense.'

She turned away from him again.

'You say he was driving a Ford Windstar.'

'That's right.'

'He pulled out of the garage in that vehicle, right?'

'Yes.'

'Did you see the license plate?'

'No.'

'Hmm. Why do you think he did that?'

'Did what?'

'Parked in the garage.'

'I have no idea. Maybe so no one would see his car.'

'Yeah, okay, that adds up.'

Charlaine took her husband's hand again. She remembered the last time they'd held hands. Two months ago, when they went to see a romantic comedy with Meg Ryan. Strangely enough Mike was a sucker for 'chick flicks.' His eyes welled up during bad romance movies. In real life, she could only remember seeing him cry once, when his father died. But at movies Mike sat in the dark and you would see a little quake in the face and then, yes, the tears would start. That night he reached out and took her hand, and what Charlaine remembered most – what tormented her now – was being unmoved. Mike had tried to interlace their fingers, but she shifted hers just enough to block him. That was how little it meant to Charlaine, nothing really, this overweight man with the comb-over reaching out to her.

'Could you please leave now?' she asked Perlmutter.

'You know I can't.'

She closed her eyes.

'I know about your tax problem.'

She stayed still.

'In fact, you called H&R Block this morning about it, isn't that right? That's where Mr. Sykes worked.'

She didn't want to let go of the hand, but it felt as though Mike was pulling away.

'Mrs. Swain?'

'Not here,' Charlaine said to Perlmutter. She let the hand drop and stood. 'Not in front of my husband.'

22

Nursing home residents are always in and happy to have a visitor. Grace called the number and a perky woman answered.

'Starshine Assisted Living!'

'I'd like to know about visiting hours,' Grace said.

'We don't have them!' She spoke in exclamations.

'Excuse me?'

'No visiting hours. You can visit anytime, twenty-four-seven.'

'Oh. I'd like to visit Mr. Robert Dodd.'

'Bobby? Well, let me connect you to his room. Oh wait, it's eight. He'll be at exercise class. Bobby likes to keep in shape.'

'Is there a way I can make an appointment?'

'To visit?'

'Yes.'

'No need, just stop by.'

The drive would take her a little under two hours. It would be better than trying to explain over the phone, especially in light of the fact that she didn't have a clue what she wanted to ask him about. The elderly are better in person anyway.

'Do you think he'll be in this morning?'

'Oh sure. Bobby stopped driving two years ago. He'll be here.'

'Thank you.'

'My pleasure.'

At the breakfast table, Max dug his hand deep into the box of Cap'n Crunch. The sight – her child going for the toy – made her pause. It was all so normal. Children sense things. Grace knew that. But sometimes, well, sometimes children are wonderfully oblivious. Right now she was grateful for that.

'You already got the toy out,' she said.

Max stopped. 'I did?'

'So many boxes, so crummy a toy.'

'What?'

The truth was, she had done the same thing when she was a kid – digging to get the worthless prize. Come to think of it, with the same cereal. 'Never mind.'

She sliced up a banana and mixed it in with the cereal. Grace always tried to be sneaky here, gradually adding more banana and less of the Cap'n. For a while she added Cheerios – less sugar – but Max quickly caught on.

'Emma! Get up now!'

A groan. Her daughter was too young to start with the trouble-getting-out-of-bed bit. Grace hadn't pulled that until she was in high school. Okay, maybe middle school. But certainly, definitely, not when she was eight. She thought about her own parents, dead for so long now. Sometimes one of the kids did something that reminded Grace of her mother or father. Emma pursed her lips so much like Grace's mom that Grace sometimes froze in place. Max's smile was like her dad's. You could see the genetic echo, and Grace never knew if it was a comfort or a painful reminder.

'Emma, now!'

A sound. Might have been a child getting out of bed.

Grace started making one lunch. Max liked to buy it at school and Grace was all for the ease of that. Making lunches in the morning was a pain in the ass. For a while Emma would buy the school lunch too, but something recently grossed her out, some indiscernible smell in the cafeteria that caused an aversion so strong Emma would gag. She ate outside, even in the cold, but the smell, she soon realized, was also in the food. Now she stayed in the cafeteria and brought a Batman lunchbox with her.

'Emma!'

'I'm here.'

Emma wore her standard gym-rat garb: maroon athletic shorts, blue high-top Converse all-stars, and a New Jersey Nets jersey. Total clash, which may have been the point. Emma wouldn't wear anything the least bit feminine. Putting on a dress usually required a negotiation of Middle East sensitivity, with often an equally violent result.

'What would you like for lunch?' Grace asked.

'Peanut butter and jelly.'

Grace just stared at her.

Emma played innocent. 'What?'

'You've been attending this school for how long now?'

'Huh?'

'Four years, right? One year of kindergarten. And now you're in third grade. That's four years.'

'So?'

'In all that time how many times have you asked me for peanut butter in school?'

'I don't know.'

'Maybe a hundred?'

Shrug.

'And how many times have I told you that your school doesn't allow peanut butter because some children might have an allergic reaction?'

'Oh yeah.'

'Oh yeah.' Grace checked the clock. She had a few Oscar Mayer 'Lunchables,' a rather disgustingly processed premade lunch, that she kept around for emergencies – i.e., no time or desire to fix a lunch. The kids, of course, loved them. She asked Emma softly if she'd like one – softly because if Max heard, that would be the end of buying lunch. Emma graciously accepted it and jammed it into the Batman lunchbox.

They sat down to breakfast.

'Mom?'

It was Emma. 'Yep.'

'When you and Dad got married.' She stopped.

'What about it?'

Emma started again. 'When you and Dad got married – at the end, when the guy said now you may kiss the bride ...'

'Right.'

'Well' – Emma cocked her head and closed one eye – 'did you have to?'

'Kiss him?'

'Yeah.'

'Have to? No, I guess not. I wanted to.'

'But do you have to?' Emma insisted. 'I mean, can't you just high-five instead?'

'High-five?'

'Instead of kiss. You know, turn to each other and high-five.' She demonstrated.

'I guess. If that's what you want.'

'That's what I want,' Emma said firmly.

Grace took them to the bus stop. This time she did not follow the bus to school. She stayed in place and bit down on her lower lip. The calm façade was slipping off again. Now that Emma and Max were gone, that would be okay.

When she got back to the house, Cora was awake and at the computer and groaning.

'Can I get you something?' Grace asked.

'An anesthesiologist,' Cora said. 'Straight preferred but not required.'

'I was thinking more like coffee.'

'Even better.' Cora's fingers danced across the keyboard. Her eyes narrowed. She frowned. 'Something's wrong here.'

'You mean with the e-mails off our spam, right?'

'We're not getting any replies.'

'I noticed that too.'

Cora sat back. Grace moved next to her and started biting a cuticle. After a few seconds, Cora leaned forward. 'Let me try something.' She brought up an e-mail, typed something in, sent it.

'What was that all about?'

'I just sent an e-mail to our spam address. I want to see if it arrives.'

They waited. No e-mail appeared.

'Hmm.' Cora leaned back. 'So either something is wrong with the mail system ...'

'Or?'

'Or Gus is still ticked about that small wee-wee line.'

'How do we find out which?'

Cora kept staring at the computer. 'Who were you on the phone with before?'

'Bob Dodd Senior's nursing home. I'm going to pay him a visit this morning.'

'Good.' Cora's eyes stayed on the screen.

'What is it?'

'I want to check something out,' she said.

'What?'

'Nothing probably, just something with the phone bills.' Cora started typing again. 'I'll call you if I learn anything.'

Perlmutter left Charlaine Swain with the Bergen County sketch artist. He had forced the truth out of her, thereby unearthing a tawdry secret that would have

116

been better left deep in the ground. Charlaine Swain had been right to keep it from him. It offered no help. The revelation was, at best, a sleazy and embarrassing distraction.

He sat with a doodle pad, wrote the word 'Windstar' and spent the next fifteen minutes circling it.

A Ford Windstar.

Kasselton was not a sleepy small town. They had thirty-eight cops on the payroll. They worked robberies. They checked on suspicious cars. They kept the school drug problems – suburban white-kid drugs – under control. They worked vandalism cases. They dealt with congestion in town, illegal parking, car accidents. They did their best to keep the urban decay of Paterson, a scant three miles from the border of Kasselton, at a safe distance. They answered too many false alarms emanating from the technological mating call of too many overpriced motion detectors.

Perlmutter had never fired his service revolver, except on a range. He had, in fact, never drawn his weapon in the line of duty. There had only been three deaths in the last three decades that fell under the possible heading of 'suspicious' and all three perpetrators were caught within hours. One was an ex-husband who got drunk and decided to profess his undying love by planning to kill the woman he purportedly adored before turning the shotgun on himself. Said ex-husband managed to get the first part right – two shotgun blasts to the ex's head – but like everything else in his pathetic life, he messed up the second part. He had only brought two shells. An hour later he was in custody. Suspicious Death Two was a teenage bully stabbed by a skinny, tormented elementary-school victim. The skinny kid served three years in juvie, where he learned the real meaning of being bullied and tormented. The final case was of a man dying of cancer who begged his wife of forty-eight years to end his suffering. She did. She got parole and Perlmutter suspected that it was worth it to her.

As for gunshots, well, there had been plenty in Kasselton but almost all were self-inflicted. Perlmutter wasn't much on politics. He wasn't sure of the relative merits of gun control, but he knew from personal experience that a gun bought for home protection was more likely – much, much, much more likely – to be used by the owner to commit suicide than to ward off a home invasion. In fact, in all his years in law enforcement, Perlmutter had never seen a case where the home gun had been used to shoot, stop, or scare away an intruder. Suicides by handguns, well, they were more plentiful than anyone wanted to let on.

Ford Windstar. He circled it again.

Now, after all these years, Perlmutter had a case involving attempted murder, bizarre abduction, unusually brutal assault – and, he suspected, much more. He started doodling again. He wrote the name *Jack Lawson* in the top left-hand corner. He wrote the name *Rocky Conwell* in the top right-hand corner. Both men, possibly missing, had crossed a toll plaza in a neighboring state at the same time. He drew a line from one name to the other.

Connection One.

Perlmutter wrote out Freddy Sykes's name, bottom left. The victim of a grievous assault. He wrote *Mike Swain* on the bottom right. Shot, attempted murder. The connection between these two men, Connection Two, was obvious. Swain's wife had seen the perpetrator of both acts, a stout Chinese guy she made sound like the Son of Odd Job from the old James Bond film.

But nothing really connected the four cases. Nothing connected the two disappearing men to the work of Odd Job's offspring. Except perhaps for one thing:

The Ford Windstar.

Jack Lawson had been driving a blue Ford Windstar when he disappeared. Mini Odd Job had been driving a blue Ford Windstar when he left the Sykes residence and shot Swain.

Granted this was a tenuous connection at best. Saying 'Ford Windstar' in this suburb was like saying 'implant' at a strip club. It wasn't much to go on, but when you add in the history of this town, the fact that stable fathers do not really just go missing, that this much activity never happens in a town like Kasselton ... no, it wasn't a strong tie, but it wasn't far off for Perlmutter to draw a conclusion:

All of this was related.

Perlmutter had no idea how this was all related, and he really didn't want to think about it too much quite yet. Let the techies and lab guys do their jobs first. Let them scour the Sykes residence for fingerprints and hairs. Let the artist finish the sketch. Let Veronique Baltrus, their resident computer weenie and an honest-to-God knockout, sift through the Sykes computer. It was simply too early to make a guess.

'Captain?'

It was Daley.

'What's up?'

'We found Rocky Conwell's car.'

'Where?'

'You know the Park-n-Ride on Route 17?'

Perlmutter took off his reading glasses. 'The one down the street?'

Daley nodded. 'I know. It doesn't make sense. We know he left the state, right?'

'Who found it?'

'Pepe and Pashaian.'

'Tell them to secure the area,' he said, rising. 'We'll check the vehicle out ourselves.'

23

Grace threw on a Coldplay CD for the ride, hoping it'd distract her. It did and it didn't. On one level she understood exactly what was happening to her with no need for interpretation. But the truth, in a sense, was too stark. To face it straight on would paralyze. That was where the surrealism probably derived from – self-preservation, the need to protect and even filter what one saw. Surrealism gave her the strength to go on, to pursue the truth, to find her husband, as opposed to the eye of reality, stark and naked and alone, which made her want to crouch into a small ball or maybe scream until they took her away.

Her cell phone rang. She instinctively glanced at the display before hitting the hands-free. Again, no, not Jack. It was Cora. Grace picked up and said, 'Hey.'

'I won't classify the news as bad or good, so let me put it this way. Do you want the weird news first or the really weird news?'

'Weird.'

'I can't reach Gus of the small wee-wee. He won't answer his calls. I keep getting his voice mail.'

Coldplay started singing, appropriately enough, a haunting number entitled 'Shiver.' Grace kept both hands on the wheel, perfectly placed at ten and two o'clock. She stayed in the middle lane and drove exactly the speed limit. Cars flew by on both her right and left.

'And the really weird news?'

'Remember how we tried to see the calls from two nights ago? I mean, the ones Jack might have made?'

'Right.'

'Well, I called the cell phone company. I pretended I was you. I assumed you wouldn't mind.'

'Correct assumption.'

'Right. Anyway, it didn't matter. The only call Jack's made in the past three days was to your cell phone yesterday.'

'The call he made when I was at the police station.'

'Right.'

'So what's weird about that?'

'Nothing. The weird part was on your home phone.'

Silence. She stayed on the Merritt Parkway, her hands on the wheel at ten and two o'clock.

'What about it?'

'You know about the call to his sister's office?' Cora asked.

'Yeah. I found that one by hitting redial.'

'And his sister – what's her name again?'

'Sandra Koval.'

'Sandra Koval, right. She told you that she wasn't there. That they never talked.'

'Yes.'

'The phone call lasted nine minutes.'

A small shudder skipped through Grace. She forced her hands to stay at two and ten. 'Ergo she lied.'

'It would seem.'

'So what did Jack say to her?'

'And what did she say back?'

'And why did she lie about it?'

'Sorry to have to tell you,' Cora said.

'No, it's good.'

'How do you figure?'

'It's a lead. Before this, Sandra was a dead end. Now we know she's somehow involved.'

'What are you going to do about it?'

'I don't know,' Grace said. 'Confront her, I guess.'

They said good-bye and Grace hung up. She drove a little farther, trying to run the scenarios through her head. 'Trouble' came on the CD player. She pulled into an Exxon station. New Jersey didn't have self-serve, so for a moment Grace just sat in her car, not realizing that she had to fill it up herself.

She bought a bottle of cold water at the station's mini-mart and dropped the change into a charity can. She wanted to think this through some more, this connection to Jack's sister, but there wasn't time for finesse here.

Grace remembered the number of the Burton and Crimstein law firm. She took out her phone and pressed in the digits. Two rings later she asked to be connected to Sandra Koval's line. She was surprised when Sandra herself said, 'Hello?'

'You lied to me.'

There was no reply. Grace walked back toward her car.

'The call lasted nine minutes. You talked to Jack.'

More silence.

'What's going on, Sandra?'

'I don't know.'

'Why did Jack call you?'

'I'm going to hang up now. Please don't try to contact me again.'

'Sandra?'

'You said he called you already.'

'Yes.'

'My advice is to wait until he calls again.'

'I don't want your advice, Sandra. I want to know what he said to you.'

'I think you should stop.'

'Stop what?'

'You're on a cell phone?'

'Yes.'

'Where are you?'

'I'm at gas station in Connecticut.'

120

'Why?'

'Sandra, I want you to listen to me.' There was a burst of static. Grace waited for it to pass. She finished filling the tank and grabbed her receipt. 'You're the last person to talk to my husband before he disappeared. You lied to me about it. You still won't tell me what he said to you. Why should I tell you anything?'

'Fair point, Grace. Now you listen to me. I'm going to leave you with one last thought before I hang up: Go home and take care of your children.'

The line went dead. Grace was back in the car now. She hit redial and asked to be connected to Sandra's office. Nobody answered. She tried again. Same thing. So now what? Try to show up in person again?

She pulled out of the gas station. Two miles later Grace saw a sign that said STARSHINE ASSISTED LIVING CENTER. Grace was not sure what she'd been expecting. The nursing home of her youth, she guessed, those one-level edifices of plain brick, the purest form of substance-over-style that, in a perverse way, reminded her of elementary schools. Life, alas, was cyclical. You start in one of those plain brick buildings, you end there. Turn, turn, turn.

But the Starshine Assisted Living Center was a three-story faux Victorian hotel. It had the turrets and the porches and the bright yellow of the painted ladies of old, all set against a ghastly aluminum siding. The grounds were manicured to the point where everything looked a tad too done, almost plastic. The place was aiming for cheery but it was trying too hard. The whole effect reminded Grace of Epcot Center at Disney World – a fun reproduction but you'd never mistake it for the real thing.

An old woman sat on a rocking chair on the front porch. She was reading the paper. She wished Grace a good morning and Grace did likewise. The lobby too tried to force up memories of a hotel from a bygone era. There were oil paintings in gaudy frames that looked like the kind of thing you'd buy at one of those Holiday Inn sales where everything was $19.99. It was obvious that they were reproductions of classics, even if you had never seen Renoir's *Luncheon of the Boating Party* or Hopper's *Nighthawks*.

The lobby was surprisingly busy. There were elderly people, of course, lots of them, in various states of degeneration. Some walked with no assistance, some shuffled, some had canes, some had walkers, some had wheelchairs. Many seemed spry; others slept.

The lobby was clean and bright but still had that – Grace hated herself for thinking like this – old-people smell, the odor of a sofa turning moldy. They tried to cover it up with something cherry, something that reminded Grace of those dangling tree fresheners in gypsy cabs, but there are some smells that you can never mask.

The singular young person in the room – a woman in her mid-twenties – sat behind a desk that was again aiming for the era but looked like something just bought at the Bombay Company. She smiled up at Grace.

'Good morning. I'm Lindsey Barclay.'

Grace recognized the voice from the phone. 'I'm here to see Mr. Dodd.'

'Bobby's in his room. Second floor, room 211. I'll take you.'

She rose. Lindsey was pretty in a way that only the young are, with that enthusiasm and smile that belong exclusively to the innocent or the cult recruiter.

'Do you mind taking the stairs?' she asked.

'Not at all.'

Many of the residents stopped and said hello. Lindsey had time for every one of them, cheerfully returning each greeting, though Grace the cynic couldn't help but wonder if this was a bit of a show for the visitor. Still Lindsey knew all the names. She always had something to say, something personal, and the residents seemed to appreciate that.

'Seems like mostly women,' Grace noted.

'When I was in school, they told us the national ratio in assisted living is five women for every one man.'

'Wow.'

'Yes. Bobby jokes that he's waited his whole life for that kind of odds.'

Grace smiled.

She waved a hand. 'Oh, but he's all talk. His wife – he calls her "his Maudie" – died almost thirty years ago. I don't think he's looked at a woman since.'

That silenced them. The corridor was done up in forest green and pink, the walls lined with the familiar – Rockwell prints, dogs playing poker, black-and-whites from old movies like *Casablanca* and *Strangers on a Train*. Grace limped along. Lindsey noticed it – Grace could tell the way she cut quick glances – but like most people, she said nothing.

'We have different neighborhoods at Starlight,' Lindsey explained. 'That's what we call the corridors like this. Neighborhoods. Each has a different theme. The one we're in now is called Nostalgia. We think the residents find it comforting.'

They stopped at a door. A nameplate on the right said 'B. Dodd.' She knocked on the door. 'Bobby?'

No reply. She opened the door anyway. They stepped into a small but comfortable room. There was a tiny kitchenette on the right. On the coffee table, ideally angled so that you could see it from both the door and the bed, was a large black-and-white photograph of a stunning woman who looked a bit like Lena Horne. The woman in the picture was maybe forty but you could tell that the picture was old.

'That's his Maudie.'

Grace nodded, lost for a moment in this image in the silver frame. She thought again about 'her Jack.' For the first time she allowed herself to consider the unthinkable: Jack might never come home. It was something she'd been avoiding from the moment she'd heard the minivan start up. She might never see Jack again. She might never hold him. She might never laugh at one of his corny jokes. She might never – and this was apropos to think here – grow old with him.

'Are you okay?'

'Fine.'

'Bobby must be up with Ira on Reminiscence. They play cards.'

They began to back out of the room. 'Is Reminiscence another, uh, neighborhood?'

'No. Reminiscence is what we call our third floor. It's for our residents with Alzheimer's.'

'Oh.'

'Ira doesn't recognize his own children, but he still plays a mean game of poker pinochle.'

They were back in the hall. Grace noticed a cluster of images next to Bobby

Dodd's door. She took a closer look. It was one of those box frames people use to display trinkets. There were army medals. There was an old baseball, brown with age. There were photographs from every era of the man's life. One photograph was of his murdered son, Bob Dodd, the same one she'd seen on the computer last night.

Lindsey said, 'Memory box.'

'Nice,' Grace said, because she didn't know what else to say.

'Every patient has one by their door. It's a way to let everyone know about you.'

Grace nodded. Summing up a life in a twelve-by-eight box frame. Like everything else about this place, it managed to be both appropriate and creepy at the exact same time.

To get to the Reminiscence floor you had to use an elevator that worked by a coded numeric keypad. 'So the residents don't wander,' Lindsey explained, which again fit into the 'making sense yet giving the willies' style of this place.

The Reminiscence floor was comfortable, well appointed, well staffed, and terrifying. Some residents were functional, but most wilted in wheelchairs like dying flowers. Some stood and shuffled. Several muttered to themselves. All had that glazed, hundred-yard stare.

A woman deep into her eighties jangled her keys and started for the elevator.

Lindsey asked, 'Where are you going, Cecile?'

The old woman turned toward her. 'I have to pick up Danny from school. He'll be waiting for me.'

'It's okay,' Lindsey said. 'School won't be out for another two hours.'

'Are you sure?'

'Of course. Look, let's have some lunch and then you can pick up Danny, okay?'

'He has piano lessons today.'

'I know.'

A staff member came over and steered Cecile away. Lindsey watched her go. 'We use validation therapy,' she said, 'with our advanced Alzheimer's patients.'

'Validation therapy?'

'We don't argue with them or try to make them see the truth. I don't, for example, tell her that Danny is now a sixty-two-year-old banker with three grandchildren. We just try to redirect them.'

They walked down a corridor – no, 'neighborhood' – filled with life-size dolls of babies. There was a changing table and teddy bears.

'Nursery neighborhood,' she said.

'They play with dolls?'

'Those that are more high functioning. It helps them prepare for visits from great-grandchildren.'

'And the others?'

Lindsey kept walking. 'Some think they're young mothers. It helps soothe them.'

Subconsciously, or maybe not, they picked up the pace. A few seconds later, Lindsey said, 'Bobby?'

Bobby Dodd rose from the card table. The first word that came to mind: Dapper. He looked sprightly and fresh. He had dark black skin, thick wrinkles like something you might see on an alligator. He was a snappy dresser in a tweed jacket, two-tone loafers, red ascot with matching hanky. His gray hair was cropped close and slicked down.

His manner was upbeat, even after Grace explained that she wanted to talk to him about his murdered son. She looked for some signs of devastation – a wetness in the eye, a tremor in the voice – but Bobby Dodd showed nothing. Okay, yes, Grace was dealing in heavy generalities, but could it be that death and big-time tragedy did not hit the elderly as hard as the rest of us? Grace wondered. The elderly could be easily agitated by the little stuff – traffic delays, lines at airports, poor service. But it was as if the big things never quite reached them. Was there a strange selfishness that came with age? Was there something about being closer to the inevitable – having that perspective – that made one either internalize, block, or brush off the big calamities? Can frailty not handle the big blows, and thus a defense mechanism, a survival instinct, runs interference?

Bobby Dodd wanted to help, but he really didn't know much. Grace could see that almost right away. His son had visited twice a month. Yes, Bob's stuff had been packed up and sent to him, but he hadn't bothered opening it.

'It's in storage,' Lindsey told Grace.

'Do you mind if I look through it?'

Bobby Dodd patted her leg. 'Not at all, child.'

'We'll need to ship it to you,' Lindsey said. 'The storage facility is off site.'

'It's very important.'

'I can have it overnighted.'

'Thank you.'

Lindsey left them alone.

'Mr. Dodd –'

'Bobby, please.'

'Bobby,' Grace said. 'When was the last time your son visited you?'

'Three days before he was killed.'

The words came quickly and without thought. She finally saw a flicker behind the façade, and she wondered about her earlier observations, about old age making tragedy less hurtful – or does it merely make the mask more deft?

'Did he seem different at all?'

'Different?'

'More distracted, anything like that.'

'No.' Then: 'Or at least I didn't notice, if he did.'

'What did you talk about?'

'We never have much to say. Sometimes we talk about his momma. Most of the time we just watch TV. They got cable here, you know.'

'Did Jillian come with him?'

'No.'

He said that too quickly. Something in his face closed down.

'Did she ever come?'

'Sometimes.'

'But not the last time?'

'That's right.'

'Did that surprise you?'

'That? No, *that*' – big emphasis – 'didn't surprise me.'

'What did?'

124

He looked off and bit his lower lip. 'She wasn't at the funeral.'

Grace thought that she must have heard wrong. Bobby Dodd nodded as if he could read her thoughts.

'That's right. His own wife.'

'Were they having marital issues?'

'If they were, Bob never said anything to me.'

'Did they have any children?'

'No.' He adjusted the ascot and glanced away for a moment. 'Why are you bringing this all up, Mrs. Lawson?'

'Grace, please.'

He did not reply. He looked at her with eyes that spoke of wisdom and sadness. Maybe the answer to elderly coldness is far simpler: Those eyes had seen bad. They didn't want to see more.

'My own husband is missing,' Grace said. 'I think, I don't know, I think they're connected.'

'What's your husband's name?'

'Jack Lawson.'

He shook his head. The name meant nothing to him. She asked if he had a phone number or any idea how she could contact Jillian Dodd. He shook his head again. They headed to the elevator. Bobby didn't know the code, so an orderly escorted them down. They rode from floor three to one in silence.

When they reached the door, Grace thanked him for his time.

'Your husband,' he said. 'You love him, don't you?'

'Very much.'

'Hope you're stronger than me.' Bobby Dodd walked away then. Grace thought of that silver-framed picture in his room, of his Maudie, and then she showed herself out.

24

Perlmutter realized that they had no legal right to open Rocky Conwell's car. He pulled Daley over. 'Is DiBartola on duty?'

'No.'

'Call Rocky Conwell's wife. Ask her if she had a set of keys to the car. Tell her we found it and want her permission to go through it.'

'She's the ex-wife. Does she have any standing?'

'Enough for our purposes,' Perlmutter said.

'Okay.'

It took Daley no time. The wife cooperated. They stopped by the Maple Garden apartments on Maple Street. Daley ran up and retrieved the keys. Five minutes later they pulled into the Park-n-Ride.

There was no reason to be suspicious of foul play. If anything, finding the car here, at this depot, would lead one to the opposite conclusion. People parked here so that they could go elsewhere. One bus whisked the weary to the heart of midtown Manhattan. Another brought you to the northern tip of the famed isle, near the George Washington Bridge. Other buses took you to the three nearby major airports – JFK, LaGuardia, Newark Liberty – and ultimately anywhere in the world. So no, finding Rocky Conwell's car did not lead one to suspect foul play.

At least, not at first.

Pepe and Pashaian, the two cops who were watching the car, had not seen it. Perlmutter's eyes slid toward Daley. Nothing on his face either. They all looked complacent, expecting this would lead to a dead end.

Pepe and Pashaian hoisted their belts and sauntered toward Perlmutter. 'Hey, Captain.'

Perlmutter kept his eyes on the car.

'You want us to start questioning the ticket agents?' Pepe asked. 'Maybe one of them remembers selling Conwell a ticket.'

'I don't think so,' Perlmutter said.

The three younger men caught something in their superior's voice. They looked at each other and shrugged. Perlmutter did not explain.

Conwell's vehicle was a Toyota Celica. A small car, old model. But the size and age didn't really matter. Neither did the fact that there was rust along the wheel trims, that two hubcaps were gone, that the other two were so dirty you could not tell where metal ended and rubber began. No, none of that bothered Perlmutter.

He stared at the back of the car and thought about those small-town sheriffs in horror movies, you know the ones, where something is very wrong, where townspeople start acting strangely and the body count keeps rising and the sheriff, that good, smart, loyal, out-of-his-league law enforcement officer, is powerless

126

to do anything about it. That was what Perlmutter felt now because the back of the car, the trunk area, was low.

Much too low.

There was only one explanation. Something heavy was in the trunk.

It could be anything, of course. Rocky Conwell had been a football player. He probably lifted weights. Maybe he was transferring a set of dumbbells. The answer could be as simple as that, good old Rocky moving his weights. Maybe he was bringing them back to the garden apartment on Maple Street, the one where his ex lived. She had worried about him. They were reconciling. Maybe Rocky loaded his car – okay, not his whole car, just his trunk, because Perlmutter could see that there was nothing in the backseat – anyway, maybe he loaded it up to move back in with her.

Perlmutter jangled the keys as he moved closer to the Toyota Celica. Daley, Pepe, and Pashaian hung back. Perlmutter glanced down at the set of keys. Rocky's wife – he thought that her name was Lorraine but he couldn't be sure – had a Penn State football helmet key chain. It looked old and scraped up. The Nittany Lion was barely visible. Perlmutter wondered what she thought about when she looked at the key chain, why she still used it.

He stopped at the trunk and sniffed the air. Not a hint. He put the key in the lock and turned. The trunk's lock popped open, the sound echoing. He began to lift the trunk. The air escaping was almost audible. And now, yes, the smell was unmistakable.

Something large had been squished into the trunk, like an oversize pillow. Without warning it sprang free like a giant jack-in-the-box. Perlmutter jumped back as the head fell out first, smacking the pavement hard.

Didn't matter, of course. Rocky Conwell was already dead.

25

Now what?

Grace was starved for one thing. She drove over the George Washington Bridge, took the Jones Road exit, and stopped to grab a bite at a Chinese restaurant called, interestingly enough, Baumgart's. She ate in silence, feeling as lonely as she had ever felt, and tried to hold herself together. What had happened? The day before yesterday – was it really only then? – she had picked up photographs at Photomat. That was all. Life was good. She had a husband she adored and two wonderful, inquisitive kids. She had time to paint. They all had their health, enough money in the bank. And then she had seen a photograph, an old one, and now ...

Grace had almost forgotten about Josh the Fuzz Pellet.

He was the one who developed the roll of film. He was the one who mysteriously left the store not long after she picked up the pictures. He had to be the one, she was sure, who put that damn photograph in the middle of her pack.

She grabbed her cell phone, asked directory assistance for the number of the Photomat in Kasselton, and even paid the extra fee to be directly connected. On the third ring, the phone was picked up.

'Photomat.'

Grace said nothing. No question about it. She would recognize that bored yah-dude slur anywhere. It was Fuzz Pellet Josh. He was back at the store.

She considered just hanging up, but maybe, somehow, that would – she didn't know – tip him off somehow. Make him run. She changed her voice, added a little extra lilt, and asked what time they closed.

'Like, six,' Fuzz Pellet told her.

She thanked him, but he had hung up. The check was already on the table. She paid and tried not to sprint to her car. Route 4 was wide open. She sped past the plethora of malls and found a parking spot not far from the Photomat. Her cell phone rang.

'Hello?'

'It's Carl Vespa.'

'Oh, hi.'

'I'm sorry about yesterday. About springing Jimmy X on you like that.'

She debated telling him about Jimmy's late night visit, decided now was not the time. 'It's okay.'

'I know you don't care, but it looks like Wade Larue is going to get released.'

'Maybe it's the right thing,' she said.

'Maybe.' But Vespa sounded far from convinced. 'You sure you don't need any protection?'

'Positive.'

'If you change your mind ...'

'I'll call.'

There was a funny pause. 'Any word from your husband?'

'No.'

'Does he have a sister?'

Grace changed hands. 'Yes. Why?'

'Her name Sandra Koval?'

'Yes. What does she have to do with this?'

'I'll talk to you later.'

He hung up. Grace stared at the phone. What the hell was that all about? She shook her head. It would be useless to call back. She tried to refocus.

Grace grabbed her purse and hurry-limped toward the Photomat. Her leg hurt. Walking was a chore. It felt as though someone were on the ground clinging to her ankle and she had to drag him along. Grace kept moving. She was three stores away when a man in a business suit stepped in her path.

'Ms. Lawson?'

A weird thought struck Grace as she looked at this stranger: His sandy hair was nearly the same color as his suit. It almost looked liked they were both made from the same material.

'May I help you?' she said.

The man reached into his coat pocket and pulled out a photograph. He held it up to her face so that she could see it. 'Did you post this on the Web?'

It was the cropped mystery photograph of the blonde and the redhead.

'Who are you?'

The sandy-haired man said, 'My name is Scott Duncan. I'm with the U.S. attorney's office.' He pointed to the blonde, the one who'd been looking up at Jack, the one with the X across her face.

'And this,' Scott Duncan said, 'is a picture of my sister.'

26

Perlmutter had broken the news to Lorraine Conwell as gently as he could.

He had delivered bad news plenty of times. Usually it involved car accidents on Route 4 or the Garden State Parkway. Lorraine Conwell had exploded into tears when he told her, but now the numb had seeped in and dried her eyes.

The stages of grief: Supposedly the first is denial. That was wrong. The first is just the opposite: Total acceptance. You hear the bad news and you understand exactly what is being said to you. You understand that your loved one – your spouse, your parent, your child – will never come home, that they are gone for good, that their life is over, and that you will never, ever, see them again. You understand that in a flash. Your legs buckle. Your heart gives out.

That was the first step – not just acceptance, not just understanding, but total truth. Human beings are not built to withstand that kind of hurt. That then is when the denial begins. Denial floods in quickly, salving the wounds or at least covering them. But there is still that moment, mercifully quick, the real Stage One, when you hear the news and stare into the abyss, and horrible as it is, you understand everything.

Lorraine Conwell sat ramrod. There was a quiver in her lips. Her eyes were dry. She looked small and alone and it took all Perlmutter had not to put his arms around her and pull her in close.

'Rocky and me,' she said. 'We were going to get back together.'

Perlmutter nodded, encouraging.

'It's my fault, you know. I made Rocky leave. I shouldn't have.' She looked up at him with those violet eyes. 'He was different when we met, you know? He had dreams then. He was so sure of himself. But when he couldn't play ball any more, it just ate away at him. I couldn't live with that.'

Perlmutter nodded again. He wanted to help her out, wanted to stay in her company, but he really did not have time for the unabridged life story. He needed to move this along and get out of here. 'Was there anyone who wanted to hurt Rocky? Did he have enemies or anything like that?'

She shook her head. 'No. No one.'

'He spent time in prison.'

'Yes. It was stupid. He got into a fight in a bar. It got out of hand.'

Perlmutter looked over at Daley. They knew about the fight. They were already on that, seeing if his victim had sought late revenge. It seemed doubtful.

'Was Rocky working?'

'Yes.'

'Where?'

'In Newark. He worked at the Budweiser plant. The one near the airport.'

'You called our office yesterday,' Perlmutter said.

She nodded, her eyes staring straight ahead.

'You spoke to an Officer DiBartola.'

'Yes. He was very nice.'

Right. 'You told him that Rocky hadn't come home from work.'

She nodded.

'You called in the early morning. You said he'd been working the night before.'

'That's right.'

'Did he work a night shift at the plant?'

'No. He'd taken a second job.' She squirmed a little. 'It was off the books.'

'Doing what?'

'He worked for this lady.'

'Doing what?'

She used one finger to wipe a tear. 'Rocky didn't talk about it much. He delivered subpoenas, I think, stuff like that.'

'Do you know the lady's name?'

'Something foreign. I can't pronounce it.'

Perlmutter did not need to think about it long. 'Indira Khariwalla?'

'That's it.' Lorraine Conwell looked up at him. 'You know her?'

He did. It had been a long time, but yes, Perlmutter knew her very well.

Grace had handed Scott Duncan the photograph, the one with all five people in it. He could not stop staring, especially at the image of his sister. He ran his finger over her face. Grace could barely look at him.

They were back at Grace's house now, sitting in the kitchen. They had been talking for the better part of half an hour.

'You got this two days ago?' Scott Duncan asked.

'Yes.'

'And then your husband ... He's this one, right?' Scott Duncan pointed to Jack's image.

'Yes.'

'He ran off?'

'He vanished,' she said. 'He didn't run off.'

'Right. You think he was, what, kidnapped?'

'I don't know what happened to him. I only know he's in trouble.'

Scott Duncan's eyes stayed on the old photograph. 'Because he gave you some kind of warning? Something about needing space?'

'Mr. Duncan, I'd like to know how you came across this picture. And how you found me, for that matter.'

'You sent it out via some kind of spam. Someone recognized the picture and forwarded it to me. I traced back the spammer and put a little pressure on him.'

'Was that why we didn't receive any answers?'

Duncan nodded. 'I wanted to talk to you first.'

'I've told you everything I know. I was on my way to confront the guy in the Photomat when you showed up.'

'We'll question him, don't worry about that.'

He couldn't take his eyes off the picture. She had done all the talking. He had told her nothing, except that the woman in the photograph was his sister.

131

Grace pointed at the crossed-out face. 'Tell me about her,' she said.

'Her name was Geri. Does her name mean anything to you?'

'I'm sorry, it doesn't.'

'Your husband never mentioned her? Geri Duncan.'

'Not that I remember.' Then: 'You said was.'

'What?'

'You said was. Her name *was* Geri.'

Scott Duncan nodded. 'She died in a fire when she was twenty-one years old. In her dorm room.'

Grace froze. 'She went to Tufts, right?'

'Yes. How did you know?'

Now it made sense – why the girl's face had seemed familiar. Grace hadn't known her, but there had been pictures in the newspapers at the time. Grace had been undergoing physical therapy and ripping through way too many periodicals. 'I remember reading about it. Wasn't it an accident? Electrical fire or something?'

'That was what I thought. Until three months ago.'

'What changed?'

'The U.S. attorney's office captured a man who goes by the name Monte Scanlon. He's a hired assassin. His job was to make it look like an accident.'

Grace tried to take it in. 'And you just learned this three months ago?'

'Yes.'

'Did you investigate?'

'I'm still investigating, but it's been a long time.' His voice was softer now. 'Not many clues after all these years.'

Grace turned away.

'I found out that Geri was dating a boy at the time, a local kid named Shane Alworth. The name mean anything to you?'

'No.'

'You're sure?'

'Pretty sure, yeah.'

'Shane Alworth had a rap sheet, nothing serious, but I checked him out.'

'And?'

'And he's gone.'

'Gone?'

'No sign of him. I can't find work records for him. I can't find any sign of a Shane Alworth on the tax payroll. I can't find any hit on his social security number.'

'For how long?'

'How long has he been gone?'

'Yes.'

'I've gone back ten years. Nothing.' Duncan reached into his coat pocket and pulled out another photograph. He handed it to Grace. 'Recognize him?'

She took a long look at the photograph. No question about it. It was the other guy in her photograph. She looked up at him for confirmation. Duncan nodded.

'Creepy, huh?'

'Where did you get this?' she asked.

'From Shane Alworth's mother. She claims her son lives in a small town in

Mexico. That he's a missionary or something and that's why his name doesn't pop up. Shane also has a brother who lives in St. Louis. Works as a psychologist. He backs up what the mother said.'

'But you don't buy it.'

'Do you?'

Grace put the mystery photograph on the table. 'So we know about three people in this photograph,' she said, more to herself than Duncan. 'We have your sister, who was murdered. We have her boyfriend, Shane Alworth, the guy over here. He's missing. We have my husband, who disappeared right after seeing this photograph. That about right?'

'Pretty much.'

'What else did the mother say?'

'Shane was unreachable. He was in the Amazon jungle, she thought.'

'The Amazon jungle? In Mexico?'

'Her geography was fuzzy.'

Grace shook her head and pointed at the picture. 'So that leaves the other two women. Any clue who they are?'

'No, not yet. But we know more now. The redhead, we should get a bead on her pretty soon. The other one, the one with her back to the camera, I don't know if we'll ever know.'

'Did you learn anything else?'

'Not really. I've had Geri's body exhumed. That took some time to arrange. A full autopsy is being done, see if they can find any physical evidence, but it's a long shot. This' – he held up the picture from the Web – 'this is the first real lead I've had.'

She didn't like the pitch of hope in his voice. 'It might just be a picture,' she said.

'You don't believe that.'

Grace put her hands on the table. 'Do you think my husband had something to do with your sister's death?'

Duncan rubbed his chin. 'Good question,' he said.

She waited.

'Something to do with it, probably. But I don't think he killed her, if that's what you're asking. Something happened to them a long time ago. I don't know what. My sister was killed in a fire. Your husband ran overseas, I guess. France, you said?'

'Yes.'

'And Shane Alworth, too. I mean, it's all connected. It has to be.'

'My sister-in-law knows something.'

Scott Duncan nodded. 'You said she's a lawyer?'

'Yes. With Burton and Crimstein.'

'That's not good. I know Hester Crimstein. If she doesn't want to tell us anything, I won't be able to apply much pressure.'

'So what do we do?'

'We keep shaking the cage.'

'Shaking the cage?'

He nodded. 'Shaking cages is the only way you make progress.'

'So we should start with shaking Josh at the Photomat,' Grace said. 'He's the one who gave me that photograph.'

Duncan stood. 'Sounds like a plan.'

'You're going there now?'

'Yes.'

'I'd like to come along.'

'Let's go then.'

'As I live and breathe. Captain Perlmutter. To what do I owe the pleasure?'

Indira Khariwalla was small and wizened. Her dark skin – she was, as her name implied, from India, more specifically Bombay – had started to harden and thicken. She was still attractive but not the exotic temptress she had been in her heyday.

'Been a long time,' he said.

'Yes.' The smile, once a dazzler, took great effort now, almost cracking the skin. 'But I'd prefer not to rehash the past.'

'Me either.'

When Perlmutter started working in Kasselton, he had been partnered with a veteran a year from retirement named Steve Goedert, a great guy. They struck up a deep friendship. Goedert had three kids, all grown, and a wife named Susan. Perlmutter did not know how Goedert met Indira, but they started up. Susan found out.

Fast-forward past the ugly divorce.

Goedert had no money left once the lawyers were through with him. He ended up working as a private investigator but with a twist: He specialized in infidelity. Or at least that was what he claimed. To Perlmutter's thinking it was a scam – entrapment at its very worst. He would use Indira as bait. She would approach the husband, lure him in, and then Goedert would take pictures. Perlmutter told him to stop. Fidelity was not a game. It was not a prank, testing a man like that.

Goedert must have known it was wrong. He hit the bottle pretty good and never came out. He too had a gun in his house, and in the end he too did not use it to stop a home invasion. After his death, Indira struck out on her own. She took over the agency, keeping Goedert's name on the door.

'A long time ago,' she said softly.

'Did you love him?'

'None of your business.'

'You ruined his life.'

'Do you really think I can wield that kind of power over a man?' She shifted in her chair. 'What can I do for you, Captain Perlmutter?'

'You have an employee named Rocky Conwell.'

She did not respond.

'I know he's off the books. I don't care about that.'

Still nothing. He slapped down a crude Polaroid of Conwell's dead body.

Indira's eyes flicked to it, ready to dismiss, and then stared there. 'Dear Lord.'

Perlmutter waited, but Indira said nothing. She stared for a little while longer and then let her head drop back.

'His wife says he worked for you.'

She nodded.

'What did he do?'

'Night shifts.'

'What did he do on the night shifts?'

'Mostly repossession. He did a little subpoena work too.'

'What else?'

She said nothing.

'There was stuff in his car. We found a long-range camera and a pair of binoculars.'

'So?'

'So was he doing surveillance?'

She looked at him. There were tears in her eyes. 'You think he was killed on the job?'

'It's a logical assumption, but I won't know for certain until you tell me what he was doing.'

Indira looked away. She began to rock in the chair.

'Was he working a job the night before last?'

'Yes.'

More silence.

'What was he doing, Indira?'

'I can't say.'

'Why not?'

'I have clients. They have rights. You know the drill, Stu.'

'You're not a lawyer.'

'No, but I can work for one.'

'Are you saying this case was attorney work product?'

'I'm not saying anything.'

'You want to take another look at that photograph?'

She almost smiled. 'You think that will make me talk?' But Indira did take another look. 'I don't see any blood,' she said.

'There wasn't any.'

'He wasn't shot?'

'Nope. No gun, no knife.'

She looked confused. 'How was he killed?'

'I don't know yet. He's on the table. But I have a guess, if you want to hear it?'

She didn't. But she nodded slowly.

'He suffocated.'

'You mean like he was garroted?'

'Doubtful. There are no ligature marks on the neck.'

She frowned. 'Rocky was huge. He was strong as an ox. It had to be poison, something like that.'

'I don't think so. The M.E. said there was substantial damage to the larynx.'

She looked confused.

'In other words, his throat was crushed like an egg-shell.'

'You mean he was strangled by hand?'

'We don't know.'

'He was too strong for that,' she said again.

'Who was he following?' Perlmutter asked.

'Let me make a call. You can wait in the hall.'

He did. The wait was not long.

When Indira came out, her voice was clipped. 'I can't speak to you,' she said.

'I'm sorry.'

'Attorney's orders?'

'I can't speak to you.'

'I'll be back. I'll get a warrant.'

'Good luck,' she said, turning away. And Perlmutter thought that maybe she meant it.

27

Grace and Scott Duncan headed back to the Photomat. Her heart sank when they entered and she saw no Fuzz Pellet.

Assistant Manager Bruce was there. He puffed out his chest. When Scott Duncan flashed his badge, the chest deflated. 'Josh is out on lunch break,' he said.

'Do you know where?'

'He usually goes to the Taco Bell. It's right down the block.'

Grace knew it. She hurried out first, afraid to lose his scent again. Scott Duncan followed. As soon as she entered the Taco Bell, the fragrance of lard rising up to assault her, she spotted Josh.

Equally important, Josh spotted her. His eyes widened.

Scott Duncan stood at her side. 'That him?'

Grace nodded.

Fuzz Pellet Josh sat alone. His head was tilted down, his hair hanging in front of his face like a curtain. His expression – and Grace guessed that he only had this one – was sullen. He bit into the taco as if it insulted his favorite grunge group. The earphones were jammed into place. The cord fell into the sour cream. Grace hated to sound like an old biddy, but having this kind of music plugged directly into the brain all day could not be good for a person. Grace enjoyed music. When she was alone, she would turn the music up, sing along, dance, whatever. So it wasn't the music or even the volume. But what did it do to the mental health of a young mind to have music, probably angry and harsh, pounding in the ears all the time? An aural confinement, solitary walls of sound, to paraphrase Elton John, inescapable. No life noises let in. No talking. An artificial soundtrack to your life.

It could not be healthy.

Josh lowered his head, pretending he didn't see them. She watched him as they approached. He was so young. He looked pitiful, sitting there alone like that. She thought about his hopes and dreams and how he already looked set on the road of life-long disappointments. She thought about Josh's mother, about how she must have tried and how she must worry. She thought about her own son, her little Max, and about how she'd handle it if he started slipping in this direction.

She and Scott Duncan stopped in front of Josh's table. He took another bite and then slowly looked up. The music coming from his earphones was so loud that Grace could actually make out the lyrics. Something about bitches and ho's. Scott Duncan took the lead. She let him.

'Do you recognize this lady?' Scott asked.

Josh shrugged. He lowered the volume.

'Take those off,' Scott said. 'Now.'

He did as he was told, but he took his time.

'I asked you if you recognized this lady.'

Josh glanced in her direction. 'Yeah, I guess.'

'How do you know her?'

'From where I work.'

'You work at the Photomat, correct?'

'Yeah.'

'And Ms. Lawson here. She's a customer.'

'That's what I said.'

'Do you remember the last time she was in the store?'

'No.'

'Think.'

He shrugged.

'Does two days ago sound about right?'

Another shrug. 'Could be.'

Scott Duncan had the envelope from the Photomat. 'You developed this roll of film, correct?'

'You say so.'

'No, I'm asking you. Look at the envelope.'

He did. Grace stayed still. Josh had not asked Scott Duncan who he was. He had not asked them what they wanted. She wondered about that.

'Yeah, I developed that roll.'

Duncan took out the photograph with his sister in it. He put it on the table. 'Did you put this picture in Ms. Lawson's packet?'

'No,' Josh said.

'You sure?'

'Positive.'

Grace waited a beat. She knew that he was lying. She spoke for the first time. 'How do you know?' she asked.

They both looked at her. Josh said, 'Huh?'

'How do you develop rolls?'

He said, 'Huh?' again.

'You put the roll in that machine,' Grace said. 'They come out in a pile. Then you put the pile in an envelope. Isn't that right?'

'Yeah.'

'Do you look at every picture you develop?'

He said nothing. He looked around as if asking for help.

'I've seen you work,' Grace said. 'You read your magazines. You listen to your music. You do not check through all the pictures. So my question is, Josh, how do you know what pictures were in that pile?'

Josh glanced at Scott Duncan. No help there. He turned back to her. 'It's weird, that's all.'

Grace waited.

'That picture looks like it's a hundred years old or something. It's the right size, but that ain't Kodak paper. That's what I meant. I'd never seen it before.' Josh liked that. His eyes lit up, warming to his lie. 'Yeah, see, that's what I thought he meant. When he said did I put it in. Did I ever see it before?'

Grace just looked at him.

'Look, I don't know what goes through that machine. But I've never seen that print. That's all I know, okay?'

'Josh?'

It was Scott Duncan. Josh turned toward him.

'That picture ended up in Ms. Lawson's pack of pictures. Do you have any idea how that happened?'

'Maybe she took the picture.'

'No,' Duncan said.

Josh gave another elaborate shrug. He must have had very powerful shoulders from all the work they got.

'Tell me how it works,' Duncan said. 'How you develop the pictures.'

'It's like she said. I put the film into the machine. It does the rest. I just set the size and the count.'

'Count?'

'You know. One print from each negative, two prints, whatever.'

'And they come out in a pile?'

'Yeah.'

Josh was more relaxed now, on comfortable ground.

'And then you put them in an envelope?'

'Right. Same envelope the customer filled out. Then I file it in alphabetical order. That's it.'

Scott Duncan looked over at Grace. She said nothing. He took out his badge. 'Do you know what this badge means, Josh?'

'No.'

'It means I work for the U.S. attorney's office. It means I can make your life miserable if you cross me. Do you understand?'

Josh looked a little scared now. He managed a nod.

'So I'm going to ask you one more time: Do you know anything about this photograph?'

'No. I swear.' He looked around. 'I gotta get back to work now.'

He stood. Grace blocked his path. 'Why did you leave work early the other day?'

'Huh?'

'About an hour after I picked up my roll of film, I went back to the store. You were gone. And the next morning too. So what happened?'

'I got sick,' he said.

'Yeah?'

'Yeah.'

'Feeling better now?'

'Guess so.' He started pushing past her.

'Because,' Grace went on, 'your manager said you had a family emergency. Is that what you told him?'

'I gotta get back to work,' he said, and this time he pushed past her and nearly ran out the door.

Beatrice Smith was not home.

Eric Wu broke in without any trouble. He checked through the house. No one was there. With the gloves still on Wu flicked on the computer. Her software PIM – a fancy term for a date and phone book – was Time & Chaos. He opened it and checked her calendar.

Beatrice Smith was visiting her son, the doctor, in San Diego. She'd be home in two days – far enough away to save her life. Wu considered that, the fickle winds of fate. He couldn't help it. He glanced through Beatrice Smith's calendar two months in the past and two months in the future. There were no overnight trips. If he had come at any other time, Beatrice Smith would be dead. Wu liked to think about things like that, about how it was often the little things, the unconscious things, the things we can't know or control, that alter our lives. Call it fate, luck, odds, God. Wu found it fascinating.

Beatrice Smith had a two-car garage. Her tan Land Rover took up the right side. The left side was empty. There was an oil stain on the ground. This, Wu figured, had been where Maury parked his car. She kept it empty now – Wu couldn't help but think of Freddy Sykes's mother – as if it was his side of the bed. Wu parked there. He opened the back. Jack Lawson looked shaky. Wu untied his legs so he could walk. The hands remained bound at the wrist. Wu led him inside. Jack Lawson fell twice. The blood had not fully circulated through the legs. Wu held him up by the scruff of his shirt.

'I'm taking the gag off,' Wu said.

Jack Lawson nodded. Wu could see it in his eyes. Lawson was broken. Wu had not hurt him much – not yet anyway – but when you spend enough time in the dark, alone with your thoughts, your mind turns inward and feasts. That was always a dangerous thing. The key to serenity, Wu knew, was to keep working, keep moving forward. When you're moving, you don't think about guilt or innocence. You don't think about your past or your dreams, your joys or disappointments. You just worry about survival. Hurt or be hurt. Kill or be killed.

Wu removed the gag. Lawson did not plead and beg or ask questions. That stage was over. Wu tied his legs to a chair. He searched the pantry and refrigerator. They both ate in silence. When they finished, Wu washed off the dishes and cleaned up. Jack Lawson stayed tied to the chair.

Wu's cell phone rang. 'Yes.'

'We have a problem.'

Wu waited.

'When you picked him up, he had a copy of that photograph, right?'

'Yes.'

'And he said there were no other copies?'

'Yes.'

'He was wrong.'

Wu said nothing.

'His wife has a copy of the picture. She's flashing it everywhere.'

'I see.'

'Will you take care of it?'

'No,' Wu said. 'I can't return to the area.'

'Why not?'

Wu did not respond.

'Forget I asked that. We'll use Martin. He has the information on her children.'

Wu said nothing. He did not like the idea, but he kept it to himself.

The voice on the phone said, 'We'll take care of it,' before hanging up.

28

Grace said, 'Josh is lying.'

They were back on Main Street. Clouds threatened, but for now humidity ruled the day. Scott Duncan gestured a few stores up with his chin. 'I could use a Starbucks,' he said.

'Wait. You don't think he's lying?'

'He's nervous. There's a difference.'

Scott Duncan pulled open the glass door. Grace entered. There was a line at Starbucks. There always seemed to be a line at Starbucks. The sound system played something old from a female warbly blues singer, a Billie Holiday or Dinah Washington or Nina Simone. The song ended and a girl-with-acoustic-guitar came on, Jewel or Aimee Mann or Lucinda Williams.

'What about his inconsistencies?' she asked.

Scott Duncan frowned.

'What?'

'Does our friend Josh look like the type who willingly cooperates with authority?'

'No.'

'So what would you expect him to say?'

'His boss said that he had a family emergency. He told us he was sick.'

'It is an inconsistency,' he agreed.

'But?'

Scott Duncan gave an exaggerated shrug, mimicking Josh. 'I've worked a lot of cases. You know what I've learned about inconsistencies?'

She shook her head. In the background the milk did that froth thing, the machine making a noise like a car-wash vacuum.

'They exist. I'd be more suspicious if there weren't a few. The truth is always fuzzy. If his story had been clean, I'd be more concerned. I'd wonder if he rehearsed it. Keeping a lie consistent isn't that difficult, but in this guy's case, if you asked him what he ate for breakfast twice he'd mess it up.'

They moved forward in line. The *barista* asked for a drink order. Duncan looked at Grace. She ordered a venti iced Americano, no water. He nodded and said, 'Make that two.' He paid using one of those Starbucks debit cards. They waited for the drinks at the bar.

'So you think he was being truthful?' Grace asked.

'I don't know. But nothing he said raised much of a red flag.'

Grace wasn't so sure. 'It had to be him.'

'Why?'

'There was no one else.'

They picked up their drinks and found a table near the window. 'Run it through for me,' he said.

'Run what?'

'Go back. You picked up the pictures. Josh handed them to you. Did you look at them right away?'

Grace's eyes went up and to the right. She tried to remember the details. 'No.'

'Okay, so you took the packet. Did you stick it in your purse or something?'

'I held it.'

'And then what?'

'I got in my car.'

'The packet was still with you?'

'Yes.'

'Where?'

'On the console. Between the two front seats.'

'Where did you go?'

'To pick up Max from school.'

'Did you stop on the way?'

'No.'

'Were the pictures in your possession the whole time?'

Grace smiled in spite of herself. 'You sound like I'm checking in for a flight.'

'They don't ask that anymore.'

'It's been a while since I flew anywhere.' She smiled stupidly and realized why she had taken this inane detour in their conversation. He did too. She had spotted something – something she really didn't want to pursue.

'What?' he asked.

She shook her head.

'I might not have been able to tell if Josh was hiding something. You, however, make for an easier interrogation. What is it?'

'Nothing.'

'Come on, Grace.'

'The pictures were never out of my possession.'

'But?'

'Look, this is a waste of time. I know it was Josh. It had to be.'

'But?'

She took a deep breath. 'I'm just going to say this once, so we can dismiss it and get on with our lives.'

Duncan nodded.

'There was one person who *may* – I stress the word *may* – have had access.'

'Who?'

'I was sitting in the car waiting for Max. I opened the envelope and looked at the first few pictures. Then my friend Cora got in.'

'Got in your car?'

'Yes.'

'Where?'

'The passenger seat.'

'And the pictures were on the console next to it?'

'No, not anymore.' Her voice cracked now with annoyance. She was not enjoying this. 'I just told you. I was looking at them.'

'But you put them down?'

'Eventually, yeah, I guess.'

'On the console?'

'I guess. I don't remember.'

'So she had access.'

'No. I was there the whole time.'

'Who got out first?'

'We both got out at the same time, I think.'

'You limp.'

She looked at him. 'So?'

'So getting out must be something of an effort.'

'I do fine.'

'But come on, Grace, work with me here. It's possible – I'm not saying likely, I'm saying possible – that while you were stepping out, your friend could have slipped that picture into the envelope.'

'Possible, sure. But she didn't.'

'No way?'

'No way.'

'You trust her that much?'

'Yes. But even if I didn't, I mean, think about it. What was she doing – carrying around this picture in the hopes I'd have a packet of developed photos in my car?'

'Not necessarily. Maybe her plan was to plant it in your pocketbook. Or in the glove compartment. Or under the seat, I don't know. Then maybe she saw the roll of film and –'

'No.' Grace held up a hand. 'We're not going there. It's not Cora. It's a waste to even start down this road.'

'What's her last name?'

'It's not important.'

'Tell me that and I'll drop it.'

'Lindley. Cora Lindley.'

'Okay,' he said. 'I'll drop it.' But he was jotting on a small pad.

'Now what?' Grace asked.

Duncan checked his watch. 'I have to go back to work.'

'What should I do?'

'Search your house. If your husband was hiding something, maybe you'll get lucky.'

'Your suggestion is to spy on my husband?'

'Shake the cages, Grace.' He started for the car. 'Sit tight. I'll be back to you soon, promise.'

29

Life does not stop.

Grace had to do some food shopping. That might sound odd considering the circumstances. Her two children, she was sure, would gladly survive on a steady diet of delivered pizzas, but they still needed the basics: milk, orange juice (the kind with calcium and never, ever, pulp), a dozen eggs, sandwich meats, a couple of boxes of cereal, loaf of bread, box of pasta, a Prego sauce. Stuff like that. It might even feel good, food shopping. Doing the mundane, doing something so numbingly normal, would surely be, if not comforting, mildly therapeutic.

She hit the King's on Franklin Boulevard. Grace held no supermarket loyalties. Her friends had favorites and would never dream of shopping elsewhere. Cora liked the A&P in Midland Park. Her neighbor liked the Whole Foods in Ridgewood. Other acquaintances favored the Stop & Shop in Waldwick. Grace's selection was more haphazard because, to put it plainly, no matter where you shopped, Tropicana Orange Juice was Tropicana Orange Juice.

In this case the King's was the closest to Starbucks. Decision made.

She grabbed a cart and pretended that she was just an average citizen having an average day. That didn't last long. She thought about Scott Duncan, his sister, what that all meant.

Where, Grace wondered, do I go from here?

First off, the purported 'Cora Connection' – Grace dismissed it. There was simply no way. Duncan did not know Cora. His job was to be suspicious. Grace knew better. Cora was out there, no question about it, but that was what had drawn Grace to her in the first place. They had met at a school concert when the Lawsons first moved to town. While their kids butchered the holiday standards, they'd both been forced to stand in the lobby because neither of them had arrived early enough to secure a seat. Cora had leaned over and whispered, 'I had an easier time getting front row for Springsteen.' Grace had laughed. And so, slowly, it began.

But forget that. Forget Grace's own biased viewpoint. What possible motive could Cora have? The smart money was still on Fuzz Pellet Josh. Yes, he would naturally be nervous. Yes, he was probably antiauthority. But there was more there, Grace was sure of it. So forget Cora. Concentrate on Josh. Figure an angle on that.

Max was on a bacon kick. There was some newfangled premade bacon he'd had at a friend's house during a play-date. He wanted her to buy it. Grace was checking the health claims. Like the rest of the country she was concentrating more on lowering the carb intake. This stuff had none. No carbs at all. Enough sodium to salt a large body of water. But no carbs.

She was checking the ingredients – an interesting potpourri of words she'd need to look up – when she felt, actually felt, someone's eyes on her. Still holding the box at eye level, she slowly shifted her gaze. Down the corridor, near the bologna and salami display, a man stood and openly stared at her. There was no one else in the aisle. He was average height, maybe five-ten or so. A razor hadn't glided across his face in at least two days. He wore blue jeans, a maroon T-shirt, and a shiny black Members Only windbreaker. His baseball cap had a Nike swoosh on it.

Grace had never seen the man before. He stared at her for another moment before he spoke. His voice was barely a whisper.

'Mrs. Lamb,' the man said to her. 'Room 17.'

For a moment the words did not register. Grace just stood there, unable to move. It wasn't that she hadn't heard him – she had – but his words were so out of context, so out of place coming from this stranger's lips, that her brain could not really comprehend the significance.

At first anyway. For a second or two. Then it all flooded in ...

Mrs. Lamb. Room 17 ...

Mrs. Lamb was Emma's teacher. Room 17 was Emma's classroom.

The man was already on the move, hurrying down the aisle.

'Wait!' Grace shouted. 'Hey!'

The man turned the corner. Grace went after him. She tried to pick up speed but the limp, that damn limp, kept her in check. She reached the end of the aisle, coming out on the back wall by the chicken parts. She looked left and right.

No sign of the man.

Now what?

Mrs. Lamb. Room 17 ...

She moved to her right, checking down the aisles as she went. Her hand slid into her pocketbook, fumbled a bit, touched down on her cell phone.

Stay calm, she told herself. Call the school.

Grace tried to pick up the pace, but her leg dragged like a lead bar. The more she hurried, the more pronounced the limp became. When she really tried to run, she resembled Quasimodo heading up the belfry. Didn't matter, of course, what she looked like. The problem was function: She wasn't moving fast enough.

Mrs. Lamb. Room 17 ...

If he's done anything to my baby, if he's so much as looked at her wrong...

Grace reached the last aisle, the refrigerated section that housed the milk and eggs, the aisle farthest from the entrance so as to encourage impulse buy. She started toward the front of the store, hoping that she'd find him when she doubled back. She fiddled with her phone as she moved, no easy task, scrolling through her saved phone numbers to see if she had the school's.

She didn't.

Damn. Grace bet those other mothers, the good mothers, the ones with the perky smiles and ideal after-school projects – she bet they had the school's phone number preprogrammed into their speed dial.

Mrs. Lamb. Room 17 ...

Try directory assistance, stupid. Dial 411.

She hit the digits and the send button. When she reached the end of the aisle, she looked down the row of cashiers.

No sign of the man.

On the phone the thunder-deep voice of James Earl Jones announced: 'Verizon Wireless four-one-one.' Then a ding. A woman's voice now: 'For English please stay on the line. *Para espanol, por favor numero dos.*'

And it was then, listening to this Spanish option, that Grace spotted the man again.

He was outside the store now. She could see him through the plate glass window. He still wore the cap and the black windbreaker. He was strolling casually, too casually, whistling even, swinging his arms. She was about to start moving again when something – something in the man's hand – made her blood freeze.

It couldn't be.

Again it did not register immediately. The sight, the stimuli the eye was sending to the brain, would not compute, the information causing some sort of short circuit. Again not for long. Only for a second or two.

Grace's hand, the one with the phone in it, dropped to her side. The man kept walking. Terror – terror unlike anything she had ever experienced before, terror that made the Boston Massacre feel like an amusement park ride – hardened and banged against her chest. The man was almost out of sight now. There was a smile on his face. He was still whistling. His arms were still swinging.

And in his hand, his right hand, the hand closest to the window, he held a Batman lunchbox.

30

'Mrs. Lawson,' Sylvia Steiner, the principal of Willard School, said to Grace in that voice that principals use when dealing with hysterical parents, 'Emma is fine. So is Max.'

By the time Grace had made it to the door at King's, the man with the Batman lunchbox was gone. She started screaming, started asking for help, but her fellow shoppers looked at her as if she'd escaped from the county mental facility. There was no time to explain. She did her limp-run to her car, called the school while driving a speed that would have intimidated an Andretti, and burst straight into the main office.

'I spoke to both of their teachers. They're in class.'

'I want to see them.'

'Of course, that's your right, but may I make a suggestion?'

Sylvia Steiner spoke so damn slowly that Grace wanted to reach her hand down her throat and rip the words out.

'I'm sure you've had a terrible fright, but take a few deep breaths. Calm yourself first. You'll scare your children if they see you like this.'

Part of Grace wanted to grab her patronizing, smug, over-coiffed 'do and pull it off her head. But another part of her, a bigger part, realized that the woman was speaking the truth.

'I just need to see them,' Grace said.

'I understand. How about this? We can peek in on them from the window at the door. Would that work for you, Mrs. Lawson?'

Grace nodded.

'Come on then, I'll escort you.' Principal Steiner shot the woman working the desk a look. The woman at the desk, Mrs. Dinsmont, did everything she could not to roll her eyes. Every school has a seen-it-all woman like this at the front desk. State law or something.

The corridors were explosions of color. The artwork of children always broke Grace's heart. The pieces were like snapshots, a moment that is forever gone, a life-post, never to be repeated. Their artistic abilities will mature and change. The innocence will be gone, captured only in fingerpaint or coloring out of the lines, in uneven handwriting.

They reached Max's classroom first. Grace put her face to the glass. She spotted her son immediately. Max's back was to her, his face tilted up. He sat cross-legged in a circle on the floor. His teacher, Miss Lyons, was in a chair. She was reading a picture book, holding it up so the children could see it, while she read.

'Okay?' Principal Steiner asked.

Grace nodded.

They continued down the corridor. Grace saw number 17 ...

Mrs. Lamb. Room 17 ...

... on the door. She felt a fresh shiver and tried not to hurry. Principal Steiner, she knew, had noticed the limp. The leg ached in a way it hadn't in years. She peered through the glass. Her daughter was there, right where she should be. Grace had to fight back the tears. Emma had her head down. The eraser end of her pencil was in her mouth. She chewed on it, deep in thought. Why, Grace wondered, do we find such poignancy in watching our children when they don't know we're there? What exactly are we trying to see?

So now what?

Deep breaths. Calm. Her children were okay. That was the key thing. Think it through. Be rational.

Call the police. That was the obvious move.

Principal Steiner faked a cough. Grace looked at her.

'I know this is going to sound nuts,' Grace said, 'but I need to see Emma's lunchbox.'

Grace expected a look of surprise or exasperation, but no, Sylvia Steiner just nodded. She did not ask why – had in fact not questioned her bizarre behavior in any way. Grace was grateful.

'All the lunchboxes are kept in the cafeteria,' she explained. 'Each class has their own bucket. Would you like me to show you?'

'Thank you.'

The buckets were all lined up in grade order. They found the big blue bucket marked 'Susan Lamb, Room 17' and started going through it.

'What does it look like?' Principal Steiner asked.

Just as she was about to reply Grace saw it. Batman. The word *POW!* in yellow caps. She slowly lifted it into view. Emma's name was written on the bottom.

'Is that it?'

Grace nodded.

'A popular one this year.'

It took all her effort not to clutch the lunchbox to her chest. She put it back as though it were Venetian glass. They headed back to the main office in silence. Grace was tempted to pull the kids out of school. It was two-thirty. They'd be let out in a half an hour anyway. But no, that wouldn't work. That would probably just freak them out. She needed time to think, to consider her response, and when she thought about it, weren't Emma and Max safest right here, surrounded by others?

Grace thanked the principal again. They shook hands.

'Is there anything else I can do?' the principal asked.

'No, I don't think so.'

Grace left then. She stood outside on the walk. She closed her eyes for a moment. The fear was not so much dissolving as solidifying, turning into pure, primitive rage. She could feel the heat running up her neck. That bastard. That bastard had threatened her daughter.

Now what?

The police. She should call them. That was the obvious move. The phone was in her hand. She was about to dial when a simple thought stopped her: What exactly would she say?

Hi, I was in the supermarket today, see, and this man near the bologna section?

Well, he whispered the name of my kid's teacher. Right, teacher. Oh, and her class-room number. Yes, at the bologna section, right there with the Oscar Mayer meats. And then the man ran off. But, I saw him later with my daughter's lunchbox. Outside the supermarket. What was he doing? Just walking, I guess. Well, no, it wasn't really Emma's lunchbox. It was the same kind. Batman. No, he didn't make any overt threats. Sorry? Yes, I'm the same woman who said her husband had been kidnapped yesterday. Right, then my husband called and said he needed space. Yep, that was me, the same hysterical broad ...

Was there another option?

She ran it through again. The police already thought she was a whack job. Could she convince them otherwise? Perhaps. What would the cops do anyway? Would they assign a man full time to watch her children? Doubtful, even if she could somehow make them understand the urgency.

Then she remembered Scott Duncan.

He was with the U.S. attorney's office. That was like being a federal cop, right? He would have pull. He would have power. And most of all he would believe her.

Duncan had given her his cell number. She checked her pocket for it. Came up empty. Had she left it in the car? Probably. Didn't matter. He told her that he was heading back to work. The U.S. attorney's office was in Newark, she figured. Either that or Trenton. Trenton was too far a ride. Better to try Newark first. He should be there by now.

She stopped walking and turned to face the school. Her children were inside. Weird thought, but there it was. They spent their days here, away from her in this bastion of brick, and part of Grace found that oddly overwhelming. She dialed directory assistance and asked for the U.S. attorney's office in Newark. She spent the extra thirty-five cents to have the operator dial it for her.

'U.S. attorney for the state of New Jersey.'

'Scott Duncan, please.'

'Hold.'

Two rings and a woman answered. 'Goldberg,' she said.

'I'm looking for Scott Duncan.'

'What case?'

'Pardon?'

'What case is this in reference to?'

'No case. I just need to speak with Mr. Duncan.'

'May I ask what it's about?'

'It's a personal matter.'

'Sorry, I can't help you. Scott Duncan doesn't work here anymore. I'm covering most of his cases. If I can help you with that...'

Grace pulled the phone away from her ear. She looked at it as though from afar. She clicked the end button. She got into her car and again watched the brick building that currently housed her children. She watched it for a very long time, wondering if there was anyone she could truly trust, before deciding what to do.

She lifted the phone back into view. She pressed in the number.

'Yes?'

'This is Grace Lawson.'

Three seconds later, Carl Vespa said, 'Is everything okay?'

'I changed my mind,' Grace said. 'I do need your help.'

31

'His name is Eric Wu.'

Perlmutter was back at the hospital. He had been working on getting a warrant compelling Indira Khariwalla to tell him who her client was, but the county prosecutor was running into more interference than expected. In the meantime the lab boys were doing their thing. The fingerprints had been sent down to the NCIC, and now, if Daley was to be believed, they had an ID on the perp.

'Does he have a record?' Perlmutter asked.

'He was let out of Walden three months ago.'

'For?'

'Armed assault,' Daley said. 'Wu cut a deal on that Scope case. I called and asked around. This is one very bad man.'

'How bad?'

'Poop-in-your-pants bad. If ten percent of the rumors about this guy are true, I'm sleeping with my Barney the Dinosaur night-lite on.'

'I'm listening.'

'He grew up in North Korea. Orphaned at a young age. Spent time working for the state inside prisons for political dissidents. He has a talent with pressure points or something, I don't know. That's what he did with that Sykes guy, some kung-fu crap, practically severed his spine. One story I heard, he kidnapped some guy's wife, worked on her for like two hours. He calls the husband and tells him to listen up. The wife starts screaming. Then she tells him, the husband, that she hates his guts. Starts cursing him. That's the last thing the husband ever hears.'

'He killed the woman?'

Daley's face had never looked so solemn. 'That's just it. He didn't.'

The room's temperature dropped ten degrees. 'I don't understand.'

'Wu let her go. She hasn't spoken since. Just sits and rocks someplace. The husband comes near her, she freaks out and starts screaming.'

'Jesus.' Perlmutter felt the chill ease through him. 'You got an extra night-lite?'

'I got two, yeah, but I'm using both.'

'So what would this guy want with Freddy Sykes?'

'Not a clue.'

Charlaine Swain appeared down the corridor. She had not left the hospital since the shooting. They had finally gotten her to talk to Freddy Sykes. It had been a strange scene. Sykes kept crying. Charlaine had tried to get information. It'd worked to some extent. Freddy Sykes seemed to know nothing. He had no idea who his assailant was or why anyone would want to hurt him. Sykes was just a small-time accountant who lived alone – he seemed to be on no one's radar.

'It's all linked,' Perlmutter said.

'You have a theory?'

'I have some of it. Strands.'

'Let's hear.'

'Start with the E-ZPass records.'

'Okay.'

'We have Jack Lawson and Rocky Conwell crossing that exit at the same time,' Perlmutter said.

'Right.'

'I think now we know why. Conwell was working for a private investigator.'

'Your friend India Something.'

'Indira Khariwalla. And she's hardly a friend. But that's not important. What makes sense here, the only thing that makes sense really, is that Conwell was hired to follow Lawson.'

'Ipso facto, the E-ZPass timing explained.'

Perlmutter nodded, trying to put it together. 'So what happened next? Conwell ends up dead. The M.E. says he probably died that night before midnight. We know he crossed the tollbooth at 10:26 P.M. So sometime soon after that, Rocky Conwell met up with foul play.' Perlmutter rubbed his face. 'The logical suspect would be Jack Lawson. He realizes he's being followed. He confronts Conwell. He kills him.'

'Makes sense,' Daley said.

'But it doesn't. Think about it. Rocky Conwell was six-five, two-sixty, and in great shape. You think a guy like Lawson could have killed him like that? With his bare hands?'

'Sweet Jesus.' Daley saw it now. 'Eric Wu?'

Perlmutter nodded. 'It adds up. Somehow Conwell met up with Wu. Wu killed him, stuffed his body into a trunk, and left him at the Park-n-Ride. Charlaine Swain said that Wu was driving a Ford Windstar. Same model and color as Jack Lawson's.'

'So what's the connection between Lawson and Wu?'

'I don't know.'

'Maybe Wu works for him.'

'Could be. We just don't know. What we do know, however, is that Lawson's alive – or at least he was alive after Conwell was killed.'

'Right, because he called his wife. When she was at the station. So what happened next?'

'Damned if I know.'

Perlmutter watched Charlaine Swain. She just stood down the hall, staring through the window of her husband's room. Perlmutter considered going over, but really, what could he say?

Daley jostled him and they both turned to see Officer Veronique Baltrus walk off the elevator. Baltrus had been with the department three years. She was thirty-eight, with tousled black hair and a constant tan. She was in a regulation police uniform that somehow hugged as much as anything with a belt and holster could, but in her off-hours she preferred Lycra workout clothes or anything that revealed the flat tan of her stomach. She was petite, with dark eyes, and every guy in the station, even Perlmutter, had a thing for her.

Veronique Baltrus was both exquisitely beautiful and a computer expert – an interesting albeit heart-racing combination. Six years ago she had been working for a bathing suit retailer in New York City when the stalking began. The stalker would call her. He would send e-mails. He would harass her at work. His main weapon was the computer, the best bastion for the anonymous and gutless. The police did not have the manpower to hunt him down. They also believed that this stalker, whoever he was, would probably not take it to the next level.

But he did.

On a calm fall evening Veronique Baltrus was savagely attacked. Her assailant got away. But Veronique recovered. Already good with computers, she now upped her ability and became an expert. She used her new knowledge to hunt down her assailant – he continued to send her e-mails discussing an encore – and bring him to justice. Then she quit her job and became a police officer.

Now, even though Baltrus wore a uniform and worked a regular shift, she was the county's unofficial computer expert. Nobody in the department but Perlmutter knew her back story. That was part of the deal when she applied for the job.

'You got something?' he asked her.

Veronique Baltrus smiled. She had a nice smile. Perlmutter's 'thing' for her was different than the rest of the guys'. It was not built simply on lust. Veronique Baltrus was the first woman to make him feel something since Marion's death. He wouldn't take it anywhere. It would be unprofessional. It would be unethical. And truth be told, Veronique was waaaaay out of his league.

She gestured down the corridor toward Charlaine Swain. 'We might have to thank her.'

'How so?'

'Al Singer.'

That, Sykes had told Charlaine, was the name Eric Wu used when he pretended to be making a delivery. When Charlaine asked who Al Singer was, Sykes jolted a little and denied knowing any Mr. Singer. He said he opened the door anyway out of curiosity. Perlmutter said, 'I thought Al Singer was a fake name.'

'Yes and no,' Baltrus said. 'I went through Mr. Sykes's computer pretty thoroughly. He'd signed up for an online dating service and had been corresponding fairly regularly with a man named Al Singer.'

Perlmutter made a face. 'A gay dating service?'

'Bisexual, actually. That a problem?'

'No. So Al Singer was, what, his online lover?'

'Al Singer doesn't exist. It was an alias.'

'Isn't that common online, especially at a gay dating service? Using an alias?'

'It is,' Baltrus agreed. 'But here's my point. Your Mr. Wu pretended to make a delivery. He used that name, Singer. How would Wu know about Al Singer unless ...?'

'You saying Eric Wu is Al Singer?'

Baltrus nodded, rested her hands on her hips. 'That would be my guess, sure. Here's what I think: Wu goes online. He uses the name Al Singer. He meets some people – potential victims – that way. In this case, he meets Freddy Sykes. He breaks into his home and assaults him. My guess is, he would have eventually killed Sykes.'

'You think he's done this before?'

'Yes.'

'So he's, what, some kind of serial bisexual basher?'

'That I don't know. But it fits the action I'm seeing on the computer.'

Perlmutter thought about it. 'Does this Al Singer have any other online partners?'

'Three more.'

'Have any of them been assaulted?'

'Not yet, no. They're all healthy.'

'So what makes you think it's serial?'

'It's too early to say for sure one way or the other. But Charlaine Swain did us a huge favor. Wu was using Sykes's computer. He probably planned on destroying it before he left, but Charlaine flushed him out before he had time. I'm piecing it together now, but there's definitely another online persona in there. I don't know the name yet, but he's working out of yenta-match.com. Jewish singles.'

'How do we know it's not Freddy Sykes?'

'Because whoever accessed this page did so in the past twenty-four hours.'

'So it had to be Wu.'

'Yes.'

'I still don't get it. Why would he go to another online dating service?'

'To find more victims,' she said. 'Here's how I think it works: This Wu has a bunch of different names and personas at a bunch of different dating sites. Once he, shall we say, uses one, like Al Singer, he won't dip into that dating pool again. He used Al Singer to get to Freddy Sykes. He'd have to know that an investigator could track that down.'

'So he stops using Al Singer.'

'Right. But he's been using other aliases at other sites. So he's ready for his next victim.'

'Do you have any of the other names yet?'

'Getting close,' Baltrus said. 'I just need a warrant for yenta-match.com.'

'You think a judge will grant it?'

'The only identity we know Wu accessed recently is the one at the yenta-match site. I think he was seeking out his next victim. If we can get a list of what name he used and who he contacted ...'

'Keep digging.'

'Will do.'

Veronique Baltrus hurried out. Wrong as it felt – he was, after all, her superior – Perlmutter watched her go with a longing that made him remember Marion.

32

Ten minutes later Carl Vespa's driver – the infamous Cram – met Grace two blocks away from the school.

Cram arrived on foot. Grace did not know how or where his car was. She'd just been standing there, looking at the school from afar, when she felt the tap on her shoulder. She leapt, her heart pounding. When she turned and saw his face, well, the sight was hardly a comforting one.

Cram arched an eyebrow. 'You rang?'

'How did you get here?'

Cram shook his head. Up close, now that she was able to get a really good look at him, the man was even more hideous than she remembered. His skin was pockmarked. His nose and mouth looked like an animal's snout, what with the sea-predator smile locked on autopilot. Cram was older than she'd thought, probably nearing sixty. He was wiry though. He had the wild-eyed look she'd always associated with serious psychosis, but there was a comfort to that element of danger right now, the kind of guy you'd want next to you in a foxhole and nowhere else.

'Tell me everything,' Cram said.

Grace started with Scott Duncan and moved on to arriving at the supermarket. She told him what the unshaven man had said to her, about him darting down the aisle, about him carrying the Batman lunchbox. Cram chewed on a toothpick. He had thin fingers. His nails were too long.

'Describe him.'

She did as best she could. When she was done, Cram spit out the toothpick and shook his head. 'For real?' he said.

'What?'

'A Members Only jacket? What is this, 1986?'

Grace did not laugh.

'You're safe now,' he said. 'Your children are safe.'

She believed him.

'What time do they get out?'

'Three o'clock.'

'Fine.' He squinted at the school. 'Christ, I hated this place.'

'You went here?'

Cram nodded. 'A Willard graduate, 1957.' She tried to picture him as a little boy coming to this school. The image would not hold. He started walking away.

'Wait,' she said. 'What do you want me to do?'

'Pick up your kids. Bring them home.'

'Where will you be?'

Cram upped the grin. 'Around.' And then he was gone.

Grace waited by the fence. The mothers began to flock in, gather, chat. Grace folded her arms, trying to give off a 'keep away' vibe. There were days she could participate in the clatter. This was not one of them.

The cell phone rang. She put it to her ear and said hello.

'You get the message now?'

The voice was male and muffled. Grace felt her scalp tingle. 'Stop looking, stop asking questions, stop flashing the picture. Or we'll take Emma first.'

Click.

Grace did not scream. She would not scream. She put the phone away. Her hands shook. She looked down at them as if they belonged to someone else. She couldn't stop the shake. Her children would be coming out soon. She jammed her hands into her pockets and tried to force up a smile. It wouldn't come. She bit her lower lip and made herself not cry.

'Hey, you okay?'

Grace startled at the voice. It was Cora.

'What are you doing here?' Grace asked. The words came out with too sharp a snap.

'What do you think? I'm picking up Vickie.'

'I thought she was with her father.'

Cora looked puzzled. 'Just for last night. He dropped her off at school this morning. Jesus, what the hell happened?'

'I can't talk about it.'

Cora did not know how to react to that one. The bell sounded. Both women turned away. Grace did not know what to think. She knew that Scott Duncan was wrong about Cora – more than that, she now knew that Scott Duncan was a liar – and yet, once voiced, the suspicion about her friend would not leave. She couldn't flick it away.

'Look, I'm just scared, okay?'

Cora nodded. Vickie appeared first. 'If you need me ...'

'Thank you.'

Cora moved away without another word. Grace waited alone, searching for the familiar faces in the stream of children pouring through the door. Emma stepped into the sunshine and shielded her eyes. When she spotted her mother, Emma's face broke into a smile. She waved.

Grace suppressed a cry of relief. Her fingers snaked through the chain-link, gripping hard, holding herself back so she wouldn't sprint over and scoop Emma into her arms.

When Grace, Emma, and Max reached home, Cram was already standing on their front stoop.

Emma looked a question at her mother, but before Grace could respond, Max sprinted up the walk. He stopped dead in front of Cram and craned his neck to look up at the sea-predator smile.

'Hey,' Max said to Cram.

'Hey.'

Max said, 'You were the guy driving that big car, right?'

'Right.'

'That cool? Driving that big car?'

'Very.'

'I'm Max.'

'I'm Cram.'

'Cool name.'

'Yeah. Yeah, it is.'

Max made a fist and held it up. Cram made one too and then they touched knuckles-against-knuckles in some newfangled high-five. Grace and Emma came up the walk.

'Cram is a family friend,' Grace said. 'He's going to help me a little.'

Emma did not like it. 'Help with what?' She aimed her 'eeuw gross' face in Cram's direction, which, under the circumstances, was both understandable and rude, but this was hardly the time for a correction. 'Where's Daddy?'

'He's on a business trip,' Grace said.

Emma did not say another word. She stepped into the house and ran upstairs.

Max squinted up at Cram. 'Can I ask you something?'

'Sure,' Cram said.

'Do all your friends call you Cram?'

'Yes.'

'Just Cram?'

'One word.' He wiggled his eyebrows. 'Like Cher or Fabio.'

'Who?'

Cram chuckled.

'Why do they call you that?' Max asked.

'Why do they call me Cram?'

'Yeah.'

'My teeth.' He opened his mouth wide. When Grace worked up the courage to look, she was greeted with a sight that resembled the mad experiment of a very deranged orthodontist. The teeth were all crammed together on the left, almost stacked. It looked like there were too many of them. Empty pockets of coarse pink where teeth should have been lined the right side of his mouth. 'Cram,' he said. 'You see?'

'Whoa,' Max said. 'That's so cool.'

'You want to know how my teeth got this way?'

Grace took that one. 'No, thank you.'

Cram glanced at her. 'Good answer.'

Cram. She took another look at the too-small teeth. Tic Tac might have been a more apt name.

'Max, you have homework?'

'Aw, Mom.'

'Now,' she said.

Max looked at Cram. 'Scram,' he said. 'We'll talk later.'

They shared another fist-knuckle salute before Max darted off with the abandon of a six-year-old. The phone rang. Grace checked the Caller ID. It was Scott Duncan. She decided to let the machine pick that one up – more important that she talk to Cram. They moved into the kitchen. There were two men sitting at the table. Grace pulled up short. Neither of the men looked up at her. They were whispering to each other. Grace was about to say something, but Cram signaled her to step outside.

'Who are they?'

'They work for me.'

'Doing?'

'Don't worry about it.'

She did, but right now there were more pressing matters. 'I got a call from the guy,' she said. 'On my cell phone.' She told him what the voice on the phone had said. Cram's expression did not change. When she finished, he pulled out a cigarette.

'You mind if I smoke?'

She told him to go ahead.

'I won't do it in the house.'

Grace looked around. 'Is that why we're out here?'

Cram did not reply. He lit the cigarette, drew a deep breath, let the smoke pour out of both nostrils. Grace looked toward the neighbor's yard. There was no one in sight. A dog barked. A lawn mower ripped through the air like a helicopter.

Grace looked at him. 'You've threatened people, right?'

'Yup.'

'So if I do what he says – if I stop – do you think they'll leave us alone?'

'Probably.' Cram took a puff so deep it looked like a doobie toke. 'But the real question is, why do they want you to stop?'

'Meaning?'

'Meaning you must have been getting close. You must have struck a nerve.'

'I can't imagine how.'

'Mr. Vespa called. He wants to see you tonight.'

'What about?'

Cram shrugged.

She looked off again.

'You ready for some more bad news?' Cram asked.

She turned to him.

'Your computer room. The one in the back.'

'What about it?'

'It's bugged. One listening device, one camera.'

'A camera?' She couldn't believe this. 'In my house?'

'Yeah. Hidden camera. It's in a book on the shelf. Fairly easy to spot if you're looking for it. You can get one at any spy shop. You've probably seen them online. You hide it in a clock or a smoke detector, that kind of thing.'

Grace tried to take this in. 'Someone is spying on us?'

'Yup.'

'Who?'

'No idea. I don't think it's the cops. It's a little too amateur for that. My boys have given the rest of the house a quick sweep. Nothing else so far.'

'How long...' She tried to comprehend what he was telling her. 'How long has the camera and – listening device, did you say? – how long have they been here?'

'No way to know. That's why I dragged you out here. So we could talk freely. I know you've been hit with a lot, but you're ready to deal with this now?'

She nodded, though her head was swimming.

'Okay, first off. The equipment. It's not all that sophisticated. It only has a range of maybe a hundred feet. If it's a live feed, it goes to a van or something. Have you noticed any vans parked on the street for long periods of time?'

'No.'

'I didn't think so. It probably just goes to a video recorder.'

'Like a VCR?'

'Exactly like a VCR.'

'And it has to be within a hundred feet of the house?'

'Yep.'

She looked around as if it might be in the garden. 'How often would they need to change tape?'

'Every twenty-four hours tops.'

'Any idea where it is?'

'Not yet. Sometimes they keep the recorder in the basement or garage. They probably have access to the house, so they can fetch the tape and put in a new one.'

'Wait a second. What do you mean, they have access to the house?'

He shrugged. 'They got that camera and bug in somehow, right?'

The rage was back now, rising, smoldering behind her eyes. Grace started looking at her neighbors. Access to the house. Who had access to the house? she asked herself. And a small voice replied ...

Cora.

Uh-uh, no way. Grace shook it off. 'So we need to find that recorder.'

'Yes.'

'And then we wait and watch,' she said. 'We see who picks up the tape.'

'That's one way of doing it,' Cram said.

'You have a better suggestion?'

'Not really.'

'Then, what, we follow the guy, see where it leads?'

'That's a possibility.'

'But ...?'

'It's risky. We could lose him.'

'What would you do?'

'If it were up to me, I'd grab him. I'd ask him some hard questions.'

'And if he refused to answer?'

Cram still wore the sea-predator smile. It was always a horrific sight, this man's face, but Grace was getting used to it. She also realized that he was not intentionally scaring her; whatever had been done to his mouth had made that become his permanent, natural expression. It spoke volumes, that face. It rendered her question rhetorical.

Grace wanted to protest, to tell him that she was civil and that they would handle this legally and ethically. But instead she said, 'They threatened my daughter.'

'So they did.'

She looked at him. 'I can't do what they asked. Even if I wanted to. I can't just walk away and leave it alone.'

He said nothing.

'I have no choice, do I? I have to fight them.'

'I don't see any other way.'

'You knew that all along.'

Cram cocked his head to the right. 'So did you.'

His cell phone went off. Cram flipped it open but did not speak, not even a hello. A few seconds later he snapped the phone shut and said, 'Someone is pulling up the drive.'

She looked out the screen door. A Ford Taurus came to a stop. Scott Duncan stepped out and approached the house.

'You know him?' Cram asked.

'That,' she said, 'is Scott Duncan.'

'The guy who lied about working for the U.S. attorney?'

Grace nodded.

'Maybe,' Cram said, 'I'll stick around.'

They remained outside. Scott Duncan stood next to Grace. Cram had stepped away. Duncan kept sneaking glances at Cram. 'Who is that?'

'You don't want to know.'

Grace gave Cram a look. He got the hint and headed back inside. She and Scott Duncan were alone now.

'What do you want?' she asked.

Duncan picked up on her tone. 'Something wrong, Grace?'

'I'm just surprised you got out of work already. I figured it'd be busier at the U.S. attorney's office.'

He said nothing.

'Cat got your tongue, Mr. Duncan?'

'You called my office.'

She touched her nose with her index finger, indicating a direct hit. Then: 'Oh wait, correction: I called the United States attorney's office. Apparently you don't work there.'

'It's not what you think.'

'How enlightening.'

'I should have told you up front.'

'Do tell.'

'Look, everything I said was true.'

'Except the part about working for the United States attorney. I mean, that wasn't true, was it? Or was Ms. Goldberg lying?'

'Do you want me to explain or not?'

Now his voice had a little steel. Grace gestured for him to continue.

'What I told you was true. I worked there. Three months ago this killer, this Monte Scanlon, he insisted on seeing me. No one could understand why. I was a low-level lawyer on political corruption. Why would a hit man insist on talking only to me? That was when he told me.'

'That he killed your sister.'

'Yes.'

She waited. They moved toward the porch furniture and sat down. Cram stood in a window watching them. He let his gaze wander toward Scott Duncan, hang there for a few heavy seconds, survey the grounds, go back to Duncan.

'He looks familiar,' Duncan said, gesturing toward Cram. 'Or maybe I'm flash-ing back to the Pirates of the Caribbean ride at Disney World. Shouldn't he have an eye patch?'

Grace shifted in her seat. 'You were telling me about why you lied?'

Duncan ran his hand through the sandy hair. 'When Scanlon said the fire was no accident ... You can't understand what it did to me. I mean, one moment my life was one thing. The next ...' He snapped his finger with a magician's flourish. 'It wasn't so much that everything was different now – it was more like the past fifteen years had all been different. Like someone had gone back in time and changed one event and it changed everything else. I wasn't the same guy. I wasn't a guy whose sister died in a tragic fire. I was a guy whose sister had been murdered and never avenged.'

'But now you have the killer,' Grace said. 'He confessed.'

Duncan smiled, but there was no joy there. 'Scanlon said it best. He was just a weapon. Like a gun. I wanted the person who pulled the trigger. It became an obsession. I tried to do it part-time, you know, work my job while searching for the killer. But I started to neglect my cases. So my boss, she strongly suggested I take a leave.' He looked up at her.

'Why didn't you just tell me?'

'I didn't think it would be a great opening line, you know, telling you I was forced out like that. I still have connections in the office. I still have friends in law enforcement. But just so we're clear, everything I'm doing is off the books.'

Their eyes locked. Grace said, 'You're still holding something back.'

He hesitated.

'What is it?'

'We should get one thing straight.' Duncan stood, did the run through the sandy hair bit again, turned away from her. 'Right now we're both trying to find your husband. It's a temporary alliance. The truth is, we have separate agendas. I won't lie to you. What happens after we find Jack, well, do we both want the truth?'

'I just want my husband.'

He nodded. 'That's what I mean about separate agendas. About our alliance being temporary. You want your husband. I want my sister's killer.'

He looked at her now. She understood.

'So now what?' Grace asked.

He took out the mystery photograph and held it up. There was a hint of a smile on his face.

'What?'

Scott Duncan said, 'I know the name of the redhead in the photograph.' She waited.

'Her name is Sheila Lambert. Attended Vermont University the same time as your husband' – he pointed at Jack and then slid his finger to the right – 'and Shane Alworth.'

'Where is she now?'

'That's just the thing, Grace. No one knows.'

She closed her eyes. A shudder ran through her.

'I sent the photograph up to the school. A retired dean identified her. I ran a full check, but she's gone. There is no sign of Sheila Lambert's existence over the past decade – no payroll tax, no social security number hit, nothing.'

'Just like with Shane Alworth.'

'Exactly like Shane.'

Grace tried to put it together. 'Five people in the photograph. One, your sister, was murdered. Two others, Shane Alworth and Sheila Lambert, haven't been heard of in years. The fourth, my husband, ran overseas and is missing now. And the last one, well, we still don't know who she is.'

Duncan nodded.

'So where do we go from here?'

'You remember I said I talked to Shane Alworth's mother?'

'The one with the fuzzy Amazonian geography.'

'When I visited her the first time, I didn't know about this picture or your husband or any of that. I want to show her the picture now. I want to gauge her reaction. And I want you there.'

'Why?'

'I just have a feeling, that's all. Evelyn Alworth is an old woman. She's emotional and I think she's scared. I went in there the first time as an investigator. Maybe, I don't know, but maybe if you go in as a concerned mother, something will shake loose.'

Grace hesitated. 'Where does she live?'

'A condo in Bedminster. Shouldn't take us more than thirty minutes to get there.'

Cram came back into view. Scott Duncan nodded toward him.

'So what's with that scary guy?' Duncan asked.

'I can't go with you now.'

'Why not?'

'I have the kids. I can't just leave them here.'

'Bring them along. There's a playground right there. We won't take long.'

Cram came to the door now. He beckoned with his hand for Grace. She said, 'Excuse me' and headed toward Cram. Scott Duncan stayed where he was.

'What is it?' she asked Cram.

'Emma. She's upstairs crying.'

Grace found her daughter in classic cry position – facedown on her bed, pillow over her head. The sound was muted. It had been a while since Emma had cried like this. Grace sat on the edge of the bed. She knew what was coming. When Emma could speak, she asked where Daddy was. Grace told her that he was on a business trip. Emma said that she didn't believe her. That it was a lie. Emma demanded to know the truth. Grace repeated that Jack was just on a business trip. That everything was fine. Emma pushed. Where was he? Why hadn't Daddy called? When was he coming home? Grace made up rationales that sounded pretty believable in her ears – he was really busy, he was traveling in Europe, London right now, didn't know how long he'd be gone, he had called but Emma had been sleeping, remember that London is in a different time zone.

Did Emma buy it? Who knew?

Child-rearing experts – those namby-pamby, lobotomy-voiced Ph.D.s on cable TV – would probably tsk-tsk, but Grace was not one of those tell-kids-everything parents. Above all else a mother's job was to protect. Emma was not old enough to handle the truth. Plain and simple. Deception was a necessary part of parenting. Of course Grace could be wrong – she knew that – but the old adage is true: Kids don't come with instructions. We all mess up. Raising a child is pure impromptu.

A few minutes later she told Max and Emma to get ready. They were going for a ride. Both children grabbed their Game Boys and piled into the back of the car. Scott Duncan moved toward the passenger seat. Cram cut him off.

'Problem?' Duncan said.

'I want to talk to Ms. Lawson before you go. Stay here.'

Duncan snapped a sarcastic salute. Cram gave him a look that could have held back a weather front. He and Grace stepped into the back room. Cram closed the door.

'You know you shouldn't go with him.'

'Maybe not. But I have to.'

Cram chewed on his lower lip. He didn't like it, but he understood. 'Do you carry a purse?'

'Yes.'

'Let me see it.'

She showed it to him. Cram pulled a gun out of his waist. It was small, almost toylike. 'This is a Glock nine-millimeter, model 26.'

Grace held up her hands. 'I don't want that.'

'Keep it in your purse. You can also wear it in an ankle holster but you'll need long pants.'

'I've never fired a gun in my life.'

'Experience is overrated. You aim for the middle of the chest, you squeeze the trigger. It's not complicated.'

'I don't like weapons.'

Cram shook his head.

'What?'

'Maybe I'm mistaken, but didn't somebody threaten your daughter today?'

That made her pause. Cram put the gun in her purse. She did not fight him.

'How long are you going to be gone?' Cram asked.

'Couple of hours, tops.'

'Mr. Vespa will be here at 7 P.M. He says it's important that he speaks to you.'

'I'll be here.'

'You sure you trust this Duncan guy?'

'I'm not sure. But I think we're safe with him.'

Cram nodded. 'Let me add a little insurance on that front.'

'How?'

Cram said nothing. He escorted her back. Scott Duncan was on his cell phone. Grace did not like what she saw on Duncan's face. He finished up his call when he spotted them.

'What?'

Scott Duncan shook his head. 'Can we go now?'

Cram walked toward him. Duncan did not back down, but there was definitely an understandable flinch. Cram stopped directly in front of him, stuck out his hand, wiggled his fingers. 'Let me see your wallet.'

'Pardon me?'

'Do I look like the kind of guy who enjoys repeating himself?'

Scott Duncan glanced at Grace. She nodded. Cram still had the fingers wiggling. Duncan handed Cram his wallet. Cram brought it over to a table and sat down. He quickly rifled through the contents, taking notes.

'What are you doing?' Duncan asked.

'While you're gone, Mr. Duncan, I'm going to learn everything about you.' He looked up. 'If Ms. Lawson is harmed in any way, my response will be' – Cram stopped, looked up as though searching for the word – 'disproportionate. I make myself clear?'

Duncan looked at Grace. 'Who the hell is this guy?'

Grace was already moving toward the car door. 'We'll be fine, Cram.'

Cram shrugged, tossed Duncan his wallet. 'Have a delightful drive.'

No one talked for the first five minutes of the ride. Max and Emma used their headphones with the Game Boys. Grace had bought the headphones recently because the beeps and buzzes and Luigi shouting 'Mamma Mia!' every two minutes gave her a headache. Scott Duncan sat next to her with his hands in his lap.

'So who was on the phone?' Grace asked.

'A coroner.'

Grace waited.

'Remember how I told you that I had my sister's body exhumed?' he said.

'Yes.'

'The police didn't really see a need for it. Too expensive. I understand, I guess. Anyway I paid for it myself. I know this person, used to work for a country M.E., who does private autopsies.'

'And he's the one who called you?'

'It's a she. Her name is Sally Li.'

'And?'

'And she says she needs to see me right away.' Duncan looked over at her. 'Her office is in Livingston. We can hit it on the way back.' He turned back away. 'I'd like you to come with me, if that's okay.'

'To a morgue?'

'No, nothing like that. Sally does the actual autopsy work at St. Barnabas Hospital. This is just an office where she does her paperwork. There's a waiting room we can stick the kids in.'

Grace did not reply.

The Bedminster condos were generic, which, when you're talking about condos, is something of a repetition in terms. They had the prefab light-brown aluminum siding, three levels, garages underneath, every building identical to the one to its right and to its left and behind it and in front of it. The complex was huge and sprawling, a khaki-coated ocean stretching as far as the eye could see.

For Grace, the route here had been familiar. Jack drove by this on his way to work. They had, for a very brief moment, debated moving into this condo development. Neither Jack nor Grace was particularly good with their hands or enjoyed fix-the-old-home shows on cable. Condos held that appeal – you pay a monthly fee, you don't worry about the roof or an addition or the landscaping or any of that. There were tennis courts and a swimming pool and, yes, a playground for children. But in the end there was just so much conformity one could take. Suburbia is already a subworld of sameness. Why add insult to injury by making your physical abode conform too?

Max spotted the complicated, brightly hued playground before the car had come to a complete stop. He was raring to sprint for the swing set. Emma looked more bored with the prospect. She held onto her Game Boy. Normally Grace would have protested – Game Boy in the car only, especially when the alternative was fresh air – but again now did not seem the time.

Grace cupped her hand over her eyes as they started moving away. 'I can't leave them alone.'

'Mrs. Alworth lives right here,' Duncan said. 'We can stay in the doorway and watch them.'

They approached the door on the first level. The playground was quiet. The air was still. Grace inhaled deeply and smelled the freshly cut grass. They stood side-by-side, she and Duncan. He rang the bell. Grace waited by the door, feeling oddly like a Jehovah's Witness.

A cackling voice not unlike the witch in an old Disney film said, 'Who is it?'

'Mrs. Alworth?'

Again the cackle: 'Who is it?'

'Mrs. Alworth, it's Scott Duncan.'

'Who?'

'Scott Duncan. We spoke a few weeks ago. About your son, Shane.'

'Go away. I have nothing to say to you.'

Grace picked up an accent now. Boston area.

'We could really use your help.'

'I don't know nothing. Go away.'

'Please, Mrs. Alworth, I need to talk to you about your son.'

'I told you. Shane lives in Mexico. He's a good boy. He helps poor people.'

'We need to ask about some of his old friends.' Scott Duncan looked at Grace, nodded for her to say something.

'Mrs. Alworth,' Grace said.

The cackle was more wary now. 'Who's that?'

'My name is Grace Lawson. I think my husband knew your son.'

There was silence now. Grace turned away from the door and watched Max and Emma. Max was on a corkscrew slide. Emma sat cross-legged and played the Game Boy.

Through the door, the cackling voice asked, 'Who's your husband?'

'Jack Lawson.'

Nothing.

'Mrs. Alworth?'

'I don't know him.'

Scott Duncan said, 'We have a picture. We'd like to show it to you.'

The door opened. Mrs. Alworth wore a housedress that couldn't have been manufactured after the Bay of Pigs. She was in her mid-seventies, heavyset, the kind of big aunt who hugs you and you disappear in the folds. As a kid you hate the hug. As an adult you long for it. She had varicose veins that resembled sausage casing. Her reading glasses dangled against her enormous chest from a chain. She smelled faintly of cigarette smoke.

'I don't have all day,' she said. 'Show me this picture.'

Scott Duncan handed her the photograph.

For a long time the old woman said nothing.

'Mrs. Alworth?'

'Why did someone cross her out?' she asked.

'That was my sister,' Duncan said.

164

She flicked a glance his way. 'I thought you said you were an investigator.'

'I am. My sister was murdered. Her name was Geri Duncan.'

Mrs. Alworth's face went white. Her lip started to tremble. 'She's dead?'

'She was murdered. Fifteen years ago. Do you remember her?'

She seemed to have lost her bearings. She turned to Grace and snapped, 'What do you keep looking at?'

Grace was facing Max and Emma. 'My children.' She gestured toward the playground. Mrs. Alworth followed suit. She stiffened. She seemed lost now, confused.

'Did you know my sister?' Duncan asked.

'What does this have to do with me?'

His voice was stern now. 'Yes or no, did you know my sister?'

'I can't remember. It was a long time ago.'

'Your son dated her.'

'He dated a lot of girls. Shane was a handsome boy. So was his brother, Paul. He's a psychologist in Missouri. Why don't you leave me alone and talk to him?'

'Try to think.' Scott's voice rose a notch. 'My sister was murdered.' He pointed to the picture of Shane Alworth. 'That's your son, isn't it, Mrs. Alworth?'

She stared down at the strange photograph for a long time before nodding. 'Where is he?'

'I told you before. Shane lives in Mexico. He helps poor people.'

'When was the last time you spoke with him?'

'Last week.'

'He called you?'

'Yes.'

'Where?'

'What do you mean where?'

'Did Shane call you here?'

'Of course. Where else would he call?'

Scott Duncan took a step closer. 'I checked your phone records, Mrs. Alworth. You haven't gotten or made an international call in the past year.'

'Shane uses one of those phone cards,' she said too quickly. 'Maybe the phone companies don't pick those up, how I should know?'

Duncan took another step closer. 'Listen to me, Mrs. Alworth. And please listen closely. My sister is dead. There is no sign of your son anywhere. This man here' – he pointed to the picture of Jack – 'her husband, Jack Lawson, he's also missing. And this woman over here' – he pointed to the redheaded girl with the spaced-out eyes – 'her name is Sheila Lambert. There's been no sign of her for at least ten years.'

'This has got nothing to do with me,' Mrs. Alworth insisted.

'Five people in the photograph. We've been able to identify four of them. They're all gone. One we know is dead. For all we know, they all are.'

'I told you. Shane is –'

'You're lying, Mrs. Alworth. Your son graduated Vermont University. So did Jack Lawson and Sheila Lambert. They must have been friends. He dated my sister; we both know that. So what happened to them? Where is your son?'

Grace put a hand on Scott's arm. Mrs. Alworth was staring out now toward the playground, at the children. Her bottom lip was quivering. Her skin was ashen.

Tears ran down both cheeks. She looked as if she'd fallen into a trance. Grace tried to step in her line of vision.

'Mrs. Alworth,' she said gently.

'I'm an old woman.'

Grace waited.

'I don't have nothing to say to you people.'

Grace said, 'I'm trying to find my husband.' Mrs. Alworth was still staring at the playground. 'I'm trying to find their father.'

'Shane is a good boy. He helps people.'

'What happened to him?' Grace asked.

'Leave me alone.'

Grace tried to meet the older woman's gaze, but the focus was gone from her eyes. 'His sister' – Grace gestured toward Duncan – 'my husband, your son. Whatever happened affected us all. We want to help.'

But the old woman shook her head and turned away. 'My son doesn't need your help. Now go away. Please.' She stepped back into her house and closed the door.

33

When they were back in the car, Grace said, 'When you told Mrs. Alworth you checked her phone records for international calls ...'

Duncan nodded. 'It was a bluff.'

The children were plugged back into their Game Boys. Scott Duncan called the coroner. She was waiting for them.

Grace said, 'We're getting closer to the answer, aren't we?'

'I think so.'

'Mrs. Alworth might be telling the truth. I mean, as far as she knows.'

'How do you figure?' he asked.

'Something happened years ago. Jack ran away overseas. Maybe Shane Alworth and Sheila Lambert did too. Your sister, for whatever reason, hung around and ended up dead.'

He did not reply. His eyes were suddenly moist. There was a tremor in the corner of his mouth.

'Scott?'

'She called me. Geri. Two days before the fire.'

Grace waited.

'I was running out the door. You have to understand. Geri was a bit of a kook. She was always so melodramatic. She said she had to tell me something important, but I figured it could wait. I figured it was about whatever new thing she was into – aromatherapy, her new rock band, her etchings, whatever. I said I'd call her back.'

He stopped, shrugged. 'But I forgot.'

Grace wanted to say something, but nothing came to her. Words of comfort would probably do more harm than good right now. She took hold of the wheel and glanced in the rearview mirror. Emma and Max both had their heads lowered, their thumbs working the buttons on the tiny console. She felt that overwhelmed thing coming on, that pure blast in the middle of normalcy, the bliss from the everyday.

'Do you mind if we stop at the coroner's now?' Duncan asked.

Grace hesitated.

'It's about a mile away. Just turn right at the next light.'

In for a penny, Grace thought. She drove. He gave directions. A minute later he pointed up ahead. 'It's that office building on the corner.'

The medical office seemed dominated by dentists and orthodontists. When they opened the door, there was that antiseptic smell Grace always associated with a voice telling her to rinse and spit. An ophthalmology group called Laser Today was listed for the second floor. Scott Duncan pointed to the name 'Sally Li,

MD.' The directory said she was on the lower level.

There was no receptionist. The door chimed when they entered. The office was properly sparse. The furniture consisted of two distressed couches and one flickering lamp that wouldn't muster a price tag at a garage sale. The lone magazine was a catalogue of medical examiner tools.

An Asian woman, mid-forties and exhausted, stuck her head through the door of the inner office. 'Hey, Scott.'

'Hey, Sally.'

'Who's this?'

'Grace Lawson,' he said. 'She's helping me.'

'Charmed,' Sally said. 'Be with you in a sec.'

Grace told the kids that they could keep playing their Game Boys. The danger of video games was that they shut the world out. The beauty of video games was that they shut the world out.

Sally Li opened the door. 'Come on in.'

She wore clean surgical scrubs with high heels. A pack of Marlboros was jammed into the breast pocket. The office, if you could call it that, had that Early American Hurricane look going for it. There were papers everywhere. They seemed to be cascading off her desk and bookshelves, almost like a waterfall. Pathology textbooks were open. Her desk was old and metal, something bought at an old elementary school garage sale. There were no pictures on it, nothing personal, though a really big ashtray sat front and center. Magazines, lots of them, were stacked high all over the place. Some of the stacks had already collapsed. Sally Li had not bothered to clean them up. She dropped herself in the chair behind her desk.

'Just knock that stuff to the floor. Sit.'

Grace removed the papers from the chair and sat. Scott Duncan did the same. Sally Li folded her hands and put them on her lap.

'You know, Scott, that I'm not much with bedside manner.'

'I know.'

'The good thing is, my patients never complain.'

She laughed. No one else did.

'Okay, so now you see why I don't get dates.' Sally Li picked up a pair of reading glasses and started shuffling through files. 'You know how the really messy person is always so well organized? They always say something like, 'It might look like untidy but I know where everything is.' That's crap. I don't know where ... Wait, here it is.'

Sally Li pulled out a manila file.

'Is that my sister's autopsy?' Duncan asked.

'Yep.'

She slid it toward him. He opened it. Grace leaned in next to him. On the top were the words DUNCAN, GERI. There were photographs too. Grace spotted one, a brown skeleton lying on a table. She turned away, as if she'd been caught invading someone's privacy.

Sally Li had her feet on the desk, her hands behind her head. 'Look, Scott, you want me to go through the rigmarole of how amazing the science of pathology has become, or do you want me to bottom-line it?'

'Skip the rigmarole.'

'At the time of her death, your sister was pregnant.'

Duncan's body convulsed as if she'd hit him with a cattle prod. Grace did not move.

'I can't tell you how long. No more than four, five months.'

'I don't understand,' Scott said. 'They must have done an autopsy the first time around.'

Sally Li nodded. 'I'm sure.'

'Why didn't they see it then?'

'My guess? They did.'

'But I never knew ...'

'Why would you? You were, what, in law school? They may have told your mom or dad. But you were just a sibling. And her pregnancy has nothing to do with the cause of death. She died in a dorm fire. The fact that she was pregnant, if they knew, would be deemed irrelevant.'

Scott Duncan just sat there. He looked at Grace and then back at Sally Li. 'You can get DNA from the fetus?'

'Probably, yeah. Why?'

'How long will it take you to run a paternity test?'

Grace was not surprised by the question.

'Six weeks.'

'Any way to rush it?'

'I might be able to get some kind of rejection earlier. In other words, rule people out. But I can't say for sure.'

Scott turned to Grace. She knew what he was thinking. She said, 'Geri was dating Shane Alworth.'

'You saw the picture.'

She had. The way Geri looked up at Jack. She had not known the camera was on her. They were all still getting ready to pose. But what was captured, the look on Geri Duncan's face, well, it was the way you look at someone who is much more than a friend.

'Let's run the test then,' Grace said.

34

Charlaine was holding Mike's hand when his eyes finally fluttered open.

She screamed for a doctor, who declared, in a moment of true obviousness, that this was a 'good sign.' Mike was in tremendous pain. The doctor put a morphine pump on him. Mike did not want to go back to sleep. He grimaced and tried to ride it out. Charlaine stayed bedside and held his hand. When the pain got bad, he squeezed hard.

'Go home,' Mike said. 'The kids need you.'

She shushed him. 'Try to rest.'

'Nothing you can do for me here. Go home.'

'Shh.'

Mike began to drift off. She looked down at him. She remembered the days at Vanderbilt. The range of emotions overwhelmed her. There was love and affection, sure, but what troubled Charlaine right now – even as she held his hand, even as she felt a strong bond with this man who shared her life, even as she prayed and made deals with a God she'd ignored for far too long – was that she knew that these feelings would not last. That was the terrible part. In the middle of this intensity Charlaine knew that her feelings would ebb away, that the emotions were fleeting, and she hated herself for knowing that.

Three years ago Charlaine attended a huge self-help rally at Continental Arena in East Rutherford. The speaker had been dynamic. Charlaine loved it. She bought all the tapes. She started doing exactly what he said – making goals, sticking to them, figuring out what she wanted from life, trying to put things in perspective, organizing and restructuring her priorities so that she could achieve – but even as she went through the motions, even as her life began to change for the better, she knew that it would not last. That this would all be a temporary change. A new regimen, an exercise program, a diet – that was how this felt too.

It would not be happily ever after.

The door behind her opened. 'I hear your husband woke up.'

It was Captain Perlmutter. 'Yes.'

'I was hoping to talk to him.'

'You'll have to wait.'

Perlmutter took another step into the room. 'Are the children still with their uncle?'

'He took them to school. We want things to feel normal for them.' Perlmutter moved next to her. She kept her eyes on Mike. 'Have you learned anything?' she asked.

'The man who shot your husband. His name is Eric Wu. Does that mean anything to you?'

She shook her head. 'How did you figure that out?'

'His fingerprints in Sykes's house.'

'Has he been arrested before?'

'Yes. In fact he's on parole.'

'What did he do?'

'He was convicted of assault and battery, but it's believed that he's committed a number of crimes.'

She was not surprised. 'Violent crimes?'

Perlmutter nodded. 'Can I ask you something?'

She shrugged.

'Does the name Jack Lawson mean anything to you?'

Charlaine frowned. 'Does he have two kids at Willard?'

'Yes.'

'I don't know him personally, but Clay, my youngest, is still at Willard. I see his wife sometimes when we do pickups.'

'That would be Grace Lawson?'

'I think that's her name. Pretty woman. She has a daughter named Emma, I think. She's a year or two behind my Clay.'

'Do you know her at all?'

'Not really, no. I see her at the school holiday concert, stuff like that. Why?'

'It's probably nothing.'

Charlaine frowned. 'You just picked that name out of a hat?'

'Early conjecture,' he said, trying to dismiss it. 'I also wanted to thank you.'

'For?'

'For talking to Mr. Sykes.'

'He didn't tell me much.'

'He told you that Wu used the name Al Singer.'

'So?'

'Our computer expert found that name on Sykes's computer. Al Singer. We think Wu used that alias for an online dating service. That's how he met Freddy Sykes.'

'He used the name Al Singer?'

'Yes.'

'It was a gay dating service then?'

'Bisexual.'

Charlaine shook her head and came close to chuckling. *Ain't that something?* She looked at Perlmutter, daring him to laugh. He was stone-faced. They both looked down at Mike again. Mike started. He opened his eyes and smiled at her. Charlaine smiled back and smoothed his hair. He closed his eyes and drifted back to sleep.

'Captain Perlmutter?'

'Yes.'

'Please leave,' she said.

35

While waiting for Carl Vespa to arrive, Grace started picking up the bedroom. Jack, she knew, was a great husband and father. He was smart, funny, loving, caring, and devoted. To counter that, God had blessed him with the organization skills of a citrus beverage. He was, in sum, a slob. Nagging him about it – and Grace had tried – did no good. So she stopped. If living happily was about compromise, this seemed to her like a pretty good one to make.

Grace had long ago given up on Jack clearing out the pile of magazines next to his bed. His post-shower wet towel never ended up back on the rack. Not every article of clothing made it to its ultimate destination. Right now, there was a T-shirt draped half-in, half-out of the hamper as if it'd been shot trying to escape.

For a moment Grace just stared down at the T-shirt. It was green with the word FUBU plastered across the front, and it might have one day been in vogue. Jack bought it for $6.99 at T.J. Maxx, a discount clothing store where hip goes to die. He'd put it on with a pair of too-baggy shorts. He stood in front of the mirror and started wrapping his arms around his body in a bizarre variety of ways.

'What are you doing?' Grace had asked him.

'Gangsta poses. Yo, whatchya think?'

'That I should get you seizure medication.'

'Phat,' he said. 'Bling-bling.'

'Right. Emma needs a ride to Christina's.'

'Word. Dawg. Hit dat.'

'Please go. Immediately.'

Grace picked up the shirt now. She had always been cynical about the male species. She was guarded with her feelings. She did not open up easily. She had never believed in love at first sight – she still didn't – but when she met Jack, the attraction had been immediate, flutters in her stomach, and deny it now as much as she wanted, a small voice had told her right then and there, first meeting, that this was the man she was going to marry.

Cram was in the kitchen with Emma and Max. Emma had recovered from her earlier histrionics. She had recovered the way only kids can – fast and with very little residue. They were all eating fish sticks, Cram included, and ignoring the side dish of peas. Emma was reading a poem to Cram. Cram was a great audience. His laugh was the kind that not only filled a room but pushed against the panes of glass. You heard it, you had to either smile or cringe.

There was still time before Carl Vespa arrived. She didn't want to think about Geri Duncan, her death, her pregnancy, the way she looked at Jack in that damned photograph. Scott Duncan had asked her what she ultimately wanted. She'd said her husband back. That was still very much the case. But maybe, with all that was happening, she needed the truth too.

With that in mind Grace headed downstairs and flipped on the computer. She brought up Google and typed in 'Jack Lawson.' Twelve hundred hits. Too many to do any good. She tried 'Shane Alworth.' Hmm, no hits. Interesting. Grace tried 'Sheila Lambert.' Hits about a woman basketball player with the same name. Nothing relevant. Then she began trying combinations.

Jack Lawson, Shane Alworth, Sheila Lambert, and Geri Duncan: These four people were together in this picture. They had to be linked in some other way. She tried various combinations. She tried one first name, one last name. Nothing of interest popped. She was still typing, going through the useless 227 hits on the words 'Lawson' and 'Alworth' when the phone rang.

Grace looked at the Caller ID and saw it was Cora. She picked up. 'Hey.'

'Hey.'

'I'm sorry,' Grace said.

'Don't worry about it. Bitch.'

Grace smiled and kept hitting the down arrow. The hits were useless.

'So do you still want my help?' Cora asked.

'Yeah, I guess.'

'Enthusiasm. I love that. Okay, fill me in.'

Grace kept it vague. She trusted Cora, but she didn't want to have to trust her. Yeah, that made little sense. It was like this: If Grace's life were in jeopardy, she'd call Cora immediately. But if the kids were in danger ... well, she'd hesitate. The scary thing was, she probably trusted Cora more than anybody, which was to say that she had never felt more isolated in her life.

'So you're putting the names through search engines?' Cora asked.

'Yes.'

'Any relevant hits so far?'

'Not a one.' Then: 'Wait, hold on.'

'What?'

But now again, trust or no trust, Grace wondered what would be the point in telling Cora more than she needed to know. 'I gotta run. I'll call you back.'

'Okay. Bitch.'

Grace hung up and stared at the screen. Her pulse started giddying up, just a little faster now. She had pretty much used up all the name combinations when she'd remembered an artist friend name Marlon Coburn. He was constantly complaining because his name was misspelled. Marlon would be spelled Marlin or Marlan or Marlen and Coburn would be Cohen or Corburn. Anyway Grace figured she'd give it a go.

The fourth 'typo' combo she tried was 'Lawson' and 'Allworth' – two Ls instead of one.

There were three hundred hits – neither name was that uncommon – but it was the fourth one that jumped out at her. She looked at the top line first:

Crazy Davey's Blog

Grace knew vaguely that a blog was a sort of public diary. People wrote down their random thoughts. Other people, for some odd reason, enjoyed reading them. A diary used to be about being private. Now it was about trying to be shrill enough to reach the masses.

The little sample bit under the link line read:

'... John Lawson on keyboards and Sean Allworth who was wicked on guitar ...'

John was Jack's real name. Sean was pretty close to Shane. Grace clicked the link. The page was forever long. She went back, clicked 'cache.' When she returned to the page, the words Lawson and Allworth would be highlighted. She scrolled down and found an entry from two years ago:

April 26

Hey, gang. Terese and I took a weekend up in Vermont. We stayed at the Westerly's bed and breakfasts. It was great. They had a fireplace and at night we played checkers ...

Crazy Davey went on and on. Grace shook her head. Who the hell read this nonsense? She skipped three more paragraphs.

That night I went with Rick, an old college bud, to Wino's. It's an old college bar. Total dump. We used to go when we went to Vermont University. Get this, we played Condom Roulette like the old days. Ever play? Every guy guesses a color – there's Hot Red, Stallion Black, Lemon Yellow, Orange Orange. Okay, the last two are jokes, but you get the point. There's this condom dispenser in the bathroom. It's still there! So each guy puts a buck on the table. One guy gets a quarter and buys a condom. He brings it to the table. You open it and whammo, if it's your color, you win! Rick guessed the first one right. He bought us a pitcher. The band that night sucked. I remembered hearing a group when I was a freshman named Allaw. There were two chicks in that band and two guys. I remember one chick played drums. The guys were John Lawson on keyboards and Sean Allworth who was wicked on guitar. That was how they got the name, I think. Allworth and Lawson. Combine it into Allaw. Rick never heard of them. Anyway we finished up the pitcher. A couple of hot chicks came in but they ignored us. We started feeling old ...

That was it. Nothing more.

Grace did a search for 'Allaw.' Nothing.

She tried more combinations. Nothing else. Only this one mention in a blog. Crazy Davey had gotten both Shane's first and last name wrong. Jack had gone by Jack, well, for as long as Grace had known him, but maybe he was John back then. Or maybe the guy remembered it wrong or saw it written down.

But Crazy Davey had mentioned four people – two women, two men. There were five people in the picture, but the one woman, the one who was pretty much a blur near the edge of the photograph – maybe she wasn't part of the group. And what had Scott said about his sister's last phone call?

I figured it was about whatever new thing she was into – aromatherapy, her new rock band ...

Rock band. Could that be it? Was it a picture of a rock group?

She searched Crazy Davey's site for a phone number or a full name. There was only an e-mail. Grace hit the link and typed quickly:

'I need your help. I have a very important question about Allaw, the band you saw in college. Please call me collect.'

She listed her phone number and then hit the send button.

So what does this mean?

She tried to put it together in a dozen different ways. Nothing fit. A few minutes later the limousine pulled up the driveway. Grace glanced out the window. Carl Vespa was here.

He had a new driver now, a mammoth muscleman with a crewcut and matching scowl who did not look half as dangerous as Cram. She bookmarked Crazy Davey's blog before heading down the corridor to open the door.

Vespa stepped in without saying hello. He still looked natty, still wearing a blazer that seemed to have been tailored by the gods, but the rest of him looked strangely unruly. His hair was always unkempt – that was his look – but there is a fine line between unkempt and not touched at all. It had crossed that line. His eyes were red. The lines around his mouth were deeper, more pronounced.

'What's wrong?'

'Somewhere we can talk?' Vespa asked.

'The kids are with Cram in the kitchen. We can use the living room.'

He nodded. From a distance they heard Max's full-bodied laugh. The sound made Vespa pull up. 'Your son is six, right?'

'Yes.'

Vespa smiled now. Grace did not know what he was thinking, but the smile broke her heart. 'When Ryan was six, he was into baseball cards.'

'Max is into Yu-Gi-Oh!'

'Yu-Gi-what?'

She shook her head to indicate that it wasn't worth explaining.

He went on: 'Ryan used to play this game with his cards. He'd break them up into teams. Then he'd lay them out on the carpet like it was a ball field. You know, the third baseman – Graig Nettles back then – actually playing third, three guys in the outfield – he even kept the extra pitchers in a bullpen out in right field.'

His face glowed in the memory. He looked at Grace. She smiled at him, as gently as she could, but the mood still burst. Vespa's face fell.

'He's getting released on probation.'

Grace said nothing.

'Wade Larue. They're rushing his release. He'll be out tomorrow.'

'Oh.'

'How do you feel about it?'

'He's been in jail for almost fifteen years,' she said.

'Eighteen people died.'

She did not want to have this conversation with him. That number – eighteen – was not relevant. Just one mattered. Ryan. From the kitchen Max laughed again. The sound shredded the room. Vespa kept his face steady but Grace could see something going on inside of him. A roiling. He did not speak. He did not have to, the thoughts obvious: Suppose it had been Max or Emma. Would she rationalize it as a stoned loser getting high and panicking? Would she be so quick to forgive?

'Do you remember that security guard, Gordon MacKenzie?' Vespa asked.

Grace nodded. He had been the hero of the night, finding a way to open up two locked emergency exits.

'He died a few weeks ago. He had a brain tumor.'

175

'I know.' They had given Gordon MacKenzie the biggest spread in the anniversary pieces.

'Do you believe in life after death, Grace?'

'I don't know.'

'How about your parents? Will you see them one day?'

'I don't know.'

'Come on, Grace. I want to know what you think.'

Vespa's eyes bored into hers. She shifted in her seat. 'On the phone. You asked if Jack had a sister.'

'Sandra Koval.'

'Why did you ask me that?'

'In a minute,' Vespa said. 'I want to know what you think. Where do we go when we die, Grace?'

She could see that it would be useless to argue with him. There was a wrong vibe here, something out of sorts. He was not asking as a friend, a father figure, out of curiosity. There was challenge in his voice. Anger even. She wondered if he'd been drinking.

'There's a Shakespeare quote,' she said. 'From Hamlet. He says that death is – and I think I have the quote right – "an undiscovered country from whose borne no traveler returns."'

He made a face. 'In other words, we don't have a clue.'

'Pretty much.'

'You know that's crap.'

She didn't say anything.

'You know that there's nothing. That I will never see Ryan again. It's just too hard for people to accept. The weak-minded invent invisible gods and gardens and reunions in paradise. Or some, like you, won't buy into that nonsense, but it's still too painful to admit the truth. So you come up with this "how can we know?" rationale. But you do know, Grace, don't you?'

'I'm sorry, Carl.'

'For what?'

'I'm sorry that you're in pain. But please don't tell me what I believe.'

Something happened to Vespa's eyes. They expanded for a moment and it was almost as if something behind them exploded. 'How did you meet your husband?'

'What?'

'How did you meet Jack?'

'What does that have to do with anything?'

He took a quick step closer. A threatening step. He looked down at her, and for the first time Grace knew that all the stories, all the rumors about what he was, what he did, they were true. 'How did you two meet?'

Grace tried not to cringe. 'You already know.'

'In France?'

'Right.'

He stared at her hard.

'What's going on, Carl?'

'Wade Larue is getting out.'

'So you said.'

176

'Tomorrow his lawyer is holding a press conference in New York. The families will be there. I want you there.'

She waited. She knew there was more.

'His lawyer was terrific. She really dazzled the parole board. I bet she'll dazzle the press too.'

He stopped and waited. Grace was puzzled for a few moments, but then something cold started in the center of her chest and spread through her limbs. Carl Vespa saw it. He nodded and stepped back.

'Tell me about Sandra Koval,' he said. 'Because, see, I can't understand how your sister-in-law, of all people, ended up representing someone like Wade Larue.'

36

Indira Khariwalla waited for the visitor.

Her office was dark. All the private detection was done for the day. Indira liked sitting with the lights out. The problem with the West, she was convinced, was overstimulation. She fell prey to it too, of course. That was the thing. No one was above it. The West seduced you with stimulation, a constant barrage of color and light and sound. It never stopped. So whenever possible, especially at the end of the day, Indira liked to sit with the lights off. Not to meditate, as one might assume because of her heritage. Not sitting in lotus position with her thumbs and forefingers making two circles.

No, just darkness.

At 10 P.M., there was a light rap on the door. 'Come on in.'

Scott Duncan entered the room. He did not bother turning on the light. Indira was glad. It would make this easier.

'What's so important?' he asked.

'Rocky Conwell was murdered,' Indira said.

'I heard about that on the radio. Who is he?'

'The man I hired to follow Jack Lawson.'

Scott Duncan said nothing.

'Do you know who Stu Perlmutter is?' she continued.

'The cop?'

'Yes. He visited me yesterday. He asked about Conwell.'

'Did you claim attorney-client?'

'I did. He wants to get a judge to compel me to answer.'

Scott Duncan turned away.

'Scott?'

'Don't worry about it,' he said. 'You don't know anything.'

Indira was not so sure. 'What are you going to do?'

Duncan stepped out of the office. He reached behind him, grabbed the knob, and started closing the door behind him. 'Nip this in the bud,' he said.

37

The press conference was at 10 a.m. Grace took the children to school first. Cram drove. He wore an oversized flannel shirt left untucked. He had a gun under it, she knew. The children hopped out. They said good-bye to Cram and hurried away. Cram shifted the car into gear.

'Don't go yet,' Grace said.

She watched until they were safely inside. Then she nodded that it was okay for the car to start moving again.

'Don't worry,' Cram said. 'I have a man watching.'

She turned to him. 'Can I ask you something?'

'Shoot.'

'How long have you been with Mr. Vespa?'

'You were there when Ryan died, right?'

The question threw her. 'Yes.'

'He was my godson.'

The streets were quiet. She looked at him. She had no idea what to do. She could not trust them – not with her children, not after she'd seen Vespa's face last night. But what choice did she have? Maybe she should try the police again, but would they really be willing or able to protect them? And Scott Duncan, well, even he had admitted that their alliance only went so far.

As if reading her thoughts, Cram said, 'Mr. Vespa still trusts you.'

'And what if he decides he doesn't anymore?'

'He'd never hurt you.'

'You're that sure?'

'Mr. Vespa will meet us in the city. At the press conference. You want to listen to the radio?'

The traffic was not bad, considering the hour. The George Washington Bridge was still crawling with cops, a hangover from September 11 that Grace could not get over. The press conference was being held at the Crowne Plaza Hotel near Times Square. Vespa told her that there'd been talk about conducting it in Boston – that would seem more appropriate – but someone in the Larue camp realized that it might be too emotionally jarring to return so close to the scene. They also hoped that fewer family members would show up if it were held in New York.

Cram dropped her off on the sidewalk and headed into the lot next door. Grace stood on the street for a moment and tried to gather herself. Her cell phone sounded. She checked the Caller ID. The number was unfamiliar. Six-one-seven area code. That was the Boston area, if she remembered correctly.

'Hello?'

'Hi. This is David Roff.'

She was near Times Square in New York. People were, of course, everywhere. No one seemed to be talking. No horns were honking. But the roar in her ear was still deafening. 'Who?'

'Uh, well, I guess you might know me better as Crazy Davey. From my blog. I got your e-mail. Is this a bad time?'

'No, not at all.' Grace realized that she was shouting to be heard. She stuck a finger in her free ear. 'Thanks for calling me back.'

'I know you said to call collect, but I got some new phone service where all long distance is included, so I figured what the hell, you know.'

'I appreciate it.'

'You made it sound kind of important.'

'It is. On your blog you mentioned a band named Allaw.'

'Right.'

'I'm trying to find out anything I can about them.'

'I figured that, yeah, but I don't think I can really help you. I mean, I just saw them that one night. Me and some buddies got totally wasted, spent the whole night there. We met some girls, did a lot of dancing, did a lot more drinking. We talked to the band afterward. That's why I remember it so well.'

'My name is Grace Lawson. My husband was Jack.'

'Lawson? That was the lead guy, right? I remember him.'

'Were they any good?'

'The band? Truth is, I don't remember, but I think so. I remember having a blast and getting wasted. Had a hangover that still makes me cringe to this day. You trying to put a surprise together for him?'

'A surprise?'

'Yeah, like a surprise party or a scrapbook about his old days.'

'I'm just trying to find out anything I can about the people in the group.'

'I wish I could help. I don't think they lasted that long. Never heard them again, though I know they had another gig at the Lost Tavern. That was in Manchester. That's all I know, I'm sorry.'

'I appreciate your calling me back.'

'Sure, no problem. Oh wait. This might be fun trivia for a scrapbook.'

'What's that?'

'The gig Allaw played in Manchester? They opened for Still Night.'

Waves of pedestrians rushed past her. Grace huddled near a wall, trying to avoid the masses. 'I'm not familiar with Still Night.'

'Well, only real music buffs would be, I guess. Still Night didn't last too long either. At least not in that incarnation.' There was a static crackle, but Grace still heard Crazy Davey's next words too clearly: 'But their lead singer was Jimmy X.'

Grace felt her grip on the phone go slack.

'Hello?'

'I'm still here,' Grace said.

'You know who Jimmy X is, right? "Pale Ink"? The Boston Massacre?'

'Yes.' Her voice sounded very far away. 'I remember.'

Cram came out of the parking lot. He spotted her face and picked up his pace again. Grace thanked Crazy Davey and hung up. She had his number on her cell phone now. She could always call him back.

'Everything okay?'

She tried to shake it off, this feeling of cold. It wouldn't happen. She managed to utter, 'Fine.'

'Who was that?'

'You my social secretary now?'

'Easy.' He held up both hands. 'Just asking.'

They headed inside the Crowne Plaza. Grace tried to process what she had just heard. A coincidence. That was all. A bizarre coincidence. Her husband had played in a bar band in college. So had a zillion other people. He happened to play on the same bill once as Jimmy X. Again so what? They were both in the same area at around the same time. This would have been at least a year, probably two, before the Boston Massacre. And Jack might not have mentioned it to her because he figured that it was irrelevant and might, in any case, upset his wife. A Jimmy X concert had traumatized her. It had left her partially crippled. So he maybe didn't see a need to mention that slight connection.

No big deal, right?

Except that Jack had never even mentioned playing in a band. Except that the members of Allaw were all now either dead or missing.

She tried to gather some of the pieces. When exactly had Geri Duncan been murdered anyway? Grace had been undergoing physical therapy when she read about the fire. That meant it probably happened a few months after the massacre. Grace would need to check the exact date. She would need to check the entire time line because, let's face it, there was no way the Allaw–Jimmy X connection was a coincidence.

But how did it work? Nothing about it made sense.

She ran it through one more time. Her husband plays in a band. One time the band plays at the same time as a band featuring Jimmy X. A year or two later – depending on if Jack had been a senior or a year postgrad – the now famous Jimmy X plays a concert that she, young Grace Sharpe, attends. She gets injured in a melee that night. Another three years pass. She meets Jack Lawson on an entirely different continent and they fall in love.

It didn't mesh.

The elevator dinged on the ground level. Cram said, 'You sure you're okay?'

'Groovy,' she said.

'Still twenty minutes until the press conference begins. I figured it would be better if you went alone, try to grab your sister-in-law beforehand.'

'You're a fount of ideas, Cram.'

The doors opened. 'Third floor,' he said. Grace stepped inside and let the elevator swallow her whole. She was alone. There would not be much time. She took out her cell phone and the card Jimmy X had given her. She pressed in the number and hit send. It went immediately into his voice mail. Grace waited for the beep:

'I know about Still Night playing with Allaw. Call me.'

She left her number and hung up. The elevator came to a stop. When she stepped off, there was one of those black signs with the changeable white letters, the kind that tell you in what room the Ratzenberg bar mitzvah or Smith-Jones wedding is being held. This one read: 'Burton-Crimstein Press Conference.' Advertising the firm. She followed the arrow to a door, took a deep breath, and pushed it open.

The whole thing was like one of those courthouse movie scenes – that pinnacle cinematic moment when the surprise witness bursts through the double doors. When Grace walked in, there was that sort of collective gasp. The room hushed. Grace felt lost. She glanced around and what she saw made her head spin. She took a step back. The faces of grief, older but no more at peace, swirled about her. There they were again – the Garrisons, the Reeds, the Weiders. She flashed back to the early days at the hospital. She had seen everything through the haze of Halcion, as if through a shower curtain. It felt the same today. They approached in silence. They hugged her. None of them said a word. They didn't have to. Grace accepted the embraces. She could still feel the sadness emanating from them.

She saw the widow of Lieutenant Gordon MacKenzie. Some said that he had been responsible for pulling Grace to safety. Like most true heroes, Gordon MacKenzie rarely talked about it. He claimed not to remember what he did exactly, that yes, he opened doors and pulled people out, but that it was more out of reaction than anything approaching bravery.

Grace gave Mrs. MacKenzie an extra long hug.

'I'm sorry for your loss,' Grace said.

'He found God.' Mrs. MacKenzie held on. 'He's with Him now.'

There was really nothing to say to that, so Grace just nodded. She let her go and looked over the woman's shoulder. Sandra Koval had entered the room from the other side. She spotted Grace at almost the same moment and a strange thing happened. Her sister-in-law smiled, almost as if she'd expected this. Grace stepped away from Mrs. MacKenzie. Sandra tilted her head, signaling her to step forward. There was a velvet rope. A security guard stepped in her way.

'It's okay, Frank,' Sandra said. He let Grace pass.

Sandra led the way. She hurried down a corridor. Grace limped behind, unable to catch up. No matter. Sandra stopped and opened a door. They stepped into a huge ballroom. Waiters busily laid out the silverware. Sandra led her to a corner. She grabbed two chairs and turned them so that they faced each other.

'You don't seem surprised to see me,' Grace said.

Sandra shrugged. 'I figured you were following the case in the news.'

'I wasn't.'

'Doesn't matter, I guess. Until two days ago you didn't know who I was.'

'What's going on, Sandra?'

She did not answer right away. The tinkling of the silverware provided background music. Sandra let her gaze wander toward the waiters in the center room.

'Why are you representing Wade Larue?'

'He was charged with a crime. I'm a criminal defense lawyer. It's what I do.'

'Don't patronize me.'

'You want to know how I stumbled upon this particular client, is that it?'

Grace said nothing.

'Isn't it obvious?'

'Not to me.'

'You, Grace.' She smiled. 'You're the reason I represent Mr. Larue.'

Grace opened her mouth, closed it, started again. 'What are you talking about?'

'You never really knew about me. You just knew that Jack had a sister. But I knew all about you.'

'I'm still not following.'

'It's simple, Grace. You married my brother.'

'So?'

'When I learned you were going to be my sister-in-law, I was curious. I wanted to learn about you. Makes sense, right? So I had one of my investigators do a background check. Your paintings are wonderful, by the way. I bought two. Anonymously. They're in my home out in Los Angeles. Spectacular stuff, really. My older daughter, Karen – she's seventeen – loves them. She wants to be an artist.'

'I don't see what this has to do with Wade Larue.'

'Really?' Her voice was strangely cheerful. 'I've worked criminal defense since I graduated law school. I started by working with Burton and Crimstein in Boston. I lived there, Grace. I knew all about the Boston Massacre. And now my brother had fallen in love with one of the Massacre's major players. It piqued my curiosity even more. I started reading up on the case – and guess what I realized?'

'What?'

'That Wade Larue had been railroaded by an incompetent lawyer.'

'Wade Larue was responsible for the death of eighteen people.'

'He fired a gun, Grace. He didn't even hit anyone. The lights went out. People were screaming. He was under the influence of drugs and alcohol. He panicked. He believed – or at least, honestly imagined – that he was in imminent danger. There was no way, no way at all, that he could have known what the outcome would be. His first lawyer should have cut a deal. Probation, eighteen months away tops. But no one really wanted to work this case. Larue was sent to jail to rot. So yes, Grace, I read about him because of you. Wade Larue had been shafted. His old attorney screwed him and ran.'

'So you took the case?'

Sandra Koval nodded. 'Pro bono. I came to him two years ago. We started preparing for the parole hearing.'

Something clicked. 'Jack knew, didn't he?'

'That I don't know. We don't talk, Grace.'

'Are you still going to tell me you didn't talk to him that night? Nine minutes, Sandra. The phone company says the call lasted nine minutes.'

'Jack's call had nothing to do with Wade Larue.'

'What did it have to do with?'

'That photograph.'

'What about it?'

Sandra leaned forward. 'First you answer a question for me. And I need the truth here. Where did you get that picture?'

'I told you. It was in my packet of film.'

Sandra shook her head, not believing her. 'And you think the guy from Photomat stuck it in there?'

'I don't know anymore. But you still haven't explained – what about the picture made him call you?'

Sandra hesitated.

'I know about Geri Duncan,' Grace said.

'You know what about Geri Duncan?'

'That she's the girl in the picture. And that she was murdered.'

That made Sandra sit up. 'She died in a fire. It was an accident.'

Grace shook her head. 'It was set intentionally.'

'Who told you that?'

'Her brother.'

'Wait, how do you know her brother?'

'She was pregnant, you know. Geri Duncan. When she died in that fire, she was carrying a baby.'

Sandra stopped and looked up in horror. 'Grace, what are you doing?'

'I'm trying to find my husband.'

'And you think this is helping?'

'You told me yesterday you didn't know anyone in the picture. But you just admitted you knew Geri Duncan, that she died in a fire.'

Sandra closed her eyes.

'Did you know Shane Alworth or Sheila Lambert?'

Her voice was soft. 'Not really, no.'

'Not really. So their names are not totally unfamiliar to you?'

'Shane Alworth was a classmate of Jack's. Sheila Lambert, I think, was a friend from a sister college or something. So what?'

'Did you know that the four of them played together in a band?'

'For a month maybe. Again so what?'

'The fifth person in the picture. The one with her head turned. Do you know who she is?'

'No.'

'Is it you, Sandra?'

She looked up at Grace. 'Me?'

'Yes. Is it you?'

There was a funny look on Sandra's face now. 'No, Grace, it's not me.'

'Did Jack kill Geri Duncan?'

The words just came out. Sandra's eyes opened as if she'd been slapped. 'Are you out of your mind?'

'I want the truth.'

'Jack had nothing to do with her death. He was overseas already.'

'So why did the picture freak him out?'

She hesitated.

'Why, dammit?'

'Because he didn't know Geri was dead until then.'

Grace looked confused. 'Were they lovers?'

'Lovers,' she repeated, as if she'd never heard the word before. 'That's a pretty mature term for what they were.'

'Wasn't she dating Shane Alworth?'

'I guess. But they were all just kids.'

'Jack was fooling around with his friend's girlfriend?'

'I don't know how friendly Jack and Shane were. But yes, Jack slept with her.'

Grace's head began to whirl. 'And Geri Duncan got pregnant.'

'I don't know anything about that.'

'But you know she's dead.'

'Yes.'

'And you know Jack ran away.'

'Before she died.'

'Before she was pregnant?'

'I just told you. I never knew she was pregnant.'

'And Shane Alworth and Sheila Lambert, they're both missing too. You want to tell me it's all a coincidence, Sandra?'

'I don't know.'

'So what did Jack say when he called you?'

She let loose a deep sigh. Her head dropped. She was silent for a while.

'Sandra?'

'Look, that picture has to be, what, fifteen, sixteen years old? When you just gave it to him like that, out of the blue ... how did you think he'd react? With Geri's face crossed out. So Jack went to the computer. He did a Web search – I think he used the *Boston Globe*'s archives. He found out she's been dead this whole time. That was why he called me. He wanted to know what happened to her. I told him.'

'Told him what?'

'What I knew. That she died in a fire.'

'Why would that make Jack run out?'

'That I don't know.'

'What made him run overseas in the first place?'

'You have to let this go.'

'What happened to them, Sandra?'

She shook her head. 'Forget the fact that I'm his attorney and that it's protected. It is simply not my place. He's my brother.'

Grace reached out and took Sandra's hands in hers. 'I think he's in trouble.'

'Then what I know can't help him.'

'They threatened my children today.'

Sandra closed her eyes.

'Did you hear what I said?'

A man in a business suit leaned into the room. He said, 'It's time, Sandra.' She nodded and thanked him. Sandra pulled her hands away, stood, smoothed out the lines of her suit.

'You have to stop this, Grace. You have to go home now. You have to protect your family. It's what Jack would want you to do.'

38

The threat at the supermarket had not taken.

Wu was not surprised. He had been raised in an environment that stressed the power of men and the subordination of women, but Wu had always found it to be more hope than truth. Women were harder. They were more unpredictable. They handled physical pain better – he knew this from personal experience. When it came to protecting their loved ones, they were far more ruthless. Men would sacrifice themselves out of machismo or stupidity or the blind belief that they would be victorious. Women would sacrifice themselves without self-deception.

He had not been in favor of making the threat in the first place. Threats left enemies and uncertainty. Eliminating Grace Lawson earlier would have been routine. Eliminating her now would be riskier.

Wu would have to return and handle the job himself.

He was in Beatrice Smith's shower, dyeing his hair back to its original color. Wu usually wore it bleached blond. He did this for two reasons. The first reason was basic: He liked the way it looked. Vanity, perhaps, but when Wu looked in the mirror he thought the surfer-blond, gel-spiked style worked on him. Reason two, the color – a garish yellow – was useful because it was what most people remembered. When he brought his hair back to its natural state of everyday Asian-black, flattened it down, when he changed his clothes from the modern hip style to something more conservative, donned a pair of wire-rimmed spectacles, well, the transformation was very effective.

He grabbed Jack Lawson and dragged him down into the basement. Lawson did not resist. He was barely conscious. He was not doing well. His mind, already stretched, had perhaps snapped. He would not survive much longer.

The basement was unfinished and damp. Wu remembered the last time he'd been in a similar setting, out in San Mateo, California. The instructions had been specific. He had been hired to torture a man for exactly eight hours – why eight Wu had never learned – and then break bones in both the man's legs and arms. Wu had manipulated the broken bones so that the jagged edges sat next to nerve bundles or near the surface of the skin. Any movement, even the slightest, would cause excruciating pain. Wu locked the basement and left the man by himself. He checked up on him once a day. The man would plead, but Wu would just stare silently. It took eleven days for the man to die of starvation.

Wu found a strong pipe and chained Lawson to it. He also cuffed his arms behind his back around a support wall. He put the gag back into his mouth.

Then he decided to test the binds.

'You should have gotten every copy of that photograph,' Wu whispered.

Jack Lawson's eyes rolled up.

'Now I'll have to pay your wife a visit'

Their gazes locked. A second passed, no more, and then Lawson sprang to life. He began to flail. Wu watched him. Yes, this would be a good test. Lawson struggled for several minutes, a fish dying on the line. Nothing gave way.

Wu left him alone then, still fighting his chains, to find Grace Lawson.

39

Grace did not want to stay for the press conference.

Being in the same room with all these mourners ... She didn't like to use the term 'aura,' but it seemed to fit. The room had a bad aura. Shattered eyes stared at her with a yearning that was palpable. Grace understood, of course. She was no longer the conduit to their lost children – too much time had passed for that. Now she was the survivor. She was there, alive and breathing, while their children rotted in the grave. On the surface there was still affection, but beneath that Grace could feel rage at the unfairness of it all. She had lived – their children had not. The years had offered no reprieve. Now that Grace had children of her own, she understood in a way that would have been impossible fifteen years ago.

She was about to slide out the back door when a hand took firm hold of her wrist. She turned and saw it was Carl Vespa.

'Where are you going?' he asked.

'Home.'

'I'll give you a ride.'

'That's okay. I can hire a car.'

His hand, still on her wrist, tightened for a brief moment and again Grace thought she saw something detonate behind his eyes. 'Stay,' he said.

It was not a request. She searched his face, but it was oddly calm. Too calm. His demeanor – so off with the surroundings, so different from the flash of fury she'd seen last night – frightened her anew. Was this really the man she was trusting with her children's lives?

She sat next to him and watched Sandra Koval and Wade Larue take to the podium. Sandra pulled the microphone closer and started up with the standard clichés about forgiveness and starting over and rehabilitation. Grace watched the faces around her shut down. Some cried. Some pursed their lips. Some visibly shook.

Carl Vespa did none of that.

He crossed his legs and leaned back. He surveyed the proceedings with a casualness that scared her more than the worst scowl. Five minutes into Sandra Koval's statement, Vespa's eyes shifted toward Grace. He saw that she'd been watching him. Then he did something that made her shiver.

He winked at her.

'Come on,' he whispered. 'Let's get out of here.'

With Sandra still talking, Carl Vespa rose and headed for the door. Heads turned and there was a brief hush. Grace followed. They took the elevator down in silence. The limousine was right out front. The big burly guy was in the driver's seat.

'Where's Cram?' Grace asked.

'On an errand,' Vespa said, and Grace thought she saw the trace of a smile. 'Tell me about your meeting with Ms. Koval.'

Grace recounted her conversation with her sister-in-law. Vespa stayed silent, gazing out the window, his index finger gently tapping his chin. When she finished, he asked, 'Is that everything?'

'Yes.'

'Are you sure?'

She did not like the lilt in his tone.

'What about your recent' – Vespa looked up, scanning for the word – 'visitor?'

'You mean Scott Duncan?'

Vespa had the oddest grin. 'You are aware, of course, that Scott Duncan works for the U.S. attorney's office.'

'Used to,' she corrected.

'Yes, used to.' His voice was too relaxed. 'What did he want with you?'

'I told you.'

'Did you?' He shifted in his chair, but he still did not face her. 'Did you tell me everything?'

'What's that supposed to mean?'

'Just a question. Was this Mr. Duncan your only recent visitor?'

Grace did not like how this was going. She hesitated.

'Nobody else you'd like to tell me about?' he continued.

She tried to search his face for a clue, but he kept it turned away from her. What was he talking about? She mulled it over, replayed the past few days ...

Jimmy X?

Could Vespa somehow know about Jimmy stopping by after his concert? It was possible, of course. He had found Jimmy in the first place – it would stand to reason that he'd have someone following him. So what should Grace do here? Would saying something now just compound the issue? Maybe he didn't know about Jimmy. Maybe opening her mouth now would just get her in deeper trouble.

Play it vague, she thought. See where it goes. 'I know I asked for your help,' she said, her tone deliberate. 'But I think I'd like to handle this on my own now.'

Vespa finally turned toward her and faced her full. 'Really?'

She waited.

'Why is that, Grace?'

'Truth?'

'Preferably.'

'You're scaring me.'

'You think I'd harm you?'

'No.'

'Then?'

'I just think it might be best –'

'What did you tell him about me?'

The interruption caught her off guard. 'Scott Duncan?'

'Is there anyone else you talked to about me?'

'What? No.'

'So what did you say to Scott Duncan about me?'

'Nothing.' Grace tried to think. 'What could I tell him anyway?'

'Good point.' He nodded, more to himself than at Grace. 'But you were never very specific on why Mr. Duncan paid you this visit.' Vespa folded his hands and put them on his lap. 'I'd very much like to know the details.'

She didn't want to tell him – didn't want him involved anymore – but there was no way to avoid it. 'It's about his sister.'

'What about her?'

'Do you remember the girl crossed out in that picture?'

'Yes.'

'Her name was Geri Duncan. She was his sister.'

Vespa frowned. 'And that's why he came to you?'

'Yes.'

'Because his sister was in the photograph?'

'Yes.'

He sat back. 'So what happened to her, this sister?'

'She died in a fire fifteen years ago.'

Vespa surprised Grace then. He didn't ask a follow-up question. He didn't ask for clarification. He simply turned away and stared out the window. He did not speak again until the car pulled into the driveway. Grace opened the door to get out, but there was some kind of locking system on it, like the safety lock she'd used when the kids were small, and she could not open it from the inside. The burly driver came around and took hold of the door handle. She wanted to ask Carl Vespa what he planned on doing now, if he'd indeed leave them alone, but his body language was wrong.

Calling him in the first place had been a mistake. Telling him she wanted him out of this may have compounded it.

'I'll keep my men on until you pick up the children from school,' he said, still not facing her. 'Then you'll be on your own.'

'Thank you.'

'Grace?'

She looked back at him.

'You should never lie to me,' he said.

His voice was ice. Grace swallowed hard. She wanted to argue, to tell him that she hadn't, but she worried that it would sound too defensive – protesting too much. So she simply nodded.

There were no good-byes. Grace headed up the walk alone. Her step teetered from something more than the limp.

What had she done?

She wondered about her next step. Her sister-in-law had said it best: Protect the children. If Grace were in Jack's shoes, if she had gone missing for whatever reason, that would be what she'd want. *Forget me*, she'd tell him. *Keep the children safe.*

So now, like it or not, Grace was out of the rescue business. Jack was on his own.

She'd pack now. She'd wait until three o'clock, until school was let out, and then she'd pick up the children and drive to Pennsylvania. She'd find a hotel where you didn't need a credit card. Or a B&B. Or a rooming house. Whatever. She'd call the police, maybe that Perlmutter even. She'd tell him what was going on. But first she needed her children. Once they were safe, once she had them in her car and was on the road, she'd be okay.

She reached her front door. There was a package on the step. She bent down and picked it up. The box had a *New Hampshire Post* logo on it. The return address read: Bobby Dodd, Sunrise Assisted Living.

It was Bob Dodd's files.

40

Wade Larue sat next to his lawyer, Sandra Koval.

He wore brand-new clothes. The room did not smell of prison, that horrid combination of decay and disinfectant, of fat guards and urine, of stains that never come out, and that in and of itself was a strange adjustment. Prison becomes your world, getting out an impossible daydream, like imagining life on other planets. Wade Larue had gone inside at the age of twenty-two. He was now thirty-seven. That meant he had spent pretty much all his adult years inside that place. That smell, that horrid smell, was all he knew. Yes, he was still young. He had, as Sandra Koval repeated mantralike, his whole life in front of him.

It didn't feel like that right now.

Wade Larue's life had been ruined by a school play. Growing up in a small town in Maine everyone agreed that Wade had the acting chops. He was a crummy student. He was not much of an athlete. But he could sing and dance and, most important, he had what one local reviewer called – this after seeing Wade star as Nathan Detroit in *Guys and Dolls* sophomore year – 'supernatural charisma.' Wade had that something special, that intangible that separated talented wannabes from the real deals.

Before his senior year of high school, Mr. Pearson, the high-school play director, called Wade into his office to tell him about his 'impossible dream.' Mr. Pearson had always wanted to put on *Man of La Mancha*, but he never had a student, not until now, who could handle the role of Don Quixote. Now, for the first time, he wanted to give it a go with Wade.

But come September Mr. Pearson moved away and Mr. Arnett took over as director. He held tryouts – usually a formality for Wade Larue – but Mr. Arnett was hostile. To the shock of everyone in town he ended up picking Kenny Thomas, a total no-talent, to play Don Quixote. Kenny's father was a bookie and Mr. Arnett, rumor had it, was into him for over twenty grand. You do the math. Wade was offered the role of the barber – one song! – and ended up quitting.

Here was how naive Wade was: He thought that his quitting would cause a town-wide uproar. High schools are made up of types. The handsome quarterback. The basketball captain. The school president. The lead in every school play. He thought the townsfolk would rally against the injustice that had befallen him. But no one said a thing. At first, Wade figured that they were scared of Kenny's father and his possible mob connections, but the truth was far simpler: They didn't care. Why should they?

It is so easy to inch your way into foul territory. The line is so thin, so flimsy. You just step over it, just for a second, and sometimes, well, sometimes you can't make your way back. Three weeks later Wade Larue got drunk, broke into the school, and vandalized the sets for the play. He was caught by the police and suspended from school.

And so the slide began.

Wade ended up taking too many drugs, moving to Boston to help sell and distribute, grew paranoid, carried a gun. And now here he was, sitting at this podium, a famous felon blamed for the death of eighteen people.

The faces glaring up at him were familiar from his trial fifteen years ago. Wade knew most of the names. At the trial they would stare with a combination of grief and bewilderment, still woozy from the sudden blow. Wade had understood back then, sympathized even. Now, fifteen years later, the glares were more hostile. Their grief and bewilderment had crystallized into a purer cut of anger and hate. At the trial, Wade Larue had avoided the glares. But no more. He kept his head up. He met their eyes. His sympathy, his understanding, had been decimated by their lack of forgiveness. He had never meant to hurt anyone. They knew that. He had apologized. He had paid a huge price. They, these families, still chose hate.

To hell with them.

Sandra Koval waxed eloquent from the seat next to him. She spoke of apologies and forgiveness, of turning corners and transformations, of understanding and the human desire for a second chance. Larue tuned her out. He spotted Grace Lawson sitting next to Carl Vespa. He should have felt tremendous fear seeing Vespa in the flesh, but no, he was beyond that now. When Wade was first put in prison, he had been badly beaten – first by people working for Vespa and then by those hoping to curry favor. Guards included. There had been no escape from the constant fear. Fear, like the smell, had become a natural part of him, his world. Maybe that explained why he was immune to it now.

Larue eventually made friends at Walden, but prison is no character-builder, despite what Sandra Koval was now telling this audience. Prison strips you down to your barest state, the state of nature, and what you do to survive is never pretty. No matter. He was out now. That was in the past. You move on.

But not quite yet.

The room was beyond silent, a vacuuming feel, as if the very air had been sucked out of it. The families all sat there, unmoved both physically and emotionally. But there was no energy there. They were hollow entities, devastated and powerless. They could not hurt him. Not anymore.

Without warning Carl Vespa rose. For a second – no longer than that – Sandra Koval was thrown. Grace Lawson stood too. Wade Larue could not understand why they were together. It made no sense. He wondered if it changed anything, if he would soon meet Grace Lawson.

Did it matter?

When Sandra Koval finished, she leaned over to him and whispered, 'Come on, Wade. You can take the back way out.'

Ten minutes later, out on the streets of Manhattan, Wade Larue was free for the first time in fifteen years.

He stared up at the skyscrapers. Times Square was his first destination. It would be noisy and crowded with people – real, live nonconvicts. Larue did not want solitude. He did not crave green grass or trees – you could see those from his prison cell in the sticks of Walden. He wanted lights and sounds and people, real people, not prisoners, and yes, perhaps, the company of a good (or better, bad) woman.

But that would have to wait. Wade Larue checked his watch. It was almost time.

He started west on Forty-third Street. There was still a chance to back out of this. He was achingly close to the Port Authority bus terminal. He could hop on a bus, any bus, and start anew someplace. He could change his name, maybe his face a little, and try out for local theater. He was still young. He still had the chops. He still had that supernatural charisma.

Soon, he thought.

He needed to clear this up. Put it behind him. When he was being released, one of the prison counselors had given him the standard lecture about this being either a new start or a bad end, it was all up to him. The counselor was right. Today he would either put this all behind him or he would die. Wade doubted that there would be an in between.

Up ahead he saw a black sedan. He recognized the man leaning against the side, his arms crossed. It was the mouth you couldn't forget, the way the teeth were all twisted together. He had been the first to beat Larue all those years ago. He wanted to know what had happened the night of the Boston Massacre. Larue had told him the truth: He didn't know.

Now he did.

'Hey, Wade.'

'Cram.'

Cram opened the door. Wade Larue slid into the back. Five minutes later they were on the West Side Highway heading toward the endgame.

41

Eric Wu watched the limousine pull up to the Lawson residence.

A large man who looked like anything but a chauffeur stepped out of the car, pulled his jacket together hard so he could work the button, and opened the back door. Grace Lawson stepped out. She headed for her front door without saying good-bye or looking behind her. The large man watched her pick up a package and go inside. Then he got back in the car and pulled out.

Wu wondered about him, the large man. Grace Lawson, he'd been told, might have protection now. She had been threatened. Her children had been threatened. The large chauffeur was not with the police. Wu was certain of that. But he was no simple driver either.

Best to be cautious.

Keeping a good distance away, Wu began to circle the perimeter. The day was clear, the foliage bursting with green. There were many places to hide. Wu did not have binoculars – it would have made the task easier – but that was not important. He spotted one man within minutes. The man was stationed behind the detached garage. Wu crept closer. The man was communicating with a cell phone walkie-talkie. Wu listened. He only picked up snippets, but it was enough. There was someone in the house too. Probably another man on the perimeter, on the other side of the street.

This was not good.

Wu could still handle it. He knew that. But he would have to strike fast. He would first have to know the exact location of the other perimeter man. He would take one out with his hands and one with the gun. He would need to rush the house. It could be done. There would be lots of bodies. The man inside could be tipped off. But it could be done.

Wu checked his watch. Twenty minutes until three.

He started circling back toward the street when the back door of the Lawson home opened. Grace stepped out. She had a suitcase. Wu stopped and watched. She put the suitcase in the trunk. She went back inside. She came out with another suitcase and a package – the same one, he thought, that he'd seen her pick up at the front door.

Wu hurried back to the car he was using – ironically enough, her Ford Windstar, though he'd switched license plates at the Palisades Mall and slapped on some bumper stickers to draw attention away from that fact. People remembered bumper stickers more than license plates or even makes. There was one about him being a proud parent of an honor roll student. A second, for the New York Knicks, read ONE TEAM, ONE NEW YORK.

Grace Lawson got behind the wheel of her car and started it up. Good, Wu thought. It would be much easier to grab her wherever she stopped. His instructions were clear. Find out what she knows. Get rid of the body. He put the Windstar in gear but kept his foot on the brake. He wanted to see if anyone else followed. No one pulled out after her. Wu kept his distance.

There were no other tails.

The men had been ordered to protect the house, he guessed, not her. Wu wondered about the suitcases, about where she might be headed, about how long this journey might take. He was surprised when she started taking small side streets. He was even more surprised when she pulled to a stop near a schoolyard.

Of course. It was nearing three o'clock. She was picking up her children from school.

He thought again about the suitcases and what they might mean. Was her intention to pick up her children and take a trip? If that was the case, it might be someplace far away. It might be hours before she stopped.

Wu did not want to wait hours.

On the other hand she might head straight back home, back into the protection of the two men on the perimeter and the one in the house. That was not good either. He would have the old set of problems, plus, in either case, children would now be involved. Wu was neither bloodthirsty nor sentimental. He was pragmatic. Grabbing a woman whose husband had already run off may raise suspicions and even police involvement, but if you add dead bodies, possibly two dead children, the attention becomes nearly intolerable.

No, Wu realized. It would be best to grab Grace Lawson here and now. Before the children came out of the schoolyard.

That did not give him much time.

Mothers began to congregate and mingle, but Grace Lawson stayed in her car. She seemed to be reading something. The time was 2:50 P.M. That gave Wu ten minutes. Then he remembered the earlier threat. They had told her that they would take her children. If that was the case, it was entirely possible that there were men watching the school too.

He had to check fast.

It didn't take long. The van was parked a block away, at the end of a cul-de-sac. So obvious. Wu considered the possibility that there was more than one. He did a quick scan and saw nothing. No time anyway. He had to strike. The school would be letting out in five minutes. Once the kids were present, it would complicate everything exponentially.

Wu had dark hair now. He put on gold-framed glasses. He had the loose-fitting casual clothes. He tried to make himself look timid as he was walked toward the van. He looked around as if lost. He moved straight to the back door and was about to open it when a bald man with a sweaty brow popped his head out.

'What do you want, pal?'

The man was dressed in a blue velour sweat suit. There was no shirt under the jacket, just mounds of chest hair. He was big and gruff. Wu reached out with his right hand and cupped the back of the man's head. He snapped his arm forward and planted his left elbow deep in the man's adam's apple. The throat simply collapsed. The entire windpipe gave way like a brittle branch. The man went down, his body thrashing like a fish on the dock. Wu pushed him deeper into the van and slid inside.

There was the same cell phone walkie-talkie, a pair of binoculars, a gun. Wu jammed the weapon into his waist. The man still thrashed. He would not live much longer.

Three minutes until the bell rang.

Wu locked the van's door behind him and hurried out. He made it back to the street where Grace Lawson was parked. Mothers lined the fence in anticipation of school being let out. Grace Lawson was out of her car now, standing by herself. That was good.

Wu walked toward her.

On the other side of the schoolyard, Charlaine Swain was thinking about chain reactions and falling dominoes.

If she and Mike hadn't had problems.

If she had not started up that perverted dance with Freddy Sykes.

If she had not looked out that window when Eric Wu was there.

If she had not opened the hide-a-key and called the police.

But right now, as she passed the playground, the dominoes were falling more in the present: If Mike had not woken up, if he had not insisted she take care of the children, if Perlmutter had not asked her about Jack Lawson, well, without all of that, Charlaine would not have been looking in Grace Lawson's direction.

But Mike had insisted. He had reminded her that the children needed her. So here she was. Picking up Clay from school. And Perlmutter had indeed asked Charlaine if she knew Jack Lawson. So when Charlaine arrived at the schoolyard, it was natural, if not inevitable, that she would start scanning the grounds for the man's wife.

That was how Charlaine came to be looking at Grace Lawson.

She had even been tempted to approach – hadn't that been part of the reason she had agreed to pick up Clay in the first place? – but then she saw Grace pick up her cell phone and start talking into it. Charlaine decided to keep her distance.

'Hi, Charlaine.'

A woman, a popular yappy mom who had never deigned to give Charlaine the time before, now stood before her with a look of feigned concern. The newspaper had not mentioned Mike's name, just that there was a shooting, but small towns and gossip and all that.

'I heard about Mike. Is he okay?'

'Fine.'

'What happened?'

Another woman sidled up to her right. Two others began to mosey over. Then two more. They came from every direction now, these approaching mothers, getting in her way, almost blocking Charlaine's view.

Almost.

For a moment Charlaine could not move. She stood frozen, watching as he approached Grace Lawson.

He had changed his appearance. He wore glasses now. His hair wasn't blond anymore. But there was no doubt. It was the same man.

It was Eric Wu.

From more than a hundred feet away Charlaine felt the shiver when Wu put his hand on Grace Lawson's shoulder. She saw him bend down and whisper something into her ear.

And then she saw Grace Lawson's whole body go rigid.

Grace wondered about the Asian man walking toward her.

She figured that he would just walk by her. He was too young to be a parent. Grace knew most of the teachers. He wasn't one of them. He was probably a new student teacher. That was probably it. She really did not give him much thought. Her mind was concerned with other things.

She had packed enough clothes for a few days anyway. Grace had a cousin who lived near Penn State, smack in the middle of Pennsylvania. Maybe she would drive out there. Grace had not called ahead to see. She did not want to leave any trail.

After throwing clothes in the suitcases, she had closed the door to her bedroom. She took out the small gun Cram had given her and set it on the bed. For a long time she just stared at it. She had always been fervently anti-gun. Like most rational people she was scared of what a weapon like this could do lying around the house. But Cram had put it succinctly yesterday: Hadn't her children been threatened?

The trump card.

Grace wrapped the nylon ankle holster around her good leg. It felt itchy and uncomfortable. She changed into jeans with a small flare at the bottom. The gun was covered now, but there was some room down there. There was still a small bulge in the area, but no more so than if she were wearing a boot.

She grabbed the box of Bob Dodd files from his office at the *New Hampshire Post* and drove to the school. She had a few minutes now, so she stayed in the car and started going through it. Grace had no idea what she expected to find. There were plenty of desk knickknacks – a small American flag, a Ziggy coffee mug, a return address stamper, a small Lucite paperweight. There were pens, pencils, erasers, paperclips, whiteout, thumbtacks, Post-it notes, staples.

Grace wanted to skip past that stuff and dive into the files, but the pickings were slim. Dodd must have done all his work on a computer. She found a few diskettes, all unmarked. Maybe there would be a clue on one of those. She'd check when she got access to a computer.

As for paperwork, all she found was press clippings. Articles written by Bob Dodd. Grace skimmed through them. Cora had been right. His stories were mostly small-time exposés. People would write in with a complaint. Bob Dodd would investigate. Hardly the sort of stuff that gets you killed, but who knows? The little things have a way of rippling.

She was just about to give up – had given up really – when she located the desk photo in the bottom. The frame was facedown. More out of curiosity than anything else she flipped the frame over and took a look. The photograph was a classic vacation shot. Bob Dodd and his wife Jillian stood on a beach, both smiling with dazzling white teeth, both wearing Hawaiian shirts. Jillian had red hair. Her eyes were widely spaced apart. Grace suddenly understood Bob Dodd's involvement. It had nothing to do with the fact that he was a reporter.

His wife, Jillian Dodd, was Sheila Lambert.

Grace closed her eyes and rubbed the bridge of her nose. Then she carefully put everything back in the package. She stuck it in the backseat and slipped out of the car. She needed time to think and put it together.

The four members of Allaw – it all came back to them. Sheila Lambert, Grace now knew, had stayed in the country. She had changed her identity and gotten married. Jack had taken off for a small village in France. Shane Alworth was either dead or in parts unknown – maybe, as his mother suggested, helping the poor in Mexico. Geri Duncan had been murdered.

Grace checked her watch. The bell would ring in a few minutes. She felt the buzz of her cell phone on her belt. 'Hello?'

'Ms. Lawson, this is Captain Perlmutter.'

'Yes, Captain, what can I do for you?'

'I need to ask you some questions.'

'I'm picking up my children at school right now.'

'Would you like me to come by your house? We can meet there.'

'They'll be out in two more minutes. I'll swing by the station.' A sense of relief rushed over her. This half-baked idea of running off to Pennsylvania – that might be too much. Maybe Perlmutter knew something. Maybe, with all she now knew about that picture, he would finally believe her. 'Will that be okay?'

'That'll be fine. I'll be here waiting.'

The very moment Grace snapped the receiver closed, she felt a hand touch down on her shoulder. She turned. The hand belonged to the young Asian man. He bent his head toward her ear.

'I have your husband,' he whispered.

42

'Charlaine? Are you okay?'

It was the popular yappy mother. Charlaine ignored her.

Okay, Charlaine, think.

What, she wondered, would the dumb heroine do? That was how she'd try to play it in the past – imagine what the waif would do and do the opposite.

C'mon, c'mon...

Charlaine tried to battle through the near-paralyzing fear. She had not expected to see this man ever again. Eric Wu was wanted. He had shot Mike. He had assaulted Freddy and held him captive. The police had his fingerprints. They knew who he was. They would send him back to prison. So what was he doing here?

Who cares, Charlaine? Do something.

The answer was a no-brainer: Call the police.

She reached into her pocketbook and pulled out her Motorola. The mothers were still barking like small dogs. Charlaine flipped the phone open.

It was dead.

Typical, and yet it made sense. She had used it during the chase. She had left it on all this time. The phone was two years old. The damn thing was always going dead. She glanced back across the schoolyard. Eric Wu was talking to Grace Lawson. They both began to walk away.

The same woman asked again: 'Is something wrong, Charlaine?'

'I need to use your cell phone,' she said. 'Now.'

Grace just stared at the man.

'If you come with me quietly, I will take you to your husband. You will see him. You will be back in an hour. But the school bell rings in one minute. If you do not come with me, I will take out a gun. I will shoot your children. I will shoot random children. Do you understand?'

Grace could not speak.

'You don't have much time.'

She found her voice. 'I'll go with you.'

'You drive. Just walk calmly with me. Please do not make the mistake of trying to signal someone. I will kill them. Do you understand?'

'Yes.'

'You may be wondering about the man assigned to protect you,' he went on. 'Let me assure you that he will not interfere.'

'Who are you?' Grace asked.

'The bell is about to ring.' He looked off, a tiny smile on his lips. 'Do you want me to be here when your children come out?'

Scream, Grace thought. Scream like a lunatic and start running. But she could see the bulge of the gun. She could see the man's eyes. This was no bluff. He meant it. He would kill people.

And he had her husband.

They began to walk to her car, side by side, like two friends. Grace's eyes darted about the playground. She spotted Cora. Cora gave her a puzzled look. Grace did not want to risk it. She looked away.

Grace kept walking. They reached her car. She had just unlocked the doors when the school bell rang.

The yappy woman rummaged through her purse. 'We have a terrible calling plan. Hal is so cheap sometimes. We run out of minutes in the first week and then we need to watch ourselves the rest of the month.'

Charlaine looked at the other faces. She did not want to cause a panic, so she kept her voice even. 'Please, does anyone have a phone I can borrow?'

She kept her eyes on Wu and Lawson. They were across the street, by Grace's car now. She saw Grace use one of those remote controls to unlock the doors. Grace stood by the driver's door. Wu was by the passenger's. Grace Lawson made no move to run away. It was hard to see her face, but she didn't look as if she was being coerced.

The bell sounded.

The mothers all turned toward the doors, a Pavlovian response, and waited for their children to emerge.

'Here, Charlaine.'

One of the mothers, eyes on the school door, handed Charlaine her cell phone. Charlaine tried not to grab it too quickly. She was raising it to her ear when she glanced over at Grace and Wu one more time. She stopped cold.

Wu was staring directly at her.

When Wu saw that woman again, he started for his gun.

He was going to shoot her. Right here. Right now. Right in front of everyone.

Wu was not a superstitious man. He realized that the odds of her being here were reasonable. She had children. She lived in the area. There must have been two or three hundred mothers here. It would make sense that she would be one of them.

But he still wanted to kill her.

On the superstitious side, he would kill this demon.

On the practical side, he would prevent her from calling the police. He would also cause a panic that would allow him to escape. If he shot her, everyone would run toward the fallen woman. It would be the ideal diversion.

But there were problems too.

First, the woman stood at least a hundred feet away. Eric Wu knew his strengths and weaknesses. In hand-to-hand he had no equal. With a gun, he was merely decent. He might only wound or, worse, miss altogether. Yes, there would be a panic, but without a body falling, it might not be the sort of diversion he wanted.

His real target – the reason he was here – was Grace Lawson. He had her now. She was listening to him. She was pliable because she still held out hope that her family could survive this. If she were to see him fire a shot, standing as she was out of his reach, there was a chance that Grace Lawson would panic and bolt.

'Get in,' he said.

Grace Lawson opened her car door. Eric Wu stared at the woman across the schoolyard. When their eyes met, he slowly shook his head and gestured toward his waist. He wanted her to understand. She had crossed him before and he had fired. He would do so again.

He waited until the woman lowered the phone. Still keeping his eyes on her, Wu slid into the car. They pulled out and disappeared down Morningside Drive.

43

Perlmutter sat across from Scott Duncan. They were in the captain's office at the station. The air-conditioning was on the fritz. Dozens of cops in full uniform all day and no air-conditioning – the place was starting to reek.

'So you're on leave from the U.S. attorney's office,' Perlmutter said.

'That's correct,' Duncan replied. 'I'm working in private practice right now.'

'I see. And your client hired Indira Khariwalla – check that, you hired Ms. Khariwalla on behalf of a client.'

'I will neither confirm nor deny that.'

'And you won't tell me if your client wanted Jack Lawson followed. Or why.'

'That's correct.'

Perlmutter spread his hands. 'So what exactly do you want, Mr. Duncan?'

'I want to know what you've learned about Jack Lawson's disappearance.'

Perlmutter smiled. 'Okay, let me make sure I have this straight. I'm supposed to tell you everything I know about a murder and missing person investigation, even though your client may very well be involved. You, in turn, are supposed to tell me squat. That about cover it?'

'No, that's not correct.'

'Well, help me here.'

'This has nothing to do with a client.' Duncan crossed his ankle over his knee. 'I have a personal involvement in the Lawson case.'

'Come again?'

'Ms. Lawson showed you the photograph.'

'Right, I remember.'

'The girl with her face crossed out,' he said, 'was my sister.'

Perlmutter leaned back and whistled low. 'Maybe you should start at the beginning.'

'It's a long story.'

'I'd say I have all day, but that would be a lie.'

As if proving the point, the door flew open. Daley jammed his head in.

'Line two.'

'What is it?'

'Charlaine Swain. She says she just saw Eric Wu at the schoolyard.'

Carl Vespa stared at the painting.

Grace was the artist. He owned eight of her paintings, though this was the one that moved him most. It was, he suspected, a portrait of Ryan's last moments. Grace's memory of that night was hazy. She hated to sound pompous about it, but this vision – this seemingly ordinary painting of a young man somehow on the verge of a nightmare – had come to her in something of an artistic trance. Grace Lawson claimed that she dreamed about that night. That, she said, was the only place that the memories existed.

Vespa wondered.

His home was in Englewood, New Jersey. The block had at one time been old money. Now Eddie Murphy lived at the end of the street. A power forward for the New Jersey Nets was two houses down. Vespa's property, once owned by a Vanderbilt, was sprawling and secluded. In 1988 Sharon, his then-wife, had torn down the turn-of-the-century stone edifice and built what was then considered modern. It had not aged well. The house looked like a bunch of glass cubes, stacked haphazardly. There were too many windows. The house got ridiculously hot in the summer. It looked and felt like a damn greenhouse.

Sharon was gone now too. She had not wanted the house in the divorce. She really did not want very much at all. Vespa did not try to stop her. Ryan had been their main connection, in his death more than life. That was never a healthy thing.

Vespa checked the security monitor for the driveway. The sedan was pulling up.

He and Sharon had wanted more children, but it was not to be. Vespa's sperm count was too low. He told no one, of course, subtly implying that the fault lay with Sharon. Awful to say now, but Vespa believed that if they had more children, if Ryan had at least one sibling, it would have made the tragedy, if not easier, at least bearable. The problem with tragedy is that you have to go on. There is no choice. You cannot just pull off the road and wait it out – much as you might want to. If you have other children you understand that right away. Your life may be over, but you get out of bed for others.

Put simply, there was no reason for him to get out of bed anymore.

Vespa headed outside and watched the sedan come to a stop. Cram got out first, a cell phone glued to his ear. Wade Larue followed. Larue did not look frightened. He looked oddly at peace, gazing at the lush surroundings. Cram mumbled something to Larue – Vespa couldn't hear what he said – and then started up the stairs. Wade Larue wandered away as if he was on retreat.

Cram said, 'We got a problem.'

Vespa waited, following Wade Larue with his eyes.

'Richie is not answering his radio.'

'Where was he stationed?'

'In a van near the kids' school.'

'Where is Grace?'

'We don't know.'

Vespa looked at Cram.

'It was three o'clock. We knew she'd gone to pick up Emma and Max. Richie was supposed to tail her from there. She got to the school, we know that. Richie radioed that in. Since then, nothing.'

'Did you send someone over?'

'Simon went to check on the van.'

'And?'

'It's still there. Parked in the same spot. But there are cops in the area now.'

'What about the kids?'

'We don't know yet. Simon thinks he sees them in the schoolyard. But he does-n't want to get too close with the cops around.'

Vespa closes his fists. 'We have to find Grace.'

Cram said nothing.

'What?'

Cram shrugged. 'I think you have it wrong, that's all.'

Neither one of them said anything after that. They stood and watched Wade Larue. He strolled the grounds, cigarette in tow. From the top of the property there was a magnificent view of the George Washington Bridge and, behind it, the distant skyline of Manhattan. It had been there that Vespa and Cram had watched the smoke billow as if from Hades when the towers fell. Vespa had known Cram for thirty-eight years. Cram was the best with a gun or a knife Vespa had ever seen. He scared people with little more than a glance. The vilest men, the most violent psychotics, begged for mercy before Cram even touched them. But on that day, standing silently in the yard, watching the smoke not dissipate, Vespa had seen even Cram break down and cry.

They looked over at Wade Larue.

'Did you talk to him at all?' Vespa asked.

Cram shook his head. 'Not a word.'

'He looks pretty calm.'

Cram said nothing. Vespa started toward Larue. Cram stayed where he was. Larue did not turn around. Vespa stopped about ten feet away and said, 'You wanted to see me?'

Larue kept staring out at the bridge. 'Beautiful view,' he said.

'You're not here to admire it.'

He shrugged. 'Doesn't mean I can't.'

Vespa waited. Wade Larue did not turn around. 'You confessed.'

'Yes.'

'Did you mean it?' Vespa asked.

'At the time? No.'

'What does that mean, at the time?'

'You want to know if I fired those two shots that night.' Wade Larue finally turned and faced Vespa full. 'Why?'

'I want to know if you killed my boy.'

'Either way I didn't shoot him.'

'You know what I mean.'

'Can I ask you something?'

Vespa waited.

'Are you doing this for you? Or your son?'

Vespa thought about that. 'It's not for me.'

'Then your son?'

'He's dead. It won't do him any good.'

'Who then?'

'It doesn't matter.'

'It does to me. If it's not about you or your son, why do you still need revenge?'

'It needs to be done.'

Larue nodded.

'The world needs balance,' Vespa went on.

'Yin and yang?'

'Something like that. Eighteen people died. Someone has to pay.'

'Or the world is out of balance?'

'Yes.'

Larue took out a pack of cigarettes. He offered one to Vespa. Vespa shook his head.

'Did you fire those shots that night?' Vespa asked.

'Yes.'

That was when Vespa exploded. His temper was like that. He went from zero to uncontrolled rage in a snap. There was an adrenaline rush, like a thermometer spiking up in a cartoon. He cocked his fist and smashed it into Larue's face. Larue went down hard on his back. He sat up, put his hand to his nose. There was blood. Larue smiled at Vespa. 'That give you balance?'

Vespa was breathing hard. 'It's a start.'

'Yin and yang,' Larue said. 'I like that theory.' He wiped his face with his forearm. 'Thing is, this universal balancing act – does it stretch across generations?'

'What the hell is that supposed to mean?'

Larue smiled. There was blood on his teeth. 'I think you know.'

'I'm going to kill you. You know that.'

'Because I did something bad? So I should pay a price?'

'Yes.'

Larue got to his feet. 'But what about you, Mr. Vespa?'

Vespa tightened his fists, but the adrenaline rush was quieting.

'You've done bad. Did you pay the price?' Larue cocked his head. 'Or did your son pay it for you?'

Vespa hit Larue deep in the gut. Larue folded. Vespa punched him in the head. Larue fell again. Vespa kicked him in the face. Larue was flat on his back now. Vespa took a step closer. Blood dripped out of Larue's mouth, but the man still laughed. The only tears were on Vespa's face, not Larue's.

'What are you laughing at?'

'I was like you. I craved revenge.'

'For what?'

'For being in that cell.'

'That was your fault.'

Larue sat up. 'Yes and no.'

Vespa took a step back. He looked behind him. Cram stood perfectly still and watched. 'You said you wanted to talk.'

'I'll wait till you're done beating me.'

'Tell me why you called.'

Wade Larue sat up, checked his mouth for blood. He seemed almost happy to see it. 'I wanted vengeance. I can't tell you how badly. But now, today, when I got out, when I was suddenly free ... I don't want that anymore. I spent fifteen years in prison. But my sentence is over. Your sentence, well, the truth is yours will never end, will it, Mr. Vespa?'

'What do you want?'

Larue stood. He walked over to Vespa. 'You're in such pain.' His voice was soft now, as intimate as a caress. 'I want you to know everything, Mr. Vespa. I want you to learn the truth. This has to end. Today. One way or another. I want to live my life. I don't want to look over my shoulder. So I'm going to tell you what I know. I'm going to tell you everything. And then you can decide what you need to do.'

'I thought you said you fired those shots.'

Larue ignored that. 'Do you remember Lieutenant Gordon MacKenzie?'

The question surprised Vespa. 'The security guard. Of course.'

'He visited me in prison.'

'When?'

'Three months ago.'

'Why?'

Larue smiled. 'That balance thing again. Making things right. You call it yin and yang. MacKenzie called it God.'

'I don't understand.'

'Gordon MacKenzie was dying.' Larue put his hand on Vespa's shoulder. 'So before he went, he needed to confess his sins.'

44

The gun was in Grace's ankle holster.

She started up the car. The Asian man sat next to her. 'Head up the road and turn left.'

Grace was scared, of course, but there was an odd calmness too. Something about being in the eye of the storm, she guessed. Something was happening. There was a potential to find answers here. She tried to prioritize.

First: Get him far away from the children.

That was the number one thing here. Emma and Max would be fine. The teachers stayed outside until all the children were picked up. When she didn't show, they would give an impatient sigh and bring them to the office. That old battleaxe of a receptionist, Mrs. Dinsmont, would gleefully cluck her tongue about the neglectful mother and make the children wait. There had been an incident about six months ago when Grace got caught up by construction and arrived late. She'd been wracked with guilt, picturing Max waiting like a scene from *Oliver Twist*, but when she got there he was in the office coloring a picture of a dinosaur. He wanted to stay.

The school was out of sight now. 'Turn right.'

Grace obeyed.

Her captor, if that's what you wanted to call him, had said that he was taking her to Jack. She did not know if that was true or not, but she somehow suspected that it was. She was sure, of course, that he was not doing this out of the goodness of his heart. She had been warned. She had gotten too close. He was dangerous – she didn't need to see the gun in his waistband to know that. There was a crackle around him, an electricity, and you knew, just knew, that this man always left devastation in his path.

But Grace desperately needed to see where this led. She had her gun in the ankle holster. If she stayed smart, if she was careful, she would have the element of surprise. That was something. So for now she would go along. There was really no alternative anyway.

She was worried about working the gun and the holster. Would the gun come out smoothly? Would the gun really just fire when she pulled the trigger? Did you really just aim and pull? And even if she could get the gun from the holster in time – something doubtful with the way this guy was watching her – what would she do? Point it at him and demand he take her to Jack?

She couldn't imagine that working.

She couldn't just shoot him either. Forget the ethical dilemma or the question of if she'd be brave enough to pull the trigger. He, this man, might be her only connection to Jack. If she killed him, where would that leave her? She'd have silenced her only solid clue, maybe her only chance, to find Jack.

Better to wait and play it out. As if she had a choice.

'Who are you?' Grace asked.

Total stone face. He took hold of her purse and emptied the contents into his lap. He went through it, sifting and tossing items into the backseat. He found her cell phone, removed the battery, threw it in the back.

She kept peppering him with questions – where is my husband, what do you want with us – but he continued to ignore her. When they reached a stoplight, the man did something that she did not expect.

He rested his hand on her bad knee.

'Your leg was damaged,' he said.

Grace was not sure how to respond to this. His touch was light, almost feathery. And then without warning his fingers dug down with steel talons. They actually burrowed beneath the kneecap. Grace buckled. The tips of the man's fingers disappeared into the hollow where the knee meets the shinbone. The pain was so sudden, so enormous, that Grace could not even scream. She reached out and grabbed his fingers, tried to pry them out of her knee, but there was absolutely no give. His hand felt like a concrete block.

His voice was barely a whisper. 'If I dig in a little more and then pull...'

Her head was swimming. She was close to losing consciousness.

'...I could tear your kneecap right off.'

When the light turned green, he let go. Grace nearly collapsed in relief. The whole incident had probably taken less than five seconds. The man looked at her. There was the smallest hint of a smile on his face.

'I'd like you to stop talking now, okay?'

Grace nodded.

He faced forward. 'Keep driving.'

Perlmutter called in the APB. Charlaine Swain had had the good sense to get both the make and license plate. The car was registered to Grace Lawson. No surprise there. Perlmutter was in an unmarked car now, heading toward the school. Scott Duncan was with him.

'So who is this Eric Wu?' Duncan asked.

Perlmutter debated what to tell him but saw no reason to hold this back. 'To date we know he broke into a house, assaulted the owner in such a way as to leave him temporarily paralyzed, shot another man, and my guess is, he killed Rocky Conwell, the guy who was following Lawson.'

Duncan had no response.

Two other police cars were already on the scene. Perlmutter did not like that – marked cars at a school. They'd had the good sense, at least, to not use their sirens. That was something. The parents picking up offspring reacted in two ways. Some hurried their kids to their cars, hands on their shoulders, shielding them as though from gunfire. Others let curiosity rule the day. They walked over, oblivious or in a state of denial that there could be any danger in so innocent a setting.

Charlaine Swain was there. Perlmutter and Duncan hurried toward her. A young uniformed cop named Dempsey was asking her questions and taking notes. Perlmutter shooed him away and asked, 'What happened?'

Charlaine told him about coming to school, keeping an eye out for Grace Lawson because of what he, Perlmutter, had said. She told him about seeing Eric Wu with Grace.

'There was no overt threat?' he asked.

Charlaine said, 'No.'

'So she might have gone him with him voluntarily.'

Charlaine Swain flicked a glance at Scott Duncan, then back to Perlmutter. 'No. She didn't go voluntarily.'

'How do you know?'

'Because Grace came alone to pick up her kids,' Charlaine said.

'So?'

'So she wouldn't just voluntarily leave them like that. Look, I couldn't call you guys right away when I saw him. He was able to make me freeze from across a schoolyard.'

Perlmutter said, 'I'm not sure I understand.'

'If Wu could do that to me from that far away,' Charlaine said, 'imagine what he'd be able to do to Grace Lawson when he was right next to her, whispering in her ear.'

Another uniformed officer named Jackson came sprinting over to Perlmutter. His eyes were wide and Perlmutter could see he was trying everything he could not to panic. The parents picked up on it too. They took a step away.

'We found something,' Jackson said.

'What?'

He leaned in closer so no one would overhear. 'A van parked two blocks away. I think you should come see this.'

She should use the gun now.

Grace's knee throbbed. It felt as if someone had set off a bomb inside the joint. Her eyes were wet from holding back tears. She wondered if she'd be able to walk when they stopped.

She sneaked glances at the man who had hurt her so. Whenever she did, he was watching her, that bemused look still on his face. She tried to think, tried to organize her thoughts, but she kept flashing back to his hand on her knee.

He had been so casual about causing her such pain. It would have been one thing if he'd been emotional about it, one way or the other, if he'd been moved to either ecstasy or revulsion, but there had been nothing there. Like hurting someone was paperwork. No strain, no sweat. His boast, if you want to call it that, had not been idle: If he'd so desired, he could have twisted off her kneecap like a bottle top.

They had crossed the state line and were in New York now. She was on Interstate 287 heading toward the Tappan Zee Bridge. Grace did not dare speak. Her mind, naturally enough, kept going back to the children. Emma and Max would have come out of the school by now. They would have looked for her. Would they have been brought to the office? Cora had seen Grace in the schoolyard. So had several other mothers, Grace was sure. Would they say or do something?

This was all irrelevant and, more than that, a waste of mental energy. Nothing she could do about it. Time to concentrate on the task at hand.

Think about the gun.

Grace tried to rehearse in her mind how it would go. She would reach down with both hands. She would pull her cuff up with her left and grab the weapon with her right. How was it strapped in? Grace tried to remember. There was a strip covering the top, wasn't there? She had snapped it into place. It kept the gun secure, so it wouldn't jerk around. She'd have to unsnap that. If she just tried to pull the gun free, it would get caught.

Okay, good. Remember that: Unsnap first. Then pull.

She thought about timing. The man was incredibly strong. She had seen that. He probably had a fair amount of experience with violence. She would have to wait for an opportunity. First – and this was obvious – she couldn't be driving when she made her move. They would either need to be at a stoplight or parked or... or better, wait until they were getting out of the car. That might work.

Second, the man would have to be distracted. He watched her a lot. He was also armed. He had a weapon in his waistband. He would be able to draw it out far faster than she could. So she had to make sure that he was not looking at her – that his attention was, in some way, diverted.

'Take this exit.'

The sign read ARMONK. They had only been on 287 for maybe three or four miles. They were not going to be crossing the Tappan Zee Bridge. She had thought that perhaps the bridge would have provided another opportunity. There were tollbooths there. She could have tried to escape or somehow signal the toll worker, though she couldn't imagine that working. Her captor would be watching her if they'd pulled up to the tollbooth. He would, she bet, have put his hand on her knee.

She veered to the right and up the ramp. She began to work it out in her head again. When you really thought about it, Grace's best bet would be to wait until they reached their destination. For one thing, if indeed he really was taking her to Jack, well, Jack would be there, right? That made some sense.

But more than that, when they stopped the car, they would both have to get out. Obvious, yes, but it would provide an opportunity. He would get out on his side. She would get out on hers.

This could be her diversion.

Again she started rehearsing it in her head. She would open the car door. As she swung her legs out, she'd pull up the cuff. Her legs would be on the ground and blocked by the car. He wouldn't see. If she timed it right, he would be getting out on his side of the car at the same time. He'd turn his back. She'd be able to pull out the weapon.

'Take the next right,' he said. 'And then the second left.'

They were moving through a town Grace didn't know. There were more trees here than in Kasselton. The houses looked older, more lived-in, more private.

'Pull into the driveway over there. Third on the left.'

Grace's hands stayed tight on the wheel. She pulled into the driveway. He told her to stop in front of the house.

She took a breath and waited for him to open the door and get out.

Perlmutter had never seen anything like it.

The guy in the van, an overweight man with a standard issue mafiosa sweat suit, was dead. His last few moments had not been pleasant. The big man's neck was, well, flat, totally flat, as if a steamroller had somehow managed to roll over only the man's throat, leaving his head and torso intact.

Daley, never one at a loss for words, said, 'Serious grossness.' Then he added, 'He looks familiar.'

'Richie Jovan,' Perlmutter said. 'Works low level for Carl Vespa.'

'Vespa?' Daley repeated. 'He's involved in this?'

Perlmutter shrugged. 'This has to be Wu's handiwork.'

Scott Duncan was turning white. 'What the hell is going on?'

'It's simple, Mr. Duncan.' Perlmutter turned to face him. 'Rocky Conwell worked for Indira Khariwalla, a private investigator you hired. The same man – Eric Wu – murdered Conwell, killed this poor schmuck, and was last seen driving away from that school with Grace Lawson.' Perlmutter moved toward him. 'You want to tell us what's going on now?'

Another police car screeched to a stop. Veronique Baltrus came flying out. 'Got it.'

'What?'

'Eric Wu at yenta-match.com. He was using the name Stephen Fleisher.' She sprinted over to them, the raven hair tied back in a tight bun. 'Yenta-match sets up Jewish widows and widowers. Wu had three online flirtations going on at the same time. One woman is from Washington, DC. Another lives in Wheeling, West Virginia. And the last one, a Beatrice Smith, resides in Armonk, New York.'

Perlmutter broke into a run. No doubt, he thought. That was where Wu had gone. Scott Duncan followed. The ride to Armonk would take no more than twenty minutes.

'Call the Armonk Police Department,' he shouted to Baltrus. 'Tell them to send every available unit right away.'

45

Grace waited for the man to get out.

The lot was wooded so that the house was hard to see from the road. There were cathedral points and lots of deck space. Grace could see an aging barbecue. There were a string of lights, the old lantern kind, but the lanterns were weathered and torn. There was a rusted swing set in the back, like ruins from another era. There had been parties here once. A family. People who liked to entertain friends. The house had the feel of a ghost town: you expected tumbleweeds to roll past.

'Turn off the ignition.'

Grace ran it over again. Open the door. Swing the legs out. Pull out the gun. Take aim ...

And then what? Tell him to put his hands up? Just shoot him in the chest? What?

She flicked off the ignition and waited for him to get out first. He reached for the door handle. She readied herself. His eyes were on the front door of the house. She slid her hand down a little.

Should she go for it now?

No. Wait until he starts getting out. Don't hesitate. Any hesitation and she would lose the edge.

The man stopped with his hand on the handle. Then he turned around, made a fist, and hit Grace so hard in the lower ribs she thought the whole cage would cave in like a bird's nest. There was a thud and a crack.

Pain exploded across Grace's side.

She thought that her whole body would simply give out. The man grabbed her head with one hand. With the other he traced his hand down the side of her rib cage. His index finger came to rest on the spot he'd just hit, at the bottom of the rib cage.

His voice was gentle. 'Please tell me how you got that picture.'

She opened her mouth but nothing came out. He nodded as if he'd expected that. His hand dropped off her. He opened the car door and got out. Grace was dizzy from the pain.

The gun, she thought. Get the goddamn gun!

But he was already on the other side of the car. He opened her door. His hand took hold of her neck, his thumb on one side, his index finger on the other. He squeezed the pressure points and started to lift. Grace tried to stay with him. The movement jarred her ribs. It felt like someone had jammed a screwdriver between two bones and was jerking it up and down.

He dragged her out by the neck. Every step was a new adventure in pain. She tried not to breathe. When she did, even that slight expansion of the ribs made the tendons feel like they were being freshly ripped. He yanked her toward the house. The front door was unlocked. He turned the knob, pushed it open, and tossed her inside. She fell hard, nearly passing out.

'Please tell me how you got that picture.'

He slowly moved toward her. Fear cleared her head. She talked fast.

'I picked up a packet of film at the Photomat,' she began.

He nodded in the way someone does when they are not listening. He kept coming closer. Grace kept talking and tried to scoot back. There was nothing on his face, a man going about a mundane task, planting seeds, hammering a nail, putting in a buy order, whittling wood.

He was on her now. She tried to struggle but he was ridiculously strong. He lifted her enough to flip her onto her stomach. The ribs banged against the floor. A different pain, a new pain, seared through her. Her vision started going hazy. They were still in the front foyer. He straddled her back. She tried to kick, but there was nothing behind it. He pinned her down.

Grace couldn't move.

'Please tell me how you got that picture.'

She felt the tears coming, but she would not let herself cry. Stupid. Macho. But she would not cry. She said it again, about going to the Photomat, and getting that packet. Still straddling her back, his knees on the other side of her hips, he put his index finger on the damaged bottom of the rib cage. Grace tried to buck. He found the spot where it hurt the most and rested the tip of his finger right there. For a moment he did not do anything. She bucked more. She flung her head back and forth. She flailed. He just waited a second. Then another.

And then he jammed the finger between two broken ribs.

Grace screamed.

The voice unchanged: 'Please tell me how you got that picture.'

Now she did cry. He let her. She started explaining again, changing her words, hoping it would sound more believable, more convincing. He did not say a word.

He rested the index finger on the damaged rib again.

That was when a cell phone rang.

The man sighed. He put his hands on her back and lifted himself off. The ribs screamed again. Grace heard a whimpering sound and realized that it was coming from her. She made herself stop. She managed to glance over her shoulder. He kept his eyes on her, took the phone from his pocket, snapped it open.

'Yes.'

One thought in her head: Go for the gun.

He stared down at her. She almost didn't care. Going for the gun right now would be suicide, but her thoughts were base – escape the pain. Whatever the cost. Whatever the risk. Escape the pain.

The man kept the phone by his ear.

Emma and Max. Their faces floated toward her in something of a haze. Grace encouraged the vision. And something odd happened then.

Lying there, still on her stomach, her cheek pressed to the floor, Grace smiled. Actually smiled. Not from feelings of maternal warmth, though that might be part of it, but with specific memory.

When she was pregnant with Emma, she told Jack that she wanted to do natural childbirth and that she did not want to take any drugs. She and Jack dutifully attended Lamaze class every Monday night for three months. They practiced breathing techniques. Jack would sit behind her and rub her belly. He would go 'hee hee hoo hoo.' She would copy him. Jack even bought a shirt that read 'Coach' on the front and 'Team Healthy Baby' on the back. He wore a whistle around his neck.

When the contractions began, they rushed to the hospital all prepared, all ready for their hard work to pay off dividends. Once there, Grace felt a stronger contraction. They started doing their breathing. Jack would go 'hee hee hoo hoo.' Grace would follow suit. It worked wonderfully well right up until the very moment Grace started to, well, started to feel pain.

Then the insanity of their plan – when did 'breathing' become a euphemism for 'painkiller'? – became apparent. It washed away the macho idiocy of 'taking the hurt,' a concept idiotically male in the first place, and reason, calm reason, finally came to her.

She reached out then, grabbed a part of Jack's anatomy, pulled him close so he could hear her. She told him to find an anesthesiologist. Now. Jack said he would, the moment she released said anatomy. She obliged. He ran and found an anesthesiologist. But by then it was too late. The contractions were too far along.

And the reason Grace was smiling now, some eight years after the fact, was that the pain that day was at least this bad, probably worse. She had taken it. For her daughter. And then, miraculously, she had been willing to risk it again for Max.

So bring it on, she thought.

Maybe she was delirious. Nothing maybe about it. She was. But she didn't care. The smile stayed in place. Grace could see Emma's beautiful face. She saw Max's face too. She blinked and they were gone. But that didn't matter anymore. She looked at the cruel man on the phone.

Bring it on, you sick son of a bitch. Bring it on.

He finished with his phone call. He moved back toward her. She was still on her stomach. He straddled her again. Grace closed her eyes. Tears squeezed out of them. She waited.

The man took hold of both of her hands and pulled them behind her back. He wrapped duct tape around them and stood. He pulled her so that she was on her knees, her hands bound behind her back. The ribs ached but the pain was manageable for now.

She looked up at him.

He said, 'Don't move.'

He turned away and left her alone then. She listened. She heard a door open and then the sound of footsteps.

He was heading down into the basement.

She was alone.

Grace struggled to free her arms, but they were wrapped tightly. No way to reach the gun. She debated trying to stand and run, but that would be futile at best. The position of her arms, the searing pain in her ribs, and of course, the fact that she was a major gimp under the best of circumstances – add it up and it didn't look like a sound alternative.

But could she slip her hands under herself?

If she could do that, if she could get her hands, even bound, to the front of her body, she could go for the gun.

It was a plan.

Grace had no idea how long he'd be gone – not long, she figured – but she had to chance it.

Her shoulders rolled back in their sockets. Her arms straightened. Every movement – every breath – set the ribs afire. She fought through it. She stood and bent at the waist. She forced her hands down.

Progress.

Still standing, she bent the knees and squirmed. She was getting close. Footsteps again.

Damn, he was heading back up the stairs.

She was caught in the middle, her bound hands under her buttocks.

Hurry, dammit. One way or the other. Put the hands back behind her or keep going.

She chose to keep going. Keep going forward.

This was going to end here and now.

The footsteps were slow. Heavier. It sounded like he was dragging something with him.

Grace pushed harder. Her hands were stuck. She bent more at the waist and knees. The pain made her head swim. She closed her eyes and swayed. She pulled up, willing to dislocate her shoulders if it would help her get through.

The footsteps stopped. A door closed. He was here.

She forced her arms through. It worked. They came out in front of her.

But it was too late. The man was back. He stood in the room, not five feet from her. He saw what she had done. But Grace did not notice that. She was, in fact, not looking at the man's face at all. She stared openmouthed at the man's right hand.

The man let go. And there, falling to the floor by his side, was Jack.

46

Grace dove toward him.

'Jack? Jack?'

His eyes were closed. His hair was matted to his forehead. Her hands were still bound, but she was able to hold his face. Jack's skin was clammy. His lips were dry and caked over. There was duct tape around his legs. A handcuff hung around his right wrist. She could see scabs on his left wrist. It had been cuffed too, for a long time judging by the marks.

She called his name again. Nothing. She lowered her ear to his mouth. He was breathing. She could see that. Shallow, but he was breathing. She shifted around and put his head in her lap. Her rib pain screamed but that was irrelevant now. He lay flat on his back, her lap his pillow. Her mind fell back to the grape groves in that vineyard in Saint-Emilion. They'd been together about three months by then, totally infatuated, jammed neatly in that sprint-across-the-park, thumping-of-the-heart-whenever-you-see-the-person stage. She packed some pâté, some cheese, wine of course. The day had been sun-kissed, the sky the kind of blue that made you believe in the angels. They'd lain down on a red tartan blanket, his head in her lap like this, she stroking his hair. She'd spent more time staring at him than the natural wonders that surrounded them. She'd traced his face with her fingers.

Grace made her voice soft, tried to ease up on the panic.

'Jack?'

His eyes fluttered open. His pupils were too large. It took him a moment to focus, and then he saw her. For a moment his caked lips cracked into a smile. Grace wondered if he too was flashing back to that same picnic. Her heart burst, but she managed to smile back. There was a serene moment, no more, and then reality flooded in. Jack's eyes widened in panic. The smile vanished. His face crumbled into anguish.

'Oh God.'

'It's okay,' she said, even though that was about as dumb a statement as one could make under the circumstances.

He was trying not to cry. 'I'm so sorry, Grace.'

'Shhh, it's okay.'

Jack's eyes searched like beacons, finding their captor. 'She doesn't know any-thing,' he said to the man. 'Let her go.'

The man took a step closer. He bent down on his haunches. 'If you speak again,' he said to Jack, 'I will hurt her. Not you. Her. I will hurt her very badly. Do you understand?'

Jack closed his eyes and nodded.

He stood back up. He kicked Jack off her lap, grabbed Grace by the hair, and pulled her to a standing position. With his other hand he clutched Jack by the neck.

'We need to take a ride,' he said.

47

Perlmutter and Duncan had just gotten off the Garden State Parkway at Interstate 287, no more than five miles from the house in Armonk, when the call was radioed in:

'They were here – Lawson's Saab is still in the driveway – but they're gone now.'

'How about Beatrice Smith?'

'Nowhere in sight. We just got here. We're still checking the residence.'

Perlmutter thought about it. 'Wu would figure that Charlaine Swain would report seeing him. He'd know he had to get rid of the Saab. Do you know if Beatrice Smith had a car?'

'Not yet, no.'

'Is there any other car in the driveway or garage?'

'Hold on.' Perlmutter waited. Duncan looked at him. Ten seconds later: 'No other car.'

'Then they took hers. Find out the make and license plate. Get an APB out right away.'

'Okay, got it. Wait, hold on a second, Captain.' He was gone again.

Scott Duncan said, 'Your computer expert. She thought that Wu was maybe a serial killer.'

'She thought it was a possibility.'

'You don't believe it though.'

Perlmutter shook his head. 'He's a pro. He doesn't pick victims for jollies. Sykes lived alone. Beatrice Smith is a widow. Wu needs a place to stay and operate. This is how he finds those places.'

'So he's a gun for hire.'

'Something like that.'

'Any thoughts on who he's working for?'

Perlmutter held the wheel. He took the Armonk exit. They were only about a mile away now. 'I was hoping you or your client might have an idea.'

The radio crackled. 'Captain? You still there?'

'I am.'

'One car registered to Mrs. Beatrice Smith. A tan Land Rover. License plate 472-JXY.'

'Get an APB out on it. They can't be far.'

48

The tan Land Rover stayed on side roads. Grace had no idea where they were headed. Jack was lying on the floor of the backseat. He had passed out. His legs were duct-taped together. His hands were cuffed behind him. Grace's hands were still bound in front of her. Her captor, she figured, had seen no reason to make her put them back.

In the backseat Jack groaned like a wounded animal. Grace looked at their captor, his placid face, one hand on the wheel like a father taking the family out for a Sunday drive. She ached. Every breath was a reminder of what he'd done to her ribs. Her knee felt as if it'd been ripped apart by shrapnel.

'What did you do to him?' she asked.

She tensed, awaiting the blow. She almost didn't care. She was beyond that. But the man did not lash out. He did not stay silent either. He pointed with his thumb toward Jack.

'Not as much,' he said, 'as he did to you.'

She stiffened. 'What the hell is that supposed to mean?'

Now, for the first time, she saw a genuine smile. 'I think you know.'

'I don't have the slightest idea,' she said.

He still smiled, and maybe, somewhere deep inside of her, the gnawing started to grow. She tried to cast it off, tried to concentrate on getting out of this, on saving Jack. She asked, 'Where are you taking us?'

He did not reply.

'I said –'

'You're brave,' he interrupted.

She said nothing.

'Your husband loves you. You love him. It makes this easier.'

'Makes what easier?'

He glanced toward her. 'You both may be willing to risk pain. But are you willing to let me hurt your husband?'

She did not reply.

'The same thing I said to him: If you talk again, I won't hurt you. I'll hurt him.'

The man was right. It worked. She kept silent. She gazed out the window and let the trees blur. They veered onto a two-lane highway. Grace had no idea where. The area was rural. She could see that. They took two more roads and now Grace knew where they were – the Palisades Parkway heading south, back down toward New Jersey.

The Glock was still in the ankle holster.

The feel of it was constant now. The weapon seemed to be calling to her, mocking her, so close and yet out of reach.

Grace would have to figure a way to get to it. There was no other choice. This man was going to kill them. She was sure of that. He wanted some information first – the origin of that photograph, for one thing – but once he had it, once he realized that she was telling the truth on that score, he would kill them both.

She had to go for the gun.

The man kept sneaking glances at her. There was no opening. She thought about it. Wait until he stopped the car? She had tried that before – it hadn't worked. Just go for it? Just pull it out and take her chances? A possibility but she really did not think she'd be fast enough. Pulling up the leg cuff, unsnapping that safety strap, getting her hand around the gun, withdrawing it... all before he reacted?

No way.

She debated the slow approach. Lower her hands a little to the side. Try to work her cuff up a bit at a time. Pretend like she had an itch.

Grace shifted in her seat and looked down at her leg. And that was when she felt her heart slam into her throat ...

Her cuff had ridden up.

The ankle holster. It was visible now.

Panic spread through her. She cut a glance at her captor, hoping that he hadn't seen it. But he had. His eyes suddenly widened. He was looking right at her leg.

Now or never.

But even as she reached, Grace could see that she had no chance. There was simply no way to get there in time. Her captor put his hand on her knee again and squeezed. Pain blasted violently through her, nearly knocking her unconscious. She screamed. Her body went rigid. Her hands dropped, useless now.

He had her.

She turned toward him, looked into his eyes, saw nothing. Then, without warning, there was movement coming from behind him. Grace gasped.

It was Jack.

Somehow he had risen up from the backseat like an apparition. The man turned, more curious than concerned. After all, Jack's hands and legs were bound. He was totally spent. What harm could he do?

Wild-eyed and looking something like an animal, Jack reared back his head and whipped it forward. The surprise caught the man off guard. Jack's forehead connected with the man's right cheek. The sound was a deep, hollow clunk. The car shrieked to a stop. The man let go of Grace's knee.

'Run, Grace!'

It was Jack's voice. Grace fumbled for the gun. She unsnapped the safety strap. But the man was back up again. He used one hand to grab Jack's neck. With the other he went after her knee again. She pulled away. He tried again.

Grace knew that there was no time to get the gun. Jack could no longer help. He had used up everything, sacrificed himself, for that one blow.

It would all be for nothing.

The man punched Grace in the ribs again. Hot knives blasted through her. Nausea swam through her stomach and head. She felt consciousness start ebbing away.

She couldn't hang on ...

Jack tried to thrash away, but he was little more than a nuisance. The man squeezed Jack's neck. Jack made a sound and went still.

The man reached for her again. Grace grabbed the door handle.

His hand clasped her arm.

She could not move.

Jack's lifeless head slid down the man's shoulder. It stopped on the forearm. And there, with his eyes closed, Jack opened his mouth and bit down hard.

The man howled and released his grip. He started shaking his arm, trying to get Jack off. Jack clenched his jaw and hung on like a bulldog. The man slammed his free palm into Jack's head. Jack slumped off.

Grace pulled the door handle, leaned her body against it.

She fell out of the car and landed on the pavement. She rolled away, anything to get farther away from her captor. She actually rolled into the other lane of the highway. A car swerved past her.

Get the gun!

She reached down again. The safety strap was off. She turned toward the car. The man was getting out. He pulled up his shirt. Grace saw his gun. She saw him reaching for it. Grace's own gun came loose.

There was no question now. There was no ethical dilemma. There was no thought about maybe yelling out a warning, telling him to freeze, asking him to put his hands on his head. There was no moral outrage. There was no culture, no humanity, no years of civilization or breeding.

Grace pulled the trigger. The gun went off. She pulled it again. And again. The man staggered. She pulled it again. The sound of sirens grew. And Grace fired again.

49

Two ambulances arrived. One whisked Jack away before Grace could even see him. Two paramedics worked on her. They were in constant motion, asking questions as they worked, but their words did not register. She was strapped to a stretcher and wheeled toward the ambulance. Perlmutter was there now.

'Where are Emma and Max?' she asked.

'At the station. They're safe.'

An hour later Jack was in surgery. That was all they would tell her. He was in surgery.

The young doctor ran a battery of tests on Grace. The ribs were indeed cracked, but there was nothing you could really do for cracked ribs. The doctor wrapped them with an Ace bandage and gave her a shot. The pain began to subside. An orthopedic surgeon checked out her knee and just shook his head.

Perlmutter came into her room and asked a lot of questions. For the most part Grace answered. On some subjects she was intentionally vague. It wasn't that she wanted to keep anything from the police. Or maybe, well, maybe she did.

Perlmutter was pretty vague too. Her dead captor's name was Eric Wu. He had been in prison. In Walden. That did not surprise Grace. Wade Larue had been in Walden too. It was all linked. That old photograph. Jack's group, Allaw. The Jimmy X Band. Wade Larue. And yes, even Eric Wu.

Perlmutter deflected most of her questions. She did not push it. Scott Duncan was in the room too. He stayed in the corner and did not speak.

Grace asked, 'How did you know I was with this Eric Wu?'

Perlmutter clearly did not mind answering this one. 'Do you know Charlaine Swain?'

'No.'

'Her son Clay goes to Willard.'

'Okay, right. I've met her.'

Perlmutter filled her in on Charlaine Swain's own ordeal at the hands of Eric Wu. He was expansive on the subject, purposefully, Grace thought, so that he could keep mum about the rest of it. Perlmutter's cell phone rang. He excused himself and headed into the corridor. Grace was alone with Scott Duncan.

'What are they thinking?' she asked.

Scott came closer. 'The popular theory is that Eric Wu was working for Wade Larue.'

'How do they figure?'

'They know you went to Larue's press conference today, so that's link one. Wu and Larue were not only in Walden at the same time, but they were cellmates for three months.'

223

'Link two,' she said. 'So what do they think Larue was after?'

'Revenge.'

'On?'

'On you, for starters. You testified against him.'

'I testified at his trial, but not really against him. I don't even remember the stampede.'

'Still. There is a solid link between Eric Wu and Wade Larue – we checked the prison phone records, they've been in touch – and there is a solid link between Larue and you.'

'But even if Wade Larue was out for vengeance, why not take me? Why take Jack?'

'They think maybe Larue was trying to hurt you by hurting your family. Make you suffer.'

She shook her head. 'And that weird photograph arriving? How do they figure that into the mix? Or your sister's murder? Or Shane Alworth or Sheila Lambert? Or Bob Dodd getting killed in New Hampshire?'

'It is a theory,' Duncan said, 'with lots of holes. But remember – and this plugs most of them – they don't see all these connections the way we do. My sister may have been murdered fifteen years ago, but that doesn't have anything to do with now. Neither does Bob Dodd, a reporter who was shot gangland style. For now they're keeping it simple: Wu gets out of jail. He grabs your husband. Maybe he would have grabbed others, who knows?'

'And the reason he didn't just kill Jack?'

'Wu was holding him until Wade Larue is released.'

'Which was today.'

'Right, today. Then Wu grabs you both. He was taking you to Larue when you escaped.'

'So Larue could, what, kill us himself?'

Duncan shrugged.

'That doesn't make sense, Scott. Eric Wu broke my ribs because he wanted to know how I got that photograph. He stopped because he got an unexpected call. Then he suddenly packed us in that car. None of that was planned.'

'Perlmutter just learned all that. They may now alter their theory.'

'And where is Wade Larue anyway?'

'No one seems to know. They're searching for him.'

Grace dropped back on her pillow. Her bones felt so damned heavy. The tears started flooding her eyes. 'How bad is Jack?'

'Bad.'

'Is he going to live?'

'They don't know.'

'Don't let them lie to me.'

'I won't, Grace. But try to get some sleep, okay?'

In the corridor Perlmutter spoke to the captain of the Armonk Police Department, Anthony Dellapelle. They were still combing through the home of Beatrice Smith.

'We just checked the basement,' Dellapelle said. 'Someone was kept locked up down there.'

'Jack Lawson. We know that.'

Dellapelle paused and said, 'Maybe.'

'What's that supposed to mean?'

'There's still a set of handcuffs against a pipe.'

'Wu unlocked him. He probably left them there.'

'That could be. There's also blood down there – not much of it, but it's fairly fresh.'

'Lawson had some cuts on him.'

There was a pause.

'What's going on?' Perlmutter asked.

'Where are you right now, Stu?'

'Valley Hospital.'

'How long would it take you to get here?'

'Fifteen minutes with the sirens,' Perlmutter said. 'Why?'

'There's something else down here,' Dellapelle said. 'Something you might want to see for yourself.'

At midnight Grace pulled herself out of bed and started down the corridor. Her children had visited briefly. Grace insisted that they let her get out of bed for that. Scott Duncan bought her some regular clothes – an Adidas sweat suit – because she did not want to greet her children in a hospital gown. She took a major pain injection so as to quiet the screaming in her ribs. Grace wanted the children to see that she was all right, that she was safe, that they were safe. She put on a brave face that lasted right up until the moment she saw that Emma had brought her poetry journal. Then she started crying.

You can only be strong for so long.

The children were spending the night in their own beds. Cora would stay in the master bedroom. Cora's daughter, Vickie, would sleep in the bed next to Emma. Perlmutter had assigned a female cop to stay the night too. Grace was grateful.

The hospital was dark now. Grace managed to stand upright. It took her forever. The hot scream was back in her ribs. Her knee felt more like shards of shattered glass than a joint.

The corridor was quiet. Grace had a specific destination in mind. Someone would try to stop her, she was sure, but that didn't really concern her. She was determined.

'Grace?'

She turned toward the female voice, readying to do battle. But that wouldn't be the case here. Grace recognized the woman from the playground. 'You're Charlaine Swain.'

The woman nodded. They moved toward each other, eyes locked, sharing something neither one of them could really articulate.

'I guess I owe you a thanks,' Grace said.

'Vice versa,' Charlaine said. 'You killed him. The nightmare is over for us.'

'How is your husband?' Grace asked.

'He's going to be fine.'

Grace nodded.

Charlaine said, 'I hear yours isn't doing well.' They were both beyond phony platitudes. Grace appreciated the honesty.

'He's in a coma.'

'Have you seen him?'

'I'm going there now.'

'Sneaking in?'

'Yes.'

Charlaine nodded. 'Let me help you.'

Grace leaned on Charlaine Swain. The woman was strong. The corridor was empty. In the distance they heard the sharp clack of heels on tile. The lights were low. They passed an empty nurse station and got into the elevator. Jack was on the third floor, in intensive care. Having Charlaine Swain with her felt oddly right to Grace. She could not say why.

This particular section of the intensive care unit had four rooms with glass walls. A nurse sat in the middle, thus able to monitor them all at once, but right now, only one room had a patient in it.

They both pulled up. Jack was in the bed. The first thing Grace noticed was that her powerful husband, the gruff six-two hunk who'd always made her feel safe, looked so small and fragile in that bed. She knew that it was her imagination. It had only been two days. He had lost some weight. He had been totally dehydrated. But that wasn't what this was.

Jack's eyes were closed. He had a tube coming out of his throat. There was another tube in his mouth. Both were taped with white adhesive. Yet another tube was in his nose. Still another in his right arm. There was an IV. There were machines surrounding him, straight out of some futuristic nightmare.

Grace felt herself starting to fall. Charlaine held her up. Grace steadied herself and moved toward the door.

The nurse said, 'You can't go in there.'

'She just wants to sit with him,' Charlaine said. 'Please.'

The nurse glanced around then back at Grace. 'Two minutes.'

Grace let go of Charlaine. Charlaine pushed opened the door for her. Grace went in alone. There were beeps and dings and a hellish sound like drops of water being sucked up a straw. Grace sat down next to the bed. She did not reach for Jack's hand. She did not kiss Jack's cheek.

'You're going to love the last verse,' Grace said.

She opened Emma's journal and started reading:

'Baseball, baseball,
Who's your best friend?
Is it the bat,
Who hits your rear end?'

Grace laughed and turned the page, but the next page – in fact, the rest of the journal – was blank.

50

A few minutes before Wade Larue died, he thought he had finally found true peace.

He had let vengeance go. He no longer needed to know the full truth. He knew enough. He knew where he was to blame and where he was not. It was time to put it behind him.

Carl Vespa had no choice. He would never be able to recover. The same was true for that awful swirl of faces – that blur of grief – he had been forced to see in the courtroom and again today at the press conference. Wade had lost time. But time is relative. Death is not.

He had told Vespa all he knew. Vespa was a bad man, no doubt about it. The man was capable of unspeakable cruelty. Over the past fifteen years Wade Larue had met a lot of people like that, but few were that simple. With the exception of full-blown psychopaths, most people, even the most evil, have the ability to love someone, to care about them, to make connections. That was not inconsistent. That was simply human.

Larue spoke. Vespa listened. Sometime in the middle of his explanation, Cram appeared with a towel and ice. He handed it to Larue. Larue thanked him. He took the towel – the ice would be too bulky – and dabbed the blood off his face. Vespa's blows no longer hurt. Larue had dealt with much worse over the years. When you've had enough of beatings, you go one way or the other – you fear them so much that you will do anything to avoid them, or you just ride them out and realize that this too shall pass. Somewhere during his incarceration Larue had joined that second camp.

Carl Vespa did not say a word. He did not interrupt or ask for clarification. When Larue finished Vespa stood there, his face unchanged, waiting for more. There was nothing. Without a word Vespa turned and left. He nodded at Cram. Cram started toward him. Larue lifted his head. He would not run. He was through with running.

'Come on, let's go,' Cram said.

Cram dropped him off in the center of Manhattan. Larue debated calling Eric Wu, but he knew that would be pointless at this stage. He started toward the Port Authority bus terminal. He was ready now for the rest of his life to begin. He was going to head to Portland, Oregon. He wasn't sure why. He had read about Portland in prison and it seemed to fit the bill. He wanted a big city with a liberal feel. From what he'd read, Portland sounded like a hippy commune that had turned into a major metropolis. He might get a fair shake out there.

He would have to change his name. Grow a beard. Dye his hair. He didn't think it would take that much to change him, to help him escape the past fifteen years.

Naïve to think it, yes, but Wade Larue still thought that an acting career was a possibility. He still had the chops. He still had the supernatural charisma. So why not give it a go? If not, he'd get a regular job. He wasn't afraid of a little hard work. He'd be in a big city again. He'd be free.

But Wade Larue didn't go to the Port Authority bus station.

The past still had too strong a pull. He couldn't go quite yet. He stopped a block away. He saw the buses churning out to the viaduct. He watched for a moment and then turned to the row of pay phones.

He had to make one last phone call. He had to know one last truth.

Now, an hour later, the barrel of a gun was pressed against that soft hollow under his ear. It was funny what you thought of a moment before death. The soft hollow – that was one of Eric Wu's favorite pressure-point spots. Wu had explained to him that knowing the location was fairly meaningless. You could not just stick your finger in there and push. That might hurt, but it would never incapacitate an opponent.

That was it. That pitiful thought, beyond pitiful, was Wade Larue's last before the bullet entered his brain and ended his life.

51

Dellapelle led Perlmutter into the basement. There was enough light, but Dellapelle still used the flashlight. He pointed it at the floor.

'There.'

Perlmutter stared down at the concrete and felt a fresh chill.

'You thinking what I'm thinking?' Dellapelle asked him.

'That maybe' – Perlmutter stopped, trying to figure this into the equation – 'that maybe Jack Lawson wasn't the only one being held down here.'

Dellapelle nodded. 'So where is the other guy?'

Perlmutter did not say anything. He just stared at the floor. Someone had indeed been held down. Someone who found a pebble and scratched two words into the floor, all in caps. A name actually, another person from that strange photograph, a name he'd just heard from Grace Lawson:

'SHANE ALWORTH.'

Charlaine Swain stayed to help Grace back to her room. Their silence was comfortable. Grace wondered about that. She wondered about a lot of things. She wondered why Jack had run away all those years ago. She wondered why he'd never touched that trust fund, why he let his sister and father control his percentage. She wondered why he'd run away not long after the Boston Massacre. She wondered about Geri Duncan and why she ended up dead two months later. And she wondered, perhaps most of all, if meeting Jack in France that day, if falling in love with him, had been more than just a coincidence.

She no longer wondered if it was all connected. She knew that it was. When they reached Grace's room, Charlaine helped her get back into bed. She turned to go.

'Do you want to stay a few minutes?' Grace asked.

Charlaine nodded. 'I'd like that.'

They talked. They started with what they had in common – children – but it was clear neither one of them wanted to stay on the subject long. An hour passed in a moment. Grace was not sure what they'd even discussed exactly. Just that she was grateful.

At nearly two in the morning the hospital phone next to Grace rang. For a moment they both just stared at it. Then Grace reached over and picked it up.

'Hello?'

'I got your message. About Allaw and Still Night.'

She recognized the voice. It was Jimmy X.

'Where are you?'

'In the hospital. I'm downstairs. They won't let me up.'

'I'll be down in a minute.'

The hospital lobby was quiet.

Grace was not sure how to handle this. Jimmy X sat with his forearms resting against his thighs. He didn't look up as she hobbled toward him. The reception-ist read a magazine. The security guard whistled softly. Grace wondered if the guard would be able to protect her. She suddenly missed that gun.

She stopped in front of Jimmy X, stood over him, and waited. He looked up. Their eyes met and Grace knew. She didn't know the details. She barely knew the outline. But she knew.

His voice was almost a plea. 'How did you learn about Allaw?'

'My husband.'

Jimmy looked confused.

'My husband is Jack Lawson.'

His jaw dropped. 'John?'

'That's what he went by back then, I guess. He's upstairs right now. He may very well die.'

'Oh God.' Jimmy buried his face in his hands.

Grace said, 'You know what always bothered me?'

He did not reply.

'Your running away. It doesn't happen very much – a rock star just giving up like that. There are rumors about Elvis or Jim Morrison, but that's because they're dead. There was that movie, *Eddie and the Cruisers,* but that was a movie. In real-ity, well, like I said before, the Who didn't run away after Cincinnati. The Stones didn't after Altamont Speedway. So why, Jimmy? Why did you run?'

He kept his head low.

'I know about the Allaw connection. It's just a matter of time before someone puts it together.'

She waited. He dropped his hands away from his face and rubbed them together. He looked toward the security guard. Grace almost took a step back, but she held her ground.

'Do you know why rock concerts used to always start so late?' Jimmy asked.

The question threw her. 'What?'

'I said ...'

'I heard what you said. No, I don't know why.'

'It's because we're so wasted – drunk, stoned, whatever – that our handlers need time to get us sobered up enough to perform.'

'Your point being?'

'That night I nearly passed out from cocaine and alcohol.' His gaze drifted off then, his eyes red. 'That's why there was such a long delay. That was why the crowd got so impatient. If I had been sober, if I had taken the stage on time...' He let his voice drift off with a 'who knows' shrug.

She didn't want excuses anymore. 'Tell me about Allaw.'

'I can't believe it.' He shook his head. 'John Lawson is your husband? How the hell did that happen?'

She didn't have an answer. She wondered if she ever would. The heart, she knew, was strange terrain. Could that have been part of the initial attraction, something subconscious, a knowing that they had both survived that terrible night? She flashed back to meeting Jack on that beach. Had it been fate, preordained – or planned? Did Jack want to meet the woman who had come to embody the Boston Massacre?

'Was my husband at the concert that night?' she asked.

'What, you don't know?'

'We can play this two ways, Jimmy. One, I can pretend I know everything and just want confirmation. But I don't. I may never know the truth, if you don't tell me. You may be able to keep your secret. But I'll keep looking. So will Carl Vespa and the Garrisons and the Reeds and the Weiders.'

He looked up, his face so like a child's.

'But two – and I think this is more important – you can't live with yourself anymore. You came to my house needing absolution. You know it's time.'

He lowered his head. Grace heard the sobs. They wracked his body. Grace did not say a word. She did not put a hand on his shoulder. The security guard glanced over. The receptionist looked up from her magazine. But that was all. This was a hospital. Adults weeping were hardly foreign in this environment. They both looked away. A minute later Jimmy's sobs started to quiet. His shoulders no longer shook.

'We met at a gig in Manchester,' Jimmy said, wiping his nose with his sleeve. 'I was with a group called Still Night. There were four bands on the roster. One of them was Allaw. That's how I met your husband. We hung out backstage, getting stoned. He was charming and all, but you have to understand. For me the music was everything. I wanted to make *Born to Run*, you know. I wanted to change the landscape of music. I ate, slept, dreamed, shat music. Lawson didn't take it too seriously. The band was fun, that's all. They had some decent songs, but the vocals and arrangement were totally amateur. Lawson didn't have any grand illusions about making it big or anything.'

The security guard was whistling again. The receptionist had her nose back in the magazine. A car drove up to the entrance. The guard headed outside and pointed toward the ER.

'Allaw broke up a few months later, I think. So did Still Night. But Lawson and I stayed in touch. When I started up the Jimmy X Band, I almost thought of asking him to join.'

'Why didn't you?'

'I didn't think he was that good a musician.'

Jimmy stood so suddenly that he startled Grace. She took a step back. She kept her eyes on him, still searching to make eye contact, as if that alone could keep him in place.

'Yeah, your husband was at the concert that night. I got him five tickets in the front pit. He brought some of his old band members with him. He even brought a couple backstage.'

He stopped then. They stood there. He looked off and for a moment Grace feared that she was losing him.

'Do you remember who they were?' she asked.

'The old band members?'

'Yes.'

'Two girls. One had this bright red hair.'

Sheila Lambert. 'Was the other girl Geri Duncan?'

'I never knew her name.'

'How about Shane Alworth? Was he there?'

'Was that the guy on keyboard?'

'Yes.'

'Not backstage. I only saw Lawson and the two girls.'

He shut his eyes.

'What happened, Jimmy?'

His face sagged and he suddenly looked older. 'I was pretty wasted. I could hear the crowd. Twenty thousand strong. They would chant my name. They would clap. Anything to get the concert started. But I could barely move. My manager came in. I told him I'd need more time. He left. I was alone. And then Lawson and those two chicks came into the room.'

Jimmy blinked and looked at Grace. 'Is there a cafeteria in this place?'

'It's closed.'

'I could use a cup of coffee.'

'Tough.'

Jimmy started pacing.

Grace asked, 'What happened after they came in the room?'

'I don't know how they got backstage. I never gave them passes. But all of a sudden Lawson comes up to me and is all "hey how's it going?" I was happy to see him, I guess. But then, I don't know, something went really wrong.'

'What?'

'Lawson. He went crazy. I don't know, he must have been higher than I was. He started pushing me, making threats. He shouted that I was a thief.'

'A thief?'

Jimmy nodded. 'It was all nonsense. He said...' He finally stayed still and met her eyes. 'He said I stole his song.'

'What song?'

'"Pale Ink."'

Grace could not move. The tremor started moving down her left side. There was a flutter in her chest.

'Lawson and that other guy, Alworth, wrote this song for Allaw called "Invisible Ink." That was pretty much the only similarity between the songs. That part of the title. You know the lyrics to 'Pale Ink,' right?'

She nodded. She didn't even try to speak.

'"Invisible Ink" had a similar theme, I guess. Both about how fragile memory can be. But that was it. I told John that. But he was just out of his mind. Whatever I said just pissed him off more. He kept pushing me. One of the girls, she had this really dark hair, was egging him on too. She started saying they'd break my legs or something. I called for help. Lawson punched me. You remember the reports that I was injured in the melee?'

She nodded again.

'I wasn't. It was your husband. He hit my jaw, and then he jumped me. I tried to push him off. He started shouting how he was going to kill me. It was, I don't know, the whole thing was surreal. He said he was going to cut me up.'

The flutter expanded and grew cold. Grace was holding her breath. This couldn't be. Please, this just couldn't be.

'By now it was just so out of hand, one of the girls, the redhead, told him to calm down. It's not worth it, she said. She pleaded with him to forget it. But he wasn't listening. He just smiled at me and then ... then he took out a knife.'

Grace shook her head.

'He said he was going to stab me in the heart. You remember how I said I was stoned out of my mind? Well, that sobered me up. You want to sober someone up? Threaten to stick a knife in their chest.' He went quiet again.

'What did you do?'

Had she spoken? Grace wasn't sure. The voice sounded like hers, but it seemed as though it'd come from someplace else, someplace tinny and distant.

Jimmy's face, lost in the memory, went slack. 'I wasn't going to just let him stab me. So I jumped him. He dropped the knife. We started wrestling. The girls were screaming now. They came over and tried to pull us apart. And then, when we were on the floor like that, I heard a gunshot.'

Grace was still shaking her head. Not Jack. Jack wasn't there that night, no way, no chance at all ...

'It was so loud, you know. Like the gun was behind my ear or something. All hell broke loose then. There were screams. And then there were two, maybe three more shots. Not in the room. They were from far away. I heard more screams. Lawson stopped moving. There was blood on the floor. He'd been hit in the back. I pushed him off and then I saw that security guard, Gordon MacKenzie, still pointing his gun.'

Grace closed her eyes. 'Wait a second. Are you telling me Gordon MacKenzie fired the first shot?'

Jimmy nodded. 'He heard the commotion, heard me calling for help and...' Again his voice trailed off. 'We just stared at each other for a second. The girls were screaming, but by now they were being drowned out by the crowd. That sound, I don't know, people talk about the most terrible sound, like maybe it's a wounded animal, but I've never heard anything that comes close to the sound of fear and panic. But you know that.'

She didn't. The head trauma had wiped out the memory. But she nodded so that he'd keep talking.

'Anyway, MacKenzie stood there for a second, stunned. And then he just ran. The two girls grabbed Lawson and started dragging him out.' He shrugged. 'You know the rest, Grace.'

She tried to take it all in. She tried to understand the implications, tried to fit it into her own reality. She had been standing yards away from all this, the other side of the stage. Jack. Her husband. He'd been right there. How could that be?

'No,' she said.

'No what?'

'No, I don't know the rest, Jimmy.'

He said nothing.

'The story didn't end there. Allaw had four members. I've been checking out the time line. Two months after the stampede someone hired a hit man to kill one of the members, Geri Duncan. My husband, the one who you say attacked you, ran overseas, shaved his beard, and started going by Jack. According to Shane Alworth's mother, he's overseas too, but I think she's lying about that. Sheila Lambert, the redhead, changed her name. Her husband was recently murdered and she disappeared again.'

Jimmy shook his head. 'I don't know anything about any of that.'

'You think it's all just a big coincidence?'

'No, I guess not,' Jimmy said. 'Maybe they were scared of what would happen if the truth came out. You remember what it was like those first few months – everyone wanting blood. They could have gone to jail, maybe worse.'

Grace shook her head. 'And what about you, Jimmy?'

'What about me?'

'Why did you keep this secret all these years?'

He said nothing.

'If what you just told me is true, you didn't do anything wrong. You were the one attacked. Why didn't you just tell the police what happened?'

He opened his mouth, closed it, tried again. 'This was bigger than me. Gordon MacKenzie was part of it, too. He came out the hero, remember? If the world ever learned that he fired that first shot, what do you think would have happened to him?'

'Are you saying you lied all these years to protect Gordon MacKenzie?'

He didn't reply.

'Why, Jimmy? Why didn't you say anything? Why did you run away?'

His eyes started shifting. 'Look, I told you everything I know. I'm going home now.'

Grace moved closer. 'You did steal that song, didn't you?'

'What? No.'

But she saw it now. 'That was why you felt responsible. You stole that song. If you hadn't, none of this would have happened.'

He just kept shaking his head. 'That's not it.'

'That's why you ran away. It wasn't just that you were stoned. You stole the song that made you. That was where it all started. You heard Allaw play in Manchester. You liked their song. You stole it.'

He shook his head, but there was nothing behind it. 'There were similarities ...'

And another thought struck her with a deep, hard pang: 'How far would you go to keep your secret, Jimmy?'

He looked at her.

'"Pale Ink" became even bigger after the stampede. That album ended up selling millions. Who has that money?'

He shook his head. 'You're wrong, Grace.'

'Did you already know I was married to Jack Lawson?'

'What? Of course not.'

'Is that why you came by my house that night? Were you trying to figure out what I knew?'

He kept shaking his head, tears on his cheeks. 'That's not true. I never meant to hurt anyone.'

'Who killed Geri Duncan?'

'I don't know anything about that.'

'Was she going to talk? Is that what happened? And then, fifteen years later, someone goes after Sheila Lambert aka Jillian Dodd, but her husband gets in the way. Was she going to talk, Jimmy? Did she know you were back?'

'I have to go.'

She stepped in his path. 'You can't run away again. There's been too much of that.'

234

'I know,' he said, his voice a plea. 'I know that better than anyone.'

He pushed past her and ran outside. Grace was tempted to yell, 'Stop! Grab him!' but she doubted the whistling guard would be able to do much. Jimmy was already outside, almost out of sight. She limped after him.

Gunshots – three of them – shattered the night. There was the squeal of tires. The receptionist dropped her magazine and picked up the phone. The security guard stopped whistling and sprinted toward the door. Grace hurried behind him.

When Grace got outside, she saw a car shoot down the exit ramp and disappear into the night. Grace had not seen who was in the car. But she thought she knew. The security guard bent down over the body. Two doctors ran out, nearly knocking Grace down. But it was too late.

Fifteen years after the stampede began, the Boston Massacre claimed its most elusive victim.

52

Maybe, Grace thought, we are not supposed to know the entire truth. And maybe the truth does not matter.

There were plenty of questions in the end. Grace thought that she would never know all the answers. Too many of the players were dead now.

Jimmy X, real name James Xavier Farmington, died from three gunshot wounds to the chest.

Wade Larue's body was found near the Port Authority Bus Terminal in New York City less than twenty-four hours after his release. He'd been shot in the head at point-blank range. There was only one significant clue: A reporter for the New York *Daily News* managed to follow Wade Larue after he left the press conference at the Crowne Plaza. According to the reporter, Larue got into a black sedan with a man fitting Cram's description. That was the last time anyone saw Larue alive.

No arrests have been made, but the answer seemed clear.

Grace tried to understand what Carl Vespa had done. Fifteen years had passed, and his son was still dead. Weird to put it that way, but maybe it was apropos. For Vespa, nothing had changed. Time had not been enough.

Captain Perlmutter would try to make a case against him. But Vespa was pretty good about covering his tracks.

Both Perlmutter and Duncan came to the hospital after Jimmy was killed. Grace told them everything. There was nothing to hide anymore. Perlmutter mentioned almost in passing that the words *Shane Alworth* had been scratched into the concrete floor.

'So what does that mean?' Grace asked.

'We're checking the physical evidence, but maybe your husband wasn't alone in that basement.'

It made sense, Grace guessed. Fifteen years later they were all coming back. Everyone in that photograph.

At four in the morning Grace was back in her hospital bed. Her room was dark when the door opened. A silhouette slid in quietly. He thought that she was asleep. For a moment Grace didn't say anything. She waited until he was in the chair again, just like fifteen years ago, before she said, 'Hello, Carl.'

'How are you feeling?' Vespa asked.

'Did you kill Jimmy X?'

There was a long pause. The shadow did not move. 'What happened that night,' he said at last. 'It was his fault.'

'It's hard to know.'

Vespa's face was no more than a shadow. 'You see too many shades of gray.'

Grace tried to sit up, but her rib cage would not cooperate. 'How did you find out about Jimmy?'

'From Wade Larue,' he said.

'You killed him too.'

'Do you want to make accusations, Grace, or do you want to know the truth?'

She wanted to ask if that was all he wanted, the truth, but she knew the answer. The truth would never be enough. Vengeance and justice would never be enough.

'Wade Larue reached out to me the day before he was released,' Vespa said. 'He asked if we could talk.'

'Talk about what?'

'He wouldn't say. I had Cram pick him up in the city. He came out to my house. He started in with some touchy-feely crap about understanding my pain. He said he was suddenly all at peace with himself, that he didn't want vengeance anymore. I didn't want to hear any of that. I wanted him to get to the point.'

'Did he?'

'Yes.' The shadow was still again. Grace debated reaching for the light switch and decided against it. 'He told me that Gordon MacKenzie had visited him in prison three months ago. Do you know why?'

Grace nodded, seeing it now. 'MacKenzie had terminal cancer.'

'Right. He was still hoping to buy a last-minute ticket to the Promised Land. All of a sudden he can't live with what he's done.' Vespa cocked his head and smiled. 'Amazing how that happens right before you're going to die anyway, isn't it? Ironic timing when you think about it. He confesses when there is no personal cost, and hey, if you buy into that confess-and-forgive nonsense, there could be a big upside.'

Grace knew not to comment. She stayed still.

'Anyway, Gordon MacKenzie took the blame. He was working the backstage entrance. He let some pretty young thing distract him. He said that Lawson and two girls sneaked past him. You know all this, don't you?'

'Some of it.'

'You know that MacKenzie shot your husband?'

'Yes.'

'And that's what started the riot. MacKenzie met up with Jimmy X after the whole thing went down. They both agreed to keep it quiet. They worried a little about Jack's injury or if those girls were going to come forward, but hey, those three had plenty to lose too.'

'So everyone just kept quiet.'

'Pretty much. MacKenzie became a hero. He got a job with the Boston police from that. He rose to captain. All off his heroics from that night.'

'So what did Larue do after MacKenzie confessed all this?'

'What do you think? He wanted the truth to come out. He wanted vengeance and exoneration.'

'So why didn't Larue tell anyone?'

'Oh, he did.' Vespa smiled. 'Three guesses who.'

Grace saw it. 'He told his lawyer.'

Vespa spread his hands. 'Give the lady a kewpie doll.'

'But how did Sandra Koval convince him to keep quiet?'

'Oh, this part is brilliant. Somehow – and let's give the lady credit – she did what was best for her client *and* her brother.'

'How?'

'She told Larue that he'd have a better chance of getting out on parole if he didn't tell the truth.'

'I don't understand.'

'You don't know much about parole, do you?'

She shrugged.

'You see, the parole board doesn't want to hear that you're innocent. They want to hear your mea culpas. If you want to get out, you have to hang your head in shame. You did wrong, you tell them. You've accepted blame – that's the first step toward rehabilitation. If you keep insisting you're innocent, you're not going to get better.'

'Couldn't MacKenzie testify?'

'He was too ill by then. You see, Larue's innocence wasn't the parole board's concern. If Larue wanted to take that route, he'd have to request a new trial. It would take months, maybe years. According to Sandra Koval – and she was telling the truth here – Larue's best chance of getting out was to admit his guilt.'

'And she was right,' Grace said.

'Yes.'

'And Larue never knew that Sandra and Jack were brother and sister?'

Again Vespa spread his hands. 'How would he?'

Grace shook her head.

'But, you see, it's not over for Wade Larue. He still wants vengeance and exoneration. He just knows he'll have to wait until he's out of jail. The question is, how? He knows the truth, but how will he prove it? Who will, pardon the expression, feel his wrath? Who is really to blame for what happened that night?'

Grace nodded as something else fell into place. 'So he went after Jack.'

'The one who pulled the knife, yep. So Larue got his old prison buddy Eric Wu to grab your husband. Larue's plan was to hook up with Wu the moment he got released. He'd make Jack tell the truth, film it, and then, he wasn't sure, but probably kill him.'

'Find exoneration and then commit murder?'

Vespa shrugged. 'He was angry, Grace. He might have ended up just beating him up or breaking his legs. Who knows?'

'So what happened?'

'Wade Larue had a change of heart.'

Grace frowned.

'You should have heard him talk about it. His eyes were so clear. I'd just punched him in the face. I'd kicked him and threatened his life. But the peace on his face ... it just stayed there. The moment Larue was free, he realized that he would be able to get past it.'

'What do you mean, past it?'

'Exactly that. His punishment was in the past. He could never really be exonerated because he wasn't blameless. He fired shots in the middle of the crowd. That raised the hysteria level. But more than that, it was like he told me: He was truly free. Nothing was left to tie him to the past. He was no longer in prison, but my son would always be dead. You see?'

'I think so.'

'Larue just wanted to live his life. He was also afraid of what I'd do to him.

So he wanted to trade. He told me the truth. He gave me Wu's number. And in exchange, I'd leave him alone.'

'So it was you who called Wu?'

'Actually Larue made the call. But yes, I spoke to him.'

'And you told Wu to bring us to you?'

'I didn't realize you were there. I thought it was just Jack.'

'What was your plan, Carl?'

He said nothing.

'Would you have killed Jack too?'

'Does it matter anymore?'

'And what would you have done with me?'

He took his time. 'There were things that made me wonder,' he said.

'About?'

'About you.'

Seconds passed. There were footsteps in the corridor. A stretcher with a squeaky wheel rolled past the door. Grace listened to the sound recede. She tried to slow her breath.

'Here you were nearly killed in the Boston Massacre – yet you end up marrying the man responsible for it all. I also know that Jimmy X came to visit your house after we saw him at that rehearsal. You never told me about that. And then there's the fact that you remember so little of what happened. Not just that night, but for almost a week before.'

She tried to keep her breaths even. 'You thought –'

'I didn't know what to think. But now maybe I do. I think your husband is a good man who made a terrible mistake. I think he ran away after the stampede. I think he felt guilty. That was why he wanted to meet you. He saw the press reports and wanted to know you were okay. Maybe he even planned on apologizing. So he found you on the beach in France. And then he fell in love with you.'

She closed her eyes and leaned back.

'It's over now, Grace.'

They sat in silence. There was nothing else to say. A few minutes later Vespa stole out, silent as the night.

53

But it wasn't over.

Four days passed. Grace got better. She went home that first afternoon. Cora and Vickie stayed with them. Cram came by that first day too, but Grace asked him to leave. He nodded and complied.

The media went crazy, of course. They only knew bits and pieces, but the fact that the notorious Jimmy X had resurfaced only to be murdered had been enough to send them into a total state of derangement. Perlmutter set up a patrol car in front of Grace's house. Emma and Max still went to school. Grace spent most of her days in the hospital with Jack. Charlaine Swain kept her company a lot.

Grace thought about the photograph that started it all. She now figured that one of the four members of Allaw had found a way to get it in her packet. Why? That was harder to answer. Perhaps one of them realized that the eighteen ghosts would never sleep.

But then there was the question of timing: Why now? Why after fifteen years?

There was no shortage of possibilities. It could have been the release of Wade Larue. It could have been the death of Gordon MacKenzie. It could have been all the anniversary coverage. But most likely, what made the most sense, was that the return of Jimmy X set everything in motion.

Who really was to blame for what happened that tragic night? Was it Jimmy for stealing the song? Jack for attacking him? Gordon MacKenzie for firing a weapon under those circumstances? Wade Larue for illegally carrying a gun, panicking, and firing more shots into an already frenzied crowd? Grace did not know. Small ripples. All of this carnage had not started with some big conspiracy. It had started with two small-time bands playing some dive in Manchester.

There were still holes, of course. Lots of them. But they would have to wait.

There are some things more important than the truth.

Now, right now, Grace stared at Jack. He lay still in his hospital bed. His doctor, a man named Stan Walker, sat next to her. Dr. Walker folded his hands and used his gravest voice. Grace listened. Emma and Max waited in the corridor. They wanted to be there. Grace didn't know what to do. What was the call on this one?

She wished that she could ask Jack.

She did not want to ask him why he had lied to her for so long. She did not want an explanation for what he had done that terrible night. She did not want to ask him how he'd happened by her on the beach that day, if he had been intentionally seeking her out, if that was why they fell in love. She didn't want to ask Jack any of that.

240

She only wanted to ask him one last question: Did he want his children by his bedside when he died?

In the end Grace let them stay. The four of them gathered as a family for the last time. Emma cried. Max sat there, his eyes trained on the tile floor. And then, with a gentle tug at her heart, Grace felt Jack leave for good.

54

The funeral was a major blur. Grace usually wore contact lenses. She took them off that day and did not wear her glasses. Everything seemed a little easier to handle in the blur. She sat in the front pew and thought about Jack. She did not picture him in the vineyards or on the beach anymore. The sight she remembered best, the sight she would always carry with her, was Jack holding Emma after she was born, the way his big hands held the little wonder, carrying her as if afraid she'd break, scared he might hurt her, the way he turned to Grace and looked at her in pure awe. That was what she saw.

The rest, all she now knew about his past, was white noise.

Sandra Koval came to the funeral. She stayed in the back. She apologized that their father could not come. He was elderly and ill. Grace said that she understood. The two women did not embrace. Scott Duncan was there. So were Stu Perlmutter and Cora. Grace had no idea how many people showed up. She didn't much care either. She held her two children and fought her way through it.

Two weeks later the children went back to school. There were issues, of course. Both Emma and Max were suffering separation anxieties. That was normal, she knew. Grace walked them into school. She was there before the bell rang to pick them up. They were hurting. That, Grace knew, was the price you paid for having a kind and loving father. The hurt never goes away.

But now it was time to end this.

Jack's autopsy.

Some would say that the autopsy, when she read and understood it, was what sent Grace's world off kilter again. But that really wasn't it. The autopsy was merely independent confirmation of what she already knew. Jack had been her husband. She had loved him. They had been together for thirteen years. They had two children together. And while he had clearly kept secrets, there were some things a man cannot hide.

Some things must truly remain on the surface.

So Grace knew.

She knew his body. She knew his skin. She knew every muscle on his back. So she really did not need the autopsy. She did not need to see the results of the full-exterior examination to tell her what she already knew.

Jack had no major scars.

And that meant that – despite what Jimmy had said, despite what Gordon MacKenzie had told Wade Larue – Jack had never been shot.

First Grace visited the Photomat and found Fuzz Pellet Josh. Then she drove back down to Bedminster, to the condominium development where Shane Alworth's mother resided. After that, she plowed through the legal work on Jack's family trust. Grace knew a lawyer from Livingston who now worked as a sports agent in Manhattan. He set up plenty of trusts for his wealthy athletes. He went through the paperwork and explained enough for her to understand.

And then, when she had all the facts pretty much down, she visited Sandra Koval, her dear sister-in-law, at the offices of Burton and Crimstein in New York City.

Sandra Koval did not meet her in the reception area this time. Grace was inspecting the photo gallery, stopping again at the shot of the wrestler, Little Pocahontas, when a peasant-bloused woman told her to come this way. She led Grace down the corridor and into the exact same conference room where she and Sandra had first talked a lifetime ago.

'Ms. Koval will be with you shortly.'

'Great.'

She left her alone. The room was set up exactly the same as last time, except now there was a yellow legal pad and a Bic pen in front of each seat. Grace did not want to sit. She did her own version of a pace, more a limp-pace, and ran it over in her head again. Her cell phone buzzed. She spoke briefly and then snapped it off. She kept it close. Just in case.

'Hi, Grace.'

Sandra Koval swept into the room like a turbulent weather front. She headed straight for the little refrigerator, opened it and peered inside.

'Can I get you something to drink?'

'No.'

With her head still in the mini-fridge, she asked, 'How are the children?'

Grace did not reply. Sandra Koval dug out a Perrier. She twisted the top off and sat.

'So what's up?'

Should she test the temperature with her toe or just jump in? Grace chose the latter. 'You didn't take on Wade Larue as a client because of me,' she began without preamble. 'You took him on because you wanted to stay close to him.'

Sandra Koval poured the Perrier into a glass. 'That might – hypothetically – be true.'

'Hypothetically?'

'Yes. I may, in a hypothetical world, have represented Wade Larue to protect a certain family member. But if I had, I would have still made sure that I represented my client to the best of my ability.'

'Two birds with one stone?'

'Perhaps.'

'And the certain family member. That would be your brother?'

'It would be possible.'

'Possible,' Grace said. 'But that wasn't what happened here. You weren't out to protect your brother.'

Their eyes met.

'I know,' Grace said.

'Oh?' Sandra took a sip. 'Then why don't you clue me in.'

'You were, what, twenty-seven years old? Fresh out of law school and working as a criminal lawyer?'

'Yes.'

'You were married. Your daughter was two years old. You were on your way to a promising career. And then your brother messed it all up for you. You were there that night, Sandra. At the Boston Garden. You were the other woman back-stage, not Geri Duncan.'

'I see,' she said without a trace of worry. 'And you know this how?'

'Jimmy X said one woman was a redhead – that's Sheila Lambert – and the other, the one who was egging Jack on, had dark hair. Geri Duncan was a blonde. You, Sandra, had dark hair.'

She laughed. 'And that's supposed to be proof of something?'

'No, not in and of itself. I'm not even sure it's relevant. Geri Duncan was prob-ably there too. She might have been the one who distracted Gordon MacKenzie so you three could sneak backstage.'

Sandra Koval gave her a vague wave of the hand. 'Go on, this is interesting.'

'Shall I just get to the heart of the matter?'

'Please do.'

'According to both Jimmy X and Gordon MacKenzie, your brother was shot that night.'

'He was,' Sandra said. 'He was in the hospital for three weeks.'

'Which hospital?'

There was no hesitation, no eye twitch, no give at all. 'Mass General.'

Grace shook her head.

Sandra made a face. 'Are you telling me you checked every hospital in the Boston area?'

'No need,' Grace said. 'There was no scar.'

Silence.

'You see, the bullet wound would have left a scar, Sandra. It's simple logic. Your brother was shot. My husband had no scar. There's only one way that can be so.' Grace put her hands on the table. They were quaking.

'I was never married to your brother.'

Sandra Koval said nothing.

'Your brother, John Lawson, was shot that day. You and Sheila Lambert helped drag him out during the melee. But his wounds were lethal. At least I hope they were, because the alternative is that you killed him.'

'And why would I do that?'

'Because if you took him to a hospital, they would have to report the shoot-ing. If you showed up with a dead body – or even if you just dumped him on the street – someone would investigate and realize where and how he was shot. You, the promising lawyer, were terrified. I bet Sheila Lambert was too. The world went crazy when this happened. The Boston DA – hell, Carl Vespa – was on tele-vision demanding blood. So were all the families. If you got caught up in that, you'd be arrested or worse.'

Sandra Koval stayed quiet.

'Did you call your father? Did you ask him what to do? Did you contact one of your old criminal clients to help you? Or did you just get rid of the body on your own?'

244

She chuckled. 'You have some imagination, Grace. Can I ask you something now?'

'Sure.'

'If John Lawson died fifteen years ago, who did you marry?'

'I married *Jack* Lawson,' Grace said. 'Who used to be known as Shane Alworth.'

Eric Wu hadn't held two men in the basement, Grace now realized. Just one. One who had sacrificed himself to save her. One who probably knew that he was going to die and wanted to scratch out some last truth in the only way left to him.

Sandra Koval almost smiled. 'That's a hell of a theory.'

'One that will be easy to prove.'

She leaned back and folded her arms. 'I don't understand something about your scenario. Why didn't I just hide my brother's body and pretend he ran away?'

'Too many people would ask questions,' Grace said.

'But that's what happened to Shane Alworth and Sheila Lambert. They just disappeared.'

'True enough,' Grace admitted. 'And maybe the answer has to do with your family trust.'

That made Sandra's face freeze. 'The trust?'

'I found the papers on the trust in Jack's desk. I took them to a friend who's a lawyer. It seems your grandfather set up six trusts. He had two children and four grandchildren. Forget the money for a second. Let's talk about voting power. All of you got equal voting shares, divided six ways, with your father getting the extra four percent. That way your side of the family kept control of the business, fifty-two percent to forty-eight. But – and I'm not good with this stuff so bear with me – Grandpa wanted to keep it all in the family. If any of you died before the age of twenty-five, the voting power would be divided equally among the five survivors. If your brother died the night of the concert, for example, that would mean that your side of the family, you and your father, would no longer hold a majority position.'

'You're out of your mind.'

'Could be,' Grace said. 'But tell me, Sandra. What drove you? Was it fear of being caught – or were you worried about losing control of the family business? Probably a combination of both. Either way, I know you got Shane Alworth to take your brother's place. It'll be easy to prove. We'll dig up old pictures. We can run a DNA test. I mean, it's over.'

Sandra started drumming the table with her fingertips. 'If that's true,' she said, 'the man you loved lied to you all these years.'

'That's true no matter what,' Grace said. 'How did you get him to cooperate anyway?'

'That question is supposed to be rhetorical, right?'

Grace shrugged. 'Mrs. Alworth tells me that they were dirt poor. His brother Paul couldn't afford college. She was living in a dump. But my guess is, you made a threat. If one member of Allaw went down for this, they all would. He probably thought he had no choice.'

'Come on, Grace. Do you really think a poor kid like Shane Alworth could pull off being my brother?'

'How hard would it be? You and your father helped, I'm sure. Getting an ID would be no problem. You had your brother's birth certificate and the pertinent paperwork. You just say he had his wallet stolen. Screening was easier back then. He'd have gotten a new driver's license, new passport, whatever. You found a new trust lawyer in Boston – my friend noticed the change from the one in Los Angeles – someone who wouldn't know what John Lawson looked like. You, your dad, and Shane go in to his office together, all with proper ID – who would question that? Your brother had already graduated from Vermont University, so it wasn't like he'd have to show up there with a new face. Shane could go overseas now. If someone bumped into him, well, he'd go by Jack and just say he was another John Lawson. It's not an uncommon name.'

Grace waited.

Sandra folded her arms. 'Is this the part where I'm supposed to crack and confess everything?'

'You? No, I don't think so. But come on, you know it's over. It won't be any problem to prove that my husband wasn't your brother.'

Sandra Koval took her time. 'That may well be,' she said, her words coming out more measured now. 'But I'm not sure I see any crime here.'

'How's that?'

'Let's say – again hypothetically – that you're right. Let's say I did get your husband to pretend to be my brother. That was fifteen years ago. There's a statute of limitations. My cousins might try to fight me on the trust issue, but they wouldn't want the scandal. We'd work it out. And even if what you said is true, my crime was hardly a big one. If I was at the concert that night, well, in the early days of that rabid frenzy, who could blame me for being scared?'

Grace's voice was soft. 'I wouldn't blame you for that.'

'Right, so there you go.'

'And at first you didn't really do anything that terrible. You went to that concert seeking justice for your brother. You confronted a man who stole a song your brother and his friend wrote. That's not a crime. Things went wrong. Your brother died. There was nothing you could do to bring him back. So you did what you thought best. You played the terrible hand you were dealt.'

Sandra Koval opened her arms. 'Then what do you want here, Grace?'

'Answers, I guess.'

'It seems as if you already got some of those.' Then she raised her index finger and added, 'Hypothetically speaking.'

'And maybe I want justice.'

'What justice? You just said yourself that what happened was understandable.'

'That part,' Grace said, her voice still soft. 'If it ended there, yeah, I'd probably just walk away. But it didn't.'

Sandra Koval sat back and waited.

'Sheila Lambert was scared too. She knew that her best move would be to change her name and disappear. You all agreed to disperse and stay silent. Geri Duncan, she stayed where she was. That was okay, at first. But then Geri found out she was pregnant.'

Sandra just shut her eyes.

'When he agreed to be John Lawson, Shane, my Jack, had to cut all ties and go overseas. Geri Duncan couldn't find him. A month later she learns that she's pregnant. She's desperate to find the father. So she came to see you. She probably wanted to start new. She wanted to tell the truth and have her baby with a clean slate. You knew my husband. He would never turn his back on her if she insisted on having a child. Maybe he'd want to wipe the slate clean too. And then what would happen to you, Sandra?'

Grace looked down at her hands. They were still shaking.

'So you had to silence Geri. You're a criminal defense attorney. You repped criminals. And one of them helped you find a hit man named Monte Scanlon.'

Sandra said, 'You can't prove any of this.'

'The years pass,' Grace went on. 'My husband is now Jack Lawson.' Grace stopped and remembered what Carl Vespa had said about Jack Lawson seeking her out. Something there still didn't mesh. 'We have children now. I tell Jack I want to go back stateside. He doesn't want to. I push him on it. We have kids. I want to be back in the United States. That's my fault, I guess. I wish he had just told me the truth –'

'And how would you have reacted, Grace?'

She thought about it. 'I don't know.'

Sandra Koval smiled. 'Neither, I guess, did he.'

It was, Grace knew, a fair point, but this was not the time for that sort of contemplation. She pressed on. 'We ended up moving to New York. But I don't know what happened next, Sandra, so you're going to have to help me with this part. I think what with the anniversary and with Wade Larue coming free, Sheila Lambert – or maybe even Jack – decided it was time to tell the truth. Jack never slept well. Maybe they both needed to ease their guilt, I don't know. You couldn't go along with that, of course. They might be granted forgiveness but not you. You had Geri Duncan killed.'

'And again I ask: The proof of that is ...?'

'We'll get to that,' Grace said. 'You've lied to me from the start, but you did tell the truth about one thing.'

'Oh goodie.' The sarcasm was thick now. 'What was that?'

'When Jack saw that old picture in the kitchen, he did look up Geri Duncan on the computer. He found out she'd died in a fire, but he suspected it was no accident. So he called you. That was the nine-minute phone call. You were afraid he was about to crack, so you knew that you had to strike fast. You told Jack that you'd explain everything but not over the phone. You set up a meet off the New York Thruway. Then you called Larue and told him that this would be a perfect time to get his revenge. You figured Larue would have Wu kill Jack, not hold him like that.'

'I don't have to listen to this.'

But Grace did not stop. 'My big mistake was showing you the photograph that first day. Jack didn't know I'd made a copy. There it was, a photograph of your dead brother and his new identity for all the world to see. You needed to keep me quiet too. So you sent that guy, the one with my daughter's lunchbox, to scare me off. But I didn't listen. So you used Wu. He was supposed to find out what I knew and then kill me.'

'Okay, I've had enough.' Sandra Koval stood. 'Get out of my office.'

'Nothing to add?'

'I'm still waiting for proof.'

'I don't really have any,' Grace said. 'But maybe you'll confess.'

She laughed at that one. 'What, you don't think I know you're wired? I haven't said or done one thing that'll incriminate me.'

'Look out the window, Sandra.'

'What?'

'The window. Look down at the sidewalk. Come on, I'll show you.'

Grace limped toward the huge picture window and pointed down. Sandra Koval moved warily, as if she expected that Grace would push her through it. But that wasn't it. That wasn't it at all.

When Sandra Koval looked down, a small gasp escaped her lips. On the sidewalk below them, pacing like two lions, were Carl Vespa and Cram. Grace turned away and started for the door.

'Where are you going?' Sandra asked.

'Oh,' Grace said. She wrote something down on a piece of paper. 'This is Captain Perlmutter's phone number. You have your choice. You can call and leave with him. Or you can take your chances with the sidewalk.'

She put the piece of paper on the conference table. And then, without looking back, Grace left the room.

Epilogue

Sandra Koval chose to call Captain Stuart Perlmutter. She then lawyered up. Hester Crimstein, the legend herself, was going to represent her. It would be a tough case to make, but the DA thought, because of certain developments, that he could do it.

One of those developments was the return of Allaw's redheaded member, Sheila Lambert. When Sheila read about the arrest – and the media appeal for her help – she came forward. The man who shot her husband fit the description of the man who threatened Grace at the supermarket. His name was Martin Brayboy. He'd been caught and had agreed to testify for the prosecution.

Sheila Lambert also told prosecutors that Shane Alworth had been at the concert that night but that he had decided at the last minute not to go backstage and confront Jimmy X. Sheila Lambert wasn't sure why he'd changed his mind, but she speculated that Shane realized John Lawson was too high, too wired, too willing to snap.

Grace was supposed to find comfort in that, but she's not sure she did.

Captain Stuart Perlmutter had hooked up with Scott Duncan's old boss, Linda Morgan, the U.S. attorney. They managed to turn one of the men from Carl Vespa's inner circle. Rumor has it they'll be arresting him soon, though it will be hard to nail him on Jimmy X's murder. Cram called Grace one afternoon. He told her Vespa wasn't fighting back. He stayed in bed a lot. 'It's like watching a slow death,' he told her. She didn't really want to hear it.

Charlaine Swain brought Mike home from the hospital. They returned to their regularly scheduled lives. Mike is back at work. They watch TV together now instead of in separate rooms. Mike still falls asleep early. They've upped their lovemaking somewhat, but it's all too self-conscious. Charlaine and Grace have become close friends. Charlaine never complains but Grace can see the desperation. Something, Grace knows, will soon give.

Freddy Sykes is still recuperating. He put his house up for sale and is buying a condo in Fair Lawn, New Jersey.

Cora remained Cora. Enough said on that subject.

Evelyn and Paul Alworth, Jack's – or in this case, she should say, Shane's – mother and brother, have also come forward. Over the years Jack had used the trust money to pay for Paul's schooling. When he started working with Pentocol Pharmaceuticals, Jack moved his mother into that condominium development so they could be closer. They had lunch together at the condo at least once a week. Both Evelyn and Paul wanted very much to be a part of the children's lives – they were, after all, Emma and Max's grandmother and uncle – but they understood that it would be best to take it slow.

As for Emma and Max, they handled the tragedy in very different ways.

Max likes to talk about his father. He wants to know where Daddy is, what heaven is like, if Daddy really sees them. He wants to be assured that his father can still observe the key events of his young life. Grace tries to answer him the best she can – tries to sell it, as it were – but her words have the stilted hollow of the dubious. Max wants Grace to make up 'Jenny Jenkins' rhymes with him in the tub, like Jack used to do, and when she does, Max laughs and he sounds so much like his father that Grace thinks her heart might explode right then and there.

Emma, her father's princess, never talks about Jack. She does not ask questions. She does not look at photographs or reminisce. Grace tries to facilitate her daughter's needs, but she is never sure what approach to take. Psychiatrists talk about opening up. Grace, who has suffered her share of tragedies, is not so sure. There is, she's learned, something to be said for denial, for severing and compartmentalizing.

Strangely enough, Emma seems happy. She's doing well in school. She has lots of friends. But Grace knows better. Emma never writes poetry anymore. She won't even look at her journal. She insists now on sleeping with her door shut. Grace stands outside her daughter's bedroom at night, often very late, and sometimes she thinks she hears soft sobs. In the morning, after Emma goes to school, Grace checks her daughter's room.

Her pillow is always wet.

People naturally assume that if Jack were still alive, Grace would have a lot of questions for him. That's true, but she no longer cares about the details of what a stoned, scared kid of twenty did in the face of that devastation and aftermath. In hindsight he should have told her. But then again suppose he had? Suppose Jack had told her right in the beginning? Or a month into their relationship? A year? How would she have reacted? Would she have stayed? She thinks about Emma and Max, about the simple fact that they are here, and the road untraveled brings a shiver.

So late at night, when Grace lies alone in their too-large bed and talks to Jack, feeling very strange because, really, she doesn't believe he's listening, her questions are more basic: Max wants to sign up for the Kasselton traveling soccer team, but isn't he too young for that kind of commitment? The school wants to put Emma in an accelerated English program, but will that put too much pressure on her? Should we still go to Disney World in February, without you, or will that be too painful a reminder? And what, Jack, should I do about those damn tears on Emma's pillow?

Questions like that.

Scott Duncan came by a week after Sandra's arrest. When she opened the door, he said, 'I found something.'

'What?'

'This was in Geri's stuff,' Duncan said.

He handed her a beat-up cassette. There was no label on it but faintly, in black ink, someone had written: ALLAW.

They moved silently into the den. Grace stuck the cassette in her player and pressed the play button.

'Invisible Ink' was the third song.

There were similarities to 'Pale Ink.' Would a court of law have found Jimmy guilty of plagiarism? It would be a close call, but Grace figured that the answer, after all these years, was probably no. There were plenty of songs that sounded alike. There was also a fine line between influence and plagiarism. 'Pale Ink,' it seemed to her, probably straddled that blurry line.

So much that went wrong did – straddled a blurry line, that is.

'Scott?'

He did not turn toward her.

'Don't you think it's time we cleared the air?'

He nodded slowly.

She was not sure how to put this. 'When you found out your sister was murdered, you investigated with a passion. You left your job. You went all out.'

'Yes.'

'It wouldn't have been hard to find out she had an old boyfriend.'

'Not hard at all,' Duncan agreed.

'And you would have found out that his name was Shane Alworth.'

'I knew about Shane before all this. They dated for six months. But I thought Geri had died in a fire. There was no reason to follow up with him.'

'Right. But now, after you talked to Monte Scanlon, you did.'

'Yes,' he said. 'It was the first thing I did.'

'You learned that he'd disappeared right around the time of your sister's murder.'

'Right.'

'And that made you suspicious.'

'To put it mildly.'

'You probably, I don't know, checked his old college records, his old high school records even. You talked to his mom. It wouldn't have taken much. Not when you're looking for it.'

Scott Duncan nodded.

'So you knew, before we even met, that Jack was Shane Alworth.'

'Yes,' he said. 'I knew.'

'You suspected him of killing your sister?'

Duncan smiled, but there was no joy in it. 'A man is dating your sister. He breaks up with her. She's murdered. He changes identity and disappears for fifteen years.' He shrugged. 'What would you think?'

Grace nodded. 'You told me you like to shake the cages. That was the way to make progress in a case.'

'Right.'

'And you knew that you couldn't just ask Jack about your sister. You had nothing on him.'

'Right again.'

'So,' she said, 'you shook the cage.'

Silence.

'I checked with Josh at the Photomat,' Grace said.

'Ah. How much did you pay him?'

'A thousand dollars.'

Duncan snorted. 'I only paid him five hundred.'

'To put that picture in my envelope.'

'Yes.'

The song changed. Allaw was now singing a song about voices and wind. Their sound was raw, but there was potential there too.

'You cast suspicion on Cora to distract me from pressuring Josh.'

'Yes.'

'You insisted I go with you to see Mrs. Alworth. You wanted to see her reaction when she saw her grandchildren.'

'More cage shaking,' he agreed. 'Did you see the look in her eyes when she saw Emma and Max?'

She had. She just hadn't known what it meant or why Mrs. Alworth ended up living in a condo right on Jack's route to work. Now, of course, she did. 'And because you were forced to take a leave, you couldn't use the FBI for surveillance. So you hired a private detective, the one who used Rocky Conwell. And you put that camera in our house. If you were going to shake the cage, you'd need to see how your suspect would react.'

'All true.'

She thought of the end result. 'A lot of people died because of what you did.'

'I was investigating my sister's murder. You can't expect me to apologize for that.'

Blame, she thought again. So much of it to go around. 'You could have told me.'

'No. No, Grace, I could never trust you.'

'You said our alliance was temporary.'

He looked at her. There was something dark there now. 'That,' he said, 'was a lie. We never had an alliance.'

She sat up and turned the music down.

'You don't remember the massacre, do you, Grace?'

'That's not uncommon,' she said. 'It's not amnesia or anything like that. I was hit so hard in the head I was in a coma.'

'Head trauma,' he said with a nod. 'I know all about it. I've seen in it lots of cases. The Central Park jogger, for one. Most cases, like yours, you don't even remember the days before it.'

'So?'

'So how did you get into the front pit that night?'

The question, coming out of nowhere like that, made her sit up. She searched his face for a give. There was none. 'What?'

'Ryan Vespa, well, his father scalped the ticket for four hundred bucks. The members of Allaw got them from Jimmy himself. The only way to get up there was to shell out a ton of dough or know someone.' He leaned forward. 'How did you get into that front pit, Grace?'

'My boyfriend got tickets.'

'That would be Todd Woodcroft? The one who never visited you at the hospital?'

'Yes.'

'You sure about that? Because before you said you don't remember.'

She opened her mouth and then closed it. He leaned closer.

'Grace, I talked to Todd Woodcroft. He didn't go to the concert.'

Something inside her chest lurched to the side. Her body went cold.

'Todd didn't visit you because you'd broken up with him two days before the show. He thought it'd be weird. And you know what, Grace? Shane Alworth broke up with my sister on that same day. Geri never went to the concert. So who do you think Shane took instead?'

Grace shivered and felt the tremor spread. 'I don't understand.'

He pulled out the photograph. 'This is the original Polaroid I had blown up and put into your envelope. My sister wrote the date on the back. The picture was taken the day before the concert.'

She shook her head.

'That mystery woman on the far right, the one we can barely see? You thought it was Sandra Koval. Well, maybe, Grace – just maybe – that's you.'

'No ...'

'And maybe, while we're looking for more people to blame, maybe we should wonder about the pretty girl who distracted Gordon MacKenzie so the others could get to Jimmy X. We know it wasn't my sister or Sheila Lambert or Sandra Koval.'

Grace kept shaking her head, but then she flashed back to that day at the beach, the first time she laid eyes on Jack, that feeling, that instant grab of the gut. Where had that come from? It was the kind of thing you feel ...

... when you've met someone before.

The strangest sort of déjà-vu. The kind where you've already connected with someone, gotten that first head rush of infatuation. You hold hands, and when the turmoil begins, there's that stomach-dropping feel of his hand slipping from yours ...

'No,' Grace said, more firmly now. 'You got it wrong. It can't be. I'd have remembered that.'

Scott Duncan nodded. 'You're probably right.'

He stood and popped the cassette out of the machine. He handed it to her. 'This is all just crazy conjecture. I mean, for all we know, maybe that mystery woman was the reason Shane didn't go backstage. Maybe she talked him out of it. Or maybe he realized that there was something more important right there, in that front pit, than anything he could find in a song. Maybe, even three years later, he made sure he found it again.'

Scott Duncan left then. Grace stood and headed into her studio. She had not painted since Jack's death. She put the cassette into her portable player and pressed the play button.

She picked up a brush and tried to paint. She wanted to paint him. She wanted to paint Jack – not John, not Shane. Jack. She thought it would come out muddled and confused, but that wasn't what happened at all. The brush soared and danced across the canvas. She started thinking again about how we can never know everything about our loved ones. And maybe, if you think about it hard, we don't even know everything about ourselves.

The cassette ended. She rewound it and started it again. She worked in a delirious and delightful frenzy. Tears ran down her cheeks. She did not brush them away. At some point she glanced at a clock. Soon it would be time to stop. School would be letting out. She had to get the kids. Emma had piano today. Max had traveling-team soccer practice.

Grace grabbed her purse and locked the door behind her.

Acknowledgments

The author wishes to thank the following for their technical expertise: Mitchell F. Reiter, MD, Chief, Division of Spine Surgery, UMDNJ (aka 'Cuz'); David A. Gold, MD; Christopher J. Christie, United States attorney for the state of New Jersey; Captain Keith Killion of the Ridgewood Police Department; Steven Miller, MD, Director of Pediatric Emergency Medicine, Children's Hospital of New York Presbyterian; John Elias; Anthony Dellapelle (the non-fictional one); Jennifer van Dam; Linda Fairstein; and Craig Coben (aka 'Bro'). As always, if there are errors, technical or otherwise, the fault is with these people. I'm tired of being the fall guy.

A nod of gratitude to Carole Baron, Mitch Hoffman, Lisa Johnson, and all at Dutton and Penguin Group USA; Jon Wood, Malcolm Edwards, Susan Lamb, Juliet Ewers, Nicky Jeanes, Emma Noble and the gang at Orion; Aaron Priest, Lisa Erbach Vance, Bryant and Hil (for helping me over that first hump), Mike and Taylor (for helping me over the second one), and Maggie Griffin.

Characters in this book may share a name with people I know, but they are still completely fictional. In fact, this entire novel is a work of fiction. That means I make stuff up.

A special thanks to Charlotte Coben for Emma's poems. All rights reserved, as they say.

The Innocent

In memory of Steven Z. Miller

To those of us fortunate enough to have been
    his friend –
We try to be thankful for the time we had,
    But it's so damn hard

And to Steve's family, especially Jesse, Maya T,
    and Nico –
When we're strong enough, we will talk about
    your father
Because he was the best man we've ever known

Prologue

You never meant to kill him.

Your name is Matt Hunter. You are twenty years old. You grew up in an upper-middle-class suburb in northern New Jersey, not far from Manhattan. You live on the poorer side of town, but it's a pretty wealthy town. Your parents work hard and love you unconditionally. You are a middle child. You have an older brother whom you worship, and a younger sister whom you tolerate.

Like every kid in your town, you grow up worrying about your future and what college you will get into. You work hard enough and get good, if not spectacular, grades. Your average is an A minus. You don't make the top ten percent but you're close. You have decent extracurricular activities, including a stint as treasurer of the school. You are a letterman for both the football and basketball team – good enough to play Division Three but not for a financial scholarship. You are a bit of a wiseass and naturally charming. In terms of popularity, you hover right below the top echelon. When you take your SATs, your high scores surprise your guidance counselor.

You shoot for the Ivy Leagues, but they are just a little out of your reach. Harvard and Yale reject you outright. Penn and Columbia waitlist you. You end up going to Bowdoin, a small elite college in Brunswick, Maine. You love it there. The class sizes are small. You make friends. You don't have a steady girlfriend, but you probably don't want one anyway. In your sophomore year, you start on the varsity football team as a defensive back. You play JV basketball right off the bat, and now that the senior point guard has graduated, you have a serious chance of getting valuable minutes.

It is then, heading back to campus between the first and second semester of your junior year, that you kill someone.

You have a wonderfully hectic holiday break with your family, but basketball practice beckons. You kiss your mother and father good-bye and drive back to campus with your best friend and roommate, Duff. Duff is from Westchester, New York. He is squat with thick legs. He plays right tackle on the football team and sits the bench for basketball. He is the biggest drinker on campus – Duff never loses a chugging contest.

You drive.

Duff wants to stop at UMass in Amherst, Massachusetts, on the way up. A high school buddy of his is a member of a wild frat there. They are having a huge party.

You're not enthusiastic, but you're no party pooper. You are more comfortable with smaller gatherings where you pretty much know everyone. Bowdoin has about 1,600 students. UMass has nearly 40,000. It is early January and freezing cold. There is snow on the ground. You see your breath as you walk into the frat house.

You and Duff throw your coats on the pile. You will think about that a lot over the years, that casual toss of the coats. If you'd kept the coat on, if you'd left it in the car, if you'd put it anyplace else . . .

But none of that happened.

The party is okay. It is wild, yes, but it feels to you like a forced wild. Duff's friend wants you both to spend the night in his room. You agree. You drink a fair amount – this is a college party, after all – though not nearly as much as Duff. The party winds down. At some point you both go to get your coats. Duff is holding his beer. He picks up his coat and swings it over his shoulder.

That is when some of his beer spills.

Not a lot. Just a splash. But it's enough.

The beer lands on a red Windbreaker. That's one of the things you remember. It was freezing cold outside, in the teens, and yet someone was wearing just a Windbreaker. The other thing you will never shake from your mind is that a Windbreaker is waterproof. The spilled beer, little as it was, would not harm the coat. It would not stain. It could so easily be rinsed away.

But someone yells, 'Hey!'

He, the owner of the red Windbreaker, is a big guy but not huge. Duff shrugs. He does not apologize. The guy, Mr. Red Windbreaker, gets in Duff's face. This is a mistake. You know that Duff is a great fighter with a short fuse. Every school has a Duff – the guy you can never imagine losing a fight.

That's the problem, of course. Every school has a Duff. And once in a while your Duff runs into their Duff.

You try to end it right there, try to laugh it off, but you have two serious beer-marinated headcases with reddening faces and tightening fists. A challenge is issued. You don't remember who made it. You all step outside into the frigid night, and you realize that you are in a heap of trouble.

The big guy with the red Windbreaker has friends with him.

Eight or nine of them. You and Duff are alone. You look for Duff's high school friend – Mark or Mike or something – but he is nowhere to be found.

The fight begins quickly.

Duff lowers his head bull-like and charges Red Windbreaker. Red Windbreaker steps to the side and catches Duff in a headlock. He punches Duff in the nose. Still holding Duff in the headlock, he punches him again. Then again. And again.

Duff's head is down. He is swinging wildly and with no effect. It is somewhere around the seventh or eighth punch that Duff stops swinging. Red Windbreaker's friends start cheering. Duff's arms drop to his sides.

You want to stop it, but you are not sure how. Red Windbreaker is going about his work methodically, taking his time with his punches, using big windups. His buddies are cheering him on now. They *ooh* and *ahh* with each splat.

You are terrified.

Your friend is taking a beating, but you are mostly worried about yourself. That shames you. You want to do something, but you are afraid, seriously afraid. You can't move. Your legs feel like rubber. Your arms tingle. And you hate yourself for that.

Red Windbreaker throws another punch straight into Duff's face. He releases the headlock. Duff drops to the ground like a bag of laundry. Red Windbreaker kicks Duff in the ribs.

You are the worst sort of friend. You are too scared to help. You will never forget that feeling. Cowardice. It is worse than a beating, you think. Your silence. This awful feeling of dishonor.

Another kick. Duff grunts and rolls onto his back. His face is streaked with crimson red. You will learn later that his injuries were minor. Duff will have two black eyes and numerous bruises. That will be about it. But right now he looks bad. You know that he would never stand by and let you take a beating like this.

You can stand it no longer.

You jump out of the crowd.

All heads turn toward you. For a moment nobody moves. Nobody speaks. Red Windbreaker is breathing hard. You see his breath in the cold. You are shaking. You try to sound rational. Hey, you say, he's had enough. You spread your arms. You try the charming smile. He's lost the fight, you say. It's over. You've won, you tell Red Windbreaker.

Someone jumps you from behind. Arms snake around you, wrapping you in a bear hug.

You are trapped.

Red Windbreaker comes at you now. Your heart is beating against your chest like a bird in too small a cage. You reel your head back. Your skull crashes into someone's nose. Red Windbreaker is closer now. You duck out of the way. Someone else comes out of the crowd. He has blond hair, his complexion ruddy. You figure that he is another one of Red Windbreaker's pals.

His name is Stephen McGrath.

He reaches for you. You buck away like a fish on a hook. More are coming at you. You panic. Stephen McGrath puts his hands on your shoulders. You try to break free. You spin frantically.

That is when you reach out and grab his neck.

Did you lunge at him? Did he pull you or did you push him? You don't know. Did one of you lose your footing on the sidewalk? Was the ice to blame? You will flash back to this moment countless times, but the answer will never be clear.

Either way, you both fall.

Both of your hands are still on his neck. On his throat. You don't let go.

You land with a thud. The back of Stephen McGrath's skull hits the sidewalk curb. There is a sound, an awful hell-spawned crack, something wet and too hollow and unlike anything you have heard before.

The sound marks the end of life as you know it.

You will always remember it. That awful sound. It will never leave you.

Everything stops. You stare down. Stephen McGrath's eyes are open and unblinking. But you know already. You know by the way his body went suddenly slack. You know by that awful hell-spawned crack.

People scatter. You do not move. You do not move for a very long time.

It happens fast then. Campus security arrives. Then the police. You tell them what happened. Your parents hire a hotshot lawyer from New York City. She tells you to plead self-defense. You do.

And you keep hearing that awful sound.

The prosecutor scoffs. Ladies and gentlemen of the jury, he says, the defendant happened to slip with his hands wrapped around Stephen McGrath's throat?

Does he really expect us to believe that?

The trial does not go well.

Nothing matters to you. You once cared about grades and playing time. How pathetic. Friends, girls, pecking order, parties, getting ahead, all that stuff. They are vapors. They have been replaced by the awful sound of that skull cracking against stone.

At the trial, you hear your parents cry, yes, but it is the faces of Sonya and Clark McGrath, the victim's parents, that will haunt you. Sonya McGrath glares at you throughout the proceedings. She dares you to meet her eye.

You can't.

You try to hear the jury announce the verdict, but those other sounds get in the way. The sounds never cease, never let up, even when the judge looks down sternly and sentences you. The press is watching. You will not be sent to a soft white-boy country-club prison. Not now. Not during an election year.

Your mother faints. Your father tries to be strong. Your sister runs out of the courtroom. Your brother, Bernie, stands frozen.

You are put in handcuffs and taken away. Your upbringing does little to prepare you for what lies ahead. You have watched TV and have heard all the tales of prison rape. That does not happen – no sexual assault – but you are beaten with fists during your first week. You make the mistake of identifying who did it. You get beaten twice more and spend three weeks in the infirmary. Years later, you will still sometimes find blood in your urine, a souvenir from a blow to the kidney.

You live in constant fear. When you are let back into the general population, you learn that the only way you can survive is to join a bizarre offshoot of the Aryan Nation. They do not have big ideas or a grandiose vision of what America should be like. They pretty much just love to hate.

Six months into your incarceration your father dies of a heart attack. You know that it's your fault. You want to cry, but you can't.

You spend four years in prison. Four years – the same amount of time most students spend in college. You are just shy of your twenty-fifth birthday. They say you've changed, but you're not really sure.

When you walk out, you step tentatively. As if the ground below your feet might give. As if the earth might simply cave in on you at any time.

In some ways you will always walk like that.

Your brother, Bernie, is at the gate to meet you. Bernie just got married. His wife, Marsha, is pregnant with their first child. He puts his arms around you. You can almost feel the last four years shed away. Your brother makes a joke. You laugh, really laugh, for the first time in so long.

You were wrong before – your life did not end on that cold night in Amherst. Your brother will help you find normalcy. You will even meet a beautiful woman down the road. Her name is Olivia. She will make you enormously happy.

You will marry her.

One day – nine years after you walk through those gates – you will learn that your beautiful wife is pregnant. You decide to buy camera phones to stay in constant touch. While you're at work, that phone rings.

Your name is Matt Hunter. The phone rings a second time. And then you answer it. . . .

264

nine years later

1

Reno, Nevada
April 18

The doorbell jangled Kimmy Dale out of her dreamless sleep.

She stirred in her bed, groaned, checked the digital clock next to her bed.

11:47 a.m.

Despite it being solidly midday, the trailer remained night-dark. That was how Kimmy liked it. She worked nights and was a light sleeper. Back in her Vegas headlining days it had taken years of testing shades, blinds, curtains, shutters, sleeping blindfolds, before she found a combination that could truly keep the branding-iron Nevada sun from niggling at her slumber. The Reno rays were less relentless, but they still searched and exploited even the smallest sliver.

Kimmy sat up in her king-size bed. The television, a no-name model she'd bought used when a local motel finally decided to upgrade, was still on with the volume off. The images floated ghostly in some distant world. She slept alone right now, but that was a condition in constant flux. There was a time when each visitor, each prospective mate, brought hope with them to this bed, brought a this-could-be-the-one optimism that, in hindsight, Kimmy realized, bordered on the delusional.

There was no such hope anymore.

She rose slowly. The swelling on her chest from her most recent cosmetic surgery ached with the movement. It was her third procedure in the area, and she wasn't a kid anymore. She hadn't wanted to do it, but Chally, who thought he had an eye for such things, had insisted. Her tips were getting low. Her popularity was waning. So she agreed. But the skin in that area had become too stretched out from past surgical abuse. When Kimmy laid on her back, the damn things fell to the side and looked like fish eyes.

The doorbell rang again.

Kimmy looked down at her ebony legs. Thirty-five years old, never had a baby, but the varicose veins were growing like feeding worms. Too many years on her feet. Chally would want those worked on too. She was still in shape, still had a pretty great figure and terrific ass, but hey, thirty-five is not eighteen. There was some cellulite. And those veins. Like a damn relief map.

She stuck a cigarette in her mouth. The book of matches came from her current place of employment, a strip joint called the Eager Beaver. She had once been a headliner in Vegas, going by the stage name Black Magic. She did not long for those days. She did not, in truth, long for any days.

Kimmy Dale threw on a robe and opened her bedroom door. The front room

267

had no sun protection. The glare assaulted her. She shielded her eyes and blinked. Kimmy did not have a lot of visitors – she never tricked at home – and figured that it was probably a Jehovah's Witness. Unlike pretty much everybody else in the free world, Kimmy did not mind their periodic intrusions. She always invited the religiously rapt into her home and listened carefully, envious that they had found something, wishing she could fall for their line of bull. As with the men in her life, she hoped that this one would be different, that this one would be able to convince her and she'd be able to buy into it.

She opened the door without asking who it was.

'Are you Kimmy Dale?'

The girl at the door was young. Eighteen, twenty, something like that. Nope, not a Jehovah's Witness. Didn't have that scooped-out-brain smile. For a moment Kimmy wondered if she was one of Chally's recruits, but that wasn't it. The girl wasn't ugly or anything, but she wasn't for Chally. Chally liked flash and glitter.

'Who are you?' Kimmy asked.

'That's not important.'

'Excuse me?'

The girl lowered her eyes and bit on her lower lip. Kimmy saw something distantly familiar in the gesture and felt a small ripple in her chest.

The girl said, 'You knew my mother.'

Kimmy fiddled with the cigarette. 'I know lots of mothers.'

'My mother,' the girl said, 'was Candace Potter.'

Kimmy winced when she said that. It was north of ninety degrees, but she suddenly tightened her robe.

'Can I come in?'

Did Kimmy say yes? She couldn't say. She stepped to the side, and the girl pushed her way past.

Kimmy said, 'I don't understand.'

'Candace Potter was my mother. She put me up for adoption the day I was born.'

Kimmy tried to keep her bearings. She closed the trailer door. 'You want something to drink?'

'No, thank you.'

The two women looked at each other. Kimmy crossed her arms.

'Not sure what you want here,' she said.

The girl spoke as if she'd been rehearsing. 'Two years ago I learned that I was adopted. I love my adopted family, so I don't want you to get the wrong idea. I have two sisters and wonderful parents. They've been very good to me. This isn't about them. It's just that . . . when you find out something like this, you need to know.'

Kimmy nodded, though she wasn't sure why.

'So I started digging for information. It wasn't easy. But there are groups who help adopted kids find their birth parents.'

Kimmy plucked the cigarette out of her mouth. Her hand was shaking. 'But you know that Candi – I mean, your mother – Candace . . .'

'. . . is dead. Yes, I know. She was murdered. I found out last week.'

Kimmy's legs started to feel a little rubbery. She sat. Memories rushed back in and they stung.

Candace Potter. Known as 'Candi Cane' in the clubs.

'What do you want from me?' Kimmy asked.

'I spoke to the officer who investigated her murder. His name is Max Darrow. Do you remember him?'

Oh, yes, she remembered good ol' Max. Knew him even before the murder. At first Detective Max Darrow had barely gone through the motions. Talk about low priority. Dead stripper, no family. Another dying cactus on the landscape, that was all Candi was to Darrow. Kimmy had gotten involved, traded favors for favors. Way of the world.

'Yeah,' Kimmy said, 'I remember him.'

'He's retired now. Max Darrow, I mean. He says they know who killed her, but they don't know where he is.'

Kimmy felt the tears coming to her eyes. 'It was a long time ago.'

'You and my mom were friends?'

Kimmy managed to nod. She still remembered it all, of course. Candi had been more than a friend to her. In this life you don't find too many people you can truly count on. Candi had been one – maybe the only one since Mama died when Kimmy was twelve. They had been inseparable, Kimmy and this white chick, sometimes calling themselves, professionally at least, Pic and Sayers from the old movie *Brian's Song*. And then, like in the movie, the white friend died.

'Was she a prostitute?' the girl asked.

Kimmy shook her head and told a lie that felt like truth. 'Never.'

'But she stripped.'

Kimmy said nothing.

'I'm not judging her.'

'What do you want then?'

'I want to know about my mother.'

'It doesn't make any difference now.'

'It does to me.'

Kimmy remembered when she first heard the news. She'd been onstage out near Tahoe doing a slow number for the lunch crowd, the biggest group of losers in the history of mankind, men with dirt on their boots and holes in their hearts that staring at naked women only made bigger. She hadn't seen Candi for three days running, but then again Kimmy had been on the road. Up there, on that stage, that was where she first overheard the rumors. She knew something bad had gone down. She'd just prayed it hadn't involved Candi.

But it had.

'Your mother had a hard life,' Kimmy said.

The girl sat rapt.

'Candi thought we'd find a way out, you know? At first she figured it'd be a guy at the club. They'd find us and take us away, but that's crap. Some of the girls try that. It never works. The guy wants some fantasy, not you. Your mother learned that pretty quick. She was a dreamer but with a purpose.'

Kimmy stopped, looked off.

'And?' the girl prompted.

'And then that bastard squashed her like she was a bug.'

The girl shifted in her chair. 'Detective Darrow said his name was Clyde Rangor?'

Kimmy nodded.

'He also mentioned a woman named Emma Lemay? Wasn't she his partner?'

'In some things, yeah. But I don't know the details.'

Kimmy did not cry when she first heard the news. She was beyond that. But she had come forward. She risked everything, telling that damn Darrow what she knew.

Thing is, you don't take too many stands in this life. But Kimmy would not betray Candi, even then, even when it was too late to help. Because when Candi died, so did the best parts of Kimmy.

So she talked to the cops, especially Max Darrow. Whoever did this – and yeah, she was sure it was Clyde and Emma – could hurt her or kill her, but she wouldn't back down.

In the end, Clyde and Emma had not confronted her. They ran instead.

That was ten years ago now.

The girl asked, 'Did you know about me?'

Kimmy nodded slowly. 'Your mother told me – but only once. It hurt her too much to talk about it. You have to understand. Candi was young when it happened. Fifteen, sixteen years old. They took you away the moment you popped out. She never even knew if you were a boy or girl.'

The silence hung heavy. Kimmy wished that the girl would leave.

'What do you think happened to him? Clyde Rangor, I mean.'

'Probably dead,' she said, though Kimmy didn't believe it. Cockroaches like Clyde don't die. They just burrow back in and cause more hurt.

'I want to find him,' the girl said.

Kimmy looked up at her.

'I want to find my mother's killer and bring him to justice. I'm not rich, but I have some money.'

They were both quiet for a moment. The air felt heavy and sticky. Kimmy wondered how to put this.

'Can I tell you something?' she began.

'Of course.'

'Your mother tried to stand up to it all.'

'Up to what?'

Kimmy pressed on. 'Most of the girls, they surrender. You see? Your mother never did. She wouldn't bend. She dreamed. But she could never win.'

'I don't understand.'

'Are you happy, child?'

'Yes.'

'You still in school?'

'I'm starting college.'

'College,' Kimmy said in a dreamy voice. Then: 'You.'

'What about me?'

'See, you're your mother's win.'

The girl said nothing.

'Candi – your mother – wouldn't want you mixed up in this. Do you understand?'

'I guess I do.'

'Hold on a second.' Kimmy opened her drawer. It was there, of course. She didn't have it out anymore, but the photograph was right on top. She and Candi smiling out at the world. Pic and Sayers. Kimmy looked at her own image and realized that the young girl they'd called Black Magic was a stranger, that Clyde Rangor might as well have pummeled her body into oblivion too.

'Take this,' she said.

The girl held the picture as if it were porcelain.

'She was beautiful,' the girl whispered.

'Very.'

'She looks happy.'

'She wasn't. But she would be today.'

The girl put her chin up. 'I don't know if I can stay away from this.'

Then maybe, Kimmy thought, you are more like your mother than you know.

They hugged then, made promises of staying in touch. When the girl was gone, Kimmy got dressed. She drove to the florist and asked for a dozen tulips. Tulips had been Candi's favorite. She took the four-hour trip to the graveyard and knelt by her friend's grave. There was no one else around. Kimmy dusted off the tiny headstone. She had paid for the plot and stone herself. No potter's grave for Candi.

'Your daughter came by today,' she said out loud.

There was a slight breeze. Kimmy closed her eyes and listened. She thought that she could hear Candi's voice, silenced so long, beg her to keep her daughter safe.

And there, with the hot Nevada sun pounding on her skin, Kimmy promised that she would.

2

'A camera phone,' Matt Hunter muttered with a shake of his head.

He looked up for divine guidance, but the only thing looking back was an enormous beer bottle.

The bottle was a familiar sight, one Matt saw every time he stepped out of his sagging two-family with the shedding paint job. With its crown 185 feet in the air, the famed bottle dominated the skyline. Pabst Blue Ribbon used to have a brewery here, but they abandoned it in 1985. Years ago, the bottle had been a glorious water tower with copper-plated steel plates, glossy enamel, and a gold stopper. At night spotlights would illuminate the bottle so that Jerseyites could see it from miles around.

But no more. Now the color looked beer-bottle brown but it was really rust red. The bottle's label was long gone. Following its lead, the once-robust neighborhood around it had not so much fallen apart as slowly disintegrated. Nobody had worked in the brewery for twenty years. From the eroding ruins, one would think it would have been much longer.

Matt stopped on the top step of their stoop. Olivia, the love of his life, did not. The car keys jangled in her hand.

'I don't think we should,' he said.

Olivia did not break stride. 'Come on. It'll be fun.'

'A phone should be a phone,' Matt said. 'A camera should be a camera.'

'Oh, that's deep.'

'One gizmo doing both . . . it's a perversion.'

'Your area of expertise,' Olivia said.

'Ha, ha. You don't see the danger?'

'Er, nope.'

'A camera and a phone in one' – Matt stopped, searching for how to continue – 'it's, I don't know, it's interspecies breeding when you think about it, like one of those B-movie experiments that grows out of control and destroys all in its path.'

Olivia just stared at him. 'You're so weird.'

'I'm not sure we should get camera phones, that's all.'

She hit the remote and the car doors unlocked. She reached for the door handle. Matt hesitated.

Olivia looked at him.

'What?' he asked.

'If we both had camera phones,' Olivia said, 'I could send you nudies when

272

you're at work.'

Matt opened the door. 'Verizon or Sprint?'

Olivia gave him a smile that made his chest thrum. 'I love you, you know.'

'I love you too.'

They were both inside the car. She turned to him. He could see the concern and it almost made him turn away. 'It's going to be okay,' Olivia said. 'You know that, right?'

He nodded and feigned a smile. Olivia wouldn't buy it, but the effort would count toward something.

'Olivia?' he said.

'Yes?'

'Tell me more about the nudies.'

She punched his arm.

But Matt's unease returned the moment he entered the Sprint store and started hearing about the two-year commitment. The salesman's smile looked somehow satanic, like the devil in one of those movies where a naïve guy sells his soul. When the salesman whipped out a map of the United States – the 'non-roaming' areas, he informed them, were in bright red – Matt started to back away.

As for Olivia, there was simply no quelling her excitement, but then again his wife had a natural lean toward the enthusiastic. She was one of those rare people who find joy in things both large and small, one of those traits that demonstrates, certainly in their case, that opposites do attract.

The salesman kept jabbering. Matt tuned him out, but Olivia gave the man her full attention. She asked a question or two, just out of formality, but the salesman knew that this one was not only hooked, lined, and sinkered but fried up and halfway down the gullet.

'Let me just get the paperwork ready,' Hades said, slinking away.

Olivia gripped Matt's arm, her face beaming. 'Isn't this fun?'

Matt made a face.

'What?'

'Did you really use the word "nudie"?'

She laughed and leaned her head against his shoulder.

Of course Olivia's giddiness – and nonstop beaming – was due to much more than the changing of their mobile phone service. Purchasing the camera phones was merely a symbol, a signpost, of what was to come.

A baby.

Two days ago, Olivia had taken a home pregnancy test and, in a move Matt found oddly loaded with religious significance, a red cross finally appeared on the white stick. He was stunned silent. They had been trying to have a child for a year – pretty much since they first got married. The stress of continuous failure had turned what had always been a rather spontaneous if not downright magical experience into well-orchestrated chores of temperature taking, calendar markings, prolonged abstinence, concentrated ardor.

Now that was behind them. It was early, he warned her. Let's not get ahead of ourselves. But Olivia had a glow that could not be denied. Her positive mood was a force, a storm, a tide. Matt had no chance against it.

That was why they were here.

Camera phones, Olivia had stressed, would allow the soon-to-be threesome to share family life in a way their parents' generation could never have envisioned. Thanks to the camera phone, neither of them would miss out on their child's life-defining or even mundane moments – the first step, the first words, the average play-date, what-have-you.

That, at least, was the plan.

An hour later, when they returned to their half of the two-family home, Olivia gave him a quick kiss and started up the stairs.

'Hey,' Matt called after her, holding up his new phone and arching an eyebrow. 'Want to try out the, uh, video feature?'

'The video only lasts fifteen seconds.'

'Fifteen seconds.' He considered that, shrugged, and said, 'So we'll extend foreplay.'

Olivia understandably groaned.

They lived in what most would consider a seedy area, in the strangely comforting shadow of the giant beer bottle of Irvington. When he was fresh out of prison, Matt had felt he deserved no better (which worked neatly because he could afford little better) and despite protestations from family, he began renting space nine years ago. Irvington is a tired city with a large African-American population, probably north of eighty percent. Some might reach the obvious conclusion about guilt over what he'd had to be like in prison. Matt knew that such things were never so simple, but he had no better explanation other than he couldn't yet return to the suburbs. The change would have been too fast, the land equivalent of the bends.

Either way, this neighborhood – the Shell gas station, the old hardware store, the deli on the corner, the winos on the cracked sidewalk, the cut-throughs to Newark Airport, the tavern hidden near the old Pabst brewery – had become home.

When Olivia relocated from Virginia, he figured that she'd insist on moving to a better neighborhood. She was used to, he knew, if not better, definitely different. Olivia grew up in the small hick town of Northways, Virginia. When Olivia was a toddler, her mother ran off. Her father raised her alone.

On the elderly side for a new dad – her father was fifty-one when Olivia was born – Joshua Murray worked hard to make a home for him and his young daughter. Joshua was the town doctor of Northways – a general practitioner who worked on everything from six-year-old Mary Kate Johnson's appendix to Old Man Riteman's gout.

Joshua was, according to Olivia, a kind man, a gentle and wonderful father who doted on his only true relative. There was just the two of them, father and daughter, living in a brick town house off Main Street. Dad's medical office was attached, on the right side off the driveway. Most days, Olivia would sprint home after school so that she could help out with the patients. She would cheer up scared kids or gab with Cassie, the long-time receptionist/nurse. Cassie was a 'sorta nanny' too. If her father was too busy, Cassie cooked dinner and helped Olivia with her homework. For her part, Olivia worshipped her father. Her dream – and yes, she thought now that it sounded hopelessly naïve – had been to become a doctor and work with her father.

But during Olivia's senior year of college, everything changed. Her father, the only family Olivia had ever known, died of lung cancer. The news took Olivia's legs out from under her. The old ambition of going to medical school – following in her father's footsteps – died with him. Olivia broke off her engagement to her college sweetheart, a premed named Doug, and moved back to the old house in Northways. But living there without her father was too painful. She ended up selling the house and moving to an apartment complex in Charlottesville. She took a job with a computer software company that required a fair amount of travel, which was, in part, how she and Matt rekindled their previously too-brief relationship.

Irvington, New Jersey, was a far cry from either Northways or Charlottesville, Virginia, but Olivia surprised him. She wanted them to stay in this place, seedy as it was, so that they could save the money for the now-under-contract dream house.

Three days after they bought the camera phones, Olivia came home and headed straight upstairs. Matt poured a glass of lime-flavored seltzer and grabbed a few of those cigar-shaped pretzels. Five minutes later he followed her. Olivia wasn't in the bedroom. He checked the small office. She was on the computer. Her back was to him.

'Olivia?'

She turned to him and smiled. Matt had always disdained that old cliché about a smile lighting up a room, but Olivia could actually do that – had that whole 'turn the world on with her smile' thing going on. Her smile was contagious. It was a startling catalyst, adding color and texture to his life, altering everything in a room.

'What are you thinking?' Olivia asked him.

'That you're smoking hot.'

'Even pregnant?'

'Especially pregnant.'

Olivia hit a button, and the screen vanished. She stood and gently kissed his cheek. 'I have to pack.'

Olivia was heading to Boston on a business trip.

'What time is your flight?' he asked.

'I think I'm going to drive.'

'Why?'

'A friend of mine miscarried after a plane ride. I just don't want to chance it. Oh, and I'm going to see Dr. Haddon tomorrow morning before I go. He wants to reconfirm the test and make sure everything is all right.'

'You want me to go?'

She shook her head. 'You have work. Come next time, when they do a sonogram.'

'Okay.'

Olivia kissed him again, her lips lingering. 'Hey,' she whispered. 'You happy?'

He was going to crack a joke, make another double entendre. But he didn't. He looked straight into those eyes and said, 'Very.'

Olivia moved back, still holding him steady with that smile. 'I better pack.'

Matt watched her walk away. He stayed in the doorway for another moment. There was a lightness in his chest. He was indeed happy, which scared the hell out of him. The good is fragile. You learn that when you kill a boy. You learn that when you spend four years in a maximum-security facility.

The good is so flimsy, so tenuous, that it can be destroyed with a gentle puff. Or the sound of a phone.

Matt was at work when the camera phone vibrated.

He glanced at the caller ID and saw that it was Olivia. Matt still sat at his old partner desk, the kind where two people face each other, though the other side had been empty for three years now. His brother, Bernie, had bought the desk when Matt got out of prison. Before what the family euphemistically called 'the slip,' Bernie had big ideas for the two of them, the Hunter Brothers. He wanted nothing to change now. Matt would put those years behind him. The slip had been a bump in the road, nothing more, and now the Hunter Brothers were back on track.

Bernie was so convincing that Matt almost started to believe it.

The brothers shared that desk for six years. They practiced law in this very room – Bernie lucrative corporate while Matt, barred from being a real attorney because he'd been a convicted felon, handled the direct opposite, neither lucrative nor corporate. Bernie's law partners found the arrangement odd, but privacy was something neither brother craved. They had shared a bedroom for their entire childhood, Bernie on the top bunk, a voice from above in the dark. Both longed for those days again – or at least, Matt did. He was never comfortable alone. He was comfortable with Bernie in the room.

For six years.

Matt put both palms on the mahogany top. He should have gotten rid of the desk by now. Bernie's side had not been touched in three years, but sometimes Matt still looked across and expected to see him.

The camera phone vibrated again.

One moment Bernie had it all – a terrific wife, two terrific boys, the big house in the burbs, partnership in a big law firm, good health, loved by everyone – the next his family was throwing dirt on his grave and trying to make sense of what happened. A brain aneurysm, the doctor said. You walk around with it for years and then, bam, it ends your life.

The phone was on 'Vibrate-Ring.' The vibrate ended and the ringer started playing the old TV Batman song, the one with the clever lyrics that basically consisted of going nah-nah-nah for a while and then shouting 'Batman!'

Matt pulled the new camera phone off his belt.

His finger hovered over the answer button. This was sort of weird. Olivia, despite being in the computer business, was terrible with all things technical. She'd rarely used the phone and when she did, well, she knew Matt was at the office. She'd call him on his landline.

Matt pressed down on the answer button, but the message appeared telling him that a photograph was 'incoming.' This, too, was curious. For all her initial excitement, Olivia had not yet learned how to use the camera feature.

His intercom sounded.

Rolanda – Matt would call her a secretary or assistant but then she'd hurt him – cleared her throat. 'Matt?'

'Yes.'

'Marsha is on line two.'

Still looking at the screen, Matt picked up the office phone to talk to his sister-in-law, Bernie's widow.

'Hey,' he said.

'Hey,' Marsha said. 'Is Olivia still in Boston?'

'Yep. In fact, right now, I think she's sending me a photo on our new cell phone.'

'Oh.' There was a brief pause. 'Are you still coming out today?'

In another move signaling familyhood, Matt and Olivia were closing on a house not far from Marsha and the boys. The house was located in Livingston, the town where Bernie and Matt grew up.

Matt had questioned the wisdom of returning. People had long memories. No matter how many years passed, he would always be the subject of whispers and innuendo. On the one hand, Matt was long past caring about that petty stuff. On the other, he worried about Olivia and about his upcoming child. The curse of the father visited upon the son and all that.

But Olivia understood the risks. This was what she wanted.

More than that, the somewhat high-strung Marsha had – he wondered what euphemism to use here – issues. There had been a brief breakdown a year after Bernie's sudden death. Marsha had 'gone to rest' – another euphemism – for two weeks while Matt moved in and took care of the boys. Marsha was fine now – that was what everyone said – but Matt still liked the idea of staying close.

Today was the physical inspection of the new house. 'I should be out in a little while. Why, what's up?'

'Could you stop by?'

'Stop by your place?'

'Yes.'

'Sure.'

'If it's a bad time . . .'

'No, of course not.'

Marsha was a beautiful woman with an oval face that sometimes looked sad-sack, and a nervous upward glance as if making sure the black cloud was in place. That was a physical thing, of course, no more a true reflection on her personality than being short or scarred.

'Everything all right?' Matt asked.

'Yeah, I'm fine. It's no big deal. It's just . . . Could you take the kids for a couple of hours? I got a school thing and Kyra's going to be out tonight.'

'You want me to take them out for dinner?'

'That would be great. But no McDonald's, okay?'

'Chinese?'

'Perfect,' she said.

'Cool, I'm there.'

'Thanks.'

The image started coming in on the camera phone.

'I'll see you later,' he said.

She said good-bye and hung up.

Matt turned his attention back to the cell phone. He squinted at the screen. It was tiny. Maybe an inch, no more than two. The sun was bright that day. The curtain was open. The glare made it harder to see. Matt cupped his hand around the tiny display and hunched his body so as to provide shade. It worked somewhat.

A man appeared on the screen.

Again it was hard to make out details. He looked in his mid-thirties – Matt's age – and had really dark hair, almost blue. He wore a red button-down shirt. His hand was up as though waving. He was in a room with white walls and a gray-sky window. The man had a smirk on his face – one of those knowing, I'm-better-than-you smirks. Matt stared at the man. Their eyes met and Matt could have sworn he saw something mocking in them.

Matt did not know the man.

He did not know why his wife would take the man's photograph.

The screen went black. Matt did not move. That seashell rush stayed in his ears. He could still hear other sounds – a distant fax machine, low voices, the traffic outside – but it was as though through a filter.

'Matt?'

It was Rolanda Garfield, said assistant/secretary. The law firm had not been thrilled when Matt hired her. Rolanda was a tad too 'street' for the stuffed shirts at Carter Sturgis. But he'd insisted. She had been one of Matt's first clients and one of his painfully few victories.

During his stint in prison, Matt managed to accrue enough credits to get his BA. The law degree came not long after his release. Bernie, a powerhouse at his uber-Newark law firm of Carter Sturgis, figured that he'd be able to convince the bar to make an exception and let his ex-con brother in.

He had been wrong.

But Bernie was not easily discouraged. He then persuaded his partners to take Matt in as a 'paralegal,' a wonderful all-encompassing term that, for the most part, seemed to mean 'scut work.'

The partners at Carter Sturgis didn't like it, at first. No surprise, of course. An ex-con at their white-shoe law firm? That simply wouldn't do. But Bernie appealed to their purported humanity: Matt would be good for public relations. He would show that the firm had heart and believed in second chances, at least in theoretical spin. He was smart. He would be an asset. More to the point, Matt could take on the large bulk of the firm's pro bono cases, freeing the partners to gouge the deep pockets without the distraction of the underclass.

The two closers: Matt would work cheap – what choice did he have? And Brother Bernie, a major-league rainmaker, would walk if they didn't agree.

The partners considered the scenario: Maybe do good and help yourself? It was the kind of logic upon which charities are built.

Matt's eyes stayed on the blank phone screen. His pulse did a little two-step. Who, he wondered, is that guy with the blue-black hair?

Rolanda put her hands on her hips. 'Earth to doofus,' she said.

'What?' Matt snapped out of it.

'You okay?'

'Me? I'm fine.'

Rolanda gave him a funny look.

The camera phone vibrated again. Rolanda stood with her arms crossed. Matt looked back at her. She did not get the hint. She rarely did. The phone vibrated again and then the Batman theme started up.

'Aren't you going to answer that?' Rolanda said.

He glanced down at the phone. The caller ID blinked out his wife's phone number again.

'Yo, Batman.'

'I'm on it,' Matt said.

His thumb touched on the green send button, lingering there for a moment before it pressed down. The screen lit up anew.

A video appeared now.

The technology was improving, but the shaky video display usually had a quality two steps below the Zapruder film. For a second or two, Matt had trouble focusing in on what was happening. The video would not last long, Matt knew. Ten, fifteen seconds tops.

It was a room. He could see that. The camera panned past a television on a console. There was a painting on the wall – Matt couldn't tell of what – but the overall impression led him to conclude that it was a hotel room. The camera stopped on the bathroom door.

And then a woman appeared.

Her hair was platinum blonde. She wore dark sunglasses and a slinky blue dress. Matt frowned.

What the hell was this?

The woman stood for a moment. Matt had the impression she did not know the camera was on her. The lens moved with her. There was a flash of light, sun bursting in through the window, and then everything came back into focus.

When the woman walked toward the bed, he stopped breathing.

Matt recognized the walk.

He also recognized the way she sat on the bed, the tentative smile that followed, the way her chin tilted up, the way she crossed her legs.

He did not move.

From across the room he heard Rolanda's voice, softer now: 'Matt?'

He ignored her. The camera was put down now, probably on a bureau. It was still aiming at the bed. A man walked toward the platinum blonde. Matt could only see the man's back. He was wearing a red shirt and had blue-black hair. His approach blocked the view of the woman. And the bed.

Matt's eyes started to blur. He blinked them back into focus. The LCD screen on the camera started to darken. The images flickered and disappeared and Matt was left sitting there, Rolanda staring at him curiously, the photographs on his brother's side of the desk still in place, and he was sure – well, pretty sure, the screen was only an inch or two, right? – that the woman in the strange hotel room, the woman in the slinky dress on the bed, that she was wearing a platinum-blonde wig and that she was really a brunette and that her name was Olivia and she was his wife.

3

Newark, New Jersey
June 22

Essex County homicide investigator Loren Muse sat in her boss's office.

'Wait a second,' she said. 'Are you telling me that the nun had breast implants?'

Ed Steinberg, the Essex County prosecutor, sat behind his desk rubbing his bowling-ball gut. He had that kind of build that from the back you wouldn't even know he was heavy, just that he had a flat ass. He leaned back and put his hands behind his head. The shirt was yellow under the armpits. 'So it appears, yeah.'

'But she died of natural causes?' Loren said.

'That's what we thought.'

'You don't think that anymore?'

'I don't think anything anymore,' Steinberg said.

'I could make a crack here, boss.'

'But you won't.' Steinberg sighed and put on his reading glasses. 'Sister Mary Rose, a tenth-grade social studies teacher, was found dead in her room at the convent. No signs of struggle, no wounds, she's sixty-two years old. Apparently a standard death – heart, stroke, something like that. Nothing suspicious.'

'But?' Loren added.

'But there's been a new development.'

'I think the word is "augmentation."'

'Stop it, you're killing me.'

Loren turned both palms up. 'I still don't see why I'm here.'

'How about that you're the greatest homicide investigator in the naked, uh, county?'

Loren made a face.

'Yeah, didn't think that'd fly. This nun' – Steinberg lowered the reading glasses again – 'taught at St. Margaret's High.' He looked at her.

'So?'

'So you were a student there, right?'

'And again I say: So?'

'So the Mother Superior has some juice with the brass. She requested you.'

'Mother Katherine?'

He checked the sheet. 'That's her name.'

'You're kidding, right?'

'Nope. She called in a favor. Requested you by name.'

Loren shook her head.

'You know her, I assume?'

'Mother Katherine? Only because I was constantly being sent to her office.'

'Wait, you weren't an easy kid?' Steinberg put his hand to his heart. 'Tattoo me shocked.'

'I still don't see why she'd want me.'

'Maybe she thought you'd be discreet.'

'I hated that place.'

'Why?'

'You didn't go to Catholic school, did you?'

He lifted his nameplate on his desk and pointed to the letters one at a time. 'Steinberg,' he read to her slowly. 'Note the Stein. Note the Berg. See those names much in church?'

Loren nodded. 'Right, then it'd be like explaining music to the deaf. What prosecutor will I be reporting to?'

'Me.'

That surprised her. 'Directly?'

'Directly and only. Nobody else is on this, understood?'

She nodded. 'Understood.'

'You ready then?'

'Ready for what?'

'Mother Katherine.'

'What about her?'

Steinberg stood and sauntered around his desk. 'She's in the next room. She wants to talk to you privately.'

When Loren Muse was a student at St. Margaret's School for Girls, Mother Katherine was twelve feet tall and approximately one hundred years old. The years had shrunk her down and reversed the aging process – but not by a lot. Mother Katherine had worn the full habit when Loren was at St. Margaret's. Now she was decked out in something undeniably pious, though far more casual. The clerical answer to Banana Republic, Loren guessed.

Steinberg said, 'I'll leave you two alone.'

Mother Katherine was standing, her hands folded in preprayer position. The door closed. Neither of them said anything. Loren knew this technique. She would not talk first.

As a sophomore at Livingston High School, Loren had been labeled a 'problem student' and sent to St. Margaret's. Loren was a petite thing back then, just five feet tall, and she hadn't grown much in the ensuing years. The other investigators, all males and oh so clever, called her Squirt.

Investigators. You get them started, they'll shred you with the cutting lines.

But Loren hadn't always been one of the so-called troubled youth. When she was in elementary school, she was that tiny tomboy, that spunky spark plug of a girl who kicked ass in kickball and would sooner die than don anything in the pink family. Her father worked a variety of blue-collar jobs, mostly involving trucking. He was a sweet, quiet man who made the mistake of falling for a woman far too beautiful for him.

The Muse clan lived in the Coventry section of Livingston, New Jersey, a slice of suburbia well beyond their social and economic means. Loren's mother, the ravishing and demanding Mrs. Muse, had insisted because, dammit, she deserved it.

No one – but no one – was going to look down on Carmen Muse.

She pushed Loren's father, demanding he work harder, take out more loans, find a way to keep up, until – exactly two days after Loren turned fourteen years old – Dad blew his brains out in their detached two-car garage.

In hindsight her father was probably bipolar. She understood that now. There was a chemical imbalance in his brain. A man kills himself – it's not fair to blame others. But Loren did. She blamed her mother. She wondered what her sweet, quiet father's life would have been like had he married someone less high maintenance than Carmen Valos of Bayonne.

Young Loren took the tragedy as one might expect: She rebelled like mad. She drank, smoked, hung out with the wrong crowd, slept around. It was, Loren knew, grossly unfair that boys with multiple sex partners are revered while girls who do the same are dumb sluts. But the truth was – and Loren hated to admit this – for all the comforting feminist rationalizations, Loren knew that her level of promiscuity was adversely (though directly) related to her self-esteem. That is, when her self-worth was low, her, uh, easiness factor rose. Men didn't seem to suffer the same fate, or if they did, they hid it better.

Mother Katherine broke the stalemate. 'It's nice to see you, Loren.'

'Same here,' Loren said in a tentative voice that was so not like her. Gee, what next? Would she start biting her fingernails again? 'Prosecutor Steinberg said you wanted to talk to me?'

'Should we sit?'

Loren shrugged a suit-yourself. They both sat. Loren folded her arms and slid low in her chair. She crossed her feet. It occurred to her that she had gum in her mouth. Mother Katherine's face pinched up in disapproval. Not to be cowed, Loren picked up the pace so that the discreet chew turned into something more like a bovine mastication.

'Do you want to tell me what's going on?'

'We have a delicate situation here,' Mother Katherine began. 'It requires . . .' She looked up as if asking the Big Guy for a little assistance.

'Delicacy?' Loren replied.

'Yes. Delicacy.'

'Okay,' Loren said, dragging out the word. 'This is about the nun with the boob job, right?'

Mother Katherine closed her eyes, opened them again. 'It is. But I think you're missing the point.'

'Which is?'

'We had a wonderful teacher pass away.'

'That would be Sister Mary Rose.' Thinking: Our Lady of the Cleavage.

'Yes.'

'Do you think she died of natural causes?' Loren asked.

'I do.'

'So?'

'This is very tough to talk about.'

'I'd like to help.'

'You were a good girl, Loren.'

'No, I was a pain in the ass.'

Mother Katherine smothered a smile. 'Well, yes, that too.'

Loren returned the smile.

'There are different kinds of troublemakers,' Mother Katherine said. 'You were rebellious, yes, but you always had a good heart. You were never cruel to others. That, for me, has always been the key. You often got in trouble because you were sticking up for someone weaker.'

Loren leaned forward and surprised herself: She took the nun's hand. Mother Katherine too seemed startled by the gesture. Her blue eyes looked into Loren's.

'Promise me you will keep what I'm about to tell you to yourself,' Mother Katherine said. 'It's very important. In this climate especially. Even the whiff of scandal –'

'I won't cover anything up.'

'Nor would I want you to,' she said, now giving her the theologically offended tone. 'We need to get to the truth. I seriously considered the idea of just' – she waved her hand – 'of just letting this go. Sister Mary Rose would have been buried quietly and that would have been the end of it.'

Loren kept her hand on the nun's. The older woman's hand was dark, like it was made of balsam wood. 'I'll do my best.'

'You must understand. Sister Mary Rose was one of our best teachers.'

'She taught social studies?'

'Yes.'

Loren searched the memory banks. 'I don't remember her.'

'She joined us after you graduated.'

'How long had she been at St. Margaret's?'

'Seven years. And let me tell you something. The woman was a saint. I know the word is overused, but there is no other way to describe her. Sister Mary Rose never asked for glory. She had no ego. She just wanted to do what was right.'

Mother Katherine took back her hand. Loren leaned back and recrossed her legs. 'Go on.'

'When we – by we, I mean two sisters and myself – when we found her in the morning, Sister Mary Rose was in her nightclothes. She, like many of us, was a very modest woman.'

Loren nodded, trying to encourage.

'We were upset, of course. She had stopped breathing. We tried mouth-to-mouth and chest compressions. A local policeman had recently visited to teach the children about lifesaving techniques. So we tried it. I was the one who did the chest compressions and. . . .' Her voice trailed off.

'. . . And that was when you realized that Sister Mary Rose had breast implants?'

Mother Katherine nodded.

'Did you mention this to the other sisters?'

'Oh, no. Of course not.'

Loren shrugged. 'I don't really understand the problem,' she said.

'You don't?'

'Sister Mary Rose probably had a life before she became a nun. Who knows what it was like?'

'That's just it,' Mother Katherine said. 'She didn't.'

'I'm not sure I follow.'

'Sister Mary Rose came to us from a very conservative parish in Oregon. She was orphaned and joined the convent when she was fifteen years old.'

Loren considered that. 'So you had no idea that . . . ?' She made halfhearted back-and-forth gestures in front of her own chest.

'Absolutely no idea.'

'How do you explain it then?'

'I think' – Mother Katherine bit her lip – 'I think Sister Mary Rose came to us under false pretenses.'

'What sort of false pretenses?'

'I don't know.' Mother Katherine looked up at her expectantly.

'And,' Loren said, 'that's where I come in?'

'Well, yes.'

'You want me to find out what her deal was.'

'Yes.'

'Discreetly.'

'That would be my hope, Loren. But we need to find the truth.'

'Even if it's ugly?'

'Especially if it's ugly.' Mother Katherine rose. 'That's what you do with the ugly of this world. You pull it into God's light.'

'Yeah,' Loren said. 'Into the light.'

'You're not a believer anymore, are you, Loren?'

'I never was.'

'Oh, I don't know about that.' Loren stood, but Mother Katherine still towered over her. Yep, Loren thought, twelve feet tall. 'Will you help me?'

'You know I will.'

4

Seconds passed. Matt Hunter guessed it was seconds. He stared at the phone and waited. Nothing happened. His mind was in deep freeze. It came out and when it did, he longed for the deep freeze to return.

The phone. He turned it over in his hand, studying it as if he'd never seen it before. The screen, he reminded himself, was small. The images were jerky. The tint and color were off. The glare had also been a problem.

He nodded to himself. Keep going.

Olivia was not a platinum blonde.

Good. More, more . . .

He knew her. He loved her. He was not the best catch. He was an ex-con with few bright prospects. He had a tendency to withdraw emotionally. He did not love or trust easily. Olivia, on the other hand, had it all. She was beautiful. She was smart, had graduated summa cum laude from the University of Virginia. She even had some money her father left her.

This wasn't helping.

Yes. Yes, it was because, despite all that, Olivia had still chosen him – the ex-con with zero prospects. She had been the first woman he'd told about his past. No other had hung around long enough for it to become an issue.

Her reaction?

Well, it hadn't been all flowers. Olivia's smile – that drop-you-to-your-knees pow – had dimmed for a moment. Matt wanted to stop right there. He wanted to walk away because there was no way he could handle being responsible for dimming, even for a brief moment, that smile. But the flicker hadn't lasted long. The beam soon returned to full wattage. Matt had bitten down on his lip in relief. Olivia had reached across the table and taken his hand and, in a sense, had never let it go.

But now, as Matt sat here, he remembered those first tentative steps when he left the prison, the careful ones he took when he blinked his eyes and stepped through the gate, that feeling – that feeling that has never totally left him – that the thin ice beneath him could crack at any time and plunge him into the freezing water.

How does he explain what he just saw?

Matt understood human nature. Check that. He understood subhuman nature. He had seen the Fates curse him and his family enough to come up with an explanation or, if you will, an anti-explanation for all that goes wrong: In sum, there is no explanation.

The world is neither cruel nor joyous. It is simply random, full of particles hurtling, chemicals mixing and reacting. There is no real order. There is no pre-ordained cursing of the evil and protecting of the righteous.

Chaos, baby. It's all about chaos.

And in the swirl of all that chaos, Matt had only one thing – Olivia.

But as he sat in his office, eyes still on that phone, his mind wouldn't let it go. Now, right now, at this very second . . . what was Olivia doing in that hotel room?

He closed his eyes and sought a way out.

Maybe it wasn't her.

Again: the screen, it was small. The video, it was jerky. Matt kept going with that, running similar rationalizations up the flagpole, hoping one would fly.

None did.

There was a sinking feeling in his chest.

Images flooded in. Matt tried to battle them, but they were overwhelming. The guy's blue-black hair. That damned knowing smirk. He thought about the way Olivia would lean back when they made love, biting her lower lip, her eyes half closed, the tendons in her neck growing taut. He imagined sounds too. Small groans at first. Then cries of ecstasy . . .

Stop it.

He looked up and found Rolanda still staring at him.

'Was there something you wanted?' he asked.

'There was.'

'And?'

'I've been standing here so long, I forget.'

Rolanda shrugged, spun, left the office. She did not close the door behind her.

Matt stood and moved to the window. He looked down at a photograph of Bernie's sons in full soccer gear. Bernie and Marsha had used this picture for their Christmas card three years ago. The frame was one of those faux bronze numbers you get at Rite-Aid or a similar drugstore-cum-frame store. In the photograph Bernie's boys, Paul and Ethan, were five and three and smiled like it. They don't smile like that anymore. They were good kids, well-adjusted and all, but there was still an inescapable, underlying sadness. When you looked closely, the smiles were more cautious now, a wince in the eye, a fear of what else might be taken from them.

So what to do now?

The obvious, he decided. Call Olivia back. See what's what.

It sounded rational on one level and ridiculous on another. What did he really think would happen here? Would the first sound he heard be his wife breathing heavily, a man's laughter in the background? Or did he think Olivia would answer with her usual sunny voice and then – what? – he'd say, 'Hi, hon, say, what's up with the motel?' – in his mind's eye it was no longer a hotel room, but now a dingy no-tell motel, changing the *h* to an *m* adding a whole new significance – 'and the platinum wig and the smirking guy with the blue-black hair?'

That didn't sound right.

He was letting his imagination run away with him. There was a logical explanation for all this. Maybe he couldn't see it yet, but that didn't mean it wasn't there. Matt remembered watching those TV specials about how magicians did their tricks. You watched the trick and you couldn't fathom the answer and once they showed it to you, you wondered how you could have been so stupid to miss it the first time. That was what this was like.

Seeing no other option, Matt decided to call.

Olivia's cell was programmed into his speed dial in the number one spot. He

286

pressed down on the button and held it. The phone began to ring. He stared out the window and saw the city of Newark. His feelings for this city were, as always, mixed. You see the potential, the vibrancy, but mostly you see the decay and shake your head. For some reason he flashed back to the day Duff had visited him in prison. Duff had started bawling, his face red, looking so like a child. Matt could only watch. There was nothing to say.

The phone rang six times before going into Olivia's voice mail. The sound of his wife's animated voice, so familiar, so . . . *his,* made his heart stutter. He waited patiently for Olivia to finish. Then the beep sounded.

'Hey, it's me,' he said. He could hear the tautness in his tone and fought against it. 'Could you give me a call when you have a second?' He paused. He usually ended with a perfunctory 'love you,' but this time he hit the end button without adding what had always come so naturally.

He kept looking out the window. In prison what eventually got to him was not the brutality or the repulsion. Just the opposite. It was when those things became the norm. After a while Matt started to like his brothers in the Aryan Nation – actually enjoyed their company. It was a perverse offshoot of the Stockholm syndrome. Survival is the thing. The mind will twist to survive. Anything can become normal. That was what made Matt pause.

He thought about Olivia's laugh. How it took him away from all that. He wondered now if that laugh was real or just another cruel mirage, something to mock him with kindness.

Then Matt did something truly strange.

He held the camera phone out in front of him, arm's distance, and snapped a picture of himself. He didn't smile. He just looked into the lens. The photograph was on the little screen now. He looked at his own face and was not sure what he saw.

He pressed her phone number and sent the picture to Olivia.

5

Two hours passed. Olivia did not call back.

Matt spent those two hours with Ike Kier, a pampered senior partner who wore his gray hair too long and slicked back. He came from a wealthy family. He knew how to network and not much else, but sometimes that was enough. He owned a Viper and two Harley-Davidsons. His nickname around the office was Midlife, short for Midlife Crisis.

Midlife was bright enough to know that he was not that bright. He thus used Matt a lot. Matt, he knew, was willing to do most of the heavy lifting and stay behind the scenes. This allowed Midlife to maintain the big corporate client relationship and look good. Matt cared, he guessed, but not enough to do anything about it.

Corporate fraud may not be good for America, but it was damned profitable for the white-shoe, white-collar law firm of Carter Sturgis. Right now they were discussing the case of Mike Sterman, the CEO of a big pharmaceutical company called Pentacol, who'd been charged with, among other things, cooking the books to manipulate stock prices.

'In sum,' Midlife said, giving the room his best you-the-jury baritone, 'our defense will be . . . ?' He looked to Matt for the answer.

'Blame the other guy,' Matt said.

'Which other guy?'

'Yes.'

'Huh?'

'We blame whoever we can,' Matt said. 'The CFO' – Sterman's brother-in-law and former best friend – 'the COO, the C Choose-Your-Favorite-Two-Letter Combination, the accounting firm, the banks, the board, the lower-level employees. We claim some of them are crooks. We claim some of them made honest mistakes that steamrolled.'

'Isn't that contradictory?' Midlife asked, folding his hands and lowering his eyebrows. 'Claiming both malice and mistakes?' He stopped, looked up, smiled, nodded. Malice and mistakes. Midlife liked the way that sounded.

'We're looking to confuse,' Matt said. 'You blame enough people, nothing sticks. The jury ends up knowing something went wrong, but you don't know where to place the blame. We throw facts and figures at them. We bring up every possible mistake, every uncrossed *t* and undotted *i*. We act like every discrepancy is a huge deal, even if it's not. We question everything. We are skeptical of everyone.'

'And what about the bar mitzvah?'

Sterman had thrown his son a two-million-dollar bar mitzvah, featuring a chartered plane to Bermuda where both Beyoncé and Ja Rule performed. The videotape – actually, it was a surround-sound DVD – was going to be shown to the jury.

'A legitimate business expense,' Matt said.

'Come again?'

'Look who was there. Executives from the big drug chains. Top buyers. Government officials from the FDA who approve drugs and give out grants. Doctors, researchers, whatever. Our client was wining and dining clients – a legit American business practice since before the Boston Tea Party. What he did was for the good of the company.'

'And the fact that the party was for his son's bar mitzvah?'

Matt shrugged. 'It works in his favor, actually. Sterman was being brilliant.'

Midlife made a face.

'Think about it. If Sterman had said, "I'm throwing a big party to win over important clients," well, that wouldn't have helped him develop the relationships he was looking for. So Sterman, that sly genius, went with something more subtle. He invites his business associates to his son's bar mitzvah. They are caught off guard now. They find it sweet, this family guy inviting them to something personal rather than hitting them up in some stuffy business venue. Sterman, like any brilliant CEO, was creative in his approach.'

Midlife arched an eyebrow and nodded slowly. 'Oh, I like that.'

Matt had figured as much. He checked his cell phone, making sure it was still powered up. It was. He checked to see if there were any messages or missed calls. There were none.

Midlife rose. 'We'll do more prep tomorrow?'

'Sure,' Matt said.

He left. Rolanda stuck her head in the door. She looked down the hall in the direction of Midlife, faked sticking a finger down her throat, and made a gagging noise. Matt checked the time. Time to get moving.

He hurried out to the firm's parking lot. His gaze wandered, focusing on nothing and everything. Tommy, the parking lot attendant, waved to him. Still dazed, Matt may have waved back. His spot was in the back, under the dripping pipes. The world was about the pecking order, he knew, even in parking lots.

Someone was cleaning a green Jag belonging to one of the founding partners. Matt turned. One of Midlife's Harleys was there, covered by a see-through tarp. There was a tipped-over shopping cart. Three of the four wheels had been ripped off the cart. What would someone want with three shopping-cart wheels?

Matt's eyes drifted over the cars on the street, mostly gypsy cabs, and noticed a gray Ford Taurus because the license plate was MLH-472, and Matt's own initials were MKH, pretty close, and things like that were distractions.

But once in his car – once alone with his thoughts – something new started gnawing at him.

Okay, he thought, trying his best to stay rational. Let's assume the worst – that what he saw on the camera phone were the opening moments of a tryst of some kind.

Why would Olivia send it to him?

What would be the point? Did she want to get caught? Was this a cry for help? That didn't really add up.

But then he realized something else: Olivia hadn't sent it.

289

It had come from her phone, yes, but she – assuming that was Olivia with the platinum wig – didn't seem to realize that the camera was on her. He remembered thinking that. She was the subject of the film – the filmee, if you will, not the filmer.

So who sent it? Was it Mr. Blue-Black Hair? If so, then who snapped the first picture, the one of Blue-Black? Had he taken it himself?

Answer: No.

Blue-Black had his palm up as if waving. Matt remembered the backside of a ring on his finger – or what he thought was a ring. He really wasn't up for looking at the picture again. But he thought about it. Could that have been a wedding band? No, the ring was on the right hand.

Either way, who had taken Blue-Black's picture?

Olivia?

Why would she send it to him? Or was the picture sent to him inadvertently? Like maybe someone hit the wrong number on the speed dial?

It seemed unlikely.

Was there a third person in the room?

Matt couldn't see it. He mulled it over some more, but nothing came together. Both calls had originated from his wife's phone. Got that. But if she was having an affair, why would she want him to know?

Answer – and yes, his reasoning was getting circular – she wouldn't.

So who would?

Matt thought again of the cocky smirk on Blue-Black's face. And his stomach roiled. When he was younger, he used to feel too much. Strange to imagine it now, but Matt had been too sensitive. He'd cry when he lost a basketball game, even a pickup game. Any slight would stay with him for weeks. All of that changed the night Stephen McGrath died. If prison teaches you one thing, it's how to deaden yourself. You show nothing. Ever. You never allow yourself anything, even an emotion, because it will either be exploited or taken away. Matt tried that now. He tried to deaden the sinking feeling in the pit of his belly.

He couldn't do it.

The images were back now, terrible ones blended in with achingly wonderful memories, the memories hurting most of all. He remembered a weekend he and Olivia had spent at a Victorian B&B in Lenox, Massachusetts. He remembered spreading pillows and blankets in front of the fireplace in the room and opening a bottle of wine. He remembered the way Olivia held the stem of the glass, the way she looked at him, the way the world, the past, his tentative, fearful steps all faded away, the way the fire reflected off her green eyes, and then he would think of her like that with another man.

A new thought hit him then – one so awful, so unbearable he nearly lost control of his car:

Olivia was pregnant.

The light turned red. Matt almost drove through it. He slammed on the brakes at the last moment. A pedestrian, already starting across the street, jumped back and waved his fist at him. Matt kept both hands on the wheel.

Olivia had taken a long time to conceive.

They were both in their mid-thirties and in Olivia's mind the clock was ticking. She so badly wanted to start a family. For a long time their attempts at conception hadn't gone well. Matt had started to wonder – and not just idly – if the fault lay with him. He had taken some pretty good beatings in prison. During his third week there, four men had pinned him down and spread-eagled his legs while a fifth kicked him hard in the groin. He had nearly passed out from the pain.

Now suddenly Olivia was pregnant.

He wanted to shut down his brain, but it wouldn't happen. Rage started to seep in. It was better, he thought, than the hurt, than the awful gut-wrenching ache of having something he cherished ripped away from him again.

He had to find her. He had to find her now.

Olivia was in Boston, a five-hour journey from where he now was. Screw the house inspection. Just drive up, have it out with her now.

Where was she staying?

He thought about that. Had she told him? He couldn't remember. That was another thing about having cell phones. You don't worry so much about things like that. What difference did it make if she was staying at the Marriott or the Hilton? She was on a business trip. She would be moving about, out at meetings and dinners, rarely in her room.

Easiest, of course, to reach her by cell phone.

So now what?

He had no idea where she was staying. And even if he did, wouldn't it make more sense to call first? For all he knew, that might not even be her hotel room he'd seen on the camera phone. It might have belonged to Blue-Black Hair. And suppose he did know the hotel. Suppose he did show up and pounded on the door and then, what, Olivia would open it in a negligee with Blue-Black standing behind her, a towel wrapped around his waist? Then what would Matt do? Beat the crap out of him? Point and shout 'Aha!'?

He tried calling her on the camera phone again. Still no answer. He didn't leave another message.

Why hadn't Olivia told him where she was staying?

Pretty obvious now, isn't it, Matt ol' boy?

The red curtain came down over his eyes.

Enough.

He tried her office, but the call went directly into her voice mail: '*Hi, this is Olivia Hunter. I'll be out of the office until Friday. If this is important, you can reach my assistant, Jamie Suh, by pressing her extension, six-four-four –*'

That was what Matt did. Jamie answered on the third ring.

'Olivia Hunter's line.'

'Hey, Jamie, it's Matt.'

'Hi, Matt.'

He kept his hands on the wheel and talked using a hands-free, which always felt weird – like you're a crazy person chatting with an imaginary friend. When you talk on a phone, you should be holding one. 'Just got a quick question for you.'

'Shoot.'

'Do you know what hotel Olivia's staying in?'

There was no reply.

'Jamie?'

'I'm here,' she said. 'Uh, I can look it up, if you want to hold on. But why don't you just call her cell? That's the number she left if any client had an emergency.'

He was not sure how to reply to that without sounding somehow desperate. If he told her he had tried that and got the message, Jamie Suh would wonder why he couldn't simply wait for her to reply. He wracked his brain for something that sounded plausible.

'Yeah, I know,' he said. 'But I want to send her flowers. You know, as a surprise.'

'Oh, I see.' There was little enthusiasm in her voice. 'Is it a special occasion?'

'No.' Then he added extra-lamely: 'But hey, the honeymoon is still on.' He laughed at his own pitiful line. Not surprisingly, Jamie did not.

There was a long silence.

'You still there?' Matt said.

'Yes.'

'Could you tell me where she's staying?'

'I'm looking it up now.' There was the tapping sound of her fingers on a keyboard. Then: 'Matt?'

'Yes.'

'I have another call coming in. Can I call you back when I find it?'

'Sure,' he said, not liking this at all. He gave her his cell phone number and hung up.

What the hell was going on?

His phone vibrated again. He checked the number. It was the office. Rolanda didn't bother with hellos.

'Problem,' she said. 'Where are you?'

'Just hitting seventy-eight.'

'Turn around. Washington Street. Eva is getting evicted.'

He swore under his breath. 'Who?'

'Pastor Jill is over there with those two beefy sons of hers. They threatened Eva.'

Pastor Jill. A woman who got her religious degree online and sets up 'charities' where the youth can stay with her as long as they cough up enough in food stamps. The scams run on the poor are beyond reprehensible. Matt veered the car to the right.

'On my way,' he said.

Ten minutes later he pulled to a stop on Washington Street. The neighborhood was near Branch Brook Park. As a kid Matt used to play tennis here. He played competitively for a while, his parents schlepping him to tournaments in Port Washington every other weekend. He was even ranked in the boys' fourteen-and-under division. But the family stopped coming to Branch Brook way before that. Matt never understood what happened to Newark. It had been a thriving, wonderful community. The wealthier eventually moved out during the suburban migration of the fifties and sixties. That was natural, of course. It happened everywhere. But Newark was abandoned. Those who left – even those who traveled just a few miles away – never looked back. Part of that was the riots in the late sixties. Part of that was simple racism. But there was something more here, something worse, and Matt didn't know exactly what it was.

He got out of the car. The neighborhood was predominantly African American. So were most of his clients. Matt wondered about that. During his prison stint, he heard the 'n'-word more often than any other. He had said it himself, to fit in at first, but it became less repulsive as time went on, which of course was the most repulsive thing of all.

In the end he'd been forced to betray what he had always believed in, the liberal suburban lie about skin color not mattering. In prison, skin color was all that mattered. Out here, in a whole different way, it mattered just as much.

His gaze glided over the scenery. It got snagged on an interesting chunk of graffiti. On a wall of chipped brick, someone had spray-painted two words in four-foot-high letters:

BITCHES LIE!

Normally Matt would not stop and study something like this. Today he did. The letters were red and slanted. Even if you couldn't read, you could feel the rage here. Matt wondered about the creator – what inspired him to write this. He wondered if this act of vandalism had diluted the creator's wrath – or been the first step toward greater destruction.

He walked toward Eva's building. Pastor Jill's car, a fully loaded Mercedes 560, was there. One of her sons stood guard with his arms crossed, his face set on scowl. Matt's eyes started their sweep again. The neighbors were out and about. One small child of maybe two sat atop an old lawn mower. His mother was using it as a stroller. She muttered to herself and looked strung out. People stared at Matt – a white man was not unfamiliar here but still a curiosity.

Pastor Jill's sons glared as he approached. The street went quiet, like in a Western. The people were ready for a showdown.

Matt said, 'How are you doing?'

The brothers might have been twins. One kept up the stare. The other started loading Eva's belongings into the trunk. Matt did not blink. He kept smiling and walking.

'I'd like you to stop that now.'

Crossed-Tree-Trunk-Arms said, 'Who are you?'

Pastor Jill came out. She looked over at Matt and scowled too.

'You can't throw her out,' Matt said.

Pastor Jill gave him the high-and-mighty. 'I own this residence.'

'No, the state owns it. You claim it's charitable housing for the city's youths.'

'Eva didn't follow the rules.'

'What rules are those?'

'We are a religious institution. We have a strict moral code here. Eva here broke it.'

'How?'

Pastor Jill smiled. 'I'm not sure that's any of your concern. May I ask your name?'

Her two sons exchanged a glance. One put down Eva's stuff. They turned toward him.

Matt pointed at Pastor Jill's Mercedes. 'Sweet wheels.'

The brothers frowned and strolled toward him. One cracked his neck as he strutted. The other opened and closed fists. Matt felt his blood hum. Strangely enough the death of Stephen McGrath – the 'slip' – hadn't made him fearful of violence. Perhaps if he had been more aggressive that night, not less . . . but that wasn't what mattered now. He had learned a valuable lesson about physical confrontations: You can predict nothing. Sure, whoever lands the first blow usually wins. The bigger man was usually victorious too. But once it got going, once the red tornado took hold of the combatants, anything could happen.

The Neck Cracker said, 'Who are you?' again.

Matt would not risk it. He sighed and took out his camera phone. 'I'm Bob Smiley, Channel Nine News.'

That stopped them.

He pointed the camera in their direction and pretended to turn it on. 'If you don't mind, I'm going to film what you're doing here. The Channel Nine News van will be here for clearer shots in three minutes.'

The brothers looked back at their mother. Pastor Jill's face broke into a beatific albeit phony smile.

'We're helping Eva move,' she said. 'To better quarters.'

'Uh huh.'

'But if she'd rather just stay here . . .'

'She'd rather stay here,' Matt said.

'Milo, move her things back into the apartment.'

Milo, the Neck Cracker, gave Matt the fish eye. Matt held up the camera. 'Hold that pose, Milo.' Milo and Fist Flex started to take the stuff out of the van. Pastor Jill hurried to her Mercedes and waited in the back. Eva looked down at Matt from the window and mouthed a thank-you. Matt nodded and turned away.

It was then, turning away, not really looking at anything, that Matt saw the gray Ford Taurus.

The car was idling about thirty yards behind him. Matt froze. Gray Ford Tauruses were plentiful, of course, perhaps the most popular car in the country. Seeing two in a day would hardly be uncommon. Matt figured that there was probably another Ford Taurus on this very block. Maybe two or three. And he would not be surprised to learn that another one might even be gray.

But would it have a license plate that started with MLH, so close to his own initials of MKH?

His eyes stayed glued to the license plate.

MLH-472.

The same car he'd seen outside his office.

Matt tried to keep his breathing even. It could, he knew, be nothing more than a coincidence. Taking a step back, that was indeed a strong possibility. A person could see the same car twice in a day. He was only, what, half a mile away from his office. This was a fairly congested neighborhood. There was no big shock here.

On a normal day – check that: On pretty much *any* other day – Matt would have let that logic win him over.

But not today. He hesitated, but not for very long. Then he headed toward the car.

'Hey,' Milo shouted, 'where you going?'

'Just keep unloading, big man.'

Matt hadn't moved five steps when the front wheels of the Ford Taurus started to angle themselves to move out of the spot. Matt hurried his pace.

Without warning, the Taurus jumped forward and cut across the street. The white taillights came on and the car jerked back. Matt realized that the driver planned on making a K turn. The driver hit the brake and turned the steering wheel hard and fast. Matt was only a few feet from the back window.

Matt yelled, 'Wait!' – as if that would do any good – and broke into a sprint. He leapt in front of the car.

Bad move.

The Taurus's tire grabbed gravel, made a little shriek, and shot toward him.

There was no slowdown, no hesitation. Matt jumped to the side. The Taurus accelerated. Matt was off the ground now, horizontal. The bumper clipped his ankle. A burst of pain exploded through the bone. The momentum swung Matt around in midair. He landed face-first and tucked into a roll. He ended up on his back.

For a few moments Matt lay there blinking into the sunlight. People gathered around him. 'You all right?' someone asked. He nodded and sat up. He checked his ankle. Bruised hard but no break. Someone helped him to his feet.

The whole thing – from the moment he saw the car to the moment it tried to run him down – had maybe taken five, maybe ten seconds. Certainly no more. Matt stared off.

Someone had been – at the very least – following him.

He checked his pocket. The cell phone was still there. He limped back toward Eva's apartment. Pastor Jill and her sons were gone. He checked to make sure Eva was okay. Then he got into his own car and took a deep breath. He thought about what to do and realized that the first step was fairly obvious.

He dialed her private line number. When Cingle answered, he asked, 'You in your office?'

'Yup,' Cingle said.

'I'll be there in five minutes.'

6

As soon as county homicide investigator Loren Muse opened her apartment door, the waft of cigarette smoke attacked. Loren let it. She stood there and sucked in a deep breath.

Her garden apartment was on Morris Avenue in Union, New Jersey. She never understood the term 'garden.' The place was a pit – all brick, no personality, and nothing resembling green. This was New Jersey's version of purgatory, a way station, the place people stayed on the way up or down economic and social ladders. Young couples lived here until they could afford the house. Unlucky pensioners returned here after the kids flew the coop.

And, of course, single women on the verge of old-maidhood who worked too hard and entertained too little – they ended up here too.

Loren was thirty-four years old, a serial dater who, to quote her cigarette-toting mother who was currently on the couch, 'never closed the sale.' The cop-thing worked like that. It initially attracted men and then sent them scurrying when the commitment-aka-expiration date approached. She was currently dating a guy named Pete whom her mother labeled a 'total loser,' and Loren had trouble arguing with that assessment.

Her two cats, Oscar and Felix, were nowhere in sight, but that was normal. Her mother, the lovely Carmen Valos Muse Brewster Whatever, lay sprawled on the couch watching *Jeopardy!* She watched the show nearly every day and had never gotten a question right.

'Hey,' Loren said.

'This place is a pigsty,' her mother said.

'Then clean it. Or better yet, move out.'

Carmen had recently split with Husband Four. Her mother was a good-looking woman – far better looking than the plain daughter who'd taken after her suicidal father. Still sexy, though now it was in a sort of sloppy-seconds way. Her looks were starting to droop, but she still landed better dates than Loren. Men loved Carmen Valos Muse Etcetera.

Carmen turned back to the television and took another deep puff of the cigarette.

Loren said, 'I told you a thousand times not to smoke in here.'

'You smoke.'

'No, Ma, I quit.'

Carmen turned the big browns in her direction, blinking seductively out of habit.

'You quit?'

'Yes.'

'Oh, come on. Two months? That's not quitting.'

'It's five months.'

'Still. Didn't you smoke in here?'

'So?'

'So what's the big deal? It's not like the smell is gone or anything. It's not like this is one of those fancy no-smoking hotel rooms. Right?'

Her mother gave her the familiar judgmental eye, sizing Loren up the way she always did and finding her wanting the way she always did. Loren waited for the inevitable 'just trying to help' beauty tip: Your hair could use some shape, you should wear something clingier, why do you have to look like a boy, have you seen the new push-up bras at Victoria's Secret, would a little makeup kill you, short girls should never go out without heels . . .

Carmen's mouth opened and the phone rang.

'Hold that thought,' Loren said.

She picked up the receiver.

'Yo, Squirt, it's *moi*.'

'*Moi*' was Eldon Teak, a sixty-two-year-old Caucasian grandfather who only listened to rap music. Eldon was also the Essex County medical examiner.

'What's up, Eldon?'

'You catch the Stacked Nun case?'

'That's what you're calling it?'

'Until we come up with something funnier. I liked Our Lady with the Valley or Mount Saint Mountains, but no one else did.'

She gently rubbed her eyes with an index finger and thumb. 'You got something for me?'

'I do.'

'Like?'

'Like the death wasn't accidental.'

'She was murdered?'

'Yup. Pillow over the face.'

'God, how the hell did they miss that?'

'How the hell did who miss that?'

'Wasn't she originally listed as death by natural causes?'

'Yes.'

'Well, Eldon, see, that's what I mean when I say, how the hell did they miss that?'

'And I asked you who you meant.'

'Whoever originally examined her.'

'No one originally examined her. That's the point.'

'Why not?'

'You're kidding, right?'

'No. I mean, shouldn't that have shown up right away?'

'You watch too much TV. Every day zillions of people die, right? Wife finds the husband dead on the floor. You think we do an autopsy? You think we check to see if it's murder? Most of the time cops don't even come in. My old man croaked, what, ten years ago. My mom called the funeral home, a doc declares him dead, they pick him up. That's how it normally works, you know that. So here a nun dies, looks like natural causes to anyone who doesn't know exactly what to look for. I would have never gotten her on the table if your Mother Superior doesn't say something.'

'You sure it was a pillow?'

'Yup. Pillow in her room, matter of fact. Plenty of fibers in the throat.'

'How about under her fingernails?'

'They're clean.'

'Isn't that unusual?'

'Depends.'

Loren shook her head, tried to put it together. 'You have an ID?'

'An ID on what?'

'On the victim?'

'I thought she was Sister Silicon or something. What do we need an ID for?'

Loren checked her watch. 'How much longer are you in the office?'

'Another two hours,' Eldon Teak said.

'I'm on my way.'

7

Here is how you find your soul mate.

It is spring break your freshman year of college. Most of your friends head down to Daytona Beach, but your high school bud Rick has a mother in the travel business. She gets you super-low rates to Vegas, so you and six friends go for a five-night stay at the Flamingo Hotel.

On the last night, you head to a nightclub at Caesars Palace because you hear it's supposed to be a great hangout for coeds on vacation. The nightclub, no surprise, is noisy and crowded. There is too much neon. It is not your scene. You are with your friends, trying to hear them over the loud crush of music, when you look across the bar.

That is when you see Olivia for the first time.

No, the music doesn't stop or segue to angelic harps. But something happens to you. You look at her and feel it in your chest, a warm twang, and you can see that she feels it too.

You are normally shy, not good with approaches, but tonight you can do no wrong. You make your way over to her and introduce yourself. We all have special nights like this, you think. You're at a party and you see a beautiful girl and she's looking at you and you start talking and you just click in a way that makes you think about lifetimes instead of one-nights.

You talk to her. You talk for hours. She looks at you as if you're the only person in the world. You go somewhere quieter. You kiss her. She responds. You start to make out. You make out all night and have no real desire to push it any further. You hold her. You talk some more. You love her laugh. You love her face. You love everything about her.

You fall asleep in each other's arms, fully clothed, and you wonder if you will ever be this happy again. Her hair smells like lilacs and berries. You will never forget that smell.

You'd do anything to make this last, but you know it won't. These sorts of interactions aren't built for the long term. You have a life, and Olivia has a 'serious' boy-friend, a fiancé really, back home. This isn't about that. It is about the two of you, your own world, for just too brief a time. You pack a small life span into that night, a complete cycle of courtship, relationship, breakup into those few hours.

In the end, you will go back to your life and she'll go back to hers.

You don't bother trading phone numbers – neither one of you wants to pretend like that – but she takes you to the airport and you passionately kiss good-bye. Her eyes are wet when you release her. You return to school.

You go on, of course, but you never quite forget her or that night or the way it felt to kiss her or the smell of her hair. She stays with you. You think of her. Not every day, maybe not even every week. But she's there. The memory is something you take out every now and then, when you're feeling alone, and you don't know if it comforts or stings.

You wonder if she ever does the same.

Eleven years pass. You don't see her in all that time.

You are no longer the same person, of course. The death of Stephen McGrath had set you off the rails. You have spent time in prison. But you're free now. Your life has been given back to you, you guess. You work at the Carter Sturgis law firm.

One day you sign onto the computer and Google her name.

You know it is stupid and immature. You realize that she probably married the fiancé, has three or four kids by now, maybe taken her husband's name. But this is harmless. You will take it no further. You are simply curious.

There are several Olivia Murrays.

You search a little deeper and find one that might be her. This Olivia Murray is the sales director for DataBetter, a consulting business that designs computer systems for small-to-midsize companies. DataBetter's Web site has employee biographies. Hers is brief but it does mention that she is a graduate of the University of Virginia. That was where your Olivia Murray was going when you met all those years ago.

You try to forget about it.

You are not one who believes in fate or kismet – just the opposite – but six months later, the partners at Carter Sturgis decide that the firm's computer system needs to be overhauled. Midlife knows that you learned about computer programming during your tenure in prison. He suggests that you be on the committee to develop a new office network. You suggest several firms come in and make bids.

One of those firms is DataBetter.

Two people from DataBetter arrive at the offices of Carter Sturgis. You are in a panic. In the end, you fake an emergency and don't attend the presentation. That would be too much – showing up like that. You let the other three men on the committee handle the interview. You stay in your office. Your leg shakes. You bite your nails. You feel like an idiot.

At noon, there is a knock on your office door.

You turn and Olivia is there.

You recognize her right away. It hits you like a physical blow. The warm twang is back. You can barely speak. You look at her left hand. At her ring finger.

There is nothing there.

Olivia smiles and tells you that she's here at Carter Sturgis doing a presentation. You try to nod. Her company is bidding to set up the firm's computer systems, she says. She spotted your name on the list of people who were supposed to be at the meeting and wondered if you were the same Matt Hunter she met all those years ago.

Still stunned, you ask her if she wants to grab a cup of coffee. She hesitates but says yes. When you rise and walk past her, you smell her hair. The lilacs and berries are still there, and you worry that your eyes will well up.

You both gloss over the phony catch-up preliminaries, which, of course, works well for you. Over the years she has thought about you too, you find out. The fiancé is long gone. She has never been married.

Your heart soars even as you shake your head. You know that this is all too impossible. Neither of you believes in concepts like love at first sight.

But there you are.

In the weeks that follow you learn what true love is. She teaches it to you. You eventually tell her the truth about your past. She gets over it. You get married. She becomes pregnant. You are happy. You both celebrate the news by buying matching camera phones.

And then, one day, you get a call and see the woman you met during that long-ago spring break – the only woman you ever loved – in a hotel room with another man.

Why the hell would someone be following him?

Matt kept his hands steady on the wheel as his head spun with possibilities. He sorted through them. Nothing stuck.

He needed help, big-time. And that meant visiting Cingle.

He was going to be late for his appointment with the home inspector. He didn't much care. Suddenly the future he had allowed himself to imagine – house, picket fence, the always-beautiful Olivia, the 2.4 kids, the Lab retriever – seemed frighteningly unrealistic. More fooling himself, he guessed. A convicted murderer returning to the suburbs he grew up in and raising the ideal family – it suddenly sounded like a bad sitcom pitch.

Matt called Marsha, his sister-in-law, to tell her he wouldn't get out there until later, but her machine picked up. He left a message and pulled into the lot.

Housed in a building of sleek glass not far from Matt's office is MVD – Most Valuable Detection, a large private-eye firm Carter Sturgis uses. By and large Matt was not a huge fan of private detectives. In fiction they were pretty cool dudes. In reality they were, at best, retired (emphasis on the 'tired') cops and at worst, guys who couldn't become cops and thus are that dangerous creation known as the 'cop wannabe.' Matt had seen plenty of wannabes working as prison guards. The mixture of failure and imagined testosterone produced volatile and often ugly consequences.

Matt sat in the office of one of the exceptions to this rule – the lovely and controversial Ms. Cingle Shaker. Matt didn't think that was her real name, but it was the one she used professionally. Cingle was six feet tall with blue eyes and honey-colored hair. Her face was fairly attractive. Her body caused heart arrhythmia – a total, no-let-up traffic-stopper. Even Olivia said 'Wow' when she met her. Rumor had it that Cingle had been a Rockette at Radio City Music Hall, but that the other girls complained that she ruined their 'symmetry.' Matt did not doubt it.

Cingle had her feet up on her desk. She had on cowboy boots that added another two inches to her height and dark jeans that fit like leggings. Up top, she wore a black turtleneck that on some women would be considered clingy but on Cingle could legitimately draw a citation for indecency.

'It was a New Jersey plate,' Matt told her for the third time. 'MLH-472.'

Cingle hadn't moved. She rested her chin in the L made by her thumb and index finger. She stared at him.

'What?' Matt said.

'What client am I supposed to bill for this?'

'No client,' he said. 'You bill me.'

'This is for you then.'

'Yes.'

'Hmm.' Cingle dropped her feet to the floor, stretched back, smiled. 'So this is personal?'

'Man,' Matt said, 'you are good. I tell you to bill *me*, that it's for *me*, and bang, you figure out that it's personal.'

'Years of detecting, Hunter. Don't be intimidated.'

Matt tried to force up a smile.

She kept her eyes on him. 'Want to hear one of the ten rules from the Cingle Shaker Book of Detection?'

'No, not really.'

'Rule Six: When a man asks you to look up a license plate for personal reasons, it can be only one of two things. One' – Cingle raised a finger – 'he thinks his wife is cheating and he wants to know who with.'

'And two?'

'There's no two. I lied. There's only one.'

'That's not it.'

Cingle shook her head.

'What?'

'Ex-cons usually lie better.'

He let that one alone.

'Okay, so let's say I believe you. Why, pray tell, do we want me to trace this down?'

'It's personal. Remember? Bill *me*, for *me*, personal?'

Cingle stood up, waaay up, and put her hands on her hips. She glared down at him. Unlike Olivia, Matt did not say 'Wow' out loud, but maybe he thought it.

'Think of me as your religious advisor,' she said. 'Confession is good for the soul, you know.'

'Yeah,' Matt said. 'Religion. That's what comes to mind.' He sat up. 'Will you just do this for me?'

'Okeydokey.' She stared at him another beat. Matt did not cringe. Cingle sat back down and threw her feet back on the desk. 'The standing up with the hands on the hips. That usually weakens a guy.'

'I'm stone.'

'Well, yes, that's part of it.'

'Ha, ha.'

She gave him the curious look again. 'You love Olivia, right?'

'I'm not getting into this with you, Cingle.'

'You don't have to answer. I've seen you with her. And her with you.'

'So you know then.'

She sighed. 'Give me the plate number again.'

He did. This time Cingle wrote it down.

'Shouldn't take more than an hour. I'll call you on your cell.'

'Thanks.' He started for the door.

'Matt?'

He turned back toward her.

'I've had some experience in stuff like this.'

'I'm sure.'

302

'Opening this door.' Cingle held up the slip of paper with the license plate. 'It's kinda like trying to break up a fight. Once you jump in, you don't know what could happen.'

'Gee, Cingle, that's pretty subtle.'

She spread her arms. 'Subtlety ended for me the day I hit puberty.'

'Just do this for me, okay?'

'I will.'

'Thank you.'

'But' – she put up her index finger – 'should you feel the need to take it further, I want you to promise to let me help.'

'I won't take it further,' he said, and the look on her face told him all he needed to know about how much she believed him.

Matt was just entering his old hometown of Livingston when his cell phone rang again. It was Jamie Suh, Olivia's assistant, finally calling back. 'Sorry, Matt, I can't find a hotel contact.'

'How can that be?' he snapped without thinking.

There was too long a pause.

He tried to backtrack. 'I mean, doesn't she usually leave one? Suppose there was an emergency.'

'She has her cell phone.'

He didn't know what to say.

'And most of the time,' Jamie went on, 'I book the hotel for her.'

'You didn't this time?'

'No.' Then she hurriedly added: 'But that's not unusual or anything. Olivia does it herself sometimes too.'

He didn't know what to make of that. 'Have you heard from her today?'

'She called in this morning.'

'Did she say where she was going to be?'

There was another pause. Matt knew that his behavior would be considered beyond the scope of normal husbandly curiosity, but he figured it was worth the risk.

'She just said she had some meetings. Nothing specific.'

'Okay, if she calls back –'

'I'll tell her you're looking for her.'

Then Jamie hung up.

Another memory struck him. He and Olivia had a huge fight, one of those no-holds-barred verbal brawls where you know you're wrong and you just keep pushing. She ran out in tears and didn't call for two days. Two full days. He would call, she wouldn't answer. He searched, but he couldn't find her. It punched a huge hole in his heart. That was what he remembered right now. The idea that she would never come back to him hurt so much he could barely breathe.

The home inspector was just finishing up when he arrived at the house. Nine years ago Matt walked out of jail after serving four years for killing a man. Now, incredible as it might seem, he was on the verge of buying a home, sharing it with the woman he loved, raising a child.

He shook his head.

The house was part of a suburban tract built in 1965. Like most of Livingston, the area used to be a farm. All the houses were pretty much the same, but if that discouraged Olivia, she hid it pretty well. She'd stared at the house with a nearly religious fervor and whispered, 'It's perfect.' Her enthusiasm had swept away any doubts he'd had about moving back.

Matt stood on what would soon be his front yard and tried to imagine himself living here. It felt odd. He didn't belong here anymore. He had known that until, well, until Olivia. Now he was back.

Behind him a police cruiser pulled up. Two men got out. The first one was in uniform. He was young and in shape. He gave Matt the cop squint. The second man was in plainclothes.

'Hey, Matt,' the man in the brown suit called out. 'Long time, no see.'

It had been a long time, since Livingston High at least, but he recognized Lance Banner right away.

'Hi, Lance.'

Both men slammed their doors closed as if they'd coordinated the move. The uniform crossed his arms and remained silent. Lance moved toward Matt.

'You know,' Lance said, 'I live on this street.'

'That a fact.'

'It is.'

Matt said nothing.

'I'm a detective on the force now.'

'Congrats.'

'Thanks.'

How long had he known Lance Banner? Since second grade, at least. They were never friends, never enemies. They played on the same Little League team for three years running. They shared a gym class in eighth grade and a study hall junior year of high school. Livingston High School had been big – six hundred kids per grade. They'd simply traveled in different circles.

'How's it been going for you?' Lance asked.

'Super.'

The home inspector stepped outside. He had a clipboard. Lance said, 'How's it look, Harold?'

Harold looked up from his clipboard and nodded. 'Pretty solid, Lance.'

'You sure?'

Something in his tone made Harold take a step back. Lance looked back at Matt.

'We have a nice neighborhood here.'

'It's why we picked it.'

'You really think it's a good idea, Matt?'

'What's that, Lance?'

'Moving back.'

'Done my time.'

'And you think that's the end of it?'

Matt didn't say anything.

'That boy you killed. He's still dead, isn't he?'

'Lance?'

'I'm Detective Banner now,' he said.

'Detective Banner, I'm going inside now.'

'I read all about your case. I even called a couple of cop buddies, got the whole scoop on what happened.'

Matt looked at him. The man had gray flecks in his eyes. He had put on weight. His fingers kept itching and Matt didn't like the way he smiled at him. Lance Banner's family had worked this land as farmers. His grandfather or maybe it was his great-grandfather had sold the land for a song. The Banners still considered Livingston their town. They were the soil here. The father drank too much. So did Lance's two dull brothers. Lance, on the other hand, always hit Matt as being pretty sharp.

'Then you know it was an accident,' Matt said.

Lance Banner nodded slowly. 'Could be.'

'So why the hard time, Lance?'

'Because you're an ex-con.'

'You think I should have gone to prison?'

'Tough call,' he said, rubbing his chin. 'But from what I read, I think you got a bad break.'

'So?'

'So you did. Go to prison, I mean.'

'I don't understand.'

'Society wants to peddle that rehabilitation crap on the public, hey, that's fine with me. But I' – he pointed to himself – 'know better. And you' – he turned the finger toward Matt – 'know better.'

Matt said nothing.

'You may have gone into that place an okay guy. But you want to tell me you're the same man now?'

Matt knew that there was no right answer to that one. He turned and started toward the door.

Lance said, 'Maybe your home inspector will find something. Give you a way to back out.'

Matt went inside and finished up with the inspector. There were several issues – some pipe problem, one overloaded breaker – but they were all small. He and Harold finished up, and Matt started for Marsha's house.

He pulled into the tree-lined street where his nephews and sister-in-law – was she still considered a sister-in-law after your brother died? 'Ex' certainly didn't sound right – resided. The boys, Paul and Ethan, were on the front lawn rolling in the leaves. Their babysitter, Kyra, was with them. Kyra Walsh was a recent freshman-transfer taking summer classes at William Paterson University. She rented a room above Marsha's garage. Kyra had come highly recommended from someone at Marsha's church, and while Matt had been initially skeptical of the whole idea of a live-in babysitter (nonetheless a college student) it seemed to be working great. Kyra ended up being a pretty terrific kid, a fresh-faced burst of needed sunshine from one of the 'I' states in the Midwest, he could never remember which one.

Matt stepped out of the car. Kyra shaded her eyes with one hand and waved with the other. She smiled as only the young can. 'Hi, Matt.'

'Hey, Kyra.'

The boys heard his voice and turned their heads like dogs hearing their owner rummaging for treats. They sprinted at him, calling, 'Uncle Matt! Uncle Matt!'

Matt felt a sudden lightness in his chest. A smile played with the corner of his lips as the boys rushed him. Ethan grabbed hold of Matt's right leg. Paul aimed for the midsection.

'McNabb back to pass,' Matt said, doing his best Greg Gumbel impression. 'Look out! Strahan breaks through the line and has a leg . . .'

Paul stopped. 'I want to be Strahan!' he demanded.

Ethan would have none of that. 'No, I want to be Strahan!'

'Hey, you both can be Strahan,' Matt said.

The two youngsters squinted at their uncle as if he were the slow kid sitting in the back. 'You can't have two Michael Strahans,' Paul said.

'Yeah,' his brother chimed in.

Then they lowered their shoulders and hit him again. Matt performed a near Pacino-esque performance of a quarterback about to be sacked. He stutter-stepped, he looked desperately for imaginary receivers, he pump-faked a pass with his invisible football, and ultimately he went down in a slow-motion heap.

'Woo-hoo!' The boys stood, high-fived each other, bumped chests. Matt groaned into a sitting position. Kyra was smothering a giggle.

Paul and Ethan were still doing a celebration dance when Marsha appeared at the door. She looked, Matt thought, very nice. She wore a dress and makeup. Her hair had that carefully mussed thing going on. The car keys were already jiggling in her hand.

When Bernie died, Matt and Marsha had both been so devastated, so desperate, that they tried to knit something together where Matt could maybe take over as husband and father.

It was a disaster.

Matt and Marsha had waited a proper amount of time – six months – and then one night, without discussing it but knowing what was about to happen, they both got drunk. Marsha made the first move. She kissed him, kissed him hard, and then she started to sob. That had been the end.

Before 'the slip,' Matt's family had been strangely blessed or maybe just bless-edly naïve. Matt had been twenty years old and all four of his grandparents were alive and in good health – two in Miami, two in Scottsdale. Tragedy had visited other families, but the Hunters had been left alone. The slip changed all that. It left them ill prepared for what followed.

Tragedy sort of works this way: Once it snakes its way in, it cuts down all your defenses and allows its brethren easy access to feed. Three of his four grandparents died during Matt's stint in prison. The burden killed his father and sapped his mother. Mom fled to Florida. Their sister ran west to Seattle. Bernie had the aneurysm.

Just like that, they were all gone.

Matt stood up. He waved to Marsha. She waved back. Kyra said, 'Is it okay if I go?'

Marsha nodded. 'Thanks, Kyra.'

'No problem.' Kyra slipped on the backpack. 'Bye, Matt.'

'Bye, kiddo.'

Matt's cell phone rang. The caller ID told him it was Cingle Shaker. He signaled to Marsha that he needed to take it. She gestured for him to go ahead. Matt moved toward the curb and picked it up.

'Hello.'

'Got some info on the license plate,' Cingle said.

'Go ahead.'

'It's a rental. Avis at Newark Airport.'

'So does that mean it's a dead end?'

'For most private investigators, most definitely. But you're dealing with a near legend in the business.'

'Near?'

'I'm trying to be modest.'

'Doesn't work on you, Cingle.'

'Yeah, but the effort is there. I called a contact at the airport. He ran it down for me. The car was rented by one Charles Talley. You know him?'

'No.'

'I figured the name might mean something to you.'

'It doesn't.'

'You want me to check this Talley guy out?'

'Yes.'

'Call you back.'

She hung up. Matt started to lower the phone when he spotted the same police cruiser turning onto the block. It slowed as it passed Marsha's house. The uniformed cop who'd been with Lance eyed him. Matt eyed him back and felt his face flush.

Paul and Ethan stood and watched the cruiser. Matt turned back to Marsha. She saw it too. He tried to smile and wave it off. Marsha frowned.

That was when his phone rang again.

Still watching Marsha, Matt put the phone to his ear without checking the caller ID.

'Hello,' he said.

'Hi, hon, how was your day?'

It was Olivia.

8

Television shows, Loren knew, had convinced people that cops commonly meet with medical examiners in a morgue over a corpse. In reality that pretty much never happens. Loren was grateful for that. She was not squeamish or any of that, but she wanted death to be a constant shock to her. She didn't make jokes at the scene. She didn't try to block or use other defense mechanisms to look past it. For Loren a morgue is too matter-of-fact, too casual, too mundane about murder.

Loren was about to open Eldon's office door when Trevor Wine, a fellow homicide investigator, stepped out. Trevor was overweight and old-school. He tolerated Loren as one might a cute pet that sometimes pees on the good carpet.

'Hey, Squirt,' he said to her.

'You catch a homicide?'

'Yup.' Trevor Wine pulled up his belt. He had that weird kind of fat where you can never get the waist to perch and stay. 'Gunshot victim. Two to the head at close range.'

'Robbery, gang, what?'

'Maybe a robbery, definitely not a gang. The vic was a retired white guy.'

'Where did you find the body?'

'Near the Hebrew cemetery off Fourteenth Avenue. We think he's a tourist.'

'A tourist in that neighborhood?' Loren made a face. 'What's there to see?'

Trevor faked a laugh and put a meaty hand on her shoulder. 'I'll let you know when I know.' He didn't add 'little lady' but he might as well have. 'See you later, Squirt.'

'Yeah, later.'

He moved away. Loren opened the door.

Eldon sat at his desk. He wore a pair of clean scrubs. Eldon always wore scrubs. His office had absolutely no personality or color. When Eldon first took the job he wanted to change that, but when people came into this room to hear the details of the death, they wanted nothing stimulating any of the senses. So Eldon shifted the décor into neutral.

'Here,' Eldon said, 'catch.'

He tossed her something. Instinctively Loren caught it. It was a plastic bag, filmy and yellow. There was some sort of gel inside it. Eldon held a matching bag in his hand.

'Is this . . . ?'

Eldon nodded. 'A well-used and thus well-soiled breast implant.'

'Can I just say for the record, "Eeuw"?'

'You may.'

Loren held the bag up to the light and frowned. 'I thought implants were clear.'

'They start off that way – at least the saline ones.'

'These aren't saline?'

'Nope. Silicone. And they've been marinating in bosom for well over a decade.'

Loren tried not to make a face. There was some sort of gel inside them. Eldon arched an eyebrow and started to knead the implant.

'Cut that out.'

He shrugged. 'Anyway, these belong to your Sister of the Immaculate Hooters.'

'And you're showing them to me because . . . ?'

'Because they offer us clues.'

'I'm listening.'

'First off, they're silicone.'

'So you said.'

'Remember, what, five, ten years ago when they had the big cancer scare?'

'The implants were leaking.'

'Right. So the companies were forced to move to saline.'

'Aren't some people moving back now to silicone?'

'Yes, but the point remains: These are old. Very old. Well over a decade.'

She nodded. 'Okay, good, that's a start.'

'There's more.' Eldon took out a magnifying glass. He flipped one of the implants over. 'See this here?'

Loren took the magnifying glass. 'It's a tag.'

'See that number over on the bottom?'

'Yes.'

'That's the serial number. This is true with pretty much any surgical implant – knees, hips, breasts, pacemaker, whatever. The device has to have a serial number.'

Loren nodded. 'And the manufacturer keeps records.'

'Exactly.'

'So if we call the manufacturer and give them the serial number . . .'

'We learn the real name of Mother with the Superiors.'

Loren looked up. 'Thanks.'

'There's a problem.'

She sat back.

'The company that made the implants was named SurgiCo. They went under eight years ago.'

'And their records?'

Eldon shrugged. 'We're trying to look into it. Look, it's late. We won't get anything tonight. I'm hoping to find out what happened to the records in the morning.'

'Okay. Anything else?'

'You asked why there were no fibers under her fingernails.'

'Yes.'

'We're still running a full tox report. It could be that she was drugged, but I don't think that was it.'

'You have another theory.'

'I do.'

'What's that?'

Eldon leaned back and crossed his legs. He turned to the side and stared at the wall. 'There was slight bruising along both inner biceps.'

Loren's eyes narrowed. 'I'm not following.'

'If a man were very strong and, uh, knowledgeable, he could sneak up on a sleeping woman,' he began, his voice almost singsong, as if he were talking to a child. 'He might flip the woman onto her back – or maybe she slept that way. He'd straddle her chest, pin her arms down with his knees – that, if he was careful and professional, could be done so as to leave very little bruising – and then he'd smother her with a pillow.'

The room dropped ten degrees. Loren's voice was barely a whisper. 'You think that's what happened here?'

'We have to wait for the full tox,' Eldon said, turning away from the wall and looking directly at her. 'But yeah. Yeah, I think that's what happened here.'

She said nothing.

'There's one more thing that backs my theory up. It could help us.' Eldon put a photograph on the desk. A headshot of the nun. Her eyes were closed as if she were expecting a facial. She'd been in her early sixties, but the lines had all been smoothed away in death. 'You know anything about fingerprints on the skin?'

'Just that they're hard to pick up.'

'Nearly impossible, if you don't catch the corpse right away. Most of the major studies are telling us to try to pick up the fingerprints at the crime scene if possible. At a minimum the lab guys should make sure the body is glue fumed right away to preserve the prints before the vic is packed away.'

Forensic detail was not Loren's forte. 'Uh huh.'

'Well, it was too late for that with our Dying Nun here.' He looked up. 'Get it? Dying Nun instead of Flying Nun?'

'It's like I'm hanging with Chris Rock here. Go on.'

'Right, so I'm trying something experimental. We got lucky that the corpse wasn't refrigerated. The condensation that builds up on the skin throws the whole thing out of whack. Anyway, I thought about going with the polyethylene terephthalate semirigid sheet. That's the one we use based on the fact that static electricity attracts dust particles – '

'Whoa.' Loren held up her palm in the classic stop gesture. 'Let's skip the CSI casting call. Did you get prints off the body?'

'Yes and no. I found smudges on both temples, one looks like a thumb, the other might be a ring finger.'

'On her temples?'

Eldon nodded. He took off his glasses, gave them a wipe down, put them back on the end of his nose, pushed up. 'I think the perp grabbed her face with one hand. Palmed it like a basketball player – with the heel of his hand on her nose.'

'Jesus.'

'Yeah. Then I think he pushed her head down as he climbed on top.'

'But the fingerprints. Can you get any kind of ID off them?'

'Doubtful. We have partials at best. It'll never be enough for court, but there's this new software that helps you, I don't know, fill in the blanks, if you will. If you find somebody, I might get enough to confirm or eliminate.'

'That might help.'

He stood. 'I'll get on it now. Probably take a day, maybe two. I'll let you know when I have more.'

'Okay,' Loren said. 'Anything else?'

It was like a shadow fell over his face.

'Eldon?'

'Yeah,' he said. 'There's something else.'

'I don't like the way you said that.'

'I don't like saying it, believe me. But I think whoever did this did more than just smother her.'

'What do you mean?'

'You know anything about stun guns?'

'Some.'

'I think they used one.' He swallowed. 'In her.'

'When you say "in her," do you mean –'

'I mean exactly what you think,' he said, interrupting her. 'Hey, I'm a product of Catholic school too, okay?'

'Are there burn marks?'

'Faint. But if you know what you're doing – and especially in an area that sensitive – you really shouldn't leave them. It was also a one-prong stunner, if that helps. Most, like the police-issue stun guns, have two prongs. I'm still running tests, but my guess is, she died in a lot of pain.'

Loren closed her eyes.

'Hey, Squirt?'

'What?'

'Do me a favor,' Eldon said. 'Nail this son of a bitch, will ya?'

9

Olivia said, 'Hi, hon, how was your day?'

Matt just held the phone.

'Matt?'

'I'm here,' he said.

The police cruiser was gone now. Matt looked behind him. Marsha stood on the front step with her hands on her hips. Paul was chasing Ethan, both of them shrieking with laughter.

'So,' Olivia said, as if it were just another day, 'where are you?'

'At Marsha's.'

'Everything okay?'

'I'm just taking the boys out to dinner.'

'Not McDonald's again. Those fries are so unhealthy.'

'Right.'

Tentative steps. The ground giving way. Matt held the phone, thinking: *You don't just jump up and scream, 'Aha, caught ya!'*

'So anything going on?' Olivia asked.

'Not much,' he said. Kyra was getting in her car. She gave him a big smile and waved good-bye. He gestured back with his chin. 'I called you before,' Matt said with as much nonchalance as he could muster.

'You did?'

'Yes.'

'When?'

'Around noon.'

'Really?'

'No, I'm making it up. Yes, really.'

'Well, that's weird.'

'Why?'

'I didn't hear the phone ring.'

'Maybe you were out of range,' he tried, giving her an out.

'Maybe,' she said slowly.

'I left a message.'

'Hold on.' There was a pause. 'Wait, it says here "three missed calls."'

'That would be me.'

'I'm sorry, honey. I know this sounds ridiculous but I still get confused about how to retrieve messages. My old phone's code was six-seven-six and then I hit a star, but I don't think that works on this one.'

'It doesn't,' Matt said. 'Your new code is the last four digits of your phone number and then you hit the pound key.'

'Oh, right. I usually just check the missed calls log.'

Matt closed his eyes. He could not believe how inane and ordinary this all felt.

'Where have you been?' he asked.

'What?'

'When I called. Where were you?'

'Oh, I was at a seminar.'

'Where?'

'What do you mean, where? I'm in Boston.'

'What was it on?'

'Some new surfing tool to guard against employees using the Web for personal use. You can't imagine the amount of work hours lost on the Internet.'

'Uh huh.'

'Listen, I have to run. I'm meeting some people for dinner.'

'Anyone I know?'

'Nope, no one you know.' Olivia sighed with a little too much flair. 'Check that: No one you'd even *want* to know.'

'Boring?'

'Very.'

'What hotel are you staying at?'

'Didn't I tell you?'

'No.'

'The Ritz. But I'll be in and out. You're better off getting me on the cell phone.'

'Olivia?'

'Oh,' she said. 'Hold up a second.'

There was a long pause. Marsha crossed the lawn, approaching him. She signaled to her car, asking if it was okay if she took off. He waved that it was fine. Ethan and Paul, tired of running around in circles, headed toward him. Ethan grabbed his right leg, Paul his left. Matt made a face and pointed to the phone, as if they'd get the meaning that he was otherwise occupied. They didn't.

Olivia said, 'There's a picture on my phone. Which button do I press again?'

'The one on the right side.'

'Hold on. Here it comes.' Then: 'Hey, it's you. Dang, I married a handsome devil.'

Matt couldn't help but smile – and that just made it hurt more. He loved her. He could try to soften the blow, but there was no way he could escape it. 'It would be wrong for me to argue with you,' he said.

'Not your best smile though. Heck, no smile at all. And next time, take your shirt off.'

'You too,' he said.

She laughed but it wasn't as let-go as usual.

'Better yet' – Matt added and then the next words: were they planned? – 'why not wear a platinum-blonde wig?'

Silence.

This time he broke it. 'Olivia?'

'I'm here.'

'Before. When I called you.'

'Yes?'

'I was calling you back.'

As if sensing the tenseness, the boys let go of his legs. Paul tilted his head at Ethan.

'But I didn't call you,' Olivia said.

'Yes, you did. I mean, I got a call from your phone.'

'When?'

'Right before I called.'

'I don't understand.'

'There was a picture on the line. Of a man with dark hair. And then there was a video.'

'A video?'

'You were in a room. At least it looked like you. Except you were wearing a platinum-blonde wig.'

More silence. Then: 'I don't know what you're talking about.'

Did he believe her? He so wanted to, so wanted to just drop it . . .

'Earlier today,' he said, 'right before I left you that message, I got a call from your cell phone. It was a camera call –'

'No, I understand that, but . . .'

'But what?'

'Oh, wait,' Olivia said. 'That might explain something.'

Paul and Ethan had started running in dizzying circles again. They were out of control and a little too close to the street. Matt put his hand over the mouthpiece and called them back.

'Explain what?' he asked.

'I think . . . well, I don't really understand why I didn't get your first call. I'm in range. I looked on the missed calls log and you know what? Jamie called too. I never heard that one either.'

'So?'

'So I'm thinking. The guys at these seminars. They're all jokers. Maybe one of them played a prank.'

'A prank.'

'Okay, during this seminar? I fell asleep. It was boring as hell. When I woke up, my purse had been moved. Not a lot. But now that I think about it, it was definitely moved. I didn't think much about it at the time.'

'And now you think . . . ?'

'That, yeah, they took it and did something with it and then put it back. I don't know, I guess that's crazy too.'

Matt didn't know what to make of this, but Olivia's tone did not ring true. 'When are you coming home?'

'Friday.'

He switched hands. 'I'll come up.'

'Don't you have work?'

'Nothing that can't keep.'

'But,' she said, and her voice dropped a little, 'isn't tomorrow your, uh, Thursday at the museum?'

He had almost forgotten about it.

'You can't miss that.'

In three years he never had. For a long time Matt had told no one about his every-other-Thursday rendezvous at the museum. People would never understand. There was a bond there, a draw built on necessity and secrecy. It was hard to say more. Those meetings were simply too important.

But he still said, 'I can put it off.'

'You shouldn't, Matt. You know that.'

'I can fly up right now –'

'There's no need. I'll be home the day after tomorrow.'

'I don't want to wait.'

'I'm crazy busy with stuff here anyway. Look, I have to go. We'll talk about this later, okay?'

'Olivia?'

'Friday,' she said. 'I love you.'

And then she hung up.

10

'Uncle Matt?'

Paul and Ethan were safely ensconced in the backseat. It had taken Matt the better part of fifteen minutes to secure the car booster seats into place. Who the hell had designed these things – NASA?

'What's up, partner?'

'You know what McDonald's has right now?'

'I already told you. We're not going to McDonald's.'

'Oh, I know. I'm just saying.'

'Uh huh.'

'You know what McDonald's has right now?'

'No,' Matt said.

'You know the new *Shrek* movie?'

'Yes.'

'They got *Shrek* toys,' Paul said.

'He means McDonald's does,' Ethan chipped in.

'Is that a fact?'

'And they're free.'

'They're not free,' Matt said.

'They are so. It's in the Happy Meal.'

'Which are overpriced.'

'Overwhat?'

'We're not going to McDonald's.'

'Oh, we know.'

'We were just saying.'

'They got free toys, is all.'

'From the new *Shrek* movie.'

'Remember when we saw the first *Shrek* movie, Uncle Matt?'

'I remember,' he said.

'I like Donkey,' Ethan said.

'Me too,' Matt agreed.

'Donkey is the toy this week.'

'We're not going to McDonald's.'

'I'm just saying.'

''Cause Chinese is good too,' Paul said.

'Even though they don't got toys.'

'Yeah, I like spare ribs.'

'And dim sum.'

'Mom likes the string beans.'

'Ugh. You don't like string beans, do you, Uncle Matt?'

'They're good for you,' Matt said.

Ethan turned to his brother. 'That means no.'

Matt smiled, tried to push away the day. Paul and Ethan were good for that.

They arrived at Cathay, an old-fashioned Chinese restaurant with the retro classics like chow mein and egg foo young, cracked vinyl booths, and a grumpy old woman at the front counter who watched you eat as if fearing you'd pocket the utensils.

The food was greasy, but that was as it should be. The boys ate a ton. At McDonald's, they picked. They managed maybe half a burger and a dozen fries. Here they cleaned the plate. Chinese restaurants would be well served by handing out movie tie-in toys.

Ethan, as always, was animated. Paul was a bit more reserved. They had been raised in pretty much the exact manner, the same gene pool, and yet they couldn't be more different. Ethan was the cutup. He never sat still. He was messy and lively and shunned affection. When Paul colored, he always stayed in the lines. He got frustrated when he made a mistake. He was thoughtful, a good athlete, and liked to cuddle.

Nature waaay over nurture.

They stopped at Dairy Queen on the ride home. Ethan ended up wearing more soft vanilla than he consumed. When he pulled into the driveway Matt was surprised to see that Marsha wasn't back yet. He took them inside – he had a key – and gave them a bath. It was eight o'clock.

Matt put on an episode of *The Fairly OddParents*, which was pretty funny on an adult level, and then convinced the boys using negotiating skills picked up in legal pleadings across the state to get into bed. Ethan was afraid of the dark, so Matt turned on the SpongeBob night-light.

Matt checked his watch. Eight thirty. He didn't mind staying later, but he was getting a little worried.

He headed into the kitchen. The latest works of art by Paul and Ethan hung on the refrigerator by magnets. There were photographs, too, in acrylic frames that never seemed to hold the photos in place. Most were halfway slipping out. Matt carefully slid the images back where they belonged.

Near the top of the fridge, too high for the children to reach (if not see?) there were two photographs of Bernie. Matt stopped and stared at his brother. After a while he turned away and picked up the kitchen phone. He dialed Marsha's cell.

Marsha had caller ID and answered, 'Matt? I was just about to call you.'

'Hey.'

'Are you at the house?'

'We are. And the boys are bathed and in bed.'

'Wow, you're good.'

'I thank you.'

'No, I thank you.'

No one spoke for a moment.

Matt asked, 'Do you need me to stay awhile?'

'If it's okay.'

'No problem. Olivia's still in Boston.'

'Thank you,' she said, and there was something in her voice.

He switched ears. 'Uh, what time do you think you'll be getting –'

'Matt?'

'Yes.'

'I lied to you before.'

He said nothing.

'I didn't have a school meeting.'

He waited.

'I'm out on a date.'

Not sure what to say to that, Matt went with the reliable 'Oh.'

'I should have told you before.' She lowered her voice. 'It's not a first date either.'

His eyes found his brother's in the photograph on the refrigerator. 'Uh huh.'

'I've been seeing someone. It's been almost two months now. The boys don't know anything about it, of course.'

'You don't have to explain to me.'

'Yeah, Matt. Yeah, I do.'

He said nothing.

'Matt?'

'I'm here.'

'Would you mind spending the night?'

He closed his eyes. 'No,' he said. 'I don't mind at all.'

'I'll be home before the boys wake up.'

'Okay.'

He heard a sniffle then. She was crying.

'It's okay, Marsha.'

'Really?'

'Yeah,' he said. 'I'll see you in the morning.'

'I love you, Matt.'

'I love you too.'

He hung up the phone. It was a good thing, Marsha going out. It was a very good thing. But his eyes drifted back toward his brother. Unfair and wrong as it was, Matt couldn't help but think that his brother had never seemed more gone.

11

Everyone seems to have this terrifying dream where you are suddenly about to take the final exam in a class you haven't attended all semester. Matt did not. Instead, in a strangely similar vein, he dreamed that he was back in prison. He had no idea what he'd done to get back there. There was no memory of a crime or a trial, just the sense that he had somehow messed up and that this time he would never get out.

He'd wake up with a start. He'd be sweating. There'd be tears in his eyes. His body would quake.

Olivia had grown used to it. She would wrap her arms around him and whisper that it was okay, that nothing could hurt him anymore. She had bad dreams of her own, his lovely wife, but she never seemed to need or want that sort of comfort.

He slept on the couch in the den. The upstairs guest room had a pullout queen-size bed that somehow felt too big when he was sleeping alone. Now, as he stared up in the dark, feeling more alone than he had since Olivia walked into his office, Matt actually feared sleep. He kept his eyes open. At four in the morning Marsha's car pulled into the driveway.

When he heard the key in the door, Matt closed his eyes and pretended to be asleep on the couch. Marsha tiptoed over and kissed him on the forehead. The smell of shampoo and soap wafted from her. She had showered, wherever she had been. He wondered if she had showered alone. He wondered why he cared.

She moved into the kitchen. Still feigning sleep, Matt slowly opened one eye. Marsha was making lunch for the boys. She spread jelly with a too-practiced hand. There were tears on her cheek. Matt kept still. He let her finish in peace and listened to her gentle footsteps pad up the stairs.

At 7 a.m., Cingle called him.

'I tried your home number,' she said. 'You weren't there.'

'I'm at my sister-in-law's.'

'Oh.'

'Just babysitting my nephews.'

'Did I ask?'

He rubbed his face. 'So what's up?'

'You coming into the office?'

'Yeah, a little later. Why?'

'I found your follower, Charles Talley.'

He sat all the way up. 'Where?'

'Let's talk about this in person, okay?'

'Why?'

'I need to do a little more research.'

'On what?'

'On Charles Talley. I'll meet you at your office at noon, okay?'

He had his Thursday rendezvous at the museum anyway. 'Yeah, okay.'

'And Matt?'

'What?'

'You said this was personal? Whatever it is with Talley?'

'Yes.'

'Then you're in deep doo-doo.'

Matt was a member of the Newark Museum. He flashed his membership card but there was no need. The guards at the door knew him by now. He nodded and entered. Very few people roamed the hall this time of the morning. Matt headed to the art gallery in the west wing. He passed the museum's newest piece, a colorful canvas by Wosene Worke Kosrof, and took the steps to the second floor.

She was the only one there.

He could see her way down at the end of the corridor. She was standing where she always stood – in front of the painting by Edward Hopper. Her head was tilted ever so slightly to the left. She was a very attractive woman, nearing sixty, almost six feet tall, high cheekbones, the kind of blonde hair only the wealthy seem to possess. As always she looked smart and tailored and polished.

Her name was Sonya McGrath. She was the mother of Stephen McGrath, the boy Matt had killed.

Sonya always waited by the Hopper. The painting was called *Sheridan Theater* and managed to catch pure desolation and despair in a picture of a movie theater. It was amazing. There were famous images depicting the ravages of war, of death, of destruction, but there was something in this seemingly simple Hopper, something in this near-empty theater balcony that spoke to both of them in ways no other image ever had.

Sonya McGrath heard him approach but she didn't turn away from the picture. Matt passed Stan, the security guard who always worked this floor on Thursday mornings. They exchanged a quick smile and nod. Matt wondered what Stan must think of his quiet trysts with this attractive older woman.

He stood next to her and looked at the Hopper. It worked like a bizarre mirror. He saw them as the two isolated figures – he Hopper's usher, she the lone patron. For a long time they didn't speak. Matt glanced at Sonya McGrath's profile. He had seen a photograph of her in the paper once, the Sunday *New York Times* Style section. Sonya McGrath was something of a socialite. In the photograph, her smile dazzled. He had never seen that smile in person – wondered, in fact, if it could exist anywhere but on film.

'You don't look so good,' Sonya said.

She was not looking at him – had not, as far as he could tell, yet glanced his way – but he nodded anyway. Sonya faced him full.

Their relationship – though the term 'relationship' didn't seem to capture it – began a few years after Matt got out of prison. His phone would ring, he would pick it up, and there would be no one there. No hang-up. No words. Matt thought that maybe he could hear breathing, but mostly there was pure silence.

Somehow Matt knew who was on the other end.

The fifth time she called, Matt took several deep breaths before working up the courage to speak. 'I'm sorry,' he said.

There was a long silence. Then Sonya replied, 'Tell me what really happened.'

'I did. In court.'

'Tell me again. Everything.'

He tried. He took a long time. She stayed silent. When he finished she hung up.

The next day she called again. 'I want to tell you about my son,' she said without preamble.

And she did.

Matt now knew more than he really wanted to know about Stephen McGrath. He was no longer merely a kid who stepped into a fight, the log jammed onto the track that sent Matt Hunter's life off the rails. McGrath had two younger sisters who adored him. He loved playing guitar. He was a little hippy-ish – he got that, Sonya said with a trace of a laugh, from his mother. He was a great listener, that was what his friends always said. If they had a problem, they went to Stephen. He never needed to be the center of attention. He was content on the sidelines. He would laugh at your joke. He had gotten in trouble only once in his life – the police caught him and some buddies drinking behind the high school – but he had never gotten into a fight, not even as a kid, and seemed deathly afraid of physical violence.

During that same phone call, Sonya asked him, 'Did you know that Stephen didn't know any of the boys in the fight?'

'Yes.'

She started to cry then. 'So why did he step in?'

'I don't know.'

They first met in person here at the Newark Museum three years ago. They had coffee and barely spoke. A few months later, they stayed for lunch. It became a steady thing, every other Thursday morning in front of the Hopper. Neither of them had ever missed one.

At first they told no one. Sonya's husband and daughters would never understand. Of course neither of them understood it either. Matt could never explain why these meetings meant so much to him. Most would assume that he did it purely out of guilt, that he did it for her or for redemption or something like that. But that wasn't the case at all.

For two hours – that's how long their meetings lasted – Matt felt strangely free because he ached and hurt and felt. He didn't know what she got out of it, but he assumed that it was something similar. They talked about that night. They talked about their lives. They talked about the tentative steps, the feeling that the ground could give way at any time. Sonya never said, 'I forgive you.' She never said that it wasn't his fault, that it was an accident, that he served his time.

Sonya started down the corridor. Matt stared at the painting another second or two and then followed. They moved back downstairs and into the museum's atrium. They grabbed coffee and sat at their usual table.

'So,' she said. 'Tell me what's going on.'

She didn't say this to be polite or as an icebreaker. This was not about how-are-you-fine-and-you? Matt told her everything. He told this woman, Sonya McGrath, things he told no one else. He never lied to her, never fudged or edited.

When he was done, Sonya asked, 'Do you think Olivia is having an affair?'

'The evidence seems pretty clear.'

'But?'

'But I've learned that evidence rarely gives you the full picture.'

Sonya nodded. 'You should call her again,' she said.

'I did.'

'Try the hotel.'

'I did.'

'Not there?'

'She wasn't registered.'

'There are two Ritz-Carltons in Boston.'

'I tried them both.'

'Ah.' She sat back and put her hand on her chin. 'So you know that, in some way, Olivia is not being truthful.'

'Yes.'

Sonya considered that. She had never met Olivia, but she knew more about Matt's relationship with her than anyone. She looked off.

'What?' he said.

'I'm just trying to find a plausible reason for her behavior.'

'And?'

'And so far I've come up with nothing.' She shrugged and took a sip of her coffee. 'I've always found your relationship with Olivia an oddity.'

'How so?'

'The way you hooked up ten years after a one-night stand.'

'It wasn't a one-night stand. We didn't sleep together.'

'Which may be the point.'

'I don't get what you mean.'

'If you slept together, well, the spell might have been broken. People claim that making love is the most intimate thing in the world. In truth, it's probably the opposite.'

He waited.

'Well, this is an odd coincidence,' she said.

'Why's that?'

'Clark is having an affair.'

Matt didn't ask her if she was sure or how she knew. He simply said, 'I'm sorry.'

'It's not what you think.'

He said nothing.

'It has nothing to do with what happened to our son.'

Matt tried to nod.

'We like to blame Stephen's death for all our problems. He's become our big life's-not-fair card. But the reason behind Clark's affair is far more basic.'

'That being?'

'He's horny.'

She smiled. Matt tried to smile back.

'Oh, did I mention that she's young? The girl Clark is sleeping with?'

'No.'

'Thirty-two. We have a daughter that age.'

'I'm sorry,' Matt said again.

'Don't be. It's the flip side of what we said before. About intimacy and sex.'

'How so?'

'The truth is, like most women my age, I have very little interest in sex. Yes, I know *Cosmo* and the like will tell you differently, what with all that nonsense about men peaking at nineteen and women in their thirties. But in reality, men are always hornier. Period. To me sex no longer has anything to do with intimacy. Clark, on the other hand, needs it. So that's all she is to him, this young girl. Sex. A release. A physical need.'

'And that doesn't bother you?'

'It's not about me.'

Matt said nothing.

'When you think about it, it's simple: Clark needs something that I have no interest in providing. So he goes elsewhere.' Sonya saw the look on his face. She sighed, put her hands on her thighs. 'Let me give you an example. If Clark loved, say, poker and I didn't want to play . . .'

'Come on, Sonya. That's not the same thing.'

'Oh, but isn't it?'

'Sex and poker?'

'Okay, fine, let's keep it on the physically pleasing. A professional massage. Clark gets rubdowns at his club every week from a masseur named Gary –'

'That's not the same thing either.'

'But don't you see? It is. Sex with this girl isn't about intimacy. It's just a physical thing. Like a back rub or a handshake. So shouldn't it be okay with me?'

Sonya looked up at him and waited.

'It wouldn't be okay with me,' Matt said.

There was a small smile on her lips. Sonya liked mind games. She liked a challenge. He wondered if she meant what she said or if she was merely testing him. 'So what are you going to do?' she asked him.

'Olivia comes home tomorrow.'

'You think you can wait till then?'

'I'm going to try.'

Her eyes stayed on him.

'What?' he asked.

'We can't escape it, can we? I thought . . .' She stopped.

'You thought what?'

Their eyes locked. 'I know it's a terrible cliché, but it all felt like a nightmare. The news about Stephen. The trial. I kept expecting to wake up and find it was all some cruel joke, that everything was okay.'

He'd felt the same way. He was stuck in a bad dream, waiting for the *Candid Camera* climax when Stephen would show up unharmed and smiling.

'But now the world feels like the opposite, doesn't it, Matt?'

He nodded.

'Instead of believing the bad is a nightmare from which you'll awaken,' she went on, 'you think it's the good that's an illusion. And that's what this call on your camera phone did. It woke you from the good dream.'

He could not speak.

'I know that I'll never get past what happened,' Sonya McGrath said. 'It's simply not possible. But I thought . . . I hoped maybe you could.'

Matt waited for her to say more. She did not. She rose suddenly, as if she had said too much. They headed together for the exit. Sonya kissed him on the cheek and when they hugged, they both held on longer than usual. He could, as always, feel the devastation emanating from her. Stephen's death was there, in every moment, in every gesture. He sat with them, their forever companion.

'If you need me,' she whispered, 'you call. Anytime.'

'I will.'

He watched her walk away. He thought about what she had said, about the fine line between the good dreams and the bad, and then, when she finally disappeared around the corner, he turned away.

12

When Matt reached Rolanda's desk, she said, 'Cingle's waiting in your office.'

'Thanks.'

'Midlife wants me to buzz him the very second you arrive.' Rolanda looked up. 'Have you arrived yet?'

'Give me five.'

She turned back to the computer terminal and started typing. Matt entered. Cingle Shaker was standing looking at the window. 'Nice view,' she said.

'You think?'

'Nah. That's just my idea of small talk.'

'You're very good at it,' he said.

'I thought you were just a paralegal.'

'I am.'

'So why the fancy digs?'

'It was my brother's.'

'So?'

'So Bernie was a big rainmaker here.'

'So?' Cingle turned toward him. 'I don't want to sound cold, but he's dead.'

'I think you were being hard on yourself before. You really are good at this small talk stuff.'

'No, I mean, he's been dead for, what, three years now? I can't believe they let an ex-con paralegal keep a space like this.'

He smiled. 'I knew what you meant.'

'So what gives?'

'Maybe they're being respectful to my brother's memory.'

'Attorneys?' Cingle made a face. 'Please.'

'Actually,' he said, 'I think they like having me around.'

'Because you're such a nice guy?'

'Because of the ex-con angle. I'm a fun oddity.'

Cingle nodded. 'Kinda like having a lesbian couple at your hoity-toity soiree.'

'Something like that, but even more exotic. It's funny. In some ways I'm the ultimate curiosity. Whenever they're drunk, they all ask me, on the sly, of course, what it's really like for a guy like them to go to the' – he made quote marks with his fingers – 'Big House.'

'You're like a local celebrity.'

'In a bizarre way, yeah.'

'And that's why they don't throw you out of the office?'

He shrugged.

'They might also be afraid of you,' Cingle said. 'You already killed one man with your bare hands.'

He sighed and took his seat. Cingle took hers.

'Sorry,' she said.

He waved her off. 'What's up?'

Cingle crossed her long legs. It was for effect, he knew that, but he wondered if it had become something of an unconscious move on her part. 'So tell me,' she said. 'Why did you want the license plate traced?'

He spread his hands. 'Do we really have to go through the meaning of "personal" again?'

'Only if you want me to tell you what I know.'

'So you're resorting to blackmail now?'

But he could see that she was serious.

'I think he was following me,' Matt said.

'Why do you think that?'

'Why do you think? I went a few places, his car was there.'

'And you just happened to pick up on that?'

'His license plate was close to my initials.'

'Excuse me?'

Matt explained about the license plate, about the three letters being similar to his own initials, about the way the car raced off when he approached. Cingle listened without moving.

When Matt finished, Cingle asked, 'So why is Charles Talley following you, Matt?'

'I don't know.'

'No idea at all?'

He did not repeat himself. He knew all about men who doth protest too much. Silence was the best response here.

'Talley has a record.'

Matt was tempted to say 'So do I,' but he knew better. Having a record – a record worth Cingle's attention – meant something. The fact that it didn't in Matt's case only proved the rule by the exception. Matt didn't like thinking that way – hadn't Lance Banner used that same prejudice? – but you'd be hard-pressed to argue with the reality.

'Assault,' Cingle said. 'He used brass knuckles. Didn't kill the poor bastard but scrambled his brains to the point where it would have been more merciful if he had.'

Matt thought about that, tried to make it fit. 'How long did he get?'

'Eight years.'

'Long time.'

'Not his first charge. And Talley was far from a model prisoner.'

Matt tried to put it together. Why would this guy be following him?

'Do you want to see what he looks like?' Cingle asked.

'You have a picture?'

'His mug shot, yeah.'

Cingle wore a blue blazer with jeans. She reached into the inner jacket pocket, plucked out the photographs, and sent Matt's world spinning all over again.

How the . . . ?

He knew that her eyes were on him, gauging his reaction, but he couldn't help it. When he saw the two mug shots – the classic front view and turn-to-the-side profile – he nearly gasped out loud. His hands gripped the desk. It felt as though he were in free fall.

'So you recognize him,' Cingle said.

He did. The same smirk. The same blue-black hair.

Charles Talley was the man from the camera phone.

13

Loren Muse walked through a time machine.

Revisiting St. Margaret's, her high school alma mater, the clichés applied: The corridors seemed tighter, the ceilings seemed lower, the lockers seemed smaller, the teachers shorter. But others things, the important stuff, did not change too much. Loren fell into a time portal as she entered. She felt the high school tingle in her belly, the constant state of insecurity, the need for both approval and rebellion churned inside of her.

She knocked on Mother Katherine's door.

'Come in.'

There was a young girl sitting in the office. She wore the same school uniform that Loren had so many years ago, the white blouse and tartan skirt. God, she'd hated that. The girl had her head down, clearly post-Mother Katherine berate. Her stringy hair hung down in front of her face like a beaded curtain.

Mother Katherine said, 'You may go now, Carla.'

Shoulders slumped, head still lowered, Carla slinked off. Loren nodded as she passed, as if to say, I feel for ya, sister. Carla did not meet her eye. She closed the door behind her.

 as though she could read Loren's mind. There were stacks of bracelets, all different colors, on her desk. When Loren pointed to them, the bemusement vanished.

'Those bracelets belong to Carla?' Loren asked.

'Yes.'

A dress code violation, Loren thought, fighting off the desire to shake her head. Man, this place will never change.

'You haven't heard about this?' Mother Katherine asked.

'Heard about what?'

'The bracelet' – she took a deep breath – 'game.'

Loren shrugged.

Mother Katherine closed her eyes. 'It's a recent . . . the word would be fad, I believe.'

'Uh huh.'

'The different bracelets . . . I don't even know how to say this . . . the different colors represent certain acts of a sexual nature. The black one, for example, is supposed to be . . . uh, for one thing. Then the red one . . .'

Loren held her hand up. 'I think I get the picture. So the girls wear them as some kind of, I don't know, level of achievement?'

'Worse.'

Loren waited.

'You're not here about this.'

'Tell me anyway.'

'Girls like Carla wear the bracelets around the boys. If the boy can grab the bracelet off the girl's arm, she must then, well, perform the act that corresponds with the bracelet color.'

'Please tell me you're kidding.'

Mother Katherine gave her a look as heavy as the ages.

'How old is Carla?' Loren asked.

'Sixteen.' Mother Katherine pointed to another set of bracelets as if afraid to touch them. 'But I took this set off an eighth grader.'

There was nothing to say to that.

Mother Katherine reached behind her. 'Here are the phone logs you requested.'

The building still had that chalk-dust musk Loren had always associated, until just now, with a certain sort of adolescent naïveté. Mother Katherine handed her a small stack of papers.

'Eighteen of us share three phones,' Mother Katherine said.

'Six of you to a phone, then?'

Mother Katherine smiled. 'And they say we don't teach math anymore.'

Loren looked at Christ on the cross behind the Mother Superior's head. She remembered an old joke, one she heard when she first got here. A boy is getting all Ds and Fs in math so his parents send him to Catholic school. On his first report card, his parents are shocked to see their son getting straight As. When his parents ask him why, he says, 'Well, when I went into the chapel and saw that guy nailed to a plus sign, I knew they were serious.'

Mother Katherine cleared her throat. 'May I ask a question?'

'Shoot.'

'Do they know how Sister Mary Rose died?'

'They're still running tests.'

Mother Katherine waited.

'That's all I can tell you right now.'

'I understand.'

Now it was Loren who waited. When Mother Katherine turned away, Loren said, 'You know more than you're saying.'

'About?'

'About Sister Mary Rose. About what happened to her.'

'Have you learned her identity yet?'

'No. But we will. Before the end of the day, I'd bet.'

Mother Katherine straightened her back. 'That would be a good start.'

'And there's nothing else you want to tell me?'

'That's correct, Loren.'

Loren waited a beat. The old woman was ... lying would be too strong a word. But Loren could smell evasion. 'Did you go through these calls, Mother?'

'I did. I had the five sisters who shared the phone with her go through them too. Most were to family members, of course. They called siblings, parents, some friends. There were some to local businesses. They order pizza sometimes. Chinese food.'

'I thought nuns had to eat, uh, convent food.'

'You thought wrong.'

'Fair enough,' Loren said. 'Any numbers that stuck out?'

'Just one.'

Mother Katherine's reading glasses dangled from a chain. She slid them onto the end of her nose and beckoned for the sheets. Loren handed them back to her. She studied the first page, licked her finger, moved to the second. She took out a pen and circled something.

'Here.'

She gave the sheet back to Loren. The number had a 973 area code. That would put it in New Jersey, no more than thirty miles from here. The call had been made three weeks ago. It lasted six minutes.

Probably nothing.

Loren spotted the computer on the credenza behind Mother Katherine's desk. It was weird to think about, the Mother Superior surfing the Web, but it truly seemed as though there were very few holdouts anymore.

'May I borrow your computer?' Loren asked.

'Of course.'

Loren tried a simple Google search on the phone number. Nothing.

'Are you looking up the number?' Mother Katherine asked.

'I am.'

'According to the link on the Verizon Web page, the number is unlisted.'

Loren looked back at her. 'You tried already?'

'I looked up all the numbers.'

'I see,' Loren said.

'Just to be certain nothing was overlooked.'

'That was very thorough of you.'

Mother Katherine nodded, kept her head high. 'I assume that you have sources to track down unlisted numbers.'

'I do.'

'Would you like to see Sister Mary Rose's quarters now?'

'Yes.'

The room was pretty much what you'd expect – small, stark, white walls of swirling concrete, one large cross above a single bed, one window. Very dormitory. The room had all the warmth and individuality of a Motel Six. There was almost nothing of a personal nature, nothing that told you anything about the room's inhabitant, almost as if that were Sister Mary Rose's goal.

'The crime-scene technicians will be here in about an hour,' Loren said. 'They'll need to dust for prints, check for hairs, that kind of thing.'

Mother Katherine's hand went slowly to her mouth. 'Then you do think Sister Mary Rose was . . . ?'

'Don't read into it, okay?'

Her cell phone trilled. Loren picked it up. It was Eldon Teak.

'Yo, sweetums, you coming by today?' he asked.

'In an hour,' she said. 'Why, what's up?'

'I found the current owner of our silicone breast manufacturer. SurgiCo is now part of the Lockwood Corporation.'

'The huge one in Wilmington?'

'Somewhere in Delaware, yeah.'

'Did you give them a call?'

'Yes.'

'And?'

'And it did not go well.'

'How's that?'

'I told them we had a dead body, a serial number on a breast implant, and that we needed an ID.'

'And?'

'They won't release the information.'

'Why not?'

'I don't know. They blathered on and on and used the term "medical privacy" a whole lot.'

'That's bullsh –' Mother Katherine's lips pursed. Loren caught herself. 'I'll get a court order.'

'They're a big company.'

'They'll cave on this. They just want legal protection.'

'It'll take time.'

She thought about that. Eldon had a point. The Lockwood Corporation was out of state. She'd probably need a federal court judge to issue a subpoena.

'Something else,' Eldon said.

'What?'

'At first they seemed to have no problem with any of it. I called down, spoke to someone, she was going to look up the serial number for me. I'm not saying it's routine, but it really shouldn't be a big issue.'

'But?'

'But then some lawyer with a bigwig-sounding name called back and gave me a very terse no.'

Loren thought about it. 'Wilmington's only, what, two hours from here?'

'The way you drive, maybe fifteen minutes.'

'I'm thinking of testing out that theory. You have the name of Mr. Bigwig Lawyer?'

'I got it here somewhere. Oh, wait, yes, Randal Horne of Horne, Buckman and Pierce.'

'Call Mr. Horne. Tell him I'm driving down to serve his ass a subpoena.'

'You don't have a subpoena.'

'You don't know that.'

'Oh, right.'

She hung up and placed another call. A woman answered the phone. Loren said, 'I need an unlisted number looked up.'

'Name and badge number, please.'

Loren gave it. Then she read the unlisted phone number Sister Mary Rose had called.

'Please hold,' the woman said.

Mother Katherine pretended to be busy. She looked in the air, then across the room. She fiddled with her prayer beads. Through the phone Loren heard fingers clacking a keyboard. Then: 'Do you have a pen?'

Loren grabbed a stubby golf pencil from her pocket. She took a gas receipt and flipped it over. 'Go ahead.'

'The number you requested is listed to a Marsha Hunter at Thirty-eight Darby Terrace, Livingston, New Jersey.'

14

'Matt?'

He stared at the mug shots of Charles Talley. That same damn knowing smirk, the one he'd seen in that picture on his cell phone. Matt had the falling sensation again, but he held on.

Cingle said, 'You know him, don't you?'

'I need you to do me a favor,' he said.

'I don't do favors. This is my job. You're being billed for this, you know.'

'Even better.' He looked up at Cingle. 'I want you to find me everything you can on Charles Talley. I mean, everything.'

'And what would I be looking for?'

Good question. Matt wondered how to play it.

'Just tell me,' Cingle said.

Matt took out his cell phone. He hesitated, but really, what was the point in trying to keep it a secret anymore? He flipped it open, hit the camera function, and pressed the back arrow until the photograph of Charles Talley, the one taken in that hotel room, came up. It was the same man, no question. He stared at it for a moment.

'Matt?'

His words were slow, deliberate. 'Yesterday I got a call from Olivia's camera phone.' He handed it to her. 'This was on it.'

Cingle reached for the camera phone. Her eyes found the screen. Matt watched them widen in surprise. Her eyes shifted back and forth between the mug shots and the image on the small display. Finally she looked up at him.

'What the hell is this?'

'Hit the forward button,' he said.

'The one on the right here?'

'Yes. It'll take you to the video that came in right after the picture.'

Cingle's face was a mask of concentration. When the video finished she said, 'If I hit this replay button, will it run again?'

'Yes.'

Cingle did. She played the short video two more times. When she was done, Cingle carefully put the camera on the desktop. 'You have an explanation for this?' she asked.

'Nope.'

Cingle thought about it. 'I've only met Olivia once.'

'I know.'

'I can't tell if that was her or not.'

'I think it is.'

'Think?'

'It's hard to make out the face.'

Cingle gnawed on her lower lip. She reached behind, grabbed her purse, started rummaging through it.

'What?' he asked.

'You're not the only one who's technically savvy,' Cingle said.

She pulled out a small handheld computer, not much bigger than Matt's phone. 'A Palm Pilot?'

'A high-end pocket PC,' she corrected. Cingle pulled out a cord. She plugged one end into the phone, one end into the pocket PC. 'You mind if I download the picture and video?'

'Why?'

'I'll take them back to the office. We have all kinds of software to blow the images up frame by frame, enhance them, make a solid analysis.'

'This stays between us.'

'Understood.' Two minutes later, the pictures were downloaded. Cingle handed the phone back to Matt. 'One more thing.'

'I'm listening.'

'Learning all we can about our friend Charles Talley may not get us what we need.' She leaned forward. 'We need to start drawing lines. We need to find a connection between Talley and . . .'

'Olivia,' he finished for her.

'Yes.'

'You want to investigate my wife.'

She sat back, recrossed the legs. 'If this was just a run-of-the-mill hot-sheet affair, it would probably be unnecessary. I mean, maybe they just met. Maybe they hooked up at a bar, I don't know. But Talley is tailing you. He's also sending you pictures, throwing it in your face.'

'Meaning?'

'Meaning there's something more here,' Cingle said. 'Let me ask you something and don't take offense, okay?'

'Okay.'

She shifted in her chair. Her every move, intentional or not, came across as a double entendre. 'What do you really know about Olivia? Her background, I mean.'

'I know everything – where she's from, where she went to school –'

'How about family?'

'Her mother ran off when she was a baby. Her father died when she was twenty-one.'

'Siblings?'

'None.'

'So her father raised her alone?'

'Basically. So?'

Cingle kept going. 'Where did she grow up?'

'Northways, Virginia.'

Cingle wrote it down. 'She went to college there, right?'

Matt nodded. 'She went to UVA.'

'What else?'

'What do you mean, what else? What else is there? She's worked for DataBetter Associates for eight years. Her favorite color is blue. She has green eyes. She reads more than any human being I know. Her guilty pleasure is corny Hallmark movies. And – at the risk of making you vomit – when I wake up and Olivia is next to me, I know, *know,* that there is no luckier man on the planet. You writing this down?'

The door to his office burst open. They both turned toward it. Midlife stepped in. 'Oh, sorry, didn't mean to interrupt.'

'No, that's okay,' Matt said.

Midlife looked at his watch, making a full production out of it. 'I really need to go over the Sterman case with you.'

Matt nodded. 'I was just about to call you anyway.'

They both looked at Cingle. She rose. Midlife unconsciously adjusted his tie and patted his hair.

'Ike Kier,' he said, sticking out his hand.

'Yeah,' Cingle said, managing not to roll her eyes. 'Charmed.' She looked at Matt. 'We'll talk.'

'Thank you.'

She looked at him a second longer than necessary and spun toward the door. Midlife moved out of her wake. After she left, Midlife took her seat, whistled, and said, 'Who in heaven is that?'

'Cingle Shaker. She works for MVD.'

'You mean she's a private dick?'

Midlife laughed at his own joke. When Matt didn't join in, he segued it into a cough and crossed his legs. His gray hair was neatly parted. Gray hair works on lawyers – a full head of it anyway. It gave them a certain gravitas with jurors.

Matt opened his desk drawer and pulled out the Sterman file. The two talked for three hours about the case, about the prelim, about what the DA might offer. They had just about talked themselves out when Matt's camera phone rang. He checked the caller ID. The screen spelled out: 'Unavailable.' Matt put the phone to his ear.

'Hello?'

'Hey.' It was a man whispering. 'Guess what I'm doing to your wife right now?'

15

For Loren Muse, there was no escaping déjà vu today.

She pulled up to the home of Marsha Hunter at 38 Darby Terrace in Livingston, New Jersey. Livingston had been Loren's hometown. Growing up, she'd decided, was never easy. Adolescence is a war zone, no matter where you live. Comfortable towns like Livingston are supposed to cushion the blows. For those who belonged, maybe it did. For Loren, this was where she lived when her father decided that he really, truly did not belong anywhere, not even with his daughter.

Livingston had all the trappings: great schools, great sports programs, great Kiwanis Club, great PTA, great high school productions. When Loren grew up here, the Jewish kids dominated the honor roll. Now it was the Asians and Indians, the next generation of immigrants, the new hungry ones. It was that kind of place. You come out here, you buy the house, you pay the taxes, you get the American dream.

But you know what they say: Be careful what you wish for.

She knocked on the door to Marsha Hunter's home. Loren hadn't figured the connection between this single mom, a rarity in Livingston, and Sister Mary Rose – other than a six-minute phone call. She probably should have done some checking first, a little background work, but there was no time. So here she stood, on the front stoop in the bright sunshine, when the door opened.

'Marsha Hunter?'

The woman, attractive in a plain way, nodded. 'Yes, that's right.'

Loren held up her identification. 'I'm Investigator Loren Muse from the Essex County prosecutor's office. I'd like a moment of your time.'

Marsha Hunter blinked, confused. 'What's this about?'

Loren tried a disarming smile. 'Could I come in a moment?'

'Oh, yes. Of course.'

She stepped back. Loren entered the home and whammo, another hit of déjà vu. Such a sameness to the interiors. In here it could be any year between 1964 and now. There was no change. The television might be fancier, the carpet a little less plush, the colors more muted, but that feeling of falling back into her old bizarro-kid-world dimension still hung in the air.

She checked the walls, looking for a cross or Madonna or some hint of Catholicism, something that might easily explain the phone call from the faux Sister Mary Rose. There was nothing hinting at any religion. Loren noticed a folded sheet and blanket on the edge of the couch, as if someone had recently slept there.

There was a young woman in the room, maybe twenty years old, and two boys no more than eight or nine. 'Paul, Ethan,' their mother said, 'this is Investigator Muse.' The well-trained boys dutifully shook Loren's hands, both going so far as to make eye contact.

The smaller one – Ethan, she thought – said, 'Are you a policeman?'

'Woman,' Loren replied automatically. 'And the answer is, sorta. I'm an investigator in the county prosecutor's office. That's like being a police officer.'

'You got a gun?'

'Ethan,' Marsha said.

Loren would have responded, would have shown it to him, but she knew that some mothers freaked about things like that. Loren understood it – anything to prevent Precious from understanding violence – but the gun-denial step was a woefully inadequate long-term tactic.

'And this is Kyra Sloan,' Marsha Hunter said. 'She helps me look after the kids.'

The young woman named Kyra waved from across the room, picking up some kind of toy. Loren waved back.

'Kyra, do you mind taking the boys outside for a little while?'

'Sure.' Kyra turned to the boys. 'How about a game of Wiffle ball, guys?'

'I'm up first!'

'No, you were up first last time! It's my turn!'

They headed outside, still debating the batting order. Marsha turned toward Loren. 'Is something wrong?'

'No, not at all.'

'So why are you here?'

'This is just a routine follow-up to an ongoing investigation.' It was a lot of vague malarkey, but Loren had found this particular brand fairly efficient.

'What investigation?'

'Mrs. Hunter –'

'Please. Call me Marsha.'

'Fine, sorry. Marsha, are you Catholic?'

'Excuse me?'

'I don't mean to pry. This isn't really a religious question. I'm just trying to see if you're in any way associated with St. Margaret's parish in East Orange.'

'St. Margaret's?'

'Yes. Are you a member?'

'No. We're with St. Philomena's in Livingston. Why would you ask that?'

'Are you associated in any way with St. Margaret's?'

'No.' Then: 'What do you mean associated?'

Loren kept going, not wanting to lose the rhythm. 'Do you know anybody attending the school?'

'St. Margaret's? No, I don't think so.'

'Do you know any of the teachers there?'

'I don't think so.'

'How about Sister Mary Rose?'

'Who?'

'Do you know any of the nuns at St. Margaret's?'

'No. I know several at St. Phil's, but no Sister Mary Rose.'

'So the name Sister Mary Rose means nothing to you?'

'Nothing at all. What is this about?'

Loren kept her eyes on the woman's face, searching for a mythical 'tell.' Nothing was showing up, but that didn't mean much.

'Do you and your children live here alone?'

'Yes. Well, Kyra has a room above the garage, but she's from out of state.'

'But she lives here?'

'She rents a room and helps out. She's taking classes at William Paterson University.'

'Are you divorced?'

'A widow.'

Something in the way Marsha Hunter said it made a piece or two tumble into place. Not all of them by any means. Not even enough yet. Loren almost kicked herself. She should have done some background work.

Marsha crossed her arms. 'What is this about anyway?'

'A Sister Mary Rose recently passed away.'

'And she worked at this school?'

'Yes, she was a teacher. At St. Margaret's.'

'I still don't see how –'

'When we were going through the phone logs, we found a call she'd made that we couldn't quite explain.'

'She called here?'

'Yes.'

Marsha Hunter looked perplexed. 'When?'

'Three weeks ago. June second to be exact.'

Marsha shook her head. 'It could have been a wrong number.'

'For six minutes?'

That made Marsha pause. 'What day again?'

'June second. Eight p.m.'

'I can check my calendar, if you'd like.'

'I'd like that very much, thank you.'

'It's upstairs. I'll be right back. But I'm sure none of us talked to this sister.'

'None of us?'

'Excuse me?'

'You said, "us." Who did you mean?'

'I don't know. Anyone in the house, I guess.'

Loren didn't comment on that. 'Do you mind if I ask your baby-sitter a few questions?'

Marsha Hunter hesitated. 'I guess that wouldn't be a problem.' She forced up a smile. 'But the boys will throw a fit if you use the word "baby" in front of them.'

'Understood.'

'I'll be right back.'

Loren headed through the kitchen toward the back door. She glanced out the window. Kyra was pitching underhand to Ethan. He swung wildly and missed. Kyra took a step in closer and bent lower and pitched again. This time, Ethan made contact.

Loren turned away. She was almost at the back door when something made her pull up.

The refrigerator.

Loren wasn't married, didn't have kids, didn't grow up in one of those sweet happy homes, but if there was anything more Americana – more family – than the front of a refrigerator she did not know what it was. Her friends had refrigerators like this. She didn't, and she realized how pitiful that was. Loren had two cats and no real family, unless you wanted to count her melodramatic and self-involved mother.

But in most American homes, if you wanted to find the personal, this – your refrigerator front – was where you looked. There was kid artwork. There were essays from school, all adorned with stars for mediocrity that passed for excellence. There were preprinted birthday invitations, one to a party at something called the Little Gym, the other to the East Hanover bowling alley. There were forms for class trips, child vaccinations, a soccer league.

And, of course, there were family snapshots.

Loren had been an only child and no matter how often she saw them – this magnetized swirl of smiles – it always seemed slightly unreal to her, like she was watching a bad TV show or reading a corny greeting card.

Loren stepped toward the photograph that had caught her eye. More pieces started to pour into place now.

How could she have missed this?

She should have put it together right away. Hunter. The name wasn't rare but it wasn't overly common either. Her eyes scanned the other pictures, but they kept coming back to the first one, the one on the left taken at what looked like a baseball game. Loren was still staring at the picture when Marsha returned.

'Is everything okay, Inspector Muse?'

Loren startled up at the voice. She tried to conjure up the details, but only a sketch came to mind. 'Did you find your calendar?'

'There's nothing there. I really don't remember where I was that day.'

Loren nodded and turned back to the refrigerator. 'This man' – she pointed and looked back at Marsha – 'this is Matt Hunter, right?'

Marsha's face closed like a metal gate.

'Mrs. Hunter?'

'What do you want?'

There had been hints of warmth before. There were none now.

'I knew him,' Loren said. 'A long time ago.'

Nothing.

'In elementary school. We both went to Burnet Hill.'

Marsha crossed her arms. She was having none of it.

'How are you two related?'

'He's my brother-in-law,' Marsha said. 'And a good man.'

Right, sure, Loren thought. *A real prince.* She'd read about the manslaughter conviction. Matt Hunter had served time at a max-security facility. Serious hard time, as she recalled. She remembered the folded blanket and sheets on the couch.

'Does Matt visit here a lot? I mean, he's the boys' uncle and all.'

'Inspector Muse?'

'Yes?'

'I'd like you to leave now.'

'Why's that?'

'Matt Hunter is not a criminal. What happened was an accident. He has more than paid for it.'

339

Loren kept quiet, hoping she'd go on. She didn't. After a few moments she realized that this line of questioning would probably not take her anywhere. Better to try a less defensive route.

'I liked him,' Loren said.

'Excuse me?'

'When we were kids. He was nice.'

That was true enough. Matt Hunter had been a pretty good guy, another Livingston wanna-fit-in who probably shouldn't have tried so hard.

'I'll leave now,' Loren said.

'Thank you.'

'If you learn anything about that phone call on June second –'

'I'll let you know.'

'Do you mind if I speak to your sitter on the way out?'

Marsha sighed, shrugged.

'Thank you.' Loren reached for the door.

Marsha called out, 'Can I ask you something?'

Loren faced her.

'Was this nun murdered?'

'Why would you ask that?'

Marsha shrugged again. 'It's a natural question, I guess. Why else would you be here?'

'I can't discuss details with you. I'm sorry.'

Marsha said nothing. Loren opened the door and headed into the yard. The sun was still high, the long days of June. The boys ran and played with such wonderful abandonment. Adults could never play like that. Never in a million years. Loren remembered her tomboy youth, the days when you could play Running Bases for hours and never, not for a second, be bored. She wondered if Marsha Hunter ever did that, ever came out and played Running Bases with her sons, and thinking about that Loren felt another pang.

No time for that now.

Marsha would be watching from the kitchen window. Loren needed to do this fast. She approached the girl – what was her name? Kylie, Kyra? Kelsey? – and waved.

'Hi.'

The girl cupped her hands over her eyes and blinked. She was pretty enough, with blonde highlights that you can only find in youth or a bottle. 'Hi.'

Loren didn't waste time with preamble. 'Does Matt Hunter come over a lot?'

'Matt? Sure.'

The girl had answered without hesitation. Loren muffled a smile. Ah, youth.

'How often?'

Kyra – that was definitely the name – shifted now, slightly more wary, but she was still young. As long as Loren remained the authority figure, she'd talk. 'I don't know. Few times a week, I guess.'

'Good guy?'

'What?'

'Matt Hunter. Is he a good guy?'

Kyra gave a huge smile. 'He's great.'

'Good with the kids?'

'The best.'

Loren nodded, feigning disinterest. 'Was he here last night?' she asked as casually as she could.

But now Kyra cocked her head to the side. 'Didn't you ask Mrs. Hunter these questions?'

'I'm just reconfirming. He was here, right?'

'Yeah.'

'All night?'

'I was in the city with some friends. I don't know.'

'There were sheets on the couch. Who stayed on it?'

She gave a shrug. 'I guess it was Matt.'

Loren risked a glance behind her. Marsha Hunter disappeared from the window. She'd be moving toward the back door now. The girl would not remember June 2. Loren had enough for now, though she didn't have a clue what it meant.

'Do you know where Matt lives?'

'In Irvington, I think.'

The back door opened. Enough, Loren thought. Finding Matt Hunter shouldn't be a problem. She smiled and started away then, trying not to give Marsha a reason to call and warn her brother-in-law. She tried to walk away as casually as possible. She waved a good-bye at Marsha. Marsha's return wave was slow.

Loren hit the driveway and headed toward her car, but another face from her distant past – wow, this case was turning into a bad episode of *Loren Muse, This Is Your Life* – stood by her car. He leaned against the hood, a cigarette dangling from his lips.

'Hey, Loren.'

'As I live and breathe,' she said. 'Detective Lance Banner.'

'In the flesh.' He tossed the cigarette onto the ground and stomped on it.

She pointed to the stub. 'I may write you up for that.'

'I thought you were county homicide.'

'Cigarettes kill. Don't you read the carton?'

Lance Banner gave her a crooked smile. His car, an obvious unmarked police vehicle, was parked across the street. 'Been a long time.'

'That firearm safety convention in Trenton,' Loren said. 'What, six, seven years ago?'

'Something like that.' He folded his arms, kept leaning against her hood. 'You here on official business?'

'I am.'

'It involve a former school chum of ours?'

'It might.'

'Wanna tell me about it?'

'Wanna tell me why you're here?'

'I live near here.'

'So?'

'So I spotted a county vehicle. Figured I might be able to be of some assistance.'

'How's that?'

'Matt Hunter wants to move back to town,' Lance said. 'He's closing on a house not far from here.'

341

Loren said nothing.

'Does that work into your case?'

'I don't see how.'

Lance smiled and opened the car door. 'Why don't you tell me what's going on? Maybe we can figure out how together.'

16

'Hey, guess what I'm doing to your wife right now?'

Matt held the phone to his ear.

The man whispered, 'Matt? You still there?'

Matt said nothing.

'Yo, Matt, did you tattle on me? I mean, did you tell the wife about me sending you those pictures?'

He couldn't move.

'Because Olivia is being much more protective with her phone. Oh, she won't stop doing me. That ain't gonna happen. She's addicted, you know what I'm saying?'

Matt's eyes closed.

'But all of a sudden she says she wants to be more careful. So I'm wondering, you know, guy to guy here, did you say something? Let her in on our little secret?'

Matt's hand clamped down so hard he thought the phone might crack in his hand. He tried to take in deep breaths, but his chest kept hitching up. He found his voice and said, 'When I find you, Charles Talley, I'm going to rip off your head and crap down your neck.'

Silence.

'You still there, Charles?'

The voice on the phone was a whisper. 'Gotta run. She's coming back.'

And then he was gone.

Matt told Rolanda to cancel his afternoon appointments.

'You don't have any appointments,' she said.

'Don't be a wiseass.'

'You want to tell me what's wrong?'

'Later.'

He started home. The camera phone was still in his hand. He waited until he pulled up to their place off Main Street in Irvington. The already-sparse grass had pretty much died in the recent drought – there had been no rainfall on the East Coast for three weeks. In suburbs like Livingston, the lushness of one's lawn is taken seriously. Banning it, sitting by idly as one's green deadened to brown, was worthy of a good neighborly teeth-gnashing over the new Weber Genesis Gold B backyard grill. Here, in Irvington, nobody cared.

Lawns were a rich man's game.

Matt and Olivia lived in a declining two-family held together by aluminum siding. They had the right side of the dwelling; the Owens, an African-American family of five, had the left. Both sides had two bedrooms and one and a half baths.

He took the stoop two steps at a time. When he got inside he hit the speed-dial-one spot for Olivia. It went into her voice mail again. He wasn't surprised.

He waited for the beep.

'I know you're not at the Ritz,' Matt said. 'I know it was you in the blonde wig. I know it wasn't a big joke. I even know about Charles Talley. So call me and explain.'

He hung up and looked out the window. There was a Shell gas station on the corner. He watched it. His breaths were coming in shallow gulps. He tried to slow them down. He grabbed a suitcase from the closet, threw it on the bed, started stuffing his clothes into it.

He stopped. Packing a suitcase. A stupid and histrionic move. Cut it out.

Olivia would be home tomorrow.

And if she wasn't?

No use thinking about it. She would be home. It would all come together, one way or the other, in a few hours.

But he was no longer above snooping. He started in Olivia's drawers. He barely hated himself for doing it. That voice on the phone had set him off. Best-case scenario now: Olivia was hiding something from him. He might as well find out what.

But he found nothing.

Not in the drawers, not in the closets. He thought about other possible hiding spots when he remembered something.

The computer.

He headed upstairs and hit the power switch. The computer booted up, came to life. It seemed to take an inordinate amount of time. Matt's right leg started shaking up and down. He put his palm on the knee to slow it down.

They'd finally gotten a cable modem – dial-ups going the way of the Betamax – and he was on the Web in seconds. He knew Olivia's password, though he had never dreamed of using it like this. He logged onto her e-mail and scanned the messages. The new stuff held no surprises. He tried the old mail.

The directory was empty.

He tried looking under her 'Sent Mail' folder. Same thing – everything had been deleted. He tried the section called 'Deleted Mail.' It too had been cleaned out. He checked through the browser's 'History,' hoping to see where Olivia had last surfed. That, too, had been erased.

Matt sat back and drew an obvious conclusion: Olivia had been covering her tracks. And the obvious follow-up question was: Why?

There was one more area to check: the cookies.

People often erased their surfing history or their mailbox, but the cookies were something different. If Olivia had wiped out the cookies, Matt would automatically know something had gone awry. His Yahoo! home page wouldn't automatically come up, for instance. Amazon wouldn't know who he was. A person trying to cover their tracks would not want that.

Clearing out the cookies would be too noticeable.

He went through Explorer and found the folder that held the Web's cookies. There were tons of them. He clicked the date button, thereby putting them in date order, the most recent at the top. His eyes ran down them. Most of them he recognized – Google, OfficeMax, Shutterfly – but there were two unfamiliar domains. He wrote them down, minimized the Explorer window, went back to the Web.

He typed in the first address and hit return. It was for the *Nevada Sun News* – a newspaper that required you to sign up in order to access the archives. The paper's home office was in Las Vegas. He checked the 'personal profile.' Olivia had signed up using a fake name and e-mail address. No surprise there. They both did that, to prevent spam and protect privacy.

But what had she been looking up?

There was no way to tell.

Strange, maybe, but the second Web address was far more so.

It took a while for the Web to recognize what he'd typed in. The address bounced from one spot to another before finally landing on something called:

Stripper-Fandom.com.

Matt frowned. There was a warning on the home page that nobody under the age of eighteen should continue. That didn't bode well. He clicked the enter icon. The pictures that appeared were, as one might expect, provocative. Stripper-Fandom was an 'appreciation' site for . . .

. . . for female strippers?

Matt shook his head. There were countless thumbnails of topless women. He clicked one. There were biographies listed for each girl:

Bunny's career as an exotic dancer started in Atlantic City, but with her impressive dance moves and slinky costumes, she quickly rose to stardom and moved to Vegas. 'I love it out here! And I love rich men!' Bunny's specialty is wearing bunny ears and doing a hop-dance using the pole . . .

Matt clicked the link. An e-mail address came up, in case you wanted to write Bunny and request rates for a 'private audience.' It actually said that – private audience. Like Bunny was the pope.

What the hell was going on here?

Matt searched through the stripper fan site until he could take no more. Nothing jumped out at him. Nothing fell into place. He just felt more confused. Maybe the site meant nothing at all. Most of the strippers were from the Vegas area. Maybe Olivia had gotten there by clicking an advertising link at that Nevada newspaper. Maybe the link wasn't even marked as a stripper site and just led there.

But why was she on a Nevada newspaper site in the first place? Why had she erased all her e-mails?

No answer.

Matt thought about Charles Talley. He Googled the name. Nothing interesting came up. He shut down the browser and moved back downstairs, that whisper from the phone call still echoing in his head, shredding all reason:

'Hey, guess what I'm doing to your wife right now?'

Time to get some air. Air and something more potent.

He headed outside and started for South Orange Avenue. From the Garden State Parkway, you couldn't miss the giant brown beer bottle rising up and dominating the skyline. But when you traveled this section of the GSP, the other thing you noticed – maybe even more than the old water tank – was the sprawling cemetery on both sides of the road. The parkway cut smack through the middle of a burial ground. You were encased left and right by unending rows of weather-beaten gravestones. But the effect of driving through was not so much splitting a cemetery in half as much as zipping it together, of making something whole. And there, in the not-so-far distance, this strange giant beer bottle stood, high in the air, a silent sentinel guarding or maybe mocking the buried inhabitants.

The damage to the brewery was somewhat mystifying. Every window was only partially broken, not fully smashed, as if someone had taken the time to throw one rock and only one rock at every single window in the twelve-story structure. Shards lay everywhere. Every opening was a yawning, jangled threat. The combination of erosion and pride, the strong skeleton against the missing-teeth shattered-eye look from the broken glass, gave the place a strange downtrodden-warrior bearing.

Soon they would tear the old factory down and build an upscale mall. Just what Jersey needed, he thought – another mall.

Matt turned down the alley and headed for the faded red door. The tavern did not have a name on it. There was one window with a Pabst Blue Ribbon neon sign in it. Like the brewery – like this city? – the sign no longer lit up.

Matt opened the door, forcing sunlight into a place bathed in darkness. The men – there was only one woman here right now and she'd hit you if you called her a lady – blinked like bats who'd had a flashlight shined on them. There was no jukebox playing, no music at all. The conversations were kept as low as the lights.

Mel was still behind the bar. Matt hadn't been here in, what, two, three years at least, but Mel still knew him by name. The tavern was a classic dive. You see them everywhere across the United States. Men – mostly, anyway – finishing up whatever job they grinded out were now looking to get a buzz on. If that included some boasting or banter, so be it, but places like this were much more about inebriation than consolation or conversation.

Before his stint in prison Matt would have never gone into a dump like Mel's. He now liked rougher spots. He was not sure why. The men in here were big with undefined muscle. They wore flannel shirts in the fall and winter, and bowling-gut-emphasizing T-shirts in the spring and summer. They wore jeans year-round. There weren't many fights in here, but you didn't walk in a place like this unless you knew how to use your fists.

Matt took a seat on a stool. Mel nodded at him. 'Beer?'

'Vodka.'

Mel poured him one. Matt held the glass, looked at it, shook his head. Drinking away his problems. Could he be a bigger cliché? He threw back the vodka and let the warmth coast through him. He nodded for another, but Mel was already on the case. Matt threw that one back too.

He started to feel better. Or to say the same thing in another way: He started to feel less. His eyes slowly swerved from side to side. He felt, as he did in most places, slightly out of place – a spy in enemy territory. He was not really comfortable anywhere anymore – his old softer world or his new hardened one. So he straddled both. Truth was, he was only comfortable – pitiful as it sounded – when he was with Olivia.

Damn her.

Third shot down the hatch. The buzzing started in the base of his skull.

Yo, check out the big man throwing back the booze.

He already felt a bit wobbly. He wanted that. Just make it go away, he thought.

Not forever. He wasn't drinking away the blues. He was postponing them, for just one more night, just until Olivia came home and explained to him why she was in a motel room with another man, why she lied about it, why the guy knew that he had told her about the pictures.

Like that. The little things.

He pointed for another. Mel, rarely one to converse or hand out advice, poured. 'You're a beautiful man, Mel.'

'Hey, thanks, Matt. I get that a lot, but it still means something, you know?'

Matt smiled and looked at the glass. Just for a night. Just let it go.

A big moose came back from the can, accidentally bumping into Matt as he walked past. Matt startled to, gave the moose the eye. 'Watch it,' Matt said.

The moose grunted an apology, diffusing the moment. Matt was almost disappointed. One would think he'd be smarter – that Matt, better than anyone, knew the danger in fisticuffs of any sort – but not tonight. Nope, tonight fisticuffs would be most welcome, yes indeed.

Screw the consequences, right?

He looked for Stephen McGrath's ghost. He often sat on the next bar stool. But Stephen was nowhere to be found tonight. Good.

Matt was not a good drinker. He knew that. He could not hold his liquor. He was already past buzzed and nearing inebriation. The key, of course, was knowing when to stop – maintaining the high without the aftermath. It was a line many people tried to find. It was a line most tripped over.

Tonight he really didn't care about the line.

'Another.'

The word came out slurred. He could hear it. It was hostile too. The vodka was making him angry or, more likely, letting him be. He was actually hoping for trouble now, even while he feared it. The anger was making him focus. Or at least that was what he wanted to believe. His thinking was no longer muddled. He knew what he wanted. He wanted to hit someone. He wanted a physical confrontation. It didn't matter if he crushed someone or someone crushed him.

He didn't care.

Matt wondered about this – this taste for violence. About its origins. Maybe his old chum Detective Lance Banner was right. Prison changes you. You go in one guy, even if you're innocent, but you come out . . .

Detective Lance Banner.

The keeper of the Livingston gate, the dumb hick bastard.

Time passed. It was impossible to say how much. He eventually signaled for Mel to come over and total him up. When he hopped off the stool, the inside of Matt's skull screamed in protest. He grabbed the bar, got his bearings. 'Later, Mel.'

'Good seeing you, Matt.'

He weaved his way out, one name ringing repeatedly in his head.

Detective Lance Banner.

Matt remembered an incident in second grade when he and Lance had both been seven. During a recess game of Four Squares – the dumbest game since Tetherball – Lance's pants had split. What made it worse, what made it one of those wholly horrifying childhood incidents, was that Lance had not worn underwear that day. A nickname had been born, one that Lance hadn't been able to shake until middle school: 'Keep It in Your Pants, Lance.'

347

Matt laughed out loud.

Then Lance's voice came back to him: *'We have a nice neighborhood here.'*

'That so?' Matt said out loud. 'Do all the kids wear underwear now, Lance?'

Matt laughed again at his own joke. The noise echoed in the tavern, but nobody looked up.

He pushed the door open. It was night now. He stumbled down the street, still cracking up at his own joke. His car was parked near his house. A couple of his quasi-neighbors stood near it, both drinking out of brown paper bags.

One of the two . . . *homeless* was the politically correct term they used nowadays, but these guys preferred the old standby *winos*, called out to him. 'Yo, Matt.'

'How are you, Lawrence?'

'Good, man.' He held out the bag. 'Need a swig?'

'Nah.'

'Yo.' Lawrence made a waving motion with his hand. 'Looks like you been having your fill anyway, huh?'

Matt smiled. He reached into his pocket and peeled off a twenty. 'You two get some of the good stuff. On me.'

A broad smile broke out on Lawrence's face. 'Matt, you's all right.'

'Yeah. Yeah, I'm very special.'

Lawrence laughed at that one like it was a Richard Pryor special. Matt waved and walked away. He dug into his pocket and pulled out his car keys. He looked at the keys in his hand, at the car, and then he stopped.

He was plastered.

Matt was irrational right now. He was stupid. He'd love to beat the hell out of someone – Lance Banner being number two on his list (Charles Talley was number one, but Matt didn't know how to find him) – but he was not *that* stupid. He wouldn't drive in this condition.

Lawrence said, 'Yo, Matt, you wanna hang with us?'

'Maybe later, guys.'

Matt spun around and headed back toward Grove Street. The number 70 bus hit Livingston. He waited at the stop, swaying with the wind. He was the only one there. Most of the people were traveling from the other direction – exhausted domestics trudging back from the wealthier environs to their far more humble abodes.

Welcome to the flip side of the burbs.

When bus 70 pulled up, Matt watched the tired women descend, zombielike. Nobody spoke. Nobody smiled. Nobody was there to greet them.

The bus ride was maybe ten miles, but what a ten miles. You went from the decay of Newark and Irvington and suddenly it was like you hit another universe. The change happened in a snap. There was Maplewood and Milburn and Short Hills and finally Livingston. Matt thought again about distance, about geography, about the truly thinnest of lines.

Matt rested his head against the bus window, the vibration working like a strange massage. He thought about Stephen McGrath and that terrible night in Amherst, Massachusetts. He thought about his hands around Stephen's neck. He wondered how hard he squeezed. He wondered if he could have let go as they fell, if that would have made a difference. He wondered if maybe, just maybe, he gripped the neck even tighter.

He wondered about that a lot.

Matt got off at the circle on Route 10 and walked toward Livingston's favorite watering hole, the Landmark. The lot on Northfield Avenue was chock full of minivans. Matt sneered. No thin line here. This was not Mel's. This was a god-damn wussy bar, if ever he saw one. He pushed open the door.

Lance Banner would be here.

The Landmark was, of course, nothing like Mel's. It was brightly lit. It was loud. Outkast sang about roses smelling like boo-boo – safe ghetto music. There was no cracked vinyl, no peeling paint, no sawdust on the floor. The Heineken signs worked. So did the Budweiser clock, complete with moving Clydesdales. Very little hard liquor was being served. Pitchers of beer lined the tables. At least half the men were dressed in softball uniforms with various sponsors – Friendly's Ice Cream, Best Buy, Burrelle's Press Clipping – and enjoying a post-rec-league-game celebration with teammates and opponents alike. There was a smattering of college kids home on break from Princeton or Rutgers or – gasp – maybe Matt's almost alma mater, Bowdoin.

Matt stepped inside and when he did, nobody turned around. Not at first. Everyone was laughing. Everyone was boisterous and red-faced and healthy. Everyone talked at the same time. Everyone smiled and swore too casually and looked soft.

And then he saw his brother, Bernie.

Except, of course, it wasn't Bernie. Bernie was dead. But man, it looked like him. At least from the back. Matt and Bernie used to come here with fake IDs. They'd laugh and be boisterous and talk at the same time and swear too casually. They'd watch those other guys, the rec-league softball players, and listen to them talk about their kitchen additions, their careers, their kids, their boxes at Yankee Stadium, their experiences coaching Little League, the lamentations over their declining sex lives.

As Matt stood there, thinking about his brother, the energy of the place shifted. Someone recognized him. A ripple began. Murmurs followed and heads turned. Matt looked around for Lance Banner. He didn't see him. He spotted the table with the cops – you could just tell that was what they were – and recognized one of them as the cop-kid Lance had braced him with yesterday.

Still heavily under the influence, Matt tried to keep his walk steady. The cops gave their best laser glares as he approached. The glares didn't faze him. Matt had seen much worse. The table grew silent as he approached the cop-kid.

Matt stopped in front of him. The kid did not step back. Matt tried not to sway.

'Where's Lance?' Matt asked.

'Who wants to know?'

'Good one.' Matt nodded. 'Say, who writes your lines?'

'What?'

'"Who wants to know?" That's funny stuff, really. I mean, I'm standing in front of you, I'm asking you directly, and you come up, bang, on the spot, no time to think, with, "Who wants to know?"' Matt moved in closer. 'I'm standing right here – so who the hell do you think wants to know?'

Matt heard the sound of chair legs scraping the floor, but he didn't look away. The cop-kid glanced toward his buddies, then back at Matt. 'You're drunk.'

'So?'

He got into Matt's face now. 'So you want me to haul your ass downtown and give you a Breathalyzer?'

'One' – Matt raised his index finger – 'Livingston's police station is not downtown. It's more midtown. You've been watching too many repeats of *NYPD Blue*. Two, I'm not driving, numbnuts, so I'm not sure what a Breathalyzer is supposed to do for you. Three, while we're on the subject of breath and you standing in my face and all, I have mints in my pocket. I'm going to slowly reach for them so you can have one. Or even the whole pack.'

Another cop stood. 'Get out of here, Hunter.'

Matt turned toward him and squinted. It took him a second to recognize the ferret-faced man. 'My God, it's Fleisher, right? You're Dougie's little brother.'

'Nobody wants you here.'

'Nobody . . . ?' Matt turned from one man to the other. 'Are you guys for real? You going to run me out of town now? You' – Matt snapped, pointed – 'Fleisher's little brother, what's your first name?'

He didn't answer.

'Never mind. Your brother Dougie was the biggest pothead in my class. He dealt to the whole school. We called him Weed, for crying out loud.'

'You talking trash about my brother?'

'I'm not talking trash. I'm talking truth.'

'You want to spend the night in jail?'

'For what, asswipe? You going to arrest me on some trumped-up charge? Go ahead. I work for a law firm. I'll sue your ass back to the high school equivalency exam you probably never passed.'

More chair scrapes. Another cop stood. Then another. Matt's heart started doing a quick two-step. Someone reached and grabbed his wrist. Matt pulled away. His right hand formed a fist.

'Matt?'

This voice was gentle and struck a distant chord deep inside of him. Matt glanced behind the bar. Pete Appel. His old friend from high school. They'd played together at the Riker Hill Park. The park was a converted Cold War missile base. He and Pete used to play rocket ships on the cracked concrete launch pads. Only in New Jersey.

Pete smiled at him. Matt relaxed the fist. The cops all stayed in place.

'Hey, Pete.'

'Hey, Matt.'

'Good to see you, man.'

'You too,' Pete said. 'Look, I'm getting off now. Why don't I give you a lift home, okay?'

Matt looked at the cops. Several were red-faced, ready to go. He turned back to his old friend. 'That's okay, Pete. I'll find my way.'

'You sure?'

'Yeah. Look, man, sorry if I caused you any trouble.'

Pete nodded. 'Good to see you.'

'You too.'

Matt waited. Two of the cops made a space. He did not look back as he walked out into the lot. He sucked in the night air and started down the street. Soon he broke into a run.

He had a specific destination in mind.

17

Lance Banner was still smiling at Loren. 'Come on, get in,' he said. 'We'll talk.'

She took one more look at Marsha Hunter's house and then slid into the passenger seat. Lance started driving around the old neighborhood.

'So,' he said, 'what did you want with Matt's sister-in-law?'

She swore Lance to secrecy but still tossed him only the bare bones – that she was investigating the suspicious death of Sister Mary Rose, that they weren't sure that there was even a murder yet, that Sister Mary Rose had possibly placed a phone call to Marsha Hunter's residence. She did not tell him about the implants or the fact that they didn't know the nun's real identity.

For his part, Lance informed her that Matt Hunter was married now, that he currently worked as a 'low-level, shat-upon' paralegal in his brother's old law firm. Matt Hunter's wife, Lance said, was from Virginia or Maryland, he couldn't remember which. Lance also added, with a little too much enthusiasm, that he would be happy to help Loren look into this case.

Loren told him not to bother, that this was her investigation, that if he thought of something he should let her know. Lance nodded and drove her back to her own car.

Before Loren stepped out, she said, 'Do you remember him? I mean, as a kid?'

'Hunter?' Lance frowned. 'Yeah, sure, I remember him.'

'He seemed like a pretty straight shooter.'

'So do a lot of killers.'

Loren reached for the door handle, shaking her head. 'You really believe that?'

Lance said nothing.

'I read something the other day,' Loren said. 'I don't remember the details, but the basic premise was that by the age of five, much of our future self is determined: how well we'll do in schools, if we'll grow up to be a criminal, our capacity to love. You buy that, Lance?'

'Don't know,' he said. 'Don't much care.'

'You've caught a lot of bad guys, right?'

'Yeah.'

'You ever look into their past?'

'Sometimes.'

'Seems to me,' Loren said, 'that I always find something. There's usually a pretty obvious case of past psychosis or trauma. On the news, the neighbors are always like, "Gee, I didn't know that nice man was chopping up little kids – he always seemed so polite." But you go back, you ask their schoolteachers, you ask their childhood friends, they almost always tell a different story. They're never surprised.'

Lance nodded.

'So what about it?' she asked. 'You see anything in his past that makes Matt Hunter a killer?'

Lance thought about it. 'If it was all determined by the age of five, we wouldn't have jobs.'

'That's not an answer.'

'Best I can do. You try to profile based on how a third-grader played on the monkey bars, we're all screwed.'

He had a point. Either way Loren needed to keep her eye on the ball – right now that meant tracking down Matt Hunter. She got back into her car and started south. There was still time to get to Lockwood Corp. in Wilmington, Delaware, before it was too dark.

She tried to reach Matt Hunter at the law firm, but he was gone for the day. She called his house and left a message on the machine: 'Matt, this is Loren Muse. I'm an investigator with the Essex County prosecutor's office. We knew each other a lifetime ago, at Burnet Hill. Could you give me a call as soon as possible?'

She left both her mobile and office numbers before hanging up.

The usually two-hour ride to Delaware took her an hour and twenty minutes. Loren didn't use the siren, but she did keep the small detachable flashing blue light on for the entire journey. She liked speeding – what's the point in being in law enforcement if you can't drive fast and carry a gun?

Randal Horne's office was a cookie-cut attorney spread. His firm took up three floors in a warehouse of office buildings, one next to the other, an unending drone of boxed sameness.

The receptionist at Horne, Buckman and Pierce, a classic battle-ax who was comfortably past her prime, eyed Loren as if she'd recognized her from a sex offender poster. Full frown in place, the battle-ax told her to sit.

Randal Horne kept her waiting for a full twenty minutes – a classic, if not transparent, lawyer mind game. She passed the time reading the thrilling magazine selection, which consisted of various issues of *The Third Branch*, the newsletter of federal courts, and the *American Bar Association Journal.* Loren sighed. What she wouldn't give for something with Lindsay, or Colin, on the cover.

Horne finally came out to the reception area and moved so that he stood directly over her. He was younger than she'd imagined, though he had that kind of shiny face Loren usually associated with Botox or Jermaine Jackson. His hair was a little too long, slicked back and curling around the neck. His suit was impeccable, though the lapels looked a little wide. Maybe that was back in.

He skipped the introductions: 'I don't really see that we have anything to discuss, Ms. Muse.'

Randal Horne stood close to her so that she couldn't really stand. That was okay. He was trying to do the height thing with her. Loren was all of five-one as it was, so she was used to it. Part of her was tempted to smash her palm into his groin, just to get him to back up, but no, let him have his play.

The battle-ax receptionist – she looked about fifteen years too old to play the prison matron in B-movies – watched the scene play out, the hint of a smile on her dry, lipstick-caked lips.

Loren said, 'I'd like the identity of the woman who purchased the breast implants with the serial number 89783348.'

'In the first place,' Horne said, 'these are very old records. SurgiCo didn't keep the woman's name on record, only the doctor who performed the procedure.'

'Fine, that'll be enough.'

Horne crossed his arms. 'Do you have a subpoena, Detective?'

'It's on its way.'

He gave her his smuggest expression, which was saying something. 'Well then,' he said, 'I'll return to my office. Please inform Tiffany here when you have it, will you?'

The battle-ax preened, smiled widely. Loren pointed at her and said, 'You have lipstick on your teeth.' Then she turned her attention back to Randal Horne. 'Do you mind telling me why you require a subpoena?'

'There are all sorts of new patient privacy laws. We at the Lockwood Corporation believe in following them.'

'But this woman is dead.'

'Still.'

'There are no medical secrets here. We know that she had implants. We're just trying to identify the body.'

'There must be other ways, Detective.'

'We're trying, believe me. But so far . . .' Loren shrugged.

'Unfortunately that does not change our position.'

'But your position, with all due respect, seems a tad fluid, Mr. Horne.'

'I'm not sure I understand your point.'

'Hold on a sec.' Loren started pulling folded papers out of her back pockets. 'I had time on the ride down here to check the New Jersey cases. It seems that your company has always cooperated with law enforcement in the past. You released records on a cadaver found last July in Somerset County. A Mr. Hampton Wheeler, age sixty-six, had his head and fingers cut off in order to avoid identification, but the killer forgot he had a pacemaker. Your company helped the authorities ID him. There was another case —'

'Detective . . . Muse, is it?'

'Inspector.'

'Inspector Muse. I'm very busy. Please make yourself comfortable. When your subpoena arrives, please feel free to tell Tiffany.'

'Wait.' Loren glanced at the battle-ax. 'Tiffany — I mean, that can't be her real name, right?'

'If you'll excuse me . . .'

'Mr. Horne, you already know I have no subpoena coming — that I was bluffing.'

Randal Horne said nothing.

Loren looked down and spotted the issue of *The Third Branch*. She frowned and turned toward Horne. This time she did stand. 'You didn't think I was bluffing,' she said, her words coming slowly. 'You knew it.'

Horne took a step back.

'But in reality,' Loren went on, more to herself than to him, 'it could have been true. It would have been tough timing, sure, but I could have called a federal judge on my way down here. The subpoena would be a no-brainer. Any member of the bench would have rubber-stamped it in five minutes. No judge in their right mind would refuse unless . . .'

Randal Horne waited. It was almost as if he hoped she'd put it together.

'Unless someone on the federal level – the FBI or U.S. attorney's office – shut you down.'

Horne cleared his throat and checked his watch. 'I really have to go now,' he said.

'Your company was cooperating with us at first. That's what Eldon said. Suddenly you stopped. Why? Why would you suddenly change your mind unless the feds told you to?' She looked up. 'Why would the feds care about this case?'

'That isn't our concern,' he said. Horne then put his hand to his mouth as if he'd been aghast at his own indiscretion. Their eyes met and she knew that he'd done her a favor. Horne wouldn't say any more. But he had said enough.

The FBI. They were the ones who had shut her down.

And maybe Loren understood why.

Back at her car Loren ran it through her head.

Who did she know at the FBI?

She had some acquaintances there, but nobody who could help on this level. The found-a-lead tingle rushed through her. This was big, no question about it. The FBI had been looking into this case. For some reason they wanted to find whoever was pretending to be Sister Mary Rose, leaving trip wires and calling cards everywhere, even with the company who supplied her breast implants.

She nodded to herself. Sure, this was mere speculation, but it made sense. Start with the victim: Sister Mary Rose had to be some sort of fugitive or witness. Someone valuable to the FBI.

Okay, good. Go on.

A long time ago Sister Mary Rose (or whatever her real name was) ran off – hard to say how long ago, but she'd been teaching at St. Margaret's, according to Mother Katherine, for seven years. So it had to be at least that long.

Loren stopped, considered the implications. Sister Mary Rose had been a fugitive for at least seven years. Had the feds been looking for her all that time?

It added up.

Sister Mary Rose had gone into deep, deep hiding. She'd changed her identity, for certain. Probably started off in Oregon, at that conservative convent Mother Katherine had mentioned. Who knows how long she was there?

Doesn't matter. What does matter is that seven years ago, for whatever reason, she chose to come east.

Loren rubbed her hands together. Oh, this is good.

So Sister Mary Rose moves to New Jersey and starts teaching at St. Margaret's. By all accounts she's a good teacher and nun, caring and devoted, living a quiet life. Seven years pass. Maybe she thinks she's safe now. Maybe she gets careless and reaches out to someone from her old life. Whatever.

Somehow, some way, her past catches up with her. Someone learns who she is. And then someone breaks into her small convent room, tortures her, and then suffocates her with a pillow.

Loren paused, almost as if she were offering up a respectful moment of silence.

Okay, she thought, so now what?

She needed to get the identity from the feds.

How?

Only thing she could think of was classic quid pro quo: Give them something in return. But what did she have?

Matt Hunter, for one.

The feds were probably at least a day or two behind her. Would they have the phone logs yet? Doubtful. And if they did, if they knew about the call to Marsha Hunter, would they have already figured in a Matt Hunter connection?

Very doubtful.

Loren hit the highway and picked up her cell phone. It was dead. She cursed the damn thing. The greatest lie – right up there with 'the check is in the mail' and 'your call is very important to us' – is the stated battery life of a cell phone. Hers was supposed to last a week on standby. She was lucky if the cursed thing gave her thirty-six hours.

She flipped open the glove compartment and pulled out the charger. One end she jammed into the cigarette lighter, the other into her phone. The phone's LCD jumped to life and informed her that there were three messages waiting.

The first was from her mother. 'Hi, sweetheart,' Mom said in a voice strangely tender. It was her public voice, the one she usually saved for when she thought someone might overhear and thus judge her maternal skills. 'I thought I'd order us a pizza from Renato's and pick up a movie at Blockbuster – the new Russell Crowe is out on DVD – and, I don't know, maybe we could have a girls' night, just the two of us. Would you like that?'

Loren shook her head, tried not to be moved, but the tears were there, right below the surface. Her mom. Every time she wanted to write her off, to dismiss her from her life, to hold a grudge, to blame her once and for all for Dad's death, she came along and said something surprising and pulled herself back from the brink.

'Yeah,' Loren said softly in the car. 'I'd like that a lot.'

The second and third messages blew that idea out of the water. They were both from her boss, County Prosecutor Ed Steinberg, and were short and to the point. The first one said: 'Call me. Now.' The second one said: 'Where the hell are you? Call me. Doesn't matter what the hour. Disaster on the way.'

Ed Steinberg was not one for overstatement or for having people call at all hours. He was old-fashioned in that approach. Loren had his home number somewhere – not on her, unfortunately – but she had never used it. Steinberg didn't like to be bothered during off hours. His motto was: Get a life, it can wait. He was usually out of the office by five o'clock and she couldn't recall a time when she'd seen him in his office after six.

It was six thirty now. She decided to try his office line first. Thelma, his secretary, might still be there. She'd know how to reach him. After one ring, the phone was picked up by Ed Steinberg himself.

This was not a good sign.

'Where are you?' Steinberg asked.

'On the way back from Delaware.'

'Come straight back here. We got a problem.'

18

For Adam Yates it started out as another day.

At least, that was what he wanted to believe. In a larger sense, no day was ever just another for Yates – at least, not for the past ten years. Each day felt like borrowed time, waiting eternally for the proverbial ax to fall. Even now, when most rational people would conclude that he'd successfully put his past mistakes behind him, the fear still gnawed in the back of his brain, tormenting him.

Yates had been a young agent then, working undercover. Now here he was, ten years later, the SAC – Special Agent in Charge – for all of Nevada, one of the FBI's most plum positions. He had risen up the ranks. In all that time, there had not been the smallest inkling of trouble.

So heading into work that morning, it seemed to be another day.

But when his chief advisor, Cal Dollinger, walked into his office, even though neither had spoken about the incident in nearly a decade, something in his old friend's face told him that this was indeed *the* day, that all others had merely been leading up to this.

Yates glanced quickly at the photograph on his desk. It was a family shot – he, Bess, the three kids. The girls were in their teens now, and no amount of training adequately prepares a father for that. Yates stayed seated. He wore his casual uniform – khakis, no socks, brightly hued polo shirt.

Cal Dollinger stood over his desk and waited. Cal was huge – six-seven and nearly three hundred pounds. Adam and Cal went way back, having first met as eight-year-olds in Mrs. Colbert's third-grade class at Collingwood Elementary School. Some men called them Lenny and George, referring to the Steinbeck characters in *Of Mice and Men*. There might be some truth to it – Cal was big and impossibly strong – but where Lenny had a gentleness, Cal had none. He was a rock, both physically and emotionally. He could indeed kill a rabbit by petting it, but he wouldn't care much.

But their bond was even stronger than that. You go back enough years, you pull each other out of enough fires, you become like one. Cal could be cruel, no question about it. But like most violent men, it was just a question of black and white. Those in his very small white zone – his wife, his kids, Adam, Adam's family – he'd protect with his dying breath. The rest of the world was black and inanimate, a distant backdrop.

Adam Yates waited, but Cal could wait longer.

'What is it?' Adam finally asked.

Cal's eyes swept the room. He feared listening devices. He said, 'She's dead.'

'Which one?'

'The older.'

'Are you sure?'

'Her body was found in New Jersey. We ID'd her by the serial numbers on the surgical implants. She was living as a nun.'

'You're kidding.'

Cal did not smile. Cal did not kid.

'What about' – Yates didn't even want to say Clyde's name – 'him?'

Cal shrugged. 'No idea.'

'And the tape?'

Cal shook his head. It was as Adam Yates had expected. It wouldn't end easily. It would never end at all. He cast one more glance at his wife and children. He looked about his spacious office, the commendations on the wall, his nameplate on the desk. All of it – his family, his career, his entire life – seemed wispy now, like holding smoke in a hand.

'We should go to New Jersey,' he said.

19

Sonya McGrath was surprised to hear the key in the lock.

Today, more than a decade after her son's death, the photographs of Stephen were still in the same frames on the same side tables. Other photographs had been added, of course. When Michelle, Sonya's oldest daughter, got married last year, they naturally took photographs. Several were framed over the fireplace. But no pictures of Stephen had ever been taken down. They could pack away his things, repaint his room, give his clothes to charity, sell his old car, but Sonya and Clark could never touch those photographs.

Her daughter Michelle, like many brides, had chosen to do the standard group photographs before the marriage ceremony. The groom, a nice guy named Jonathan, had a large extended family. They took all the usual shots. Sonya and Clark had gamely posed – with their daughter, with their daughter and soon-to-be son-in-law, with Jonathan's parents and the new bride and groom, whatever, but they balked when the photographer called for the 'McGrath family photograph,' the one that would have consisted of Sonya and Clark and Michelle and Cora, Michelle's younger sister, because all any of them would ever see, even after this joy-filled day, was the giant hole in the 'McGrath family photograph' where Stephen still belonged.

The big house was silent tonight. It had been that way since Cora started college. Clark was 'working late again' – a euphemism for 'sleeping with the bimbette' – but Sonya didn't care. She didn't question his hours because their home was even lonelier, even more silent, when Clark was here.

Sonya swirled the brandy in the snifter. She sat alone in the new theater room, in the dark, cuing up a movie on DVD. She'd rented something with Tom Hanks – his presence, even in crummy movies, oddly comforted her – but she hadn't hit the play button yet.

God, she thought, am I really this pitiful?

Sonya had always been a popular woman. She had many true and wonderful friends. It would be easy to blame them, to say that they slowly disengaged themselves from her after Stephen's death, that they had tried to be dutiful but after a while, you can only take so much, and so they made one excuse, and then another, gradually drifting away, cutting ties.

But that would not be fair to them.

It might be true in some small part – there had certainly been a detachment of sorts – but Sonya had been far more responsible for that than any of her friends. She pushed them away. She did not want comfort. She did not want company or camaraderie or commiseration. She didn't want to be miserable either, but perhaps that was the easiest and ergo best alternative.

The front door opened.

Sonya turned on the small lamp next to her movie-theater recliner. It was dark outside, but in this airless room that didn't matter. The shades blocked out all light. She heard the footsteps in the marble foyer and then on the polished hardwood floors. They were coming toward her.

She waited.

A moment later, Clark stepped into the room. He said nothing, just stood there. She studied him for a moment. Her husband looked somehow older, or maybe it had been a long time since she had really studied the man she'd married. He'd chosen not to go distinguished gray and took to coloring his hair. The coloring was done, as with all things Clark, meticulously, but it still didn't look right. His skin had an ashen tone. He looked thinner.

'I was just going to put on a movie,' she said.

He stared at her.

'Clark?'

'I know,' he said.

He did not mean that he knew that she was putting on a movie. He meant something else entirely. Sonya did not ask for clarification. There was no need. She sat very still.

'I know about your visits to the museum,' he went on. 'I've known for a long time.'

Sonya debated how to reply. Countering with an 'I know about you too' was the obvious move, but it would be both too defensive and entirely irrelevant. This was not about an affair.

Clark stood, his hands at his sides, his fingers itching but not clenching.

'How long have you known?' she asked.

'A few months.'

'So how come you didn't say anything before now?'

He shrugged.

'How did you find out?'

'I had you followed,' he said.

'Followed? You mean like you hired a private investigator?'

'Yes.'

She crossed her legs. 'Why?' Her voice raised a notch, stung by this strange betrayal. 'Did you think I was sleeping around?'

'He killed Stephen.'

'It was an accident.'

'Really? Is that what he tells you when you have your little lunches? Do you discuss how he accidentally murdered my son?'

'Our son,' she corrected him.

He looked at her then, a look she had seen before but never directed at her. 'How could you?'

'How could I what, Clark?'

'Meet with him. Offer him forgiveness –'

'I've never offered him anything of the sort.'

'Comfort then.'

'It's not about that.'

'Then what is it about?'

'I don't know.' Sonya rose to her feet. 'Clark, listen to me: What happened to Stephen was an accident.'

He made a noise of derision. 'Is that how you comfort yourself, Sonya? By telling yourself it was an accident?'

'Comfort myself?' A dark chill ripped through her. 'There is no comfort, Clark. Not for a second. Accident, murder – Stephen is dead either way.'

He said nothing.

'It was an accident, Clark.'

'He's convinced you of that, eh?'

'Actually, just the opposite.'

'What's that supposed to mean?'

'He's no longer sure himself. He feels tremendous guilt.'

'Poor baby.' Clark made a face. 'How can you be so naïve?'

'Let me ask you something,' Sonya said, moving closer to him. 'If they fell another way, if the angle had been different or if Stephen had twisted his body and Matt Hunter had hit his head on that curb –'

'Don't even start with that.'

'No, Clark, listen to me.' She took another step. 'If it had gone another way, if Matt Hunter ended up dead and Stephen had been found on top of him –'

'I'm not in the mood to play hypotheticals with you, Sonya. None of that matters.'

'Maybe it does to me.'

'Why?' Clark countered. 'Weren't you the one who said that either way Stephen is dead?'

She said nothing.

Clark crossed the room, moving past her, keeping enough distance so that he did not so much as brush up against her. He collapsed into a chair and lowered his head into his hands. She waited.

'Do you remember the case of that mother drowning her kids in Texas?' he asked.

'What does that have to do with anything?'

'Just' – he closed his eyes for a moment – 'just bear with me, okay? Do you remember that case? This overworked mother drowned her kids in the tub. I think there were four or five of them. Awful story. The defense made an insanity plea. Her husband supported her. Do you remember, on the news?'

'Yes.'

'What did you think?'

She said nothing.

'I'll tell you what I thought,' he continued. 'I thought, who cares? I don't mean that to sound cold. I mean, what's the difference? If this mother was found insane and spent the next fifty years in a loony bin or if she was found guilty and spent the rest of her life in jail or on death row – what does it matter? Either way you killed your own children. Your life is over, isn't it?'

Sonya closed her eyes.

'That's how it is with Matt Hunter to me. He killed our son. If it was an accident or intentional, I only know that our boy is dead. The rest doesn't matter. Do you understand that?'

More than he could ever know.

Sonya felt the tears escape from her eyes. She looked at her husband. Clark was in so much pain. Just go, she wanted to say. Bury yourself in your work, in your mistress, in whatever. Just go.

'I'm not trying to hurt you,' she said.

He nodded.

'Do you want me to stop seeing him?' she asked.

'Would it matter if I did?'

She did not reply.

Clark rose and left the room. A few seconds later, Sonya heard the front door close, leaving her yet again all alone.

20

Loren Muse made even better time on the way back from Wilmington, Delaware, to Newark. Ed Steinberg was alone in his office on the third floor of the new county courthouse.

'Shut the door,' her boss said.

Steinberg looked disheveled – loose tie, collar button undone, one sleeve rolled up higher than the other – but that was pretty much his normal look. Loren liked Steinberg. He was smart and played fair. He hated the politics of the job but understood the necessity of the game. He played it well.

Loren found her boss sexy in that cuddly-bear, hairy-Vietnam-vet-on-his-Harley vein. Steinberg was married, of course, with two kids in college. Cliché but true: The good ones were always taken.

When Loren was young, her mother would warn her to wait: 'Don't get married young,' Carmen would slur through the daytime wine. Loren never consciously followed that advice, but she realized somewhere along the way that it was idiotic. The good men, the ones who wanted to commit and raise children, were scooped up early. The field became thinner and thinner as the years went by. Now Loren had to settle for what one of her friends called 'retreads' – overweight divorcées who were making up for the years of high school rejection or those still cowering from the anguish of their first marriage or those semi-decent guys who were interested – and why not? – in some young waif who'd worship them.

'What were you doing in Delaware?' Steinberg asked.

'Following a lead on our nun's identity.'

'You think she's from Delaware?'

'No.' Loren quickly explained about the implants' identification code, the initial cooperation, the stone-walling, the connection to the feds. Steinberg stroked his mustache as if it were a small pet. When she finished, he said, 'The SAC in the area is a fed named Pistillo. I'll call him in the morning, see what he can tell me.'

'Thank you.'

Steinberg stroked his mustache some more. He looked off.

'Is that what you needed to see me about?' she asked. 'The Sister Mary Rose case?'

'Yes.'

'And?'

'The lab guys dusted the nun's room.'

'Right.'

'They found eight sets of prints,' he said. 'One set matched Sister Mary Rose. Six others matched various nuns and employees of St. Margaret's. We're running those through the system, just in case, see if anybody had a record we don't know about.'

He stopped.

Loren came over to the desk and sat down. 'I assume,' she said, 'you got a hit on the eighth set?'

'We did.' His eyes met hers. 'That's why I called you back here.'

She spread her hands. 'I'm all ears.'

'The prints belong to a Max Darrow.'

She waited for him to say more. When he stayed quiet, she said, 'I assume this Darrow has a record?'

Ed Steinberg shook his head slowly. 'Nope.'

'Then how did you get a match?'

'He served in the armed forces.'

In the distance, Loren could hear a phone ring. Nobody answered it. Steinberg leaned back in his big leather chair. He tilted his chin to look up. 'Max Darrow isn't from around here,' he said.

'Oh?'

'He lived in Raleigh Heights, Nevada. It's near Reno.'

Loren considered that. 'Reno's a pretty long way from a Catholic school in East Orange, New Jersey.'

'Indeed.' Steinberg was still looking up. 'He used to be on the job.'

'Darrow was a cop?'

He nodded. 'Retired. Detective Max Darrow. Worked homicide in Vegas for twenty-five years.'

Loren tried to fit that into her earlier theory about Sister Mary Rose being a fugitive. Maybe she was from the Vegas or Reno area. Maybe she'd stumbled across this Max Darrow sometime in the past.

The next step seemed pretty obvious: 'We need to locate Max Darrow.'

Ed Steinberg's voice was soft. 'We already have.'

'How's that?'

'Darrow is dead.'

Their eyes met and something else clicked into place. She could almost see Trevor Wine pulling up his belt. How had her patronizing colleague described his murder victim?

'A retired white guy . . . a tourist.'

Steinberg nodded. 'We found Darrow's body in Newark, near that cemetery off Fourteenth Avenue. He was shot twice in the head.'

21

It finally started to rain.

Matt Hunter had stumbled from the Landmark Bar and Grill and headed back up Northfield Avenue. Nobody followed him. It was late and dark and he was drunk, but that didn't matter. You always know the streets near where you grew up.

He made the right on Hillside Avenue. Ten minutes later he arrived. The Realtor's sign was still out front, reading UNDER CONTRACT. In a few days this house would be his. He sat on the curb and stared at it. Slow raindrops the size of cherries pounded down on him.

Rain reminded him of prison. It turned the world gray, drab, shapeless. Rain was the color of jail asphalt. Since the age of sixteen Matt wore contact lenses – was wearing them now – but in prison he'd stayed with glasses and kept them off a lot. It seemed to help, making his prison surroundings a blur, more unformed gray.

He kept his eyes on the house he'd planned to buy – this 'saltbox charmer' as the ad had called it. Soon he'd move in with Olivia, his beautiful, pregnant wife, and they'd have a baby. There'd probably be more kids after that. Olivia wanted three.

There was no picket fence in the front, but there might as well have been. The basement was unfinished, but Matt was pretty good with his hands. He'd do it himself. The swing set in the back was old and rusty and would need to be thrown out. While they were two years away from purchasing a replacement, Olivia had already located the exact brand she wanted – something with cedar wood – because they guaranteed no splinters.

Matt tried to see all that – that future. He tried to imagine living inside this three-bedroom abode with the kitchen that needed updating, a roaring fire, laughter at the dinner table, the kid coming to their bed because a nightmare had scared her, Olivia's face in the morning. He could almost see it, like one of Scrooge's ghosts was showing him the way, and for a second he almost smiled.

But the image wouldn't hold. Matt shook his head in the rain.

Who had he been kidding?

He didn't know what was going on with Olivia, but one thing he knew for certain: It marked the end. The fairy tale was over. As Sonya McGrath had said, the images on the camera phone had been his wake-up call, the reality check, the 'It's all a joke on you!' moment, when deep down inside, he'd always known that.

You don't come back.

Stephen McGrath was not about to leave his side. Every time Matt started to pull away, Dead Stephen was there, catching up from behind, tapping him on the shoulder.

'I'm right here, Matt. Still with you . . .'

He sat in the rain. He idly wondered what time it was. Didn't much matter. He thought about that damned picture of Charles Talley, the mysterious man with the blue-black hair, his mocking whispers on the phone. To what end? That was what Matt could not get around or figure out. Drunk or sober, in the comfort of his home or heck, outside in the pouring rain, the drought finally over. . . .

And that was when it struck him.

Rain.

Matt turned and looked up, encouraging the drops now. Rain. Finally. There was rain. The drought had ended with a massive fury.

Could the answer be that simple?

Matt thought about it. First thing: He needed to get home. He needed to call Cingle. Didn't matter what the time. She'd understand.

'Matt?'

He hadn't heard the car pull up, but the voice, even now, even under these conditions, well, Matt couldn't help but smile. He stayed on the curb. 'Hey, Lance.'

Matt looked up as Lance Banner stepped out of a minivan.

Lance said, 'I heard you were looking for me.'

'I was.'

'Why?'

'I wanted to fight you.'

Now it was Lance's turn to smile. 'You wouldn't want to do that.'

'Think I'm afraid?'

'I didn't say that.'

'I'd kick your ass.'

'Which would only prove me right.'

'About?'

'About how prison changes a man,' Lance said. 'Because before you went in, I'd have beaten you with two broken arms.'

He had a point. Matt stayed seated. He still felt pretty wasted and didn't fight the feeling. 'You always seem to be around, Lance.'

'That I am.'

'You're just so damn helpful.' Matt snapped his fingers. 'Hey, Lance, you know who you're like now? You're like that Block Mom.'

Lance said nothing.

'Remember that Block Mom on Hobart Gap Road?' Matt asked.

'Mrs. Sweeney.'

'Right. Mrs. S. Always peering out the window, no matter what time it was. Big sourpuss on her face, complaining about the kids cutting through her yard.' Matt pointed at him. 'You're like that, Lance. You're like a great big Block Mom.'

'You been drinking, Matt?'

'Yup. That a problem?'

'Not in and of itself, no.'

'So why are you always out and about, Lance?'

He shrugged. 'I'm just trying to keep the bad out.'

'You think you can?'

Lance didn't reply to that.

'You really think that your minivans and good schools are, what, some kind of force field, warding off evil?' Matt laughed too hard at that one. 'Hell, Lance, look at me, for chrissake. I'm the poster boy proving that's a load of crap. I should be on your warn-the-teens tour, you know, like when we were in high school and the cops would make us look at some car smashed up by a drunk driver. That's what I should be. One of those warnings to the youngsters. Except I'm not sure what my lesson would be.'

'Not to get into fights, for one.'

'I didn't get in a fight. I tried to break one up.'

Lance fought back a sigh. 'You want to retry the case out here in the rain, Matt?'

'No.'

'Good. Then how about I give you a lift home?'

'Not going to arrest me?'

'Maybe another time.'

Matt took one last look at the house. 'You may be right.'

'What about?'

'About my belonging.'

'Come on, Matt, it's wet out. I'll drive you home.'

Lance came up behind him. He put his hands under Matt's armpits and lifted. The man was powerful. Matt stumbled to a wobbly stand. His head spun. His stomach gurgled. Lance helped him to the car and into the front passenger seat.

'You get sick in my car,' Lance said, 'you'll wish I arrested you.'

'Ooo, tough guy.' Matt cracked the window, enough for a breeze but not enough to let in the rain. He kept his nose near the opening like a dog. The air helped. He closed his eyes and leaned his head against the window. The glass was cool against his cheek.

'So why the drinking binge, Matt?'

'Felt like it.'

'You do that a lot? Drink yourself stupid?'

'You an AA counselor too, Lance? You know, along with your gig as the Block Mom?'

Lance nodded. 'You're right. Change of subject.'

The rain let up a little. The wipers slowed down a notch. Lance kept both hands on the wheel.

'My oldest daughter is thirteen. You believe that?'

'How many kids you got, Lance?'

'Three. Two girls and a boy.' He took one hand off the wheel and fumbled for his wallet. He extracted three photographs and handed them to Matt. Matt studied them, searching as he always did, for echoes of the parent. 'The boy. How old is he?'

'Six.'

'Looks just like you did at that age.'

Lance smiled. 'Devin. We call him Devil. He's wild.'

'Like his old man.'

'Guess, yeah.'

They fell into silence. Lance reached for the radio then decided against it. 'My daughter. The oldest. I'm thinking of putting her in Catholic school.'

'She at Heritage now?' Heritage had been the middle school they'd attended.

'Yeah, but, I don't know, she's a little wild. I heard St. Margaret's in East Orange is supposed to be good.'

Matt looked out the window.

'You know anything about it?'

'About Catholic school?'

'Yeah. Or St. Margaret's.'

'No.'

Lance had both hands on the wheel again. 'Say, do you know who went there?'

'Went where?'

'St. Margaret's.'

'No.'

'Remember Loren Muse?'

Matt did. It was that way with people you went to elementary school with, even if you never saw them after graduation. You recall the name and face instantly. 'Sure. Tomboy, hung out with us for a while. Then she kinda faded away. Her father died when we were kids, right?'

'You don't know?'

'Know what?'

'Her old man committed suicide. Blew his brains out in their garage when she was in like eighth grade. They kept it a secret.'

'God, that's awful.'

'Yeah, but she's doing okay. She works in the prosecutor's office in Newark now.'

'She's a lawyer?'

Lance shook his head. 'An investigator. But after what happened with her father, well, Loren hit a rough patch too. St. Margaret's helped, I think.'

Matt said nothing.

'But you don't know anybody who went to St. Margaret's?'

'Lance?'

'Yeah.'

'This subtlety act. It's not really playing. What are you trying to ask me here?'

'I'm asking if you know anything about St. Margaret's.'

'You want me to write your daughter a letter of recommendation?'

'No.'

'Then why are you asking me these questions?'

'How about a Sister Mary Rose? Taught social studies there. Do you know her?'

Matt shifted so that he faced Lance full on. 'Am I a suspect in some kind of crime?'

'What? We're just having a friendly conversation here.'

'I don't hear a no, Lance.'

'You have a very guilty conscience.'

'And you're still evading my question.'

'You don't want to tell how you knew Sister Mary Rose?'

Matt closed his eyes. They weren't far from Irvington now. He leaned his head back against the headrest. 'Tell me more about your kids, Lance.'

Lance did not reply. Matt closed his eyes and listened to the rain. It brought him back to what he'd been thinking before Lance Banner showed up. He needed to call Cingle as soon as he could.

Because, strangely enough, the rain could hold the key to what Olivia was doing in that hotel room.

22

Matt thanked Lance for the ride and watched him pull away.

As soon as the minivan was out of sight, he headed inside, grabbed his phone, and started dialing Cingle's cell. He checked the time. It was nearly eleven o'clock. He hoped that she was awake, but even if she wasn't, well, once he explained, she'd understand.

The phone rang four times and then went into Cingle's simple voice mail message: 'Me. You. Tone.'

Damn.

He left Cingle a message: 'Call me back, it's urgent.' He hit the button for 'other options' and plugged in his home number. Maybe she'd get the page.

He wanted to download the images from his camera phone onto his hard drive, but like a dummy he'd left the USB cord at work. He searched the computer room for the cord that came with Olivia's phone, but he couldn't find it.

It was then that he noticed the phone's message light was blinking. He picked it up and hit play. There was only one message and after the day he'd had, it hardly surprised him.

'Matt, this is Loren Muse. I'm an investigator with the Essex County prosecutor's office. We knew each other a lifetime ago, at Burnet Hill. Could you give me a call as soon as possible?'

She left two numbers – office and cell.

Matt put the phone back in its cradle. So Lance was trying to get a jump on his county counterpart. Or they were working together. Whatever. He wondered what it could be about. Lance had said something about St. Margaret's in East Orange. Something about a nun there.

What could it possibly have to do with him?

Whatever, it couldn't be good.

He didn't want to speculate. He also didn't want to get caught unawares. So he headed into the computer room and ran a classic Google search. He searched for St. Margaret's in East Orange and got too many hits. He tried to remember the nun's name. Sister Mary Something. He added that into the mix. 'Sister Mary' 'St. Margaret's' 'East Orange.'

No relevant hits.

He sat back and thought it through. Nothing came to him. He wouldn't call Loren back. Not yet. It could wait until morning. He could say that he was out drinking – Lance would back that up – and forgot to check his messages.

His head started clearing. He thought about his next move. Even though he was alone in the house, Matt checked the corridor and closed the door. Then he opened the closet door, reached toward the back, and pulled out the lockbox. The combination was 878 because those numbers had absolutely no link to his life. He'd just made them up on the spot.

Inside the lockbox was a gun.

He stared at it. The semiautomatic was a Mauser M2. Matt had bought it off the streets – it's not hard to do – when he got out of jail. He'd told no one – not Bernie, not Olivia, not Sonya McGrath. He was not sure how to explain why he owned it. One would again think that his past would have taught him the danger of such actions. It had, he supposed, but with a twist. Now that Olivia was having a baby, yes, he'd have to get rid of the gun. But he wasn't sure that he'd be able to go through with it.

The prison system has its share of critics. Most problems are obvious and, to some extent, organic, what with the fact that you are, for the most part, caging bad people with other bad people. But the one thing that was definitely true was that prison taught you all the wrong skills. You survive by being aloof, by isolating yourself, by fearing any alliance. You are not shown how to assimilate or become productive – just the opposite. You learn that no one can be trusted, that the only person you can truly count on is yourself, that you must be ready to protect yourself at all times.

Having the gun gave Matt a strange feeling of comfort.

He knew it was wrong. He knew the odds were much greater that the gun would lead to disaster rather than salvation. But there it was. And now, with the world caving in on him, he was eyeing it for the first time since he'd bought it.

The phone startled him. He quickly closed the lockbox, as if someone had suddenly entered the room, and picked up the receiver.

'Hello?'

'Guess what I was doing when you called.'

It was Cingle.

'I'm sorry,' Matt said. 'I know it was late.'

'No, no. Guess. C'mon. Okay, forget it, I'll tell you. I was putting out for Hank. He takes forever. I was getting so bored I almost picked up mid, er, thrust. But men, well, they're so sensitive, you know?'

'Cingle?'

'What's up?'

'The pictures you downloaded from my phone.'

'What about them?'

'Do you have them?'

'You mean the files? They're at the office.'

'Did you blow them up?'

'My tech guy did, but I haven't had a chance to study them.'

'I need to see them,' Matt said. 'Blown up, that is.'

'Why?'

'I have a thought.'

'Uh oh.'

'Yes, uh oh. Look, I know it's late, really late, but if you could meet me down at your office –'

'Now?'

'Yes.'

'I'm on my way.'

'I owe you.'

'Time and a half,' Cingle said. 'See you in forty-five minutes.'

He grabbed his keys – he was sober enough now to drive – jammed his cell phone and wallet into his pocket, started for the door. Then he remembered the Mauser semiautomatic. It was still on the desktop. He considered his next move.

He picked up the gun.

Here was something that they never tell you: Holding a gun feels great. On television, the average person always acts all repulsed when the gun is first handed to them. They make a face and say, 'I don't want that thing!' But the truth is, having a gun in your hand – the cold steel against your skin, the weight in your palm, the very shape, the way your hand naturally coils around the grip, the way your index finger slides into the trigger loop – it feels not only good, but right and even natural.

But no, he shouldn't.

If he somehow got caught carrying a piece, with his record, there would be huge problems. He knew that.

But he still jammed the gun into the waist of his pants.

When Matt opened his front door, she was walking up the stoop. Their eyes met.

Matt wondered if he would have recognized her had he not just heard her name from Lance and listened to the message on the machine. Hard to say. The hair was still short. That tomboyish quality remained. She looked very much the same to him. Again there was something to that – to running into adults you only knew as kids in elementary school, how you can still recognize them by seeing the small child there.

Loren Muse said, 'Hey, Matt.'

'Hey, Loren.'

'Long time.'

'Yeah.'

She managed a smile. 'Do you have a second? I need to ask you a few questions.'

23

Standing on his front stoop, Matt Hunter asked, 'Is this about that nun at St. Margaret's?'

Loren was startled by that one, but Hunter held up his hand.

'Don't get excited,' he said. 'I know about the nun because Lance already questioned me.'

She should have known. 'So you want to fill me in?'

Matt shrugged, didn't say anything. She pushed past him, stepped into his foyer, and took a look around. Books were piled everywhere. Some had fallen, looking like crumbling towers. There were framed photographs on the table. Loren studied them. She picked one up.

'This your wife?'

'Yes.'

'Pretty.'

'Yes.'

She put the picture down and turned to him. It would be corny to say that his past was written on his face, that prison had somehow not only changed the inside, but the outside as well. Loren wasn't a fan of that stuff. She didn't believe the eyes were the windows to the soul. She had seen killers with beautiful, kind eyes. She had met brilliant people who had that open-eyed vacancy thing going on. She had heard jurors say, 'I knew he was innocent the minute he walked in the court – you can just tell' and knew that it was total, awful nonsense.

But that said, there was something in Matt Hunter's stance, in the tilt of the chin maybe, in the line of the mouth. The damage, the defensiveness, emanated from him. She couldn't put her finger on why, but it was there. Even if she hadn't known that he'd served hard time after a fairly comfortable childhood, would she still feel this unmistakable vibe?

She thought the answer was yes.

Loren couldn't help but think back to Matt as a kid, a good, goofy, sweet-natured kid, and a pang of sorrow skipped through her.

'What did you tell Lance?' she asked.

'I asked him if I was a suspect.'

'A suspect in what?'

'In anything.'

'And what did he say?'

'He was evasive.'

'You're not a suspect,' she said. 'Not yet anyway.'

'Whew.'

'Was that sarcasm?'

Matt Hunter shrugged. 'Could you ask your questions quickly? I have to be someplace.'

'Have to be someplace' – she repeated, making a production of checking her watch – 'at this hour?'

'I'm something of a party animal,' he said, stepping back onto the stoop.

'I somehow doubt that.'

Loren followed. She glanced about the neighborhood. There were two men drinking out of brown paper bags and singing an old Motown classic.

'That the Temptations?' she asked.

'Four Tops,' he said.

'I always mix those two up.'

She turned back to him. He spread his hands.

'Not exactly Livingston, is it?' Matt said.

'I heard you're moving back.'

'It's a nice town to raise a family.'

'You think?'

'You don't?'

She shook her head. 'I wouldn't go back.'

'That a threat?'

'No, that's meant to be literal. I, me, Loren Muse, would never want to live there again.'

'To each his own then.' He sighed. 'We done with the small talk now?'

'Guess so.'

'Fine. So what happened to this nun, Loren?'

'We don't know yet.'

'Come again?'

'Did you know her?'

'I don't even remember what Lance told me her name was. Sister Mary Something.'

'Sister Mary Rose.'

'What happened to her?'

'She died.'

'I see. So how do I fit in?'

Loren debated how to play this. 'How do you think?'

He sighed and started to walk past her. 'Good night, Loren.'

'Wait, okay, that was dumb. Sorry.'

Matt turned back to her.

'Her phone logs.'

'What about them?'

'Sister Mary Rose made one call we can't figure out.'

Matt's face showed nothing.

'Did you know her or not?'

Matt shook his head. 'No.'

'Because the log shows that she placed a call to your sister-in-law's residence in Livingston.'

He frowned. 'She called Marsha?'

'Your sister-in-law denied receiving any calls from anyone at St. Margaret's. I also talked to that Kylie girl who rents from her.'

'Kyra.'

'What?'

'Her name is Kyra, not Kylie.'

'Right, whatever. Anyway, I know you stay there a lot. I know, in fact, that you stayed there last night.'

Matt nodded. 'So you figured – drumroll, please – that I must be the one this nun called,' he finished for her.

She shrugged. 'Makes sense.'

Matt took a deep breath.

'What?'

'Isn't this the part where I get all angry and say it only makes sense because you have a bias against an ex-con, even though he's served his time and paid his debt to society?'

That made her smile. 'What, you just want to skip the indignation? Move right to your denial?'

'It would speed things up,' he said.

'So you don't know Sister Mary Rose?'

'No. For the record, I don't know any Sister Mary Rose. I don't even think I know any nuns. I don't know anybody connected with St. Margaret's, except, well, according to Lance, you went there, so I guess the answer would be: only you. I have no idea why Sister Mary Rose would call Marsha's house or even if indeed she called Marsha's house.'

Loren decided to shift tracks. 'Do you know a man named Max Darrow?'

'Did he call Marsha too?'

'How about a straight answer, Matt? Do you know a Max Darrow from Raleigh Heights, Nevada, yes or no?'

Jolt. Loren saw it. A small one – the smallest of tells on Matt's face. But it was there – a slight widening in the eyes. He recovered in less than a second.

'No,' he said.

'Never heard of him?'

'Never. Who is he?'

'You'll read about him in the paper tomorrow. You mind telling where you were yesterday? I mean, before you got to Marsha's house.'

'Yes, I do mind.'

'How about telling me anyway?'

He looked off, closed his eyes, opened them again. 'This is beginning to sound more like a full-fledged, suspectlike interrogation, Detective Muse.'

'Inspector Muse,' she said.

'Either way, I think I've answered enough questions for tonight.'

'So you're refusing?'

'No, I'm leaving.' Now it was Matt's turn to check his watch. 'I really have to go.'

'And I assume you're not going to tell me what you're up to?'

'You assume correctly.'

Loren shrugged. 'I could always follow you.'

'I'll save you the time. I'm heading to the MVD offices in Newark. What I do once I'm inside remains my own business. Have a pleasant night.'

He started down the stairs.

'Matt?'

'What?'

'This might sound weird,' Loren said, 'but it was good seeing you. I mean, I wish it were under different circumstances.'

He almost smiled. 'Same here.'

24

Nevada, Matt thought. Loren Muse had asked him about a man from Nevada.

Twenty minutes after leaving Loren on his stoop, Matt was in Cingle's office. He'd spent the drive running the interrogation through his head. One word kept coming back to him:

Nevada.

Max Darrow, whoever the hell he was, was from Nevada.

And Olivia had been checking a Web site for a newspaper called the *Nevada Sun News*.

Coincidence?

Yeah, right.

The offices at MVD were silent. Cingle sat at her desk, wearing a black Nike sweat suit. Her hair was swept back in a long ponytail. She hit the power button to boot up the computer.

'Have you heard anything about the death of a nun at St. Margaret's?' he asked.

Cingle frowned. 'That the church in East Orange?'

'Yes. It's also a school.'

'Nope.'

'How about anything involving a man named Max Darrow?'

'Like what?'

Matt quickly explained the questions from his old classmates Lance Banner and Loren Muse. Cingle sighed and took notes. She said nothing, only raising an eyebrow when he mentioned finding a computer cookie leading to a stripper Web site. 'I'll look into it.'

'Thanks.'

She swiveled the computer monitor so they could both view it. 'Okay, so what do you want to see?'

'Can you blow up the still shot of Charles Talley that came in on my cell phone?'

She started moving the mouse and clicking. 'Let me explain something quickly.'

'I'm listening.'

'This enhancement program. Sometimes it's a miracle worker, sometimes a total piece of crap. When you take a digital picture, the quality is dependent on the pixels. That's why you get a camera with as many pixels as possible. Pixels are dots. The more dots, the clearer the picture.'

'I know all this.'

'Your camera phone has a pretty crappy pixel reading.'

'I know that too.'

'So you know that the more you blow up the image, the less clear it becomes. This software program uses some kind of algorithm – yeah, I know, big word. Put simply, it guesses what should be there based on whatever clues it comes up with. Coloring, shading, ridges, lines, whatever. It's far from exact. There's a lot of trial and error. But that said . . .'

She pulled up the picture of Charles Talley. This time Matt skipped the blue-black hair, the smirk, the entire face. He ignored the red shirt and white walls. He only had eyes for one thing.

He pointed at it. 'See this?'

Cingle put on a pair of reading glasses, squinted, looked at him. 'Yes, Matt,' she said deadpan. 'We call it a window.'

'Can you blow it up or enhance it any more?'

'I can try. Why, you think there's something out that window?'

'Not exactly. Just do it, please.'

She shrugged, placed the cursor over it, blew it up. The window now took up half the screen.

'Can you make it any clearer?'

Cingle hit something called fine tune. Then she looked at Matt. He smiled at her.

'Don't you see?'

'See what?'

'It's gray. That much I could tell on the camera phone. But now look. There are raindrops on the window.'

'So?'

'So this picture was sent to me yesterday. You see any rain yesterday? Or the day before?'

'But wait, isn't Olivia supposed to be in Boston?'

'Maybe she was, maybe she wasn't. But there hasn't been rain in Boston either. There hasn't been rain anywhere in the Northeast.'

Cingle sat back. 'So what does it mean?'

'Hold up, check something else first,' Matt said. 'Bring up the camera phone video and play it slowly.'

Cingle minimized the photograph of Charles Talley. She started clicking icons again. Matt felt the rush. His leg started shaking. His head began to clear.

The video started playing. Matt tried to watch the woman with the platinum-blonde wig. Later, maybe he'd go through it step-by-step, confirm that it was indeed Olivia. He remained fairly certain that it was. But that wasn't the issue right now.

He waited until the woman started moving, waited for the flash of light.

'Hit pause.'

Cingle was quick. She hit it with the light still there.

'Look,' he said.

Cingle nodded. 'Well, I'll be damned.'

The sun was bursting through the window.

'The photograph and the video weren't taken at the same time,' she said.

'Exactly.'

'So what happened? They downloaded the first picture onto Olivia's phone or maybe took a picture of a picture?'

'Something like that.'

'I still don't get it.'

'I'm not sure I do either. But . . . start the tape rolling again. Slow motion.'

Cingle did as he asked.

'Stop.' He looked at it. 'Blow up the guy's left hand.'

It was a shot from the palm side of the hand. Again it was blurry when she first blew it up. She used the software enhancer. The hand came more into focus.

'Just skin,' Matt said.

'So?'

'No ring or wedding band. Let's switch back to our photograph of Charles Talley.'

This one was easier. The photograph had a better resolution. The figure of Charles Talley was larger. His hand was up, palm wide open, almost as if stopping traffic.

The backside of a ring was clearly visible.

'My God,' Cingle said. 'It's a setup.'

Matt nodded.

'I mean, I don't know what's going on in this video, but they wanted you to think this Charles Talley guy was having an affair with Olivia. Do you have any idea why?'

'None. Did you find anything more on Talley?'

'Let me check my e-mail. Something should be in by now.'

While Cingle started up her online service, Matt took out his cell phone. He once again hit the speed dial for Olivia. The small warmth was back in his chest. He smiled. Yes, there were problems – Olivia was still in a hotel room with a strange man – and, okay, maybe he was still just a touch high from the remnants of vodka, but there was hope now. The curtain of doom seemed to be parting.

This time, Olivia's recorded voice sounded melodic to him. He waited for the beep and said, 'I know you didn't do anything wrong. Please call me.' He looked over at Cingle. She was pretending not to listen. 'I love you,' he finished.

'Aw, how sweet,' Cingle said.

A male voice from her computer shouted: 'You've got mail.'

'Anything?' Matt asked.

'Give me a second.' She started scanning the e-mails. 'Not much yet, but, okay, it's something. Talley has three assault convictions, arrested twice more but the cases were dropped. He was suspected – man, this guy is creepy – of beating his landlord to death. Talley last served time at a state prison called – get this – Lovelock.'

'That name rings a bell. Where is it?'

'Doesn't say. Hold on, let me do a quick search.' Cingle started typing, hit return. 'Jesus.'

'What?'

She looked up at him. 'It's in Lovelock, Nevada.'

Nevada. Matt felt the floor drop away. Cingle's cell phone chirped. She lifted it into view, read the LCD screen.

'Give me a second, okay?'

Matt might have nodded. He felt numb.

Nevada.

And then another stray thought – another wild, possible connection to

379

Nevada – came to him: During his freshman year of college, hadn't he gone with some friends to Nevada?

Las Vegas, to be more specific.

It was there, on that trip so many years ago, that he first met the love of his life. . . .

He shook his head. Uh uh, no way. Nevada is a big state.

Cingle hung up the phone and started typing on her computer.

'What?' he said.

Her eyes were still on the monitor. 'Charles Talley.'

'What about him?'

'We know where he is.'

'Where?'

She hit the return button and squinted. 'According to Mapquest, less than four miles from where you're now standing.' She took off her reading glasses and looked up at him. 'Talley has been staying at the Howard Johnson's by Newark Airport.'

25

'You sure?' Matt asked.

Cingle nodded. 'Talley's been there at least two nights. Room 515.'

Matt tried to put some of the pieces together. Nothing fit. 'Do you have the phone number?'

'The Howard Johnson's? I can look it up online.'

'Do that.'

'You're going to just call him?'

'Yes.'

'And say what?'

'Nothing yet. I just want to see if it's the same voice.'

'The same voice as what?'

'The guy who called me whispering about what he was about to do to Olivia. I just want to know if it was Charles Talley.'

'And if it was?'

'Hey, you think I have a long-term plan here?' Matt said. 'I'm barely winging it.'

'Use my phone. The caller ID is blocked.'

Matt picked up the receiver. Cingle read off the number. The operator answered on the third ring. 'Howard Johnson's, Newark Airport.'

'Room 515, please.'

'One moment.'

With the first ring his heart began to pick up its pace. The third ring was cut off midway. Then he heard a voice say, 'Yeah.'

Matt calmly replaced the receiver.

Cingle looked up at him. 'Well?'

'It's him,' Matt said. 'It's the same guy.'

She frowned, crossed her arms. 'So now what?'

'We could study the video and picture more,' Matt said.

'Right.'

'But I don't know what that would tell us. Suppose I'm wrong. Suppose it was Talley in both the video and the picture. Then we need to talk to him. Suppose it was two different men. . . .'

'We still need to talk to him,' Cingle said.

'Yes. I don't see where we have any choice. I have to go over there.'

'*We* have to go over there.'

'I'd rather go alone.'

'And I'd rather shower with Hugh Jackman,' Cingle said, standing. She took out her hair tie, tightened the ponytail, put the tie back in. 'I'm coming.'

Further argument would just delay the inevitable. 'Okay, but you stay in the car.

Man-to-man, alone, maybe I can get something out of him.'

'Fine, whatever.' Cingle was already on her way to the door. 'I'll drive.'

The ride took five minutes.

The Howard Johnson's could have been located near an uglier stretch of free-way, but not without a dumping permit. Or maybe they already had one. On one side of Frontage Road was the New Jersey Turnpike Exit 14 toll plaza. On the other side was the parking lot for Continental Airlines employees. Take Frontage Road a few hundred more feet, and you were at the Northern State Prison, con-veniently located – more convenient than the Howard Johnson's even – to Newark Airport. Perfect for the quick getaway.

Cingle pulled up to the lobby entrance.

'You sure you want to go alone?' she asked.

'Yes.'

'Give me your cell phone first,' she said.

'Why?'

'I have this friend – a financial bigwig on Park Avenue. He taught me this trick. You put on your cell phone. You call mine. You leave it on and connected. I put the mute feature on my phone. Now it's like a one-way intercom. I can hear what you say and do. If there's any trouble, just shout.'

Matt frowned. 'A financial bigwig needs to do this?'

'You don't want to know.'

Cingle took Matt's phone, dialed in her number, answered her phone. She handed his cell phone back to him. 'Attach it to your belt. If you're in trouble, just yell for help.'

'Okay.'

The lobby was empty. Not a surprise considering the hour. He heard a bell ding when the glass door slid open. The night shift receptionist, an unshaven blob who resembled an overstuffed laundry bag, staggered into view. Matt waved to him without slowing, trying to look as if he belonged. The receptionist returned the wave, staggered back.

Matt reached the elevator and pushed the call button. There was only one working elevator car. He heard it start toward him with a grunt, but it took its time coming. Images again started flashing through his head. That video. The platinum-blonde wig. He still had no idea what it all meant, no clue at all.

Yesterday Cingle had compared all this to stepping into a fight – you couldn't predict the outcome. But here he was, about to open a door literally, and in truth he had no idea what he'd find behind it.

A minute later, Matt stood in front of the door to Room 515.

The gun was still on him. He debated taking it out and hiding it behind his back, but no, if Talley saw it, this would all go wrong. Matt lifted his hand and knocked. He listened. A noise came from down the corridor, a door opening, maybe. He turned.

Nobody.

He knocked again, harder this time.

'Talley?' he shouted. 'You in there? We need to talk.'

He waited. Nothing.

'Please open up, Talley. I just want to talk to you, that's all.'

And then a voice came from behind the door, the same voice he'd heard on the phone: 'One second.'

The door to Room 515 opened.

And suddenly, standing in front of him, with that blue-black hair and knowing scowl, was Charles Talley.

Talley stood in the doorway, talking on his mobile phone. 'Right,' he said to whoever was on the other end. 'Right, okay.'

He gestured with his chin for Matt to step inside.

And that was exactly what Matt did.

26

Loren thought about the jolt.

Matt had tried to cover it, but he'd reacted to the name Max Darrow. The question was, of course, why.

She actually took up Matt's challenge and semi-followed him – that is, she drove ahead and planted herself near the offices of MVD. She knew that the owner of the private investigation firm was an ex-fed. He had a reputation for discretion, but maybe he could be squeezed.

When Matt pulled in – just as he'd said – there were two other cars in the lot. Loren wrote down the license plate numbers. It was late. There was no reason to hang around now.

Twenty minutes later, Loren arrived home. Oscar, her oldest cat, nestled up for an ear scratch. Loren obliged but the cat quickly grew bored, meowed his impatience, and crept into the dark. There was a time when Oscar would dart away, but age and bad hips had ended that. Oscar was getting old. The vet had given Loren that look during the last checkup, the one that said she'd better start preparing. Loren blocked on it. In movies, it was always the kids who were, à la Old Yeller and its subsequent ripoffs, devastated by the loss of a pet. In reality kids get bored with pets. Lonely adults feel the loss most acutely. Like Loren.

It was freezing in the apartment. The air conditioner rattled against the windowsill, dripping water and keeping the room at a good temperature to store meat. Mom was asleep on the couch. The television was still on, playing an infomercial for some contraption guaranteed to give you six-pack abs. She flicked off the air conditioner. Her mother did not budge.

Loren stood in the doorway and listened to her mother's smoke-phlegm snore. The grating sound was something of a comfort – it eased Loren's own desire to light up. Loren didn't wake her mother. She didn't fluff her pillow or pull a blanket over her. She just watched for a few moments and wondered for the umpteenth time what she felt for this woman.

Loren made herself a ham sandwich, wolfed it down over the sink in the kitchen, and poured a glass of Chablis from a jug-shaped bottle. The garbage, she saw, needed to be taken out. The bag was overflowing, not that that ever stopped her mother from trying to stuff more into it.

She ran the dish under the faucet and lifted the garbage can with a sigh. Her mother still did not stir; there was no disturbance or variance in her phlegm-snore cycle. She took the bag to the Dumpster outside. The outside air was sticky. The crickets hummed. She tossed the bag on the heap.

When she got back to her apartment her mother was awake.

'Where were you?' Carmen asked.

384

'I had to work late.'

'And you couldn't call?'

'Sorry.'

'I was worried sick.'

'Yeah,' Loren said. 'I saw how it affected your sleep.'

'What's that supposed to mean?'

'Nothing. Good night.'

'You're so inconsiderate. How could you not call? I waited and waited –'

Loren shook her head. 'I'm kinda getting tired of it, Mom.'

'Of what?'

'Your constantly berating me.'

'You want to throw me out?'

'I didn't say that.'

'But that's what you want, isn't it? To have me gone?'

'Yes.'

Carmen opened her mouth and put her hand to her chest. There was probably a time when men would react to such theatrics. Loren remembered all those
photographs of the young Carmen – so lovely, so unhappy, so sure she deserved
more.

'You'd throw out your own mother?'

'No. You asked if I wanted to. I do. But I won't.'

'Am I that horrible?'

'Just . . . just stay off my back, okay?'

'I just want you to be happy.'

'Right.'

'I want you to find someone.'

'You mean a man.'

'Yes, of course.'

Men – that was Carmen's answer to everything. Loren wanted to say, *'Yeah,
Mom, look at how ecstatically happy men have made you,'* but she bit down.

'I just don't want you to be alone,' her mother said.

'Like you,' Loren said, wishing she hadn't.

She did not wait for the response. She headed into the bathroom and started
getting ready for bed. When she came out, her mother was back on the couch.
The television was off. The air conditioner was back on.

Loren said, 'I'm sorry.'

Her mother did not reply.

'Were there any messages?' Loren asked.

'Tom Cruise called twice.'

'Fine, good night.'

'What, you think that boyfriend of yours called?'

'Good night, Mother.'

Loren headed into the bedroom and switched on the laptop. While it booted
up, she decided to check the caller ID. Nope, Pete, her new boyfriend, hadn't
called – hadn't called, for that matter, in three days. In fact, other than those that
had emanated from her office, there had been no new calls at all.

Man, that was pitiful.

Pete was a nice enough guy, on the overweight side and sort of sweaty. He worked some district job for Stop & Shop. Loren could never figure out what he did exactly, probably because it really didn't interest her much. They were nothing steady, nothing serious, the kind of relationship that just glides along, that scientific principle about a body in motion will keep moving. Any friction would pretty much stop it in its tracks.

She glanced around the room, at the bad wallpaper, the nondescript bureau, the Kmart snap-together night table.

What kind of life was this?

Loren felt old and without prospects. She considered moving out west – to Arizona or New Mexico, someplace warm and new like that. Start fresh with great weather. But the truth is, she didn't like the outdoors all that much. She liked the rain and cold because they gave her an excuse to stay inside and watch a movie or read a book guilt-free.

The computer sprang to life. She checked her e-mail. There was a message from Ed Steinberg sent within the hour:

Loren,

I don't want to get into Trevor Wine's file on Max Darrow without involving him. We'll do that in the morning. Here are the prelims. Get some sleep, I'll see you at nine a.m.

– Boss

A file was attached. She downloaded the document and decided to print it out. Reading too much on a computer monitor made her eyes ache. She grabbed the pages out of her printer and slipped under the covers. Oscar managed to jump on the bed, but Loren could see him wince from the effort. The old cat cuddled next to her. Loren liked that.

She scanned the documents and was surprised to see that Trevor Wine had already come up with a decent hypothesis for the crime. According to the notes, Max Darrow, a former detective with the Las Vegas Police Department and current resident of Raleigh Heights, Nevada, had been found dead in a rental car near the Hebrew cemetery in Newark. According to the report, Max Darrow had been staying at the Newark Airport Howard Johnson's. He had rented a car from someplace called LuxDrive. The car, a Ford Taurus, had been driven, per the speedometer, eight miles in the two days the car had been in Darrow's possession.

Loren turned to the second page. Here was where things got interesting.

Max Darrow was found shot dead in the driver's seat of the rental car. No one had called it in. A patrol car had spotted the bloodstains on the window. When Darrow was found, his pants and boxers were pulled down around his ankles. His wallet was gone. The report stated that Darrow was wearing no jewelry when found, implying that he'd probably been robbed of those items too.

According to the preliminary report – everything was still preliminary – the blood found in the car, especially the trajectory on the windshield and driver-side window, showed that Darrow had been shot while sitting in the driver's seat of the car. Splatters were also found on the inside of his pants and boxers, which would be consistent with the man having his pants pulled down before the gun fired, not after.

The working theory was obvious: Max Darrow had decided to get lucky – or more likely, to buy some 'get lucky.' He had picked up the wrong prostitute who waited for the right moment – pants down – and then rolled him. Something had gone wrong then, though it was hard to say what. Maybe Darrow, being an ex-cop, had tried to make a hero play. Maybe the prostitute was simply too strung out. Whatever, she ends up shooting and killing Darrow. She takes what she can find – wallet, jewelry – and runs.

The investigative team, in cooperation with the Newark Police Department, would squeeze the prostitution trade. Someone would know what happened. They'd talk.

Case solved.

Loren put down the report. Wine's theory made sense if you didn't know about Darrow's fingerprints being found in Sister Mary Rose's room. Still, now that Loren knew that the lead theory was crap – what did she have left? Well, for one thing, this was probably a pretty clever setup.

Play it out for a second.

You want to kill Darrow. You get in a car with him. You put a gun to his head. You tell him to drive to a sleazy part of town. You make him pull down his pants – anyone who'd ever watched any forensic TV show would know that if you pulled the pants down after the shooting, the blood splatters would show that. Then you shoot him in the head, take his money and jewelry, make it look like a robbery.

Trevor Wine had bought it.

In a vacuum Loren probably would have come to the same conclusion.

So what would be the next logical step?

She sat up in bed.

Wine's theory had been that Max Darrow had done some cruisin' and picked up the wrong girl. But if that wasn't the case – Loren was sure of that much – how did the killer get in the car with Darrow in the first place? Wouldn't it be most logical to assume that Darrow was with his killer from the beginning of his car trip?

That meant Darrow probably knew his killer. Or at least did not view him as a threat.

She checked the mileage again. Only eight miles. Assuming he used it the day before, well, that meant that he hadn't driven very far.

There was something else to consider: Another set of fingerprints had been found in Sister Mary Rose's room – more specifically, on her body.

Okay, Loren thought, suppose Darrow was working with someone else – a partner maybe. They'd stay together, right? Or near each other, at the very least.

Darrow had been staying at the Howard Johnson's.

She checked the file. The rental car company LuxDrive – they had a counter at the same hotel.

So that was where it all started. At the Howard Johnson's.

Most hotels have security cameras. Had Trevor Wine checked out the ones at the Howard Johnson's yet?

Hard to say, but it would definitely be worth it for her to check it out.

Either way, it could wait until morning, right?

She tried to sleep. She sat in bed and closed her eyes. She did this for well over an hour. From the other room, she heard her mother's snores. The case was heating up. Loren felt the buzz in her blood. She pushed back the covers and got out of bed. There was no way she could sleep. Not now. Not when there was something of a clue in the air. And tomorrow she'd have a whole new set of problems, what with Ed Steinberg calling the feds and Trevor Wine getting involved.

She might be taken off the case.

Loren threw on her sweats, grabbed her wallet and ID. She tiptoed outside, started up her car, and headed for the Howard Johnson's.

27

Nothing worse than crappy porn.

Lying in the motel room bed, that was what Charles Talley had been thinking before the phone rang. He'd been watching some weirdly edited porno on the Spectravision Pay-Per-View channel. It had cost him $12.95, but the damn movie cut out all the good stuff, all the close-ups and, well, genitalia both male and female.

What the hell is this crap?

Worse yet, the movie, in order to make up for the lost time, kept replaying over and over the same parts. So the girl would be like sliding down to her knees and then they'd show this guy's face tilting back and then they'd go back to the girl sliding down, the guy's face, the girl sliding down . . .

It was maddening.

Talley was about to call down to the front desk, give them a piece of his mind. This was the friggin' United States of America. A man has a right to watch porn in the privacy of his own hotel room. Not this chicken-ass soft stuff. Real porn. Hardcore action. This stuff, this soft porn – might as well be put on the Disney Channel.

That was when the phone rang. Talley checked his watch.

About time. He'd been waiting for this callback for hours now.

Talley reached for the phone, put it to his ear. On the screen the girl was panting the exact same way for, what, ten minutes now. This crap was beyond boring.

'Yeah.'

Click. Dial tone.

A hang-up. Talley looked at the receiver as if it might give him a second response. It didn't. He put the receiver down and sat up. He waited for the phone to ring again. After five minutes passed, he started to worry.

What was going on here?

Nothing had turned out as planned. He'd flown in from Reno, what, three days ago now? Hard to remember exactly. His assignment yesterday had been clear and easy: Follow this guy named Matt Hunter. Keep a tail on him.

Why?

He had no idea. Talley had been told where to start off – parked outside some big law office in Newark – and to follow Hunter wherever he went.

But the guy, this Matt Hunter, had spotted the tail almost immediately.

How?

Hunter was strictly an amateur. But something had gone very wrong. Hunter had made him right away. And then, worse – much worse – when Talley called him a few hours ago, Matt Hunter knew who he was.

389

He had used Talley's full name, for chrissake.

This confused Talley.

He didn't handle confusion well. He placed some calls, tried to find out what was going on, but nobody had picked up.

That confused him even more.

Talley had few talents. He knew strippers and how to handle them. He knew how to hurt people. That was pretty much it. And really, when you thought about it, those two things went together. You want to keep a strip joint running and happy, you need to know how to put on the hurt.

So when things got muddled – as they were now – that was always his fallback position. Violence. Hurting someone and hurting them bad. He had spent time in prison for only three assault beefs, but in his life Talley guessed that he'd probably beaten or maimed fifty plus. Two had died.

His preferred method of putting on the hurt involved stun guns and brass knuckles. Talley reached into his bag. First he pulled out his brand-new stun gun. It was called the Cell Phone Stun Gun. The thing looked, as the name suggested, exactly like a cell phone. Cost him sixty-nine bucks off the Web. You could take it anywhere. You could have it out and put it to your ear like you were talking and bam, you press a button and the 'antenna' on the top wallops your enemy with 180,000 volts.

Then he pulled out his brass knuckles. Talley preferred the newer designs with the wider impact area. They not only spread out your area of collision, they put less pressure on your hand when you laid into someone good.

Talley put both the stun gun and brass knuckles on the night table. He went back to his movie, still holding out hope that the porno flick would improve. Every once in a while he would glance at his weapons. There was arousal there too, no doubt about it.

He tried to think about what to do next.

Twenty minutes later, there was a knock on his hotel room door. He checked the bedside clock. It was nearly one in the morning. He quietly slid off the bed.

There was another knock now, more urgent.

He tiptoed to the door.

'Talley? You in there? We need to talk.'

He peeked through the peephole. *What the . . . ?*

It was Matt Hunter!

Panic flooded in. How the hell had Hunter tracked him down?

'Please open up, Talley. I just want to talk to you, that's all.'

Talley did not think. He reacted. He said, 'One second.'

Then he crept back toward the bed and slipped the brass knuckles on his left hand. In the right, he held the cell phone to his ear, as if he were in the middle of the conversation. He reached for the knob. Before he turned, he looked into the peephole.

Matt Hunter was still there.

Talley planned his next three moves. That was what the greats did. They planned ahead.

He would open the door, pretending he was on the phone. He would signal for Hunter to come forward. As soon as he was in range, Talley would hit him with the stun gun. He'd aim for the chest – a big target with the most surface area. At the same time he'd have the left hand prepared. With the brass knuckles, he'd use an uppercut to the ribs.

Charles Talley opened the door.

He started talking on the phone, pretending someone was on the other line. 'Right,' Talley said into the stun gun. 'Right, okay.'

He gestured with his chin for Matt Hunter to step inside.

And that was exactly what Matt Hunter did.

28

Matt hesitated in the doorway to Room 515 but not for very long.

He had no choice here. He couldn't stay in the corridor and try to talk to him. So he started to move inside. He still was not sure how to present this, what role Talley was playing. Matt had decided to play it fairly straight and see where it led. Did Talley know he was part of a setup? Was he the guy in the video – and if so, why had the other picture been taken at an earlier time?

Matt entered.

Charles Talley was still talking on his mobile phone. As the door started to close, Matt said, 'I think we can help each other out.'

And that was when Charles Talley touched his chest with the cell phone.

It felt like Matt's entire body had suddenly short-circuited. His spine jolted upright. His fingers splayed. His toes went rigid. His eyes widened.

He wanted the cell phone away. Off him. But he couldn't move. His brain shouted. His body would not listen.

The gun, Matt thought. *Get your gun.*

Charles Talley reeled back a fist. Matt could see it. Again he tried to move, tried to at least turn away, but the electrical voltage must have stopped certain brain synapses from firing. His body simply wouldn't obey.

Talley punched him in the bottom point of the rib cage.

The blow landed against the bone like a sledgehammer. The pain burst through him. Matt, already falling, dropped onto his back.

He blinked, his eyes watering, and looked up into the smiling face of Charles Talley.

The gun . . . get the damn gun. . . .

But his muscles were in spasm.

Calm yourself. Just relax. . . .

Standing over him, Talley had the cell phone in one hand. He wore brass knuckles on the other.

Matt idly wondered about his own cell phone. The one on his belt. Cingle was on the other end, listening. He opened his mouth to call out to her.

Talley hit him again with what must have been a stun gun.

The volts raced through his nervous system. His muscles, including those in his jaws, contracted and quaked uncontrollably.

His words, his cry for help, never made it out.

Charles Talley smiled down at him. He showed him the fist with the brass knuckles. Matt could only look up and stare.

In prison, some of the guards used to carry stun guns. They worked, Matt had learned, by overloading and thus disrupting the internal communication system.

The current mimics the body's own natural electrical impulses, confusing them, telling the muscles to do a great deal of work, depleting energy.

The victim is left helpless.

Matt watched Talley pull back his fist. He wanted to grab his Mauser M2 and blow the bastard away. The weapon was just there, in his waistband, but it might as well have been out of state.

The fist headed toward him.

Matt wanted simply to raise an arm, wanted to roll away, wanted to do anything. He couldn't. Talley's punch was aimed straight for Matt's chest. Matt watched as it moved as though it were in slow motion.

The knuckles smashed into his sternum.

It felt as if the bones had caved in on his heart. Like his sternum was made of Styrofoam. Matt opened his mouth in a silent, anguished scream. His air was gone. His eyes rolled back.

When Matt's eyes finally regained focus, the brass knuckles were heading toward his face.

Matt struggled, but he was weak. Too weak. His muscles still wouldn't obey. His internal communication network remained shut down. But something primitive, something base, was still there, still had enough survival instincts to at the very least turn away from the blow.

The brass knuckles scraped off the back of his skull. The skin burst open. Pain exploded in his head. His eyes closed. This time they did not reopen. From somewhere far away he heard a voice, a familiar voice, shout, 'No!' But that was probably not real. Between the electrical currents and the physical punishment, the brain's wiring was probably conjuring up all sorts of strange delusions.

There was another blow. Maybe another. Maybe there were more, but Matt was too far away to notice.

29

'Talley? You in there? We need to talk.'

Cingle Shaker perked up when she heard Matt's voice through the cell phone. The sound wasn't great, but she could make out enough.

'Please open up, Talley. I just want to talk to you, that's all.'

The reply was muffled. Too muffled to make out. Cingle tried to clear her head and concentrate. Her car sat double-parked by the front entrance. It was late. Nobody would bother her.

She debated heading inside now. That would be the smart play. Matt was on the fifth floor. If something went wrong, it would take her a while to get up there. But Matt had been fairly adamant. He felt his best chance was to brace this Talley guy alone. If she was spotted before they talked, that would only complicate matters.

But now that there was a muffled voice, Cingle could be reasonably sure that Talley was not in the lobby. In fact, from her vantage point, nobody was in the lobby.

She decided to head in.

Surveillance was far from Cingle's forte. She was simply too noticeable. She had never been a Rockette or dancer of any sort – yes, she'd heard all the rumors – but she had given up trying to dress herself down years ago. Cingle had started developing at a young age. By twelve, she could pass for eighteen. Boys loved her, girls hated her. With all the years of enlightenment, that was pretty much the norm.

Neither one of those attitudes bothered her much. What did bother her, especially at that young age, were the looks of older men, even relatives, even men she trusted and loved. No, nothing ever happened. But you learn at a young age how longing and lust can twist a mind. It is rarely pretty.

Cingle was just about in the lobby when, through the phone, she heard a strange sound.

What the hell was that?

The lobby's glass doors slid open. A little bell dinged. Cingle kept the phone pressed against her ear. Nothing. There was no sound, no talking at all.

That couldn't be good.

A sudden crashing sound came through the earpiece, startling her. Cingle picked up her pace, ran for the elevator bank.

The guy behind the desk waddled out, saw Cingle, pulled in his gut and smiled. 'May I help you?'

She pushed the call button.

'Miss?'

There was still no talking coming from the phone. She felt a chill on her neck. She had to risk it. Cingle put the phone to her mouth. 'Matt?'

Nothing.

Damn, she'd put on the mute button. She'd forgotten about that.

Yet another strange sound – a grunt maybe. Only more muffled. More choked.

Where the hell was that damn elevator?

And where the hell was that mute button?

Cingle found the mute button first. It was on the bottom right-hand corner. Her thumb fumbled before touching down. The little mute icon disappeared. She put the phone to her mouth.

'Matt?' she shouted. 'Matt, are you okay?'

Another strangled cry. Then a voice – not Matt's – said, 'Who the hell . . . ?'

From behind her, the night man asked, 'Is something wrong, miss?'

Cingle kept pressing the elevator call button. *Come on, come on . . .*

Into the phone: 'Matt, are you there?'

Click. Silence now. Absolute silence. Cingle's heart beat as though trying to break free.

What should she do?

'Miss, I really have to ask you –'

The elevator door opened. She jumped inside. The night man stuck his arm out and stopped the door from closing. Cingle's gun was in her shoulder holster. For the first time ever in the line of duty, she pulled it out.

'Let go of that door,' she said to him.

He obeyed, taking his hand away like it didn't belong to him.

'Call the police,' she said. 'Tell them you have an emergency on the fifth floor.' The doors slid closed. She pressed the five button. Matt might not be happy about that, about getting the police involved, but it was her call now. The elevator groaned and started ascending. It seemed to move one foot up, two feet down.

Cingle held the gun in her right hand. With her finger off the trigger, she repeatedly pushed the five button on the elevator console. Like that would help. Like the elevator would see that she was in a hurry and pick up speed.

Her cell phone was in her left hand. She quickly re-dialed Matt's cell phone.

No ring, just his recorded voice: 'I'm not available right now –'

Cingle cursed, pressed the end button. She positioned her body directly in front of the crack in the door so as to get out of the elevator in mid-opening and as soon as humanly possible. The elevator buzzed with each floor, a signal for the blind, and finally came to a halt with a ding.

She hunched over like a sprinter starting in the standing position. When the doors started sliding open, Cingle pried them apart with both hands and pulled herself through.

She was in the corridor now.

Cingle could only hear the footsteps, not see anyone. It sounded like someone running the other way.

'Halt!'

Whoever it was did not let up. Neither did she. Cingle ran down the hall.

How long? How long since she'd lost contact with Matt?

From down the corridor Cingle heard a heavy door bang open. Emergency door, she bet. To the stairwell.

Cingle was counting off the room numbers as she ran. When she reached Room 511, she could see far enough up ahead to see that the door to Room 515 –

two doors ahead of her – was wide open.

She debated what to do – follow whoever was running down the stairs or check in Room 515 – but only briefly.

Cingle hurried, turned the corner, gun drawn.

Matt was flat on his back, his eyes closed. He was not moving. But that wasn't the really shocking thing.

The really shocking thing was who was with him.

Cingle almost dropped her gun.

For a moment she just stood there and stared in disbelief. Then she stepped fully into the room. Matt had still not moved. Blood was pooling behind his head.

Cingle's gaze stayed locked on the other person in the room.

The person kneeling next to Matt.

The face was tearstained. The eyes were red.

Cingle recognized the woman right away.

'Olivia.'

30

Loren Muse took the Frontage Road exit off Route 78 and pulled into the Howard Johnson's lot. A car was double-parked by the front entrance.

She hit the brake.

That car, a Lexus, had been in the MVD lot less than an hour ago.

This could not be a coincidence.

She maneuvered her vehicle by the front door and snapped her gun onto her belt. The shield was already there. The handcuffs dangled off her back. She hurried toward the car. No one inside. The keys were still in the ignition. The door was unlocked.

Loren opened the Lexus's door.

Was this a legal search? She thought it might be. The keys were in plain view in the ignition. The car was unlocked. She was helping out here. That had to make it legit somehow, right?

She pulled her sleeves up over her hands, forming makeshift mittens so she wouldn't leave fingerprints. She dropped open the glove compartment and tried to paw through the paperwork. It didn't take long. It was a company car, belonging to MVD. But the paperwork from the Midas Muffler dealer showed that it had been brought in by someone named Cingle Shaker.

Loren knew the name. The guys in the county office discussed her with a tad too much zeal. Said she had a body that could knock a movie rating from PG to R.

So what was her connection to Hunter?

Loren took the car keys with her – no sense in giving Ms. Shaker a chance to run off without them having a little chat. She headed inside and approached the desk. The man behind it was breathing in uneven gulps.

'You guys are back?' he asked.

'Back?'

Not her best line of interrogation, but it was a start.

'The other cops left, what, an hour ago maybe. With the ambulance.'

'What other cops?'

'You're not with them?'

She approached him. 'What's your name?'

'Ernie.'

'Ernie, why don't you tell me what happened here?'

'It's like I told the other guys.'

'Now tell me.'

Ernie sighed dramatically. 'Okay, fine, it's like this. First this guy comes dashing into the hotel.'

'When?' Loren interrupted.

'What?'

'What time was this?'

'I don't know. Two hours ago maybe. Don't you know all this?'

'Go on.'

'So this guy, he goes into the elevator. He goes up. Couple minutes later, this big chick comes flying in and runs over to the elevator.' He coughed into his fist. 'So, you know, I call out to her. Ask her if everything is okay. You know, doing my job and all.'

'Did you ask the guy if everything was okay?'

'What? No.'

'But you asked the' – Loren made quote marks with her fingers – 'big chick?'

'Hold up a sec. She wasn't big really. She was tall. I don't want you to think she was fat or anything. Give you the wrong idea. She wasn't. Not fat at all. Just the opposite. Like a chick in one of those Amazon movies, you know?'

'Yeah, Ernie, I think I got the picture.' Sounded like Cingle Shaker. 'So you asked Miss Amazon if everything was okay?'

'Right, yeah, like that. And this girl, this *tall* girl, she pulls a gun on me – a gun! – and tells me to call the cops.'

He paused now, waiting for Loren's jaw to drop in shock.

'And that's what you did?'

'Hell, yeah. I mean, she pulled a gun on me. You believe that?'

'I'll try to, Ernie. So then what happened?'

'She's in the elevator, right? She holds the gun on me until the doors close. So then I called the cops. Like she said to do. Two Newark guys were eating next door. They were here in no time. I told them she'd gone up to the fifth floor. So they went up.'

'You said something about an ambulance?'

'They must have called for one.'

'They? You mean, the cops?'

'Nah. Well, I mean, maybe. But I think it was the women in the room who made the call.'

'What room?'

'Look, I didn't go up there. I didn't see it or anything.' Ernie's eyes narrowed into thin slits. 'This is secondhand knowledge you're asking about now. Aren't you only supposed to ask me what I actually saw or have direct knowledge of?'

'This isn't a courtroom,' she snapped. 'What was going on upstairs?'

'I don't know. Someone got beaten up.'

'Who?'

'I just said. I don't know.'

'Man, woman, black, white?'

'Oh, I see what you mean. But I don't get it. Why are you asking me? Why can't you –?'

'Just tell me, Ernie. I don't have time to make a bunch of calls.'

'Not a bunch of calls, but you could just radio the cops who were here before, the Newark guys –'

Her voice was steel. 'Ernie.'

'Okay, okay, relax. It was a man, all right? White. I'd say mid-thirties. They wheeled him out on a stretcher.'

'What happened to him?'

'Someone beat him up, I guess.'

'And this all happened on the fifth floor?'

'I guess so, yeah.'

'And you said something about women in the room. That they might have called the ambulance.'

'Yeah. Yeah, I did say that.' He smiled like he was proud of himself. Loren wanted to draw her gun too.

'How many women, Ernie?'

'What? Oh, two.'

'Was one of them the tall girl who pulled the gun on you?'

'Yeah.'

'And the other?'

Ernie looked left. He looked right. Then he leaned closer and whispered, 'I think it might have been the guy's wife.'

'The guy who got beaten up?'

'Uh huh.'

'Why do you say that?'

His voice stayed soft. 'Because she went with him. In the ambulance.'

'So why are we whispering?'

'Well, I'm trying to be whatchya call discreet.'

Loren matched the whisper. 'Why, Ernie? Why are we being whatchya call discreet?'

'Because that other woman – the wife, I mean – she's been staying here for the past two nights. He, the husband, hasn't been.' He leaned over the desk. Loren got a whiff of whatchya call chronic halitosis. 'All of a sudden the husband rushes in, there's a fight of some kind . . .' He stopped, raised both eyebrows as though the implications were obvious.

'So what happened to the Amazon girl?'

'The one who pulled the gun on me?'

'Yes, Ernie,' Loren said, fighting off her growing impatience. 'The one who pulled the gun on you.'

'The cops arrested her. Cuffed her and everything.'

'The woman you think might be the wife, the one who stayed here the past two days. You have a name?'

He shook his head. 'No, sorry, I never heard it.'

'Didn't she register?'

Ernie's eyes lit up. 'Sure. Sure, she did. And we take an imprint of a credit card and everything.'

'Great.' Loren rubbed the bridge of her nose with her index finger and thumb. 'So – shot in the dark here, Ernie – why don't you look up the name for me?'

'Yeah, sure, I can do that. Let me see.' He turned to the computer and started typing. 'I think she was in Room 522. . . . Wait, here it is.'

He turned the monitor so Loren could see.

The occupant of Room 522 was named Olivia Hunter. Loren just stared at the screen for a moment.

Ernie pointed to the letters. 'It says Olivia Hunter.'

'I can see that. What hospital did they go to?'

'Beth Israel, I think they said.'

Loren handed Ernie her card with her cell phone number on it. 'Call me if you think of anything else.'

'Oh, I will.'

Loren rushed out for the hospital.

31

Matt Hunter woke up.

Olivia's face was there.

There was no question that this was real. Matt didn't have one of those moments where you wonder if it's a dream or not. The color was drained from Olivia's face. Her eyes were red. He could see the fear and the only thing Matt could think – not about answers, not about explanations – the only thing he could think clearly is, 'How do I make it better?'

The lights were bright. Olivia's face, still beautiful, was framed by what looked like a white shower curtain. He tried to smile at her. His skull throbbed like a thumb hit with a hammer.

She was watching him. He saw her eyes well up with tears. 'I'm sorry,' she whispered.

'I'm fine,' he said.

He felt a little la-dee-dah. Painkillers, he thought. Morphine or something similar. His ribs ached but it was a dull ache. He remembered the man in the hotel room, Talley, he of the blue-black hair. He remembered the paralyzing feeling, the dropping to the floor, the brass knuckles.

'Where are we?' he asked.

'Emergency room, Beth Israel.'

He actually smiled. 'I was born here, you know.' Yep, he was definitely on something – a muscle relaxant, painkiller, something. 'What happened to Talley?' he asked.

'He ran away.'

'You were in his room?'

'No. I was down the hall.'

He closed his eyes for just a moment. That last part did not compute – she was down the hall? – so he tried to clear his mind.

'Matt?'

He blinked a few times and tried to refocus. 'You were down the hall?'

'Yes. I saw you go into his room, so I followed you.'

'You were staying at that hotel?'

Before she could reply, the curtain was pulled open. 'Ah,' the doctor said. He had an accent – Pakistani or Indian, maybe. 'How are we feeling?'

'Like a million bucks,' Matt said.

The doctor smiled at them. His name tag read PATEL. 'Your wife told me that you were assaulted – that she thought the perpetrator might have used a stun gun.'

'I guess.'

'That's good, in a way. Stun guns don't leave permanent damage.

401

They only temporarily incapacitate.'

'Yeah,' Matt said. 'I live under a lucky star.'

Patel chuckled, checked something on the chart. 'You suffered a concussion. The rib is probably cracked, but I won't know that until we do an X-ray. It doesn't matter much – bad bruise or break, you can only treat it with rest. I already gave you something for the pain. You may need more.'

'Okay.'

'I'm going to keep you overnight.'

'No,' he said.

Patel looked up. 'No?'

'I want to go home. My wife can look after me.'

Patel looked at Olivia. She nodded. He said, 'You understand I don't recommend this?'

Olivia said, 'We do.'

On TV, the doctor always fights the 'wanna-go-home' patient. Patel didn't. He simply shrugged. 'Okay, you sign the release forms, you're out of here.'

'Thanks, Doc,' Matt said.

Patel shrugged again. 'Have a nice life then.'

'You too.'

He left.

'Are the police here?' Matt asked.

'They just left, but they'll be back.'

'What did you tell them?'

'Not much,' she said. 'They assumed it was some kind of marital spat. You caught me with another man, something like that.'

'What happened to Cingle?'

'They arrested her.'

'What?'

'She drew her gun to get past the clerk at the front desk.'

Matt shook his aching head. 'We have to bail her out.'

'She said not to, that she'd take care of it.'

He started to sit up. Pain tore down the back of his skull like a hot knife.

'Matt?'

'I'm okay.'

And he was. He'd been beaten worse. Much worse. This was nothing. He could play through it. He sat all the way up and met her eyes. She looked as if she were steeling herself for a blow.

Matt said, 'This is something bad, isn't it?'

Olivia's chest hitched. The tears welling began to escape. 'I don't know yet,' she said. 'But yeah. Yeah, it's pretty bad.'

'Do we want the police involved?'

'No.' The tears had started running down her cheeks. 'Not until I tell you everything.'

He swung his feet off the bed. 'Then let's hurry the hell out of here.'

Loren counted six people on line at the ER reception desk. When she cut to the front, all six grunted their disapproval. Loren ignored them. She slammed her badge down on the desk.

'You had a patient brought in here a little while ago.'

'You're kidding.' The woman behind the desk looked up over the half-moon reading glasses and let her eyes travel over the packed waiting room. 'A patient, you say?' She chewed gum. 'Gee, I guess you caught us. We did have a patient brought in here a little while ago.'

The line snickered. Loren's face reddened.

'He was an assault victim. From Howard Johnson's.'

'Oh, him. I think he's gone.'

'Gone?'

'Checked himself out a few minutes ago.'

'Where did he go?'

The woman gave her flat eyes.

'Right,' Loren said. 'Never mind.'

Her cell phone rang. She picked it up and barked, 'Muse.'

'Uh, hi, are you the policewoman who was here before?'

Loren recognized the voice. 'Yes, Ernie. What's up?'

There was a low moan. 'You have to come back here.'

'What is it? Ernie?'

'Something happened,' he said. 'I think . . . I think he's dead.'

32

Matt and Olivia had filled out the necessary paperwork, but neither of them had a car. Matt's was still parked at the MVD lot. Olivia's was at the Howard Johnson's. They called a taxi and waited outside by the entrance.

Matt sat in a wheelchair. Olivia stood next to him. She looked straight forward, not at him. It was hot and sticky, but Olivia still stood with her arms wrapped around herself. She wore a sleeveless blouse and khaki pants. Her arms were toned and tan.

The taxi pulled up. Matt struggled to his feet. Olivia tried to help, but he waved her off. They both got into the backseat. Their bodies did not touch. They did not hold hands.

'Good evening,' the driver said, eyes in the rearview. 'Where to?'

The driver was dark-skinned and spoke with some sort of African accent. Matt gave him their address in Irvington. The driver was chatty. He was from Ghana, he told them. He had six children. Two of them lived here with him, the rest were back in Ghana with his wife.

Matt tried to be responsive. Olivia stared out her window and said nothing. At one point Matt reached for her hand. She let him take it, but it felt lifeless.

'Did you visit Dr. Haddon?' Matt asked her.

'Yes.'

'And?'

'Everything is fine. It should be a normal pregnancy.'

From the front seat, the driver said, 'Pregnancy? You're having a baby?'

'Yes, we are,' Matt said.

'Is this your first?'

'Yes.'

'Such a blessing, my friend.'

'Thank you.'

They were in Irvington now, on Clinton Avenue. Up ahead the light turned red. The driver cruised to a stop.

'We make a right here, yes?'

Matt had been glancing out the window, preparing to say yes, when something snared his gaze. Their house was indeed down the street on the right. But that wasn't what had captured his attention.

There was a police car parked on the street.

'Hold up a second,' Matt said.

'Pardon me?'

Matt cranked open the window. The police car's engine was running. He wondered about that. He looked to the corner. Lawrence the Wino was staggering with his customary brown bag, singing the old Four Tops classic 'Bernadette.'

Matt leaned out the window. 'Hey, Lawrence.'

'. . . And never find the love I've found in y –' Lawrence stopped mid-lyric. He cupped his hand over his eyes and squinted. A smile broke out on his face. He stumbled toward them. 'Matt, mah man! Look at you, all fine and fancy in a taxi.'

'Yep.'

'You been out drinking, right? I remember from before. Didn't want to drink and drive, am I right?'

'Something like that, Lawrence.'

'Whoa.' Lawrence pointed to the bandage on Matt's head. 'What happened to you? You know who you look like, with your head wrapped like that?'

'Lawrence –'

'That dude marching in that old picture, the one playing the flute. Or is it the one on the snare? I can never remember. Had his head wrapped, just like you. What was that picture called again?'

Matt tried to get him on track. 'Lawrence, do you see that cop car over there?'

'What' – he leaned closer – 'he did that to you?'

'No, nothing like that. I'm fine, really.'

Lawrence was perfectly positioned to block the car's view of Matt's face. If the cop happened to look this way, he'd probably figure Lawrence was panhandling.

'How long has he been parked there?' Matt asked.

'I don't know. Fifteen, twenty minutes maybe. Time flies by now, Matt. Older you get, the faster it goes by. You listen to Lawrence.'

'Has he gotten out of the car?'

'Who?'

'The cop.'

'Oh, sure. Knocked on your door too.' Lawrence smiled. 'Oh, I see. You in trouble, ain't you, Matt?'

'Me? I'm one of the good guys.'

Lawrence loved that one. 'Oh, I know that. You have a good night now, Matt.' He leaned into the window a little. 'You too, Liv.'

Olivia said, 'Thank you, Lawrence.'

Lawrence saw her face and paused. He looked at Matt and straightened up. His voice grew softer. 'You take care now.'

'Thanks, Lawrence.' Matt sat forward and tapped the driver. 'Change of destination.'

The driver said, 'Will I get in trouble for this?'

'Not at all. I was in an accident. They want to talk to me about how I got hurt. We'd rather wait until morning.'

The driver wasn't buying it, but he didn't seem ready to argue either. The light turned green. The taxi started up, heading straight instead of right.

'So where to?'

Matt gave him the address of MVD in Newark. He figured that they could pick up his car and find a place to go and talk. The question was, where? He checked his watch. It was three in the morning.

The driver pulled into MVD's lot. 'This is good, yes?'

'Fine, thanks.'

They got out of the car. Matt paid the man. Olivia said, 'I'll drive.'

'I'm fine.'

'Right, fine. You just got beaten up and you're high on meds.' Olivia put out her palm. 'Give me the keys.'

He did. They got into the car and started out.

'Where are we going?' Olivia asked.

'I'm going to call Marsha, see if we can crash there.'

'You're going to wake up the kids.'

He managed a small smile. 'Grenades in their pillows wouldn't wake up those two.'

'And what about Marsha?'

'She won't mind.'

But Matt suddenly hesitated. He really didn't worry about waking Marsha – there had been plenty of late-night calls over the years – but now he wondered if she would be alone tonight, if maybe he wouldn't be interrupting something. He also – and this was really weird – started worrying about something else right now.

Suppose Marsha got remarried.

Paul and Ethan were still young. Would they call the guy Daddy? Matt wasn't sure if he could handle that. More to the point, what role would Uncle Matt have in this new life, this new family? All of this was silly, of course. He was getting way ahead of himself. It was hardly the time either, what with his other problems right now. But the thoughts were there, in his head, knocking to come out of some back closet.

He pulled out his cell phone and pushed the second number on his speed dial. As they hit Washington Avenue, Matt noticed two cars going past them in the opposite direction. He turned and watched them pull into the MVD lot. The cars were from the Essex County prosecutor's office. They were the same make and model Loren had been using earlier in the evening.

This couldn't be good.

The phone was picked up on the second ring.

Marsha said, 'I'm glad you called.' If she'd been sleeping, she hid it pretty well.

'Are you alone?'

'What?'

'I mean . . . I know the kids are there –'

'I'm alone, Matt.'

'I don't mean to pry. I just want to make sure I'm not interrupting anything.'

'You're not. You never will be.'

That should have set his mind at ease, he guessed. 'Do you mind if Olivia and I crash at your place tonight?'

'Of course not.'

'It's a long story, but basically I was assaulted tonight –'

'Are you okay?'

The pain was starting to ebb back into his head and ribs. 'I got a few bumps and bruises, but I'll be fine. Thing is, the police want to ask some questions and we're just not ready for that yet.'

'Does this have anything to do with that nun?' Marsha asked.

'What nun?'

Olivia's head snapped toward him.

'There was a county investigator here today,' Marsha said. 'I should have called you, but I guess I was hoping it was no big deal. Hold on, I have her card here someplace . . .'

Matt's mind, both exhausted and scrambled, remembered now. 'Loren Muse.'

'Right, that's the name. She said a nun made a phone call to the house.'

'I know,' he said.

'Muse reached you?'

'Yes.'

'I figured she would. We were just talking and then, I don't know, she spotted your picture on the refrigerator and suddenly she starts asking Kyra and me all these questions about how often you visit.'

'Don't worry, I straightened it out. Look, we'll be there in twenty minutes.'

'I'll get the guest room ready.'

'Don't go to any trouble.'

'No trouble. I'll see you in twenty minutes.'

She hung up.

Olivia said, 'What's this about a nun?'

Matt told her about Loren's visit. Olivia's face lost even more color. By the time he finished, they were in Livingston. The roads were completely empty of both cars and pedestrians. There was no one about. The only lights coming from the homes were those downstairs lamps set on timers to fool burglars.

Olivia remained silent as she pulled into Marsha's driveway. Matt could see Marsha's silhouette through the curtain in the downstairs foyer. The light above the garage was on. Kyra was awake. He saw her look out. Matt slid down the car window and waved up to her. She waved back.

Olivia turned off the ignition. Matt checked his face in the visor mirror. He looked like hell. Lawrence was right. What with the bandage wrapped around his head, he did resemble the soldier playing the flute in Willard's *Spirit of '76.*

'Olivia?'

She said nothing.

'Do you know this Sister Mary Rose?'

'Maybe.'

She stepped out of the car. Matt did the same. The outside lights – Matt had helped Bernie install the motion detectors – snapped on. Olivia came around to him. She took his hand and held it firmly.

'Before I say anything else,' she began, 'I need you to know something.'

Matt waited.

'I love you. You are the only man I've ever loved. Whatever happens now, you have brought me a happiness and joy I once thought was impossible.'

'Olivia –'

She put her finger to his lips. 'I just want one thing. I want you to hold me. Hold me right now. Just for a minute or two. Because after I tell you the truth, I'm not sure you will ever want to hold me again.'

33

When Cingle got to the police station she used her phone call to reach her boss, Malcolm Seward, the president of Most Valuable Detection. Seward was retired FBI. He opened MVD ten years ago and was making a small fortune.

Seward was not thrilled about the late-night call. 'You pulled a gun on the guy?'

'It's not like I would have shot him.'

'How reassuring.' Seward sighed. 'I'll make some calls. You'll be out in an hour.'

'You're the best, Boss.'

He hung up.

She went back to her holding cell and waited. A tall officer unlocked the holding cell door. 'Cingle Shaker.'

'Right here.'

'Please follow me.'

'Anywhere, handsome.'

He led her down the hallway. She expected this to be it – the bail hearing, the quick release, whatever – but that wasn't the case.

'Please turn around,' he said.

Cingle cocked an eyebrow. 'Shouldn't you buy me dinner first?'

'Please turn around.'

She did. He cuffed her hands.

'What are you doing?'

He didn't speak. He escorted her outside, opened the back door of his squad car, and pushed her in.

'Where are we going?'

'The new court building.'

'The one on West Market?'

'Yes, ma'am.'

The ride was short, less than a mile. They took the elevator to the third floor. The words OFFICE OF THE ESSEX COUNTY PROSECUTOR were stenciled on the glass. There was a big trophy case by the door, the kind you see in a high school. Cingle wondered about that, about what a trophy case was doing in a prosecutor's office. You prosecute killers and rapists and drug dealers and the first thing you see when you enter is a bunch of trophies celebrating softball wins. Weird.

'This way.'

He led her through the waiting area, past the double doors. When they stopped, she peeked inside a small, windowless space. 'An interrogation room?'

He said nothing, just held the door. She shrugged and entered.

Time passed. A lot of time, actually. They had confiscated her possessions, including her watch, so she didn't really know how much. There was no one-way mirror either, like you usually see on TV. They used a camera here. There was one mounted in the corner of the wall. From the monitoring room, you could zoom the camera in or change the angle, whatever. There was one sheet of paper taped down at a funny angle. That was the guide spot, she knew, where you put the release statement so that the camera could tape you signing it.

When the door finally opened, a woman – Cingle assumed that it was a plain-clothes investigator – stepped into the room. She was a tiny thing, maybe five-one, 110 pounds tops. Sweat drenched her body. It looked like she'd just stepped out of a steam room. Her blouse stuck to her chest. There was dampness under her pits. A thin coat of perspiration made her face glisten. She wore a gun on her belt and had a manila folder in her hand.

'I'm Investigator Loren Muse,' the woman said.

Wow, that was fast. Cingle remembered the name – Muse was the one who'd questioned Matt earlier this evening.

'Cingle Shaker,' she said.

'Yes, I know. I have a few questions.'

'And I'm going to choose not to answer them right now.'

Loren was still catching her breath. 'Why's that?'

'I'm a working private investigator.'

'And who would your client be?'

'I don't have to tell you.'

'There is no such thing as PI-client privilege.'

'I'm aware of the law.'

'So?'

'So I choose not to answer any questions at this time.'

Loren dropped the manila folder on the table. It stayed closed. 'Are you refusing to cooperate with the county prosecutor's office?'

'Not at all.'

'Then please answer my question. Who is your client?'

Cingle leaned back. She stretched out her legs and crossed her ankles. 'You fall in a pool or something?'

'Oh, wait, I get it. Because I'm wet? Good one, really. Should I get a pen, you know, in case you come up with more gems?'

'No need.' Cingle pointed to the camera. 'You can just watch the tape.'

'It's not on.'

'No?'

'If I wanted to tape this, I'd have you sign the release.'

'Is anybody in the monitoring room?'

Loren shrugged, ignored the question. 'Aren't you curious about how Mr. Hunter's doing?'

Cingle didn't bite. 'Tell you what. I won't ask any questions if you don't.'

'I don't think so.'

'Look, Inspector . . . Muse, is it?'

'Yes.'

'What's the big deal here? It was a simple assault. That hotel probably has three a week.'

'Yet,' Loren said, 'it was serious enough for you to pull a gun on a man?'

'I was just trying to get upstairs before it got any more dangerous.'

'How did you know?'

'Pardon me?'

'The fight was on the fifth floor. You were outside in your car. How did you know that someone was in trouble?'

'I think we're done.'

'No, Cingle, I don't think we are.'

Their eyes met. Cingle did not like what she saw. Loren pulled out the chair and sat down. 'I've just spent the last half an hour in the stairwell of the Howard Johnson's. It's not air-conditioned. In fact, it's hot as hell. That's why I look like this.'

'Am I supposed to know what you're talking about?'

'It's not a simple assault, Cingle.'

Cingle eyed the manila folder. 'What's that?'

Loren dumped out the folder's contents. They were photographs. Cingle sighed, picked one up, froze.

'I assume you recognize him?'

Cingle stared at the two pictures. The first was a headshot. No question about it – the dead man was Charles Talley. His face looked like raw meat. The other was a full body shot. Talley was sprawled on what looked like metal steps. 'What happened to him?'

'Two shots to the face.'

'Jesus.'

'Feel like talking now, Cingle?'

'I don't know anything about this.'

'His name is Charles Talley. But you knew that, right?'

'Jesus,' Cingle said again, trying to put it together. Talley was dead. How? Hadn't he just assaulted Matt?

Loren put the pictures back in the manila folder. She folded her hands and leaned closer. 'I know you're working for Matt Hunter. I also know that right before you headed for that hotel you two met in your office for a very late-night chat. Would you care to tell me what you discussed?'

Cingle shook her head.

'Did you kill this man, Ms. Shaker?'

'What? Of course not.'

'How about Mr. Hunter? Did he kill him?'

'No.'

'How do you know?'

'Excuse me?'

'I didn't even tell you when he was killed.' Loren tilted her head. 'How could you possibly know that he wasn't involved in the man's death?'

'That's not what I meant.'

'What did you mean?'

Cingle took a breath. Loren did not.

'How about retired detective Max Darrow?'

'Who?' But Cingle remembered that name from Matt. He had asked her to check him out.

'Another dead man. Did you kill him? Or did Hunter do it?'

'I don't know what . . .' Cingle stopped, crossed her arms. 'I have to get out of here.'

'That's not going to happen, Cingle.'

'Are you charging me with something?'

'As a matter of fact, we are. You threatened a man with a loaded handgun.'

Cingle crossed her arms and tried to regain her composure. 'Old news.'

'Ah, but see, you're no longer getting sped through the system. You'll be kept overnight and arraigned in the morning. We're going to prosecute this to the full extent of the law. You'll only lose your license if it all breaks your way, but my bet is, you'll serve jail time.'

Cingle said nothing.

'Who assaulted Mr. Hunter tonight?'

'Why don't you ask him?'

'Oh, I will. Because – and this is interesting – when we found Mr. Talley's corpse he had a stun gun and a pair of brass knuckles. There was fresh blood on the brass knuckles.' Loren did that head tilt again, moving in a little closer. 'When we run a DNA test, whose blood do you think will match?'

There was a knock on the door. Loren Muse held the gaze a moment longer before she opened it. The man who escorted Cingle from the station was there. He was holding a cell phone.

'For her,' the man said, gesturing toward Cingle. Cingle looked at Loren. Loren's face gave away nothing. Cingle took the phone and put it to her ear. 'Hello?'

'Start talking.'

It was her boss, Malcolm Seward.

'It's a sensitive case.'

'I'm on the computer network now,' Seward said. 'Which case number?'

'There isn't a case number yet.'

'What?'

'With all due respect, sir, I don't feel comfortable talking with the authorities here.'

She heard Seward sigh. 'Guess who just called me, Cingle. Guess who called me at home at three in the morning.'

'Mr. Seward –'

'Actually, no, don't guess. I'll tell you because, hey, it's three in the morning and I'm too tired for games. Ed Steinberg. Ed Steinberg himself called me. Do you know who that is?'

'Yes.'

'Ed Steinberg is the Essex County prosecutor.'

'I know.'

'He's also been my friend for twenty-eight years.'

'I know that too.'

'Good, Cingle, then we're on the same wavelength here. MVD is a business. A very successful business, or so I like to think. And a big part of our effectiveness – yours and mine – depends on working with these people. So when Ed Steinberg calls me at home at three in the morning and tells me he's working on a triple homicide –'

'Hold up,' Cingle said. 'Did you say triple?'

411

'You see? You don't even know how deep this doo-doo goes. Ed Steinberg, my old pal, very much wants your cooperation. That means I, your boss, very much want your cooperation. Do I make myself clear?'

'I guess so.'

'Guess? What, am I being too subtle here, Cingle?'

'There are mitigating factors.'

'Not according to Steinberg. Steinberg tells me this all involves some ex-con. That true?'

'He works at Carter Sturgis.'

'Is he a lawyer?'

'No, he's a paralegal.'

'And he served time for manslaughter?'

'Yes, but –'

'Then there's nothing to discuss. There's no privilege here. Tell them what they want to know.'

'I can't.'

'Can't?' There was an edge in Seward's tone now. 'I don't like to hear that.'

'It's not that simple, Mr. Seward.'

'Well, then let me simplify it for you, Cingle. You have two choices: Talk or clean out your desk. Bye now.'

He hung up the phone. Cingle eyed Loren. Loren smiled at her.

'Everything all right, Ms. Shaker?'

'Peachy.'

'Good. Because as we speak, our techno people are on their way to MVD's office. They'll comb through your hard drive. They'll scrutinize every document you've got in there. Prosecutor Steinberg is right now calling back your boss. He'll find out what files you accessed recently, who you talked to, where you've been, what you've been working on.'

Cingle stood slowly, towering over Loren. Loren did not back up a step. 'I have nothing more to say.'

'Cingle?'

'What?'

'Sit your ass down.'

'I prefer to stand.'

'Fine. Then listen up because we're coming to the end of our conversation. Did you know I went to school with Matt Hunter? Elementary school, actually. I liked him. He was a good kid. And if he's innocent, nobody will be more anxious to clear his name than yours truly. But your keeping mum like this, well, Cingle, it suggests you might be hiding something. We have Talley's brass knuckles. We know Matt Hunter was at the murder scene tonight. We know he got into some kind of fight in Room 515 – that was Mr. Talley's room. We also know that Mr. Hunter was out drinking at two bars this evening. We know that the DNA test on the brass knuckles will show that the blood is Hunter's. And, of course, we know that Mr. Hunter, a convicted felon, has something of a history of getting into fights where someone ends up dead.'

Cingle sighed. 'Is there a point to this?'

'Sure is, Cingle, and here it comes: Do you really think I need your help to nail him?'

Cingle started tapping her foot, looking for a way out. 'Then what do you want from me?'

'Help.'

'Help with what?'

'Tell me the truth,' Loren said. 'That's all I ask. Hunter is already as good as indicted. Once he's in the system – him being an ex-con and all – well, you know how that'll go.'

She did. Matt would freak. He'd go nuts if they lock him up – his greatest fear come to fruition.

Loren moved a little closer. 'If you know something that might help him,' she said, 'now is the time to say it.'

Cingle tried to think it through. She almost trusted this little cop, but she knew better. That was what Muse wanted – playing good cop and bad cop in one package. Christ, an amateur could see through this charade and yet Cingle was almost ready to bite.

Key word: almost.

But Cingle also knew that once they got into her office computer, there would be huge problems. The last files she accessed were the photographs from Matt's cell phone. Pictures of the murder victim. A video of the murder victim and Matt Hunter's wife.

Those would be the final nails in any ex-con's coffin.

As Investigator Muse had pointed out, they already had enough with the physical evidence. The photographs would add one thing more: motive.

Cingle had her own career to worry about too. This had started out as a favor to a friend, just another case. But how far was she willing to go? What should she be willing to sacrifice? And if Matt had nothing to do with the murder of Charles Talley, wouldn't cooperating right from the get-go help bring the truth to light?

Cingle sat back down.

'You have something to say?'

'I want to call my lawyer,' Cingle said. 'Then I'll tell you everything I know.'

34

'I haven't charged you with anything,' Loren said.

Cingle crossed her arms. 'Let's not play semantics games, okay? I asked for my lawyer. The interview is over. The end. *El fin.*'

'If you say so.'

'I say so. Get me a phone, please.'

'You're entitled to call an attorney.'

'That's who I plan on calling.'

Loren thought about this. She didn't want Cingle warning Hunter. 'You mind if I dial the number for you?'

'Suit yourself,' Cingle said. 'I'll need a phone book though.'

'You don't know your attorney's home number by heart?'

'No, sorry.'

It took another five minutes. Loren dialed and handed her the phone. She could always check the call log later, make sure she didn't sneak another call in. She turned off the microphone and moved into the monitoring room. Cingle, wise in the ways of the camera, turned her back to the lens, just in case someone could read lips.

Loren started working the phones. First she tried the cop sitting in front of Hunter's residence in Irvington. He informed her that Matt and Olivia Hunter still weren't home. Loren knew that this was not good news. She started a quiet search because she didn't want to sound off too many alarm bells yet.

She'd need to get a subpoena for both Matt and Olivia Hunter's recent credit card transactions – run it through TRW. If they were on the run, they'd probably need to access money at an ATM or check into a motel – something.

From the monitoring screen, Loren could see that Cingle had finished her phone call. Cingle held the phone up to the camera and signaled for someone to hit the audio switch. Loren complied.

'Yes?'

Cingle said, 'My attorney is on his way.'

'Sit tight then.'

Loren switched off the intercom. She leaned back. Exhaustion was starting to set in. She was nearing the wall. She needed a little shut-eye or her brain would start going hazy. Cingle's attorney wouldn't be here for at least half an hour. She crossed her arms, threw her feet on the desk, and closed her eyes, hoping to doze for just a few minutes, just until the attorney showed.

Her cell phone rang. She startled up and put it to her ear.

It was Ed Steinberg. 'Hey.'

'Hey,' she managed.

'The private eye talking?'

'Not yet. She's waiting for her lawyer.'

'Let her wait then. Let them both wait.'

'Why, what's up?'

'The feds, Loren.'

'What about them?'

'We're meeting them in an hour.'

'Who?'

'Joan Thurston.'

That made her drop her feet to the floor. 'The U.S. attorney herself?'

'In the flesh. And some hotshot SAC from Nevada. We're meeting them at Thurston's office to discuss your phony nun.'

Loren checked the clock. 'It's four in the morning.'

'Thank you, Mistress of the Obvious.'

'No, I mean, I'm surprised you'd call the U.S. attorney that early.'

'Didn't have to,' Steinberg said. 'She called me.'

When Ed Steinberg arrived, he looked at Loren and shook his head. Her hair was frizzed out from the humidity. The sweat had dried, but she was still a mess.

'You look,' Steinberg said, 'like something I once left in the bottom of my gym locker.'

'Flattering, thank you.'

He motioned at her with both his hands. 'Can't you – I don't know – do something about your hair?'

'What, this a singles' club now?'

'Evidently not.'

The ride from the county prosecutor's office to the U.S. attorney's was three blocks. They entered via the well-guarded private underground garage. There were very few cars at this hour. The elevator dropped them on the seventh floor. The stencil on the glass read:

UNITED STATES ATTORNEY
DISTRICT OF NEW JERSEY
JOAN THURSTON
UNITED STATES ATTORNEY

Steinberg pointed at the top line and then the bottom line. 'Kinda redundant, no?'

Despite the power of the office, the waiting room was done up in Early American Dentist. The carpet was threadbare. The furniture managed to be neither fashionable nor functional. There were a dozen different issues of *Sports Illustrated* on the table and nothing else. The walls seemed to plead for a paint job. They were stained and barren, except for the photographs of past U.S. attorneys, a remarkable lesson in what not to wear and how not to pose when taking a picture for posterity.

No receptionist was sitting guard at this hour. They knocked and were buzzed into the inner sanctum. It was much nicer in here, a totally different feel and look, like they'd stepped through a wall into Diagon Alley.

They turned right and headed toward the corner office. A man – an enormous man – stood in the corridor. He had a buzz cut and a frown. He stood perfectly still and looked as if he could double as a squash court. Steinberg stuck out his hand. 'Hi, I'm Ed Steinberg, county prosecutor.'

Squash Court took the hand but he did not look happy about it. 'Cal Dollinger, FBI. They're waiting.'

That was the end of that conversation. Cal Dollinger stayed where he was. They turned the corner. Joan Thurston greeted them at the door.

Despite the early hour U.S. Attorney Joan Thurston looked resplendent in a charcoal gray business suit that seemed to have been tailored by the gods. Thurston was mid-forties and, in Loren's view, excessively attractive. She had auburn hair, broad shoulders, tapered waist. She had two sons in their early teens. Her husband worked at Morgan Stanley in Manhattan. They lived in ritzy Short Hills with a vacation home on Long Beach Island.

In short: Joan Thurston was what Loren wanted to be when she grew up.

'Good morning,' Thurston said, which felt weird because outside her windows, the skies were still night black.

She shook Loren's hand firmly, meeting her eye and softening it with a smile. She gave Steinberg a hug and buss on the cheek. 'I'd like you to meet Adam Yates. He's the FBI Special Agent in Charge of the Las Vegas office.'

Adam Yates wore freshly ironed khakis and a bright pink shirt that might be the norm on Worth Avenue in Palm Beach but not Broad Street in Newark. He wore loafers without socks, his legs too casually crossed. He had that whole Old World, came-over-on-the-Mayflower thing going on, what with the receding ash-blond hair, the high cheekbones, the eyes so ice blue she wondered if he was wearing contacts. His cologne smelled like freshly cut grass. Loren liked it.

'Please sit,' Thurston said.

Thurston had a spacious corner office. On one wall – the least noticeable wall – was a smattering of diplomas and awards. They were put out of the way, almost as if to say, 'Hey, I need to put them up but I don't like to put on airs.' The rest of the office was personal. She had photographs of her children and her husband, all of whom – big surprise – were gorgeous. Even the dog. There was a white guitar autographed by Bruce Springsteen hanging behind her head. On the bookshelf were the usual assortment of law books, along with autographed baseballs and footballs. All the local teams, of course. Joan Thurston had no photographs of herself, no news clippings, no Lucite-block awards in view.

Loren sat down carefully. She used to tuck her heels underneath her to gain a few inches, but she'd read a business self-help book about how women sabotage their own careers, and one of the rules said that a woman must never sit on her heels. It looked unprofessional. Usually Loren forgot that rule. Something about seeing Joan Thurston brought it all back.

Thurston came around and half-sat/half-leaned against the front lip of her desk. She folded her arms and focused her attention on Loren.

'Tell me what you have so far.'

Loren glanced at Ed Steinberg. He nodded.

'We have three dead people. The first, well, we don't know her real name. That's why we're here.'

'This would be Sister Mary Rose?' Thurston asked.

416

'Yes.'

'How did you stumble across her case?'

'Pardon?'

'I understand that the death was originally ruled of natural causes,' Thurston said. 'What made you look into it deeper?'

Steinberg took that one. 'The Mother Superior personally asked Investigator Muse to look into it.'

'Why?'

'Loren is an alum of St. Margaret's.'

'I understand that, but what made this Mother Superior . . . what's her name?'

'Mother Katherine,' Loren said.

'Mother Katherine, right. What made her suspect foul play in the first place?'

'I'm not sure she suspected anything,' Loren said. 'When Mother Katherine found Sister Mary Rose's body, she tried to resuscitate her with chest compressions and discovered that she had breast implants. That didn't mesh with Sister Mary Rose's history.'

'So she came to you to find out what was up?'

'Something like that, yes.'

Thurston nodded. 'And the second body?'

'Max Darrow. He was a retired Vegas police officer now residing in the Reno area.'

They all looked at Adam Yates. He stayed still. So, Loren thought, this would be the game. They'd roll over and maybe, just maybe, the feds would award them with a tiny doggie treat.

Thurston asked, 'How did you connect Max Darrow to Sister Mary Rose?'

'Fingerprints,' Loren said. 'Darrow's fingerprints were found in the nun's private quarters.'

'Anything else?'

'Darrow was found dead in his car. Shot twice at point-blank range. His pants were down around his ankles. We think the killer tried to make it look like a prostitute rolled him.'

'Fine, we can go into the details later,' Thurston said. 'Tell us how Max Darrow connects to the third victim.'

'The third victim is Charles Talley. For one thing, both Talley and Darrow lived in the Reno area. For another, they were both staying at the Howard Johnson's near Newark Airport. Their rooms were next door to one another's.'

'And that's where you found Talley's body? At the hotel?'

'Not me. A night custodian found him in the stairwell. He'd been shot twice.'

'Same as Darrow?'

'Similar, yes.'

'Time of death?'

'It's still being worked on, but sometime tonight between eleven p.m. and two a.m. The stairwell had no air-conditioning, no windows, no ventilation – it had to be over a hundred degrees in there.'

'That's why Investigator Muse here looks like that,' Steinberg said, gesturing with both hands as if he were presenting a soiled prize. 'From being in that sauna.'

Loren shot him a look and tried to hold back from smoothing her hair. 'The heat makes it more difficult for our ME to pinpoint a better time frame.'

'What else?' Thurston asked.

417

Loren hesitated. Her guess was that Thurston and Yates probably knew – or at least, could readily learn – most of what she'd already told them. So far, this had all been about getting up to speed. All that she really had left – all that she'd have that they probably wouldn't – was Matt Hunter.

Steinberg held up a hand. 'May I make a suggestion?'

Thurston turned toward him. 'Of course, Ed.'

'I don't want to have any jurisdictional hassles here.'

'Neither do we.'

'So why don't we just pool our resources on this one? Totally open communication both ways. We tell you what we know, you tell us what you know. No holding back.'

Thurston glanced at Yates. Adam Yates cleared his throat and said, 'We have no problem with that.'

'Do you know the real identity of Sister Mary Rose?' Steinberg asked.

Yates nodded. 'We do, yes.'

Loren waited. Yates took his time. He uncrossed his legs, tugged at the front of his shirt as if trying to get some air.

'Your nun – well, she's not even close to being a nun, believe me – was one Emma Lemay,' Yates said.

The name meant nothing to Loren. She looked at Steinberg. He, too, had no reaction to the name.

Yates continued: 'Emma Lemay and her partner, a cretin named Clyde Rangor, disappeared from Vegas ten years ago. We did a fairly massive search for both of them but turned up nothing. One day they were there, the next – poof – they were both gone.'

Steinberg asked, 'How did you know we found Lemay's body?'

'The Lockwood Corporation had her silicone implants marked. The NCIC now puts everything they can into the national database. Fingerprints, you know about. DNA and descriptions, those have been in there for a while. But now we're working on a national database for medical devices – any kind of joint replacements, surgical implants, colostomy bags, pacemakers – mostly to help identify Jane and John Does. You get the model number, you put it in the system. It's new, pretty experimental. We're trying it out on a select few that we're very anxious to locate.'

'And this Emma Lemay,' Loren said. 'You were anxious to locate her?'

Yates had a good smile. 'Oh, yes.'

'Why?' Loren asked.

'Ten years ago Lemay and Rangor agreed to turn on a nasty perennial RICO top-ten asswipe, guy named Tom "Comb-Over" Busher.'

'Comb-Over?'

'That's what they call him, though not to his face. Been his nickname for years, actually. Used to be, he had this comb-over going. You know, when he started going bald. But it just kept growing. So now he kinda twirls it around and around, looks like he stuck a cinnamon swirl on top of his head.'

Yates chuckled. Nobody else did.

Thurston said, 'You were talking about Lemay and Rangor?'

'Right. So anyway, we nailed Lemay and Rangor on pretty serious drug charges, pressed them like hell, and for the first time, we got someone on the inside to flip. Clyde Rangor and Comb-Over are cousins. They started working with us, taping conversations, gathering evidence. And then. . . .' Yates shrugged.

'So what do you think happened?'

'The most likely scenario was that Comb-Over got wind of what was up and killed them. But we never really bought that.'

'Why not?'

'Because there was evidence – lots of it, actually – that Comb-Over was searching for Lemay and Rangor too. Even harder than we were. For a while it was like the race was on, you know, who'd find them first. When they never turned up, well, we figured we lost the race.'

'This Comb-Over. He still on the streets?'

'Yes.'

'And what about Clyde Rangor?'

'We have no idea where he is.' Yates shifted in his chair. 'Clyde Rangor was a major whack-job. He managed a couple of strip clubs for Comb-Over and had a rep for enjoying the occasional, uh, rough session.'

'How rough?'

Yates folded his hands and placed them in his lap. 'We suspect that some of the girls didn't recover.'

'When you say didn't recover –'

'One ended up in a catatonic state. One – the last one, we think – ended up dead.'

Loren made a face. 'And you were cutting a deal with this guy?'

'What, you want us to find someone nicer?' Yates snapped.

'I –'

'Do I really need to explain to you how trading up works, Investigator Muse?'

Steinberg stepped in. 'Not at all.'

'I didn't mean to imply. . . .' Loren bit back, her face reddening, upset with herself for sounding so amateurish. 'Go on.'

'What else is there? We don't know where Clyde Rangor is, but we believe that he can still provide valuable information, maybe help us take Comb-Over down.'

'How about Charles Talley and Detective Max Darrow? Any idea how they fit in?'

'Charles Talley is a thug with a record for brutality. He handled some of the girls in the clubs, made sure they kept in line, didn't steal much, shared their, uh, tips with the house. Last we heard he was working for a dump in Reno called the Eager Beaver. Our best guess is, Talley was hired to kill Emma Lemay.'

'By this Comb-Over guy?'

'Yes. Our theory is that somehow Comb-Over found out that Emma Lemay was pretending to be this Sister Mary Rose. He sent Talley here to kill her.'

'And what about Max Darrow?' Loren asked. 'We know he was in Lemay's quarters. What was his role?'

Yates uncrossed his legs and sat up. 'For one thing, we think Darrow, though a fairly solid cop, might have been crooked.'

His voice drifted off. He cleared his throat.

'And for another,' Loren prompted.

Yates took a deep breath. 'Well, Max Darrow . . .' He looked at Thurston. She didn't nod, didn't move, but Loren got the impression that, as she had done with Steinberg, Yates was looking for an okay. 'Let's just say that Max Darrow is connected into this case in another way.'

419

They waited. Several seconds passed. Loren finally said, 'How?'

Yates rubbed his face with both hands, suddenly looking exhausted. 'I mentioned before that Clyde Rangor was into rough trade.'

Loren nodded.

'And that we think he killed his last victim.'

'Yes.'

'The victim was a small-time stripper and probable hooker, named . . . hold on, I have it here . . .' – Yates pulled a small leather notepad from his back pocket, licked his finger, flipped through the pages – 'named Candace Potter, aka Candi Cane.' He snapped the notebook shut. 'Emma Lemay and Clyde Rangor disappeared soon after her body was found.'

'And how does that fit in with Darrow?'

'Max Darrow was the homicide investigator in charge of the case.'

Everyone stopped.

'Wait a second,' Ed Steinberg began. 'So this Clyde Rangor murders a stripper. Darrow catches the case. A few days later, Rangor and his girlfriend Lemay vanish. And now, what, ten years later, we get Darrow's fingerprints at Emma Lemay's murder scene?'

'That pretty much sums it up, yes.'

There was more silence. Loren tried to digest this.

'Here's the important thing,' Yates continued, leaning forward. 'If Emma Lemay still had materials pertinent to this case – or if she left information on the whereabouts of Clyde Rangor – we believe that Investigator Muse is in the best position to find it.'

'Me?'

Yates turned toward her. 'You have a relationship with her colleagues. Lemay lived with the same group of nuns for seven years now. The Mother Superior clearly trusts you. What we need you to concentrate on is that angle – in finding out what Lemay knew or what she had.'

Steinberg looked at Loren and shrugged. Joan Thurston moved around her desk. She opened a mini-fridge. 'Anybody want a drink?' she asked.

They didn't reply. Thurston shrugged, grabbed a bottle, began to shake it. 'How about you, Adam? You want something?'

'Just a water.'

She tossed him a bottle.

'Ed? Loren?'

They both shook their heads. Joan Thurston twisted off the cap and took a deep sip. She moved back in front of her desk.

'Okay, time to stop the dance,' Thurston said. 'What else have you learned, Loren?'

Loren. Already calling her Loren. Again she checked with Steinberg. Again he nodded.

'We found several connections between all of this and an ex-con named Matt Hunter,' Loren said.

Thurston's eyes narrowed. 'Why does that name ring a bell?'

'He's local, from Livingston. His case made the papers years back. He got into a fight at a college party –'

'Oh, right, I remember,' Thurston interrupted. 'I knew his brother Bernie. Good lawyer, died much too young. I think Bernie got him a job at Carter Sturgis when he got out.'

'Matt Hunter still works there.'

'And he's involved in this?'

'There are connections.'

'Such as?'

She told them about the phone call from St. Margaret's to Marsha Hunter's residence. They did not seem all that impressed. When Loren started filling them in on what she'd learned this very night – that Matt Hunter had, in all likelihood, gotten into a fight with Charles Talley at the Howard Johnson's – they sat up. For the first time Yates started jotting notes in the leather pad.

When she finished, Thurston asked, 'So what do you make of it, Loren?'

'Truth? I don't have a clue yet.'

'We should look at this guy Hunter's time in prison,' Yates said. 'We know Talley was in the system too. Maybe they met along the way. Or maybe Hunter somehow got involved with Comb-Over's people.'

'Right,' Thurston said. 'Could be that Hunter is the one cleaning up the loose ends for Comb-Over.'

Loren kept quiet.

'You don't agree, Loren?'

'I don't know.'

'What's the problem?'

'This may sound hopelessly naïve, but I don't think Matt Hunter is working as some kind of hit man. He has a record, yes, but that's from a fight at a frat party fifteen years ago. He had no priors and has been clean ever since.'

She did not tell him that they'd gone to school together or that her 'gut' didn't like it. When other investigators used that rationale, Loren wanted to gag.

'So how do you explain Hunter's involvement?' Thurston asked.

'I don't know. It might be a more personal thing. According to the front-desk guy, his wife was staying at the hotel without him.'

'You think it's a lovers' quarrel?'

'It could be.'

Thurston looked doubtful. 'Either way, we all agree that Matt Hunter is involved?'

Steinberg said, 'Definitely.' Yates nodded hard. Loren stayed still.

'And right now,' Thurston continued, 'we have more than enough to arrest and indict. We have the fight, the call, all that. We'll get DNA soon linking him to the dead man.'

Loren hesitated. Ed Steinberg did not. 'We got enough to arrest.'

'And with Hunter's record, we can probably get a no-bail situation. We can put him in the system and keep him there for a little while, right, Ed?'

'I'd bet on it, yeah,' Steinberg said.

'Pick him up then,' Joan Thurston said. 'Let's get Hunter's ass back behind bars pronto.'

35

Matt and Olivia were alone in Marsha's guest room.

Nine years ago Matt had spent his first night as a free man in this room. Bernie had brought him home. Marsha had been outwardly polite, but looking back on it, there must have been some serious reservations. You move into a house like this to escape people like Matt. Even if you know he's innocent, even if you think he's a good guy and got a bad break, you don't want your life enmeshed with his. He is a virus, a carrier of something malevolent. You have children. You want to protect them. You want to believe, as Lance Banner did, that the manicured lawns can keep this element out.

He thought about his old college buddy Duff. At one time Matt had believed that Duff was tough. Now he knew better. Now he could kick Duff's ass around the corner without breaking a sweat. He wasn't being boastful. He didn't think that with any pride. It was just a fact of life. His buddies who thought they were tough – the Duffs of the world – man, they had no idea.

But tough as Matt had become, he'd spent his first night of freedom in this room crying. He couldn't exactly say why. He had never cried in prison. Some would say that he simply feared showing weakness in such a horrible place. That was part of it, maybe. Maybe it was just a 'saving up' outlet, that now he was crying for four years of anguish.

But Matt didn't think so.

The real reason, he suspected, had more to do with fear and disbelief. He could not accept that he was really free, that prison was really behind him. It felt like a cruel hoax, that this warm bed was an illusion, that soon they'd drag him back and lock him away forever.

He'd read how interrogators and hostage-takers try to break spirits by holding mock executions. That would work, Matt thought, but what would undoubtedly be more effective, what would unquestionably make a man crack, would be the opposite – pretending you were going to set him free. You get the guy dressed, you tell him that his release has been all arranged, you say good-bye and blindfold him and drive him around and then, when they stop and take him inside and pull off his blindfold, he finds that he is back where he started, that it was all a sick joke.

That was how it felt.

Matt sat now on the same queen-size mattress. Olivia stood with her back to him. Her head was lowered. Her shoulders were still high, still proud. He loved her shoulders, the sinew of her back, the knot of gentle muscles and supple skin.

Part of him, maybe most of him, wanted to say, 'Let's just forget it. I don't need to know. You just said that you love me. You just told me that I am the only man you ever loved. That's enough.'

When they arrived Kyra had come out and met them in the front yard. She had been concerned. Matt remembered when she first moved in over the garage. He'd noted that she was 'just like the Fonz.' Kyra had no idea what he'd been talking about. Funny what you think about when you're terrified. Marsha looked concerned too, especially when she saw Matt's bandages and noticed his tentative step. But Marsha knew him well enough to know that now was not the time for questions.

Olivia broke the silence. 'Can I ask you something?'

'Sure.'

'You said something on the phone about receiving pictures.'

'Yes.'

'May I see them, please?'

He took out his cell phone and held it up. Olivia turned and took it from him without touching his skin. He watched her face now. She concentrated in that way he knew so well. Her head tilted a little to the side, the same as it always did when something confused her.

'I don't understand this,' she said.

'Is that you?' he asked. 'With the wig?'

'Yes. But it wasn't like that.'

'Like what?'

Her eyes stayed on the camera. She hit the replay button, watched the scene again, shook her head. 'Whatever you want to think of me, I never cheated on you. And the man I met with. He was wearing a wig too. So he could look like the guy in the first picture, I guess.'

'I figured that.'

'How?'

Matt showed her the window, the gray skies, the ring on the finger. He explained about the drought and about blowing up the pictures in Cingle's office.

Olivia sat next to him on the bed. She looked so damn beautiful. 'So you knew.'

'Knew what?'

'Deep in your heart, despite what you saw here, you knew that I'd never cheat on you.'

He wanted to reach out and take her in his arms. He could see her chest hitching a little, trying to hold it together.

Matt said, 'I just need to ask you two questions before you begin, okay?'

She nodded.

'Are you pregnant?' he asked.

'Yes,' she said. 'And before you ask the second question – yes, it's yours.'

'Then I don't care about the rest. If you don't want to tell me, you don't have to. It doesn't matter. We can just run off, I don't care.'

She shook her head. 'I don't think I can run again, Matt.' She sounded so worn. 'And you can't just do that either. What about Paul and Ethan? What about Marsha?'

She was right, of course. He didn't know how to put it. He shrugged and said, 'I just don't want things to change.'

'Neither do I. And if I could come up with a way around this, I would. I'm scared, Matt. I've never been so scared in my life.'

423

She turned to him. She reached out and cupped the back of his head. She leaned forward and kissed him. She kissed him hard. He knew that kiss. It was the prelude. Despite what was happening, his body reacted, began to sing. The kiss grew hungrier. She moved closer, pressed against him. His eyes rolled back.

They turned a little, and Matt's ribs suddenly screamed. Pain shot down his side. He stiffened. His low cry chased the moment away. Olivia released him, pulled away. She lowered her eyes.

'Everything I've ever told you about me,' she said, 'was a lie.'

He did not react. He was not sure what he had expected her to say – not this – but he just sat and waited.

'I didn't grow up in Northways, Virginia. I didn't go to UVA – I didn't even go to high school. My father wasn't the town doctor – I don't know who my father was. I never had a nanny named Cassie or any of that. I made it all up.'

Outside the window a car turned onto the street, the headlights dancing against the wall as it passed. Matt just sat there, still as a stone.

'My real mother was a strung-out junkie who gave me to Child Services when I was three. She died from an OD two years later. I bounced around from foster home to foster home. You don't want to know what they were like. I did that until I ran away when I was sixteen. I ended up near Las Vegas.'

'When you were sixteen?'

'Yes.'

Olivia's voice had taken on a strange monotone now. Her eyes were clear, but she stared straight ahead, two yards past him. She seemed to be waiting for a reaction. Matt was still fumbling, trying to take this all in.

'So those stories about Dr. Joshua Murray . . . ?'

'You mean the young girl with the dead mother and the kindly father and the horses?' She almost smiled. 'Come on, Matt. I got that from a book I read when I was eight.'

He opened his mouth but nothing came out. He tried again. 'Why?'

'Why did I lie?'

'Yes.'

'I didn't really lie so much as . . .' She stopped, looked up . . . 'so much as died. I know that sounds melodramatic. But becoming Olivia Murray was more than just a fresh start. It was like I was never that other person. The foster child was dead. Olivia Murray of Northways, Virginia, took her place.'

'So everything . . .' He put his hands up. 'It was all a lie?'

'Not us,' she said. 'Not how I feel about you. Not how I act around you. Nothing about us was ever a lie. Not one kiss. Not one embrace. Not one emotion. You didn't love a lie. You loved me.'

Loved, she had said. You loved me. The past tense.

'So when we met in Las Vegas, you weren't in college?'

'No,' she said.

'And that night? At the club?'

Her eyes met his. 'I was supposed to be working.'

'I don't understand.'

'Yeah, Matt. Yeah, you do.'

He remembered the Web site. The stripper site.

'You danced?'

'Danced? Well, yes, the politically correct term is exotic dancer. All the girls use that term. But I was a stripper. And sometimes, when they made me. . . .' Olivia shook her head. Her eyes started to water. 'We'll never get past this.'

'And that night,' Matt said, a surge of anger coursing through him, 'what, I looked like I had money?'

'That's not funny.'

'I'm not trying to be funny.'

Her voice had steel in it now. 'You have no idea what that night meant to me. It changed my life. You never got it, Matt.'

'Never got what?'

'Your world,' she said. 'It's worth fighting for.'

He wasn't sure what she meant – or if he wanted to know what she meant. 'You said you were in foster homes.'

'Yes.'

'And that you ran away?'

'My last foster home encouraged this line of work. You can't imagine how badly you want to get out. So they told us where to go. My last foster mother's sister – she ran the club. She got us fake IDs.'

He shook his head. 'I still don't see why you didn't tell me the truth.'

'When, Matt?'

'When what?'

'When should I have told you? That first night in Las Vegas? How about when I came to your office? Second date? Engagement? When should I have told you?'

'I don't know.'

'It wasn't that easy.'

'It wasn't easy for me to tell you about my time in prison either.'

'My situation involves more than me,' she said. 'I made a pact.'

'What kind of pact?'

'You have to understand. I might have been able to risk it, if it was just me. But I couldn't risk it for her.'

'Who?'

Olivia looked away and didn't say anything for a long time. She took a piece of paper out of her back pocket, unfolded it slowly, and handed it to him. Then she turned her face away from him again.

Matt took the piece of paper and turned it over. It was an article printed out from the *Nevada Sun News* Web site. He read it. It didn't take long.

WOMAN SLAIN

Las Vegas, NV – Candace Potter, age 21, was found slain in a trailer park off Route 15. The cause of death was strangulation. Police would not comment about the possibility of sexual assault. Ms. Potter worked as a dancer at the Young Thangs, a nightclub on the outskirts of the city, using the stage name Candi Cane. Authorities said the investigation was ongoing and that they were following up some promising leads.

Matt looked up. 'I still don't get it.' Her face was still turned away from him. 'You promised this Candace person?'

She chuckled without humor. 'No.'

'Then who?'

'What I said before. About not really lying to you. About it being more like I died.'

Olivia turned toward him.

'That's me,' she said. 'I used to be Candace Potter.'

36

When Loren got back to the county prosecutor's office, Roger Cudahy, one of the techno guys who'd gone to Cingle's office, was sitting with his feet up on her desk, his hands folded behind his head.

'Comfy?' Loren said.

His smile was wide. 'Oh yeah.'

'Don't we look like the proverbial cat who ate the proverbial canary.'

The smile stayed. 'Not sure that proverbial applies, but again: Oh yeah.'

'What is it?'

With his hands still behind his head, Cudahy motioned toward the laptop. 'Take a look.'

'On the laptop?'

'Oh yeah.'

She moved the mouse. The darkened screen came to life. And there, filling up the entire screen, was a snapshot of Charles Talley. He was holding his hand up. His hair was blue-black. He had a cocky grin on his face.

'You got this off Cingle Shaker's computer?'

'Oh yeah. It came from a camera phone.'

'Nice work.'

'Hold up.'

'What?'

Cudahy continued to grin. 'As Bachman Turner Overdrive used to sing, you ain't seen nothing yet.'

'What?' Loren said.

'Hit the arrow key. The right one.'

Loren did it. The shaky video started up. A woman in a platinum-blonde wig came out of the bathroom. She moved toward the bed. When the video was finished, Cudahy said, 'Comments?'

'Just one.'

Cudahy put out his palm. 'Lay it on me.'

Loren slapped him five. 'Oh yeah.'

37

'It was about a year after I met you,' Olivia said.

She stood across the room. The color was back in her face. Her spine was straighter. It was as though she was gaining strength, telling him all this. For his part, Matt tried not to process yet. He just wanted to absorb.

'I was eighteen years old, but I'd already been in Vegas for two years. A lot of us girls lived in old trailers. The manager of the club, an evil man named Clyde Rangor, had a couple of acres a mile down the road. It was just desert. He put up a chain-link fence, dragged in three or four of the most beaten-down trailers you'd ever seen. And that's where we lived. The girls, they came and went, but at this time I was sharing the trailer with two people. One was new, a girl named Cassandra Meadows. She was maybe sixteen, seventeen years old. The other was named Kimmy Dale. Kimmy was away that day. See, Clyde used to send us out on road trips. We'd strip in some small town, do three shows a day. Easy money for him. Good tips for us, though Clyde kept most of that too.'

Matt needed to get his bearings, but there was just no way. 'When you started there, you were how old?' he asked.

'Sixteen.'

He tried not to close his eyes. 'I don't understand how that worked.'

'Clyde was connected. I don't really know how, but they'd find hard-up girls from foster homes in Idaho.'

'That's where you're from?'

She nodded. 'They had contacts in other states too. Oklahoma. Cassandra was from Kansas, I think. The girls would basically be funneled to Clyde's place. He'd give them fake IDs and put them to work. It wasn't difficult. We both know that nobody really cares about the poor, but little children are, at least, sympathetic. We were just sullen teenagers. We had nobody.'

Matt said, 'Okay, go on.'

'Clyde had this girlfriend named Emma Lemay. Emma was sort of a mother figure to all the girls. I know how that sounds, but when you consider what we'd had in the past, she almost made you believe it. Clyde used to beat the hell out of her. He'd just walk by, you'd see Emma flinch. I didn't realize it then, but that victimization . . . it made us relate, I guess. Kimmy and I liked her. We all talked about one day getting out – that's all we ever talked about. I told her and Kimmy about meeting you. About what that night meant to me. They listened. We all knew it would never happen, but they listened anyway.'

There was a sound from outside of the room. A tiny cry. Olivia turned toward it.

'That's just Ethan,' Matt said.

'Does he do that a lot?'

'Yes.'

They waited. The house fell silent again.

'One day I was feeling sick,' Olivia said. Her voice had again moved into a distant monotone. 'It's not like they give you nights off, but I was so nauseous I could barely stand, and, well, girls throwing up on stage didn't do much for business. Since Clyde and Emma weren't around, I checked with the guy at the door. He said I could leave. So I walked back to the Pen – that's what we called the trailer area. It was around three in the afternoon. The sun was still strong. I could almost feel my skin being baked.'

Olivia smiled wistfully then. 'You know what's odd? Well, I mean, the whole thing is odd, but you know what just struck me?'

'What?'

'The degrees. Not the temperature degrees. But the degrees that change everything. The little ifs that become the big ones. You know about those better than anyone. If you had just driven straight back to Bowdoin. If Duff hadn't spilled the beer. You know.'

'I do.'

'It's the same thing here. If I hadn't been sick. If I had just danced like I did every night. Except in my case, well, I guess different people would say different things. But I'd say my ifs saved my life.'

She was standing by the door. She eyed the knob as if she wanted to flee.

Matt said, 'What happened when you got back to the Pen?'

'The place was empty,' Olivia said. 'Most of the girls were already at the club or in town. We usually finished around three in the morning and slept to noon. The Pen was so depressing, we got the hell out of there as soon as we could. So when I came back, it was silent. I opened the door to my trailer and the first thing I saw was blood on the floor.'

He watched closely now. Olivia's breathing had deepened, but her face was smooth, untroubled.

'I called out. That was stupid, I guess. I probably should have just started screaming and ran, I don't know. Another if, right? Then I looked around. The trailers had two rooms, but they're set up backwards, so you first walk into the bedroom where the three of us slept. I had the lower bunk. Kimmy's was on the top. Cassandra, the new girl, her bed was against the far wall. Kimmy was neat as a pin. She was always getting on us about not cleaning up. Our lives were dumps, she'd say, but that didn't mean we had to live in one.

'Anyway, the place was totally trashed. The drawers had all been dumped out, clothes everywhere. And there, near Cassandra's bed, where the blood trailed off, I could see two legs on the floor. I ran over and I just pulled up short.'

Olivia looked him straight in the eye. 'Cassandra was dead. I didn't need to feel for a pulse. Her body was on its side, almost in a fetal position. Both eyes were open, staring at that wall. Her face was purple and swollen. There were cigarette burns on her arms. Her hands were still hog-tied with duct tape behind her back. You have to remember, Matt. I was eighteen years old. I may have felt older or looked older. I may have had too much life experience. But think about that. I'm standing there looking at a dead body. I was frozen. I couldn't move. Even when I heard the sounds coming from the other room, even when I heard Emma scream out, "Clyde, don't!"'

She stopped, closed her eyes, let loose a deep breath.

'I turned just in time to see a fist flying at my face. There was no time to react. Clyde didn't pull the punch at all. His knuckles landed flush on my nose. I actually heard the crack more than I felt it. My head snapped back. I fell back and landed on top of Cassandra – that was probably the worst part of all. Landing on her dead body. Her skin was all clammy. I tried to crawl off her. Blood was flowing down into my mouth.'

Olivia paused, swallowing air, trying to catch her breath. Matt had never felt more incompetent in his life. He did not move, did not say anything. He just let her gather herself.

'Clyde rushed over and looked down on me. His face . . . I mean, he usually had this smirk. I'd seen him give Emma Lemay the backside of his hand lots of times. I know this sounds foreign to you. Why didn't we act? Why didn't we do something? But his beatings weren't unusual to us. They were normal. You have to understand that. This was all any of us knew.'

Matt nodded, which felt totally inadequate, but he understood this thinking. Prisons were filled with this sort of rationale – it wasn't so much that you did something awful as that the awful was simply the norm.'

'Anyway,' Olivia went on, 'the smirk was gone. If you think rattlesnakes are mean, you never met Clyde Rangor. But now, standing over me, he looked terrified. He was breathing hard. There was blood on his shirt. Behind him – and this is a sight I'll never forget – Emma just stood with her head down. Here I was, bleeding and hurt, and I was looking past the psycho with the clenched fists at his other victim. His real victim, I guess.

'"Where's the tape?" Clyde asked me. I had no idea what he meant. He stomped down hard on my foot. I howled in pain. Then Clyde shouted, "You playing games with me, bitch? Where is it?"'

'I tried to scramble back, but I bumped up into the corner. Clyde kicked Cassandra's body out of the way and followed. I was trapped. I could hear Emma's voice in the distance, meek as a lamb, "Don't, Clyde. Please." With his eyes still on me, Clyde reeled on her. He had the full weight of his body in the blow. The back of his hand split Emma's cheek wide open. She tumbled back and out of sight. But it was enough for me. The distraction gave me the chance to act. I lashed out with my foot and managed to kick the spot right below his knee. Clyde's leg buckled. I got to my feet and rolled over the bed. See, I had a destination in mind. Kimmy kept a gun in the room. I didn't like it, but if you think I had it tough, Kimmy had it worse. So she was always armed. She had two guns. She kept this mini-revolver, a twenty-two in her boot. Even onstage. And Kimmy had another gun under her mattress.'

Olivia stopped and smiled at him.

'What?' Matt said.

'Like you.'

'What do you mean?'

'You don't think I know about your gun?'

He had forgotten all about it. He checked his pants. They'd taken them off him in the hospital. Olivia calmly opened her purse. 'Here,' she said.

She handed him the gun.

'I didn't want the police to find it and trace it back to you.'

'Thanks,' he said stupidly. He looked at the gun, tucked it away.

'Why do you keep it?' she asked.

'I don't know.'

'I don't think Kimmy did either. But it was there. And when Clyde went down, I dove for it. I didn't have much time. My kick hadn't incapacitated Clyde – it'd just bought me a few seconds. I dug my hand under the top bunk's mattress. I heard him shout, "Crazy whore, I'm gonna kill you." I had no doubt he would. I'd seen Cassandra. I'd seen his face. If he caught me, if I didn't get the gun, I was dead.'

Olivia was looking off now, her hand raised as though she were back in that trailer, digging for that gun. 'My hand was under the mattress. I could almost feel his breath on my neck. But I still couldn't find the gun. Clyde grabbed my hair. He was just starting to pull when my fingers felt the metal. I gripped for all I was worth as he tugged me back. The gun came with me. Clyde saw it. I didn't have a real grip on it. My thumb and forefinger were wrapped around the butt of the gun. I tried to snake my finger around the trigger. But Clyde was on me. He grabbed my wrist. I tried to fight him off. He was too strong. But I didn't let go. I held on. And then he dug his thumbnail into my skin. Clyde had these really long, sharp fingernails. See this?'

Olivia made a fist, tilted it back so that he could see the crescent-white scar on the underside of her wrist. Matt had noticed it before. A lifetime ago, she'd told him it was from a fall off a horse.

'Clyde Rangor did that. He dug his fingernail in so deep that he drew blood. I dropped the gun. He still had me by the hair. He flung me onto the bed and jumped on top of me. He grabbed me by the neck and began to squeeze. He was crying now. That's what I remember. Clyde was squeezing the life out of me and he was crying. Not because he cared or anything like that. He was scared. He was choking me and I could hear him pleading, "Just tell me where it is. Just tell me . . ."'

Olivia gently put her own hand up to her throat now. 'I struggled. I kicked, I flailed, but I could feel the power draining out of me. There was nothing behind my blows anymore. I could feel his thumb pushing down on my throat. I was dying. And then I heard the gun go off.'

Her hand dropped to the side. The antique clock in the dining room, a wedding gift to Bernie and Marsha, started to chime. Olivia waited, let it finish playing.

'The gun wasn't loud. It was more like the crack of a bat. I guess that's because it was a twenty-two, I don't know. For a second, Clyde's grip somehow tightened. His face looked more surprised than pained. He let go of me. I started gagging, choking. I rolled to the side, gasping for air. Emma Lemay was standing behind him. She pointed the gun at him and it was like all those years of abuse, all those beatings, they just boiled over. She didn't cower. She didn't look down. Clyde spun toward her, enraged, and she fired again, right in his face.

'Then Emma pulled the trigger one more time and Clyde Rangor was dead.'

38

Motive.

Loren now had motive. If the video was any indication, Charles Talley, a scumbag by anyone's calculations, had not only slept with Matt Hunter's wife – Loren was betting that it was Olivia Hunter in that video with the blonde wig – but he'd gone through the trouble of sending the pictures to Matt.

Mocking him.

Pissing him off.

Calling him out, if you will.

It added up. It made perfect sense.

Except too many things in this case made perfect sense at first. And then, after a few minutes, they didn't anymore. Like Max Darrow being rolled by a prostitute. Like the murder of Charles Talley looking like a common jealous-husband scenario when, if that indeed was the case, how do you explain the connection to Emma Lemay and the Nevada FBI and all the rest of the stuff she'd learned at Joan Thurston's office?

Her cell phone trilled. The number was blocked.

'Hello?'

'So what's up with this APB on Hunter?'

It was Lance Banner.

'Do you ever sleep?' she asked.

'Not in the summer. I prefer winter hibernation. Like a bear. So what's up?'

'We're looking for him.'

'Stop with all specifics, Loren. I mean, no, really, I can't handle all that detail.'

'It's a long story, Lance, and I've had a long night.'

'The APB was mainly on the Newark wire.'

'So?'

'So has anyone checked out Hunter's sister-in-law's?'

'I don't think so.'

'I live right down the block,' Lance Banner said. 'Consider me on the way.'

432

39

Neither Matt nor Olivia moved. The story had drained her. He could see that. He almost made a move to come closer, but she put up her hand.

'I saw an old picture of Emma Lemay once,' Olivia began. 'She was so beautiful. She was smart too. If anyone had the wiles to get out of this life, it was Emma. But you see, no one does. I was eighteen, Matt. And I already felt like my life was over. So there we were, me retching, Emma still holding the gun. She stared down at Clyde for a long time and simply waited for me to catch my breath. It took a few minutes. Then she turns to me, all clear-eyed, and says, "We need to hide his body"

'I remember shaking my head. I told her I didn't want any part of that. She didn't get upset or raise her voice. It was so strange. She looked so . . . serene.'

Matt said, 'She'd just slain her abuser.'

'That was part of it, sure.'

'But?'

'It was almost as if she'd been waiting for this moment. Like she knew it would one day happen. I said we should call the police. Emma shook her head, calm, in control. The gun was still in her hand. She didn't point it at me. 'We could tell them the truth," I said. "That it was self-defense. We'll show them the bruises on my neck. Hell, we'll show them Cassandra.'

Matt shifted in his seat. Olivia saw it and smiled.

'I know,' she said. 'The irony isn't lost on me. Self-defense. Like you claimed. We were both, I guess, at that same fork in the road. Maybe you didn't have a choice, what with all those people around. But even if you did, you came from a different world. You trusted the police. You thought that truth would win out. But we knew better. Emma had shot Clyde three times, once in the back, twice in the face. No one would buy self-defense. And even if they did, Clyde made big money for his mobbed-up cousin. He'd never let us live.'

'So what did you do?' he asked.

'I was confused, I guess. But Emma kept explaining the predicament. We had no choice. Not really. And that was when she hit me with her best argument.'

'What?'

'Emma said, "What if it all goes well?"'

'What if what all goes well?' Matt asked.

'What if the police believe us and Clyde's cousin leaves us alone?'

She stopped, smiled.

'I don't get it,' Matt said.

'Where would we be? Emma and me. Where would we be if it all worked out?'

Matt saw it now. 'You'd be where you were.'

'Right. This was our chance, Matt. Clyde had a hundred thousand dollars hidden at the house. Emma said we'd take it. We'd split up and run. We'd start anew. Emma already had a destination in mind. She'd been planning on leaving for years, but she never had the courage. Neither did I. Neither did any of us.'

'But now you had to.'

Olivia nodded. 'She said that if we hid Clyde, they'd figure the two of them ran off together. They'd be looking for a couple. Or they'd think they were both killed and buried together. But she needed my help. I said, "What about me? Clyde's friends know what I look like. They'll hunt me down. And how do we explain Cassandra being dead?"

'But Emma already had that covered. She said, "Give me your wallet." I dug into my pocket and pulled it out. She took out my ID – back in those days, Nevada didn't require you to have pictures on the ID – and she jammed it into Cassandra's pocket. "When is Kimmy coming back?" she asked me. In three days, I told her. Plenty of time, she said. Then she said, "Listen to me. Neither you nor Cassandra has any real family. Cassandra's mother threw her out years ago. They don't talk."

'I said, "I don't understand."

'"I've been thinking about this for years," Emma said. "Whenever he beat me. Whenever he choked me until I passed out. Whenever he said he was sorry and promised that it would never happen again and that he loved me. Whenever he told me he'd hunt me down and kill me if I ever left. What . . . what if I killed Clyde and buried him and just took the money and ran someplace I knew was safe? What if I made amends, you know, for what I'd done to you girls? You have those fantasies, don't you, Candi? About running away?"'

Matt said, 'And you did.'

Olivia held up her index finger. 'With one difference. I said before that my life already felt over. I disappeared in my books. I tried to keep upbeat. I imagined something different. Because I had something to hold on to. Look, I don't want to make too much of that night in Vegas. But I thought about it, Matt. I thought about the way you made me feel. I thought about the world you lived in. I remember everything you said – about your family, about where you grew up, about your friends and your school. And what you didn't know, what you still don't understand, is that you were describing a place I couldn't let myself imagine.'

Matt said nothing.

'After you left that night, I can't tell you how many times I thought of trying to find you.'

'Why didn't you?'

She shook her head. 'You of all people should understand shackles.'

He nodded, afraid to answer.

'Didn't matter anymore,' Olivia said. 'It was too late for any of that now. Even with shackles, like you said, we had to act. So we came up with a plan. It was simple, really. First, we rolled Clyde's body up in a blanket and dumped it in the back of the car. We padlocked the Pen. Emma knew a place. Clyde had dumped at least two bodies there, she said. Out in the desert. We buried him in a shallow grave, way out in this no-man's-land. Then Emma called the club. She made sure all the girls were made to work overtime, so that none of them would be able to go back to the Pen.

'We stopped at her place to shower. I stepped under the warm water and

434

thought, I don't know, I thought it would be weird, showering off the blood, like something out of *Macbeth*.'

A wan smile crossed her face.

'But it wasn't like that?' Matt asked.

Olivia shook her head slowly. 'I had just buried a man in the desert. At night the jackals would dig him up and feast. Carry his bones away. That's what Emma told me. And I didn't care.'

She looked at him as if daring him to challenge her.

'So what did you do next?'

'Can't you guess?'

'Tell me.'

'I . . . I mean, Candace Potter was nothing. There was no one to even notify in the event of her untimely death. Emma as her employer and almost guardian called the police. She said that one of her girls had been murdered. The police arrived. Emma showed them Cassandra's body. The ID was already in her pocket. Emma identified the body and confirmed that it belonged to one of her girls, Candace "Candi Cane" Potter. There was no next of kin. No one questioned it. Why should they? Why would anyone make something like this up? Emma and I split the money. I got over fifty grand. Can you imagine? All the girls at the club had fake IDs anyway, so getting a new one was no problem for me.'

'And you just ran off?'

'Yes.'

'What about Cassandra?' Matt asked.

'What about her?'

'Didn't anyone wonder what happened to her?'

'We had a million girls come and go. Emma told everyone she'd quit – been spooked off by the murder. Two other girls got scared and ran off too.'

Matt shook his head, trying to wrap his brain around all this. 'When I met you the first time, you used the name Olivia Murray.'

'Yes.'

'You went back to that name?'

'That was the only time I used it. With you that night. Did you ever read *A Wrinkle in Time*?'

'Sure. In fifth grade, I think.'

'When I was a kid, it was my favorite book. The protagonist was named Meg Murray. That's how I came up with the last name.'

'And Olivia?'

She shrugged. 'It sounded like the direct opposite of Candi.'

'So then what happened?'

'Emma and I made a pact. We would never tell anyone the truth – no matter what – because if one of us talked, it could lead to the death of the other. So we swore. I need you to understand how solemnly I made that promise.'

Matt was not sure what to say to that. 'Then you went to Virginia?'

'Yes.'

'Why?'

'Because it was where Olivia Murray lived. It was far away from Vegas or Idaho. I made up a background story. I took courses at the University of Virginia. I didn't officially attend, of course, but this was in the days before strict security.

I just sat in on classes. I hung out in the library and cafeteria. I met people. They just figured I was a student. A few years later, I pretended to graduate. I got a job. I never looked back or thought about Candi. Candace Potter was dead.'

'And then, what, I came along?'

'Something like that, yeah. Look, I was a scared kid. I ran away and tried to make a life for myself. A real one. And the truth is, I had no interest in meeting a man. You hired DataBetter, remember?'

Matt nodded. 'I do.'

'I'd had enough of that in my life. But then I saw you and . . . I don't know. Maybe I wanted to go back to the night we met. To some silly dream. You scoff at the idea of living out here, Matt. You don't see that this place, this town, this is the best possible world.'

'And that's why you want to move out here?'

'With you,' she said, her eyes imploring. 'Don't you see? I never bought that soul-mate stuff. You see what I've seen and . . . but maybe, I don't know, maybe our wounds work for us. Maybe the suffering gives us a better appreciation. You learn to fight for what others just take for granted. You love me, Matt. You never really believed I was having an affair. It's why you kept digging for that proof – because despite what I'm telling you here, you and you alone really know me. You're the only one. And yes, I want to move out here and raise a family with you. That's all I want.'

Matt opened his mouth, but no words came out.

'It's okay,' she said with a small smile. 'It's a lot to take in.'

'It's not that. It's just . . .' He couldn't express it. The emotions were still swirling. He needed to let them settle. 'So what went wrong?' he asked. 'After all these years, how did they find you?'

'They didn't find me,' she said. 'I found them.'

Matt was about to ask a follow-up question when another set of car headlights began to skitter across the wall. They slowed a beat too long. Matt raised his hand to quiet her for a moment. They both listened. The sound of an idling engine was faint, but it was there. No mistake.

Their eyes met. Matt moved toward the window and peeked out.

The car was parked across the street. The headlights went off. A few seconds later, so did the car engine. Matt recognized the car right away. He had, in fact, been in that car just a few hours earlier.

It belonged to Lance Banner.

40

Loren burst back into the interrogation room.

Cingle was checking out her own nails. 'Lawyer's not here yet.'

Loren just stared at her for a moment. She wondered what it must be like to look like Cingle Shaker, to have men fawn over you, to know you can pretty much do what you want with them. Loren's mother had a bit of that, but when a woman looked like Cingle Shaker, what must that be like? Would it be a good thing or bad? Would you start to rely on those assets to the detriment of your others? Loren didn't think that was the case with Cingle, but that just made her more of a threat.

'Guess what we found on your office computer?' Loren asked.

Cingle blinked. But it was enough. She knew. Loren took out the photograph of Charles Talley. She also took out a few choice stills from the video. She put them on the table in front of Cingle. Cingle barely glanced at them.

'I'm not talking,' Cingle said.

'Would you nod?'

'What?'

'I'll start talking. You can nod along if you like. Because I think it's all pretty obvious now.' Loren sat down, folded her hands, and put them on the table. 'Our lab guys said these photographs came from a camera phone. So here is how we figured it played out. Charles Talley was a bit of a sicko. We know that. He has a criminal history rather rich in violence and perversion. Anyway, he meets up with Olivia Hunter. I don't know how yet. Maybe you'll tell us when your lawyer arrives. Doesn't matter. Either way, for whatever sick reasons, he gets off on sending a photograph and video to our mutual bud Matt Hunter. Matt brings the pictures to you. You, because you're good at what you do, find out that the guy in the pictures is Charles Talley and that he is currently staying at the Howard Johnson's by Newark Airport. Or maybe you figure out that Olivia Hunter is staying there. I don't know which.'

Cingle said, 'That's not right.'

'But it's close. I don't know the details, and I don't really care why or how Hunter came to you. What is clear is that he did. That he gave you the picture and the video. That you found Charles Talley. That you both drove to confront him at the hotel. That Talley and Hunter got into a fight. That Hunter ended up injured and that Talley ended up dead.'

Cingle looked away.

'You have something to add?' Loren asked.

Loren's cell phone rang again. She pulled it out, flipped it open, and said, 'Hello.'

'It's your friendly neighborhood Lance.'

'What's up?'

'Guess where I am.'

'In front of Marsha Hunter's house?'

'Bingo. Now guess whose car is parked in her driveway.'

Loren straightened up. 'You call for backup?'

'They're on their way.'

She snapped the phone closed. Cingle's eyes were on her.

'That about Matt?'

Loren nodded. 'We're about to arrest him.'

'He's going to freak.'

Loren shrugged, waited.

Cingle bit down on a fingernail. 'You got it wrong.'

'How's that?'

'You think Charles Talley sent those pictures to Matt.'

'He didn't?'

Cingle shook her head very slowly.

'Then who did?'

'Good question.'

Loren sat back. She thought about the photograph, the one of Charles Talley. He had his hand up, almost as if he were embarrassed to have the picture taken. He hadn't shot that picture of himself.

'Doesn't matter. We'll have Matt in custody in a few minutes.'

Cingle stood. She began to pace. She folded her arms. 'Maybe,' she started again, 'the pictures are a big setup.'

'What?'

'Come on, Loren. Use your head here. Don't you think this is all a little too neat?'

'Most murder cases are.'

'Bull.'

'You find a dead man, you check his love life. You find a dead woman, you check her boyfriend or husband. It's usually just that simple.'

'Except Charles Talley wasn't Olivia Hunter's boyfriend.'

'And you figured that out how?'

'I didn't figure it out. Matt did.'

'I'm still waiting for the how.'

'Because the pictures are fakes.'

Loren opened her mouth, closed it, decided to wait her out.

'That's why Matt came to my office tonight. He wanted to blow up the pictures. He realized that they weren't what they appeared to be. He figured it out when it started to rain.'

Loren leaned back and spread her hands. 'You better explain from the beginning.'

Cingle grabbed the photograph of Charles Talley. 'Okay, see the window here, the way the sun shines through it . . . ?'

41

Lance Banner's car stayed parked across the street from Marsha's house.

'You know him?' Olivia asked Matt.

'Yes. We went to school together. He's a cop here in town.'

'He's here to ask about the assault?'

Matt did not reply. That made sense, he guessed. What with Cingle's arrest, the police probably wanted to file a full report. Or maybe Matt's name, as a victim or a witness, had gone out over a police radio and Lance had seen it. Maybe this was simply more harassment.

Either way, it really wasn't a big deal. If Lance came to the door, Matt would send him away. That was his right. They couldn't arrest a victim for not filing a timely report.

'Matt?'

He turned toward Olivia. 'You were saying that they didn't find you. That you found them.'

'Yes.'

'I'm not sure I follow.'

'That's because this is the most difficult part,' Olivia said.

He thought – no, hoped – that she was joking. He was trying to hold on, trying to compartmentalize, rationalize, or just plain block.

'I told a lot of lies,' she said. 'But this last one is the worst.'

Matt stayed by the window.

'I became Olivia Hunter. I told you that already. Candace Potter was dead to me. Except . . . except there was one part of her I could never quite give up.'

She stopped.

'What is it?' Matt asked in a soft voice.

'When I was fifteen I got pregnant.'

He closed his eyes.

'I was so scared, I hid it until it was too late. When my water broke, my foster mother brought me to a doctor's office. They had me sign a bunch of papers. There was a payment made, I don't know how much. I never saw the money. The doctor put me under. I had the baby. When I woke up . . .'

Her voice tailed off. She sort of shrugged it away and said: 'I never even knew if it was a boy or a girl.'

Matt kept his eyes on Lance's car. He felt something at his core rip away. 'What about the father?'

'He ran off when he heard I was pregnant. Broke my heart. He got killed in a car crash a couple of years later.'

'And you never knew what happened to the baby?'

'Never. Not a word. And in many ways I was okay with that. Even if I wanted to interfere in her life, I couldn't – not with my predicament. But that doesn't mean I didn't care. Or wonder what happened to her.'

There was a moment of silence. Matt turned and faced his wife.

'You said "her."'

'What?'

'Just now. First you said you didn't know if it was a boy or girl. Then you said you didn't want to interfere in *her* life and that you wondered what happened to *her.*'

Olivia said nothing.

'How long have you known you had a girl?'

'Just a few days.'

'How did you find out?'

Olivia took out another sheet of paper. 'Do you know anything about online adoption support groups?'

'No, not really.'

'There are these boards where adoptive kids can post looking for their biological parents and vice versa. I always checked. Just out of curiosity. I never thought I'd find anything. Candace Potter was long dead. Even if her child searched for her biological mother, she'd learn that and give up. Besides, I couldn't say anything anyway. I had my pact. Finding me could only bring my child harm.'

'But you checked the boards anyway?'

'Yes.'

'How often?'

'Does that matter, Matt?'

'I guess not.'

'You don't understand why I did it?'

'No, I do,' he said, though he was not sure if that was the truth. 'So what happened?'

Olivia handed him the sheet of paper. 'I found this post.'

The paper was wrinkled and had clearly been opened and closed many times. The date on the top was from four weeks ago. It read:

This is an urgent message and must be kept in strict confidence. Our daughter was adopted eighteen years ago at the office of Dr. Eric Tequesta in Meridian, Idaho, on February 12th. The birth mother's name is Candace Potter, who is deceased. We have no information on the father.

Our daughter is very sick. She desperately needs a kidney donation from a blood relative. We are searching for any blood relatives who might be a match. Please, if you are a blood relative of the late Candace Potter, please contact us at . . .

Matt kept reading and rereading the post.

'I had to do something,' Olivia said.

He nodded numbly.

'I e-mailed the parents. At first I just pretended to be an old friend of Candace Potter's, but they wouldn't release any information to me. I didn't know what to do. So I wrote again and said I was indeed a blood relative. And then it all took a weird turn.'

'How?'

'I think . . . I don't know . . . suddenly the parents got cagey. So we agreed to meet in person. We set up a time and place.'

'In Newark?'

'Yes. They even booked the room for me. I had to check in and wait for them to contact me. I did. Some man finally called and told me to go to Room 508. When I got there, the man said he needed to search my bag. That's when he took the phone out, I guess. Then he told me to change in the bathroom and put on a wig and a dress. I didn't get why, but he said we were going someplace and he did-n't want anyone recognizing either one of us. I was too afraid not to listen. He put on a wig too, a black one. When I came out he told me to sit on the bed. He walked toward me, just like you saw. When he got to the bed, he stopped and said he knew who I was. If I wanted to save my daughter's life, I'd have to transfer money to his account. I should get it ready.'

'Did you?'

'Yes.'

'How much?'

'Fifty thousand dollars.'

He nodded, feigning calm. All the money they had. 'So then what?'

'He told me he'd need more. Another fifty thousand. I told him I didn't have that kind of money. We argued. I finally said he'd get more money when I saw my daughter.'

Matt looked off.

'What?' she asked.

'Weren't you starting to wonder?'

'About?'

'If this was all a con of some sort.'

'Of course,' Olivia said. 'I read about these con men who'd pretend to find information on MIAs in Vietnam. They'd get the family to give them money to continue the search. The families wanted it to be true so badly that they couldn't see it was all a ruse.'

'So?'

'Candace Potter was dead,' she said. 'Why would someone try to con money from a dead woman?'

'Maybe someone figured out you were alive.'

'How?'

'I don't know. Emma Lemay might have said something.'

'Suppose she did. Then what? Nobody knew, Matt. The only person in Vegas I told was my friend Kimmy, but even she didn't know all that information – the date of birth, the town in Idaho, the name of the doctor. I didn't even remember the doctor's name until I saw it in that post. The only people who would know all that were my daughter or her adoptive parents. And even if it was some sort of scam, what with the wig and all, I had to follow it up. I mean, somehow my daughter had to be involved. Don't you see that?'

'I do,' he said. He also saw that her logic was somewhat flawed, but now was not the time to point that out. 'So now what?'

'I insisted on seeing my daughter. So he set up a meet. That's when I'm supposed to bring the rest of the money.'

'When?'

'Tomorrow at midnight.'

'Where?'

'In Reno.'

'Nevada?'

'Yes.'

Again Nevada. 'Do you know a man named Max Darrow?'

She said nothing.

'Olivia?'

'He was the man in the black wig. The one I met with. I knew him back in Vegas too. He used to hang at the club.'

Matt was not sure what to make of that. 'Where in Reno?'

'The address is 488 Center Lane Drive. I have a plane ticket. Darrow said I shouldn't tell anyone. If I'm not there . . . I don't know, Matt. They said they would hurt her.'

'Hurt your daughter?'

Olivia nodded. The tears were back in her eyes. 'I don't know what's going on. I don't know if she's sick or if they kidnapped her or hell, if she's somehow in on it. But she's real and she's alive and I have to go to her.'

Matt tried to take it in, but it wasn't happening. His cell phone rang. Matt automatically reached to snap it off, but then he thought better of it. At this hour it was probably Cingle. She could be in trouble, need his help. He checked the caller ID. Private number. Could be the police station.

'Hello?'

'Matt?'

He frowned. It sounded like Midlife. 'Ike, is that you?'

'Matt, I just got off the phone with Cingle.'

'What?'

'I'm on the way to the county prosecutor's office now,' Midlife said. 'They want to interrogate her.'

'She called you?'

'Yeah, I guess, but I think that had more to do with you.'

'What are you talking about?'

'She wanted to warn you.'

'About what?'

'I wrote it down, hold on. Okay, first off, you asked her about a man named Max Darrow? He's been murdered. They found him shot dead in Newark.'

Matt looked at Olivia. She said, 'What is it?'

Midlife was still talking. 'But worse, Charles Talley is dead. They found his body at the Howard Johnson's. They also found a set of bloody brass knuckles. They're running DNA tests on them now. And within the hour, they'll have the photographs off your cell phone.'

Matt said nothing.

'Do you understand what I'm telling you, Matt?'

He did. It didn't take long. They'd put it together like this: Matt, an ex-con who'd already served time for killing a man in a fight, gets these mocking photographs on his cell phone. His wife was clearly shacking up with Charles Talley. Matt used a private eye to find out where they were. He charged into the hotel late at night. There was a fight. There'd be at least one witness – the guy at the front desk. Probably a security video. They'd have physical evidence too. His DNA is probably all over the dead man.

There would be holes in their case. Matt could show them the gray window and explain about the drought. He also didn't know what time Talley had been killed, but if Matt was lucky, the murder took place when he was in the ambulance or at the hospital. Or maybe he'd have an alibi in the taxi driver. Or his wife.

Like that would hold up.

'Matt?'

'What is it?'

'The police are probably searching for you now.'

He glanced out the window. A police car pulled up next to Lance's. 'I think they already found me.'

'You want me to arrange a peaceful surrender?'

A peaceful surrender. Trust the authorities to straighten it out. Do the law-abiding thing.

That worked so well before, didn't it?

Fool me once, shame on me. Fool me twice . . .

And suppose he did come clean. Then what? They'd have to tell everything, including Olivia's past. Forget about the fact that Matt swore, *swore,* he'd never let himself go back to prison. Olivia had indeed committed a crime. She'd, at best, helped dispose of a dead body. Not to mention the fact that Max Darrow, who had also been murdered, had been blackmailing her. How would that look?

'Ike?'

'Yes.'

'If they know we communicated, you could get nailed for aiding and abetting.'

'Nah, Matt, I really can't. I'm your attorney. I'm giving you the facts and encouraging you to surrender. But what you do . . . well, I can't control that. I can only be shocked and outraged. You see?'

He did. He looked out the window again. Another squad car pulled up. He thought about being back in prison. In the window reflection, he saw Stephen McGrath's ghost. Stephen winked at him. Matt felt the tightness in his chest.

'Thanks, Ike.'

'Good luck, pal.'

Midlife hung up the phone. Matt turned to Olivia. 'What is it?' she asked.

'We have to get out of here.'

42

Lance Banner approached Marsha Hunter's front door.

Two tired uniforms were with him now. Both men had facial stubble nestled in that cusp between needing a shave and trendy, the end of an uneventful Livingston night shift. They were young guys, fairly new on the force. They walked in silence. He could hear them breathing hard. Both men had put on weight recently. Lance was not sure why that happened, why the new recruits always gained weight during their first year with the force, but he'd be hard-pressed to find examples where that didn't happen.

Lance was conflicted here. He was having second thoughts about his run-in with Matt yesterday. Whatever his past crime, whatever he may have become, Hunter had not deserved being subject to Banner's clumsy and stupid harass-ment. And it had been stupid, no question about it, intimidating a purported interloper like some redneck sheriff in a bad movie.

Last night Matt Hunter had scoffed at Lance's seemingly Pollyanna-ish attempt to keep evil out of his fair town. But Matt got it wrong. Lance wasn't naïve. He understood that there was no protective force field around the fertile suburban sprawl. That was the point. You work hard to make a life for yourself. You meet up with like-minded people and build a great community. Then you fight to keep it. You see a potential problem, you don't let it fester. You remove it. You're proactive. That was what he'd been doing with Matt Hunter. That was what men like Lance Banner did for their hometowns. They were the soldiers, the front line, the few who took night duty so that the others, including Lance's own family, could sleep soundly.

So when his fellow cops started talking about doing something, when Lance's own wife, Wendy, who had gone to school with Matt Hunter's younger sister and thought she was a 'Queen Bitch,' started getting on his case about a convicted killer moving into their neighborhood, when one of the town councilmen had offered up the sternest of suburban worries – 'Lance, do you realize what it'll do to property values?' – he had acted.

And now he wasn't sure if he regretted it or not.

He thought about his conversation with Loren Muse yesterday. She'd asked him about young Matt Hunter. Had Lance seen any early signs of psychosis there? The answer was a pretty firm no. Hunter had been soft. Lance remembered him crying at a Little League game when he dropped a fly ball. His father had com-forted him while Lance marveled at what a big baby the kid was. But – and this might seem the opposite of Loren's study on early signs of trouble – men can indeed change. It was not all decided by age five or whatever Loren had told him.

The catch was, the change was always, *always,* for the worse.

If you discover a young psychotic, he will never turn himself around and become productive. Never. But you can find plenty of guys, nice guys who grew up with the right values, quality guys who respected the law and loved thy neighbor, gentle guys who found violence abhorrent and wanted to stay on the straight and narrow – you find lots of guys like this who end up doing terrible things.

Who knew why? Sometimes it was, as in Hunter's case, just a question of bad luck, but then again it's all about luck, isn't it? Your upbringing, your genes, your life experience, conditions, whatever – they're all a crapshoot. Matt Hunter had been in the wrong place at the wrong time. That didn't matter anymore. You could see it in his eyes. You could see it in the way Hunter walked, the early gray in his hair, the way he blinked, the tightness in his smile.

Bad follows some people. It hooks into them and never lets them go.

And simple as it sounded, you don't want those people around you.

Lance knocked on Marsha Hunter's door. The two uniforms stood behind him in vee formation. The sun had begun its ascent. They listened for a sound.

Nothing.

He saw the doorbell. Marsha Hunter, he knew, had two young children. If Matt wasn't here, he'd feel bad about waking them, but that couldn't be helped. He pressed the bell and heard the chime.

Still nothing.

Just for the heck of it, Lance tried the door, hoping it might be unlocked. It wasn't.

The officer on Lance's right started shifting his feet. 'Kick it in?'

'Not yet. We don't even know if he's here.'

He rang the bell again, keeping his finger pressed against it until it rang a third time too.

The other cop said, 'Detective?'

'Give it a few more seconds,' he said.

As if on cue, the foyer light snapped on. Lance tried to look through the pebble glass, but the view was too distorted. He kept his face pressed against it searching for movement.

'Who is it?'

The female voice was tentative – understandable under the circumstances.

'It's Detective Lance Banner, Livingston Police. Could you open the door, please?'

'Who?'

'Detective Lance Banner, Livingston Police. Please open the door.'

'Just a minute.'

They waited. Lance kept peering through the pebble glass. He could make out a hazy figure coming down the stairs now. Marsha Hunter, he assumed. Her steps were as tentative as her voice. He heard a bolt slide and a chain rattle and then the door was opened.

Marsha Hunter had a bathrobe tied tightly around her waist. The robe was old and terrycloth. It looked like it belonged to a man. Lance wondered for a brief second if it had been her late husband's. Her hair was mussed. She wore no makeup, of course, and while Lance had always considered her an attractive woman, she could have used the touches.

She looked at Lance, then at the two officers at his wing, then back to Lance.

'What do you want at this hour?'

'We're looking for Matt Hunter.'

Her eyes narrowed. 'I know you.'

Lance said nothing.

'You coached my son last year in rec soccer. You have a boy Paul's age.'

'Yes, ma'am.'

'Not ma'am,' she said, her voice sharp. 'My name is Marsha Hunter.'

'Yes, I know.'

'We're your neighbors, for crying out loud.' Marsha again took in the uniformed men before returning her gaze to Lance. 'You know I live alone with two young boys,' she said, 'yet you wake us up like storm troopers?'

'We really need to talk to Matt Hunter.'

'Mommy?'

Lance recognized the boy coming down the stairs. Marsha gave Lance a baleful eye before turning to her son. 'Go to bed, Ethan.'

'But, Mom . . .'

'I'll be up in a moment. Go back to bed.' She turned back to Lance. 'I'm surprised you don't know.'

'Don't know what?'

'Matt doesn't live here,' she said. 'He lives in Irvington.'

'His car is in your driveway.'

'So?'

'So is he here?'

'What's going on?'

Another woman was at the top of the stairs.

'Who are you?' Lance asked.

'My name is Olivia Hunter.'

'Olivia Hunter as in Mrs. Matt Hunter?'

'Excuse me?'

Marsha looked back at her sister-in-law. 'He was just asking why your car is in the driveway.'

'At this hour?' Olivia Hunter said. 'Why would you want to know that?'

'They're looking for Matt.'

Lance Banner said, 'Do you know where your husband is, Mrs. Hunter?'

Olivia Hunter started to move down the stairs. Her steps, too, were deliberate. Maybe that was the tip-off. Or maybe it was her clothes. She was, after all, wearing clothes. Regular clothes. Jeans and a sweatshirt. Not nightclothes. No robe, no pajamas. At this hour.

That didn't make sense.

When Lance glanced back at Marsha Hunter, he saw it. A small tell on her face. Damn, how could he have been so stupid? The turning on the light, the walking down the stairs, the slow walk right now . . . it had all taken too long.

He spun to the uniformed cops. 'Check around back. Hurry.'

'Wait,' Olivia shouted too loudly. 'Why are your men going to the backyard?'

The cops started running – one toward the right, one to the left. Lance looked at Marsha. She stared back at him defiantly.

That was when they heard a woman's scream.

*

446

'What's going on?' Olivia asked.

'That was Midlife,' Matt said. 'Charles Talley and Max Darrow are both dead.'

'Oh, my God.'

'And unless I'm mistaken,' he continued, gesturing toward the window, 'these guys are here to arrest me for their murders.'

Olivia closed her eyes, tried to ride it out. 'What do you want to do?'

'I have to get out of here.'

'You mean, *we* have to get out of here.'

'No.'

'I'm going with you, Matt.'

'You're not the one they want. They have nothing on you. At worst they think you cheated on your husband. You just refuse to answer any questions. They can't hold you.'

'So you're just going to run?'

'I have no choice.'

'Where will you go?'

'I'll figure that out. But we can't communicate. They'll be watching the house, tapping the phone.'

'We need a plan here, Matt.'

'How about this,' he said. 'We meet up in Reno.'

'What?'

'Tomorrow at midnight. The address you said – 488 Center Lane Drive.'

'You still think there's still a chance that my daughter . . . .'

'I doubt it,' Matt said. 'But I also doubt Darrow and Talley were doing this on their own.'

Olivia hesitated.

'What?'

'How are you going to get across the country that fast?'

'I don't know. If I can't make it, we'll figure out something later. Look, it's not a great plan, but we don't have time for anything better.'

Olivia took a step forward. He felt it again in his chest, the gentle thrum. She had never looked so beautiful or vulnerable. 'Do we have time for you to say you still love me?'

'I do love you. More than ever.'

'Just like that?'

'Just like that,' he said.

'Even after . . . ?'

'Even after.'

She shook her head. 'You're too good for me.'

'Yeah, I'm a prince.'

Olivia laughed through the sob. He put his arms around her.

'We'll get into this later, but right now we need to find your daughter.'

Something she had said – about this life being worth fighting over. It resonated in him, even more than the revelations. He would fight. He would fight for both of them.

Olivia nodded, wiped her tears. 'Here. I only have twenty dollars.'

He took it. They risked a glance out the window. Lance Banner was approaching the front door, flanked by two cops. Olivia moved in front of him as if readying

447

to take a bullet.

'You sneak out back,' Olivia said. 'I'll wake up Marsha, tell her what's going on. We'll try to stall them.'

'I love you,' he said.

She gave him the crooked smile. 'Good to hear.' They kissed hard and quick. 'Don't let anything happen to you,' she said.

'I won't.'

He headed downstairs and started toward the back door. Olivia was already in Marsha's room. It wasn't right to drag Marsha into this, but what choice did they have? From the kitchen he could see another police car pull up to the front.

There was a knock on the door.

No time. Matt had something of a plan. They were not far from the East Orange Water Reservation, which was basically a forest. Matt had gone through it countless times as a child. Once inside he'd be difficult to find. He'd be able to work his way toward Short Hills Road and from there, well, suffice to say that he needed outside help.

He knew where to go.

His hand was on the back-door knob. Matt heard Lance Banner ring the bell. He turned the knob and pushed open the door.

Someone was standing right there, already in the doorway. He nearly jumped out of his skin.

'Matt?'

It was Kyra.

'Matt, what are –?'

He signaled her to stay quiet and beckoned her inside.

'What's going on?' Kyra whispered.

'What are you doing awake?'

'I – ' She shrugged. 'I saw police cars. What's going on?'

'It's a long story.'

'That investigator who came by today. She asked me about you.'

'I know.'

They both heard Marsha shout: 'Just a minute.'

Kyra's eyes widened. 'You're trying to run away?'

'It's a long story.'

Her eyes met his. He wondered what Kyra was going to do here. He didn't want to involve her. If she screamed, he would understand. She was just a kid. She had no role in any of this, no real reason to trust him.

'Go,' Kyra whispered.

He didn't wait or say thank you. He started outside. Kyra followed, veering the other way back toward her room above the garage. Matt saw the swing set he'd put up with Bernie a lifetime ago. It'd been ridiculously hot the day they assembled it. They'd both had their shirts off. Marsha had waited on the porch with beers. Bernie had wanted to put in one of those ziplines, but Marsha had nixed that, claiming, correctly in Matt's view, that they were dangerous.

What you remember.

The yard was too open – there were no trees, no bushes, no rocks. Bernie had cleared out a lot of the brush with the anticipation of putting in a swimming pool – another dream, albeit a small one, that died with him. There were white bases

448

laid out in the shape of a baseball diamond and two small soccer goals. He started to cross the yard. Kyra had gone back inside the garage.

Matt heard a commotion.

'Wait!' The voice belonged to Olivia. She was intentionally shouting so that he would hear. 'Why are your men going to the backyard?'

There was no time to hesitate. He was out in the open. Make a mad run for it? There was little choice. He sprinted into the neighbor's yard. Matt avoided the flower beds, which were a strange thing to worry about at a time like this, but he did it anyway. He risked a glance behind him.

A policeman had made the turn into the backyard.

Damn.

He hadn't been spotted. Not yet. He searched for a place to hide. The neighbors had a toolshed. Matt leaped behind it. He pressed his back against it, like he'd seen done in the movies. A pointless move. He checked his waistband.

The gun was there.

Matt risked a peek.

The cop was staring directly at him.

Or at least he appeared to be. Matt quickly pulled back. Had the cop seen him? Hard to say. He waited for someone to yell, 'Hey, he's right there, right in the next yard behind that toolshed!'

Nothing happened.

He wanted to take another look.

He couldn't risk it.

He stayed and waited.

Then he heard a voice – another cop, he guessed: 'Sam, you see some –?'

The voice cut out like a radio turned off.

Matt held his breath. He strained his ears. Footsteps? Was he hearing footsteps? He couldn't say for sure. He debated sneaking another glance. If they were on their way toward him, what harm would it do? Either way he'd be nailed.

It was too quiet back here.

If the cops were actively searching for him, they'd be calling out to one another. If they were being quiet, quiet like this, there was only one explanation.

He'd been spotted. They were sneaking up on him.

Matt listened again.

Something jangled. Like something on a policeman's belt.

No question now – they were coming for him. His heart picked up pace. He could feel it hammering in his chest. Caught. Again. He pictured what would happen: the rough handling, the handcuffs, the back of the cruiser . . .

Jail.

Fear gripped him. They were coming. They'd take him away and throw him back into that pit. They'd never listen. They'd lock him up. He was an ex-con. Another man was dead after a fight with Matt Hunter. Forget everything else. This one would be a slam dunk.

And what would happen to Olivia if he was caught?

He couldn't even explain the truth, even if he wanted to, because then she would end up in jail. And if there was one thing that terrified him more than his own incarceration . . .

Matt wasn't sure how it happened, but suddenly the Mauser M2 was in his hand.

Calm down, he told himself. We're not shooting anybody here.

But he could still use the threat, couldn't he? Except that there were several cops here, four or five at a minimum, more probably on the way. They'd draw their weapons too. Then what? Were Paul and Ethan awake?

He slid to the back part of the toolshed. He risked a peek out from the back. Two cops were no more than six feet away from him.

He had been spotted. No way around that. They were headed right toward him. There was no escape.

Matt gripped the gun and got ready to sprint when his gaze was snagged by something in Marsha's backyard.

It was Kyra.

She must have been watching the whole time. She was standing near her door at the garage. Their eyes met. Matt saw something that looked like a small smile on her face. He almost shook his head no, but he didn't.

Kyra screamed.

The scream shattered the air and rang in the ears. The two cops turned toward her – and away from him. She screamed again. The cops sprinted toward her.

'What's wrong?' one of the cops yelled.

Matt did not hesitate now. He used Kyra's diversion and sprinted in the opposite direction, toward the woods. She screamed again. Matt never looked back, not until he was deep in the trees.

43

Sitting with her feet on her desk, Loren Muse decided to call Max Darrow's widow.

It was three or four in the morning in Nevada – Loren could never remember if Nevada was two hours or three behind – but she suspected that a woman whose husband gets murdered probably sleeps uneasily.

She dialed the number. It went into voice mail. A man's voice said, 'Max and Gertie can't answer your call right now. We're probably out fishing. Leave a message, okay?'

The voice from the grave made her pause. Max Darrow, retired cop, was a human being. Simple, but you forget that sometimes. You get caught up in the details, in the puzzle pieces. A life has been lost here. Gertie will have to change that message. She and Max won't be going fishing anymore. Sounded like a small thing but it was a life, a struggle, a world now shattered.

Loren left a message with her phone number and hung up.

'Hey, what are you working on?'

It was Adam Yates, the FBI chief from Vegas. He'd driven to the county prosecutor's office with her after their meeting with Joan Thurston. Loren looked up at him. 'Just a few strange developments.'

'Such as?'

She told him about her conversation with Cingle Shaker. Yates grabbed a chair from a nearby desk. He sat, never taking his eyes off hers. He was one of those guys. Big on eye contact.

When she finished, Yates frowned. 'I just can't see how this Hunter guy fits in.'

'He should be in custody soon. Maybe we'll learn something then.'

Yates nodded, kept up with the eye contact.

Loren said, 'What?'

'This case,' Yates said. His voice was soft now. 'It means a great deal to me.'

'Any reason in particular?'

'Do you have children?' he asked.

'No.'

'Married?'

'No.'

'You gay?'

'Jesus, Yates.'

He held up his hand. 'That was stupid, sorry.'

'Why all the questions?'

'You don't have kids. I don't think you'll understand.'

'Are you for real?'

Yates held up the hand again. 'I don't mean that the way it sounded. I'm sure you're a good person and all.'

451

'Gee, thanks.'

'It's just that . . . when you have kids, it just changes things.'

'Do me a favor, Yates. Please don't give me that having-children-alters-you spiel. I listen to that crap enough from my painfully few friends.'

'It's not that.' He paused. 'Actually I think single people make better cops. You can focus.'

'Speaking of which . . .' She picked up some papers and pretended to be busy.

'Let me ask you something, Muse.'

She waited.

'When you wake up,' Yates went on, 'who's the first person you think about?'

'Excuse me?'

'Okay, it's morning. You open your eyes. You start getting out of bed. Who is the first person you think about?'

'Why don't you tell me?'

'Well, not to be insulting, but the answer is you, right? There's nothing wrong with that. You think about you. That's normal. All single people do that. You wake up and wonder what you're going to do that day. Oh, sure, you might take care of an elderly parent or something. But here's the thing. When you have a child, you are never number one again. Someone is more important than you. It changes your worldview. It has to. You think you know about protect and serve. But when you have a family . . .'

'Is there a point to this?'

Adam Yates finally stopped with the eye contact. 'I have a son. His name is Sam. He's fourteen now. When he was three years old, he got meningitis. We thought he might die. He was in the hospital in this great big bed. It was too big for him, you know? It looked like it would swallow him up. And me, I just sat next to him and watched him get worse.'

He gulped a breath and swallowed hard. Loren let him take his time.

'After a couple of hours, I picked Sam up and held him in my arms. I didn't sleep. I didn't put him down. I just kept holding him. My wife says it was three full days. I don't know. I just knew that if I kept Sam in my arms, if I kept watching him, then death couldn't take him away from me.'

Yates seemed to drift off.

Loren spoke softly. 'I still don't see the point.'

'Well, here it is,' he said, his voice back to normal. He locked eyes again. His pupils were pinpricks. 'They threatened my family.'

Yates put his hand to his face, then back down as if he wasn't sure where he wanted to put it. 'When I first started this case,' he went on, 'they set their sights on my wife and kids. So you understand.'

She opened her mouth, said nothing.

The phone on the desk rang. Loren picked it up.

Lance Banner said, 'We lost Matt.'

'What?'

'That kid who lives with them. Kyra, whatever. She started screaming and. . . . Anyway, his wife is here. She says that she was driving the car, not him, and that she doesn't know where he is.'

'That's crap.'

'I know it.'

452

'Bring her in.'

'She refuses to come.'

'Excuse me?'

'We have nothing on her.'

'She's a material witness in a murder investigation.'

'She's lawyering up. She says we either have to arrest her or let her go.'

Her cell phone chirped. Loren checked the caller ID. The call was originating from Max Darrow's house.

'I'll get back to you.' She hung up the office phone and clicked on the mobile. 'Investigator Muse.'

'This is Gertie Darrow. You left me a message?'

Loren could hear the tears in her voice. 'I'm sorry about your loss.'

'Thank you.'

'I don't mean to disturb you at such a terrible time, but I really need to ask you a few questions.'

'I understand.'

'Thank you,' Loren said. She grabbed a pen. 'Do you know why your husband was in Newark, Mrs. Darrow?'

'No.' She said it as though it was the most painful word she ever uttered. 'He told me he was visiting a friend in Florida. A fishing trip, he said.'

'I see. He was retired, yes?'

'That's right.'

'Could you tell me if he was working on anything?'

'I don't understand. What does this have to do with his murder?'

'This is just routine –'

'Please, Investigator Muse,' she interrupted, her voice up a notch. 'My husband was a police officer, remember? You're not calling me at this hour for routine questions.'

Loren said, 'I'm trying to find a motive.'

'A motive?'

'Yes.'

'But . . .' And then she quieted down. 'The other officer. The one who called before. Investigator Wine.'

'Yes. He works in my office.'

'He told me that Max was in a car, that' – there was a choke in the voice but she kept it together – 'that he had his pants down.'

Loren closed her eyes. So Wine had already told her. She understood, she guessed. In today's society of openness, you couldn't even spare a widow anymore. 'Mrs. Darrow?'

'What?'

'I think that was a setup. I don't think there was any prostitute. I think your husband was murdered for some other reason. And I think it might involve an old case of his. So I'm asking you: Was he working on anything?'

There was a brief silence. Then: 'That girl.'

'What?'

'I knew it. I just knew it.'

'I'm sorry, Mrs. Darrow. I'm not sure what you mean.'

'Max never talked about business. He never brought it home. And he was retired. She had no reason to come around.'

'Who?'

'I don't know her name. She was a young thing. Maybe twenty.'

'What did she want?'

'I told you. I don't know. But Max . . . after she left, he was like a madman. He started going through old files.'

'Do you know what the files referred to?'

'No.' Then: 'Do you really think this could have something to do with Max's murder?'

'Yes, ma'am. I think it might have everything to do with it. Does the name Clyde Rangor mean anything to you?'

'No, I'm sorry.'

'How about Emma Lemay or Charles Talley?'

'No.'

'Candace Potter?'

Silence.

'Mrs. Darrow?'

'I saw that name.'

'Where?'

'On his desk. There was a file. Must have been a month ago. I just saw the word "Potter." I remember because that was the name of the bad guy in *It's a Wonderful Life*. Remember? Mr. Potter?'

'Do you know where the file is now?'

'I'll go through the cabinets, Investigator Muse. If it's still here, I'll find it for you and call back.'

44

Matt learned how to steal cars in prison. Or at least, that was what he thought.

There was a guy named Saul two cells over who had a fetish for joyriding with stolen cars. He was about as decent a guy as you'd meet in prison. He had his demons – his seemingly more innocuous than most – but the demons did him in. He got arrested for stealing a car when he was seventeen, then again when he was nineteen. On his third go-round, Saul lost control of the vehicle and killed someone. He'd already had two priors so he got a life sentence.

'All that stuff you see on TV?' Saul had told him. 'That's all crap, unless you want a specific make. Otherwise, you don't jam the lock. You don't use tools. And you don't hot-wire. That only works on old cars anyway. And with all the alarms, you try most of that stuff, the car will lock down on you.'

'So what do you do?' Matt asked.

'You use a person's car keys. You open the door like a human being. You drive away.'

Matt made a face. 'Just like that?'

'No, not just like that. What you do is, you go to a crowded parking lot. Malls work great, though you gotta look out for the rent-a-cops circling around. Those big superstores are even better. You find an area where people won't be watching you much. You just keep walking and running your hand over a front tire or under the bumper. People leave their keys there. They also keep them in those cute magnets under the driver's-side fender. Not everyone. But hey, at least one in fifty. You do that enough, you'll find a key. *Voilà.*'

Matt wondered. His prison info was at least nine years old and perhaps obsolete. He had been on foot for more than an hour – first making his way through the woods and now keeping off main roads. When he reached the corner of Livingston Avenue, he grabbed a bus to the campus of Bergen Community College in Paramus. The ride took about an hour. Matt slept for all of it.

Bergen Community was a commuter school. There were tons of cars driven by carefree coeds. Security was almost nonexistent. Matt began his search. It took almost an hour, but as Saul promised, Matt eventually hit pay dirt in the form of a white Isuzu with a quarter tank of gas. Not bad. The keys had been hidden in one of those magnets above the front tire. Matt got into the car and drove toward Route 17. He didn't know Bergen County all that well. It might be smarter to go north over the Tappan Zee but he chose the route he knew over the George Washington Bridge.

He was on his way to Westport, Connecticut.

When he reached the GWB, he worried that the toll booth operator would recognize him – he even went so far as to rip the bandage off his head and replace it with a New York Rangers cap he found in the backseat – but that didn't happen. He switched on the radio and listened to the news – first, 1010 WINS for twenty-two minutes, then CBS 880. In the movies they always interrupt for a special bulletin when a man is at large. But neither station said anything about him. In fact, there was nothing on any of it – nothing about Max Darrow or Charles Talley or a fleeing suspect.

He needed money. He needed a place to sleep. He needed some meds. The pain had been held in check by the flow of adrenaline. That was ebbing now. He'd only slept about an hour in the past twenty-four, and the preceding night, what with the pictures on his camera phone, hadn't brought him much slumber either.

Matt checked the money. He had thirty-eight bucks. Hardly enough. He couldn't use his ATM or credit cards. The police would be able to track those down. Ditto with getting help from close friends or relatives, not that he had many he could really depend on.

There was, however, one person Matt could go to whom the police would never suspect.

When he got off at the Westport exit, he slowed down. He had never been invited here, but he knew the address. When he first got out of prison, he actually drove past this particular road several times, but he never had the courage to turn onto the block.

Now he took a right and then another and pulled slowly down the quiet, tree-lined street. His pulse started kicking up again. He checked the driveway. Her car was the only one there. He considered using his cell phone, but no, the police would be able to access that too. Maybe he should just knock. He thought about it, but in the end he decided to play it safe. He drove back toward town and spotted a pay phone. He dialed the number.

Sonya McGrath answered on the first ring. 'Hello?'

'It's me,' he said. 'Are you alone?'

'Yes.'

'I need your help.'

'Where are you?'

'I'm about five minutes from your house.'

Matt pulled into the McGraths' driveway.

There was a rusted basketball hoop near the garage. The shredded netting had not been replaced in a very long time. The hoop didn't fit in with the surroundings. It was old and unkempt where the rest of the house was so posh, so updated. For a moment Matt stopped and stared at the basketball hoop. Stephen McGrath was there. He was shooting with nice form, his eyes locked on the front rim. Matt could see the backspin on the ball. Stephen was smiling.

'Matt?'

He turned around. Sonya McGrath stood on the front step. She looked over to see where he'd been staring and her face fell.

'Tell me,' Sonya said.

He did – but as he did, he noticed the devastation in her face did not fade. He had seen her take blows like this before. She always came back, if not all the way, then enough. That wasn't happening now. Her face maintained that horrid pallor. It wouldn't change. Matt saw it, but he couldn't stop himself. He kept talking and explaining what he was doing here and somewhere along the line Matt had an almost out-of-body experience where he rose above them and actually heard what he was saying and how it must sound to her. But he still did not stop. He just kept talking while a small voice inside his brain urged him to shut the hell up. But he didn't listen. He'd trudged on, figuring that he'd somehow make it through.

But in the end, when you cut through it all, his words sounded like this: Another fight, another death.

When he finally wound down, Sonya McGrath just watched him for several seconds. Matt could feel himself wither and die under the glare.

'You want me to help you?' she said.

And there it was. So simply stated. He could hear it now, how not only ridiculous it sounded, but how outrageous. How obscene.

He didn't know what to do.

'Clark found out about our meetings,' she said.

He was going to say I'm sorry or something similar, but it didn't feel appropriate. He kept quiet now and waited.

'Clark thinks I'm after comfort. He has a point, I guess, but I don't think that's it. I think I needed closure. I think I needed to forgive you. And I can't.'

'I should go,' he said.

'You should turn yourself in, Matt. If you're innocent, they'll –'

'They'll what?' he said, his tone edgier than he'd wanted. 'I've tried that route already, remember?'

'I do.' Sonya McGrath tilted her head to the side. 'But were you innocent then, Matt?'

He looked back at the basketball hoop. Stephen had the ball in his hand. He stopped mid-shot, turned, and waited for Matt's answer.

'I'm sorry,' Matt said, turning away from them both. 'I have to go.'

45

Loren Muse's cell phone rang. It was Max Darrow's widow calling back.

'I found something,' she said.

'What?'

'It looks like an autopsy file on Candace Potter,' Gertie Darrow said. 'I mean, it is an autopsy. It's signed by the old medical examiner. I remember him. He was a very nice man.'

'What does it say?'

'It says a lot of things. Height, weight. You want me to read it all to you?'

'How about a cause of death?'

'It says something here about strangulation. It also says something about a severe beating and trauma to the head.'

That fit in with what they already had. So what had Max Darrow noticed after all these years? What had sent him to Newark, to Emma Lemay as Sister Mary Rose?

'Mrs. Darrow, do you have a fax machine?'

'There's one in Max's office.'

'Could you fax me the file?'

'Of course.'

Loren gave her the fax number.

'Investigator Muse?'

'Yes.'

'Are you married?'

Loren held back a sigh. First Yates, now Mrs. Darrow. 'No, I'm not.'

'Ever been?'

'No. Why do you ask?'

'I believed the other investigator. Mr. Wine, is it?'

'That's right.'

'What he said about Max being in the car with, well, a woman of questionable morals, as we used to say.'

'Right.'

'I just wanted to let you know.'

'Know what, Mrs. Darrow?'

'See, Max, well, he wasn't always a good husband, you know what I mean?'

'I think so,' Loren said.

'What I'm trying to say is Max had done that in the past. In a car like that. More than once. That's why I was so quick to believe. I thought you should know. Just in case this doesn't pan out.'

'Thank you, Mrs. Darrow.'

'I'll fax it over now.'

She hung up without saying anything more. Loren stood and waited by the fax machine.

Adam Yates came back with two Cokes. He offered her one, but she shook him off. 'Uh, what I said before, about not having kids –'

'Forget it,' Loren said. 'I know what you were trying to get at.'

'Still stupid of me to put it that way.'

'Yeah. Yeah, it was.'

'What's going on here?'

'Max Darrow was looking into Candace Potter's autopsy.'

Yates frowned. 'What does that have to do with this?'

'Not a clue, but I doubt it's a coincidence.'

The phone rang and the fax machines began their mating screech. The first sheet churned out slowly. There was no cover letter. That was good. Loren hated the waste of paper. She grabbed the sheet and started searching for the conclusion. In truth she read very little else in autopsy reports. Weights of livers and hearts might interest some people, but she was only interested in what they meant to her case.

Adam Yates read over her shoulder. It all seemed pretty normal.

'You see anything?' she asked.

'No.'

'Me neither.'

'This could be a dead end.'

'Probably is.'

Another sheet came in. They both started reading it.

Yates pointed midway down the right-hand column. 'What's this over here?'

There was a check mark in the middle of the body description.

Loren read it out loud: 'No ovaries, testes hidden, probable AIS.'

'AIS?'

'It stands for Androgen Insensitivity Syndrome,' Loren said. 'I had a friend in college who had it.'

'What's the relevance of that?' Yates asked.

'I'm not sure. AIS women look and feel like typical females and for all practical purposes, they're considered female. They can legally marry and adopt.' She stopped, tried to think it through.

'But?'

'But in short it means that Candace Potter was genetically male. She had testes and XY chromosomes.'

He made a face. 'You mean she was, what, a transsexual?'

'No.'

'Then, what, she was a guy?'

'Genetically, yes. But probably not in any other way. Oftentimes an AIS woman doesn't know she's any different until she reaches puberty and doesn't menstruate. It's not that uncommon. There was a Miss Teen USA a few years back who was AIS. Many believe Queen Elizabeth I and Joan of Arc and a slew of supermodels and actresses have it, but that's really nothing more than speculation. Either way you can lead a perfectly normal life. In fact, if Candace Potter was a prostitute, perverse as this sounds, it may even have benefited her.'

'Benefited her how?'

Loren looked up at him. 'Women with AIS can't get pregnant.'

46

Matt drove away. Sonya McGrath headed back inside. Their relationship, if there had ever been one, was over. It felt odd and yet, despite the honesty and raw emotion, anything built on such misery was bound to cave. It was all too fragile. They were simply two people needing something that neither could ever get.

He wondered if Sonya would call the police. He wondered if it mattered.

God, he'd been stupid to come here.

He was hurting badly. He needed to rest. But there was no time. He'd have to push through. He checked the gas gauge. It was near empty. He stopped at a nearby Shell station and used the rest of his money to fill the tank.

During his ride, he thought about the bombshell Olivia had just dropped on him. At the end of the day, as weird or naïve as this might sound, he wondered what it really changed. He still loved Olivia. He loved the way she frowned when she checked herself in the mirror, that little smile she made when she was thinking of something funny, the way she rolled her eyes when he made a clumsy double entendre, the way she tucked her feet under when she read, the way she took deep, almost cartoon breaths when she was irritated, the way her eyes welled up with tears when they made love, the way his heart pumped a little faster when she laughed, the way he'd catch her studying him when she thought he wouldn't notice, the soft way her eyes closed when she listened to a favorite song on the radio, the way her hand would just take his at any time without hesitation or embarrassment, the way her skin felt, the charge at her touch, the way she'd drape a leg over him on the lazy mornings, the way her chest felt pressed against his back when they slept, the way when she slipped out of bed in the early morning she'd kiss his cheek and make sure the blankets still covered him.

What about any of that was different now?

The truth was not always freeing. Your past was your past. He had not, for example, told her about his stint in prison to illuminate the 'real Matt' or 'take their relationship to the next level' – he told her because she would undoubtedly find out anyway. It didn't mean a thing. If he hadn't told her, wouldn't their relationship be equally strong?

Or was this all a giant rationalization?

He stopped at an ATM near Sonya's house. He had no choice now. He needed money. If she called the police, well, they'd know he'd been in this area anyway. If they traced it down, he'd be long gone by the time they arrived. He didn't want to use the credit card at a gas station. They might get his license plate number that way. As it was, if he could get the money and put distance between himself and this ATM, he figured that he'd be all right.

The ATM had a max of a thousand dollars. He took it.

Then he started thinking of a way to get to Reno.

Loren drove. Adam Yates sat in the passenger seat.

'Explain this to me again,' he said.

'I have a source. A man named Len Friedman. A year ago we found two dead women in a hooker alley, both young, both black, both had their hands cut off so that we couldn't get an ID off fingerprints. But one of the girls had a strange tattoo, a logo from Princeton University, on her inner thigh.'

'Princeton?'

'Yes.'

He shook his head.

'Anyway, we put that in the papers. The only person who came forward was this Len Friedman. He asked if she also had a rose petal tattoo on her right foot. That hadn't been released. So our interest, to put it mildly, was piqued.'

'You figured he was the perp.'

'Sure, why not? But it turns out that both women were strippers – or as Friedman calls them, erotic dancers – at a dump called the Honey Bunny in Newark. Friedman is an expert on all things stripper. It's his hobby. He collects posters, bios, personal information, real names, tattoos, birthmarks, scars, I mean everything. A full database. And not just on the local trade. I assume you've walked the Vegas Strip?'

'Sure.'

'You know how they pass out cards advertising strippers and prostitutes and whatever.'

'Hey, I live there, remember?'

She nodded. 'Well, Len Friedman collects them. Like baseball cards. He gathers information on them. He travels for weeks at a time visiting these places. He writes what some consider academic essays on the subject. He also collects historical material. He has a brassiere belonging to Gypsy Rose Lee. He has stuff that dates back more than a century.'

Yates made a face. 'He must be a lot of fun at parties.'

Loren smiled. 'You have no idea.'

'What's that supposed to mean?'

'You'll see.'

They fell into silence.

Yates said, 'I'm really sorry again. About what I said before.'

She waved him off. 'How many kids do you have anyway?'

'Three.'

'Boys, girls?'

'Two girls, one boy.'

'Ages?'

'My daughters are seventeen and sixteen. Sam is fourteen.'

'Seventeen- and sixteen-year-old girls,' Loren said. 'Yikes.'

Yates smiled. 'You have no idea.'

'You have pictures?'

'I never carry pictures.'

'Oh?'

Yates shifted in his seat. Loren glanced at him out of the corner of her eye. His posture was suddenly rigid. 'About six years ago,' he began, 'I had my wallet stolen. I know, I'm head of an FBI field office and I'm dumb enough to get pick-pocketed. Sue me. Anyway, I went nuts. Not because of the money or the credit cards. But all I kept thinking about was, some slimeball has pictures of my kids. My kids. He probably just took the cash and dumped the wallet in the garbage. But suppose he didn't. Suppose he kept the pictures. You know, for his own amusement. Maybe he, I don't know, stared at the pictures longingly. Maybe he even put his fingers on their faces, caressed them.'

Loren frowned. 'Talk about being a lot of fun at parties.'

Yates chuckled without humor. 'Anyway, that's why I never carry pictures.'

They turned off of Northfield Avenue in West Orange. It was a nicely aging town. Most of the newer burbs had landscapes that looked somehow phony, like a recent hair transplant. West Orange had lush lawns and ivy on the walls. The trees were tall and thick. The houses were not cookie-cutter – there were Tudors, next to capes, next to Mediterranean style. They were all a little past due, not in prime condition, but it all seemed to work.

There was a tricycle in the driveway. Loren pulled up behind it. They both got out. Someone had set up one of those baseball net-retrievers in the front yard. Two mitts sat in the fetal position on the grass.

Yates said, 'Your source lives here?'

'Like I said, you have no idea.'

Yates shrugged.

A woman straight out of the Suzy Homemaker handbook answered the door. She wore a checkered apron and a smile Loren usually associated with religious fervor. 'Len's in the workroom downstairs,' she said.

'Thank you.'

'Would you like some coffee?'

'No, that's okay.'

'Mom!'

A boy of maybe ten ran into the room. 'Kevin, we have guests.'

Kevin smiled like his mother. 'I'm Kevin Friedman.' He stuck out his hand and met Loren's eye. The shake was firm. He turned to Yates, who seemed startled. He shook too and introduced himself.

'Very nice to meet you,' Kevin said. 'Mom and I are making some banana bread. Would you care for a slice?'

'Maybe later,' Loren said. 'We, uh . . .'

'He's down that way,' Suzy Homemaker said.

'Right, thanks.'

They opened the basement door. Yates muttered, 'What did they do to that boy? I can't even get my kids to say hello to me, forget strangers.'

Loren muffled a laugh. 'Mr. Friedman?' she called out.

He stepped into view. Friedman's hair had gone a shade grayer since the last time she'd seen him. He wore a light blue button-down sweater and khakis. 'Nice to see you again, Investigator Muse.'

'Same here.'

'And your friend?'

'This is Special Agent in Charge Adam Yates from Las Vegas.'

Friedman's eyes lit up when he heard the location. 'Vegas! Welcome then.

Come, let's sit and see if I can help you out.'

He opened a door with a key. Inside was everything stripper. There were photographs on the wall. Documents of one kind or another. Framed panties and bras. Feathered boas and fans. There were old posters, one advertising Lili St. Cyr, and her 'Bubble Bath Dance,' another for Dixie Evans, 'The Marilyn Monroe of Burlesque,' who was appearing at the Minsky-Adams Theater in Newark. For a moment Loren and Yates just looked around and gaped.

'Do you know what that is?' Friedman gestured toward a big feathered fan he kept in a museum-style glass cube.

'A fan?' Loren said.

He laughed. 'Not just a fan. Calling this a fan would be like' – Friedman thought about it – 'like calling the Declaration of Independence a piece of parchment. No, this very fan was used by the great Sally Rand at the Paramount Club in 1932.'

Friedman waited for a reaction, didn't get one.

'Sally Rand invented the fan dance. She actually performed it in the 1934 movie *Bolero*. The fan is made from real ostrich feathers. Can you believe that? And that whip over there? It was used by Bettie Page. She was called the Queen of Bondage.'

'By her mother?' Loren couldn't resist.

Friedman frowned, clearly disappointed. Loren held up an apologetic hand. Friedman sighed and moved toward his computer.

'So I assume this involves an erotic dancer from the Vegas area?'

'It might,' Loren said.

He sat at his computer and typed something in. 'Do you have a name?'

'Candace Potter.'

He stopped. 'The murder victim?'

'Yes.'

'But she's been dead for ten years.'

'Yes, we know.'

'Most people believe she was killed by a man named Clyde Rangor,' Friedman began. 'He and his girlfriend Emma Lemay had a wonderful eye for talent. They co-managed some of the best low-rent but talent-loaded gentlemen's clubs anywhere.'

Loren sneaked a glance at Yates. Yates was shaking his head in either amazement or repulsion. It was hard to tell which. Friedman saw it too.

'Hey, some guys get into NASCAR,' Friedman said with a shrug.

'Yeah, what a waste,' Loren said. 'What else?'

'There were bad rumors about Clyde Rangor and Emma Lemay.'

'They abused the girls?'

'Sure, I mean, they were mob connected. This isn't unusual in the business, unfortunately. It really taints the overall aesthetic, you know what I mean?'

Loren said, 'Uh huh.'

'But even among thieves there is a certain code. They purportedly broke it.'

'In what way?'

'Have you seen the new commercials for Las Vegas?' Friedman asked.

'I don't think so.'

'The ones that say, "What goes on in Vegas stays in Vegas"?'

'Oh wait,' Loren said. 'I've seen them.'

'Well, gentlemen's clubs take that motto to a fanatical extreme. You never, ever tell.'

'And Rangor and Lemay told?'

Friedman's face went dark. 'Worse. I –'

'Enough,' Yates said, cutting him off.

Loren turned toward Yates. She gave him a what-gives shrug.

'Look,' Yates continued, checking his watch, 'this is all interesting, but we're a little pressed for time here. What can you tell us about Candace Potter specifically?'

'May I ask a question?' Friedman said.

'Shoot.'

'She's been dead a long time. Has there been a new development in the case?'

'There might have been,' Loren said.

Friedman folded his hands and waited. Loren took the chance.

'Did you know that Candace Potter may have been' – she decided to go with a more popular though inaccurate term – 'a hermaphrodite?'

That got him. 'Wow.'

'Yes.'

'You're sure?'

'I've seen the autopsy.'

'Wait!' Friedman shouted it in the same way an editor in an old movie would shout, 'Hold the presses!' 'You have the actual autopsy?'

'Yes.'

He licked his lips, tried not to look too anxious. 'Is there any way I can get a copy?'

'It can probably be arranged,' Loren said. 'What else can you tell us about her?'

Friedman started typing on the computer. 'The information on Candace Potter is sketchy. For the most part she went by the stage name Candi Cane, which, let's face it, is a horrible name for an exotic dancer. It's too much, you know? Too cute. You know what a good name is? Jenna Jameson, for example. You've probably heard of her. Well, Jenna started as a dancer, you know, before she got into porn. She got the name Jameson from a bottle of Irish whiskey. See? It's classier. It has more oomph, you know what I mean.'

'Right,' Loren said, just to say something.

'And Candi's solo act was not the most original either. She dressed like a hospital candy striper and carried a big lollipop. Get it? Candi Cane? I mean, talk about clichéd.' He shook his head in the manner of a teacher let down by a prized pupil. 'Professionally she'll be better remembered for a dual act where she was known as Brianna Piccolo.'

'Brianna Piccolo?'

'Yes. She worked with another dancer, a statuesque African American named Kimmy Dale. Kimmy, in the act, went by the name Gayle Sayers.'

Loren saw it. So did Yates.

'Piccolo and Sayers? Please tell me you're kidding.'

'Nope. Brianna and Gayle did a sort of exotic dance rendition of the movie *Brian's Song*. Gayle would tearfully say, "I love Brianna Piccolo," you know, like Billy Dee did on the dais in the movie. Then Brianna would be lying sick in a bed. They'd help each other undress. No sex. Nothing like that. Just an exotic artistic experience. It had great appeal to those with an interracial fetish, which, frankly, is nearly everyone. I think it was one of the finest political statements made in exotic dance, an early display of racial sensitivity. I never saw the act in person, but my understanding was that it was a moving portrayal of socioeconomic –'

'Yeah, moving, I get it,' Loren interrupted. 'Anything else?'

'Sure, of course, what do you want to know? The Sayers-Piccolo number was usually the opening act for Countess Allison Beth Weiss IV, better known as Jewish Royalty. Her act – get this – was called "Tell Mom It's Kosher." You've probably heard of it.'

A waft of banana bread was reaching them down here. The smell was wonderful, even in this appetite-reducing atmosphere. Loren tried to get Friedman back on track. 'I mean anything else about Candace Potter. Anything that can illuminate what happened to her.'

Friedman shrugged. 'She and Kimmy Dale were not only dance partners but also real-life roommates. In fact, Kimmy Dale paid for the funeral to save Candi from – pardon the unintentional pun here – a potter's grave. Candi is buried at Holy Mother in Coaldale, I think. I've visited the tombstone to pay my respects. It's quite a moving experience.'

'I bet. Do you keep track of what happens to exotic dancers after they leave the business?'

'Of course,' he said, as if she'd asked a priest if he ever went to Mass. 'That's often the most interesting part. You wouldn't believe the variety of life roads they take.'

'Right, so what happened to this Kimmy Dale?'

'She's still in the business. A true warhorse. She no longer has the looks. She's – again pardon the unintentional pun – slid down the pole, if you will. The headline days are over. But Kimmy still has a small following. What she loses in not being, say, toned or hard-bodied she makes up for in experience. She's out of Vegas though.'

'Where is she?'

'Reno, last I heard.'

'Anything else?'

'Not really,' Friedman said. Then he snapped his fingers. 'Hold on, I have something to show you. I'm quite proud of this.'

They waited. Len Friedman had three tall file cabinets in the corner. He opened the second drawer of the middle one and began to finger through it. 'The Piccolo and Sayers act. This is a rare piece and it's only a color reproduction off a Polaroid. I'd really like to find more.' He cleared his throat as he continued his search. 'Do you think, Investigator Muse, that I could get a copy of that autopsy?'

'I'll see what I can do.'

'It would really add to my studies.'

'Studies. Right.'

'Here it is.' He took out a photograph and placed it on the table in front of them. Yates looked at it and nodded. He turned to Loren and saw the expression on her face.

'What?' Yates said.

Friedman added, 'Investigator Muse?'

Not in here, Loren thought. Not a word. She stared at the late Candace Potter aka Candi Cane aka Brianna Piccolo aka the Murder Victim.

'This is definitely Candace Potter?' she managed.

'Yes.'

'You're sure?'

'Of course.'

Yates looked a question at her. Loren tried to blink it away.

Candace Potter. If this really was Candace Potter, then she wasn't a murder victim. She wasn't dead at all. She was alive and well and living in Irvington, New Jersey, with her ex-con husband Matt.

They'd had it all wrong. Matt Hunter wasn't the connection here. Things were finally starting to make some sense.

Because Candace Potter had a new alias now.

She was Olivia Hunter.

47

Adam Yates tried to maintain his cool.

They were back outside now, on the Friedmans' front lawn. That had been much too close a call. When that Friedman cuckoo had started yammering about never ever telling, well, it could have ended right there – Yates's career, his marriage, even his freedom. Everything.

Yates needed to take control.

He waited until he and Loren Muse were back in the car. Then, calmly as he could, Yates asked, 'So what was that all about?'

'Candace Potter is still alive,' Muse said.

'Pardon me?'

'She's alive and well and married to Matt Hunter.'

Yates listened to Loren's explanation. He felt his insides tremor. When she finished he asked to see the autopsy. She handed it to him.

'No photos of the victim?'

'It's not the whole file,' Loren said. 'It's just the pages that concerned Max Darrow. My guess is he somehow learned the truth – that Candace Potter hadn't been killed all these years ago. Maybe it had something to do with the fact that the real victim was an AIS female.'

'Why would Darrow have checked that now? I mean, after ten years?'

'I don't know. But we need to talk to Olivia Hunter.'

Adam Yates nodded, trying to take this in. It was impossible for him to fathom. Olivia Hunter was the dead stripper named Candace Potter. Candi Cane. She had been there that night, he was sure of it.

It was likely now, very likely, that Olivia Hunter had the videotape.

That meant he had to take Loren Muse out of the equation. Right now.

Yates glanced at the autopsy report again. Muse drove. The height, weight, and hair color matched, but the truth seemed obvious now. The real victim had been Cassandra Meadows. She'd been dead all along. He should have figured that. She wouldn't have been smart enough to vanish.

Len Friedman had been right when he talked about the honor of thieves. Yates had counted on that, he guessed, which in hindsight was beyond stupid. People in that business respect confidentiality not out of any sense of honor but because of profit. If you get a reputation for talking, you lose your clientele. Simple as that. The only thing was, Clyde Rangor and Emma Lemay had found a way to make even more money. Ergo the 'honor of thieves' nonsense went right out the window.

Yates didn't do it a lot, but over the years, he'd cheated on Bess. Yates never really considered it a big deal. It was beyond compartmentalizing – beyond the usual 'sex was one thing, making love another.' Sex with Bess was fine. Even after all these years. But a man needs more. Check all the history books – that one is a given. No great men were sexually monogamous. It was as simple and as complicated as that.

And in truth there was nothing wrong with it. Do wives really get upset if their husband occasionally watches, for example, an X-rated film? Was that a crime? An act worthy of divorce? A betrayal?

Of course not.

Hiring a prostitute was really no different. A man might use pictures or 900-lines or whatever as outside stimuli. That was all this was. Many wives understood this. Yates might even be able to explain it to Bess.

If that was all it had been.

Rangor and Lemay – they should rot in hell.

Yates had been looking for Rangor, Lemay, Cassandra, and that damn tape for ten years. Now there was a twist. At least two of them were dead. And Candace Potter was suddenly in the mix.

What did she know?

He cleared his throat and looked at Loren Muse. First step: Remove her from the case. So how to handle this . . . ? 'You said you knew Matt Hunter?'

'Yes.'

'You shouldn't do the interview with his wife then.'

Loren frowned. 'Because I used to know him?'

'Yes.'

'That was in elementary school, Adam. I don't think I've spoken to him since we were ten.'

'Still. There's a connection.'

'So?'

'So the defense can use it.'

'How?'

Yates shook his head.

'What?'

'You seem like a decent investigator, Muse. But every once in a while, your naïveté is absolutely startling.'

Her grip on the wheel tightened. He knew that his words had stung.

'Go back to the office,' he said. 'Cal and I will take over this part of the investigation.'

'Cal? Was he that lug in Joan Thurston's office this morning?'

'He's a damn good agent.'

'I'm sure.'

They fell into silence. Loren was trying to think of a way out of this. Yates waited, knowing how to work this now.

'Look, I know the way,' Loren said. 'I'll drive you to Hunter's house and stay outside in case –'

'No.'

'But I want –'

'Want?' Yates cut her off. 'Who do you think you're talking to, Investigator Muse?'

She fumed in silence.

'This is now a federal investigation. Most of this case, in fact, seems to lead back to Nevada. Either way it clearly crosses state lines and certainly pissant county lines. You're a county investigator. You get that? There's county, then state, then federal. I'll demonstrate this with a bar graph, if you'd like. But you don't give the orders here. I do. You'll go back to your office and if I deem it appropriate, I'll keep you informed of what is occurring in my investigation. Do I make myself clear?'

Loren fought to keep her voice steady. 'You wouldn't even know about Olivia Hunter being Candace Potter if it wasn't for me.'

'Oh, I see. Is that what this is about, Muse? Your ego? You want the credit? Fine, it's yours. I'll put a gold star next to your name on the board, if you like.'

'That's not what I meant.'

'That's sure as hell how it sounded to me. Naïve and a glory hound. Quite a winning combination.'

'That's not fair.'

'That's not . . .' Yates laughed. 'Are you kidding me? Fair? How old are you, Muse, twelve? This is a federal investigation into murder and racketeering and you're worried about my playing fair with a lowly county investigator? You'll drive me back to your office immediately and' – enough stick, a little carrot – 'if you want to participate in this investigation, your current assignment will be to find out anything you can on that other whore, the black one she roomed with.'

'Kimmy Dale.'

'Yes. Find out exactly where she is, what her story is, everything you can. You will not talk to her, however, without talking to me first. If you don't like it, I'll have you removed from the case. Understood?'

She responded as if there were nails in her mouth: 'Understood.'

He knew that she would take it. Loren wanted to remain in the loop. She'd settle for marginalized, hoping she'd make it back onto the center stage. Truth was, she was a damn fine investigator. Yates would try to steal her away when this was all over. He'd flatter her and let her have all the credit and then, good as she was, she probably wouldn't look too closely at the details.

At least that was what he hoped.

Because so far, those who had died had not been innocent – they'd been trying to hurt him. Loren Muse was different. He really didn't want her harmed. But as old a philosophy as it was, in the end, if it comes down to us or them, it is always us.

Loren Muse pulled the car into the lot and got out without a word. Yates let her huff off. He called Cal Dollinger, the only man he trusted with this sort of information. He quickly explained what he needed to. Cal did not need much detail.

Adam flashed on a painful memory – the hospital when Sam had meningitis. What he left out of the story he'd told Loren was Cal's part in the nightmare. Cal, too, had refused to leave the hospital. Adam's oldest friend had pulled up a stiff metal chair and stayed outside Sam's door for three straight days, not saying a word, just sitting there on guard, making certain that if Adam needed anything, he'd be ready.

'You want me to go alone?' Cal asked.

'No, I'll meet you at the Hunters' house,' Yates said, his voice soft. 'We'll get the tape. Then we end this.'

469

48

Olivia Hunter held it together until Midlife had been able to extricate her from Detective Lance Banner. Now that she was back in her own home she let her defenses down. She cried silently. Tears ran down her cheeks. Olivia could not stop them. She did not know if they came from joy, relief, fear, what. She only knew that sitting down and trying to stop them would be a waste of time.

She had to move.

Her suitcase was still at the Howard Johnson's. She simply packed another. She knew better than to wait. The police would be back. They would want answers.

She had to get to Reno right now.

She couldn't stop crying, which was unlike her yet understandable, she guessed, under the circumstances. Olivia was physically and emotionally spent. She was pregnant, for one thing. For another, she was worried about her adopted daughter. And finally, after all this time, she had told Matt the truth about her past.

The pact was over. Olivia had broken it when she responded to that online post – more than that, she had been directly responsible for the death of Emma Lemay. It was Olivia's fault. Emma had done a lot wrong in her life. She had hurt many people. Olivia knew that she'd tried to make up for it, that she'd truly spent her last years making amends. She didn't know where that put Emma on the Great Ledger in the Sky, but if anyone earned redemption, she assumed that Emma Lemay had.

But the thing Olivia could not get over, the thing that was really making the tears waterfall down her cheeks, was the look on Matt's face when she told him the truth.

It had not been what she'd imagined at all.

He should have been upset. He probably was. How could he not be? From the first time they met in Vegas, Olivia had always loved the way he looked at her – as if God had never created anything more spectacular, more – for lack of a better word – pure. Olivia naturally expected that look to vanish or at least dim once he learned the truth. She figured that his faded-blue eyes would harden, grow cold.

But that hadn't happened.

Nothing had changed. Matt had learned that his wife was a lie, that she had done things that would make most men turn away forever in disgust. And he had reacted with unconditional love.

Over the years Olivia had gained enough distance to see that her awful upbringing made her, like so many of the girls she worked with, lean toward self-destruction. Men who grew up like that, in different foster homes and under what

470

could best be described as poor situations, usually reacted with violence. That was how abused men showed rage – by striking out, with physical brutality.

Women were different. They used more subtle forms of cruelty or, as in most cases, directed the rage inward – they cannot hurt someone else so they hurt themselves. Kimmy had been like that. Olivia – no, Candi – had been like that too.

Until Matt.

Maybe it was because of the years he spent in jail. Maybe, like she said before, it had to do with their mutual wounds. But Matt was the finest man she had ever known. He truly didn't sweat the small stuff. He lived in the moment. He paid attention to what mattered. He didn't let the trappings get in the way. He ignored the superfluous and saw what was really there. It made her see past it too – at least, in herself.

Matt didn't see the ugly in her – still didn't see it! – ergo, it was not there.

But as Olivia packed, the cold hard truth was obvious. After all the years and all the pretending, she had not rid herself of that self-destructive bent. How else to explain her actions? How stupid had she been – searching online for Candace Potter like that?

Look at the damage she'd wrought. To Emma, of course. To herself, yes, but more to the point, to the only man she'd ever loved.

Why had she insisted on poking at the past?

Because, in truth, she couldn't help herself. You can read all the pro-choice, pro-adoption, pro-life arguments – over the years, Olivia had ad nauseum – but there was one basic truth: Getting pregnant is the ultimate fork in the road. Whatever you choose, you will always wonder about the path not taken. Even though she was very young, even though keeping the child would have been impossible, even though the decision was ultimately made by others, no day passed without Olivia wondering about that gigantic what-if.

No woman simply skates by that one.

There was a knock on the door.

Olivia waited. A second knock. There was no peephole, so she went to a nearby window, pushed the lace curtain to the side, and peered out.

There were two men at her door. One looked like he'd just walked out of an L.L. Bean catalogue. The second man was enormous. He wore a suit that didn't seem to fit him quite right, but then again, judging by his looks, no suit would. He had a military buzz cut and no neck.

The enormous man turned to the window and caught her eye. He nudged the smaller man. The smaller man turned too.

'FBI,' the normal-size one said. 'We'd like to speak to you for a moment.'

'I have nothing to say.'

The L.L. Bean man stepped toward her. 'I don't think that's a wise position to take, Mrs. Hunter.'

'Please refer all questions to my attorney, Ike Kier.'

The man smiled. 'Maybe we should try again.'

Olivia did not like the way he said that.

'My name is Special Agent in Charge Adam Yates from the Las Vegas office of the Federal Bureau of Investigation. This' – he gestured to the big man – 'is Special Agent Cal Dollinger. We would very much like to speak with Olivia Hunter or, if she prefers, we can arrest one Candace Potter.'

471

Olivia's knees buckled at the sound of her old name. A smile cracked the big man's rock face. He was enjoying the moment.

'Up to you, Mrs. Hunter.'

There was no choice now. She was trapped. She'd have to let them in, would have to talk.

'Let me see your identification please.'

The big man walked over toward the window. Olivia had to fight off the desire to step back. He reached into his pocket, took out his ID, slammed it hard enough against the glass to make her jump. The other man, the one named Yates, did likewise. The IDs looked legitimate, though she knew how easy it was to buy fakes.

'Slide your business card under the door. I'd like to call your office and verify who you are.'

The big man, Dollinger, shrugged, the stilted smile still locked in place. He spoke for the first time: 'Sure thing, Candi.'

She swallowed. The big man reached into his wallet, plucked out a card, slid it under the door. There was no reason to go ahead and call the number. The card had a raised seal and looked too legitimate – plus there had been no hesitation on the part of Cal Dollinger, who, according to the card, was indeed a special agent out of the Las Vegas office.

She opened the door. Adam Yates entered first. Cal Dollinger ducked in as if he were entering a teepee. He stayed by the door, hands folded in front of him.

'Nice weather we're having,' Yates said.

And then Dollinger closed the door.

49

Loren Muse fumed.

She'd been about to call Ed Steinberg and complain about Yates's treatment of her, but in the end she decided against it. Little lady can't take care of herself. Needs to call her boss for help. No, she wouldn't play into that.

She was still part of the investigation. Fine, that was all she wanted. A foot in the door. She started digging up all she could on the roommate, Kimmy Dale. It wasn't too difficult. Kimmy had a record for prostitution. Despite what people thought, prostitution was not legal in Clark County, where Las Vegas is.

One of Dale's old probation officers, an old-timer named Taylor, was in early. He remembered her.

'What can I tell you?' Taylor began. 'Kimmy Dale had a bad family history, but what girl out here doesn't? You ever listen to Howard Stern on the radio?'

'Sure.'

'Ever listen when he has strippers on? He always kinda jokingly asks, 'And you were first abused at what age?' and the thing is, they always have an answer. They always were. They sit there and say it's great getting naked and they made their own choice, blah blah, but there's always something in the background. You know what I mean?'

'I do.'

'So Kimmy Dale was another classic case. She ran away from home and started stripping when she was probably fourteen, fifteen tops.'

'Do you know where she is now?'

'She moved out to Reno. I got a home address if you want.'

'I do.'

He gave her Kimmy Dale's home address. 'Last I heard she works out of a place called the Eager Beaver, which, believe it or not, is not as classy as the name would lead you to believe.'

Eager Beaver, she thought. Wasn't that where Yates said Charles Talley worked?

Taylor said, 'Nice town, Reno. Not like Vegas. Don't get me wrong. I love Vegas. We all do. It's awful and horrible and mobbed up, but we don't leave. You know what I'm saying?'

'I'm calling you from Newark, New Jersey,' she said. 'So yeah, I know what you mean.'

Taylor laughed. 'Anyway, Reno is actually a pretty nice place to raise a family nowadays. Good weather because it's below the Sierra Nevada mountains. Used to be divorce capital of the USA and have more millionaires per capita than anywhere in the country. You ever been?'

'Nope.'

'Are you cute?'

'Adorable.'

'So come out to Vegas. I'll show you around.'

'Next plane, I'm there.'

'Wait, you're not one of those "I-hate-men" feminazis, are you?'

'Only when I don't get enough sleep.'

'So what's this about?'

Her cell phone began to ring. 'I'll fill you in later, okay? Thanks, Taylor.'

'We'll stay at the Mandalay Bay. I know a guy. You'll love it.'

'Right, soon, bye.'

She hung up and hit the answer button.

'Hello?'

Without preamble, Mother Katherine said, 'She was murdered, wasn't she?'

Loren was about to hem and haw again, but something in Mother Katherine's tone told her it would be a waste of time. 'Yes.'

'Then I need to see you.'

'Why's that?'

'I wasn't allowed to say anything before. Sister Mary Rose was very specific.'

'Specific about what?'

'Please come by my office as soon as you can, Loren. I need to show you something.'

'What can I do for you, Agent Yates?' Olivia asked.

By the door, Cal Dollinger's eyes swept the room. Adam Yates sat and rested his elbows on his thighs. 'You own a lot of books,' Yates said.

'Very observant.'

'Are they yours or your husband's?'

Olivia put her hands on her hips. 'Yes, I can see how that would be relevant, so let me clear your mind. Most of the books belong to me. Are we done?'

Yates smiled. 'You're very amusing,' he said. 'Isn't she amusing, Cal?'

Cal nodded. 'Most strippers and whores, they're bitter. But not her. She's a slice of sunshine.'

'Sunshine indeed,' Yates added.

Olivia did not like the way this was going. 'What do you want?'

'You faked your own death,' Yates said. 'That's a crime.'

She said nothing.

'That girl who really died,' he went on. 'What was her name?'

'I don't know what you're talking about.'

'Her name was Cassandra, wasn't it?' Yates leaned in a little. 'Were you the one who murdered her?'

Olivia held her ground. 'What do you want?'

'You know.'

Yates's hands tightened into fists, then relaxed. She glanced at the door. Cal remained calm, a statue.

'I'm sorry,' she said. 'I don't.'

Yates tried a smile. 'Where's the tape?'

Olivia stiffened. She flashed back to that trailer. There had been a horrible smell when she and Kimmy first moved into it, as if small animals had died in the walls. Kimmy had bought some heavy potpourri – much too perfumed. It tried to mask something that could never really be hidden. The smell came back to her now. She saw Cassandra's crumpled body. She remembered the fear on Clyde Rangor's face as he asked:

'Where's the tape?'

She tried to keep her voice from cracking. 'I don't know what you're talking about.'

'Why did you run away and change your name?'

'I needed a fresh start.'

'Just like that?'

'No,' Olivia said. 'Nothing about it was "just like that."' She stood. 'And I don't want to answer any more questions until my attorney is present.'

Yates looked up at her. 'Sit down.'

'I want you both out of here.'

'I said sit down.'

She looked over at Cal Dollinger again. Still playing statue. He had eyes with nothing behind them. Olivia did as Yates said. She sat.

'I was going to say something like, "You got a nice life here, you wouldn't want me to spoil it all for you,"' Yates began. 'But I'm not sure that will work. Your neighborhood is a cesspool. Your house is a dump. Your husband is an ex-con wanted in a triple murder.' He gave her the smile. 'One would have thought you'd have made the most of your new start, Candi. But amazingly you did just the opposite.'

He was intentionally trying to antagonize her. Olivia wouldn't let that happen. 'I'd like you both to leave now.'

'You don't care who learns your secret?'

'Please leave.'

'I could arrest you.'

That was when she decided to take the chance. Olivia put out her hands, as if ready to be cuffed. Yates did not move. He could arrest her, of course. She wasn't sure of the exact law or the statute of limitations, but she had clearly interfered with a murder investigation – she had, in fact, pretended to be the victim. It would be more than enough to hold her.

But that wasn't what Yates wanted.

Clyde's pleading voice: 'Where's the tape?'

Yates wanted something else. Something Cassandra had died for. Something Clyde Rangor had killed for. She looked into his face. The eyes were steady. His hands kept clenching and unclenching.

Her wrists were still together in front of her. She waited another second, then dropped them back to her sides. 'I don't know anything about any tapes,' she said.

Now it was Yates's turn to study her. He took his time. 'I believe you,' he said.

And for some reason the way he said it scared her more than anything else.

'Please come with us,' Yates said.

'Where?'

'I'm taking you in.'

'On what charge?'

'You want the list alphabetically?'

'I'll need to call my attorney.'

'You can call him from the precinct.'

She was not sure how to play this. Cal Dollinger took a step toward her. When she took a step back, the big man said, 'You want me to drag you out of here in cuffs?'

Olivia stopped. 'That won't be necessary.'

They headed outside. Yates took the lead. Dollinger stayed next to her. Olivia checked the streets. The giant brown beer bottle was in the sky. For some reason it gave her comfort. Yates walked ahead. He unlocked the car door, slid in, started it up. He turned back and looked at Olivia and suddenly it hit her.

She recognized him.

Names fled easily, but faces were her prisoners for life. When she'd danced it became a way of numbing herself. She'd studied the faces. She'd memorize them, classify them by their level of boredom and enjoyment, try to remember how many times they'd been there. It had been a mental exercise, a way to distract herself.

Adam Yates had been to Clyde's club.

She may have hesitated or maybe Cal Dollinger was just attuned to what was going on around him. She was about to flee, just start running until her legs gave out, but Dollinger put a firm hand on her arm. He squeezed the spot above her elbow just hard enough to get her attention. She tried to pull away, but it was like pulling your arm out of a concrete block.

She couldn't move.

They were almost at the car now. Cal picked up speed. Olivia's eyes skimmed the street, pausing on Lawrence. He was standing on the corner, swaying with another man she didn't know. Both of them had brown paper bags in their hand. Lawrence looked at her and started to raise his hand to wave.

Olivia mouthed the words: Help me.

Lawrence's face didn't change. There was no reaction at all. The other man made a joke. Lawrence laughed long and hard and slapped his thigh.

He hadn't seen her.

They approached the car. Olivia's mind raced. She did not want to get in with them. She tried to slow her walk. Dollinger gave her arm a quick, painful pinch.

'Keep moving,' the big man told her.

They reached the back door. Dollinger opened it. She tried to hold her ground, but his grip was simply too strong. He pushed her into the backseat.

'Yo, got a dollar?'

The big man took a quick glance. It was Lawrence. Dollinger started turning away, dismissing the panhandler, but Lawrence grabbed his shoulder.

'Yo, man, I'm hungry. Got a dollar?'

'Buzz off.'

Lawrence put his hands on the big man's chest. 'I'm just asking for a dollar, man.'

'Let go of me.'

'A dollar. Is that too much to –'

And that was when Dollinger let go of her arm.

Olivia hesitated but not for long. When both of Dollinger's hands gripped Lawrence by the front of his shirt, she was ready. She jumped up and started to run.

'Run, Liv!'

Lawrence didn't have to tell her twice.

Dollinger dropped Lawrence and spun around. Lawrence jumped on the big man's back. Dollinger shrugged him off like dandruff. Then Lawrence did something truly foolish. He hit Dollinger with the brown bag. Olivia could hear the clunk from the beer bottle inside. Dollinger turned around and punched Lawrence in the sternum. Lawrence went down hard.

Dollinger shouted, 'Stop! FBI!'

I don't think so, big man.

Olivia heard the car take off. The tires squealed as Yates peeled out. She glanced behind her.

Dollinger was catching up to her. And he had a gun in his hand.

Her lead was maybe fifty feet. She ran as hard as she could. This was her neighborhood. She'd have the advantage, right? She cut down a back alley. It was empty – nobody else in sight. Dollinger followed. She risked a look back. He was gaining on her and didn't look the least bit put out.

She spun forward and ran harder, pumping her arms.

A bullet whizzed by her. Then another.

Oh, God. He's shooting!

She had to get out of the alley. Had to find people. He wouldn't just shoot her in front of a lot of people.

Would he?

She veered right back onto the street. The car was there. Yates sped toward her. She rolled over a parked car and onto the sidewalk. They were at the old Pabst Blue Ribbon factory. Soon it would be gone, replaced with yet another no-personality shopping center. But right now the broken-down ruins could be a haven.

Wait, where was that old tavern?

She swerved to the left. It was down the second alley. She remembered that. Olivia did not dare look behind her, but she could hear his footsteps now. He was gaining.

'Stop!'

Like hell, she thought. The tavern. Where the hell was that tavern?

She turned right.

Bingo, there it was!

The door was on the right. She wasn't far from it. She ran hard. She grabbed the handle as Dollinger made the turn. She pulled the door open and fell inside.

'Help!'

There was one person inside. He was cleaning glasses behind the bar. He looked up in surprise. Olivia stood and quickly threw the bolt.

'Hey,' the bartender shouted, 'what's going on here?'

'Someone is trying to kill me.'

The door shook. 'FBI. Open up!'

Olivia shook her head. The bartender hesitated, then gestured toward the back room with his head. She ran for it. The bartender picked up a shotgun as Dollinger kicked the door open.

The bartender was startled by the size of the man. 'Jesus H. Christ!'

'FBI! Drop it.'

'Let's just slow down, buddy . . .'

Dollinger pointed his gun at the bartender and fired twice.

The bartender went down, leaving only a splash of blood on the wall behind him.

Oh my God oh my God oh my God!

Olivia wanted to scream.

No. Go. Hurry.

She thought about the baby inside her. It gave her the extra spurt. She dove into the back room where the bartender had gestured.

Gunfire raked the wall behind her. Olivia dropped to the floor.

She crawled toward the back door. It was made of heavy metal. There was a key in the lock. In one move she pulled the door open and twisted the key so hard that it broke in the knob. She rolled back into the sunlight. The door closed and locked automatically behind her.

She heard him twisting the knob. When that didn't work, he began to pound on the door. This time the door would not give way easily. Olivia ran, keeping off the main streets, looking out for both Yates's car and Dollinger on foot.

She saw neither. Time to get the hell out of here.

Olivia walk-jogged for another two miles. When a bus drove by, she hopped on, not much caring where it took her. She got off in the center of Elizabeth. Taxis were lined up by the depot.

'Where to?' the driver asked her.

She tried to catch her breath. 'Newark Airport, please.'

50

As Matt crossed into Pennsylvania in the white Isuzu, he was amazed at how much of what he'd thought of as useless information he'd retained from prison. Of course, prison is not the great education in all things crime many thought it was. You have to keep in mind that the inhabitants had all been, well, caught, and thus any claimed expertise had something of a shadow cast over it.

He had also never listened too closely. Criminal activities did not interest him. His plan, which he'd maintained for nine years, was to stay away from anything even remotely unlawful.

That had changed.

Saul's stolen car method had borne fruit. And now Matt remembered other law-evading lessons from his time behind bars. He stopped in the parking lot of a Great Western off Route 80. No security, no surprise. He did not want to steal another car, just a license plate. He wanted a license plate with the letter P in it. He got lucky. There was a car in the employee lot with a plate that began with the letter P. The employee car would work well, he thought. It was eleven a.m. Most places would be in early- to mid-shift by then. The employee owner would probably be inside for several more hours at a minimum.

He stopped in a Home Depot and bought thin black electric tape, the kind you use to repair phone cords. Making sure no one was watching, he ripped a strip and put it on the letter P, turning it into the letter B. It wouldn't hold up under close scrutiny, but it should be good enough to get him where he was going.

Harrisburg, Pennsylvania.

There was no choice. Matt had to get to Reno. That meant flying on an airplane. He knew that would be risky. The prison tips for evading detection, even if good in their heyday, were all pre-9/11. Security had changed a lot since then, but there were still methods. He just had to think it through, move fast, and be more than a little lucky.

First, he tried a little old-fashioned confusion and mayhem. He used a pay phone back on the New Jersey border to make flight reservations from Newark Airport to Toronto. Maybe they'd track that down and figure he was an amateur. Maybe not. He hung up, moved to another pay phone, and made his other reservation. He wrote down his booking number, hung up, and shook his head.

This was not going to be easy.

Matt pulled into the Harrisburg airport parking lot. The Mauser M2 was still in his pocket. No way he could take it with him. Matt jammed the weapon under the front passenger seat because, if things did not go as planned, he might be back. The Isuzu had served him well. He wanted to write a note to its owner, explaining what he had done and why. With luck there'd be a chance to explain in the future.

479

Now to see if his plan worked. . . .

But first, he needed sleep. He bought a baseball cap in the souvenir store. Then he found a free chair in the arrivals area, folded his arms across his chest, closed his eyes, pulled the brim low across his face. People slept in airports all the time, he figured. Why would anyone bother him?

He woke up an hour later, feeling like absolute hell. He headed upstairs to the departure level. He bought some extra-strength Tylenol and Motrin, took three of each. He cleaned up in the bathroom.

The line at the ticket sales counter was long. That was good, if the timing worked. He wanted the staff to be busy. When it was his turn, the woman behind the desk gave him that distracted smile.

'To Chicago, Flight 188,' he said.

'That flight leaves in twenty minutes,' she said.

'I know. There was traffic and –'

'May I see your picture ID, please?'

He gave her his driver's license. She typed in 'Hunter, M.' This was the moment of truth. He stood perfectly still. She frowned and typed some more. Nothing happened. 'I don't see you in here, Mr. Hunter.'

'That's odd.'

'Do you have your booking number?'

'I sure do.'

He handed the one he'd gotten when he made the reservation on the phone. She typed in the letters: YTIQZ2. Matt held his breath.

The woman sighed. 'I see the problem.'

'Oh?'

She shook her head. 'Your name is misspelled on the reservation. You're listed here as Mike, not Matt. And the last name is Huntman, not Hunter.'

'Honest mistake,' Matt said.

'You'd be surprised how often it happens.'

'Nothing would surprise me,' he said.

They shared a world-is-full-of-dopes laugh. She printed out his ticket and collected the money. Matt smiled, thanked her, and headed to the plane.

There was no nonstop from Harrisburg to Reno, but that might work in his favor. He didn't know how the airline computer system meshed with the federal government's, but two short flights would probably work better than one long one. Would the computer system pick up his name right away? Matt doubted it – or maybe hope sprang eternal. Thinking logically, the whole thing would have to take some time – gathering the information, sorting it, getting it to the right person. A few hours at a minimum.

He'd be in Chicago in one.

It sounded good in theory.

When he landed safely at O'Hare in Chicago, he felt his heart start up again. He disembarked, trying not to look conspicuous, planning an escape route in case he saw a row of police officers at the gate. But no one grabbed him when he came off the plane. He let out a long breath. So they hadn't located him – yet. But now came the tricky part. The flight to Reno was longer. If they put together what he'd done the first time, they'd have plenty of time to nail him.

So he tried something slightly different.

480

Another long line at the airline purchasing desk. Matt might need that. He waited, snaking through the velvet ropes. He watched, seeing which employee looked most tired or complacent. He found her, on the far right. She looked bored past the point of tears. She examined IDs, but there was little spark in her eyes. She kept sighing. She kept glancing around, clearly distracted. Probably had a personal life, Matt thought. Maybe a fight with the husband or her teenage daughter or who knew what?

Or maybe, Matt, she's very astute and just has a tired-looking face.

Still, what other options were there? When Matt got to the front of the line and his agent wasn't free, he faked looking for something and told the family behind him to go ahead. He did that one more time and then it was his agent's turn to say, 'Next.'

He approached as inconspicuously as possible. 'My name is Matthew Huntler.' He handed her a piece of paper with the booking number on it. She took it and started typing.

'Chicago to Reno/Tahoe, Mr. Huntler.'

'Yes.'

'ID, please.'

This was the hardest part. He had tried to set it up as smoothly as possible. M. Huntler was a member of their frequent-flier club – Matt had signed him up a few hours ago. Computers don't know from subtlety. Humans sometimes do.

He gave her his wallet. She did not look at it at first. She was still typing into the computer. Maybe he'd get lucky here. Maybe she wouldn't even check his ID.

'Any luggage to check?'

'Not today, no.'

She nodded, still typing. Then she turned toward his ID. Matt felt his stomach tumble. He remembered something Bernie had sent him by e-mail several years ago. It said:

Here's a fun test. Read this sentence:

FINISHED FILES ARE THE RESULT OF YEARS OF SCIENTIFIC STUDY COMBINED WITH THE EXPERIENCE OF YEARS.

Now count the F's in that sentence.

He had done it and ended up with four. The real answer was six. You don't see every letter. That's not how we're built. He was counting on something like that here. Hunter, Huntler. Would someone really catch the difference?

The woman said to him. 'Aisle or window.'

'Aisle.'

He'd made it. The security check went even easier – after all, Matt had already been ID'd at the counter, right? The security guard looked at his picture, at his face, but he didn't come up with the fact that the ID said Hunter while the boarding pass read Huntler. Typos are made all the time anyway. You see hundreds or thousands of boarding passes each day. You really wouldn't notice such a small thing.

Once again Matt got to his plane right as the gate was about to close. He settled into his aisle seat, closed his eyes, and didn't wake up until the pilot announced their descent into Reno.

*

The door to Mother Katherine's office was closed.

This time there was no flashback for Loren. She pounded hard on the door and put her hand on the knob. When she heard Mother Katherine say, 'Come in,' she was ready.

The Mother Superior had her back to the door. She did not turn around when Loren entered. She merely asked, 'Are you sure Sister Mary Rose was murdered?'

'Yes.'

'Do you know who did it?'

'Not yet.'

Mother Katherine nodded slowly. 'Have you learned her real identity?'

'Yes,' Loren said. 'But it would have been easier if you'd just told me.'

She expected Mother Katherine to argue, but she didn't. 'I couldn't.'

'Why not?'

'Unfortunately it was not my place.'

'She told you?'

'Not exactly, no. But I knew enough.'

'How did you figure it out?'

The old nun shrugged. 'Some of her statements about her past,' she said. 'They didn't add up.'

'You confronted her?'

'No, never. And she never told me her true identity. She said it would endanger others. But I know that it was sordid. Sister Mary Rose wanted to move past it. She wanted to make amends. And she did. She contributed much to this school, to these children.'

'With her work or with finances?'

'Both.'

'She gave you money?'

'The parish,' Mother Katherine corrected. 'Yes, she gave quite a bit.'

'Sounds like guilt money.'

Mother Katherine smiled. 'Is there any other kind?'

'So that story about chest compressions . . . ?'

'I already knew about the implants. She told me. She also told me that if someone learned who she really was, they'd kill her.'

'But you didn't think that happened.'

'It appeared to be death by natural causes. I thought it best to leave it alone.'

'What changed your mind?'

'Gossip,' she said.

'What do you mean?'

'One of our sisters confided to me that she had seen a man in Sister Mary Rose's room. I was suspicious, of course, but I couldn't prove anything. I also needed to protect the school's reputation. So I needed this investigated quietly and without my betraying Sister Mary Rose's trust.'

'Enter me.'

'Yes.'

'And now that you know she was murdered?'

'She left a letter.'

'For whom?'

Mother Katherine showed her the envelope. 'A woman named Olivia Hunter.'

Adam Yates was closing in on panic.

He parked a good distance from the old brewery and waited while Cal quickly cleaned up. The clues would be gone. Cal's weapon could not be traced. The license plates they were using would lead to nowhere. Some crazy person might identify a huge man chasing a woman but there would be no practical way of linking them with the dead bartender.

Perhaps.

No, no perhaps about it. He had been in worse scrapes. The bartender had pulled a rifle on Cal. It would have his fingerprints on it. The untraceable gun would be left behind. They would both be out of state in a matter of hours.

They would get through it.

When Cal sat in the passenger seat, Adam said, 'You messed up.'

Cal nodded. 'I did at that.'

'You shouldn't have tried to shoot her.'

He nodded again. 'A mistake,' he agreed. 'But we can't let her go. If her background comes out –'

'It's going to come out anyway. Loren Muse knows about it.'

'True, but without Olivia Hunter, it doesn't lead anyplace. If she's caught, she will try to save herself. That may mean looking into what happened all those years ago.'

Yates felt something inside him start to tear. 'I don't want to hurt anyone.'

'Adam?'

He looked at the big man.

'It's too late for that,' Dollinger said. 'Us or them, remember?'

He nodded slowly.

'We need to find Olivia,' Dollinger said. 'And I do mean we. If other agents arrest her . . .'

Yates finished it for him. 'She may talk.'

'Precisely.'

'So we call her in as a material witness,' Yates said. 'Tell them to keep an eye on the nearby airports and train stations but not to do anything until they notify us.'

Cal nodded. 'Already done.'

Adam Yates considered his options. 'Let's head back to the county office. Maybe Loren found something useful on that Kimmy Dale.'

They had driven about five minutes when the phone rang. Cal picked it up and barked, 'Agent Dollinger.'

Cal listened closely.

'Let her land. Have Ted follow her. Do not, repeat, do not, approach. I'll be on the next plane out.'

He hung up.

'What?'

'Olivia Hunter,' he said. 'She's already on a plane to Reno.'

'Reno again,' Yates said.

'Home of the deceased Charles Talley and Max Darrow.'

'And maybe the tape.' Yates made a right up ahead. 'All the signs are pointing west, Cal. I think we better get to Reno too.'

51

The taxi driver worked for a company called Reno Rides. He pulled to a full stop, shifted in park, turned around, and looked Olivia up and down. 'You sure this is the place, ma'am?'

Olivia could only stare.

'Ma'am?'

An ornate cross dangled from the taxi's rearview mirror. Prayer cards wallpapered the glove compartment.

'Is this 488 Center Lane Drive?' she asked.

'It is.'

'Then this is the place.' Olivia reached into her purse. She handed him the money. He handed her a pamphlet.

'You don't have to do this,' he said.

The pamphlet was church-affiliated. John 3:16 was on the cover. She managed to smile.

'Jesus loves you,' the driver said.

'Thank you.'

'I'll take you anywhere else you want to go. No charge.'

'It's okay,' Olivia said.

She stepped out of the taxi. The driver gave her a forlorn look. She waved as he departed. Olivia cupped a hand over her eyes. The sign of tired neon read:

EAGER BEAVER – NUDE DANCING.

Her body began to quake. Old reaction, she guessed. She had never been in this place, but she knew it. She knew the dirty pickups that littered the lot. She knew the men trudging in mindlessly, the low lights, the sticky feel of the dance pole. She headed toward the door, knowing what she'd find inside.

Matt feared prison – going back. This, right in front of her, was her prison.

Candi Cane lives another day.

Olivia Hunter had tried to exorcise Candace 'Candi Cane' Potter years ago. Now the girl was back in a big bad way. Forget what experts tell you: You can indeed wipe away the past. Olivia knew that. She could jam Candi in some back room, lock the door, destroy the key. She had almost done it – would have done – but there'd been one thing that always kept that door, no matter how hard she pushed, from closing all the way.

Her child.

A chill scrambled down her back. Oh, God, she thought. Was her daughter working here?

Please no.

It was four p.m. Still plenty of time before the midnight meeting. She could go somewhere else, find a Starbucks maybe or get a motel room, grab some sleep. She had caught a little shut-eye on the plane out here, but she could definitely use more.

When she first landed, Olivia called FBI headquarters and asked to speak to Adam Yates. When she was connected to the office of the Special Agent in Charge, she hung up.

So Yates was legit. Dollinger too, she supposed.

That meant that two FBI agents had tried to kill her.

There would be no arrest or capture. She knew too much.

The last words Clyde had said to her came back: *'Just tell me where it is. . . .'*

It was starting to make some sense. There were rumors about Clyde making tapes for blackmail. He'd probably blackmailed the wrong guy – either Yates or somebody close to them. Somehow that led him to poor Cassandra. Did she have the tapes? Was she in them?

Standing there, reading the sign about the $4.99 EAGER BEAVER BUFFET! Olivia nodded to herself.

That was it. It had to be. She started walking toward the front door.

She should wait, come back.

No.

She got a curious look at the door. Women do not come to these places alone. Every once in a while a man might bring a girlfriend. The girlfriend would be trying to show she was hip. Or maybe she had lesbian tendencies. Whatever. But women never came in alone.

Heads turned when she entered, but not as many as you'd think. People reacted slowly at places like this. The air was syrupy, languid. The lights were down. Jaws remained slack. Most patrons probably assumed that she was either a working girl on her downtime or a lesbian waiting for her lover's shift to end.

The Human League's 'Don't You Want Me' played over the sound system, a song that had been an already aged classic when Olivia had danced. Retro, she guessed, but she had always liked the track. In this place, the lyrics were supposed to be a sexy come-on, but if you listened closely, Phil Oakey, the lead singer, made you feel the pain and shock of having your heart broken. The title wasn't repeated with lust. It was repeated with shattering disbelief.

Olivia took a seat in a back booth. There were three dancers onstage right now. Two looked off at nothing. One worked a customer, feigning passion, inviting him to jam dollar bills into her G-string. The man complied. She took in the audience and realized that nothing had changed in the decade since she'd worked rooms like these. The men were of the same variety. Some had the blank faces. Some had the glazed smile. Some tried a cocky look, a swagger in their expression, as if they were somehow above it all. Others aggressively downed their beers, staring at the girls with naked hostility, as if demanding an answer to the eternal question, 'Is that all there is?'

The girls onstage were young and on drugs. You could tell. Her old roommate Kimmy had two brothers who OD'd. Kimmy wouldn't tolerate drug use. So Olivia – no, Candi – took to drinking, but Clyde Rangor had made her stop when she started stumbling onstage. Clyde as a rehab counselor. Weird, but there you have it.

The grease from the awful lunch buffet took to the air, becoming more a skin coating than a smell. Who ate that stuff? she wondered. Buffalo wings dating back to the Carter administration. Hot dogs that sit in water until, well, until they were gone. French fries so oily it makes picking them up a near impossibility. Fat men circled the dishes and piled their Styrofoam plates to dizzying heights. Olivia could almost see their arteries hardening in the dim light.

Some strip joints called themselves 'gentlemen's clubs,' and businessmen wore suits and acted above the riffraff. There was no such pretense at the Eager Beaver. This was a place where tattoos outnumbered teeth. People fought. The bouncers had bigger guts than muscle because muscle was show and these guys would seriously kick your ass.

Olivia was not scared or intimidated, but she wasn't sure what she was doing here. The girls onstage began their rotation. The dancer at the one spot went offstage. A bubbly young girl came on in the three spot. No way was she legal age. She was all legs, moving on the high heels like a colt. Her smile looked almost genuine, so Olivia figured that the life had not yet been ripped out of her.

'Get you something?'

The waitress looked at the oddity that was Olivia with a wary eye.

'Coca-Cola please.'

She left. Olivia kept her eye on the bubbly young girl. Something about her brought back memories of poor Cassandra. Just the age, she guessed. Cassandra had been far prettier. And then, as she looked at the three girls still onstage, the obvious question hit her:

Was one of these girls her daughter?

She looked at their faces for any sort of resemblance and saw none. That meant nothing, of course. She knew that. The waitress delivered the Coke. Olivia just let it sit there. There was no way she'd drink from any of these glasses.

Ten minutes later the girls rotated again. Another new girl. Probably running a five shift – three girls on, two girls off, fairly steady rotation. Could be a six shift. She wondered about Matt, about how he'd find his way out here. He had seemed so confident that he'd be able to make it, or had that been false bravado for her sake?

The dancer in the two spot worked some guy with a toupee so bad it looked like it had a zipper. Probably handing him that old favorite about working her way through school, Olivia thought. Why guys got off on the idea that a girl was a student always amazed her. Did they need a spot of purity to offset their filth?

The girl who'd been in the one spot when Olivia entered came out from the back. She approached a man who had a chicken wing sticking out of his mouth. The man dropped the chicken wing, wiped his hands on his jeans. The girl took the man by the hand and disappeared into a corner. Olivia wanted to follow her. She wanted to grab all of these girls and drag them out into the sunshine.

Enough.

She signaled to the waitress to bring over a check. The waitress broke away from a bunch of laughing locals. 'Three-fifty,' she said.

Olivia stood, reached into her purse, and took out a five. She was just about to hand it to the waitress, just about ready to leave this dark, awful place, when the dancers shifted again. A new girl came out from the back.

Olivia froze. Then a small groan, a groan of quiet, strong anguish, escaped from her lips.

The waitress said, 'Miss, you okay?'

Walking on the stage, taking the number three position.

It was Kimmy.

'Miss?'

Olivia's legs almost gave way. She sat back down. 'Get me another Coke.'

She had not touched her last one but if that bothered the waitress, she hid it pretty well. Olivia simply stared. For several seconds, she let the swirl of emotions twist through her. Regret, of course. Deep sadness to see Kimmy still up on that stage after all this time. Guilt for what Olivia had been forced to leave behind. But there was joy too at seeing her old friend. Olivia had visited a couple of Web sites in recent weeks, trying to see if Kimmy was dancing. She'd found nothing, which, Olivia had hoped, meant that Kimmy was no longer in the business. Now she could see the truth: Kimmy had just been too low-level to earn even a mention.

Olivia could not move.

Despite what one might think, it was not hard to forge friendships in that life. Most of the girls genuinely liked one another. They were like army buddies, bonding while trying to stay alive. But no one had been like Kimmy Dale. Kimmy had been her closest friend, the only one she still missed, still thought about, still wished that she could talk to. Kimmy had made her laugh. Kimmy had kept her off cocaine. Kimmy had even kept the gun in their trailer that ended up saving Olivia's life.

Olivia smiled in the dark. Kimmy Dale, the clean freak, her sometimes dance partner, her confidante.

And then the guilt and sadness roared back.

The years hadn't been kind, but then again no years ever had been to Kimmy Dale. Her skin sagged. There were lines around her mouth and eyes. A pattern of small bruises dotted her thighs. She wore too much makeup now, like the old 'hangers-on' they used to dread becoming. That had been their greatest fear: being one of the old hangers-on who couldn't see it was time to get out of the business.

Kimmy's stage dance hadn't changed – the same few steps, the moves a little slower now, more lethargic. The same high black boots she had always favored. There was a time when Kimmy would work the crowd better than anyone – she had a terrific smile – but there was no posturing anymore. Olivia kept back.

Kimmy thinks I'm dead.

How, she wondered, would Kimmy react to seeing this . . . this ghost? Olivia wondered what to do. Should she reveal herself – or just stay here in the shadows, wait another thirty minutes, slip out when she was sure Kimmy couldn't see her?

She sat there and watched her friend and considered her next step. It was obvious. Everything was coming out now. The pact with Emma was over. Yates and Dollinger knew who she was. There was no reason to hide anymore. There was no one left to protect and maybe, just maybe, there was still someone she could save.

When Kimmy was on the final leg of her rotation, Olivia waved over the waitress.

'The dancer on the right,' Olivia said.

'The black one?'

'Yeah.'

'We call her Magic.'

'Okay, good. I want a private session with her.'

The waitress cocked an eyebrow. 'You mean in the back?'

'Right. A private room.'

'Fifty bucks extra.'

'No problem,' Olivia said. She had picked up cash at the ATM in Elizabeth. She handed the girl an extra ten for her own troubles.

The waitress stuffed the bill in her cleavage and shrugged. 'Go back and to the right. Second door. It's got a B on it. I'll send Magic over in five minutes.'

It took longer. There was a couch and a bed in the room. Olivia did not sit. She stood there and waited. She was shaking. She heard people walking past her door. On the sound system, Tears for Fears noted that everybody wants to rule the world. No kidding.

There was a knock on the door.

'You in there?'

The voice. No question who it was. Olivia wiped her eyes.

'Come in.'

The door opened. Kimmy stepped inside. 'Okay, let me tell you the price –'

She stopped.

For several seconds, they both just stood there and let the tears roll down their cheeks. Kimmy shook her head in disbelief.

'It can't be . . .'

Candi – not Olivia now – finally nodded. 'It's me.'

'But . . .'

Kimmy put a hand to her mouth and began to sob. Candi spread her arms. Kimmy nearly collapsed. Candi grabbed her and held on.

'It's okay,' she said softly.

'It can't be . . .'

'It's okay,' Olivia said again, stroking her friend's hair. 'I'm here. I'm back.'

52

Loren's flight went to Reno via Houston.

She had bought the ticket with her own money. She was taking a huge chance – the kind of chance that might indeed force her to leave her job and move out to someplace like New Mexico or Arizona – but the facts were there. Steinberg needed to play it more by the book. She understood that, agreed with it on some level.

But in the end she knew that this was the only way to go.

Yates, a powerful fed, was up to something.

Her suspicions first took flight when Yates abruptly turned nasty after leaving Len Friedman's house. He had suddenly pretended to be an irrational ass – not an unusual thing for a big-time federal agent, she knew – but it just didn't ring true. It seemed forced to her. Yates feigned control, but she sensed a panic there. You could almost smell it on him.

Yates clearly did not want her to see or talk to Olivia Hunter.

Why?

And when she thought about it, what had brought on that hissy fit in the first place? She remembered something that had happened in Friedman's basement – something that had seemed small and unimportant at the time. Yates had gone out of his way to steer the conversation away from what Rangor and Lemay used to do that Friedman had referred to as 'worse' than telling on their clientele. At the time she'd just been annoyed by Yates's interruption. But then you add in the way he threw her off the case and you had . . .

Well, okay, you still had nothing.

After visiting Mother Katherine, Loren had called Yates's cell phone. She had not gotten an answer. She had tried Olivia Hunter's residence. No answer there either. And then a report came over the radio, about a murder in Irvington, in a tavern not far from where the Hunters lived. There was not much yet, but there was some talk about a huge man running down the street chasing a woman.

A huge man. Cal Dollinger, whom Yates said he was bringing with him to question Olivia Hunter, was a huge man.

Again, on its own it meant very little.

But add it to what she knew.

She'd called Steinberg then and asked, 'Do you know where Yates is?'

'No.'

'I do,' she said. 'I checked with my airport source.' Newark Airport was, after all, in Essex County. The office had several contacts there. 'He and that Goliath are on a plane heading to the Reno-Tahoe airport.'

'And I care because?'

'I'd like to follow them,' she said.

'Come again?'

'Yates is up to something.'

She told Steinberg what she knew. She could almost see him frowning.

'So let me get this straight,' her boss said. 'You think that Yates is somehow involved in all this? Adam Yates, a decorated FBI agent. Wait, no, scratch that: a dedicated Special Agent in Charge, the top fed in Nevada. You base this on – A – his mood. B, that a big person might have been seen somewhere near but not even at a murder scene in Irvington. And C, that he's flying back to his home state. That about cover it?'

'You should have heard him playing good cop-bad cop, boss.'

'Uh huh.'

'He wanted me off the case and away from Olivia Hunter. I'm telling you: Yates is bad, boss. I know it.'

'And you know what I'm going to say, right?'

Loren did. 'Gather evidence.'

'You got it.'

'Do me one favor, boss.'

'What?'

'Check on Yates's story about Rangor and Lemay turning state's witness.'

'What about it?'

'See if it's true.'

'What, you think he made that up?'

'Just check it.'

He hesitated. 'I doubt it'll do any good. I'm a county guy. That's RICO. They don't like to talk.'

'Ask Joan Thurston then.'

'She'll think I'm nuts.'

'Doesn't she already?'

'Yeah, well, that's a point,' he said. He cleared his throat. 'One more thing.'

'Yes, boss.'

'You thinking of doing something stupid?'

'Who, me?'

'As your boss, you know I won't authorize anything. But if you're off the clock and I'm none the wiser . . .'

'Say no more.'

She hung up. Loren knew that the answers were in Reno. Charles Talley worked at the Eager Beaver in Reno. Kimmy Dale did too. Now Yates and Dollinger were on their way there. So Loren made sure that she was off the clock. Then she booked a flight and rushed to the airport. Before she boarded, she made one more phone call. Len Friedman was still in his basement office.

'Hey,' Friedman said. 'Is this about getting me Candi Cane's autopsy?'

'It's yours, if you answer a few more questions. You said something about "what goes on in Vegas stays in Vegas."'

'Yes.'

'When I asked if you meant that Clyde Rangor and Emma Lemay were telling on patrons, you said, "Worse."'

There was silence.

'What did you mean, Mr. Friedman?'

'It's just something I heard,' he said.

'What?'

'That Rangor had a scheme going.'

'You mean like a blackmail scheme?'

'Yeah, something like that.'

He went quiet.

'How like that?' she asked.

'He made tapes.'

'Of?'

'Of what you think.'

'His clients having sex with women?'

Again there was a brief silence.

'Mr. Friedman?'

'Yes,' he said. 'But . . .'

'But what?'

'But' – his voice grew soft – 'I'm not sure you'd call them women.'

She frowned. 'They were men?'

'No, not like that,' Friedman said. 'Look, I don't even know if it's true. People make stuff up all the time.'

'And you think that's the case here?'

'I don't know, that's all I'm saying.'

'But you heard rumors?'

'Yes.'

'So what are these rumors?' Loren asked. 'What did Rangor have on those tapes?'

53

Matt got off the plane and hurried out of the airport. Nobody stopped him. He felt a rush. He'd done it. He'd made it to Reno with hours to spare.

He grabbed a taxi. '488 Center Lane Drive.'

They drove in silence. When they pulled up to the address, Matt stared out the window at the Eager Beaver. He paid the driver, got out, and headed inside.

Fitting, he thought to himself.

While he had not expected 488 Center Lane Drive to be a strip joint, he was not all that surprised either. Olivia was missing something in all of this. He understood that. He even understood why. She wanted to find her child. It had blinded her a bit. She couldn't see what was so obvious to him: This was about more than an adoption or even a scam to extort money.

It all came back to the pictures on his camera phone.

If you're the family with a sick daughter, you are not interested in making a husband jealous. If you're a lowlife crook after a big payday, you don't care about breaking up a marriage.

But this had to be about more than that. Matt wasn't sure what exactly, but he knew that it was something bad – something that made whoever was behind this want to drag them back to a place like this.

He headed inside and found a table in the corner. He looked around, hoping to see Olivia. He didn't. Three girls slowly undulated onstage. He tried to imagine his beautiful wife, the one who made everyone lucky enough to encounter her feel somehow blessed, up there like that. Oddly enough it wasn't that hard to picture. Rather than confusing him, something about Olivia's shocking confessions made it all click. It was why she had such a zest for things most found too ordinary, why she so badly wanted a family, a home, the life in the suburbs. She yearned for what we consider both our normalcy and our dream. He understood that better now. It made more sense to him.

That life. The life they were trying to make together. She was right: It was worth fighting for.

A waitress came by and Matt asked for coffee. He needed the caffeine fix. She brought it over. It was surprisingly good. He sipped it and watched the girls and tried to put some of the facts together. Nothing was really coming to him.

He stood and asked if there was a pay phone. The bouncer, a fat man with a pockmarked face, pointed with his thumb. Matt had a prepaid phone card. He always carried it – another holdover from what he'd learned in the pen, he guessed. The truth was, you could trace a phone card. You could find out where it came from and even who bought it. Eventually. Best example was when prosecutors traced a call made with a phone card in the Oklahoma bombing case. But

492

it took time. It could be used to prosecute, but Matt wasn't worried about that anymore.

His cell phone was off. If you keep it on, there are ways to figure out where you are. Cell-phone tracking, even without making a call, is a reality. He pressed in the digits for the 800 number, then his code, then Midlife's private line at the office.

'Ike Kier.'

'It's me.'

'Don't say anything you don't want someone else to hear.'

'Then you do the talking, Ike.'

'Olivia is okay.'

'Did they hold her?'

'No. She's, uh, gone.'

That was good to hear. 'And?'

'Hold on.' He passed the phone.

'Hey, Matt.'

It was Cingle.

'I talked to that investigator friend of yours. I hope you don't mind, but they had my ass over a barrel.'

'That's okay.'

'Nothing I said will hurt you anyway.'

'Don't worry about it,' he said.

Matt was looking off in the direction of the club's entrance. Cingle was telling him something else, something about Darrow and Talley, but there was a sudden rush in his ears.

Matt almost dropped the phone when he saw who'd just walked into the Eager Beaver.

It was Loren Muse.

Loren Muse flashed her badge at the fat guy at the door.

'I'm looking for one of your dancers. Her name is Kimmy Dale.'

The fat man just stared at her.

'Did you hear me?'

'Yeah.'

'So?'

'So your ID says New Jersey.'

'I'm still a law enforcement officer.'

The fat man shook his head. 'You're out of your jurisdiction.'

'What are you, a lawyer?'

The fat man pointed at her. 'Good one. Bye, bye now.'

'I said I'm looking for Kimmy Dale.'

'And I said you have no jurisdiction here.'

'You want me to bring someone more local?'

He shrugged. 'If that gets you off, honey, do whatever.'

'I can make trouble.'

'This.' The fat man smiled and pointed at his own face. 'This is me scared.'

Loren's cell phone rang. She took a step to the right. The music blared. She put the phone to her right ear and stuck a finger in her left. Her eyes squinted, as if that'd make the connection better.

'Hello?'

'I want to make a deal with you.'

It was Matt Hunter.

'I'm listening.'

'I surrender to you and only you. We go somewhere and wait until at least one in the morning.'

'Why one in the morning?'

'Do you think I killed Darrow or Talley?'

'You're certainly wanted for questioning.'

'I didn't ask you that. I asked you if you think I killed them.'

She frowned. 'No, Matt. I don't think you have anything to do with it. But I think your wife does. I know her real name. I know she's been hiding and running for a long time. I think that Max Darrow somehow figured out that she was still alive. I think they went after her and that somehow you got caught in the middle.'

'Olivia is innocent.'

'That,' Loren said, 'I'm not sure about.'

'My deal still stands. I surrender to you. We go somewhere else and talk this out until one in the morning.'

'Somewhere else? You don't even know where I am.'

'Yeah,' Matt said. 'I know exactly where you are.'

'How?'

She heard a click. Damn, he hung up. She was about to dial in for an immediate trace when she felt a tap on her shoulder. She turned and he was standing right there, as if he'd just materialized out of thin air.

'So,' Matt said. 'Was I smart to trust you?'

54

When the plane landed, Cal Dollinger took over. Yates was used to that. Most mistook Dollinger as the muscle and Yates as the brains. In truth theirs had always been closer to a more political partnership. Adam Yates was the candidate who stayed clean. Cal Dollinger was behind-the-scenes and willing to get nasty.

'Go ahead,' Dollinger said. 'Make the call.'

Yates called Ted Stevens, the agent they had assigned to follow Olivia Hunter.

'Hey, Ted, you still on her?' Yates asked.

'I am at that.'

'Where is she?'

'You're not going to believe this. Ms. Hunter got off the plane and headed straight to a strip joint called the Eager Beaver.'

'She still there?'

'No, she left with a black stripper. I followed them back to some dump on the west side of town.' Stevens gave him the address. Yates repeated it for Dollinger.

'So Olivia Hunter is still at the stripper's trailer,' Yates asked.

'Yes.'

'Anyone else with them?'

'Nope, just the two of them alone.'

Yates looked at Dollinger. They had discussed how to handle this, how to get Stevens off the case and set it up for what was about to occur. 'Okay, thanks, Ted, you can leave them now. Meet me at the Reno office in ten minutes.'

'Someone else picking them up?' Stevens asked.

'Not necessary,' Yates said.

'What's going on?'

'Olivia Hunter used to work the clubs for Comb-Over. We flipped her yesterday.'

'She knows a lot?'

'She knows enough,' Yates said.

'So what's she doing with the black chick?'

'Well, she promised us that she would try to convince a woman named Kimmy Dale, a black dancer who works at the Eager Beaver, to flip too. Hunter told us that Dale knows a ton. So we gave her rope, see if she was keeping her word.'

'Which it looks like she is.'

'Yeah.'

'So we're in good shape.'

Yates looked over at Dollinger. 'As long as Comb-Over doesn't find out, yeah, I think we're in real good shape. I'll meet you at the office in ten minutes, Ted. We'll talk more.'

Yates pressed the end button. They were in the concourse now, heading for the exit. He and Dollinger walked shoulder to shoulder, as they'd done since elementary school. They lived on the same block in Henderson, outside of Las Vegas. Their wives had been college roommates and were still inseparable. Dollinger's oldest son was best friends with Yates's daughter Anne. He drove her to school every morning.

'There has to be another way,' Yates said.

'There isn't.'

'We're crossing a line here, Cal.'

'We've crossed lines before.'

'Not like this.'

'No, not like this,' Cal agreed. 'We have families.'

'I know.'

'You have to do the math. On one side, you have one person. Candace Potter, an ex-stripper, probably an old coked-out whore, who was involved with lowlifes like Clyde Rangor and Emma Lemay. That's on one side of the equation, right?'

Yates nodded, knowing how this would go.

'On the other side are two families. Two husbands, two wives, three kids of yours, two of mine. You and me, we may not be that innocent. But the rest of them are. So we end one ex-hooker's life, maybe two if I can't get her away from this Kimmy Dale – or we let seven other lives, worthy lives, get destroyed.'

Yates kept his head down.

'Us or them,' Dollinger said. 'In this case, it's not even a close call.'

'I should go with you.'

'No. We need you to be at the office with Ted. You're creating our murder scenario. When Hunter's body is found, it will naturally look like a mob hit to keep an informant quiet.'

They headed outside. Night had begun to settle in now.

'I'm sorry,' Yates said.

'You've pulled my butt out of plenty of fires, Adam.'

'There has to be another way,' Yates said again. 'Tell me there's another way.'

'Go to the office,' Dollinger said. 'I'll call you when it's done.'

55

The smell of potpourri filled Kimmy's trailer.

Whenever Olivia had smelled potpourri over the past decade it brought her back to that trailer outside Vegas. Kimmy's new place still had that same smell. Olivia could feel herself start slipping back in time.

If there were train tracks nearby, this neighborhood was on the wrong side of them. The trailer had siding that seemed to be in mid-shed. Missing windows were covered with plywood. Her rusted car cowered like an abandoned dog. The driveway was oil-stained sand. But the interior, besides the aforementioned odor, was clean and what magazines would dub tastefully furnished. Nothing expensive, of course. But there were little touches. Nice throw pillows. Small figurines.

It was, in short, a home.

Kimmy grabbed two glasses and a bottle of wine. They sat on a futon couch, and Kimmy poured. The air conditioner whirred. Kimmy put her glass to the side. She reached out with both hands and gently placed them on Olivia's cheeks.

'I can't believe you're here,' Kimmy said softly.

Then Olivia told her the whole story.

It took a while. She started with being sick at the club, going back to the trailer early, Cassandra's dead body, Clyde attacking her. Kimmy listened, totally rapt. She did not say a word. She cried sometimes. She shook. But she did not interrupt.

When Olivia mentioned the online post about her daughter, she saw Kimmy go rigid.

'What?'

'I met her,' Kimmy said.

Olivia felt her stomach drop. 'My daughter?'

'She came here,' Kimmy said. 'To my house.'

'When?'

'Two months ago.'

'I don't understand. She came here? Why?'

'She said she started looking for her birth mother. You know, out of curiosity. The way kids do. I told her as nicely as I could that you were dead, but she already knew that. Said she wanted to find Clyde and avenge you, something like that.'

'How would she have known about Clyde?'

'She said – let me think a second – she said that first she went to the cop who handled your homicide.'

'Max Darrow?'

'Right, I think that's the name. She went to him. He told her that he thought Clyde killed you but that nobody knew where Clyde was.' Kimmy shook her head.

'All these years. That son of a bitch has been dead all these years?'

'Yes,' Olivia said.

'It's like hearing Satan died, you know.'

She did. 'What was my daughter's name?'

'She didn't tell me.'

'Did she look sick?'

'Sick? Oh, wait, I see. Because of that online post. No, she looked pretty healthy.' Kimmy smiled then. 'She was pretty. Not flashy. She had spunk though. Just like you. I gave her that picture. You know, the one of us from the Sayers-Pic routine. You remember that?'

'Yeah. Yeah, I do.'

Kimmy just shook her head. 'I just can't believe you're here. It's like a dream or something. I'm scared you're going to start to fade away and I'm going to wake up in this cockroach hell without you.'

'I'm here,' Olivia said.

'And you're married. And pregnant.' She shook her head some more and let loose a dazzling smile. 'I just can't believe it.'

'Kimmy, do you know a Charles Talley?'

'You mean Chally? Crazy whack-job. He works at the club now.'

'When did you last see him?'

'Oh, I don't know. Week at least.' She frowned. 'Why? What does that bastard have to do with this?'

Olivia was silent.

'What is it, Candi?'

'They're dead.'

'Who?'

'Charles Talley and Max Darrow. They were in on it somehow. I don't know. Something with my daughter coming back tipped them off. They probably wrote that post to find me.' Olivia frowned. Something felt off about that part, but for now she pushed through. 'Darrow wanted money. I gave him fifty thousand. Charles Talley was involved too.'

'You're not making sense.'

'I was supposed to meet with someone tonight,' Olivia said. 'They were supposed to show me my daughter. Only now Darrow and Chally are both dead. And someone is still looking for some tape.'

Again Kimmy's face fell. 'Tape?'

'When Clyde was beating me up, he kept asking, "Where's the tape?" And then today –'

'Wait a second.' Kimmy held up a hand. 'Clyde asked you that?'

'Yes.'

'And that's why he killed Cassandra? To find a videotape?'

'I think so, yeah. He was going nuts searching for it.'

Kimmy started biting her nails.

'Kimmy?'

But her old friend just stood and walked toward the cabinet in the corner.

'What's going on?' Olivia asked.

'I know why Clyde wanted the tape,' Kimmy said, her voice suddenly calm. She pulled open the cabinet door. 'And I know where it is.'

56

Matt led Loren to the Eager Beaver's darkened back booth. They sat down as ABC began to sing 'The Look of Love.' The room was dark. The strippers felt suddenly far away.

'You're not armed, are you?' Matt said.

'I didn't have time to get a weapon approval.'

'You're also here on your own.'

'So?'

Matt shrugged. 'If I wanted to, I could probably still knock you over and run.'

'I'm tougher than I look.'

'I don't doubt it. You were a tough kid.'

'You weren't.'

He nodded. 'So what do you know about my wife?'

'Why don't you start, Matt?'

'Because I've done all the stuff that shows trust so far,' he replied. 'You haven't.'

'Fair point.'

'So?'

Loren thought about it but not for long. There was no reason not to. She truly believed he was innocent and if she was wrong, the evidence would prove it. He wouldn't be able to talk his way out of it. Ex-cons don't have that luxury.

'I know your wife's real name is Candace Potter.'

She started talking. He did too. He interrupted with questions and follow-ups. When Loren reached the part about the Candace Potter autopsy, about the AIS woman, Matt sat up and his eyes widened.

'Say that again.'

'Max Darrow checked off the part about the victim having AIS.'

'Which you said is like being a hermaphrodite?'

'A little, yeah.'

He nodded. 'So that's how Darrow figured it out.'

'Figured out what?'

'That Candace Potter was alive. Look, my wife had a daughter when she was fifteen. The baby was put up for adoption.'

Loren started nodding. 'So somehow Darrow found that out.'

'Exactly.'

'And then he remembers the AIS from the autopsy. If Candace Potter was at one time pregnant –'

'Then it couldn't have been Candace Potter who was murdered,' Matt finished.

'Your wife is supposed to meet with her daughter here tonight?'

'At midnight, right.'

499

Loren nodded. 'That's why you made this deal with me. That one a.m. thing. So your wife would be able to keep her rendezvous with her daughter.'

'Right,' Matt said.

'Nice of you. To make that sacrifice.'

'Yeah, I'm a prince except . . .' Matt stopped. 'Oh, Christ, think about what we've been saying. It's all a setup. It has to be.'

'I'm not following.'

'Okay, let's say you're Max Darrow. Let's say you figure out that Candace Potter is still alive, that she ran off. How would you find her after all these years?'

'I don't know.'

'You'd try to draw her out, right?'

'Yeah, I guess.'

'And how? By forcing her to show herself. You might post something about her long-lost daughter being on death's door. You, if you're a cop, might be able to find out some details about the hospital, the town, the doctor. Maybe you even find out from the adopted daughter herself, I don't know.'

'Risky,' Loren said.

'Risky how?'

'What would make him think she'd still be looking up her old name like that?'

He thought about that. 'I'm not sure. But of course that's not all you do. You try to follow up on any old leads. You go back over the case step-by-step. But if she's out there, if she's got a computer like everyone else in the free world, maybe she's going to be curious and Google her old name. It's bound to happen, right?'

Loren frowned. So did Matt. The same thing kept troubling him.

'Those pictures on my camera phone,' he said.

'What about them?'

He was thinking about how to put it when the waitress popped up to their booth. 'Another drink?'

Matt took out his wallet. He plucked out a twenty-dollar bill and showed it to her. 'Do you know Kimmy Dale?'

She hesitated.

'I only want a yes or no,' Matt said. 'Twenty bucks.'

'Yes.'

He handed her the twenty and took out another.

'Is she here?'

'Just yes or no again?'

'Right.'

'No.'

He handed it to her. He took out three more. 'You get these if you tell me where she is.'

The waitress thought about it. Matt kept the money in sight.

'Kimmy might be home. I mean, it was weird. Her shift is supposed to run until eleven, but she just ran out an hour ago with some lady.'

Loren turned to him, but Matt did not blink. His face kept still. He took out another twenty. He also took out a photograph of Olivia. 'Was this the lady Kimmy left with?'

The waitress suddenly looked scared. She didn't answer. She didn't have to. Loren was already up and starting for the door. Matt dropped the dollars and followed her.

'What's up?' Matt said.

'Come on,' Loren called back. 'I already have Kimmy Dale's address.'

Kimmy put the videotape into the player. 'I should have known,' she said.

Olivia sat on the futon and waited.

'You remember that closet in the kitchen?' Kimmy asked.

'Yes.'

'Three, maybe four weeks after your murder, I bought this big vat of vegetable oil. I got on a stepladder to put it on the top shelf and behind the lip on top of the door, I saw this' – she pointed with her chin toward the screen – 'stuck up there with duct tape.'

'Have you watched it?'

'Yeah,' she said softly. 'I should have – I don't know – gotten rid of it. Given it to the police, something.'

'Why didn't you?'

Kimmy just shrugged.

'What's on it?'

She looked like she was about to explain, but then she gestured toward the screen. 'Watch.'

Olivia sat up. Kimmy paced, wringing her hands, not looking at the screen. For a few seconds there was nothing but static. Then it snapped to an all-too-familiar scene.

A bedroom.

It was filmed in black and white. The date and time were stamped in the corner. A man sat on the edge of a bed. She did not recognize him.

A male voice whispered, 'This is Mr. Alexander.'

Mr. Alexander – if that was his real name – started undressing. From stage right, a woman appeared and started to help him.

'Cassandra,' Olivia said.

Kimmy nodded.

Olivia frowned. 'Clyde was taping customers?'

'Yes,' Kimmy said. 'But with a twist.'

'What sort of twist?'

On the screen, both participants were naked. Cassandra was on top of the man now. Her back was arched. Her mouth was open. They could hear her purported cries of passion – they couldn't have sounded more fake if she'd used a cartoon voice.

'I think I've seen enough,' Olivia said.

'No,' Kimmy said, 'I don't think you have.'

Kimmy hit the fast-forward button. The onscreen activities became more hurried. Changing positions, quick shifts. It didn't take all that long. The man was done and dressed in fast-forward seconds. When he left the room, Kimmy let go of the button. The tape slowed back down to normal speed.

Cassandra moved closer to the camera. She smiled into the lens. Olivia felt her breath grow deep. 'Look at her, Kimmy. She was so young.'

Kimmy stopped pacing. She put a finger to her lips and then pointed it at the screen.

A man's voice came on. 'This is a souvenir for Mr. Alexander.'

Olivia made a face. Sounded like Clyde Rangor trying to disguise his voice.

'Did you have fun, Cassandra?'

'I had lots of fun,' Cassandra said in the flattest monotone. 'Mr. Alexander was just great.'

There was a brief pause. Cassandra licked her lips and glanced toward someone who was out of the shot, as if waiting for her cue. It came soon enough.

'How old are you, Cassandra?'

'I'm fifteen.'

'Are you sure?'

Cassandra nodded. Someone off camera handed her a sheet of paper. 'I just turned fifteen last week. Here's my birth certificate.' She put the document close to the lens. For a moment the picture was blurry, but then someone worked the focus. Cassandra held it up for nearly thirty seconds. Born at the Mercy Medical Center in Nampa, Idaho. Parents were named Mary and Sylvester. Dates were clearly visible.

'Mr. Alexander said he wanted someone fourteen,' Cassandra said, as if reading her lines for the first time, 'but then he said I'd be okay.'

The camera went back to static.

Olivia sat in silence. So did Kimmy. It took a while for the full weight of what Clyde Rangor had done to hit her.

'My God,' she said.

Kimmy nodded.

'Clyde didn't just blackmail them with prostitutes,' Olivia said. 'He set them up with underage girls. He had their birth certificates for proof. He even pretended that the johns were the ones who requested pubescent girls, but either way, even if you claim that you thought the girl was over eighteen, that's a serious crime. This guy, this Mr. Alexander, he didn't just risk being embarrassed or found out. He could be ruined. He could end up in jail.'

Kimmy nodded.

The static ended and another man appeared on the screen.

'This is Mr. Douglas,' the whispery voice said.

Olivia felt her blood go cold. 'Oh, no.'

'Candi?'

She moved closer to the screen. The man. The man on the bed. No question about it. Mr. Douglas was Adam Yates. Olivia watched transfixed. Cassandra entered the room again. She helped him undress. So that was it. That was why Clyde had gotten so desperate. He had taped an important federal officer. He probably didn't know that – not even Clyde Rangor would be that stupid – and when he tried to blackmail him, it had all gone wrong.

'You know him?' Kimmy said.

'Yeah,' Olivia said. 'We just met.'

The front door burst open. Olivia and Kimmy both spun toward the sound. Kimmy shouted, 'What the . . . ?'

Cal Dollinger closed the door behind him, pulled out his gun, and took aim.

57

Loren had rented a car.

Matt said, 'So how do you think it worked here? Darrow got the ball rolling?'

'It makes the most sense,' she agreed. 'Darrow somehow finds out about your wife having a daughter. He remembers the autopsy. Then he starts to figure out what really happened back then. He knows there was money involved. He hires some muscle to help out.'

'That would be Charles Talley?'

'Right, Talley.'

'And you think he found Olivia when she answered that post online?'

'Yes, but . . .' Loren stopped.

'What?'

'They found Emma Lemay first.'

'As Sister Mary Rose.'

'Yes.'

'How?'

'I don't know. Maybe she was trying to make amends. I mean, I got the whole story on her from the Mother Superior. Sister Mary Rose has lived a good and pious life since she changed IDs. Maybe, I don't know, maybe she saw the post too.'

'And tried to help?'

'Yes. And that might explain that six-minute phone call from St. Margaret's to your sister-in-law's house.'

'She was warning Olivia?'

'Maybe, I don't know. But they probably found Emma Lemay first. The medical examiner says they tortured her. Maybe they wanted money. Or maybe they wanted your wife's name. Whatever, Emma Lemay ends up dead. And when I try to find out her true identity, it sets off warning bells.'

'And this FBI guy. Yates. He hears them?'

'Yes. Or maybe he already knew about Lemay. Maybe he was using that as a cover to come out and get involved, I'm not sure.'

'And you think Yates is trying to cover something up?'

'I have a source who told me about this blackmail taping involving underage girls. He's not sure if they're real. But if they are, yeah, I think that somehow he's tied into all this. I think he took me off the case because I was getting too close. He's in Reno too right now.'

Matt faced front. 'How much longer?'

'Next block.'

The car had barely made the turn when Loren spotted Cal Dollinger near a

503

trailer. He was hunched down, looking through a window. She slammed on the brake. 'Damn.'

'What?'

'We need a weapon.'

'Why? What's wrong?'

'That's Yates's man. By the window.'

Dollinger stood up. They could see him reach into his jacket and pull out a gun. With a speed that defied his bulk, Dollinger moved to the door, pushed against it, and disappeared inside.

Matt did not hesitate.

'Wait, where are you going?'

He didn't look back, didn't break stride. He sprinted toward the house. He could see through the window into the trailer.

Olivia was there.

She stood up suddenly and put up her hands. Another woman – he assumed it was Kimmy Dale – was there too. She opened her mouth to scream. Dollinger was pointing the gun at them.

He fired.

Oh, no. . . .

Kimmy fell. Olivia dived from view. Matt did not let up. Dollinger stood not far from a window. Using all his momentum, realizing that time was past the point of essence, Matt leaped toward the glass. He tucked his chin and led with his forearms.

The glass shattered with surprising ease.

Matt got his legs under him. He landed and again there was no hesitation. Dollinger still had the gun. His mouth had dropped open in surprise. Matt did not want to lose that. He jumped straight at him.

It was like jumping against a cement block. Dollinger barely gave at all.

'Run!' Matt shouted.

Dollinger reacted now. He aimed his gun at Matt. Matt took hold of Dollinger's wrist with both hands. He pulled. So did Dollinger. Even though Matt was using two hands against Dollinger's one, Matt was losing the battle of strength. With his free hand, Dollinger hit Matt in the ribs with an uppercut. Matt felt his belly collapse, the air go out of him. He wanted to collapse and writhe on the floor.

But he wouldn't.

Olivia was here.

So he held on to the wrist with all he had.

Another fist slammed under his rib cage. Matt's eyes watered. He saw dark spots. He was losing consciousness, losing his grip.

A voice screamed, 'Freeze! Police! Drop your weapon!'

It was Loren Muse.

Dollinger let him go. Matt sank to the floor. But only for a second. He looked up at Dollinger. Dollinger had a funny look on his face. He glanced about the room.

Loren Muse was nowhere in sight.

Matt knew how this would go. Dollinger would wonder why she wasn't show- ing herself. He would remember that she had just flown over from Newark, that she was a county investigator, that the authorities would not let her travel with a gun.

He would realize that Loren didn't have a weapon. That she was bluffing.

Olivia was crawling toward Kimmy Dale. Matt looked over at her. Their eyes met. 'Go,' he mouthed. He looked back up at Dollinger.

Dollinger had put it together now.

He swung his aim back toward Olivia.

'No!' Matt shouted.

He bent his legs and pushed off as if they were two pistons. He knew something about real-life fights. He knew that the good big man almost always beats the good little man. But he didn't care about winning. He cared about saving his wife. He just needed to do enough so that Olivia could get free.

And Matt knew something else.

Even the biggest, strongest men have the same vulnerable spots as the rest of us.

Matt positioned his hand for a palm strike. He leaped up and smacked Dollinger in the heart of the groin. The big man made an oof noise and bent at the waist. He grabbed Matt on his way down. Matt tried to straighten. Dollinger was too big.

Vulnerable spots, he thought. Hit the vulnerable spots.

Matt reared back with his head. The skull landed on Dollinger's nose. Dollinger howled and stood up. Matt looked over at his wife.

What the . . . ?

Olivia had not run away. He couldn't believe it. She was still by Kimmy's side, working on her friend's leg, feverishly trying, he assumed, to stop the bleeding or something.

'Get out!' he shouted.

Dollinger had recovered. The gun was aimed at Matt now.

From the other end of the trailer Loren Muse let out a cry and pounced on Dollinger's back. She reached around for his face. The big man pulled back, his nose and mouth covered with blood. He threw Loren off like a bucking bronco. She landed hard against the wall. Matt jumped up.

Go for the vulnerable . . .

He tried to get Dollinger's eyes and missed. His hand slipped down. They ended up on the big man's throat.

Just like before.

Just like all those years ago, on a college campus in Massachusetts, with a boy named Stephen McGrath.

Matt didn't care.

He squeezed hard. He put his thumb on the hollow of the throat. And he squeezed some more.

Dollinger's eyes bulged. But his gun hand was free now. He raised his weapon toward Matt's head. Matt let go of the throat with one hand. He tried to deflect Dollinger's aim. The gun fired anyway. Something hot sliced into the flesh above Matt's hip.

His leg went slack. His hand dropped off Dollinger's neck.

Dollinger had the gun ready now. He looked into Matt's eyes and started to squeeze the trigger.

A shot rang out.

Dollinger's eyes bulged a little more. The bullet had hit his temple. The big man folded to the floor. Matt spun and looked at his wife.

In her hand she had a small pistol. Matt crawled over to her. They looked down. Kimmy Dale wasn't bleeding from her leg. She was bleeding from a spot just above the elbow.

'You remembered,' Kimmy said.

Olivia smiled.

Matt said, 'Remembered what?'

'Like I told you,' Olivia said, 'Kimmy always kept a gun in her boot. It just took me a few seconds to dig it out.'

58

Loren Muse sat across from Harris Grimes, the assistant director in charge who ran the FBI's Los Angeles field office. Grimes was one of the most powerful federal officers in the region, and he was not a happy man.

'You realize that Adam Yates is a friend of mine,' Grimes said.

'It's the third time you've told me,' Loren said.

They were using a room on the second floor of the Washoe Medical Center in Reno. Grimes narrowed his eyes and chewed on his lower lip. 'Are you being insubordinate, Muse?'

'I've told you what happened three times.'

'And you'll tell it again. Now.'

She did. There was a lot to cover. It took hours. The case wasn't over. There were still plenty of questions. Yates was missing. No one knew where he was. But Dollinger was dead. Loren was learning that he, too, had been well liked by his fellow agents.

Grimes stood and rubbed his chin. There were three other agents in the room, all with legal pads, all keeping their heads down and jotting away. They knew now. No one wanted to believe it, but the videotape of Yates and Cassandra spoke volumes. Grudgingly they were beginning to accept her theory. They just weren't liking it.

'You have any idea where Yates would have gone?' Grimes asked her.

'No.'

'He was last seen at our Reno office on Kietzke Lane maybe fifteen minutes before the incident at Ms. Dale's residence. He checked in with a special agent named Ted Stevens, who'd been told to trail Olivia Hunter when she arrived at the airport.'

'Right. You told me. Can I go now?'

Grimes turned his back and waved his hand. 'Get the hell out of my sight.'

She stood and walked downstairs to the emergency room on the first floor. Olivia Hunter sat by the ER receptionist.

'Hey,' Loren said.

'Hi.' Olivia managed to smile. 'I just came down to check on Kimmy.'

Olivia had suffered no real injuries. Kimmy Dale was finishing up at the other end of the corridor. Her arm was wrapped in a sling. The bullet had missed bone, but there was serious muscle and tissue damage. It would be painful and need hours of rehabilitation. But, alas, in this era of getting people out of the hospital pronto – six days after having his chest cut open Bill Clinton was reading in his backyard – they finished asking their questions and told Kimmy that she could go home but needed to 'stay in town.'

'Where's Matt?' Loren asked.

'He just came out of surgery,' Olivia said.

'Did it go okay?'

'The doctor said he'll be fine.'

The bullet from Dollinger's gun had grazed the neck of Matt's femur just below the hip joint. The doctors needed to put in a couple of bone screws. Fairly minor surgery, they said. He'd be up and out in two days.

'You should get some rest,' Olivia said.

'Can't,' Loren said. 'I'm too wired.'

'Yeah, me too. Why don't you sit with Matt in case he wakes up? I'm just going to get Kimmy settled and then I'll be right up.'

Loren took the elevator to the third floor. She sat next to Matt's bed. She thought about the case, about Adam Yates, about where he was and what he might do.

A few minutes later Matt's eyes blinked open. He looked up at her.

'Hey, hero,' Loren said.

Matt managed a smile. He turned his head to the right.

'Olivia?'

'She's downstairs with Kimmy.'

'Is Kimmy . . . ?'

'She's fine. Olivia's just helping her get settled.'

He closed his eyes. 'There's something I need you to do.'

'Why don't you rest?'

Matt shook his head. His voice was weak. 'I need you to get some phone records for me.'

'Now?'

'The camera phone,' he said. 'The picture. The video. It still doesn't add up. Why would Yates and Dollinger take those pictures?'

'They didn't. Darrow did.'

'Why . . .' He closed his eyes again. 'Why would he?'

Loren thought about that. Then Matt's eyes suddenly opened. 'What time is it?'

She checked her watch. 'Eleven thirty.'

'At night?'

'Of course at night.'

And then Loren remembered. The meeting at midnight. At the Eager Beaver. She quickly grabbed the phone and called down to the emergency room receptionist.

'This is Investigator Muse. I was down there a few moments ago with a woman named Olivia Hunter. She was waiting for a patient named Kimmy Dale.'

'Right,' the receptionist said, 'I saw you.'

'Are they still there?'

'Who, Miss Dale and Miss Hunter?'

'Yes.'

'No, they hurried out the same time you left.'

'Hurried out?'

'Into a taxi.'

Loren hung up. 'They're gone.'

'Give me the phone,' Matt said, still flat on his back. She nestled the phone next

508

to his ear. Matt gave her Olivia's cell number. The phone rang three times before he heard Olivia's voice.

'It's me,' he said.

'Are you okay?' Olivia asked.

'Where are you?'

'You know where.'

'You still think . . .'

'She called, Matt.'

'What?'

'She called Kimmy's cell. Or someone did. She said the meeting was still on, but no cops, no husbands, nobody. We're on our way over now.'

'Olivia, it has to be a setup. You know that.'

'I'll be fine.'

'Loren is on her way.'

'No. Please, Matt. I know what I'm doing. Please.'

And then Olivia hung up.

59

11:50 p.m.
The Eager Beaver
Reno, Nevada

When Olivia and Kimmy arrived, the fat man at the door pointed to Kimmy and said, 'You left early. You got hours to make up.'

Kimmy showed him her arm in a sling. 'I'm hurt.'

'What, you can't get naked with that?'

'You for real?'

'This.' He pointed to his face. 'This is me being real. Some guys get turned on by that kinda thing.'

'An arm in a cast?'

'Sure. Like the guys who get off on amputees.'

'I'm not an amputee.'

'Hey, guys get turned on by a strong wind, you know what I'm saying?' The fat man rubbed his hands together. 'I used to know a guy who got off on toe jam. Toe jam.'

'Nice.'

'So who's your friend?'

'Nobody.'

He shrugged. 'Some cop from New Jersey was asking about you.'

'I know. It's okay now.'

'I want you to go on. With that sling.'

Kimmy looked at Olivia. 'I might be better able to watch up there, you know. Like I won't be noticed.'

Olivia nodded. 'Up to you,' she said.

Kimmy disappeared into the back room. Olivia sat at a table. She did not see or notice the crowd. She did not look in the dancer's face for her daughter. There was a rushing in her head. Sadness, an overwhelming sadness, weighed her down.

Call it off, she thought. Walk away.

She was pregnant. Her husband was in the hospital. That was where her life was now. This was in the past. She should leave it there.

But she didn't do that.

Olivia thought again about how the abused always take the path of self-destruction. They simply could not stop themselves. They take it no matter what the consequences, no matter what the danger. Or maybe, as in her case, they take it for the opposite reason – because no matter how much life has tried to beat them down, they cannot let go of hope.

Wasn't there still a chance that tonight she'd be reunited with the baby she'd put up for adoption all those years ago?

The waitress came over to the table. 'Are you Candace Potter?'

There was no hesitation. 'Yes, I am.'

'I have a message for you.'

She handed Olivia a note and left. The message was short and simple:

Go to backroom B now. Wait ten minutes.

It felt like she was walking on stilts. Her head spun. Her stomach churned. She bumped into a man on the way and said, 'Excuse me,' and he said, 'Hey, baby, my pleasure.' The men with him yukked it up. Olivia kept walking. She found the back area. She found the door with the letter B on it, the same one she'd been in just a few hours ago.

She opened it and went inside. Her cell phone rang. She picked it up and said hello.

'Don't hang up.'

It was Matt.

'Are you at the club?'

'Yes.'

'Get out of there. I think I know what's going on –'

'Shh.'

'What?'

Olivia was crying now. 'I love you, Matt.'

'Olivia, whatever you're thinking, please, just –'

'I love you more than anything in the world.'

'Listen to me. Get out of –'

She closed the phone and turned the power off. She faced the door. Five minutes passed. She stayed standing, not moving, not swaying, not looking around. There was a knock on the door.

'Come in,' she said.

And the door opened.

60

Try as he might, Matt couldn't get out of bed.

'Go!' he told Loren.

She radioed the Reno Police Department and ran to her car. Loren was within two miles of the Eager Beaver when her cell phone sounded.

She picked it up and barked, 'Muse.'

'So are you still in Reno?'

It was Adam Yates. His voice was slurred.

'I am.'

'Are they all applauding your genius?'

'I'd say just the opposite.'

Yates chuckled. 'I was, alas, beloved.'

He had definitely been drinking. 'Tell me where you are, Adam.'

'I meant what I said. You know that, right?'

'Sure, Adam. I know.'

'I mean, about them threatening my family. I never said it was physical. But my wife. My kids. My job. That tape was like a big gun. A big gun they were pointing at us all, you know what I mean?'

'I do,' Loren said.

'I was working undercover, pretending to be a rich real estate dealer. So Clyde Rangor figured I was the perfect mark. I never knew the girl was underage. You need to believe that.'

'Where are you, Adam?'

He ignored her question. 'Someone called. Demanded a payoff in exchange for the tape. So Cal and me, we went to see Rangor. We leaned on him hard. Ah, who am I kidding? Cal did the leaning. He was a good man but he had a violent streak. He once beat a suspect to death. I saved his ass then. He saved my ass, I saved his. That's what makes a friend. He's dead now, isn't he?'

'Yes.'

'Damn.' He started to cry. 'Cal hurt Emma Lemay. Punched her hard in the kidney. That was his warning. We walk in and I think we're just going to talk and he starts off by spinning Lemay and pounding her back like a heavy bag. Rangor, it doesn't bother him. He beat that woman silly anyway. Better her than him, you know?'

Loren was nearly in the parking lot now.

'So Rangor pisses in his pants. Literally, I mean. He's so scared he runs to his cabinet to get the tape. Only it's gone. The girl, he says, the one in the video. Cassandra, her name is. He says she must have stolen it. He says he'll get it. Cal and me, we figure we got the fear of God in him now. He'll do what we say. Next thing we know, Rangor and Lemay and that Cassandra girl, they all disappear. Years pass. I still think about it. I think about it every day. And then we get that call from the NCIC. Lemay's body's been found. And it all comes back. Like I always knew it would.'

'Adam, it's not too late.'

'Yeah, it is.'

She pulled into the lot. 'You still have friends.'

'I know. I called them. That's why I'm calling you.'

'What?'

'Grimes is going to bury the tape.'

'What are you talking about?'

'If it gets out, it destroys my family. It'll destroy those other guys on the tape too. They were just being johns, you know.'

'You can't just bury the tape.'

'Nobody needs it anymore. Grimes and his guys will arrange it for me. They just need you to cooperate.'

And then she realized what he was about to do. Panic seized her.

'Wait, Adam, listen to me.'

'Cal and I will die in the line of fire.'

'Adam, don't. You have to listen.'

'Grimes will set it up that way.'

'Think about your kids –'

'I am. Our families will get full benefits.'

'My father, Adam.' Loren had tears on her cheeks now. 'He killed himself. Please, you don't know what this will do –'

But he wasn't listening. 'You just have to keep it to yourself, okay? You're a good investigator. One of the best. Please, for my kids.'

'Dammit, Adam, listen to me!'

'Good-bye, Loren.'

And then he hung up the phone.

Loren Muse put the car in park. She stepped outside, crying, shrieking at the skies, and in the distance, she was sure that she could hear the rumble of a gun blast.

61

The door to Backroom B opened. Olivia waited.

When Kimmy walked into the room, the two women just stared at each other. They both had tears in their eyes. Just like a few hours earlier.

But this was nothing like that.

'You knew,' Kimmy said.

Olivia shook her head. 'I thought.'

'How?'

'You acted like you didn't remember Max Darrow. He was one of your clients in the old days. But the main thing is, everyone figures Darrow put that post online. But he wouldn't have known that it'd draw me out. Only a good friend, my best friend, would know I'd still be checking up on my child.'

Kimmy stepped into the room. 'You just left me, Candi.'

'I know.'

'We were supposed to go together. I told you my dreams. You told me yours. We always helped each other out, remember?'

Olivia nodded.

'You promised me.'

'I know I did.'

Kimmy shook her head. 'All these years, I thought you were dead. I buried you, did you know that? I paid for your funeral. I mourned. I cried for months. I did things to Max for free – anything he wanted – just to make sure he tried to find your killer.'

'You have to understand. I couldn't tell. Emma and I –'

'You what?' Kimmy shouted. The sound echoed in the stillness. 'You made a promise?'

Olivia said nothing.

'I died when you died. Do you know that? The dreams. The hope about getting out of this life. It all died when you did. I lost everything. For all those years.'

'How . . . ?'

'. . . did I find out you were alive?'

Olivia nodded.

'Two days after that girl comes to my door, Max comes over. He said that he sent her – that she wasn't really your daughter. He'd just sent her to test me.'

Olivia tried to make sense of that. 'Test you?'

'Yeah. He knew we were close. He figures I know where you are. So he sets me up. He sends me some girl pretending to be your long-lost daughter. Then he watches me, sees if I'm going to call you or something. But all I do is, I go to your grave site and cry.'

'I'm so sorry, Kimmy.'

'Imagine it, okay? Imagine when Max comes to my house and shows me the autopsy. He tells me the dead girl had some kind of freak condition and couldn't possibly have kids. He tells me you aren't dead and you know what I did? I just shook my head. I didn't believe him. I mean, how could I? Candi would never do that to me, I tell him. She'd never just leave me behind like that. But Max shows me the pictures of the dead girl. It's Cassandra. I start to see the truth now. I start putting it together.'

'And you wanted revenge,' Olivia said.

'Yes. I mean . . . I did.' Kimmy shook her head. 'But it all got so crazy, you know?'

'You were the one who helped Darrow find me. You had the idea about posting on the adoption Web site. You knew I'd bite.'

'Yes.'

'So you set up that meet. At the motel.'

'Not just me. If it was just me . . .' Kimmy stopped and just stared. 'I was just so hurt, you know.'

Olivia nodded, said nothing.

'So, yeah, I wanted payback. And I wanted a big payday too. I was the one getting the new life this time. It was finally my turn. But once Max and Chally flew out to Jersey' – Kimmy shut her eyes and shook her head as if she might jar something out – 'it all just spun out of control.'

'You were trying to hurt me,' Olivia said.

Kimmy nodded.

'So first, you went after my marriage with that call to my husband's phone.'

'Max came up with that, actually. He was going to use his own camera phone, but then he realized it'd work even better if he could use yours. See, if something went wrong, Chally would be the guy on the camera phone. He'd be holding the bag. But first he needed Chally's help.'

'With Emma Lemay.'

'Right. Chally was dumb muscle. He and Max flew up to get Emma to talk. But she wouldn't give you up. No matter what they did to her. So they kept pushing. And they just pushed too far.'

Olivia closed her eyes. 'So this' – she gestured around the room – 'us being here tonight, this was to be your grand finale, right, Kimmy? You take my money. You break my heart by showing me that there is no daughter, no child. And then what?'

Kimmy said nothing for several seconds. 'I don't know.'

'Yeah, Kimmy, you do.'

She shook her head, but there was nothing behind it.

'Darrow and Chally wouldn't have let me stay alive,' Olivia said.

'Darrow,' Kimmy said softly, 'had nothing to say about it.'

'Because you killed him?'

'Yes.' She smiled. 'Do you know how many times that son of a bitch had his pants down in a car with me?'

'And that's why you killed him?'

'No.'

'Then why?'

'I needed to stop this,' Kimmy said. 'And I needed to strike first.'

'You thought he'd kill you?'

'For this kind of money, Max Darrow would kill his own mother. Yeah, I was hurt when I found out – no, it was more like . . . it was more like I was in shock. But Max, I thought he was just in this with me. But then he started running his own game too. It had to stop.'

'What do you mean?'

'Just . . .' Her whole persona emanated exhaustion. 'Just forget it,' Kimmy said. 'All that matters is, Max didn't like witnesses. I was an unreliable whore. You think he'd risk that?'

'And Charles Talley?'

'Your husband tracked him down. They got into that fight and then he ran away. Chally called me. See, I was staying on the floor below you. He was in a panic, all worried about the cops coming. He was on parole. One more offense and he was in for life. He'd do anything to avoid that. So I told him to wait in the stairwell.'

'You set it up to look like Matt killed him.'

'That had been what Max wanted all along – to set up both Chally and your husband.' She shrugged. 'I figured, might as well stick with the plan.'

Olivia looked at her old friend. She stepped closer. 'I thought about you,' she said. 'You know that.'

'I know,' Kimmy said. 'But that wasn't enough.'

'I was afraid. Emma said if they found out what we'd done, they'd hurt us all. They'd look for the tape again. We didn't have it. They'd kill us.'

'Look at me,' Kimmy said.

'I am.'

She pulled out a gun. 'Look at what I've become.'

'Kimmy?'

'What?'

'I didn't plan it like this,' Olivia said. 'I thought I would die.'

'I know that now.'

'And I'm pregnant.'

Kimmy nodded. 'I know that too.' The gun in her hand shook.

Olivia took another step closer. 'You won't kill the baby.'

Kimmy's face fell. Her voice was barely audible. 'It was the tape.'

'What was, Kimmy?' And then Olivia saw it. 'Oh. Oh, no . . . .'

'That damn tape,' Kimmy said, tears spilling down her face. 'That's what got Cassandra killed. That's what started it all.'

'Oh, God.' Olivia swallowed. 'Cassandra wasn't the one who stole it from Clyde,' she said. 'You were.'

'For us, Candi. Don't you see?' she pleaded. 'That tape was our ticket out. We were going to get a big stash of cash. We'd run away, you and me – just like we talked about. It'd be our turn, you know? And then I come home and someone's murdered you . . . .'

'All that time, all these years, you . . .' Olivia felt her heart break anew. 'You blamed yourself for my death.'

Kimmy managed a nod.

'I'm so sorry, Kimmy.'

'It hurt so bad when I found out you were alive. You understand? I loved you so much.'

Olivia did understand. You grieve, not just for the dead, but for yourself, for what might have been. You think your best friend, the one person you could dream with . . . you think she died because of you. You live with that guilt for ten years and then one day, you learn it was all a lie. . . .

'We can make it okay,' Olivia said.

Kimmy straightened up. 'Look at me.'

'I want to help.'

There was a hard rap on the door. 'Open up! Police!'

'I killed two men,' Kimmy said to her. Then she smiled – a beatific smile that brought Olivia back. 'Look at my life. It's my turn, remember? My turn to escape.'

'Please, Kimmy . . .'

But Kimmy pointed the gun to the floor and fired. There was a moment of panic and then the door burst open. Kimmy spun toward the door and aimed her gun. Olivia screamed, 'No!'

Gun blasts followed. Kimmy spun one more time, like a marionette, and then she dropped to the floor. Olivia fell to her knees and cupped her friend's head. She lowered her lips to Kimmy's ear.

'Don't . . . ,' Olivia begged.

But now, at long last, it was Kimmy's turn.

62

Two days later, Loren Muse was home in her garden apartment. She was making a ham and cheese sandwich. She grabbed two slices of bread and put them on her plate. Her mother sat on the couch in the next room, watching Entertainment Tonight. Loren heard the familiar theme music. She dug into the mayonnaise and began spreading it on the bread when she started to cry.

Loren's sobs were silent. She waited until they passed, until she could talk again.

'Mom.'

'I'm watching my program.'

Loren moved behind her mother. Carmen was munching down a bag of Fritos. Her swollen feet were propped up with a pillow on the coffee table. Loren smelled the cigarette smoke, listened to her mother's raspy breath.

Adam Yates had killed himself. Grimes would not be able to cover it up. The two girls, Ella and Anne, and the boy, Sam, the one Adam had held in the hospital to ward off death – they would know the truth. Not about the videotape. Despite Adam Yates's fear, those images would not be what haunted his children late at night.

'I always blamed you,' Loren said.

No reply. The only sound came from the television.

'Mom?'

'I heard you.'

'This man I just met. He killed himself. He had three kids.'

Carmen finally turned around.

'See, the reason I blamed you was because otherwise –' She stopped, caught her breath.

'I know,' Carmen said softly.

'How come . . .' Loren said, her voice hitching, the tears flowing freely. Her face began to crumble. 'How come Daddy didn't love me enough to want to live?'

'Oh, honey.'

'You were his wife. He could have left you. But I was his daughter.'

'He loved you so much.'

'But not enough to want to live.'

'It's not like that,' Carmen said. 'He was in so much pain. No one could save him. You were the best thing in his life.'

'You.' Loren wiped her face with her sleeve. 'You let me blame you.'

Carmen said nothing.

'You were trying to protect me.'

'You needed to find blame,' her mother said.

'So all these years . . . you took the hit.'

She thought about Adam Yates, about how much he'd loved his children, about how that hadn't been enough either. She wiped her eyes.

'I should call them,' Loren said.

'Who?'

'His children.'

Carmen nodded and spread out her hands. 'Tomorrow, okay? Right now come here. Come sit with me on the couch here.'

Loren sat on the couch. Her mother scooted over.

'It's okay,' Carmen said.

She threw the afghan over Loren. A commercial came on. Loren leaned on her mother's shoulder. She could smell the stale cigarettes, but that was comforting now. Carmen stroked her daughter's hair. Loren closed her eyes. A few seconds later, her mother began to flick the remote.

'Nothing good on,' Carmen said.

With her eyes still closed, Loren smiled and moved in even closer.

Matt and Olivia flew home that same day. Matt had a cane. He limped, but that wouldn't last much longer. When they stepped off the plane, Matt said, 'I think I should go alone.'

'No,' Olivia said. 'We do this together.'

He did not argue.

They took the same Westport exit, pulled down the same street. There were two cars in the driveway this morning. Matt looked at the basketball hoop. There was no sign of Stephen McGrath. Not today.

They headed to the door together. Olivia held his hand. He rang the bell. A minute passed. Then Clark McGrath opened the door.

'What the hell are you doing here?'

Behind him, Sonya McGrath said, 'Who is it, Clark?'

Sonya pulled up short when she saw who it was. 'Matt?'

'I squeezed too hard,' Matt said.

The grounds were hushed. There was no wind, no cars driving by, no pedestrians. It was just four people and maybe one ghost.

'I could have let go. I was so scared. And I thought Stephen was a part of it. And when we landed, I don't know anymore. I could have done better. I held on too long. I know that now. I can't tell you how sorry I am.'

Clark McGrath bit down, his face reddening. 'You think that makes it all okay?'

'No,' Matt said. 'I know it doesn't. My wife is pregnant now. So I understand better. But it has to end, right here and right now.'

Sonya said, 'What are you talking about, Matt?'

He held up a sheet of paper.

'What is that?' Sonya asked.

'Phone records.'

When Matt first woke up in the hospital, he had asked Loren to get these for him. He had maybe an inkling of a suspicion – no more than that. But something about Kimmy's revenge scheme . . . it seemed like something she could never quite pull off on her own. It seemed too focused, too anxious to destroy not only Olivia . . .

. . . but Matt as well.

'These phone records belong to a man named Max Darrow who lived in Reno, Nevada,' Matt said. 'He called your husband's line eight times in the past week.'

'I don't understand,' Sonya said. She turned to her husband. 'Clark?'

But Clark closed his eyes.

'Max Darrow was a police officer,' Matt said. 'Once he found out who Olivia was, he would have investigated her. He would have learned that her husband was a notorious ex-con. He got in contact with you. I don't know how much you paid him, Mr. McGrath, but it just made so much sense. Kill two birds with one stone. Like Darrow's partner told my wife, he was playing his own game. With you.'

Sonya said, 'Clark?'

'He should be in prison,' Clark spat at her. 'Not having lunch with you.'

'What did you do, Clark?'

Matt stepped closer. 'This is over now, Mr. McGrath. I'm going to apologize one more time for what happened. I know you won't accept it. I understand that. I'm very sorry about Stephen. But here's something I think you'll understand.'

Matt took one more step. The two men were almost nose to nose.

'If you come near my family again,' Matt said, 'I will kill you.'

Matt walked away. Olivia stayed for another second. She looked first at Clark McGrath and then at Sonya, as if hammering home her husband's words. Then she turned away and took her husband's hand and never looked back.

63

Matt drove away from the McGraths'. For a long time they sat in silence. Damien Rice's 'O' was on the car radio. Olivia leaned forward and flipped it off.

'This feels so weird,' she said.

'I know.'

'We just, what, pick up like nothing happened?'

Matt shook his head. 'I don't think so.'

'We start again?'

Matt shook his head. 'I don't think so.'

'Well, as long as we've got that cleared up.'

He smiled. 'You know something.'

'What?'

'We'll be fine.'

'I won't settle for fine.'

'Neither will I.'

'We will be,' Olivia said, 'spectacular.'

They arrived at Marsha's house. She ran out to greet them, threw her arms around them both. Paul and Ethan followed. Kyra stayed by the door, her arms folded.

'My God,' Marsha said, 'what on earth happened to you two?'

'We have a lot to tell you.'

'Your leg . . .'

Matt waved her off. 'It's fine.'

'The cane is cool, Uncle Matt,' Paul said.

'Yeah, way cool,' chimed in Ethan.

They approached the door where Kyra was standing. Matt remembered how she had helped him escape from the backyard. 'Hey, thanks for that scream.'

She blushed. 'You're welcome.'

Kyra took the boys into the yard. Matt and Olivia began to explain. Marsha listened closely. They told her everything. They did not hold back. She seemed grateful. When they were done, Marsha said, 'Let me make you both lunch.'

'You don't have to –'

'Sit.'

They did. Olivia looked off. Matt could see that there was still a giant hole.

'I already called Cingle,' he said.

'Thank you.'

'We'll find your child.'

Olivia nodded, but she didn't believe it anymore. 'I want to visit Emma's grave. Pay my last respects.'

'I understand.'

'I can't believe she ended up so close to us.'

'What do you mean?'

'That was part of our pact. We knew each other's new identities, of course. But we never communicated. I thought she was still at the parish in Oregon.'

Matt felt the tingle start in his spine. He sat up.

Olivia said, 'What's the matter?'

'You didn't know she was at St. Margaret's?'

'No.'

'But she called you.'

'What?'

'As Sister Mary Rose. There were phone records. She called you.'

Olivia shrugged. 'She could have found out where I was, I guess,' she said. 'She knew my name. Maybe she tried to reach me or warn me.'

Matt shook his head. 'Six minutes.'

'What?'

'The call lasted six minutes. And she didn't call our house. She called here.'

'I don't understand.'

And then another voice said, 'She was calling me.'

They both turned. Kyra stepped into the room. Marsha stood behind her.

Kyra said, 'I've been wondering how to tell you.'

Matt and Olivia stayed still as a stone.

'You didn't break the pact, Olivia,' Kyra said. 'Sister Mary Rose did.'

'I don't understand,' Olivia said.

'See, I always knew I was adopted,' Kyra said.

Olivia put her hand to her mouth. 'Oh, my God . . .'

'And once I started looking into it, I found out pretty fast that my birth mother had been murdered.'

A sound escaped Olivia's mouth. Matt sat stunned.

Olivia, he thought. She was from Idaho. And Kyra . . . she lived in one of those Midwestern 'I' states. . . .

'But I wanted to learn more about it. So I tracked down the policeman who investigated the death.'

'Max Darrow,' Matt said.

Kyra nodded. 'I told him who I was. He seemed to genuinely want to help. He took all the information – where I was born, the doctor, all that. He gave me Kimmy Dale's address. I visited her.'

'Wait,' Matt said, 'I thought Kimmy said –'

Kyra looked at him, but Matt stopped himself. The answer was obvious. Darrow had been controlling things again by keeping Kimmy in the dark. Why let her know that there really was a daughter in the picture? Maybe Kimmy, already emotionally unhinged, would swing the other way if she knew that the girl who visited her really was Candi's flesh and blood.

'I'm sorry,' Matt said. 'Go on.'

Kyra slowly turned back to Olivia. 'So I visited Kimmy's trailer. She was so nice. And talking to her just made me want to find out more about you. I wanted to . . . I know how this will sound, but I wanted to find your killer. So I kept digging. I kept asking around. And then I got a call from Sister Mary Rose.'

'How . . . ?'

'She was trying to help some of her old girls, I think. Make amends. She heard what I was up to. So she called me.'

'She told you I was still alive?'

'Yes. I mean, it was a total shock. I thought you'd been murdered. And then Sister Mary Rose tells me if I do what she says, I might be able to find you. But we had to play it safe, she said. I didn't want to put you in danger or anything. I just wanted . . . I just wanted a chance to get to know you.'

Matt looked at Marsha. 'You knew?'

'Not until yesterday. Kyra told me.'

'How did you happen to live here?'

'That was part luck,' Kyra said. 'I wanted to find a way to get close to you. Sister Mary Rose was going to try to get me hired at DataBetter. But then we heard Marsha needed a live-in helper. So Sister Mary Rose called someone at St. Philomena's. She gave them my name.'

Matt remembered now that Marsha had met Kyra through her church. A nun would have that kind of pull – who would question that kind of recommendation?

'I wanted to tell you,' Kyra said, her eyes only on Olivia. 'I was just looking for the right time. But then Sister Mary Rose called. Like you said. Three weeks ago. She said it was still too soon – that I shouldn't say anything until she contacted me again. I was scared, but I trusted her. So I listened. I didn't even know she'd been killed. And then the other night, when you both came here so late – I was going to tell you anyway. That's why I came back in from the garage. But Matt was running out.'

Olivia stood, opened her mouth, closed it, tried again. 'So you . . . you're my . . . ?'

'Daughter. Yes.'

Olivia took a tentative step toward Kyra. She reached out with one hand. Then, thinking better of it, she dropped it back to her side.

'Are you okay, Kyra?' Olivia asked.

Kyra smiled, a smile so heartbreakingly close to her mother's Matt wondered how he'd missed it before. 'I'm fine,' she said.

'Are you happy?'

'I am, yes.'

Olivia said nothing. Kyra took another step.

'I'm fine, really.'

And then Olivia started to cry.

Matt looked away. This wasn't about him. He heard the sobs and the shushing sounds of two people trying to comfort each other. He thought about the miles, the pain, the prison, the abuse, the years, and what Olivia had said about this life, this simple life, being worth fighting for.

Epilogue

Your name is Matt Hunter.

A year has passed.

Lance Banner has apologized to you. For several months Lance remains wary, but then one day, at a neighborhood barbecue, he asks you to be his assistant basketball coach. Your nephew, Paul, Lance reminds you with a slap on the back, is on the team too. So what do you say?

You say yes.

You bought the house in Livingston, after all. You work out of it now, consulting on legal matters for Carter Sturgis. Ike Kier is by far your biggest client. He pays you well.

All charges against Cingle Shaker were dropped. Cingle has opened her own private investigation agency called Cingler Service. Ike Kier and Carter Sturgis throw all the business they can her way. She has three investigators working for her now.

Your sister-in-law, Marsha, is now serious with a man named Ed Essey. Ed works in manufacturing. You really don't understand what he does. They plan on marrying soon. He seems nice, this Ed guy. You try to like him, but you can't. He loves Marsha though. He will take care of her. He will probably be the only father Paul and Ethan will remember. They'll be too young to remember Bernie. Maybe that's how it should be, but it kills you. You will always try to be a presence in their lives, but you will become simply an uncle. Paul and Ethan will run to Ed first.

Last time you were in the house, you looked for the picture of Bernie on the refrigerator. It was still there, but it's buried under more recent photographs and report cards and artwork.

You never hear from Sonya or Clark McGrath again.

Their son, Stephen, still visits you sometimes. Not as much as he used to. And sometimes you're even glad to see him.

After you close on the new house, Loren Muse comes over. The two of you sit in the backyard with Corona beers.

'Back in Livingston,' she says.

'Yep.'

'Happy?'

'Towns don't make you happy, Loren.'

She nods.

There is still something hanging over your head. 'What's going to happen to Olivia?' you ask.

Loren reaches into her pocket and pulls out an envelope. 'Nothing.'

'What's that?'

'A letter from Sister Mary Rose née Emma Lemay. Mother Katherine gave it to me.'

You sit up. She hands it to you. You start to read it.

'Emma Lemay put it all on herself,' Loren tells you. 'She and she alone killed Clyde Rangor. She and she alone hid his body. She and she alone lied to the authorities about the identity of the murder victim. She claimed Candace Potter didn't know anything about it. There's more, but that's the gist.'

'You think that will wash?'

Loren shrugs. 'Who's to say otherwise?'

'Thank you,' you say.

Loren nods. She puts down her beer and sits up. 'Now, you want to tell me about those phone records, Matt?'

'No.'

'You think I don't know who Darrow spoke to in Westport, Connecticut.'

'Doesn't matter. You can't prove anything.'

'You don't know that. McGrath probably sent him money. There could be a trail.'

'Let it go, Loren.'

'Wanting revenge is not a defense.'

'Let it go.'

She picks the beer back up. 'I don't need your approval.'

'True.'

Loren looks off. 'If Kyra had just told Olivia the truth in the beginning –'

'They'd probably all be dead.'

'What makes you say that?'

'Emma Lemay's phone call. She told Kyra to stay silent. And I think she had a good reason.'

'That being?'

'I think Emma – or Sister Mary Rose – knew that they were getting close.'

'You saying Lemay took the hit for all of them?'

You shrug. You wonder how they found Lemay and Lemay alone. You wonder why Lemay, if she suspected something, didn't run. You wonder how she stood up to their torture and never gave Olivia away. Maybe Lemay figured one last sacrifice would end it. She wouldn't have known they'd post something about the adoption. She probably figured that she was the only link. And if that link was permanently broken – especially by force – there'd be no way to find Olivia.

But you'll never know for sure.

Loren looks off again. 'Back in Livingston,' she says.

You both shake your head. You both sip your beers.

Over the course of the year Loren visits every once in a while. If the weather is cooperating, you two sit outside.

The sun is high on that day a year later. You and Loren are sprawled out in lawn chairs. You both have Sol beers. Loren tells you that they're better than Coronas.

You take a sip and agree.

As always, Loren looks around and shakes her head and says her usual refrain: 'Back in Livingston.'

You are in your backyard. Your wife Olivia is there, planting a flower bed. Your son Benjamin is on a mat next to her. Ben is three months old. He is making a happy cooing noise. You can hear it all the way across the yard. Kyra is in the garden too, helping her mother. She has been living with you for a year now. She plans on staying until she graduates.

So you, Matt Hunter, look at them. All three of them. Olivia feels your eyes on her. She looks up and smiles. So does Kyra. Your son makes another cooing noise.

You feel the lightness in your chest.

'Yeah,' you say to Loren with a silly grin on your face. 'Back in Livingston.'

Acknowledgments

Once again, a nod of gratitude to Carole Baron, Mitch Hoffman, Lisa Johnson, Kara Welsh, and all at Dutton, NAL, and Penguin Group USA; Jon Wood, Malcolm Edwards, Susan Lamb, Jane Wood, Juliet Ewers, Emma Noble, and the gang at Orion; Aaron Priest and Lisa Erbach Vance for all the usual stuff.

A special thanks to Senator Harry Reid of Nevada. He constantly shows me the beauty of his state and her inhabitants, even if, for the sake of drama, I end up putting my own spin on them.

The author also wishes to thank the following for their technical expertise:

- Christopher J. Christie, United States Attorney for the state of New Jersey;
- Paula T. Dow, Essex County (NJ) Prosecutor;
- Louie F. Allen, Chief of Investigators, Essex County (NJ) Prosecutor's Office;
- Carolyn Murray, First Assistant Essex County (NJ) Prosecutor;
- Elkan Abramowitz, attorney extraordinaire;
- David A. Gold, MD, surgeon extraordinaire;
- Linda Fairstein, lotsa-things extraordinaire;
- Anne Armstrong-Coben, MD, Medical Director of Covenant House Newark and just plain extraordinaire;
- And for the third straight book (and final time), Steven Z. Miller, MD, Director of Pediatric Emergency Medicine, Children's Hospital of New York-Presbyterian. You taught me about much more than medicine, my friend. I will miss you always.

Promise Me

For Charlotte, Ben, Will and Eve.
You're a handful, but you will always be my world.

1

The missing girl – there had been unceasing news reports, always flashing to that achingly ordinary school portrait of the vanished teen, you know the one, with the rainbow-swirl background, the girl's hair too straight, her smile too self-conscious, then a quick cut to the worried parents on the front lawn, micro-phones surrounding them, Mom silently tearful, Dad reading a statement with quivering lip – that girl, that missing girl, had just walked past Edna Skylar.

Edna froze.

Stanley, her husband, took two more steps before realizing that his wife was no longer at his side. He turned around. 'Edna?'

They stood near the corner of Twenty-first Street and Eighth Avenue in New York City. Street traffic was light this Saturday morning. Foot traffic was heavy. The missing girl had been headed uptown.

Stanley gave a world-weary sigh. 'What now?'

'Shh.'

She needed to think. That high school portrait of the girl, the one with the rainbow-swirl background . . . Edna closed her eyes. She needed to conjure up the image in her head. Compare and contrast.

In the photograph, the missing girl had long, mousy-brown hair. The woman who'd just walked by – woman, not girl, because the one who'd just walked by seemed older, but maybe the picture was old too – was a redhead with a shorter, wavy cut. The girl in the photograph did not wear glasses. The one who was head-ing north up Eighth Avenue had on a fashionable pair with dark, rectangular frames. Her clothes and makeup were both more – for a lack of a better word – adult.

Studying faces was more than a hobby with Edna. She was sixty-three years old, one of the few female physicians in her age group who specialized in the field of genetics. Faces were her life. Part of her brain was always working, even when far away from her office. She couldn't help it – Dr. Edna Skylar studied faces. Her friends and family were used to the probing stare, but strangers and new acquain-tances found it disconcerting.

So that was what Edna had been doing. Strolling down the street. Ignoring, as she often did, the sights and sounds. Lost in her own personal bliss of studying the faces of passersby. Noting cheek structure and mandibular depth, inter-eye distance and ear height, jaw contours and orbital spacing. And that was why, despite the new hair color and style, despite the fashionable glasses and adult makeup and clothing, Edna had recognized the missing girl.

'She was walking with a man.'

'What?'

Edna hadn't realized that she'd spoken out loud.

'The girl.'

Stanley frowned. 'What are you talking about, Edna?'

That picture. That achingly ordinary school portrait. You've seen it a million times. You see it in a yearbook and the emotions start to churn. In one fell swoop, you see her past, you see her future. You feel the joy of youth, you feel the pain of growing up. You can see her potential there. You feel the pang of nostalgia. You see her years rush by, college maybe, marriage, kids, all that.

But when that same photograph is flashed on your evening news, it skewers your heart with terror. You look at that face, at that tentative smile, at the droopy hair and slumped shoulders, and your mind goes to dark places it shouldn't.

How long had Katie – that was the name, Katie – how long had she been missing?

Edna tried to remember. A month probably. Maybe six weeks. The story had only played locally and not for all that long. There were those who believed that she was a runaway. Katie Rochester had turned eighteen a few days before the disappearance – that made her an adult and thus lowered the priority a great deal. There was supposed trouble at home, especially with her strict albeit quivering-lipped father.

Maybe Edna had been mistaken. Maybe it wasn't her.

One way to find out.

'Hurry,' Edna said to Stanley.

'What? Where are we going?'

There was no time to reply. The girl was probably a block ahead by now. Stanley would follow. Stanley Rickenback, an ob-gyn, was Edna's second husband. Her first had been a whirlwind, a larger-than-life figure too handsome and too passionate and, oh yeah, an absolute ass. That probably wasn't fair, but so what? The idea of marrying a doctor – this was forty years ago – had been a fun novelty for Husband One. The reality, however, had not sat as well with him. He had figured that Edna would outgrow the doc phase once they had children. Edna didn't – just the opposite, in fact. The truth was – a truth that had not escaped her children – Edna loved doctoring more than motherhood.

She rushed ahead. The sidewalks were crowded. She moved into the street, staying close to the curb, and sped up. Stanley tried to follow. 'Edna?'

'Just stay with me.'

He caught up. 'What are we doing?'

Edna's eyes searched for the red hair.

There. Up ahead on the left.

She needed to get a closer look. Edna broke into a full-fledged sprint now, a strange sight in most places, a nicely dressed woman in her mid-sixties sprinting down the street, but this was Manhattan. It barely registered a second glance.

She circled in front of the woman, trying not to be too obvious, ducking behind taller people, and when she was in the right place, Edna spun around. The possible-Katie was walking toward her. Their eyes met for the briefest of moments, and Edna knew.

It was her.

Katie Rochester was with a dark-haired man, probably in his early thirties. They were holding hands. She did not seem too distressed. She seemed, in fact, up until the point where their eyes met anyway, pretty content. Of course that might not mean anything. Elizabeth Smart, that young girl who'd been kid-napped out in Utah, had been out in the open with her kidnapper and never tried to signal for help. Maybe something similar was playing here.

Edna wasn't buying it.

The redheaded possible-Katie whispered something to the dark-haired man. They picked up their pace. Edna saw them veer right and down the subway stairs. The sign read c and e trains. Stanley caught up to Edna. He was about to say something, but he saw the look on her face and kept still.

'Come on,' she said.

They hurried around the front and started down the stairs. The missing woman and the dark-haired man were already through the turnstile. Edna started toward it.

'Damn it.'

'What?'

'I don't have a MetroCard.'

'I do,' Stanley said.

'Let me have it. Hurry.'

Stanley plucked the card from his wallet and handed it to her. She scanned it, moved through the turnstile, handed it back to him. She didn't wait. They'd gone down the stairs to the right. She started that way. She heard the roar of an incoming train and hurried her steps.

The brakes were squeaking to a halt. The subway doors slid open. Edna's heart beat wildly in her chest. She looked left and right, searching for the red hair.

Nothing.

Where was that girl?

'Edna?' It was Stanley. He had caught up to her.

Edna said nothing. She stood on the platform, but there was no sign of Katie Rochester. And even if there was, what then? What should Edna do here? Does she hop on the train and follow them? To where? And then what? Find the apartment or house and then call the police. . . .

Someone tapped her shoulder.

Edna turned. It was the missing girl.

For a long time after this, Edna would wonder what she saw in the girl's expression. Was there a pleading look? A desperation? A calmness? Joy, even? Resolution? All of them.

They just stood and stared at each other for a moment. The bustling crowd, the indecipherable static on the speaker, the swoosh of the train – it all disappeared, leaving just the two of them.

'Please,' the missing girl said, her voice a whisper. 'You can't tell anybody you saw me.'

The girl stepped onto the train then. Edna felt a chill. The doors slid closed. Edna wanted to do something, do anything, but she couldn't move. Her gaze remained locked on the girl's.

'Please,' the girl mouthed through the glass.

And then the train disappeared into the dark.

2

There were two teenage girls in Myron's basement. That was how it began. Later, when Myron looked back on all the loss and heartbreak, this first series of what-ifs would rise up and haunt him anew. What if he hadn't needed ice. What if he'd opened his basement door a minute earlier or a minute later. What if the two teenage girls – what were they doing alone in his basement in the first place? – had spoken in whispers so that he hadn't overheard them.

What if he had just minded his own business.

From the top of the stairs, Myron heard the girls giggling. He stopped. For a moment he considered closing the door and leaving them alone. His small soiree was low on ice, not out of it. He could come back.

But before he could turn away, one of the girls' voices wafted smoke-like up the stairwell. 'So you went with Randy?'

The other: 'Oh my God, we were like so wasted.'

'From beer?'

'Beer and shots, yeah.'

'How did you get home?'

'Randy drove.'

At the top of the stairs, Myron stiffened.

'But you said – '

'Shh.' Then: 'Hello? Is someone there?'

Caught.

Myron took the stairs in a trot, whistling as he went. Mr. Casual. The two girls were sitting in what used to be Myron's bedroom. The basement had been 'finished' in 1975 and looked it. Myron's father, who was currently lollygagging with Mom in some condo near Boca Raton, had been big on two-sided tape. The adhesive wood paneling, a look that aged about as well as the Betamax, had started to give. In some spots the concrete walls were now visible and noticeably flaking. The floor tiles, fastened down with something akin to Elmer's Glue, were buckling. They crunched beetle-like when you stepped on them.

The two girls – one Myron had known her whole life, the other he had just met today – looked up at him with wide eyes. For a moment no one spoke. He gave them a little wave.

'Hey, girls.'

Myron Bolitar prided himself on big opening lines.

The girls were both high school seniors, both pretty in that coltish way. The one sitting on the corner of his old bed – the one he met for the first time an hour ago – was named Erin. Myron had started dating Erin's mother, a widow and freelance magazine writer named Ali Wilder, two months ago. This party, here at the house Myron had grown up in and now owned, was something of a 'coming out' party for Myron and Ali as a couple.

The other girl, Aimee Biel, mimicked his wave and tone. 'Hey, Myron.'

More silence.

He first saw Aimee Biel the day after she was born at St. Barnabas Hospital. Aimee and her parents, Claire and Erik, lived two blocks away. Myron had known Claire since their years together at Heritage Middle School, less than half a mile from where they now gathered. Myron turned toward Aimee. For a moment he fell back more than twenty-five years. Aimee looked so much like her mother, had the same crooked, devil-may-care grin, it was like looking through a time portal.

'I was just getting some ice,' Myron said. He pointed toward the freezer with his thumb to illustrate the point.

'Cool,' Aimee said.

'Very cool,' Myron said. 'Ice cold, in fact.'

Myron chuckled. Alone.

With the stupid grin still on his face, Myron looked over at Erin. She turned away. That had been her basic reaction today. Polite and aloof.

'Can I ask you something?' Aimee said.

'Shoot.'

She spread her hands. 'Was this really your room growing up?'

'Indeed it was.'

The two girls exchanged a glance. Aimee giggled. Erin did likewise.

'What?' Myron said.

'This room . . . I mean, could it possibly be lamer?'

Erin finally spoke. 'It's like too retro to be retro.'

'What do you call this thing?' Aimee asked, pointing below her.

'A beanbag chair,' Myron said.

The two girls giggled some more.

'And how come this lamp has a black lightbulb?'

'It makes the posters glow.'

More laughs.

'Hey, I was in high school,' Myron said, as if that explained everything.

'Did you ever bring a girl down here?' Aimee asked.

Myron put his hand to his heart. 'A true gentleman never kisses and tells.' Then: 'Yes.'

'How many?'

'How many what?'

'How many girls did you bring down here?'

'Oh. Approximately' – Myron looked up, drew in the air with his index finger – 'carry the three . . . I'd say somewhere between eight and nine hundred thousand.'

That caused rip-roaring laughter.

'Actually,' Aimee said, 'Mom says you used to be real cute.'

Myron arched an eyebrow. 'Used to be?'

Both girls high-fived and fell about the place. Myron shook his head and grumbled something about respecting their elders. When they quieted down, Aimee said, 'Can I ask you something else?'

'Shoot.'

'I mean, seriously.'

'Go ahead.'

'Those pictures of you upstairs. On the stairwell.'

Myron nodded. He had a pretty good idea where this was going.

'You were on the cover of *Sports Illustrated*.'

'That I was.'

'Mom and Dad say you were like the greatest basketball player in the country.'

'Mom and Dad,' Myron said, 'exaggerate.'

Both girls stared at him. Five seconds passed. Then another five.

'Do I have something stuck in my teeth?' Myron asked.

'Weren't you, like, drafted by the Lakers?'

'The Celtics,' he corrected.

'Sorry, the Celtics.' Aimee kept him pinned with her eyes. 'And you hurt your knee, right?'

'Right.'

'Your career was over. Just like that.'

'Pretty much, yes.'

'So like' – Aimee shrugged – ''how did that feel?'

'Hurting my knee?'

'Being a superstar like that. And then, *bam*, never being able to play again.'

Both girls waited for his answer. Myron tried to come up with something profound.

'It sucked big-time,' he said.

They both liked that.

Aimee shook her head. 'It must have been the worst.'

Myron looked toward Erin. Erin had her eyes down. The room went quiet. He waited. She eventually looked up. She looked scared and small and young. He wanted to take her in his arms, but man, would that ever be the wrong move.

'No,' Myron said softly, still holding Erin's gaze. 'Not even close to the worst.'

A voice at the top of the stairs shouted down, 'Myron?'

'I'm coming.'

He almost left then. The next big what-if. But the words he'd overheard at the top of the stairs – *Randy drove* – kept rattling in his head. Beer and shots. He couldn't let that go, could he?

'I want to tell you a story,' Myron began. And then he stopped. What he wanted to do was tell them about an incident from his high school days. There had been a party at Barry Brenner's house. That was what he wanted to tell them. He'd been a senior in high school – like them. There had been a lot of drinking. His team, the Livingston Lancers, had just won the state basketball tournament, led by All-American Myron Bolitar's forty-three points. Everyone was drunk. He remembered Debbie Frankel, a brilliant girl, a live wire, that sparkplug who was always animated, always raising her hand to contradict the teacher, always arguing and taking the other side and you loved her for it. At midnight Debbie came over and said good-bye to him. Her glasses were low on her nose. That was what he remembered most – the way her glasses had slipped down. Myron could see that Debbie was wasted. So were the other two girls who would pile into that car.

You can guess how the story ends. They took the hill on South Orange Avenue too fast. Debbie died in the crash. The smashed-up car was put on display in front of the high school for six years. Myron wondered where it was now, what they'd eventually done to that wreck.

'What?' Aimee said.

But Myron didn't tell them about Debbie Frankel. Erin and Aimee had undoubtedly heard other versions of the same story. It wouldn't work. He knew that. So he tried something else.

'I need you to promise me something,' Myron said.

Erin and Aimee looked at him.

He pulled his wallet from his pocket and plucked out two business cards. He opened the top drawer and found a pen that still worked. 'Here are all my numbers – home, business, mobile, my place in New York City.'

Myron scribbled on the cards and passed one to each of them. They took the cards without saying a word.

'Please listen to me, okay? If you're ever in a bind. If you're ever out drinking or your friends are drinking or you're high or stoned or I don't care what. Promise me. Promise me you'll call me. I'll come get you wherever you are. I won't ask any questions. I won't tell your parents. That's my promise to you. I'll take you wherever you want to go. I don't care how late. I don't care how far away you are. I don't care how wasted. Twenty-four-seven. Call me and I'll pick you up.'

The girls said nothing.

Myron took a step closer. He tried to keep the pleading out of his voice. 'Just please . . . please don't ever drive with someone who's been drinking.'

They just stared at him.

'Promise me,' he said.

And a moment later – the final what-if? – they did.

3

Two hours later, Aimee's family – the Biels – were the first to leave.

Myron walked them to the door. Claire leaned close to his ear. 'I heard the girls were down in your old room.'

'Yep.'

She gave him a wicked grin. 'Did you tell them – ?'

'God, no.'

Claire shook her head. 'You're such a prude.'

He and Claire had been good friends in high school. He'd loved her free spirit. She acted like – for lack of a more appropriate term – a guy. When they'd go to parties, she'd try to pick someone up, usually with more success because, hey, she was an attractive girl. She'd liked muscle-heads. She'd go with them once, maybe twice, and then move on.

Claire was a lawyer now. She and Myron had messed around once, down in that very basement, on a holiday break senior year. Myron had been much more uptight about it. The next day, there had been no awkwardness for Claire. No discomfort, no silent treatment, no 'maybe we should discuss what happened.'

No encore either.

In law school Claire had met her husband, 'Erik with a *K*.' That was how he always introduced himself. Erik was thin and tightly wound. He rarely smiled. He almost never laughed. His tie was always wonderfully Windsored. Erik with a K was not the man Myron had figured Claire would end up with, but they seemed to work. Something about opposites attract, he guessed.

Erik gave him a firm handshake, made sure that there was eye contact. 'Will I see you on Sunday?'

They used to play in a pickup basketball game on Sunday mornings, but Myron had stopped going months ago. 'I won't be there this week, no.'

Erik nodded as though Myron had said something profound and started out the door. Aimee smothered a laugh and waved. 'Nice talking to you, Myron.'

'Same here, Aimee.'

Myron tried to give her a look that said, 'Remember the promise.' He didn't know if it worked, but Aimee did give him a small nod before heading down the path.

Claire kissed his cheek and whispered in his ear again. 'You look happy.'

'I am,' he said.

Claire beamed. 'Ali's great, isn't she?'

'She is.'

'Am I the greatest matchmaker ever?'

'Like something out of a bad road production of *Fiddler*,' he said.

'I'm not rushing things. But I am the greatest, aren't I? It's okay, I can take it. I'm the best ever.'

'We're still talking about matchmaking, right?'

'Fresh. I know I'm the best at the other.'

Myron said, 'Eh.'

She punched his arm and left. He watched her walk away, shook his head, smiled. In a sense, you are always seventeen years old and waiting for your life to begin.

Ten minutes later, Ali Wilder, Myron's new lady love, called for her children. Myron walked them all to the car. Jack, the nine-year-old boy, proudly wore a Celtics uniform with Myron's old number on it. It was the next step in hip-hop fashion. First there had been the retro uniforms of your favorite greats. Now, at a Web site called Big-Time-Losahs.com or something like that, they sold uniforms for players who became has-beens or never-weres, players who went bust.

Like Myron.

Jack, being only nine years old, didn't get the irony.

When they reached the car, Jack gave Myron a big hug. Unsure how to play this, Myron hugged back but kept it brief. Erin stayed back. She gave him a half-nod and slipped into the backseat. Jack followed his big sister. Ali and Myron stood and smiled at each other like a pair of newly dating doofs.

'This was fun,' Ali said.

Myron was still smiling. Ali looked up at him with these wonderful green-brown eyes. She had red-blond hair and there were still remnants of childhood freckles. Her face was wide and her smile just held him.

'What?' she said.

'You look beautiful.'

'Man, you are smooth.'

'I don't want to brag, but yes. Yes, I am.'

Ali looked back at the house. Win – real name: Windsor Horne Lockwood III – stood with arms folded, leaning against the doorframe. 'Your friend Win,' she said. 'He seems nice.'

'He's not.'

'I know. I just figured him being your best friend and all, I'd say that.'

'Win is complicated.'

'He's good-looking.'

'He knows.'

'Not my type though. Too pretty. Too rich-preppy-boy.'

'And you prefer macho he-men,' Myron said. 'I understand.'

She snickered. 'Why does he keep looking at me like that?'

'My guess? He's probably checking out your ass.'

'Good to know somebody is.'

Myron cleared his throat, glanced away. 'So you want to have dinner together tomorrow?'

'That would be nice.'

'I'll pick you up at seven.'

Ali put her hand on his chest. Myron felt something electric in the touch. She stood on tiptoes – Myron was six-four – and kissed his cheek. 'I'll cook for you.'

'Really?'

'We'll stay in.'

'Great. So it'll be, what, like a family-type thing? Get to know the kids more?'

'The kids will be spending the night at my sister's.'

'Oh,' Myron said.

Ali gave him a hard look and slipped into the driver's seat.

'Oh,' Myron said again.

She arched an eyebrow. 'And you didn't want to brag about being smooth.'

Then she drove off. Myron watched the car disappear, the dorky smile still on his face. He turned and walked back to the house. Win had not moved. There had been many changes in Myron's life – his parents' moving down south, Esperanza's new baby, the fate of his business, even Big Cyndi – but Win remained a constant. Some of the ash-blond hair around the temples had grayed a bit, but Win was still the über-WASP. The patrician lockjaw, the perfect nose, the hair parted by the gods – he stank, deservedly so, of privilege and white shoes and golfer's tan.

'Six-point-eight,' Win said. 'Round it up to a seven.'

'Excuse me?'

Win raised his hand, palm down, tilted it back and forth. 'Your Ms. Wilder. If I'm being generous, I give her a seven.'

'Gee, that means a lot. Coming from you and all.'

They moved back into the house and sat in the den. Win crossed his legs in that perfect-crease way of his. His expression was permanently set on haughty. He looked pampered and spoiled and soft – in the face anyway. But the body told another story. He was all knotted, coiled muscle, not so much wiry as, if you will, barbed-wiry.

Win steepled his fingers. Steepling looked right on Win. 'May I ask a question?'

'No.'

'Why are you with her?'

'You're kidding, right?'

'No. I want to know what precisely you see in Ms. Ali Wilder.'

Myron shook his head. 'I knew I shouldn't have invited you.'

'Ah, but you did. So let me elaborate.'

'Please don't.'

'During our years at Duke, well, there was the delectable Emily Downing. Then, of course, your soul mate for the next ten-plus years, the luscious Jessica Culver. There was the brief fling with Brenda Slaughter and alas, most recently, the passion of Terese Collins.'

'Is there a point?'

'There is.' Win opened the steeple, closed it again. 'What do all these women, your past loves, have in common?'

'You tell me,' Myron said.

'In a word: bodaciousness.'

'That's a word?'

'Smoking-hot honeys,' Win continued with the snooty accent. 'Each and every one of them. On a scale of one to ten, I would rate Emily a nine. That would be the lowest. Jessica would be a so-hot-she-singes-your-eyeballs eleven. Terese Collins and Brenda Slaughter, both near-tens.'

'And in your expert opinion . . .'

'A seven is being generous,' Win finished for him.

Myron just shook his head.

'So pray tell,' Win said, 'what is the big attraction?'

'Are you for real?'

'I am indeed.'

'Well, here's a news flash, Win. First off, while it's not really important, I disagree with your awarded score.'

'Oh? So how would you rate Ms. Wilder?'

'I'm not getting into that with you. But for one thing, Ali has the kind of looks that grow on you. At first you think she's attractive enough, and then, as you get to know her – '

'Bah.'

'Bah?'

'Self-rationalization.'

'Well, here's another news flash for you. It's not all about looks.'

'Bah.'

'Again with the *bah*?'

Win re-steepled his fingers. 'Let's play a game. I'm going to say a word. You tell me the first thing that pops in your head.'

Myron closed his eyes. 'I don't know why I discuss matters of the heart with you. It's like talking about Mozart with a deaf man.'

'Yes, that's very funny. Here comes the first word. Actually it's two words. Just tell me what pops in your head: Ali Wilder.'

'Warmth,' Myron said.

'Liar.'

'Okay, I think we've discussed this enough.'

'Myron?'

'What?'

'When was the last time you tried to save someone?'

The usual faces flashed strobelike through Myron's head. He tried to block them out.

'Myron?'

'Don't start,' Myron said softly. 'I've learned my lesson.'

'Have you?'

He thought now about Ali, about that wonderful smile and the openness of her face. He thought about Aimee and Erin in his old bedroom down in the basement, about the promise he had forced them to make.

'Ali doesn't need rescuing, Myron.'

'You think that's what this is about?'

'When I say her name, what's the first thing that comes to mind?'

'Warmth,' Myron said again.

But this time, even he knew he was lying.

Six years.

That was how long it had been since Myron had played superhero. In six years he hadn't thrown a punch. He hadn't held, much less fired, a gun. He hadn't threatened or been threatened. He hadn't cracked wise with steroid-inflated pituitary glands. He hadn't called Win, still the scariest man he knew, to back him up or get him out of trouble. In the past six years, none of his clients had been murdered – a real positive in his business. None had been shot or arrested – well, except for that prostitution beef out in Las Vegas, but Myron still claimed that was entrapment. None of his clients or friends or loved ones had gone missing.

He had learned his lesson.

Don't stick your nose in where it doesn't belong. You're not Batman, and Win is not a psychotic version of Robin. Yes, Myron had saved some innocents during his quasi-heroic days, including the life of his own son. Jeremy, his boy, was nineteen now – Myron couldn't believe that either – and was serving in the military in some undisclosed spot in the Middle East.

But Myron had caused damage too. Look what had happened to Duane and Christian and Greg and Linda and Jack. . . . But mostly, Myron could not stop thinking about Brenda. He still visited her grave too frequently. Maybe she would have died anyway, he didn't know. Maybe it wasn't his fault.

The victories have a tendency to wash off you. The destruction – the dead – stay by your side, tap you on the shoulder, slow your step, haunt your sleep.

Either way, Myron had buried his hero complex. For the past six years, his life had been quiet, normal, average – boring, even.

Myron rinsed off the dishes. He semi-lived in Livingston, New Jersey, in the same town – nay, the same house – where he was raised. His parents, the beloved Ellen and Alan Bolitar, performed aliya, returning to their people's homeland (south Florida) five years ago. Myron bought the house as both an investment, a good one, in fact, and so that his folks would have a place to return to when they migrated back during the warmer months. Myron spent about a third of his time living in this house in the burbs and two-thirds rooming with Win at the famed Dakota apartment building on Central Park West in New York City.

He thought about tomorrow night and his date with Ali. Win was an idiot, no question about that, but as usual his questions had scored a hit, if not a bull's-eye. Forget that looks stuff. That was utter nonsense. And forget the hero complex stuff too. That wasn't what this was about. But something was holding him back and yes, it had to do with Ali's tragedy. Try as he might, he couldn't shake it.

As for the hero stuff, making Aimee and Erin promise to call him – that was different. It doesn't matter who you are – the teenage years are hard. High school is a war zone. Myron had been a popular kid. He was a Parade All-American basketball player, one of the top recruits in the country, and, to trot out a favorite cliché, a true scholar-athlete. If anyone should have had it easy in high school, it would be someone like Myron Bolitar. But he hadn't. In the end, no one gets out of those years unscathed.

You just need to survive adolescence. That's all. Just get through it.

Maybe that was what he should have said to the girls.

4

The next morning Myron headed into work. His office was on the twelfth floor of the Lock-Horne Building – as in Win's name – on Park Avenue and Fifty-second Street in midtown Manhattan. When the elevator opened, Myron was greeted with a big sign – a new addition to the place – that read

MB REPS

in some funky font. Esperanza had come up with the new logo. The *M* stood for Myron. The *B* for Bolitar. The *Reps* came from the fact that they were in the business of *rep*resentation. Myron had come up with the name by himself. He would often pause after telling people that and wait for the applause to die down.

Originally, when they just worked in the sports field, the firm was called MB SportsReps instead of MB Reps. Over the past five years the company had diversified, representing actors, authors, and celebrities of various stripes. Ergo the clever shortening of the name. Getting rid of the excess, cutting away the fat. Yep, that was MB Reps right down to the name.

Myron heard the baby cry. Esperanza must be in already. He poked his head into her office.

Esperanza was breast-feeding. He immediately looked down.

'Uh, I'll come back later.'

'Stop being an ass,' Esperanza said. 'You'd think you've never seen a breast before.'

'Well, it's been a while.'

'And certainly not one this spectacular,' she added. 'Sit.'

At first, MB SportsReps had just been just Myron the super-agent and Esperanza the receptionist/secretary/Girl Friday. You may remember Esperanza during her years as the sexy, lithe professional wrestler named Little Pocahontas. Every Sunday morning on Channel 11 here in the New York area, Esperanza would take to the ring, donning a feathered headband and drool-inducing bikini of pseudosuede. Along with her partner, Big Chief Mama, known in real life as Big Cyndi, they held the intercontinental tag-team championship belt for FLOW, the Fabulous Ladies Of Wrestling. The wrestling organization had originally wanted to call itself the Beautiful Ladies Of Wrestling, but the network had trouble with the ensuing acronym.

Esperanza's current title at MB Reps was senior vice president, but she pretty much ran the sports division now.

'Sorry I missed your coming-out party,' Esperanza said.

'It wasn't a coming-out party.'

'Whatever. Hector here had a cold.'

'Is he better now?'

'He's fine.'

'So what's going on here?'

'Michael Discepolo. We need to get his contract done.'

'The Giants still dragging their feet?'

'Yes.'

'Then he'll be a free agent,' Myron said. 'I think that's probably a good move, what with the way he's been playing.'

'Except Discepolo is a loyal guy. He'd rather sign.'

Esperanza pulled Hector away from her nipple and put him on the other breast. Myron tried not to look away too suddenly. He never quite knew how to play it when a woman breast-fed in front of him. He wanted to be mature about it, but what exactly did that mean? You don't stare, but you don't divert your eyes either. How do you mine the area between those two?

'I have some news,' Esperanza said.

'Oh?'

'Tom and I are getting married.'

Myron said nothing. He felt a funny twinge.

'Well?'

'Congrats.'

'That's it?'

'I'm surprised, that's all. But really, I think that's great. When's the big day?'

'Three weeks from Saturday. But let me ask you something. Now that I'm marrying the father of my baby, am I still a fallen woman?'

'I don't think so.'

'Damn, I like being a fallen woman.'

'Well, you still had the baby out of wedlock.'

'Good point. I could run with that.'

Myron looked at her.

'What's wrong?'

'You, married.' He shook his head.

'I was never big on commitment, was I?'

'You change partners like a cineplex changes movies.'

Esperanza smiled. 'True.'

'I don't even remember you staying with the same gender for more than, what, a month?'

'The wonders of bisexuality,' Esperanza said. 'But it's different with Tom.'

'How so?'

'I love him.'

He said nothing.

'You don't think I can do it,' she said. 'Stay true to one person.'

'I never said that.'

'Do you know what bisexual means?'

'Of course,' Myron said. 'I dated a lot of bisexual women – I'd mention sex, the girl would say, "Bye."'

Esperanza just looked at him.

'Okay, old joke,' he said. 'It just . . .' Myron sort of shrugged.

'I like women and I like men. But if I make a commitment, it's to a person, not a gender. Make sense?'

'Sure.'

'Good. Now tell me what's wrong with you and this Ali Wilder.'

'Nothing's wrong.'

'Win said you two haven't done the deed yet.'

'Win said that?'

'Yes.'

'When?'

'This morning.'

'Win just came in here and said that?'

'First he made a comment about my increased cup size since giving birth, then yes, he told me that you've been dating this woman for almost two months and haven't done the nasty yet.'

'What makes him think that?'

'Body language.'

'He said that?'

'Win is good when it comes to body language.'

Myron shook his head.

'So is he right?'

'I'm having dinner at Ali's house tonight. The kids are staying with her sister.'

'She made this plan?'

'Yes.'

'And you haven't . . . ?' With Hector still feeding, Esperanza still managed to gesture the point.

'We haven't.'

'Man.'

'I'm waiting for a signal.'

'Like what, a burning bush? She invited you to her house and told you the kids would be away for the night.'

'I know.'

'That's the international signal for Jump My Bones.'

He said nothing.

'Myron?'

'Yes.'

'She's a widow – not a cripple. She's probably terrified.'

'That's why I'm taking it slow.'

'That's sweet and noble, but stupid. And it's not helping.'

'So you're suggesting . . . ?'

'A major bone jump, yes.'

5

Myron arrived at Ali's at seven p.m. The Wilders lived in Kasselton, a town about fifteen minutes north of Livingston. Myron had gone through a strange ritual before leaving his house. Cologne or no cologne? That one was easy: no cologne. Tighty-whiteys or boxers? He chose something between the two, that hybrid that was either tight boxers or long tighties. Boxer briefs, the package said. And he chose them in gray. He wore a Banana Republic tan pullover with a black T-shirt underneath. The jeans were from the Gap. Slip-on loafers from the Tod's outlet store adorned his size-fourteen feet. He couldn't be more American Casual if he tried.

Ali opened the door. The lights behind her were low. She wore a black dress with a scooped front. Her hair was pinned back. Myron liked that. Most men, they liked it when the hair came down. Myron had always been a fan of keeping it off the face.

He stared at her for another moment and then said, 'Whoa.'

'I thought you said you were smooth.'

'I'm holding back.'

'But why?'

'If I go all out in the smooth department,' Myron said, 'women all over the tri-state area begin to disrobe. I need to harness the power.'

'Lucky for me then. Come on in.'

He had never made it past her foyer before. Ali walked to the kitchen. His stomach knotted. There were family photographs on the wall. Myron did a quick scan. He spotted Kevin's face. He was in at least four different photographs. Myron didn't want to stare, but his gaze got caught on an image of Erin. She was fishing with her dad. Her smile was heartbreaking. Myron tried to picture the girl in his basement smiling like that, but it wouldn't hold.

He looked back at Ali. Something crossed her face.

Myron sniffed the air. 'What are you cooking?'

'I'm making Chicken Kiev.'

'Smells great.'

'You mind if we talk first?'

'Sure.'

They headed into the den. Myron tried to keep his head about him. He looked around for more pictures. There was a framed wedding photo. Ali's hair was too big, he thought, but maybe that was the look then. He thought that she was prettier now. That happens with some women. There was also a photograph of five men in matching black tuxedos with bow ties. The groomsmen, Myron figured. Ali followed his gaze. She walked over and picked up the group shot.

'This one is Kevin's brother,' she said, pointing to the man second on the right. Myron nodded.

'The other men worked at Carson Wilkie with Kevin. They were his best friends.'

Myron said, 'Were they – '

'All dead,' she said. 'All married, all had children.'

The elephant in the room – it was as if all hands and fingers were suddenly pointing at it.

'You don't have to do this,' Myron said.

'Yeah, Myron, I do.'

They sat down.

'When Claire first set us up,' she began, 'I told her that you'd have to raise the subject of 9/11. Did she tell you that?'

'Yes.'

'But you didn't.'

He opened his mouth, closed it, tried again. 'How was I supposed to do that exactly? Hi, how are you, I hear you're a 9/11 widow, do you want Italian or maybe Chinese?'

Ali nodded. 'Fair enough.'

There was a grandfather clock in the corner, a huge ornate thing. It chose then to start chiming. Myron wondered where Ali had gotten it, where she had gotten everything in this house, how much of Kevin was watching them now, in this house, in *his* house.

'Kevin and I started dating when we were juniors in high school. We decided to take time off during our freshman year of college. I was going to NYU. He would be off at Wharton. It would be the mature thing to do. But when we came home for Thanksgiving, and we saw each other . . .' She shrugged. 'I've never been with another man. Ever. There, I said it. I don't know if we did it right or wrong. Isn't that weird? I think we sorta learned together.'

Myron sat there. She was no more than a foot away from him. He wasn't sure of the right move here – the story of his life. He put his hand close to hers. She picked it up and held it.

'I don't know when I first realized I was ready to start dating. It took me longer than most of the widows. We talk about it, of course – the widows, I mean. We talk a lot. But one day I just said to myself, okay, now maybe it's time. I told Claire. And when she suggested you, do you know what I thought?'

Myron shook his head.

'He's out of my league, but maybe this will be fun. I thought – this is going to sound stupid and please remember I really didn't know you at all – that you'd be a good transition.'

'Transition?'

'You know what I mean. You were a pro athlete. You probably had a lot of women. I thought maybe, well, it would be a fun fling. A physical thing. And then, afterwards, maybe I'd find someone nice. Does that make sense?'

'I think so,' Myron said. 'You just wanted me for my body.'

'Pretty much, yeah.'

'I feel so cheap,' he said. 'Or is it thrilled? Let's go with thrilled.'

That made her smile. 'Please don't take offense.'

'No offense taken.' Then: 'Hussy.'

She laughed. The sound was melodic.

'So what happened to your plan?' he asked.

'You weren't what I expected.'

'That a good thing or bad?'

'I don't know. You used to date Jessica Culver. I read that in a *People* magazine.'

'I did.'

'Was it serious?'

'Yes.'

'She's a great writer.'

Myron nodded.

'She's also stunning.'

'You're stunning.'

'Not like that.'

He was going to argue, but he knew that it would sound too patronizing.

'When you asked me out, I figured that you were looking for something, I don't know, different.'

'Different how?' he asked.

'Being a 9/11 widow,' she said. 'The truth is, and I hate to admit this, but it gives me something of a warped celebrity.'

He did know. He thought about what Win had said, about that first thing that pops in your head when you hear her name.

'So I figured – again not knowing you, just knowing that you were this good-looking pro athlete who dates women who look like supermodels – I figured that I might be an interesting notch on the belt.'

'Because you were a 9/11 widow?'

'Yes.'

'That's pretty sick.'

'Not really.'

'How's that?'

'It's like I said. There's a weird sort of celebrity attached. People who wouldn't give me the time of day suddenly wanted to meet me. It still happens. About a month ago, I started playing in this new tennis league at the Racket Club. One of the women – this rich snob who wouldn't let me cut through her yard when we first moved to town – comes up to me and she's making the poo-poo face.'

'The poo-poo face?'

'That's what I call it. The poo-poo face. It looks like this.'

Ali demonstrated. She pursed her lips, frowned, and batted her eyes.

'You look like Donald Trump being sprayed with mace.'

'That's the poo-poo face. I get it all the time since Kevin died. I don't blame anyone. It's natural. But this woman with the poo-poo face comes up to me and she takes both of my hands in hers and looks me in the eyes and has this whole earnest thing going on so that I want to scream, and she says, "Are you Ali Wilder? Oh, I so wanted to contact you. How are you doing?" You get the point.'

'I do.'

She looked at him.

'What?'

'You've turned into the dating version of the poo-poo face.'

'I'm not sure I follow.'

'You keep telling me I'm beautiful.'

'You are.'

'You met me three times when I was married.'

Myron said nothing.

'Did you think I was beautiful then?'

'I try not to think that way about married women.'

'Do you even remember meeting me?'

'Not really, no.'

'And if I looked like Jessica Culver, even if I were married, you'd have remembered.' She waited.

'What do you want me to say here, Ali?'

'Nothing. But it's time to stop treating me like the poo-poo face. It doesn't matter why you first started dating me. It matters why you're here now.'

'Can I do that?'

'Do what?'

'Can I tell you why I'm here now?'

Ali swallowed and for the first time she looked unsure of herself. She made a go-ahead gesture with her hand.

He dove in. 'I'm here because I really like you – because I may be confused about a lot of things and maybe you're making a good point about the poo-poo face, but the fact is, I'm here right now because I can't stop thinking about you. I think about you all the time and when I do, I have this goofy smile on my face. It looks like this.' Now it was his turn to demonstrate. 'So that's why I'm here, okay?'

'That,' Ali said, trying to hold back a smile, 'is a really good answer.'

He was about to crack wise, but he held back. With maturity comes restraint.

'Myron?'

'Yes?'

'I want you to kiss me. I want you to hold me. I want you to take me upstairs and make love to me. I want you to do it with no expectations because I don't have any. I could dump you tomorrow and you could dump me. It doesn't matter. But I'm not fragile. I'm not going to describe the hell of the past five years, but I'm stronger than you'll ever know. If this relationship continues after tonight, you're the one who'll have to be strong, not me. This is a no-obligation offer. I know how valiant and noble you want to be. But I don't want that. All I want tonight is you.'

Ali leaned toward him and kissed him on the lips. First gently then with more hunger. Myron felt a surge go through him.

She kissed him again. And Myron felt lost.

An hour later – or maybe it was only twenty minutes – Myron collapsed and rolled onto his back.

'Well?' Ali said.

'Wow.'

'Tell me more.'

'Let me catch my breath.'

Ali laughed, snuggled closer.

'My limbs,' he said. 'I can't feel my limbs.'

'Not a thing?'

'A little tingle maybe.'

'Not so little. And you were pretty good yourself.'

'As Woody Allen once said, I practice a lot when I'm alone.'

She put her head on his chest. His racing heart started to slow. He stared at the ceiling.

'Myron?'

'Yes.'

'He'll never leave my life. He'll never leave Erin and Jack either.'

'I know.'

'Most men can't handle that.'

'I don't know if I can either.'

She looked at him and smiled.

'What?'

'You're being honest,' she said. 'I like that.'

'No more poo-poo face?'

'Oh, I wiped that off twenty minutes ago.'

He pursed his lips, frowned, and batted his eyes. 'But wait, it's back.'

She put her head back on his chest.

'Myron?'

'Yes?'

'He'll never leave my life,' she said. 'But he's not here now. Right now I think it's just the two of us.'

6

On the third floor of St. Barnabas Medical Center, Essex County investigator Loren Muse rapped on a door that read edna skylar, md, geneticist.

A woman's voice said, 'Come in.'

Loren turned the knob and entered. Skylar stood. She was taller than Loren, but most people were. Skylar crossed the room, hand extended. They both offered up firm handshakes and plenty of eye contact. Edna Skylar nodded in a sisterhood way to her. Loren had seen it before. They were both in professions still dominated by men. That gave them a bond.

'Won't you please have a seat?'

They both sat. Edna Skylar's desk was immaculate. There were manila folders, but they were stacked without any papers peeking out. The office was standard issue, dominated by a picture window that offered up a wonderful view of a parking lot.

Dr. Skylar stared intently at Loren Muse. Loren didn't like it. She waited a moment. Skylar kept staring.

Loren said, 'Problem?'

Edna Skylar smiled. 'Sorry, bad habit.'

'What's that?'

'I look at faces.'

'Uh-huh.'

'It's not important. Well, maybe it is. That's how I got into this predicament.'

Loren wanted to get to it. 'You told my boss that you have information on Katie Rochester?'

'How is Ed?'

'He's good.'

She smiled warmly. 'He's a nice man.'

'Yeah,' Loren said, 'a prince.'

'I've known him a long time.'

'He told me.'

'That's why I called Ed. We had a long talk about the case.'

'Right,' Loren said. 'And that's why he sent me here.'

Edna Skylar looked off, out the window. Loren tried to guess her age. Mid-sixties probably, but she wore it well. Dr. Skylar was a handsome woman, short gray hair, high cheekbones, knew how to sport a beige suit without coming across as too butch or overly feminine.

'Dr. Skylar?'

'Could you tell me something about the case?'

'Excuse me?'

'Katie Rochester. Is she officially listed as missing?'

'I'm not sure how that's relevant.'

Edna Skylar's eyes moved slowly back to Loren Muse. 'Do you think she met up with foul play – '

'I can't really discuss that.'

' – or do you think she ran away? When I talked to Ed, he seemed pretty sure she was a runaway. She took money out of an ATM in midtown, he said. Her father is rather unsavory.'

'Prosecutor Steinberg told you all that?'

'He did.'

'So why are you asking me?'

'I know his take,' she said. 'I want yours.'

Loren was about to protest some more, but Edna Skylar was again staring with too much intensity. She scanned Skylar's desk for family photographs. There were none. She wondered what to make of that and decided nothing. Skylar was waiting.

'She's eighteen years old,' Loren tried, treading carefully.

'I know that.'

'That makes her an adult.'

'I know that too. And what about the father? Do you think he abused her?'

Loren wondered how to play this. The truth was, she didn't like the father, hadn't from the get-go. RICO said that Dominick Rochester was mobbed up and maybe that was part of it. But there was something to reading a person's grief. On the one hand, everyone reacts differently. It was true that you really couldn't tell guilt based on someone's reaction. Some killers cried tears that'd put Pacino to shame. Others were beyond robotic. Same with the innocent. It was like this: You're with a group of people, a grenade is thrown in the middle of the crowd, you never know who is going to dive on it and who is going to dive for cover.

That said, Katie Rochester's father . . . there was something off about his grief. It was too fluid. It was like he was trying on different personas, seeing which one would look best for the public. And the mother. She had the whole shattered-eye thing going on, but had that come from devastation or resignation? It was hard to tell.

'We have no evidence of that,' Loren said in the most noncommittal tone she could muster.

Edna Skylar did not react.

'These questions,' Loren went on. 'They're a bit bizarre.'

'That's because I'm still not sure what to do.'

'About?'

'If a crime has been committed, I want to help. But . . .'

'But?'

'I saw her.'

Loren Muse waited a beat, hoping she'd say more. She didn't. 'You saw Katie Rochester?'

'Yes.'

'When?'

'It'll be three weeks on Saturday.'

'And you're just telling us now?'

Edna Skylar was looking out at the parking lot again. The sun was setting, the rays slicing in through the venetian blinds. She looked older in that light.

'Dr. Skylar?'

'She asked me not to say anything.' Her gaze was still on the lot.

'Katie did?'

Still looking off, Edna Skylar nodded.

'You talked to her?'

'For a second maybe.'

'What did she say?'

'That I couldn't tell anybody that I saw her.'

'And?'

'And that was it. A moment later she was gone.'

'Gone?'

'On a subway.'

The words came easier now. Edna Skylar told Loren the whole story, how she'd been studying faces while walking in New York, how she spotted the girl despite the appearance change, how she followed her down into the subway, how she'd vanished into the dark.

Loren wrote it all down, but fact was, this figured into what she'd believed from the beginning. The kid was a runaway. As Ed Steinberg had already told Skylar, there had been an ATM withdrawal at a Citibank in midtown near the time she vanished. Loren had seen the bank video. The face had been covered by a hood, but it was probably the Rochester girl. The father had clearly been on the over-strict side. That was how it always was with the runaways. The too-liberal parents, their kids often got hooked on drugs. The too-conservative, their kids were the runaways with the sex issues. Might be a stereotype to break it down like that, but Loren had seen very few cases that broke those rules.

She asked a few more follow-up questions. There was nothing that they could really do now. The girl was eighteen. There was no reason, from this description, to suspect foul play. On TV, the feds get involved and put a team on it. That doesn't happen in real life.

But Loren felt a niggling at the base of her brain. Some would call it intuition. She hated that. Hunches . . . that didn't really work either. She wondered what Ed Steinberg, her boss, would want to do. Nothing, probably. Their office was busy working with the U.S. Attorney on two cases, one involving a possible terrorist and the other a Newark politician on the take.

With their resources so limited, should they pursue what appeared to be an obvious runaway? It was a tough call.

'Why now?' Loren asked.

'What?'

'Three weeks, you didn't say anything. What made you change your mind?'

'Do you have children, Investigator Muse?'

'No.'

'I do.'

Loren again looked at the desk, at the credenza, at the wall. No family pictures. No sign of children or grandchildren. Skylar smiled, as if she understood what Muse was doing.

'I was a lousy mother.'

'I'm not sure I understand.'

'I was, shall we say, laissez-faire. When in doubt, I'd let it go.'

Loren waited.

'That,' Edna Skylar said, 'was a huge mistake.'

'I'm still not sure I understand.'

'Neither do I. But this time . . .' Her voice faded away. She swallowed, looked down at her hands before turning her gaze to Loren. 'Just because everything looks okay, maybe it's not. Maybe Katie Rochester needs help. Maybe this time I should do more than just let it go.'

The promise in the basement came back to haunt Myron at exactly 2:17 a.m.

Three weeks had passed. Myron was still dating Ali. It was the day of Esperanza's wedding. Ali came as his date. Myron gave away the bride. Tom – real name Thomas James Bidwell III – was Win's cousin. The wedding was small. Strangely enough, the groom's family, charter members of the Daughters of the American Revolution, was not thrilled with Tom's marriage to a Bronx-born Latina named Esperanza Diaz. Go figure.

'Funny,' Esperanza said.

'What's that?'

'I always thought I'd marry for money, not love.' She checked herself in the mirror. 'But here I am, marrying for love and getting money.'

'Irony is not dead.'

'Good thing. You're going to Miami to see Rex?'

Rex Storton was an aging movie star they were repping. 'I'm flying down tomorrow afternoon.'

Esperanza turned away from the mirror, spread her arms, and gave him a dazzling smile. 'Well?'

She was a vision. Myron said, 'Wow.'

'You think?'

'I think.'

'Come on then. Let's get me hitched.'

'Let's.'

'One thing first.' Esperanza pulled him aside. 'I want you to be happy for me.'

'I am.'

'I'm not leaving you.'

'I know.'

Esperanza looked into his face. 'We're still best friends,' she said. 'You under-stand that? You, me, Win, Big Cyndi. Nothing has changed.'

'Sure it has,' Myron said. 'Everything has changed.'

'I love you, you know.'

'And I love you.'

She smiled again. Esperanza was always so damned beautiful. She had that whole peasant-blouse fantasy thing going on. But today, in that dress, the word *luminous* was simply too weak. She had been so wild, such a free spirit, had insisted that she would never settle down with one person like this. But here she was, with a baby, getting married. Even Esperanza had grown up.

'You're right,' she said. 'But things change, Myron. And you've always hated change.'

'Don't start with that.'

'Look at you. You lived with your parents into your mid-thirties. You own your childhood home. You still spend most of your time with your college roommate, who, let's face it, can't change.'

He put up his hand. 'I get the point.'

'Funny though.'

'What?'

'I always thought you'd be the first to get married,' she said.

'Me too.'

'Win, well, like I said, let's not even go there. But you always fell in love so easily, especially with that bitch, Jessica.'

'Don't call her that.'

'Whatever. Anyway, you were the one who bought the American dream – get married, have two-point-six kids, invite friends to barbecues in the backyard, the whole thing.'

'And you never did.'

Esperanza smiled. 'Weren't you the one who taught me, *Men tracht und Gott lacht?*'

'Man, I love it when you shiksas speak Yiddish.'

Esperanza put her hand through the crook of his arm. 'That can be a good thing, you know.'

'I know.'

She took a deep breath. 'Shall we?'

'You nervous?'

Esperanza looked at him. 'Not even a little.'

'Then onward.'

Myron walked her down the aisle. He thought it would be a flattering formality, standing in for her late father, but when Myron gave Esperanza's hand to Tom, when Tom smiled and shook his hand, Myron started to well up. He stepped back and sat down in the front row.

The wedding was not so much an eclectic mix as a wonderful collision. Win was Tom's best man while Big Cyndi was Esperanza's maid of honor. Big Cyndi, her former tag-team wrestling partner, was six-six and comfortably north of three hundred pounds. Her fists looked like canned hams. She had not been sure what to wear – a classic peach maid of honor dress or a black leather corset. Her compromise: peach leather with a fringed hem, sleeveless so as to display arms with the relative dimensions and consistency of marble columns on a Georgian mansion. Big Cyndi's hair was done up in a mauve Mohawk and pinned on the top was a little bride-and-groom cake decoration.

When trying on the, uh, dress, Big Cyndi had spread her arms and twirled for Myron. Ocean tides altered course, and solar systems shifted. 'What do you think?' she asked.

'Mauve with peach?'

'It's very hip, Mr. Bolitar.'

She always called him Mister; Big Cyndi liked formality.

Tom and Esperanza exchanged vows in a quaint church. White poppies lined the pews. Tom's side of the aisle was dressed in black and white – a sea of penguins. Esperanza's side had so many colors, Crayola sent a scout. It looked like the

Halloween parade in Greenwich Village. The organ played beautiful hymns. The choir sang like angels. The setting could not have been more serene.

For the reception, however, Esperanza and Tom wanted a change of pace. They rented out an S&M nightclub near Eleventh Avenue called Leather and Lust. Big Cyndi worked there as a bouncer and sometimes, very late at night, she took to the stage for an act that boggled the imagination.

Myron and Ali parked in a lot off the West Side Highway. They passed a twenty-four-hour porn shop called King David's Slut Palace. The windows were soaped up. There was a big sign on the door that read NOW UNDER NEW MANAGEMENT.

'Whew.' Myron pointed to the sign. 'It's about time, don't you think?'

Ali nodded. 'The place had been so mismanaged before.'

When they ducked inside Leather and Lust, Ali walked around as though she were at the Louvre, squinting at the photos on the wall, checking out the devices, the costumes, the bondage material. She shook her head. 'I am hopelessly naïve.'

'Not hopelessly,' Myron said.

Ali pointed at something black and long that resembled human intestines.

'What's that?' she asked.

'Dang if I know.'

'Are you, uh, into . . . ?'

'Oh no.'

'Too bad,' Ali said. Then: 'Kidding. So very much kidding.'

Their romance was progressing, but the reality of dating someone with young kids had set in. They hadn't spent another full night together since that first. Myron had only offered up brief hellos to Erin and Jack since that party. They weren't sure how fast or slow they should go in their own relationship, but Ali was pretty adamant that they should go slow where it concerned the kids.

Ali had to leave early. Jack had a school project she'd promised to help him with. Myron walked her out, deciding to stay in the city for the night.

'How long will you be in Miami?' Ali asked.

'Just a night or two.'

'Would it make you retch violently if I say I'll miss you?'

'Not violently, no.'

She kissed him gently. Myron watched her drive off, his heart soaring, and then he headed back to the party.

Since he planned on sleeping in anyway, Myron started drinking. He was not what one would call a great drinker – he held his liquor about as well as a four-teen-year-old girl – but tonight, at this wonderful albeit bizarre celebration, he felt in the mood to imbibe. So did Win, though it took far more to get him buzzed. Cognac was mother's milk to Win. He rarely showed the effects, at least on the outside.

Tonight it didn't matter. Win's stretch limo was already waiting. It would take them back uptown.

Win's apartment in the Dakota was worth about a billion dollars and had a décor that reminded one of Versailles. When they arrived, Win carefully poured himself an obscenely priced vintage port, Quinta do Noval Nacional 1963. The bottle had been decanted several hours ago because, as Win explained, you must give vintage port time to breathe before consumption. Myron normally drank a chocolate Yoo-hoo, but his stomach was not in the mood. Plus the chocolate wouldn't have time to breathe.

Win snapped on the TV, and they watched *Antiques Roadshow*. A snooty woman with a lazy drawl had brought in a hideous bronze bust. She started telling the appraiser a story about how Dean Martin in 1950 offered her father ten thousand dollars for this wretched hunk of metal, but her daddy, she said with an insistent finger-point and matching smirk, was too wily for that. He knew that it must be worth a fortune. The appraiser nodded patiently, waited for the woman to finish, and then he lowered the boom:

'It's worth about twenty dollars.'

Myron and Win shared a quiet high five.

'Enjoying other people's misery,' Win said.

'We are pitiful,' Myron said.

'It's not us.'

'No?'

'It's this show,' Win said. 'It illuminates so much that is wrong with our society.'

'How so?'

'People aren't satisfied just to have their trinket be worth a fortune. No, it is better, far better, if they bought it on the cheap from some unsuspecting rube. No one considers the feelings of the unsuspecting yard salesman who was cheated, who lost out.'

'Good point.'

'Ah, but there's more.'

Myron smiled, sat back, waited.

'Forget greed for the moment,' Win went on. 'What really upsets us is that everybody but everybody lies on *Antiques Roadshow*.'

Myron nodded. 'You mean when the appraiser asks, "Do you have any idea what it's worth?" '

'Precisely. He asks that same question every time.'

'I know.'

'And Mr. or Mrs. Gee-Whiz act like the question caught them totally off guard – as if they'd never seen the show before.'

'It's annoying,' Myron agreed.

'And then they say something like, "Gasp-oh-gasp, I never thought of that. I have no idea what it might be worth."' Win frowned. 'I mean, please. You dragged your two-ton granite armoire to some impersonal convention center and waited in line for twelve hours – but you never, ever, not in your wildest dreams wondered what it might be worth?'

'A lie,' Myron agreed, feeling the buzz. 'It's up there with "Your call is very important to us."'

'And that,' Win said, 'is why we love when a woman like that gets slammed. The lies. The greed. The same reason why we love the boob on *Wheel of Fortune* who knows the solution but always goes for the extra spin and hits Bankrupt.'

'It's like life,' Myron pronounced, feeling the booze.

'Do tell.'

But then the door's intercom buzzed.

Myron felt his stomach drop. He checked his watch. It was one-thirty in the morning. Myron just looked over at Win. Win looked back, his face a placid pool. Win was still handsome, too handsome, but the years, the abuse, the late nights of either violence or, as with tonight, sex, were starting to show just a little.

Myron closed his eyes. 'Is that a . . . ?'

'Yes.'

He sighed, rose. 'I wish you'd told me.'

'Why?'

They'd been down that road before. There was no answer to that one.

'She's from a new place on the Upper West Side,' Win said.

'Yeah, how convenient.'

Without another word Myron headed down the corridor toward his bedroom. Win answered the door. As much as it depressed him, Myron took a peek. The girl was young and pretty. She said, 'Hi!' with a forced lilt in her voice. Win did not reply. He beckoned her to follow him. She did, teetering on too-high heels. They vanished down the corridor.

As Esperanza had noted, some things refuse to change – no matter how much you'd like them to.

Myron closed the door and collapsed onto the bed. His head swam from drink. The ceiling spun. He let it. He wondered if he was going to get sick. He didn't think so. He pushed thoughts of the girl out of his head. She left him easier than the girls used to, a change in him that was definitely not for the better. He didn't hear any noises – the room Win used (not his bedroom, of course) was soundproof – and eventually Myron closed his eyes.

The call came in on his cell phone.

Myron had it set on vibrate-ring. It rattled against his night table. He woke from his half-sleep and reached for it. He rolled over, and his head screamed. That was when he saw the bedside digital clock.

2:17 a.m.

He did not check the caller ID before he put the phone to his ear.

'Hello?' he croaked.

He heard the sob first.

'Hello?' he said again.

'Myron? It's Aimee.'

'Aimee.' Myron sat up. 'What's wrong? Where are you?'

'You said I could call.' There was another sob. 'Anytime, right?'

'Right. Where are you, Aimee?'

'I need help.'

'Okay, no problem. Just tell me where you are.'

'Oh God . . .'

'Aimee?'

'You won't tell, right?'

He hesitated. He flashed to Claire, Aimee's mother. He remembered Claire at this age and felt a funny pang.

'You promised. You promised you wouldn't tell my parents.'

'I know. Where are you?'

'Promise you won't tell?'

'I promise, Aimee. Just tell me where you are.'

7

Myron threw on a pair of sweats. His brain was a little hazy. There was still some of the drink in him. The irony did not escape him – he had told Aimee to call him because he didn't want her to get in a car with somebody who'd drank, and here he was, slightly tipsy. He tried to step back and judge his sobriety. He figured that he was okay to drive, but isn't that what every drinker thinks?

He debated asking Win, but Win was otherwise preoccupied. Win had also drunk even more, despite the sober façade. Still, he shouldn't just rush out, should he?

Good question.

The fine wooden floors in the corridor had recently been redone. Myron decided quickly to test his sobriety. He walked along one plank as though it were a straight line, as though a cop had pulled him over. He passed, but again Myron was, all modesty aside, pretty damned coordinated. He could probably pass that test whilst wasted.

Still, what choice did he have here? Even if he found someone else to drive at this hour, how would Aimee react to him showing up with a stranger? He, Myron, had been the one to make her promise to call him if such a situation were to arise. He had been the one who jammed his card with all the phone numbers into her hand. He had been the one, as Aimee had just pointed out, who swore complete confidentiality.

He had to go himself.

His car was in a twenty-four-hour lot on Seventieth Street. The gate was closed. Myron rang the bell. The attendant grudgingly pressed the button and the gate ascended.

Myron was not a big-car guy, and thus he still drove a Ford Taurus, which he dubbed the 'Chick Magnet.' A car got him from point A to point B. Period. More important to him than horsepower and V6 was having radio controls on the steering wheel, so he could constantly flip stations.

He pressed Aimee's number on the cell phone. She answered in a small voice.
'Hello?'
'I'm on my way.'
Aimee did not reply.
'Why don't you stay on the line?' he said. 'Just so I know you're okay.'
'My battery is almost dead. I want to save the power.'
'I should be there in ten, fifteen minutes tops,' Myron said.
'From Livingston?'
'I was staying in the city.'
'Oh, that's good. See you soon.'

561

She disconnected the call. Myron checked the car clock: 2:30 a.m. Aimee's parents must be worried sick. He hoped that she'd already called Claire and Erik. He was tempted to place the call himself, but no, that wasn't part of how this worked. When she got in the car, he'd encourage her to do it.

Aimee's location, he'd been surprised to hear, was midtown Manhattan. She told him that she'd wait on Fifth Avenue by Fifty-fourth. That was pretty much Rockefeller Center. What was strange about that, about an eighteen-year-old girl in the Big Apple imbibing in that area, was that midtown was dead at night. During the week, this place hustled with enterprise. On weekend days, you had the tourist trade. But on a Saturday night, there were few people on the street. New York might be the city that never sleeps, but as he hit Fifth Avenue in the upper Fifties, midtown was taking a serious nap.

He got caught at a traffic light on Fifth Avenue at Fifty-second Street. The door handle jangled, and then Aimee opened the door and slipped into the back.

'Thank you,' she said.

'You okay?'

From behind him a small voice said, 'I'm fine.'

'I'm not a chauffeur, Aimee. Sit up front.'

She hesitated, but she did as he asked. When she closed the passenger door, Myron turned to face her. Aimee stared straight out the front window. Like most teens, she'd splattered on too much makeup. The young don't need makeup, especially that much. Her eyes were red and raccoon-like. She was dressed in something teenage-tight, like a thin wrapping of gauze, the kind of thing that, even if you had the figure, you couldn't carry past the age of maybe twenty-three.

She looked so much like her mother had at that age.

'The light's green,' Aimee said.

He started driving. 'What happened?'

'Some people were drinking too much. I didn't want to drive with them.'

'Where?'

'Where what?'

Again Myron knew that midtown was not a young-people hot spot. Most hung out in bars on the Upper East Side or maybe down in the Village. 'Where were you drinking?'

'Is that important?'

'I'd like to know.'

Aimee finally turned toward him. Her eyes were wet. 'You promised.'

He kept driving.

'You promised you wouldn't ask any questions, remember?'

'I just want to make sure you're all right.'

'I am.'

Myron made a right, cutting across town. 'I'll take you home then.'

'No.'

He waited.

'I'm staying with a friend.'

'Where?'

'She lives in Ridgewood.'

He glanced at her, brought his eyes back to the road. 'In Bergen County?'

'Yes.'

562

'I'd rather take you home.'

'My parents know I'm staying at Stacy's.'

'Maybe you should call them.'

'And say what?'

'That you're okay.'

'Myron, they think I'm out with my friends. Calling them would only make them worry.'

She had a point, but Myron didn't like it. His gas light went on. He'd need to fill up. He headed up the West Side Highway and over the George Washington Bridge. He stopped at the first gas station on Route 4. New Jersey was one of only two states that did not allow you to pump your own gas. The attendant, wearing a turban and engrossed in a Nicholas Sparks novel, was not thrilled to see him.

'Ten dollars' worth,' Myron told him.

He left them alone. Aimee started sniffling.

'You don't look drunk,' Myron began.

'I didn't say I was. It was the guy who was driving.'

'But you do look,' he continued, 'like you've been crying.'

She did that teen thing that might have been a shrug.

'Your friend Stacy. Where is she now?'

'At her house.'

'She didn't go into the city with you?'

Aimee shook her head and turned away.

'Aimee?'

Her voice was soft. 'I thought I could trust you.'

'You can.'

She shook her head again. Then she reached for the door and pulled the handle. She started to get out. Myron reached for her. He grabbed her left wrist a little harder than he meant to.

'Hey,' she said.

'Aimee . . .'

She tried to pull away. Myron kept a grip on the wrist.

'You're going to call my parents.'

'I just need to know you're okay.'

She pulled at his fingers, trying to get free. Myron felt her nails on his knuckles.

'Let go of me!'

He did. She jumped out of the car. Myron started after her, but he was still wearing his seat belt. The shoulder harness snapped him back. He unbuckled and got out. Aimee was stumbling up the highway with her arms crossed defiantly.

He jogged up to her. 'Please get back in the car.'

'No.'

'I'll drive you, okay?'

'Just leave me alone.'

She stormed off. Cars whizzed by. Some honked at her. Myron followed.

'Where are you going?'

'I made a mistake. I should have never called you.'

'Aimee, just get back in the car. It's not safe out here.'

'You're going to tell my parents.'

'I won't. I promise.'

She slowed down and then stopped. More cars zoomed by on Route 4. The gas station attendant looked at them and spread his arms in a what-gives gesture. Myron held up a finger indicating that they needed a minute.

'I'm sorry,' Myron said. 'I'm just concerned for your welfare. But you're right. I made a promise. I'll keep it.'

Aimee still had her arms crossed. She squinted at him, again as only a teenager can. 'Swear?'

'I swear,' he said.

'No more questions?'

'None.'

She trudged back to the car.

Myron followed. He gave the attendant his credit card, and they drove off.

Aimee told him to take Route 17 North. There were so many malls, so many shopping centers, that it almost seemed as though it were one continuous strip. Myron remembered how his father, whenever they would drive past the Livingston Mall, would shake his head and point and moan, 'Look at all the cars! If the economy is so bad, why are there so many cars? The lot's full! Look at them all.'

Myron's mother and father were currently ensconced in a gated community outside of Boca Raton. Dad had finally sold the warehouse in Newark and now spent his days marveling at what most people had been doing for years: 'Myron, have you been to a Staples? My God, they have every kind of pen and paper there. And the price clubs. Don't even get me started. I bought eighteen screwdrivers for less than ten dollars. We go, we buy so much stuff, I always tell the man at the checkout counter, I say – oh, he laughs at this, Myron – I always say, "I just saved so much money, I'm going bankrupt."'

Myron cast a glance at Aimee. He remembered his own teenage years, the war that is adolescence, and thought about how many times he'd deceived his own parents. He'd been a good kid. He never got in trouble, got good grades, was lofted high because of his basketball skills, but he'd hidden stuff from his parents. All kids do. Maybe it was healthy. The kids who are watched all the time, who are under constant parental surveillance – those were the ones who eventually freaked out. You need an outlet. You have to leave kids room to rebel. If not, the pressure just builds until . . .

'Take that exit over there,' Aimee said. 'Linwood Avenue West.'

He did as she asked. Myron did not really know this area. New Jersey is a series of hamlets. You only knew yours well. He was an Essex County boy. This was Bergen. He felt out of his element. When they stopped at a traffic light he sighed and leaned back, and used the move to take a good hard look at Aimee.

She looked young and scared and helpless. Myron thought about that last one for a moment. Helpless. She turned and met his eyes, and there was a challenge there. Was helpless a fair assessment? Stupid as it might be to think about it, how much of a role was sexism playing here? Play the chauvinism card for a moment. If Aimee was a guy, a big high school football jock, for example, would he be this worried?

The truth was, he was indeed treating her differently because she was a girl.

Was that right – or was he getting mired in some politically correct nonsense?

'Take the next right, then a left at the end of the road.'

He did. Soon they were deep in the tangle of houses. Ridgewood was an old albeit large village – tree-lined streets, Victorians, curvy roads, hills and valleys. Jersey geography. The suburbs were puzzle pieces, interconnected, parts jammed into other parts, few smooth boundaries or right angles.

She led him up a steep road, down another, a left, then a right, then another right. Myron obeyed on autopilot, his thoughts elsewhere. His mind tried to conjure up the right words to say. Aimee had been crying earlier tonight – he was sure of that. She looked somewhat traumatized, but at her age, isn't everything a trauma? She probably had a fight with her boyfriend, the basement-mentioned Randy. Maybe ol' Randy dumped her. Guys did that in high school. They got off on breaking hearts. Made them a big man.

He cleared his throat and aimed for casual: 'Are you still dating that Randy?'

Her reply: 'Next left.'

He took it.

'The house is over there, on the right.'

'At the end of the cul-de-sac?'

'Yes.'

Myron pulled up to it. The house was hunkered down, totally dark. There were no streetlights. Myron blinked a few times. He was still tired, still more foggy-brained than he should be from the earlier festivities. He flashed to Esperanza for a moment, to how lovely she looked, and, selfish as it sounded, he wondered again how this marriage would change things.

'It doesn't look like anybody's home,' he said.

'Stacy's probably asleep.' Aimee pulled a key out. 'Her bedroom is by the back door. I always just let myself in.'

Myron shifted into park and turned off the ignition. 'I'll walk with you.'

'No.'

'How will I know you got in okay?'

'I'll wave.'

Another car pulled down the street behind them. The headlights hit Myron via the rearview mirror. He shaded his eyes. Odd, he thought, two cars on this road at this time of night.

Aimee snagged his attention. 'Myron?'

He looked at her.

'You can't tell my parents about this. They'll freak, okay?'

'I won't tell.'

'Things – ' She stopped, looked out the window toward the house. 'Things aren't so great with them right now.'

'With your parents?'

She nodded.

'You know that's normal, right?'

She nodded again.

He knew that he had to tread gently here. 'Can you tell me more?'

'Just . . . this will only strain things more. If you tell, I mean. Just don't, okay?'

'Okay.'

'Keep your promise.'

And with that, Aimee was out the door. She jogged toward the gate leading to the back. She disappeared behind the house. Myron waited. She came back out to the gate. She smiled now and waved that everything was just fine. But there was something there, something in the wave, something that didn't quite add up.

Myron was about to get out of the car, but Aimee stopped him with a shake of her head. Then she slipped back into the yard, the night swallowing her whole.

8

In the days that followed, when Myron looked back at that moment, at the way Aimee smiled and waved and vanished into the dark, he would wonder what he'd felt. Had there been a premonition, an uneasy feeling, a twinge at the base of his subconscious, something warning him, something that he just couldn't shake?

He didn't think so. But it was hard to remember.

He waited another ten minutes on that cul-de-sac. Nothing happened.

So Myron came up with a plan.

It took a while to find his way out. Aimee had led him into this suburban thicket, but maybe Myron should have dropped bread crumbs on the way. He worked rat-in-a-maze style for twenty minutes until he stumbled upon Paramus Road, which led eventually to a main artery, the Garden State Parkway.

But now, Myron had no plans to return to the apartment in New York.

It was a Saturday night – well, Sunday morning now – and if he went to the house in Livingston instead, he could play basketball the next morning before heading to the airport for his flight to Miami.

And, Myron knew, Erik, Aimee's father, played every Sunday without fail.

That was Myron's immediate, if not pathetic, plan.

So, early in the morning – too early, frankly – Myron rose and put on his shorts and T-shirt, dusted off the old knee brace, and drove over to the gym at Heritage Middle School. Before he headed inside, Myron tried Aimee's cell phone. It went immediately to her voice mail, her tone so sunny and, again, teenage, complete with a 'Like, leave your message.'

He was about to put the phone down when it buzzed in his hand. He checked the caller ID. Nothing.

'Hello?'

'You're a bastard.' The voice was muffled and low. It sounded like a young man, but it was hard to know. 'Do you hear me, Myron? A bastard. And you will pay for what you did.'

The call disconnected. Myron hit star sixty-nine and waited to hear the number. A mechanical voice gave it to him. Local area code, yes, but otherwise the number was wholly unfamiliar. He stopped the car and jotted it down. He'd check it out later.

When Myron ducked into his school, it took a second to adjust to the artificial light, but as soon he did, the familiar ghosts popped up. The gym had the stale smell of every other middle school gym. Someone dribbled a ball. A few guys laughed. The sounds were all the same – all tainted by that hollow echo.

Myron hadn't played in months because he didn't like these sort of white-collar pickup games. Basketball, the game itself, still meant so much to him. He loved it. He loved the feel of the ball on his fingertips, the way they would find the grooves on the jump shot, the arch as the ball headed for the rim, the backspin on it, the positioning for the rebound, the perfect bounce pass. He loved the split-second decision making – pass, drive, shoot – the sudden openings that lasted tenths of a second, the way the world slowed down so that you could split the seam.

He loved all that.

What he did not love was the middle-age machismo. The gym was filling up with Masters of the Universe, the wannabe alpha males who, despite the big house and fat wallet and penis-compensating sports car, still needed to beat someone at something. Myron had been competitive in his youth. Too competitive perhaps. He had been a nutjob for winning. This was, he had learned, not always a wonderful quality, though it often separated the very good from the greats, the near-pros from the pros: this desire – no, need – to better another man.

But he had outgrown it. Some of these guys – a minority for certain, but enough – had not.

When they saw Myron, the former NBA player (no matter for how short a time), they saw their chance to prove what real men they were. Even now. Even when most of them were north of forty. And when the skills are slower but the heart still hungers for glory, it can get physical and downright ugly.

Myron scanned the gym and found his reason for being there.

Erik warmed up at the far basket. Myron jogged over and called out to him.

'Erik, hey, how's it going?'

Erik turned and smiled at him. 'Good morning, Myron. Nice to see you show up.'

'I'm usually not much of a morning guy,' Myron said.

Erik tossed him the ball. Myron took a shot. It clanged off the rim.

'Late night?' Erik asked.

'Very.'

'You've looked better.'

'Gee, thanks,' Myron said. Then: 'So how are things?'

'Fine, you?'

'Good.'

Someone shouted out and the ten guys jogged toward center court. That was how it was. If you wanted to play in the first group, you have to be one of the first ten to arrive. David Rainiv, a brilliant numbers guy and CFO of some Fortune 500 company, always made up teams. He had a knack for balancing the talent and forming competitive matchups. No one questioned his decisions. They were final and binding.

So Rainiv divided up the sides. Myron was matched up against a young guy who stood six-seven. This was a good thing. The theory of men having Napoleon complexes may be debatable in the real world but not in pickup games. Little guys wanted to harm big guys – show them up in an arena usually dominated by size.

But sadly, today the exception proved the rule. The six-seven kid was all elbows and anger. He was athletic and strong but had little basketball talent. Myron did his best to keep his distance. The truth was, despite his knee and age, Myron could score at will. For a while that was what he did. It just came so naturally. It was hard to go easy. But eventually he pulled back. He needed to lose. More men had come in. It was winners-stay-on. He wanted to get off the court so he could talk to Erik.

So after they won the first three games, Myron threw one.

His teammates were not pleased when Myron dribbled off his own foot, thus losing the game. Now they'd have to sit out. They bemoaned the moment but relished the fact that they'd had a great streak going. Like it mattered.

Erik had a water bottle, of course. His shorts matched his shirt. His sneakers were neatly laced. His socks came up to the exact same spot on both ankles, both having the same size roll. Myron used the water fountain and sat next to him.

'So how's Claire?' Myron tried.

'Fine. She does a Pilates-yoga mix now.'

'Oh?'

Claire had always been into some exercise craze or another. She'd gone through the Jane Fonda leggings, the Tae Bo kicks, the Soloflex.

'That's where she is now,' Erik said.

'Taking a class?'

'Yes. During the week, she takes one at six thirty in the morning.'

'Yikes, that's early.'

'We're early risers.'

'Oh?' Myron saw an opening and took it. 'And Aimee?'

'What about Aimee?'

'Does she get up early too?'

Erik frowned. 'Hardly.'

'So you're here,' Myron said, 'and Claire is working out. Where's Aimee?'

'She slept at a friend's last night.'

'Oh?'

'Teenagers,' he said, as if that explained everything. Maybe it did.

'Trouble?'

'You have no idea.'

'Oh?'

Again with the Oh.

Erik said nothing.

'What kind?' Myron asked.

'Kind?'

Myron wanted to say *Oh* again, but he feared going to the well once too often. 'Trouble. What kind of trouble?'

'I'm not sure I understand.'

'Is she sullen?' Myron said, again trying to sound nonchalant. 'Does she not listen? Does she stay up late, blow off school, spend too much time on the Internet, what?'

'All of the above,' Erik said, but now his words came out even slower, even more measured. 'Why do you ask?'

Back up, Myron thought. 'Just making conversation.'

Erik frowned. 'Making conversation usually consists of bemoaning the local teams.'

'It's nothing,' Myron said. 'It's just . . .'

'Just what?'

'The party at my house.'

'What about it?'

'I don't know, seeing Aimee like that, I just started thinking about how tough those teenage years are.'

Erik's eyes narrowed. On the court someone had called a foul and someone was protesting the call. 'I didn't touch you!' a guy with a mustache and elbow pads shouted. Then the name-calling began – something else you never outgrow on a basketball court.

Erik's eyes were still on the court. 'Did Aimee say anything to you?' he asked.

'Like what?'

'Like anything. I remember you were in the basement with her and Erin Wilder.'

'Right.'

'What did you guys talk about?'

'Nothing. They were just goofing on me about how dated the room was.'

Now he looked at Myron. Myron wanted to look away, but he held on. 'Aimee can be,' Erik said, 'rebellious.'

'Like her mother.'

'Claire?' He blinked. 'Rebellious?'

Oh man, he should learn to shut his mouth.

'In what way?'

Myron went for the politician response: 'It depends on what you mean by rebellious, I guess.'

But Erik didn't let it slide. 'What did you mean by it?'

'Nothing. It's a good thing. Claire had edge.'

'Edge?'

Shut up, Myron. 'You know what I mean. Edge. Good edge. When you first saw Claire – that very first second – what attracted you to her?'

'Many things,' he said. 'But edge was not one of them. I had known a lot of girls, Myron. There are those you want to marry and those you just want, well, you know.'

Myron nodded.

'Claire was the one you wanted to marry. That was the first thing I thought when I saw her. And yes, I know how it sounds. But you were her friend. You know what I mean.'

Myron tried to look noncommittal.

'I loved her so much.'

Loved, Myron thought, keeping quiet this time. He'd said loved, not love.

As if reading his mind, Erik added, 'I still do. Maybe more than ever.'

Myron waited for the 'but.'

Erik smiled. 'You heard the good news, I assume?'

'About?'

'Aimee. In fact, we owe you a great big thank-you.'

'Why's that?'

'She got accepted to Duke.'

'Hey, that's great.'

'We just heard two days ago.'

'Congratulations.'

'Your recommendation letter,' he said. 'I think it pushed her over the line.'

Myron said, 'Nah,' though there was probably more truth in Erik's statement than Erik knew. Myron had not only written that letter, but he also had called one of his old teammates, who now worked in admissions.

'No, really,' Erik went on. 'There's so much competition to get into the top schools.

Your recommendation carried a lot of weight, I'm sure. So thank you.'

'She's a good kid. It was my pleasure.'

The game ended. Erik rose. 'Ready?'

'I think I'm done for today,' Myron said.

'Hurting, eh?'

'A little.'

'We're getting older, Myron.'

'I know.'

'There are more aches and pains now.'

Myron nodded.

'Seems to me you have a choice when things hurt,' Erik said. 'You can sit out – or you can try to play through the pain.'

Erik jogged away, leaving Myron to wonder if he'd still been talking about basketball.

9

Back in the car, Myron's cell phone rang again. He checked the caller ID. Again nothing. 'Hello?'

'You're a bastard, Myron.'

'Yeah, I got that the first time. Do you have any new material or are we going to follow up with that original line about me paying for what I've done?'

Click.

Myron shrugged it off. Back in the days when he used to play superhero, he had been a rather well-connected fellow. It was time to see if that still held. He checked his cell phone's directory. The number for Gail Berruti, his old contact from the telephone company, was still there. People think it's unrealistic how private eyes in TV can get phone records with a snap. The truth is, it was beyond easy. Every decent private eye has a source in the phone company. Think about how many people work for Ma Bell. Think how many of them wouldn't mind making an extra buck or two. The going rate had been five hundred dollars per billing statement, but Myron imagined the price had gone up in the past six years.

Berruti wasn't in – she was probably off for the weekend – but he left a message.

'This is a voice from your past,' Myron began.

He asked Berruti to get back to him with the trace on the phone number. He tried Aimee's cell phone again. It went to her voice mail. When he got home, he headed to the computer and Googled the number. Nothing came up. He took a quick shower and then checked his e-mail. Jeremy, his sorta-son, had written him an e-mail from overseas:

Hey, Myron –

We're only allowed to say that we're in the Persian Gulf area. I'm doing well. Mom sounds crazy. Give her a call if you can. She still doesn't understand. Dad doesn't either, but at least he pretends he does. Thanks for the package. We love getting stuff.

I got to go. I'll write more later, but I might be out of touch for a while. Call Mom, okay?

Jeremy

Myron read it again and then again, but the words didn't change. The e-mail, like most of Jeremy's, said nothing. He didn't like that 'out of touch' part. He thought about parenting, how he had missed so much of it, all of it really, and how this kid, his son, fit into his life now. It was working, he thought, at least for Jeremy. But it was hard. The kid was the biggest what-could-have-been, the biggest if-only-I'd-known, and most of the time, it just plain hurt.

Still staring at the message, Myron heard his cell phone. He cursed under his breath, but this time the caller ID told him it was the divine Ms. Ali Wilder.

Myron smiled as he answered it. 'Stallion Services,' he said.

'Sheesh, suppose it was one of my kids on the phone.'

'I'd pretend to be a horse seller,' he said.

'A horse seller?'

'Whatever they call people who sell horses.'

'What time is your flight?'

'Four o'clock.'

'You busy?'

'Why?'

'The kids will be out of the house for the next hour.'

'Whoa,' he said.

'My thoughts exactly.'

'Are you suggesting a little righteous nookie?'

'I am.' Then: 'Righteous?'

'It'll take me some time to get there.'

'Uh-huh.'

'And it'll have to be a quickie.'

'Isn't that your specialty?' she said.

'Now that hurt.'

'Only kidding. Stallion.'

He brayed. 'That's horse-speak for "I'm on my way".'

'Righteous,' she said.

But when he knocked on her door, Erin answered it. 'Hey, Myron.'

'Hey,' he said, trying not to sound disappointed.

He glanced behind her. Ali shrugged a sorry at him.

Myron stepped inside. Erin ran upstairs. Ali came closer. 'She got in late and didn't feel like going to drama club.'

'Oh.'

'Sorry about that.'

'No problem.'

'We could stand in a corner and neck,' she said.

'Can I cop a feel?'

'You better.'

He smiled.

'What?' she said.

'I was just thinking.'

'Thinking what?'

'Something Esperanza said to me yesterday,' Myron said. '*Men tracht und Gott lacht.*'

'Is that German?'

'Yiddish.'

'What does it mean?'

'Man plans, God laughs.'

She repeated it. 'I like that.'

'Me too,' he said.

He hugged her then. Over her shoulder, he saw Erin at the top of the stairs.

She was not smiling. Myron's eyes met hers and again he thought about Aimee, about how the night had swallowed her whole, and about the promise he had sworn to keep.

10

Myron had time before his flight. He grabbed a coffee at the Starbucks in the center of town. The barista who took his order had the trademark sullen attitude. As he handed Myron the drink, lifting it to the counter as though it were the weight of the world, the door behind them opened with a bang. The barista rolled his eyes as they entered.

There were six of them today, trudging in as though through deep snow, heads down, a variety of shakes. They sniffled and touched their faces. The four men were unshaven. The two women smelled like cat piss.

They were mental patients. For real. They spent most nights at Essex Pines, a psychiatric facility in the neighboring town. Their leader – wherever they walked, he stayed in front – was named Larry Kidwell. His group spent most days wandering through town. Livingstonites referred to them as the Town Crazies. Myron uncharitably thought of them as a bizarre rock group: Lithium Larry and the Medicated Five.

Today they seemed less lethargic than usual so it must be pretty close to medication time back at the Pines. Larry was extra jittery. He approached Myron and waved.

'Hey, Myron,' he said too loudly.

'What's happening, Larry?'

'Fourteen hundred eighty-seven planets on creation day, Myron. Fourteen hundred eighty-seven. And I haven't seen a penny. You know what I'm saying?'

Myron nodded. 'I hear you.'

Larry Kidwell shuffled forward. Long, stringy hair peeked out of his Indiana Jones hat. There were scars on his face. His worn blue jeans hung low, displaying enough plumber-crack to park a bike.

Myron started heading for the door. 'Take it easy, Larry.'

'You too, Myron.' He reached out to shake Myron's hand. The others in the group suddenly froze, all eyes – wide eyes, glistening-from-meds eyes – on Myron. Myron reached out his hand and clasped Larry's. Larry held on hard and pulled Myron closer. His breath, no surprise, stank.

'The next planet,' Larry whispered, 'it might be yours. Yours alone.'

'That's great to know, thanks.'

'No!' Still a whisper, but it was harsh now. 'The planet. It's slither moon. It's out to get you, you know what I'm saying?'

'I think so.'

'Don't ignore this.'

He let go of Myron, his eyes wide. Myron took a step back. He could see the man's agitation.

'It's okay, Larry.'

'Heed my warning, man. He stroked the moon slither. You understand? He hates you so bad he stroked the moon slither.'

The others in the group were total strangers, but Myron knew Larry's tragic backstory. Larry Kidwell had been two years ahead of Myron in school. He'd been immensely popular. He was an incredible guitarist, good with the girls, even dated Beth Finkelstein, the hometown hottie, during his senior year. Larry ended up being salutatorian of his class at Livingston High. He went to Yale University, his father's alma mater, and from all accounts, had a great first semester.

Then it all came apart.

What was surprising, what made it all the more horrific, was how it happened. There had been no terrifying event in Larry's life. There had been no family tragedy. There had been no drugs or alcohol or girl gone wrong.

The doctor's diagnosis: a chemical imbalance.

Who knows how you get cancer? It was the same thing with Larry. He simply had a mental disease. It started as mild OCD, then became more severe, and then, try as they might, no one could stop his slide. By his sophomore year Larry was setting up rat traps so he could eat them. He became delusional. He dropped out of Yale. Then there were suicide attempts and major hallucinations and problems of all sorts. Larry broke into someone's house because the 'Clyzets from planet three hundred twenty-six' were trying to lay a nest there. The family was home at the time.

Larry Kidwell has been in and out of psych institutes ever since. Supposedly, there are moments when Larry is entirely lucid, and it is so painful for him, realizing what he has become, that he rips at his own face – ergo the scars – and cries out in such agony that they immediately sedate him.

'Okay,' Myron said. 'Thanks for the warning.'

Myron headed out the door, shook it off. He hit Chang's Dry Cleaning next door. Maxine Chang was behind the counter. She looked, as always, exhausted and overworked. There were two women about Myron's age at the counter. They were talking about their kids and colleges. That was all anybody talked about right now. Every April, Livingston became a snow globe of college acceptances. The stakes, if you were to listen to the parents, could not have been higher. These weeks – those thick-or-thin envelopes that arrived in their mailboxes – decided how happy and successful their offspring would be for the rest of their lives.

'Ted is wait-listed at Penn but he made Lehigh,' one said.

'Do you believe Chip Thompson got into Penn?'

'His father.'

'What? Oh wait, he's an alum, right?'

'He gave them a quarter million dollars.'

'I should have known. Chip had terrible boards.'

'I heard they hired a pro to write his essays.'

'I should have done that for Cole.'

Like that. On and on.

Myron nodded at Maxine. Maxine Chang usually had a big smile for him. Not today. She shouted, 'Roger!'

Roger Chang came out of the back. 'Hey, Myron.'

'What's up, Roger?'

'You wanted the shirts boxed this time, right?'

'Right.'

'I'll be right back.'

'Maxine,' one of the women said, 'did Roger hear from schools yet?'

Maxine barely looked up. 'He made Rutgers,' she said. 'Wait-listed at others.'

'Wow, congratulations.'

'Thank you.' But she didn't seem thrilled.

'Maxine, won't he be the first in your family to go to college?' the other woman said. Her tone could only have sounded more patronizing if she'd been petting a dog. 'How wonderful for you.'

Maxine wrote up the ticket.

'Where is he wait-listed?'

'Princeton and Duke.'

Hearing his alma mater made Myron think again about Aimee. He flashed back to Larry and his spooky planet talk. Myron wasn't one for bad omens or any of that, but he didn't feel like poking the fates in the eye either. He debated trying Aimee's phone again, but what would be the point? He thought back over last night, replayed it in his head, wondered how he could have done it differently.

Roger – Myron had forgotten that the kid was already a high school senior – came back and handed him the box of shirts. Myron took them, told Roger to put them on his account, headed out the door. He still had time before his flight.

So he drove to Brenda's grave.

The cemetery still overlooked a schoolyard. That was what he could still not get over. The sun shone hard as it always seemed to when he visited, mocking his gloom. He stood alone. There were no other visitors. A nearby backhoe dug a hole. Myron remained still. He lifted his head and let the sun shine on his face. He could still feel that – the sun on his face. Brenda, of course, could not. Would never again.

A simple thought, but there you go.

Brenda Slaughter had only been twenty-six when she died. Had she survived, she'd have turned thirty-four in two weeks. He wondered where she'd be if Myron had kept his promise. He wondered if she'd be with him.

When she died, Brenda was in the middle of her residency in pediatric medicine. She was six-foot-four, stunning, African-American, a model. She was about to play pro basketball, the face and image that would launch the new women's league. There had been threats made. So Myron had been hired by the league owner to protect her.

Nice job, All-Star.

He stood and stared down and clenched his fists. He never talked to her when he came here. He didn't sit and try to meditate or any of that. He didn't conjure up the good or her laugh or her beauty or her extraordinary presence. Cars whizzed by. The schoolyard was silent. No kids were out playing. Myron did not move.

He did not come here because he still mourned her death. He came because he didn't.

He barely remembered Brenda's face anymore. The one kiss they shared . . . when he conjured it up he knew it was more imagination than memory. That was the problem. Brenda Slaughter was slipping away from him. Soon it would be as

577

though she never existed. So Myron didn't come here for comfort or to pay his respects. He came because he still needed to hurt, needed the wounds to stay fresh. He still wanted to be outraged because moving on – feeling at peace with what happened to her – was too obscene.

Life goes on. That was a good thing, right? The outrage flickers and slowly leaks away. The scars heal. But when you let that happen, your soul goes dead a little too.

So Myron stood there and clenched his fists until they shook. He thought about the sunny day they buried her – and the horrible way he had avenged her. He summoned up the outrage. It came at him like a force. His knees buckled. He tottered, but he stayed upright.

He had messed up with Brenda. He had wanted to protect her. He had pushed too hard – and in doing so he had gotten her killed.

Myron looked down at the grave. The sun was still warm on him, but he felt the shiver travel down his back. He wondered why he chose today of all days to visit, and then he thought about Aimee, about pushing too hard, about wanting to protect, and with one more shiver, he thought – no, he feared – that maybe, somehow, he had let it all happen again.

11

Claire Biel stood by the kitchen sink and stared at the stranger she called a husband. Erik was eating a sandwich carefully, his tie tucked into his shirt. There was a newspaper perfectly folded into one quarter. He chewed slowly. He wore cuff links. His shirt was starched. He liked starch. He liked everything ironed. In his closet his suits were hung four inches apart from one another. He didn't measure to achieve this. It just happened. His shoes, always freshly polished, were lined up like something in a military procession.

Who was this man?

Their two youngest daughters, Jane and Lizzie, were both wolfing down PB&J on white bread. They chatted through their sticky mouths. They made noise. Their milk sloshed into small spills. Erik kept reading. Jane asked if they could be excused. Claire said yes. They both darted toward the door.

'Stop,' Claire said.

They did.

'Plates in the sink.'

They sighed and did the eye-roll – though they were only nine and ten, they had learned from the best, their older sister. They trudged back as though through the deep snow of the Adirondacks, lifted plates that must have seemed like boulders, and somehow scaled the mountain toward the sink.

'Thank you,' Claire said.

They took off. The room was quiet now. Erik chewed quietly.

'Is there any more coffee?' he asked.

She poured some. He crossed his legs, careful not to crease his trousers. They had been married for nineteen years, but the passion had slipped out the window in under two. They were treading water now, had been treading for so long that it no longer seemed that difficult. Oldest cliché in the book was about how fast time went by, but it was true. It didn't seem like the passion had been gone that long. Sometimes, like right now, she could look at him and remember a time when just seeing him would take her breath away.

Still not glancing up, Erik asked, 'Have you heard from Aimee?'

'No.'

He straightened his arm to pull back the sleeve, checked his watch, arched an eyebrow. 'Two in the afternoon.'

'She's probably just waking up.'

'We might want to call.'

He didn't move.

'By we,' Claire said, 'do you mean me?'

'I'll do it if you want.'

She reached for the phone and dialed their daughter's cell phone. They'd gotten Aimee her own phone last year. Aimee had brought them an advertisement showing them that they could add a third line for ten dollars a month. Erik was unmoved. But, Aimee whined, all her friends – everyone! – had one, an argument that always *always* led Erik to remark, 'We are not everyone, Aimee.'

But Aimee was ready for that. She quickly changed tracks and plucked on the parental-protection heartstrings: 'If I had my own phone, I could always stay in touch. You could find me twenty-four-seven. And if there was ever an emergency . . . '

That had closed the sale. Mothers understood this basic truism: Sex and peer pressure may sell, but nothing sells like fear.

The call went to voice mail. Aimee's enthusiastic voice – she had taped her message almost immediately after getting the phone – told Claire to, like, leave a message. The sound of her daughter's voice, familiar as it was, made her ache, though she wasn't sure for what exactly.

When the beep came, Claire said, 'Hey, honey, it's Mom. Just give me a call, okay?' She hung up.

Erik still read his paper. 'She didn't answer?'

'Gee, what gave it away? Was it the part where I asked her to give me a call?'

He frowned at the sarcasm. 'Her phone probably went dead.'

'Probably.'

'She always forgets to charge it,' he said, with a shake of his head. 'Whose house was she sleeping over? Steffi's, right?'

'Stacy.'

'Right, whatever. Maybe we should call Stacy.'

'Why?'

'I want her home. She has that project due on Thursday.'

'It's Sunday. She just got into college.'

'So you think she should slack off now?'

Claire handed him the portable. 'You call.'

'Fine.'

She gave him the number. He pressed the digits and put the phone to his ear. In the background, Claire heard her younger daughters giggle. Then one shouted, 'I do not!' When the phone was picked up, Erik cleared his throat. 'Good afternoon, this is Erik Biel. I'm Aimee Biel's father. I was wondering if she was there right now.'

His face didn't change. His voice didn't change. But Claire saw his grip on the phone tighten and she felt something deep in her chest give way.

12

Myron had two semicontradictory thoughts about Miami. One, the weather was so beautiful he should move down here. Two, sun – there was too much sun down here. Everything was too bright. Even in the airport Myron found himself squinting.

This was not a problem for Myron's parents, the beloved Ellen and Al Bolitar, who wore those oversize sunglasses that looked suspiciously like welder's goggles, though without the style. They both waited for him at the airport. Myron had told them not to, that he would get a taxi, but Dad had insisted. 'Don't I always pick you up from the airport? Remember when you came back from Chicago after that big snowstorm?'

'That was eighteen years ago, Dad.'

'So? You think I forgot how to go?'

'And that was Newark Airport.'

'Eighteen minutes, Myron.'

Myron's eyes closed. 'I remember.'

'Exactly eighteen minutes.'

'I remember, Dad.'

'That's how long it took me to get from the house to Terminal A at Newark Airport. I used to time it, remember?'

'I do, yes.'

So here they were, both of them, at the airport with dark suntans and fresh liver spots. When Myron came down the escalator, Mom ran over and wrapped her arms around her boy as if this were a POW homecoming in 1974. Dad stayed in the background with that satisfied smile. Myron hugged her back. Mom felt smaller. That was how it was down here. Your parents withered and got smaller and darker, like giant shrunken heads.

Mom said, 'Let's get your luggage.'

'I have it here.'

'That's it? Just that one bag?'

'I'm only down for a night.'

'Still.'

Myron watched her face, checked her hands. When he saw the shake was more pronounced, he felt the thud in his chest.

'What?' she said.

'Nothing.'

Mom shook her head. 'You've always been the worst liar. Remember that time I walked in on you and Tina Ventura and you said nothing was going on? You think I didn't know?'

Junior year of high school. Ask Mom and Dad what they did yesterday, they won't remember. Ask them about anything from his youth, and it's like they studied replays at night.

He held up his hands in mock surrender. 'Got me.'

'Don't be such a smart guy. And that reminds me.'

They reached Dad. Myron kissed him on the cheek. He always did. You never outgrow that. The skin felt loose. The smell of Old Spice was still there, but it was fainter than usual. There was something else there, some other smell, and Myron thought it was the smell of the old. They started for the car.

'Guess who I ran into?' Mom said.

'Who?'

'Dotte Derrick. Remember her?'

'No.'

'Sure you do. She had that thing, that what-you-call-it, in her yard.'

'Oh, right. Her. With that thing.'

He had no idea what she was talking about, but this was easier.

'So anyway, I saw Dotte the other day and we start talking. She and Bob moved down here four years ago. They have a place in Fort Lauderdale, but Myron, it's really run-down. I mean, it hasn't been kept up at all. Al, what's the name of Dotte's place? Sunshine Vista, something like that, right?'

'Who cares?' Dad said.

'Thanks, Mr. Helpful. Anyway, that's where Dotte lives. And this place is awful. So run-down. Al, isn't Dotte's place run-down?'

'The point, El,' Dad said. 'Get to the point.'

'I'm getting there, I'm getting there. Where was I?'

'Dotte Something,' Myron said.

'Derrick. You remember her, right?'

'Very well,' Myron said.

'Right, good. Anyway, Dotte still has cousins up north. The Levines. Do you remember them? No reason you should, forget it. Anyway, one of the cousins lives in Kasselton. You know Kasselton, right? You used to play them in high school – '

'I know Kasselton.'

'Don't get snappy.'

Dad spread his arms to the sky. 'The point, El. Get to the point.'

'Right, sorry. You're right. When you're right, you're right. So to make a long story short – '

'No, El, you've never made a long story short,' Dad said. 'Oh, you've made plenty of short stories long. But never, ever, have you made a long story short.'

'Can I talk here, Al?'

'Like anyone could stop you. Like a large gun or big army tank – like even that could stop you.'

Myron couldn't help but smile. Ladies and gents, meet Ellen and Alan Bolitar or, as Mom liked to say, 'We're El Al – you know, like the Israeli airline?'

'So anyway, I was talking to Dotte about this and that. You know, the usual. The Ruskins moved out of town. Gertie Schwartz had gall stones. Antonietta Vitale, such a pretty thing, she married some millionaire from Montclair. That kind of thing. And then Dotte told me – Dotte told me this, by the way, not you

– Dotte said you're dating someone.'

Myron closed his eyes.

'Is it true?'

He said nothing.

'Dotte said you were dating a widow with six children.'

'Two children,' Myron said.

Mom stopped and smiled.

'What?'

'Gotcha.'

'Huh?'

'If I said two children, you might have just denied it.' Mom pointed an aha finger up in the air. 'But I knew if I said six, you'd react. So I caught you.'

Myron looked at his father. His father shrugged. 'She's been watching a lot of *Matlock* lately.'

'Children, Myron? You're dating a woman with children?'

'Mom, I'm going to say this as nicely as I can: Butt out.'

'Listen to me, Mr. Funny Guy. When children are involved, you can't just go on your merry way. You need to think about the repercussions on them. Do you understand what I'm telling you?'

'Do you understand the meaning of "butt out"?'

'Fine, do what you want.' Now she did the mock surrender. Like mother, like son. 'What do I care?'

They continued walking – Myron in the middle, Dad on his right, Mom on his left. That was how they always walked. The pace was slower now. That didn't bother him much. He was more than willing to slow down so they could keep up.

They drove to the condo and parked in the designated spot. Mom purposely took the long path past the swimming pool, so she could introduce Myron to a dizzying array of condo owners. Mom kept saying, 'You remember meeting my son?' and Myron faked remembering them back. Some of the women, many in their upper seventies, were too-well built. As Dustin Hoffman had been advised in *The Graduate*, 'Plastics.' Just a different kind. Myron had nothing against cosmetic surgery, but past a certain age, discriminatory or not, it creeped him out.

The condo was also too bright. You'd think as you got older you'd want less light, but no. His parents actually kept on the welder sunglasses for the first five minutes. Mom asked if he was hungry. He was smart enough to answer yes. She had already ordered a sloppy joe platter – Mom's cooking would be deemed inhumane at Guantánamo Bay – from a place called Tony's, which was 'just like the old Eppes Essen's' at home.

They ate, they talked, Mom kept trying to wipe the small bits of cabbage that got stuck in the corners of Dad's mouth, but her hand shook too badly. Myron met his father's eye. Mom's Parkinson's was getting worse, but they wouldn't talk to Myron about it. They were getting old. Dad had a pacemaker. Mom had Parkinson's. But their first duty was still to shield their son from all that.

'When do you have to leave for your meeting?' Mom asked.

Myron checked his watch. 'Now.'

They said good-byes, did the hug-n-kiss thing again. When he pulled away, he felt as if he were abandoning them, as if they were going to hold off the enemy on their own while he drove to safety. Having aging parents sucked; but as Esperanza, who lost both parents young, often pointed out, it was better than the alternative.

Once in the elevator, Myron checked his cell phone. Aimee had still not called him back. He tried her number again and was not surprised when it went to voice mail. Enough, he thought. He would just call her house. See what's what.

Aimee's voice came to him: '*You promised . . .*'

He dialed Erik and Claire's home number. Claire answered. 'Hello?'

'Hey, it's Myron.'

'Hi.'

'What's happening?'

'Not much,' Claire said.

'I saw Erik this morning' – man, was it really the same day? – 'and he told me about Aimee getting accepted to Duke. So I wanted to offer up my congratulations.'

'Yeah, thanks.'

'Is she there?'

'No, not right now.'

'Can I call her later?'

'Yeah, sure.'

Myron changed gears. 'Everything okay? You sound a little distracted.'

He was about to say more but again Aimee's words – '*You promised you wouldn't tell my parents*' – floated down to him.

'Fine, I guess,' Claire said. 'Look, I gotta go. Thanks for writing that recommendation letter.'

'No big deal.'

'Very big deal. The kids ranked four and seven in her class both applied and didn't get in. You were the difference.'

'I doubt it. Aimee's a great candidate.'

'Maybe, but thanks anyway.'

There was a grumbling noise in the background. Sounded like Erik.

In his mind, there was Aimee's voice again: '*Things aren't so great with them right now.*' Myron was trying to think of something else to say, a follow-up question maybe, when Claire hung up the phone.

Loren Muse had landed a fresh homicide case – double homicide, actually, two men shot outside a nightclub in East Orange. Rumor was that the killings were a hit carried out by John 'The Ghost' Asselta, a notorious hitman who'd actually been born and raised in the area. Asselta had been quiet for the past few years. If he was back, they were about to be very busy.

Loren was reviewing the ballistics report when her private line rang. She picked up and said, 'Muse.'

'Guess who?'

She smiled. 'Lance Banner, you old dog. Is that you?'

'It is.'

Banner was a police officer in Livingston, New Jersey, the suburb where they'd both grown up.

'To what do I owe the pleasure?'

'You still investigating Katie Rochester's disappearance?'

'Not really,' she said.

'Why not?'

'For one thing, there's no evidence of violence. For another, Katie Rochester is over eighteen.'

'Just barely.'

'In the eyes of the law, eighteen might as well be eighty. So officially we don't even have an investigation going on.'

'And unofficially?'

'I met with a doctor named Edna Skylar.' She recounted Edna's story, using almost the same words she'd used when she'd told her boss, county prosecutor Ed Steinberg. Steinberg had sat there for a long while before predictably concluding: 'We don't have the resources to go after such a maybe.'

When she finished, Banner asked, 'How did you get the case in the first place?'

'Like I said, there was no case, really. She's of age, no signs of violence, you know the drill. So no one was assigned. Jurisdiction is questionable anyway. But the father, Dominick, he made a lot of noise with the press, you probably saw it, and he knew someone who knows someone, and that led to Steinberg. . . .'

'And that led to you.'

'Right. The key word being *led*. As in past tense.'

Lance Banner asked, 'Do you have ten minutes to spare?'

'Did you hear about that double homicide in East Orange?'

'I did.'

'I'm the lead.'

'As in the present tense of *led*?'

'You got it.'

'I figured that,' Banner said. 'It's why I'm only asking for ten minutes.'

'Important?' she asked.

'Let's just say' – he stopped, thinking of the word – ''very odd.''

'And it involves Katie Rochester's disappearance?'

'Ten minutes max, Loren. That's all I'm asking for. Heck, I'll take five.'

She checked her watch. 'When?'

'I'm in the lobby of your building right now,' he said. 'Can you get us a room?'

'For five minutes? Sheesh, your wife wasn't kidding about your bedroom stamina.'

'Dream on, Muse. Hear that ding? I'm stepping into the elevator. Get the room ready.'

Livingston police detective Lance Banner had a crew cut. He was big with features and a build that made you think of right angles. Loren had known him since elementary school and she still couldn't get that image out of her head, of what he looked like back then. That's how it is with kids you grew up with. You always see them as second-graders.

Loren watched him hesitate when he entered, unsure how to greet her – a kiss on the cheek or a more professional handshake. She took the lead and pulled him toward her and kissed his cheek. They were in an interrogation room, and they both headed for the interrogator seat. Banner pulled up, raised both hands, sat across from her.

'Maybe you should Mirandize me,' he said.

'I'll wait until I have enough for an arrest. So what have you got on Katie Rochester?'

'No time for chitchat, eh?'

She just looked at him.

'Okay, okay, let's get to it then. Do you know a woman named Claire Biel?'

'No.'

'She lives in Livingston,' Banner said. 'She would have been Claire Garman when we were kids.'

'Still no.'

'She was older than us anyway. Four, five years probably.' He shrugged. 'I was just checking.'

'Uh-huh,' Loren said. 'Do me a favor, Lance. Pretend I'm your wife and skip the foreplay.'

'Fine, here it is. She called me this morning. Claire Biel. Her daughter went out last night and hasn't come home.'

'How old is she?'

'She just turned eighteen.'

'Any sign of foul play?'

He made a face suggesting an inner debate. Then: 'Not yet.'

'So?'

'So normally we wait a little. Like you said on the phone – over eighteen, no signs of violence.'

'Like with Katie Rochester.'

'Right.'

'But?'

'I know the parents a little. Claire was in school with my older brother. They live in the neighborhood. They're concerned, of course. But on the face of it, well, you figure the kid is just messing around. She got accepted to college the other day. Made Duke. Her first choice. She goes out partying with her friends. You know what I'm saying.'

'I do.'

'But I figure, what's the harm in doing a little checking, right? So I do the easiest thing. Just to satisfy the parents that their girl – her name is Aimee, by the way – that Aimee is okay.'

'So what did you do?'

'I ran her credit card number, see if Aimee made any charges or used an ATM.'

'And?'

'Sure enough. She took out a thousand dollars, the max, at an ATM machine at two in the morning.'

'You get the video from the bank?'

'I did.'

Loren knew that this was done in seconds now. You didn't have an old-fashioned tape anymore. The videos are digital and could be e-mailed and downloaded almost instantaneously.

'It was Aimee,' he said. 'No question about it. She didn't try to hide her face or anything.'

'So?'

'So you figure it's a runaway, right?'

'Right.'

'A slam dunk,' he went on. 'She took the money and is doing a little partying, whatever. Blowing off steam at the end of her senior year.' Banner looked off.

'Come on, Lance. What's the problem?'

'Katie Rochester.'

'Because Katie did the same thing? Used an ATM before disappearing?'

He tilted his head back and forth in a maybe-yes, maybe-no gesture. His eyes were still far away. 'It's not just that she did the same thing as Katie,' he said. 'It's that she did the *exact* same thing.'

'I'm not following.'

'The ATM machine Aimee Biel used was located in Manhattan – more specifically' – he slowed his words now – ''at a Citibank on Fifty-second Street and Sixth Avenue.'

Loren felt the chill begin at the base of her skull and travel south.

Banner said, 'That's the same one Katie Rochester used, right?'

She nodded and then she said something truly stupid: 'Could be a coincidence.'

'Could be,' he agreed.

'You got anything else?'

'We're just starting, but we pulled the logs on her cell phone.'

'And?'

'She made a phone call right after she took out the money.'

'To whom?'

Lance Banner leaned back and crossed his legs. 'Do you remember a guy a few years ahead of us – big basketball star named Myron Bolitar?'

13

Down in Miami, Myron dined with Rex Storton, a new client, at some super-huge restaurant Rex had picked out because a lot of people walked by. The restaurant was one of those chains like Bennigans or TGI Fridays or something equally universal and awful.

Storton was an aging actor, a one-time superstar who was looking for the indie role that would launch him out of Miami's Loni Anderson Dinner Theater and back into the upper echelon of La-La Land. Rex was resplendent in a pink polo with the collar turned up, white pants that a man his age just shouldn't involve himself with, and a shiny gray toupee that looked good when you weren't sitting directly across the table from it.

For years Myron had represented professional athletes only. When one of his basketball players wanted to cross over and do movies, Myron started meeting actors. A new branch of the business took root, and now he handled the Hollywood clients almost exclusively, leaving the sports management stuff to Esperanza.

It was strange. As an athlete himself, one would think that Myron would relate more to those in a similar profession. He didn't. He liked the actors more. Most athletes are singled out right away, at fairly young ages, and elevated to godlike status from the get-go. Athletes are in the lead clique at school. They get invited to all the parties. They nab all the hot girls. Adults fawn. Teachers let them slide.

Actors are different. Many of them had started out at the opposite end of the spectrum. Athletics rule in most towns. Actors were often the kids who couldn't make the team and were looking for another activity. They were often too small – ever meet an actor in real life and notice that they're tiny? – or uncoordinated. So they back into acting. Later, when stardom hits them, they are not used to the treatment. They're surprised by it. They're somewhat more appreciative. In many cases – no, not all – it makes them more humble than their athletic counterparts.

There were other factors, of course. They say that actors take to the stage to fill a void of emptiness only applause can fill. Even if true, it made thespians somewhat more anxious to please. While athletes were used to people doing their bidding and came to believe it was their due in life, actors came to that from a position of insecurity. Athletes need to win. They need to beat you. Actors need only your applause and thus your approval.

It made them easier to work with.

Again this was a complete generalization – Myron was an athlete, after all, and did not consider himself difficult – but like most generalizations, there was something to it.

He told Rex about the indie role as, to quote the pitch, 'a geriatric, cross-dressing car thief, but with a heart.' Rex nodded. His eyes continuously scanned the room, as if they were at a cocktail party and he was waiting for someone more important to come in. Rex always kept one eye toward the entrance. This was how it was with actors. Myron repped one guy who was world-renowned for detesting the press. He had battled with photographers. He had sued tabloids. He had demanded his privacy. Yet whenever Myron ate dinner with him, the actor always chose a seat in the center of the room, facing the door, and whenever someone would enter, he'd look up, just for a second, just to make sure he was recognized.

His eyes still moving, Rex said, 'Yeah, yeah, I get it. Do I have to wear a dress?'

'For some scenes, yes.'

'I've done that before.'

Myron arched an eyebrow.

'Professionally, I mean. Don't be a wiseass. And it was tastefully done. The dress must be something tasteful.'

'So, what, nothing with a plunging neckline?'

'Funny, Myron. You're a scream. Speaking of which, do I have to do a screen test?'

'You do.'

'Chrissakes, I've made eighty films.'

'I know, Rex.'

'He can't look at one of them?'

Myron shrugged. 'That's what he said.'

'You like the script?'

'I do, Rex.'

'How old is this director?'

'Twenty-two.'

'Jesus. I was already a has-been by the time he was born.'

'They'll pay for a flight to L.A.'

'First class?'

'Coach, but I think I can get you a business upgrade.'

'Ah, who am I kidding? I'd sit on the wing in only my girdle if the role was right.'

'That's the spirit.'

A mother and daughter came over and asked Rex for his autograph. He smiled grandly and puffed out his chest. He looked at the obvious mother and said, 'Are you two sisters?'

She giggled as she left.

'Another happy customer,' Myron said.

'I aim to please.'

A buxom blonde came by for an autograph. Rex kissed her a little too hard. After she sashayed away, Rex held up a piece of paper. 'Look.'

'What is it?'

'Her phone number.'

'Terrific.'

'What can I say, Myron? I love women.'

Myron looked up and to his right.

'What?'

'I'm just wondering,' Myron said, 'how your prenup will hold up.'

'Very funny.'

They ate some chicken from a deep fryer. Or maybe it was beef or shrimp. Once in the deep fryer, it all tasted the same. Myron could feel Rex's eyes on him.

'What?' Myron said.

'It's sort of tough to admit this,' Rex said, 'but I'm only alive when I'm in the spotlight. I've had three wives and four kids. I love them all. I enjoyed my time with them. But the only time I feel really myself is when I'm in the spotlight.'

Myron said nothing.

'Does that sound pathetic to you?'

Myron shrugged.

'You know what else?'

'What?'

'In their heart of hearts, I think most people are like that. They crave fame. They want people to recognize them and stop them on the streets. People say it's a new thing, what with the reality TV crap. But I think it's always been that way.'

Myron studied his pitiful food.

'You agree?'

'I don't know, Rex.'

'For me, the spotlight has dimmed a touch, you know what I'm saying? It's faded bit by bit. I was lucky. But I've met some one-hit wonders. Man, they're never happy. Not ever again. But me, with the slow fade, I could get used to it. And even now, people still recognize me. It's why I eat out every night. Yeah, that's awful to say, but it's true. And even now, when I'm in my seventies, I still dream about clawing my way back to that brightest of spotlights. You know what I'm saying?'

'I do,' Myron said. 'It's why I love you.'

'Why's that?'

'You're honest about it. Most actors tell me it's just about the work.'

Rex made a scoffing noise. 'What a load of crap. But it's not their fault, Myron. Fame is a drug. The most potent. You're hooked, but you don't want to admit it.' Rex gave him the twinkly smile that used to melt the girls' hearts. 'And what about you, Myron?'

'What about me?'

'Like I said, there's this spotlight, right? For me it faded slowly. But for you, top college basketball player in the country, on your way to a big pro career . . .'

Myron waited.

'. . . and then, *flick*' – Rex snapped his fingers – 'lights out. When you're only, what, twenty-one, twenty-two?'

'Twenty-two,' Myron said.

'So how did you cope? And I love you too, sweetums. So tell me the truth.'

Myron crossed his legs. He felt his face flush. 'Are you enjoying the new show?'

'What, the dinner theater gig?'

'Yes.'

'It's dog crap. It's worse than stripping on Route 17 in Lodi, New Jersey.'

'And you know this from personal experience?'

'Stop trying to change the subject. How did you cope?'

Myron sighed. 'Most would say I coped amazingly well.'

Rex lifted his palm to the sky and curled his fingers as if to say, *Come on, come on.* 'What exactly do you want to know?'

Rex thought about it. 'What did you do first?'

'After the injury?'

'Yes.'

'Rehab. Lots of rehab.'

'And once you realized that your basketball days were over . . . ?'

'I went back to law school.'

'Where?'

'Harvard.'

'Very impressive. So you went to law school. Then what?'

'You know what, Rex. I got my JD, opened up a sports agency, grew into a full-service agency that now represents actors and writers too.' He shrugged.

'Myron?'

'What?'

'I asked for the truth.'

Myron picked up his fork, took a bite, chewed slowly. 'The lights didn't just go out, Rex. I had a full-fledged power outage. A lifetime blackout.'

'I know that.'

'So I needed to push past it.'

'And?'

'And that's it.'

Rex shook his head and smiled.

'What?'

'Next time,' Rex said. He picked up his fork. 'You'll tell me next time.'

'You're a pain in the ass.'

'But you love me, remember?'

By the time they finished dinner and drinks, it was late. Drinking for a second night in a row. Myron Bolitar, lush of the stars. He made sure that Rex was safely back in his residence before heading to his parents' condo. He had a key. He slipped it in quietly so as to not awaken Mom and Dad. He knew that it would do no good.

The TV was on. His father sat in the living room. When Myron entered, Dad faked like he was just waking up. He wasn't. Dad always stayed awake until Myron came home. Didn't matter what time Myron returned. Didn't matter that Myron was now in his fourth decade.

Myron came up behind his father's chair. Dad turned around and gave him the smile, the one he saved only for Myron, the one that told Myron that he was the single greatest creation in this man's eyes and how could you beat that?

'Have fun?'

'Rex is a pretty cool guy,' Myron said.

'I used to like his movies.' His father nodded a few times too many. 'Sit for a second.'

'What's up?'

'Just sit, okay?'

He did. Myron folded his hands and put them in his lap. Like he was eight. 'Is this about Mom?'

'No.'

'Her Parkinson's is getting worse.'

'That's how it is with Parkinson's, Myron. It gets worse.'

'Is there anything I can do?'

'No.'

'I think I should say something, at least.'

'Don't. It's better. And what would you say that your mother doesn't already know?'

Now it was Myron's turn to nod a few times too many. 'So what do you want to talk about?'

'Nothing. I mean, your mother wants us to have a heart-to-heart.'

'What about?'

'Today's *New York Times*.'

'Excuse me?'

'There was something in it. Your mother thinks you'll be upset and that we should talk. But I don't think I'm going to do that. I think what I'm going to do instead is hand you the newspaper and let you read it for yourself and leave you alone for a while. If you want to talk, you come and get me, okay? If not, I'll give you your space.'

Myron frowned. 'Something in *The New York Times*?'

'Sunday Styles section.' Dad stood and pointed with his chin toward the pile of Sunday papers. 'Page sixteen. Good night, Myron.'

'Good night, Dad.'

His father moved down the hall. No need to tiptoe. Mom could sleep through a Judas Priest concert. Dad was the night watchman, Mom the sleepy princess. Myron stood. He picked up the Sunday Styles section, turned to page sixteen, saw the photo, and felt the stiletto pierce his heart.

The New York Times Sunday Styles was upscale gossip. The most well-read pages were for wedding announcements. And there, on page sixteen, in the top left-hand corner, was a photograph of a man with Ken-doll good looks and teeth that were too perfect to be capped. He had a Republican senator's cleft chin, and his name was Stone Norman. The article said Stone ran and operated the BMV Investment Group, a highly successful financial enterprise specializing in major institutional trades.

Snore.

The engagement announcement said that Stone Norman and his wife-to-be would be married next Saturday at Tavern on the Green in Manhattan. A reverend would preside over the ceremony. Then the newlyweds would begin their lives together in Scarsdale, New York.

More snore. Stone Snore.

But none of that was what had pierced his heart. No, what did that, what really hurt and made the knees buckle, was the woman ol' Stone was marrying, the one smiling with him in that photograph, a smile Myron still knew far too well.

For a moment Myron just stared. He reached out and brushed the bride-to-be's face with his finger. Her biography stated that she was a best-selling writer who'd been nominated for both the PEN/Faulkner and National Book Award. Her name was Jessica Culver, and though it didn't say so in the article, for more than a decade she had been the love of Myron Bolitar's life.

He just sat and stared.

Jessica, the woman he'd been sure was his soul mate, was getting married to someone else.

He had not seen her since they broke up seven years ago. Life had gone on for him. It had, of course, gone on for her. Why should he be surprised?

He put down the paper, then picked it up again. A lifetime ago Myron had asked Jessica to marry him. She had said no. They stayed together on and off for the next decade. But in the end Myron wanted to get married, and Jessica didn't. She pretty much scoffed at the bourgeois idea of it all – the suburbs, the picket fence, the children, the barbecues, the Little League games, the life Myron's parents had led.

Except now Jessica was marrying big Stone Norman and moving to the über-suburb of Scarsdale, New York.

Myron carefully folded the paper and put it on the coffee table. He stood with a sigh and headed down the corridor. He flicked off the lights as he went. He passed his parents' bedroom. The reading lamp was still on. His father faked a cough to let Myron know he was there.

'I'm fine,' he said out loud.

His father did not respond, and Myron was grateful. The man was like a master on the tightrope, managing the nearly impossible feat of showing he cared without butting in or interfering.

Jessica Culver, the love of his life, the woman he'd always believed was his destined soul mate, was getting married.

Myron wanted to sleep on that one. But sleep would not come.

14

Time to talk to Aimee Biel's parents. It was six in the morning. County investigator Loren Muse sat on her floor cross-legged. She wore shorts, and the quasi-shag carpeting made her legs itch. Police files and reports were spread out everywhere. In the center was the timetable she'd made up.

A harsh snoring came from the other room. Loren had lived alone in this same crappy apartment for more than a decade now. They called them 'garden' apartments, though the only thing that seemed to grow was a monotonous red brick. They were sturdy structures with the personality of prison cells, way stations for people on the way up or on the way down, or, for a very few, stuck in a sort of personal-life purgatory.

The snoring did not come from a boyfriend. Loren had one – a total loser named Pete – but her mother, the multimarried, once-desirable, now-flabby Carmen Valos Muse Brewster Whatever was between men and thus living with her. Her snoring had the phlegm of a lifelong smoker, mixed with a few too many years of cheap wine and tacky song.

Cracker crumbs dominated the counter. An open jar of peanut butter, the knife sticking out like Excalibur, stood in the middle like a watchtower. Loren studied the phone logs, the credit card charges, the E-ZPass reports. They painted an interesting picture.

Okay, Loren thought, let's map this out.

- 1:56 A.M.: Aimee Biel uses the 52nd Street Citibank ATM machine – the same one used by Katie Rochester three months ago. Weird.
- 2:16 A.M.: Aimee Biel places a call to the Livingston residence of Myron Bolitar. The call lasts only seconds.
- 2:17 A.M.: Aimee places a call to a mobile phone registered to Myron Bolitar. The call lasts three minutes.

Loren nodded to herself. It seemed logical that Aimee Biel had first tried Bolitar's home and when he didn't answer – that would explain the brevity of the first call – she called his mobile.

Back to it:

- 2:21 A.M.: Myron Bolitar calls Aimee Biel. This call lasts one minute.

From what they'd been able to dig up, Bolitar often stayed in New York City at the Dakota apartment of a friend named Windsor Horne Lockwood III. Lockwood was known to police; despite a ritzy, Main Line upbringing, he was a suspect in several assaults and, yes, even a couple of homicides. The man had the craziest reputation Loren had ever seen. But again, that did not seem relevant to the case at hand.

The point here was, Bolitar was probably staying at Lockwood's apartment in Manhattan. He kept his car in a nearby lot. According to the night attendant, Bolitar had taken the car out sometime around 2:30 A.M.

They had no proof yet, but Loren was fairly sure Bolitar had gone to midtown and picked up Aimee Biel. They were working on getting surveillance videos from the nearby businesses. Maybe Bolitar's car would be on one. But for now, it seemed like a fairly likely conclusion.

More from the time line:

- 3:11 A.M.: There was a credit card charge on Bolitar's Visa account from an Exxon gas station on Route 4 in Fort Lee, New Jersey, right off the George Washington Bridge.
- 3:55 A.M.: the E-ZPass on Bolitar's car showed him heading south on the Garden State Parkway, crossing the Bergen County tolls.
- 4:08 A.M.: the E-ZPass hit the Essex County tolls, showing that Bolitar was still traveling south.

That was it on the tolls. He could have gotten off at Exit 145, which would lead him to his residence in Livingston. Loren drew the route out. It made no sense. You wouldn't go up over the George Washington Bridge and then down the parkway. And even if you did, it wouldn't take forty minutes to get to the Bergen toll. It would take at most, that time of night, twenty minutes.

So where had Bolitar gone?

She went back to her time line. There was a gap of more than three hours, but at 7:18 A.M., Myron Bolitar placed a call to Aimee Biel's cell phone. No answer. He tries twice more that morning. No answer. Yesterday he called the Biels' home number. That was the only call that lasted more than a few seconds. Loren wondered if he talked to the parents.

She picked up her phone and dialed Lance Banner.

'What's up?' he asked.

'Did you tell Aimee's parents about Bolitar?'

'Not yet.'

'I think,' Loren said, 'that now might be the time.'

Myron had a new morning routine. The first thing he did was grab the newspaper and check for war casualties. He looked at the names. All of them. He made sure that Jeremy Downing wasn't listed. Then he went back and took the time to read every name again slowly. He read the rank and hometown and age. That was all they put. But Myron imagined that every dead kid listed was another Jeremy, was like that terrific nineteen-year-old kid who lives down your street, because, simple as it sounded, they were. For just a few minutes Myron imagined what that death meant, that this young, hopeful, dream-filled life was gone forever, what the parents must be thinking.

He hoped that our leaders did something similar. But he doubted it.

Myron's cell phone rang. He checked the caller ID. It read SWEET CHEEKS. That was Win's unlisted number. Myron clicked it on and said hello.

Without preamble, Win said, 'Your flight arrives at one P.M.'

'You work for the airlines now?'

'Work for the airlines,' Win repeated. 'Good one.'

'So what's up?'

'Work for the airlines,' Win said again. 'Wait, just let me savor that line for a moment. Work for the airlines. Hilarious.'

'You done?'

'Hold on, let me get a pen so I can write that one down. Work. For. The. Airlines.'

Win.

'You done now?'

'Let me try again: Your flight arrives at one P.M. I will meet you at the airport. I have two tickets to the Knicks game. We will sit courtside, probably next to Paris Hilton or Kevin Bacon. Personally, I'm pulling for Kevin.'

'You don't like the Knicks,' Myron said.

'True.'

'In fact, you don't like going to basketball games. So why . . . ?' Myron saw it. 'Damn.'

Silence.

'Since when do you read the Styles Section, Win?'

'One o'clock. Newark Airport. See you then.'

Click.

Myron hung up the phone and couldn't help but smile. That Win. What a guy.

He headed into the kitchen. His father was up and making breakfast. He said nothing about Jessica's upcoming nuptials. Mom, however, jumped from her chair, rushed over to him, gave him a look that suggested a terminal illness, asked if he was all right. He assured her that he was fine.

'I haven't seen Jessica in seven years,' he said. 'It's no big deal.'

His parents both nodded in a way that suggested that they were humoring him.

A few hours later he took off for the airport. He had tossed and turned, but in the end he really was all right with it. Seven years. They had been over for seven years. And while Jessica had been the one with the upper hand throughout most of their time together, Myron had been the one who'd finally put an end to it.

Jessica was the past. He took out his cell phone and called Ali – the present.

'I'm at Miami airport,' he said.

'How was your trip?'

Hearing Ali's voice filled him with warmth. 'It was good.'

'But?'

'But nothing. I want to see you.'

'How about around two? The kids will be out, I promise.'

'What have you got in mind?' he asked.

'The technical term would be – hold on, let me check my thesaurus – "a nooner."'

'Ali Wilder, you little vixen.'

'That I am.'

'I can't make it at two. Win is taking me to see the Knicks.'

'How about immediately following the game?' she asked.

'Man, I hate it when you play hard to get.'

'I'll take that as yes.'

'Very much so.'

'You okay?' she asked.

596

'I'm fine.'

'You sound a little funny.'

'I'm trying to sound very funny.'

'Then don't try so hard.'

There was an awkward moment. He wanted to tell her that he loved her. But it was too soon. Or maybe, with what he'd learned about Jessica, the timing was wrong. You don't want to say something like that for the first time for the wrong reason.

So instead he said, 'They're boarding my flight.'

'See you soon, handsome.'

'Wait, if I get there in the evening, will it still be a "nooner"? Wouldn't it be an "evening-er"?'

'That would take too long to say. I don't want to waste any time.'

'And on that note . . .'

'Stay safe, handsome.'

Erik Biel sat alone on the couch while his wife, Claire, chose a chair. Loren noticed that. One would think that a couple in a situation like this would sit next to each other, draw comfort from each other. The body language here suggested that both wanted to be as far away from the other as possible. It could mean a rift in the relationship. Or it could mean that this experience was so raw that even tenderness – especially tenderness – would sting like hell.

Claire Biel had served them tea. Loren really hadn't wanted any, but she learned that most people relaxed if you allow them to be in control of something, of anything, if you allow them to do something mundane or domestic. So she had accepted. Lance Banner, who remained standing behind her, had declined.

Lance was letting her take the lead. He knew them. That might help for some questioning, but she'd get the ball rolling. Loren took a sip of the tea. She let the silence work them a little – let them be the first to speak. Some might view it as cruel. It wasn't, if it helped find Aimee. If Aimee were found okay, it would be quickly forgotten. If she weren't, the discomfort from silence would be nothing compared to what they would then endure.

'Here,' Erik Biel said, 'we made a list of her close friends and their phone numbers. We've already called all of them. And her boyfriend, Randy Wolf. We spoke to him too.'

Loren took her time looking over the names.

'Have there been any developments?' Erik asked.

Erik Biel was, Loren thought, the poster boy for uptight. The mother, Claire, well, you could see the missing kid etched into her face. She hadn't slept. She was a mess. But Erik, with his starched dress shirt and tie and recently shaved face, somehow looked more harried. He was trying so hard to keep it together that you just knew that there would be no slow fray here. When it came apart, it would be ugly and maybe permanent.

Loren handed the paper to Lance Banner. She turned and sat up straight. She kept her eyes on Erik's face as she dropped the bomb: 'Do either of you know a man named Myron Bolitar?'

Erik frowned. Loren moved her gaze toward the mother. Claire Biel looked as if Loren had asked if she could lick their toilet.

'He's a family friend,' Claire Biel said. 'I've known him since junior high.'

'Did he know your daughter?'

'Of course. But what does – '

'What sort of relationship did they have?'

'Relationship?'

'Yes. Your daughter and Myron Bolitar. What sort of relationship did they have?'

For the first time since they'd entered the house, Claire slowly turned and looked to her husband for guidance. Erik too turned toward his wife. They both wore the faces of someone who'd been smacked in the gut by a two-by-four.

Erik finally spoke. 'What are you suggesting?'

'I'm not suggesting anything, Mr. Biel. I'm asking you a question. How well did your daughter know Myron Bolitar?'

Claire: 'Myron is a family friend.'

Erik: 'He wrote Aimee a recommendation letter for her college application.'

Claire nodded with vigor. 'Right. Like that.'

'Like what?'

They didn't respond.

Loren kept her voice even. 'Do they ever see each other?'

'See each other?'

'Yes. Or talk on the phone. Or maybe e-mail.' Then Loren added: 'Without you two present.'

Loren wouldn't have thought it possible, but Erik Biel's spine got even straighter. 'What the hell are you saying?'

Okay, Loren thought. They didn't know. This was no act. It was time to shift gears, check their honesty. 'When was the last time either of you spoke to Mr. Bolitar?'

'Yesterday,' Claire said.

'What time?'

'I'm not sure. Early afternoon, I think.'

'Did you call him or did he call you?'

'He called here,' Claire said.

Loren glanced at Lance Banner. Score one for the mom. That matched up with the phone records.

'What did he want?'

'To congratulate us.'

'What about?'

'Aimee got accepted to Duke.'

'Anything else?'

'He asked if he could speak to her.'

'To Aimee?'

'Yes. He wanted to congratulate her.'

'What did you say?'

'That she wasn't home. And then I thanked him for writing the recommendation.'

'What did he say?'

'He said he'd call her back.'

'Anything else?'

'No.'

Loren let that sit.

Claire Biel said, 'You can't think Myron has anything to do with this.'

Loren just stared at her, letting the silence soak in, giving her a chance to keep talking. She didn't disappoint.

'You have to know him,' Claire went on. 'He's a good man. I'd trust him with my life.'

Loren nodded and then looked at Erik. 'And you, Mr. Biel?'

His eyes were out of focus.

Claire said, 'Erik?'

'I saw Myron yesterday,' he said.

Loren sat up. 'Where?'

'At the middle school gym.' His voice was a dull ache. 'There's pickup basketball there on Sundays.'

'What time would this have been?'

'Seven thirty. Maybe eight.'

'In the morning?'

'Yes.'

Loren glanced back at Lance. He nodded slowly. He'd caught it too. Bolitar couldn't have gotten home much before five, six in the morning. A few hours later, he goes off to play basketball with the missing girl's father?

'Do you play with Mr. Bolitar every Sunday?'

'No. I mean, he used to play a bit. But he hadn't been there in months.'

'Did you talk to him?'

Erik's nod was slow.

'Wait a second,' Claire said. 'I want to know why you're asking us so many questions about Myron. What does he have to do with any of this?'

Loren ignored her, keeping her gaze on Erik Biel. 'What did you two talk about?'

'Aimee, I guess.'

'What did he say?'

'He tried to be subtle about it.'

Erik explained that Myron Bolitar had approached him and that they started talking about exercising and waking up early and then he segued into asking about Aimee, about where she was, about how troublesome teenagers could often be. 'His tone was strange.'

'How so?'

'He wanted to know *how* she was trouble. I remember he asked if Aimee was sullen, if she spent too much time on the Internet, things like that. I remember thinking it was a little odd.'

'How did he look?'

'Like hell.'

'Tired? Unshaven?'

'Both.'

'Okay, that's enough,' Claire Biel said. 'We have a right to know why you're asking all these questions.'

Loren looked up at her. 'You're a lawyer, aren't you, Mrs. Biel?'

'I am.'

'So help me out here: Where in the law does it say I have to tell you anything?'

Claire opened her mouth, closed it. Unduly harsh, Loren thought, but playing good cop/bad cop – it's not just for the perps. Witnesses too. She didn't like it, but it was damn effective.

Loren looked back at Lance. Lance picked up his cue. He coughed into his fist. 'We have some information linking Aimee with Myron Bolitar.'

Claire's eyes narrowed. 'What sort of information?'

'The night before last, at two a.m., Aimee called him. First at home. Then on his cell phone. We know Mr. Bolitar then picked up his car from a garage in the city.' Lance continued to explain the time line. Claire's face drained of color. Erik's hands tightened into fists.

When Lance finished, when they were still too dazed to ask follow-up questions, Loren leaned forward. 'Is there any way that there may have been more between Myron and Aimee than family friends?'

'Absolutely not,' Claire said.

Erik closed his eyes. 'Claire . . .'

'What?' she snapped. 'You can't possibly believe that Myron would get involved – '

'She called him right before . . .' He shrugged. 'Why would Aimee call him? Why wouldn't he say something about that when I saw him at the gym?'

'I don't know, but the idea' – she stopped, snapped her fingers – 'wait, Myron's dating a friend of mine, as a matter of fact. Ali Wilder. An adult woman, thank you very much. A lovely widow with two kids of her own. The idea that Myron could possibly . . .'

Erik squeezed his eyes shut.

Loren said, 'Mr. Biel?'

His voice was soft. 'Aimee hasn't been herself lately.'

'How so?'

Erik's eyes were still shut. 'We both dismissed it as normal teenage stuff. But the last few months, she's been secretive.'

'That is normal, Erik,' Claire said.

'It's gotten worse.'

Claire shook her head. 'You still think of her as your little girl. That's all it is.'

'You know it's more than that, Claire.'

'No, Erik, I don't.'

He closed his eyes again.

'What is it, Mr. Biel?' Loren asked.

'Two weeks ago I tried to access her computer.'

'Why?'

'Because I wanted to read her e-mail.'

His wife glared at him, but he didn't see it – or maybe he didn't care. Loren pushed ahead.

'So what happened?'

'She changed her password. I couldn't get on.'

'Because she wanted privacy,' Claire said. 'You think that's unusual? I had a diary when I was a kid. I kept it locked with a key and still hid it. So what?'

Erik went on. 'I called our Internet provider. I'm the bill payer with the master account. So they gave me the new password. Then I went online to check her e-mails.'

'And?'

He shrugged. 'They were gone. All of them. She'd deleted every one of them.'

'She knew you'd snoop,' Claire said. Her tone was a blend of anger and defensiveness. 'She was just guarding against it.'

Erik spun toward her. 'Do you really believe that, Claire?'

'Do you really believe that she's having an affair with Myron?'

Erik did not reply.

Claire spun back toward Loren and Lance. 'Have you asked Myron about the calls?'

'Not yet.'

'So what are we waiting for?' Claire started for her purse. 'Let's go now. He'll straighten this out.'

'He's not in Livingston,' Loren said. 'In fact, he flew down to Miami, not long after he played ball with your husband.'

Claire was about to ask something else, but she stopped. For the first time, Loren could see the doubt crawl into her face. Loren decided to use that. She rose.

'We'll be in touch,' Loren said.

15

Myron sat on the plane and thought about his old love, Jessica. Shouldn't he be happy for her?

She had always been fiery to the point of a pain in the ass. His mother and Esperanza hadn't liked her. His father, like a great TV anchor, played it neutral. Win yawned. In Win's eyes, women were either doable or they weren't. Jessica was most definitely doable, but after that . . . so what?

The women thought that Myron was blinded by Jessica's beauty. She could write like a dream. She was two steps beyond passionate. But they were different. Myron wanted to live like his parents. Jessica sneered at that idyllic nonsense. It was a constant tension that both kept them apart and drew them to each other.

Now Jessica was marrying some Wall Street dude named Stone. Big Stone, Myron thought. Rolling Stone. The Stoner. Smokin' Stone. The Stone Man.

Myron hated him.

What had become of Jessica?

Seven years, Myron. It changes a person.

But that much?

The plane landed. He checked his phone while the plane taxied toward the terminal. There was a text message from Win:

YOUR PLANE JUST LANDED.
PLEASE FILL IN YOUR OWN WITTICISM ABOUT MY WORKING FOR THE AIRLINES. I'M WAITING BY THE LOWER LEVEL CURB.

The plane slowed as it approached the gate. The pilot asked everybody to stay in their seats with their belts fastened. Almost everybody ignored that request. You could hear the belts clack open. Why? What did people gain from that extra second? Was it that we just liked to defy rules?

He debated calling Aimee's cell phone again. That might be overkill. How many calls could he make, after all? The promise had also been pretty clear. He would drive her anywhere. He would not ask questions. He would not tell her parents. It should hardly surprise him that after such a venture, Aimee would not want to talk to him for a few days.

He got off the plane and was starting toward the exit when he heard someone call out, 'Myron Bolitar?'

He turned. There were two of them, a man and a woman. The woman had been the one who called his name. She was small, not much over five feet. Myron was six-four. He towered over her. She did not seem intimidated. The man with her sported a military cut. He also looked vaguely familiar.

The man had a badge out. The woman did not.

'I'm Essex County investigator Loren Muse,' she said. 'This is Livingston police detective Lance Banner.'

'Banner,' Myron said automatically. 'You Buster's brother?'

Lance Banner almost smiled. 'Yeah.'

'Good guy, Buster. I played hoops with him.'

'I remember.'

'How's he doing?'

'Good, thanks.'

Myron did not know what was going on, but he'd had experience with law enforcement. Out of habit more than anything else, he reached for his cell phone and pressed the button. It was his speed dial. It would reach Win. Win would hit the mute button and listen in. This was an old trick of theirs, one Myron hadn't employed in years, and yet there he was, with police officers, falling into the old routines.

From his past run-ins with the law, Myron had learned a few basic truisms that could be summed up thusly: Just because you haven't done anything wrong doesn't mean you're not in trouble. Best to play it with that knowledge.

'We'd like you to come with us,' Loren Muse said.

'May I ask what this is about?'

'We won't take much of your time.'

'I got Knicks tickets.'

'We'll try not to interfere with your plans.'

'Courtside.' He looked at Lance Banner. 'Celebrity row.'

'Are you refusing to come with us?'

'Are you arresting me?'

'No.'

'Then before I agree to go with you, I'd like you to tell me what it's about.'

Loren Muse did not hesitate this time. 'It's about Aimee Biel.'

Whack. He should have seen it coming, but he didn't. Myron staggered back a step. 'Is she all right?'

'Why don't you come with us?'

'I asked you – '

'I heard you, Mr. Bolitar.' She turned away from him now and started heading down toward the exit. 'Why don't you come with us so we can discuss this further?'

Lance Banner drove. Loren Muse rode shotgun. Myron sat in the backseat.

'Is she okay?' Myron asked.

They would not reply. He was being played, Myron knew that, but he didn't much care. He wanted to know about Aimee. The rest was irrelevant.

'Talk to me, for crying out loud.'

Nothing.

'I saw her Saturday night. You know that already, right?'

They did not respond. He knew why. The ride was mercifully short. That explained their silence. They wanted his admissions on record. It was probably taking all of their willpower not to say anything, but soon they would have him in an interrogation room and put it all on tape.

They drove into the garage and led him to an elevator. They got off on the eighth floor. They were in Newark, the county courthouse. Myron had been here before. They brought him into an interrogation room. There was no mirror and thus no one-way glass. That meant a camera was doing the surveillance.

'Am I under arrest?' he asked.

Loren Muse tilted her head. 'What makes you say that?'

'Don't play these games with me, Muse.'

'Please have a seat.'

'Have you done any checking on me yet? Call Jake Courter, the sheriff in Reston. He'll vouch for me. There are others.'

'We'll get to that in a moment.'

'What happened to Aimee Biel?'

'You mind if we film this?' Loren Muse asked.

'No.'

'Do you mind signing a waiver?'

It was a Fifth Amendment waiver. Myron knew better than to sign it – he was a lawyer, for Chrissake – but he pushed past that. His heart hammered in his chest. Something had happened to Aimee Biel. They must think he either knew something or was involved. The faster this moved along and they eliminated him, the better for Aimee.

'Okay,' Myron said. 'Now what happened to Aimee?'

Loren Muse spread her hands. 'Who said anything happened to her?'

'You did, Muse. When you braced me at the airport. You said, "It's about Aimee Biel." And because, while I don't like to brag, I have amazing powers of deduction, I deduced that two police officers didn't stop me and say it was about Aimee Biel because she sometimes pops her gum in class. No, I deduced that something must have happened to her. Please don't shun me because I have this gift.'

'You finished?'

He was. He got nervous, he started talking.

Loren Muse took out a pen. There was already a notebook on her desk. Lance Banner stood and remained silent. 'When was the last time you saw Aimee Biel?'

He knew better than to ask what happened again. Muse was going to play it her way.

'Saturday night.'

'What time?'

'I guess between two and three a.m.'

'So this would have been Sunday morning rather than Saturday night?'

Myron bit back the sarcastic rejoinder. 'Yes.'

'I see. Where did you last see her?'

'In Ridgewood, New Jersey.'

She wrote that down on a legal pad. 'Address?'

'I don't know.'

Her pen stopped. 'You don't know?'

'That's right. It was late. She gave me directions. I just followed them.'

'I see.' She sat back and dropped the pen. 'Why don't you start at the beginning?'

The door behind them flew open. All heads spun to the door. Hester Crimstein stomped in as though the very room had whispered an insult and she wanted to call it out. For a moment no one moved or said anything.

Hester waited a beat, spread her arms, put her right foot forward, and shouted, 'Ta-da!'

Loren Muse raised an eyebrow. 'Hester Crimstein?'

'We know each other, sweetie?'

'I recognize you from TV.'

'I'll be happy to sign autographs later. Right now I want the camera off and I want you two' – Hester pointed at Lance Banner and Loren Muse – 'out of here, so I can chat with my client.'

Loren stood. They were eye-to-eye, both about the same height. Hester had the frizzy hair. Loren tried to stare her down. Myron almost laughed. Some would call famed criminal attorney Hester Crimstein as mean as a snake, but most would consider that slanderous to the snake.

'Wait,' Hester said to Loren. 'Wait for it. . . .'

'Excuse me?'

'Any second now, I'm going to pee in my pants. From fear, I mean. Just wait. . . .'

Myron said, 'Hester . . .'

'Shh, you.' Hester shot him a glare and made a *tsk-tsk* noise. 'Signing a waiver and talking without your lawyer. What kind of dope are you?'

'You're not my lawyer.'

'Shh again, you.'

'I'm representing myself.'

'You know the expression "A man who represents himself has a fool for a client"? Change "fool" to 'total brain-dead numbskull.'"

Myron wondered how Hester had gotten there so quickly, but the answer was obvious. Win. As soon as Myron had hit his cell phone, as soon as Win heard the voices of the cops, he would have found Hester and gotten her there.

Hester Crimstein was one of the country's top defense attorneys. She had her own cable show called *Crimstein on Crime*. They'd become friends when Hester had helped Esperanza with a murder rap a few years back.

'Hold up.' Hester looked back at Loren and Lance. 'Why are you two still here?'

Lance Banner took a big step forward. 'He just said you're not his lawyer.'

'Your name again, handsome?'

'Livingston police detective Lance Banner.'

'Lance,' she said. 'Like in what I use to get rid of a boil? Okay, Lance, here's some advice: The step forward was a nice move, very commanding, but you need to stick out your chest more. Make your voice a little deeper and add a scowl. Like this: "Yo, chickie, he just said you're not his lawyer." Try it.'

Myron knew that Hester wouldn't simply go away. He also knew that he probably didn't want her to. He wanted to cooperate, of course, get this over with, but he also wanted to know what the hell had happened to Aimee.

'She's my lawyer,' Myron said. 'Please give us a minute.'

Hester gave them a satisfied smirk that you know they both wanted to slap off her face. They turned for the doors. Hester gave them a five-finger toodle-oo wave. When they were both out the door, she closed it and looked up at the camera. 'Turn it off now.'

'It probably is,' Myron said.

'Yeah, sure. Cops never play games with that.'

She took out her cell phone.

'Who are you calling?' he asked.

'Do you know why they have you in here?'

'It has something to do with a girl named Aimee Biel,' Myron said.

'That much I know already. But you don't know what happened to her?'

'No.'

'That's what I'm trying to find out. I got my local investigator working on it. She's the best, knows everybody in this office.' Hester put the phone to her ear. 'Yeah, Hester here. What's up? Uh-huh. Uh-huh.' Hester listened without taking notes. A minute later, she said, 'Thanks, Cingle. Keep digging and see what they got.'

Hester hung up. Myron shrugged a *well?* at her.

'This girl – her last name is Biel.'

'Aimee Biel,' Myron said. 'What about her?'

'She's missing.'

Myron felt the thump again.

'It seems she never came home on Saturday night. She was supposed to sleep at a friend's house. She never arrived. Nobody knows what happened to her. Apparently there are phone records linking you to the girl. Other stuff too. My investigator is trying to find out what exactly.'

Hester sat down. She looked across the table at him. 'So okay, bubbe, tell Aunt Hester everything.'

'No,' Myron said.

'What?'

'Look, you have two choices here. You can stay while I talk to them right now or I can fire you.'

'You should talk to me first.'

'We can't waste the time. You have to let me tell them everything.'

'Because you're innocent?'

'Of course I'm innocent.'

'And the police never ever *ever* arrest the wrong man.'

'I'll risk it. If Aimee is in trouble, I can't have them wasting time on me.'

'I disagree.'

'Then you're fired.'

'Don't get all Trump on me. I'm advising you, that's all. You're the client.'

She rose, opened the door, called them back in. Loren Muse moved past her and sat back down. Lance took his post in the corner. Muse was red-faced, probably upset with herself for not questioning him in the car before Hester's arrival.

Loren Muse was about to say something, but Myron stopped her by raising his palm.

'Let's get to it,' Myron said to them. 'Aimee Biel is missing. I know that now. You've probably pulled our phone logs, so you know she called me around two in the morning. I'm not sure what else you have so far, so let me help you out. She asked for a ride. I picked her up.'

'Where?' Loren asked.

'Midtown Manhattan. Fifty-second and Fifth, I think. I took the Henry Hudson to the GWB. Do you have the credit card charge for the gas station?'

'Yes.'

'Then you know we stopped there. We continued down Route 4 to Route 17 and then to Ridgewood.' Myron saw a change in their posture. He had missed something, but he pressed on. 'I dropped her off at a house on the end of a cul-de-sac. Then I drove home.'

'And you don't remember the address, is that correct?'

'That's correct.'

'Anything else?'

'Like?'

'Like why did Aimee Biel call you in the first place?'

'I'm a friend of the family.'

'You must be a close friend.'

'I am.'

'So why you? I mean, first she called your house in Livingston. Then she went to your cell phone. Why did she call you and not her parents or an aunt or an uncle or even a school friend?' Loren lifted her palms to the sky. 'Why you?'

Myron's voice was soft. 'I made her promise.'

'Promise?'

'Yes.'

He explained about the basement, about hearing the girls talk about driving with a drunk kid, about making them promise – and as he did, he could see their faces change. Even Hester's. The words, the rationale, rang hollow in his own ears now, and yet he couldn't put his finger on why. His explanation went on a little too long. He could hear the defensiveness in his voice.

When he was done, Loren asked, 'Have you ever made this promise before?'

'No.'

'Never?'

'Never.'

'No other helpless or inebriated girls you volunteered to chauffeur around?'

'Hey!' Hester wouldn't let that pass. 'That's a total mischaracterization of what he said. And the question was already asked and answered. Move on.'

Loren shifted in her seat. 'How about young boys? You ever make any boys promise to call you?'

'No.'

'So just girls?'

'Just *these* two girls,' Myron said. 'It wasn't like I planned it.'

'I see.' Loren rubbed her chin. 'How about Katie Rochester?'

Hester said, 'Who's that?'

Myron ignored that. 'What about her?'

'Did you ever make Katie Rochester promise to call you when she was drunk?'

'Again that's a total mischaracterization of what he said,' Hester jumped in. 'He was trying to prevent them from drinking and driving.'

'Right, sure, he's a hero,' Loren said. 'Ever do anything like that with Katie Rochester?'

'I don't even know Katie Rochester,' Myron said.

'But you've heard the name.'

'Yes.'

'In what context?'

'On the news. So what's the deal, Muse – I'm a suspect in every missing persons case?'

Loren smiled. 'Not every.'

Hester leaned toward Myron and whispered in his ear. 'I don't like this, Myron.'

Neither did he.

Loren continued: 'So you've never met Katie Rochester?'

He couldn't help his lawyer training. 'Not to my knowledge.'

'Not to your knowledge. Then whose knowledge would it be?'

'Objection.'

'You know what I mean,' Myron said.

'How about her father, Dominick Rochester?'

'No.'

'Or her mother, Joan? Ever meet her?'

'No.'

'No,' Loren repeated, 'or not to your knowledge?'

'I meet lots of people. I don't remember them all. But the names ring no bells.'

Loren Muse looked down at the table. 'You said you dropped Aimee off in Ridgewood?'

'Yes. At her friend Stacy's.'

'At her friend's?' That got Loren's attention. 'You didn't mention that before.'

'I'm mentioning it now.'

'What's Stacy's last name?'

'Aimee didn't say.'

'I see. Did you meet this Stacy?'

'No.'

'Did you walk Aimee to the front door?'

'No, I stayed in the car.'

Loren Muse faked a puzzled look. 'Your promise to protect her didn't extend from the car to the front door?'

'Aimee asked me to stay in the car.'

'Who opened the door to the house then?'

'Nobody.'

'Aimee just let herself in?'

'She said that Stacy was probably asleep and that she always lets herself in the back door.'

'I see.' Loren rose. 'Let's go then.'

'Where are you taking him?' Hester asked.

'To Ridgewood. Let's see if we can find this cul-de-sac.'

Myron stood with her. 'Can't you just find Stacy's address from Aimee's parents?'

'We already know Stacy's address,' Loren said. 'The problem is, Stacy doesn't live in Ridgewood. She lives in Livingston.'

16

When Myron headed out of the interrogation room, he spotted Claire and Erik Biel in an office down the corridor. Even from the distance and through the reflection in the plate glass window, Myron could see the strain. He stopped.

'What's the problem?' Loren Muse asked.

He gestured with his chin. 'I want to talk to them.'

'And say what exactly?'

He hesitated.

'Do you want to waste time explaining yourself,' Loren Muse asked, 'or do you want to help us find Aimee?'

She had a point. What would he say right now anyway? 'I didn't harm your daughter? I just drove her to some house in Ridgewood because I didn't want her to drive with a drunk kid'? What good would that do?

Hester kissed him goodbye. 'Keep your trap shut.'

He looked at her.

'Fine, whatever. Just call me if they arrest you, okay?'

'Okay.'

Myron took the elevator to the garage with Lance Banner and Loren Muse. Banner took one car and started out. Myron looked a question at Loren.

'He's going ahead to get a local to accompany us.'

'Oh.'

Loren Muse moved over to a squad car, complete with the perp cage in the back. She opened the back door for Myron. He sighed and slid in. She took the driver's seat. There was a laptop attached to the console. She started typing into it.

'So what now?' Myron asked.

'Can I have your mobile phone?'

'Why?'

'Just give it to me.'

He handed it to her. She scanned through the call log and then dropped it on the front passenger's seat.

'When exactly did you call Hester Crimstein?' she asked.

'I didn't.'

'Then how – '

'Long story.'

Win would not want his name mentioned.

'It doesn't look good,' she said. 'Calling a lawyer so quickly.'

'I don't much care how it looks.'

'No, I guess you don't.'

'So what's next?'

'We drive to Ridgewood. We try to figure out where you purportedly dropped off Aimee Biel.'

They started moving.

'I know you from somewhere,' Myron said.

'I grew up in Livingston. When I was a kid, I went to some of your high school basketball games.'

'That's not it,' he said. He sat up. 'Wait, did you handle that Hunter case?'

'I was' – she paused – ''involved.'

'That's it. The Matt Hunter case.'

'You know him?'

'I went to school with his brother Bernie. I was at his funeral.' He sat back. 'So what's next? Are you getting a warrant for my house, my car, what?'

'Both.' She checked her watch. 'They're being served now.'

'You'll probably find evidence that Aimee was in both. I told you about the party, about being in my basement. And I told you I drove her the night before.'

'All very neat and convenient, yes.'

Myron closed his eyes. 'Are you going to take my computer too?'

'Of course.'

'I have a lot of private correspondence on it. Client information.'

'They'll be careful.'

'No, they won't. Do me a favor, Muse. Inspect the computer yourself, okay?'

'You trust me? I'm almost flattered.'

'Okay, look, cards on the table,' Myron said. 'I know I'm a good suspect.'

'Really? Why? Because you were the last person who saw her? Because you're a single ex-jock who lives alone in his childhood home and picks up teenage girls at two in the morning?' She shrugged. 'Why would you be a suspect?'

'I didn't do it, Muse.'

She kept her eyes focused on the road.

'What is it?' Myron asked.

'Tell me about the gas station.'

'The . . .' And then he saw it. 'Oh.'

'Oh what?'

'What do you have – a surveillance video or the attendant's testimony?'

She said nothing.

'Aimee got mad at me because she thought I'd tell her parents.'

'Why would she think that?'

'Because I kept asking her questions – where she'd been, who she'd been with, what happened.'

'And you'd promised to take her wherever she wanted, no questions asked.'

'Right.'

'So why were you reneging?'

'I wasn't reneging.'

'But?'

'She didn't look right.'

'How's that?'

'She wasn't in a part of the city where kids would go to drink at that hour. She didn't look drunk. I didn't smell booze on her. She looked more upset than anything else. So I thought I'd try to find out why.'

'And she didn't like that?'

'Right. So at the gas station, Aimee jumped out of the car. She wouldn't get back in until I promised I wouldn't ask any more questions or tell her parents. She said' – Myron frowned, hating to betray this sort of confidence – 'she said that there were problems at home.'

'With Mom and Dad?'

'Yes.'

'What did you say?'

'That that was normal.'

'Man,' Loren said, 'you are good. What other nuggets did you offer? "Time heals all wounds"?'

'Give me a break, Muse, will you?'

'You're still my prime suspect, Myron.'

'No, I'm not.'

She lowered her eyebrows. 'Excuse me?'

'You're not this stupid. Neither am I.'

'What's that supposed to mean?'

'You've known about me since last night. So you made some calls. Who did you talk to?'

'You mentioned Jake Courter earlier.'

'You know him?'

Loren Muse nodded.

'And what did Sheriff Courter say about me?'

'That in the tri-state area, you've caused more ass discomfort than hemorrhoids.'

'But that I didn't do it, right?'

She said nothing.

'Come on, Muse. You know I couldn't be this stupid. Phone records, credit card charges, E-ZPass, an eyewitness at the gas station . . . it's overkill. Plus you know my story will pan out. The phone records show that Aimee called me first. That fits in with what I'm telling you.'

They drove in silence for a while. The car radio buzzed. Loren picked it up. Lance Banner said, 'I got a local with me. We're good to go.'

'I'm almost there,' she said. Then to Myron: 'What exit did you take – Ridgewood Avenue or Linwood?'

'Linwood.'

She repeated it into the microphone. She pointed at the green sign through the windshield. 'Linwood Avenue West or East?'

'Whichever one says Ridgewood.'

'That would be west.'

He sat back. She took the ramp. 'Do you remember how far away from here?'

'I'm not sure. We drove straight for a while. Then we started making a lot of turns. I don't remember.'

Loren frowned. 'You don't hit me as the forgetful type, Myron.'

'Then I got you fooled.'

'Where were you before she called?'

'At a wedding.'

'Drink much?'

'More than I should have.'

'Were you drunk when she called?'

'I probably would have passed a Breathalyzer.'

'But you were, shall we say, feeling it?'

'Yes.'

'Ironic, don't you think?'

'Like an Alanis Morissette song,' he said. 'I have a question for you.'

'I'm not really into answering your questions, Myron.'

'You asked me if I knew Katie Rochester. Was that just routine – two missing girls – or do you have a reason to believe that their disappearances are related?'

'You're kidding, right?'

'I just need to know – '

'Squat. You need to know squat. Now walk me through it again. Everything. What Aimee said, what you said, the phone calls, the drop-off, everything.'

He did. On the corner of Linwood Avenue, Myron noticed a Ridgewood police car slide in behind them. Lance Banner sat in the passenger seat.

'They coming along for jurisdiction?' Myron asked.

'More like protocol. Do you remember where you drove from here?'

'I think we turned right by that big pool.'

'Okay. I have a map up on the computer. We'll try to find the cul-de-sacs and see what happens.'

Myron's hometown of Livingston was nouveau and Jewish-y, former farmland converted into look-alike clusters of split-levels, with one big mall. Ridgewood was old Victorians and WASPy, lusher landscapes, and a true town center with restaurants and shops. The houses in Ridgewood were built in a variety of eras. Trees lined both sides of the streets, age tilting them toward the center to form a protective canopy. There was less sameness here.

Was this street familiar?

Myron frowned. He couldn't say. Not much sameness during the day, but at night, it all looked woodsy. Loren headed down a cul-de-sac. Myron shook his head. Then another and another. The roads twisted seemingly without reason or plan, like something in an abstract painting.

More dead ends.

'You said before that Aimee didn't seem drunk,' Loren said.

'That's right.'

'How did she seem?'

'Distraught.' He sat up. 'I was thinking that maybe she'd broken up with her boyfriend. I think his name is Randy. Have you talked to him yet?'

'No.'

'Why not?'

'I need to explain myself to you?'

'It's not that, but a girl vanishes, you investigate – '

'There wasn't an investigation. She's of age, no signs of violence, missing only a few hours . . .'

'Enter me.'

'Exactly. Claire and Erik called her friends, of course. Randy Wolf, the boyfriend, wasn't supposed to see her last night. He stayed home with his parents.'

Myron frowned. Loren Muse spotted it in the rearview mirror. 'What?' she asked.

'Saturday night at the end of his senior year,' he said, 'and Randy stays home with his mommy and daddy?'

'Do me a favor, Bolitar. Just look for the house, will you?'

As soon as she made the turn, Myron felt the pang of déjà vu. 'On the right. At the end of the cul-de-sac.'

'That's it?'

'I'm not sure yet.' Then: 'Yeah. Yeah, this is it.'

She pulled up to it and parked. The Ridgewood police car parked behind them. Myron looked out the window. 'Move up a few yards.'

Loren did as he asked. Myron kept his eyes on the house.

'Well?'

He nodded. 'This is it. She opened that gate on the side of the house.' He almost added *That was the last time I saw her,* but he held back.

'Wait in the car.'

She got out. Myron watched. She headed over and talked to Banner and a cop with Ridgewood police logos on his uniform. They chatted and gestured toward the house. Then Loren Muse started up the walk. She rang the doorbell. A woman answered it. Myron couldn't see her at first. Then she stepped outside. Nope, not familiar. She was slim. Her blond hair peeked out from a baseball cap. She looked like she'd just finished a workout.

The two women talked for a full ten minutes. Loren kept glancing back at Myron as if she feared he'd try to escape. Another minute or two passed. Loren and the woman shook hands. The woman went back inside and closed the door. Loren walked back to the car and opened the back door.

'Show me where Aimee walked.'

'What did she say?'

'What do you think she said?'

'That she never heard of Aimee Biel.'

Loren Muse touched her index finger to her nose and then pointed at him.

'This is the place,' Myron said. 'I'm sure of it.'

Myron traced her path. He stopped at the gate. He remembered how Aimee had stood here. He remembered her wave, that there was something there, something that bugged him.

'I should have . . .' He stopped. No point. 'She went in here. She disappeared from sight. Then she came back and waved that I should leave.'

'And you did?'

'Yes.'

Loren Muse looked in the backyard before she walked him back to another squad car. 'They'll drive you home.'

'Can I have my cell phone?'

She tossed it to him. Myron got into the back of the car. Banner started it up. Myron took hold of the door handle.

'Muse?'

'What?'

'There was a reason she picked this house,' Myron said.

He closed the door. They drove off in silence. Myron watched that gate, watched it grow smaller until finally it, like Aimee Biel, was gone.

17

Dominick Rochester, the father of Katie, sat at the head of the dining-room table. His three boys were there too. His wife, Joan, was in the kitchen. That left two empty chairs – hers and Katie's. He chewed his meat and stared at the chair, as if willing Katie to appear.

Joan came out of the kitchen. She had a platter of sliced roast beef. He gestured toward his near-empty plate, but she was already on it. Dominick Rochester's wife stayed home and took care of the house. None of that working-woman crap. Dominick wouldn't have it.

He grunted a thank-you. Joan returned to her seat. The boys were all chowing down in silence. Joan smoothed her skirt and picked up her fork. Dominick watched her. She used to be so damned beautiful. Now she was glassy-eyed and meek. She hunched over in a permanent cower. She drank too much during the day, although she thought he didn't know. No matter. She was still the mother of his children and kept in line. So he let it slide.

The phone rang. Joan Rochester leaped to her feet, but Dominick signaled her to sit with a wave of his hand. He wiped his face as though it were a windshield and rose from his seat. Dominick was a thick man. Not fat. Thick. Thick neck, thick shoulders, thick chest, thick arms and thighs.

The last name Rochester – he hated that. His father had changed it because he wanted to sound less ethnic. But his old man was a weakling and a loser. Dominick thought about changing it back, but that would look weak too. Like maybe he worried too much about what other people would think. In Dominick's world, you never showed weakness. They had walked all over his father. Made him shut down his barbershop. Poked fun at him. His father thought he could rise above it. Dominick knew better.

You bust heads or you get your head busted. You don't ask questions. You don't reason with them – at least, not at first. At first, you bust heads. You bust heads and take licks until they respect you. Then you reason with them. You show them you're willing to take a hit. You let them see you're not afraid of blood, not even your own. You want to win, you smile right through your blood. That gets their attention.

The phone rang again. He checked the caller ID. The number was blocked, but most people who called here didn't like people to know their business. He was still chewing when he lifted the receiver.

The voice on the other end said, 'I have something for you.'

It was his contact at the county prosecutor's office. He swallowed the meat. 'Go ahead.'

'There's another missing girl.'

That got his attention.

'She's from Livingston too. Same age, same class.'

'Name?'

'Aimee Biel.'

The name didn't mean anything to him, but he really didn't know Katie's friends very well. He put his hand over the mouthpiece. 'Any of you know a girl named Aimee Biel?'

No one said anything.

'Hey, I asked a question here. She'd be Katie's year.'

The boys shook their heads. Joan didn't move. His eyes met hers. She shook her head slowly.

'There's more,' his contact said.

'Like what?'

'They found a link to your daughter.'

'What kind of link?'

'I don't know. I've just been eavesdropping. But I think it has something to do with where they both went missing. Do you know a guy named Myron Bolitar?'

'The old basketball star?'

'Yeah.'

Rochester had seen him a few times. He also knew that Bolitar had had run-ins with some of Rochester's nastier colleagues.

'What about him?'

'He's involved.'

'How?'

'He picked up the missing girl in midtown Manhattan. That's the last time she was seen. She used the same ATM as your Katie.'

He felt a jolt. 'He what?'

Dominick's contact explained a bit more, about how this Bolitar guy had driven Aimee Biel back over to Jersey, how a gas station attendant saw them arguing, and how she just disappeared.

'The police talk to him?'

'Yeah.'

'What did he say?'

'I don't think very much. He lawyered up.'

'He . . .' Dominick felt a red swirl build in his head. 'Son of a bitch. Did they arrest him?'

'No.'

'Why not?'

'Not enough yet.'

'So, what, they just let him walk?'

'Yeah.'

Dominick Rochester didn't say anything. He got very quiet. His family noticed. They all went very still, afraid to move. When he finally spoke again, his voice was so calm, his family held their breaths.

'Anything else?'

'That's it for now.'

'Keep digging.'

Dominick hung up the phone. He turned toward the table. His whole family was watching him.

Joan said, 'Dom?'

'It was nothing.'

He felt no need to explain. This didn't involve them. It was his job to handle stuff like this. The father was the soldier, the one who kept vigil so that his family could sleep untroubled.

He headed to the garage. Once inside, he closed his eyes and tried to smother the rage. It wouldn't happen.

Katie . . .

He eyed the metal baseball bat. He remembered reading about Bolitar's injured knee. If he thought that hurt, if he thought a mere knee injury was pain . . .

He made some calls, did a little background. In the past, Bolitar had gotten in trouble with the Ache brothers, who ran New York. Bolitar was supposedly a tough guy, good with his fists, who hung out with a psycho named Windsor Something.

Taking on Bolitar would not be easy.

But it wouldn't be all that difficult either. Not if Dominick got the best.

His cell phone was a throwaway, the kind you can buy in cash with a false name and toss away after you use up your minutes. No way to trace it back to him. He grabbed a fresh one off the shelf. For a moment he just held it and debated his next move. His breathing was labored.

Dominick had busted his share of heads in his day, but if he dialed this number, if he did indeed call the Twins, he was crossing a line he'd never gone near before.

He thought about his daughter's smile. He thought about how she had to wear braces when she was twelve and how she wore her hair and the way she used to look at him, a long time ago, when she was a little girl and he was the most powerful man in the world.

Dominick pressed the digits. After this call, he would have to get rid of the phone. That was one of the Twins' rules, and when it came to those two, it didn't matter who you were, didn't matter how tough or how hard you'd scraped to buy this fancy house in Livingston, you don't mess around with the Twins.

The phone was answered on the second ring. No hello. No greeting at all. Just silence.

Dominick said, 'I'm going to need both of you.'

'When?'

Dominick picked up the metal bat. He liked the weight of it. He thought about this Bolitar guy, this guy who drove off with a missing girl and then lawyered up, who was free now and probably watching TV or enjoying a nice meal.

No way you let that slide. Even if you gotta bring in the Twins.

'Now,' Dominick Rochester said. 'I need you both now.'

18

When Myron arrived back at his house in Livingston, Win was already there. Win was sprawled out in a chaise longue on the front lawn. His legs were crossed. He wore khakis sans socks, a blue shirt, a Lilly Pulitzer tie of dizzying green. Some people could wear anything and make it work. Win was one of those people.

He had his face tilted to the sun, eyes closed. He did not open them as Myron approached.

'Do you still want to go to the Knicks game?' Win asked.

'I think I'll pass.'

'You mind if I take someone else then?'

'No.'

'I met a girl at Scores last night.'

'She's a stripper?'

'Please.' Win held up a finger. 'She's an erotic dancer.'

'Career woman. Nice.'

'Her name is Bambi, I think. Or maybe Tawny.'

'Is that her real name?'

'Nothing about her is real,' Win said. 'By the way, the police were here.'

'Searching the place?'

'Yes.'

'They take my computer?'

'Yes.'

'Damn.'

'Fret not. I arrived before them and backed up your personal files. Then I erased the hard drive.'

'You,' Myron said. 'You're good.'

'The best,' Win said.

'Where did you back it up?'

'USB hard drive on my key chain,' he said, dangling it, his eyes still closed. 'Kindly move to the right a little. You're blocking my sun.'

'Has Hester's investigator learned anything new?'

'There was an ATM charge on young Ms. Biel's card,' Win said.

'Aimee took out cash?'

'No, a library book. Yes, cash. Apparently, Aimee Biel picked up a thousand dollars at an ATM machine a few minutes before she called you.'

'Anything else?'

'Like?'

'They're linking this to another disappearance. A girl named Katie Rochester.'

'Two girls disappearing from the same area. Of course they're going to link them.'

Myron frowned. 'I think there's something else.'

Win opened one eye. 'Trouble.'

'What?'

Win said nothing, just kept staring. Myron turned and followed his gaze and felt his stomach drop.

It was Erik and Claire.

For a moment no one moved.

Win said, 'You're blocking my sun again.'

Myron saw Erik's face. There was rage there. Myron started toward them, but something made him stop. Claire put her hand on her husband's arm. She whispered something in his ear. Erik closed his eyes. She stepped toward Myron, her head high. Erik stayed back.

Claire walked toward Myron's door. He slid toward her.

Myron said, 'You know I didn't – '

'Inside.' Claire kept walking toward his front door. 'I want you to tell me everything when we're inside.'

Essex County prosecutor Ed Steinberg, Loren's boss, was waiting for her when she got back to the office.

'Well?'

She filled him in. Steinberg was a big man, soft in the middle, but he had that wanna-squeeze-him, teddy-bear thing going on. Of course he was married. It had been so long since Loren had met a desirable man who wasn't.

When she finished, Steinberg said, 'I did a little more checking up on Bolitar. Did you know he and his friend Win used to do some work with the feds?'

'There were rumors,' she said.

'I spoke to Joan Thurston.' Thurston was the U.S. Attorney for the State of New Jersey. 'A lot of it is hush-hush, I guess, but in sum, everyone thinks Win is several fries short of a Happy Meal – but that Bolitar is pretty straight.'

'That's the vibe I got too,' Loren said.

'You believe his story?'

'Overall, yeah, I guess I do. It's just too crazy. Plus, as he sort of pointed out himself, would a guy with his experience be dumb enough to leave so many clues behind?'

'You think he's being framed?'

Loren made a face. 'That doesn't jibe much either. Aimee Biel called him herself. She'd have to be in on it, I guess.'

Steinberg folded his hands on his desk. His sleeves were rolled up. His forearms were big and covered with enough hair to count as fur. 'Then odds are, what, she's a runaway?'

'Odds are,' Loren said.

'And the fact that she used the same ATM as Katie Rochester?'

She shrugged. 'I don't think it's a coincidence.'

'Maybe they know each other.'

'Not according to either set of parents.'

'That doesn't mean anything,' Steinberg said. 'Parents don't know *bupkus* about their kids. Trust me here, I had teenage daughters. The moms and dads who claim they know everything about their kids usually know the least.' He shifted in his chair. 'Nothing found in the search of Bolitar's home or car?'

'They're still going through it,' Loren said. 'But what can they find? We know she was in the house and in the car.'

'The locals handled the search?'

She nodded.

'Then let's let the locals handle the rest of it. We really don't even have a case yet anyway – the girl is of age, right?'

'Right.'

'Good, then it's settled. Give it to the locals. I want you concentrating on these homicides in East Orange.'

Steinberg told her more about the case. She listened and tried to focus. This was a biggie, no doubt about it. A double murder. Maybe a major hit man back in the area. It was the kind of case she loved. It would take up all her time. She knew that. And she knew the odds. Aimee Biel had withdrawn cash before she called Myron. That meant that she had probably not been abducted, that she was probably just fine – and that either way, Loren Muse really shouldn't be involved anymore.

They say worrying and grief make you age, but with Claire Biel it was almost the opposite. Her skin was drawn tight around her cheekbones – so tight the blood seemed to stop flowing. There were no lines on her face. She was pale and almost skeletal.

Myron flashed back to an ordinary memory. Study hall, senior year. They would sit and talk and he would make her laugh. Claire was normally quiet, often subdued. She spoke with a soft voice. But when he got her going, when he worked in all her favorite routines from stupid movies, Claire would laugh so hard she'd start to cry. Myron wouldn't stop. He loved her laugh. He loved to see the pure joy when she let go like that.

Claire stared at him. Every once in a while you try to trace your life back to a time like that, when everything was so good. You try to go back and figure out how it started and the path you'd taken and how you ended up here, if there was a moment you could go back to and somehow alter and *poof*, you wouldn't be here, you'd be someplace better.

'Tell me,' Claire said.

He did. He started with the party at his house, overhearing Aimee and Erin in the basement, the promise, the late-night phone call. He went through it all. He told her about the stop at the gas station. He even told her about Aimee talking about how things weren't great with her parents.

Claire's posture stayed rigid. She said nothing. There was a quake near her lips. Every once in a while she would close her eyes. There would be a slight wince, as if she spotted a coming blow but was unwilling to defend herself from it.

Neither spoke when he finished. Claire did not ask any follow-up questions. She just stood there and looked very frail. Myron took a step toward her, but he could see right away it was the wrong move.

'You know I'd never hurt her,' he said.

She did not reply.

'Claire?'

'Do you remember that time we met up at Little Park by the circle?'

Myron waited a beat. 'We met up there a lot, Claire.'

'At the playground. Aimee was three years old. The Good Humor truck came along. You bought her a Toasted Almond Fudge.'

'Which she hated.'

Claire smiled. 'You remember?'

'I do.'

'Do you remember what I was like that day?'

He thought about it. 'I don't know what you're trying to get at.'

'Aimee didn't know her limits. She would try everything. She wanted to go on that high slide. There was a big ladder. She was too young for it. Or at least that's what I thought. She was my first child. I was so afraid all the time. But I couldn't stop her. So I let her climb the ladder, but I would stay right behind her, remember? You made a crack about it.'

He nodded.

'Before she was born, I swore I'd never be one of those overprotective parents. Swore it. But Aimee is climbing up this ladder and I'm right behind her, my hands poised behind her butt. Just in case. Just in case she slipped because wherever you are, even someplace as innocent as a playground, all a parent imagines is the worst. I kept picturing her tiny foot missing a step. I kept seeing her fingers slipping off those rails and her little body tipping back and then she'd land on her head wrong and her neck would be at a bad angle . . .'

Her voice faded away.

'So I stayed behind her. And I was ready for anything.'

Claire stopped and stared at him.

'I'd never hurt her,' Myron said.

'I know,' she said softly.

He should have felt relief at that. He didn't. There was something in her tone, something that kept him on the hook.

'You wouldn't harm her, I know that.' Her eyes flared up. 'But you're not blameless either.'

He had no idea what to say to that.

'Why aren't you married?' she asked.

'What the hell does that have to do with anything?'

'You're one of the nicest, sweetest men I know. You love kids. You're straight. So why aren't you married yet?'

Myron held back. Claire was in shock, he told himself. Her daughter was missing. She was just lashing out.

'I think it's because you bring destruction, Myron. Wherever you go, people get hurt. I think that's why you've never been married.'

'You think – what? – that I'm cursed?'

'No, nothing like that. But my little girl is gone.' Her voice was slow now, one weighted word at a time. 'You were the last to see her. You promised that you would protect her.'

He just stood there.

'You could have told me,' she said.

'I promised – '

'Don't,' she said, holding up her hand. 'That's no excuse. Aimee wouldn't have ever known. You could have pulled me aside and said, "Look, I told Aimee that she could call me if she had a problem." I'd have understood that. I'd have even liked it, because then I would have still been there for her, like with the ladder. I would have been able to protect her because that's what a parent does. A parent, Myron, not a family friend.'

He wanted to defend himself, but the arguments wouldn't come.

'But you didn't do that,' she went on, her words raining down on him. 'Instead you promised that you wouldn't tell her parents. Then you drove her somewhere and dropped her off, but you didn't watch out for her like I would have. Do you understand that? You didn't take care of my baby. And now she's gone.'

He said nothing.

'What are you going to do about that?' she asked.

'What?'

'I asked you what you're going to do about it.'

He opened his mouth, closed it, tried again. 'I don't know.'

'Yeah, you do.' Suddenly Claire's eyes seemed focused and clear. 'The police are going to do one of two things. I can see it already. They're backing away. Aimee took money out of an ATM machine before she called you. So they're either going to dismiss her as a runaway or they're going to think you were involved. Or both. You helped her run maybe. You're her boyfriend. Either way, she's eighteen. They're not going to look hard. They're not going to find her. They'll have other priorities.'

'What do you want me to do?'

'Find her.'

'I don't save people. You yourself pointed that out.'

'Then you better start now. My daughter is gone because of you. I hold you accountable.'

Myron shook his head. But she was having none of it.

'You made her promise. Right here in this house. You made her promise. Now you do the same, dammit. Promise me you'll find my baby. Promise me you'll bring her home.'

And a moment later – the truly final what-if? – Myron did.

621

19

Ali Wilder had finally stopped thinking long enough about Myron's impending visit to call her editor, a man she generously referred to as Caligula.

'I just don't get this paragraph, Ali.'

She bit back a sigh. 'What about it, Craig?' Craig was the name her editor used when he introduced himself, but Ali was sure his real name was Caligula.

Before 9/11, Ali had a solid job with a major magazine in the city. After Kevin's death, there was no way she could keep it. Erin and Jack needed her home. She took a sabbatical and then became a freelance journalist, mostly writing for magazines. At first, everyone offered her jobs. She refused them out of what she now saw as stupid pride. She hated getting the 'pity' assignments. She felt above it. She now regretted that.

Caligula cleared his throat, making a production about it, and read her paragraph out loud: 'The closest town is Pahrump. Picture Pahrump, rhymes with dump, as what's left on the road if a buzzard ate Las Vegas and spit out the bad parts. Tackiness as art form. A bordello is made to look like a White Castle restaurant, which seems like a bad pun. Signs with giant cowboys compete with signs for fireworks stores, casinos, trailer parks, and beef jerky. All the cheese is American singles.'

After a meaningful pause, Caligula said, 'Let's start with the last line.'

'Uh-huh.'

'You say that the only cheese in the town is American singles?'

'Yes,' Ali said.

'Are you sure?'

'Pardon me?'

'I mean, did you go to the supermarket?'

'No.' Ali started gnawing on a fingernail. 'It's not a statement of fact. I'm trying to give you a feel for the town.'

'By writing untruths?'

Ali knew where this was going. She waited. Caligula did not disappoint.

'How do you know, Ali, they don't have some other kind of cheese in this town? Did you check all the supermarket shelves? And even if you did, did you consider the fact that maybe someone shops in a neighboring town and brings other cheese into Pahrump? Or that maybe they order by mail service? Do you understand what I'm saying?'

Ali closed her eyes.

'We print that, about the American singles being the only cheese in town, and suddenly we get a call from the mayor and he says, "Hey, that's not true. We have tons of varieties here. We have Gouda and Swiss and cheddar and provolone – "'

'I get the point, Craig.'

' 'And Roquefort and blue and mozzarella – ' '

'Craig . . .'

' – and heck, what about cream?'

'Cream?'

'Cream cheese, for crying out loud. That's a kind of cheese, right? Cream cheese. Even a hickville place would have cream cheese. You see?'

'Right, uh-huh.' More gnawing on the nail. 'I see.'

'So that line has to go.' She could hear his pen go through it. 'Now let's talk about the line before that, the one about trailer parks and beef jerky.'

Caligula was short. Ali hated short editors. She used to joke about it with Kevin. Kevin had always been her first reader. His job was to tell her that whatever she had scribbled out was brilliant. Ali, like most writers, was insecure. She needed to hear his praise. Any criticism while she wrote paralyzed her. Kevin understood. So he would rave. And when she battled with her editors, especially those short of sight and stature like Caligula, Kevin always took her side.

She wondered if Myron would like her writing.

He had asked to see some of her pieces, but she'd been putting it off. The man had dated Jessica Culver, one of the top novelists in the country. Jessica Culver had been reviewed on the front page of *The New York Times Book Review*. Her books had been short-listed for every major literary award. And as if that weren't enough, as if Jessica Culver didn't have it all over Ali Wilder professionally, the woman was ridiculously gorgeous.

How could Ali possibly stack up against that?

The doorbell rang. She checked her watch. Too early for Myron.

'Craig, can I call you back?

Caligula sighed. 'Fine, okay. In the meantime I'll just tweak this a bit.'

She winced when he said that. There was an old joke about being left on a deserted island with an editor. You are starving. All you have left is a glass of orange juice. Days pass. You are near death. You are about to drink the juice when the editor grabs the glass from your hand and pees into it. You look at him, stunned. 'There,' the editor says, handing you the glass. 'It just needed a little tweaking.'

The bell rang again. Erin galloped down the stairs and yelled, 'I'll get it.'

Ali hung up. Erin opened the door. Ali saw her go rigid. She hurried her step. There were two men at the door. They both held police badges.

'May I help you?' Ali said.

'Are you Ali and Erin Wilder?'

Ali's legs went rubbery. No, this wasn't a flashback of how she learned about Kevin. But there was still some sort of déjà vu here. She turned to her daughter. Erin's face was white.

'I'm Livingston police detective Lance Banner. This is Kasselton detective John Greenhall.'

'What's this about?'

'We'd like to ask you both a few questions, if we might.'

'What about?'

'Can we come in?'

'I'd like to know why you're here first.'

Banner said, 'We'd like to ask a few questions about Myron Bolitar.'

Ali nodded, trying to figure this through. She turned to her daughter. 'Erin, head upstairs for a little while and let me talk to the officers, okay?'

'Actually, uh, ma'am?'

It was Banner.

'Yes?'

'The questions we want to ask,' he said, stepping through the door and motioning with his head toward Erin. 'They're for your daughter, not you.'

Myron stood in Aimee's bedroom.

The Biel house was walking distance from his. Claire and Erik had driven ahead of him. Myron talked to Win a few minutes, asked him if he could help track down whatever the police had on both Katie Rochester and Aimee. Then he followed on foot.

When Myron entered the house, Erik was already gone.

'He's driving around,' Claire said, leading him down the corridor. 'Erik thinks if he goes to where she hangs out, he can find her.'

They stopped in front of Aimee's door. Claire opened it.

'What are you looking for?' she asked.

'Damned if I know,' Myron said. 'Did Aimee know a girl named Katie Rochester?'

'That's the other missing girl, right?'

'Yes.'

'I don't think so. In fact, I asked her about it, you know, when she was on the news?'

'Right.'

'Aimee said she'd seen her around but she didn't know her. Katie went to middle school at Mount Pleasant. Aimee went to Heritage. You remember how it is.'

He did. By the time they both got to high school, their cliques were solidified.

'Do you want me to call around and ask her friends?'

'That might be helpful.'

Neither of them moved for a moment.

Claire asked, 'Should I leave you alone in here?'

'For now, yeah.'

She did. She closed the door behind her. Myron looked around. He had told the truth – he didn't have a clue what he was looking for here – but he figured that it would be a good first step. This was a teenage girl. She had to keep secrets in her room, right?

It also felt right, being here. From the moment he'd made the promise to Claire, his entire perspective began to shift. His senses felt strangely attuned. It had been a while since he'd done this – investigate – but the memory muscle jumped in and took effect. Being in the girl's room brought it all back to him. In basketball, you need to get into the zone to do your best. Doing this kind of thing, there was a similar feel. Being here, in the victim's room, did that. Put him in the zone.

There were two guitars in the room. Myron didn't know anything about instruments, but one was clearly electric, the other acoustic. There was a poster of Jimi Hendrix on the wall. Guitar picks were encased in Lucite blocks. Myron read through them. They were collector's picks. One belonged to Keith Richards – others to Nils Lofgren, Eric Clapton, Buck Dharma.

Myron almost smiled. The girl had good taste.

The computer was already on, a screen saver of a fish tank rolling by. Myron wasn't a computer expert, but he knew enough to get started. Claire had given him Aimee's password and told him about Erik going through the e-mail. He checked it anyway. He brought up AOL and signed on.

Yep, all the e-mail had been deleted.

He hit Windows Explorer and put her files in date order, to see what she had worked on most recently. Aimee had been writing songs. He thought about that, about this creative young woman, about where she was now. He scanned through the most recent word processing documents. Nothing special. He tried checking her downloads. There were some recent photographs. He opened them. Aimee with a bunch of school pals, he guessed. Nothing obviously special about them either, but maybe he'd have Claire take a look.

Teens, he knew, were huge with instant messaging online. From the relative calm of their computers, they had conversations with dozens of people sometimes at the same time. Myron knew plenty of parents who whined about this, but in his day, they'd spent hours tying up the phone gossiping with one another. Was IMing any worse?

He brought up her buddy list. There were at least fifty screen names like SpazaManiacJack11, MSG Watkins, and YoungThangBlaine742. Myron printed them out. He'd let Claire and Erik go through them with one of Aimee's friends, see if there was a name that didn't belong, that none of them knew about. It was a long shot, but it would keep them busy.

He let go of the computer mouse and started to search the old-fashioned way. The desk came first. He went through her drawers. Pens, papers, note cards, spare batteries, a smattering of computer software CDs. Nothing personal. There were several receipts from a place called Planet Music. Myron checked the guitars. They had Planet Music stickers on the back.

Big wow.

He moved to the next drawer. More nothing.

In the third drawer, Myron saw something that made him stop. He reached down and gently lifted it into view. He smiled. Protected in a plastic sleeve . . . it was Myron's rookie basketball card. He stared at his younger self. Myron remembered the photo shoot. He had done several dumb poses – taking a jump shot, pretending to pass, the old-fashioned triple-threat position – but they'd settled for one of him bending down and dribbling. The background was an empty arena. In the picture he wore his green Boston Celtics jersey – one of maybe five times he got to wear it in his entire life. The card company had printed up several thousand before his injury. They were collector's items now.

It was nice to know Aimee had one, though he wondered what the police might make of it.

He put it back in the drawer. His fingerprints would be on it now, but then again they would be all over the room. Didn't matter. He pressed on. He wanted to find a diary. That was what you always saw in the movies. The girl writes a diary, and it talks about her secret boyfriend and double life and all that. That worked in fiction. It wasn't happening for him in reality.

He hit an undergarments drawer. He felt yucky but he persevered. If she was going to hide anything, this could be the place. But there was nothing. Her tastes seemed on the wholesome side for a teenage girl. Tank tops were as bad as it got. Near the bottom, however, he found something particularly racy. He pulled it into view. There was a tag on it from a mall lingerie store called Bedroom Rendezvous. It was white, sheer, and looked like something out of a nurse fantasy. He frowned and wondered what to make of it.

There was a smattering of bobble-head dolls. An iPod with white earbuds was lounged out on the bed. He checked the tunes. She had Aimee Mann on there. He took that as a small victory. He'd given her Aimee Mann's *Lost in Space* a few years back, thinking the first name might pique her interest. Now he could see that she had five of Aimee Mann's CDs. He liked that.

There were photographs stuck onto a mirror. They were all group pictures – Aimee with a slew of girlfriends. There were two of the volleyball team, one in classic team pose, another a celebration shot taken after they'd won the counties. There were several pictures of her high school rock band, Aimee playing lead guitar. He looked at her face while she played. Her smile was heartbreaking, but what girl that age doesn't have a heartbreaking smile?

He found her yearbook. He started paging through it. Yearbooks had come a long way since he'd graduated. For one thing, they included a DVD. Myron would watch it, he guessed, if he had the time. He looked up Katie Rochester's entry. He'd seen that photograph before, on the news. He read about her. She'd miss hanging with Betsy and Craig and Saturday nights at the Ritz Diner. Nothing significant. He turned to Aimee Biel's page. Aimee mentioned a whole bunch of her friends; her favorite teachers, Miss Korty and Mr. D; her volleyball coach, Mr. Grady; and all the girls on the team. She ended with, 'Randy, you've made the past two years so special. I know we'll be together always.'

Good ol' Randy.

He checked out Randy's entry. He was a good-looking kid with wild, almost Rastafarian curls. He had a soul patch and a big white smile. He talked mostly about sports in his write-up. He mentioned Aimee too, how much she'd 'enriched' his time in high school.

Hmm.

Myron thought about that, looked again at the mirror, and for the first time wondered if perhaps he'd stumbled across a clue.

Claire opened the door. 'Anything?'

Myron pointed to the mirror. 'This.'

'What about it?'

'How often do you come in this room?'

She frowned. 'A teenager lives here.'

'Would that mean rarely?'

'Pretty much never.'

'Does she do her own laundry?'

'She's a teenager, Myron. She does nothing.'

'So who does it?'

'We have a live-in. Her name is Rosa. Why?'

'The photographs,' he said.

'What about them?'

'She has a boyfriend named Randy, right?'

'Randy Wolf. He's a sweet kid.'

'And they've been together awhile?'

'Since sophomore year. Why?'

Again he gestured to the mirror. 'There are no pictures of him. I looked all over the room. No photos of him anywhere. That's why I was asking about when you were last in the room.' He looked back at her. 'Did there used to be?'

'Yes.'

He pointed to several blank spots on the bottom of the mirror. 'This all looks out of sequence, but I bet she removed the pictures from here.'

'But they just went to the prom together, what, three nights ago.'

Myron shrugged. 'Maybe they had a big fight there.'

'You said Aimee looked emotional when you picked her up, right?'

'Right.'

'Maybe they'd just broken up,' Claire said.

'Could be,' Myron said. 'Except she hasn't been home since then, and the photographs on the mirror are gone. That would imply that they broke up at least a day or two before I picked her up. One more thing.'

Claire waited. Myron showed her the lingerie from Bedroom Rendezvous. 'Have you seen this before?'

'No. You found it in here?'

Myron nodded. 'Bottom of the drawer. It looks unworn. The tag is still on it.'

Claire went quiet.

'What?'

'Erik was telling the police how Aimee's been acting strangely lately. I fought him on it, but the truth is, she has. She's grown very secretive.'

'Do you know what else struck me about this room?'

'What?'

'Forgetting this lingerie – which might be relevant and might be nothing – the opposite of what you just said: There is almost nothing secretive in here. I mean, she's a high school senior. There should be something, right?'

Claire considered that. 'Why do you think that is?'

'It's like she's working hard to hide something. We need to check other places where she might have kept personal stuff, someplace that you and Erik wouldn't think to snoop. Like her school locker maybe.'

'Should we do that now?'

'I think it'd be better to talk to Randy first.'

She frowned. 'His father.'

'What about him?'

'His name is Jake. Big Jake, everyone calls him. He's bigger than you. And the wife is a flirt. Last year Big Jake got into a fight at one of Randy's football games. Beat this poor guy senseless in front of his kids. He's a total putz.'

'Total?'

'Total.'

'Whew.' Myron pantomimed wiping the sweat off his brow. 'A partial putz, I mind. A total putz – that's my bag.'

20

Randy Wolf lived in the new Laurel Road section. The brand-new estates of brushed brick had more square footage than Kennedy Airport. There was a faux wrought-iron gate. The gate was open enough for Myron to walk through. The grounds were over-landscaped, the lawn so green it looked like someone had gone overboard with spray paint. There were three SUVs parked in the driveway. Next to them, gleaming from a fresh waxing and seemingly perfect sun placement, sat a little red Corvette. Myron started humming the matching Prince tune. He couldn't help it.

The familiar whack of a tennis ball drifted in from the backyard. Myron headed toward the sound. There were four lithe ladies playing tennis. They all wore ponytails and tight tennis whites. Myron was a big fan of women in tennis whites. One of the lithe ladies was about to serve when she noticed him. She had great legs, Myron observed. He checked again. Yep, great.

Ogling tan legs probably wasn't a clue, but why chance it?

Myron waved and gave the woman serving his best smile. She returned it and signaled to the ladies to excuse her for a moment. She jogged toward him. Her dark ponytail bounced. She stopped very close to him. Her breathing was deep. Sweat made the tennis whites cling. It also made them a little see-through – again Myron was just being observant – but she didn't seem to care.

'Something I can do for you?'

She had one hand on her hip.

'Hi, my name is Myron Bolitar.'

Commandment Four from the Bolitar Book on Smoothness: Wow the ladies with a dazzling first line.

'Your name,' she said. 'It rings a bell.'

Her tongue moved around a lot when she talked.

'Are you Mrs. Wolf?'

'Call me Lorraine.'

Lorraine Wolf had that way of speaking where everything sounded like a double entendre.

'I'm looking for your son, Randy.'

'Wrong reply,' she said.

'Sorry.'

'You were supposed to say that I looked too young to be Randy's mother.'

'Too obvious,' Myron said. 'An intelligent woman like you would have seen right through that.'

'Nice recovery.'

'Thanks.'

The other ladies gathered by the net. They had towels draped around their necks and were drinking something green.

'Why are you looking for Randy?' she asked.

'I need to talk to him.'

'Well, yes, I figured that out. But maybe you could tell me what this is about?'

The back door opened with an audible bang. A large man – Myron was six-four, two-fifteen and this guy had at least two inches and thirty pounds on him – stepped out the door.

Big Jake Wolf, Myron deducted, was in da house.

His black hair was slicked back. He had a mean squint going.

'Wait, isn't that Steven Seagal?' Myron asked, sotto voce.

Lorraine Wolf smothered a giggle.

Big Jake stomped over. He kept glaring at Myron. Myron waited a few seconds, then he winked and gave Big Jake the Stan Laurel, five-finger wave. Big Jake did not look pleased. He marched to Lorraine's side, put his arm around her, tugged her tight against his hip.

'Hi, honey,' he said, his eyes still on Myron.

'Well, hi, back!' Myron said.

'I wasn't talking to you.'

'Then why were you looking at me?'

Big Jake frowned and pulled his wife closer. Lorraine cringed a little, but she let him. Myron had seen this act before. Raging insecurity, he suspected. Jake released his glare long enough to kiss his wife's cheek before retightening his grip. Then he started glaring again, holding his wife firmly against his side.

Myron wondered if Big Jake was going to pee on her to mark his territory.

'Go back to your game, honey. I'll handle this.'

'We were just finishing anyway.'

'Then why don't you ladies go inside and have a drink, hmm?'

He let her go. She looked relieved. The ladies walked down the path. Myron again checked their legs. Just in case. The women smiled at him.

'Hey, what are you looking for?' Big Jake snapped.

'Potential clues,' Myron said.

'What?'

Myron turned back to him. 'Never mind.'

'So what do you want here?'

'My name is Myron Bolitar.'

'So?'

'Good comeback.'

'What?'

'Never mind.'

'You some kind of comedian?'

'I prefer the term "comic actor." Comedians are always typecast.'

'What the . . . ?' Big Jake stopped, got his bearings. 'You always do this?'

'Do what?'

'Stop by uninvited?'

'It's the only way people will have me,' Myron said.

Big Jake squinted a little more. He wore tight jeans and a silk shirt that had one too many buttons open. There was a gold chain enmeshed in chest hair. 'Stayin'

Alive' wasn't playing in the background, but it should have been.

'Wild stab in the dark here,' Myron said. 'The red Corvette. It's yours, right?'

He glared some more. 'What do you want?'

'I'd like to speak to your son, Randy.'

'Why?'

'I'm here on behalf of the Biel family.'

That made him blink. 'So?'

'Are you aware that their daughter is missing?'

'So?'

'That "so" line. It never gets old, Jake, really. Aimee Biel is missing and I'd like to ask your son about it.'

'He has nothing to do with that. He was home Saturday night.'

'Alone?'

'No. I was with him.'

'How about Lorraine? Was she there too? Or was she out for the evening?'

Big Jake didn't like Myron using his wife's first name. 'None of your business.'

'Be that as it may, I'd still like to talk to Randy.'

'No.'

'Why not?'

'I don't want Randy mixed up in this.'

'In what?'

'Hey,' he pointed at Myron, 'I don't like your attitude.'

'You don't?' Myron gave him the wide game-show-host smile and waited. Big Jake looked confused. 'Is this better? Rosier, am I right?'

'Get out.'

'I would say, "Who's going to make me," but really, that would be sooo expected.'

Big Jake smiled and stepped right up to Myron. 'You wanna know who's going to make you?'

'Wait, hold on, let me check the script.' Myron mimed flipping pages. 'Okay here it is. I say, "No, who?" Then you say, "I am."'

'Got that straight.'

'Jake?'

'What?'

'Are any of your children home?' Myron asked.

'Why? What's that gotta do with anything?'

'Lorraine, well, she already knows you're a little man,' Myron said, not moving an inch, 'but I'd hate to beat your ass in front of your kids.'

Jake's breathing turned into a snort. He didn't back up, but he was having trouble holding the eye contact. 'Ah, you ain't worth it.'

Myron rolled his eyes, but he bit back the that's-the-next-line-in-the-script rejoinder. Maturity.

'Anyway, my son broke up with that slut.'

'By slut, you mean . . . ?'

'Aimee. He dumped her.'

'When?'

'Three, four months ago. He was done with her.'

'They went to the prom together last week.'

'That was for show.'

630

'For show?'

He shrugged. 'I'm not surprised any of this happened.'

'Why do you say that, Jake?'

'Because Aimee was no good. She was a slut.'

Myron felt his blood tick. 'And why do you say that?'

'I know her, okay? I know the whole family. My son has a bright future. He's going to Dartmouth in the fall, and I want nothing getting in the way of that. So listen to me, Mr. Basketball. Yeah, I know who you are. You think you're such hot stuff. Big, tough basketball stud who never made it to the pros. Big-time All-American who crapped out in the end. Who couldn't hack it once the going got tough.'

Big Jake grinned.

'Wait, is this the part where I break down and cry?' Myron asked.

Big Jake put his finger on Myron's chest. 'You just stay the hell away from my son, you understand me? He has nothing to do with that slut's disappearance.'

Myron's hand shot forward. He grabbed Jake by the balls, and squeezed. Jake's eyes flew open. Myron positioned his body so that nobody could see what he was doing. Then he leaned in so he could whisper in Jake's ear.

'We're not going to call Aimee that anymore, are we, Jake? Feel free to nod.'

Big Jake nodded. His face was turning purple. Myron closed his eyes, cursed himself, let go. Jake sucked in a deep breath, staggered back, dropped to one knee. Myron felt like a dope, losing control like that.

'Hey, look, I'm just trying to – '

'Get out,' Jake hissed. 'Just . . . just leave me alone.'

And this time, Myron obeyed.

From the front seat of a Buick Skylark, the Twins watched Myron walk down the Wolfs' driveway.

'There's our boy.'

'Yep.'

They weren't really twins. They weren't even brothers. They didn't look alike. They did share a birthday, September 24, but Jeb was eight years older than Orville. That was part of how they got the name – having the same birthday. The other was how they met: at a Minnesota Twins baseball game. Some would claim that it was a sadistic turn of fate or ridiculously bad star alignment that brought them together. Others would claim that there was a bond there, two lost souls that recognized a kindred spirit, as if their streak of cruelty and psychosis were some kind of magnet that drew them to each other.

Jeb and Orville met in the bleachers at the Dome in Minneapolis when Jeb, the older Twin, got into a fight with five beer-marinated head cases. Orville stepped in and together they put all five in the hospital. That was eight years ago. Three of the guys were still in comas.

Jeb and Orville stayed together.

These two men, both life-loners, neither married, never in a long-term relationship, became inseparable. They moved around from city to city, town to town, always leaving havoc in their wake. For fun, they would enter bars and pick fights and see how close they could come to killing a man without actually killing him.

When they destroyed a drug-dealing motorcycle gang in Montana, their rep was cemented.

Jeb and Orville did not look dangerous. Jeb wore an ascot and smoking jacket. Orville had the Woodstock thing going on – a ponytail, scruffy facial hair, pink-tinted glasses, and a tie-dyed shirt. They sat in the car and watched Myron.

Jeb began singing, as he always did, mixing English songs with his own Spanish interpretation. Right now he was singing the Police's 'Message in a Bottle.'

'I hope that someone gets my, I hope that someone gets my, I hope that someone gets my, *mensaje en una botella* . . .'

'I like that one, dude,' Orville said.

'Thank you, *mi amigo.*'

'Man, you were younger, you should do that *American Idol.* That Spanish thing. They'd love that. Even that Simon judge who hates everything.'

'I love Simon.'

'Me too. The dude is far out.'

They watched Myron get into his car.

'So, like, what do you think he was doing at this house?' Orville asked.

Singing: 'You ask me if our love would grow, *yo no se, yo no se.*'

'The Beatles, right?'

'Bingo.'

'And *yo no se.* I don't know.'

'Right again.'

'Groovy.' Orville checked the car's clock. 'Should we call Rochester and tell him what's shaking?'

Jeb shrugged. 'Might as well.'

Myron Bolitar started driving. They followed. Rochester picked up on the second ring.

'He, like, left that house,' Orville said.

Rochester said, 'Keep following him.'

'Your dollars,' Orville said with a shrug. 'But I think it's a waste, man.'

'He may give you a clue where he stashed the girls.'

'If we, like, snatch his ass now, he'll give us all the clues he knows.'

There was a moment of hesitation. Orville smiled and gave Jeb a thumbs-up sign.

'I'm at his house,' Rochester said. 'That's where I want you to take him.'

'Are you at or in?'

'At or in what?'

'His house.'

'I'm outside. In my car.'

'So you don't know if he's got a plasma TV.'

'What? No, I don't know.'

'If we're going to be working him awhile, it'd be righteous if he had one. In case it gets to be a drag, you know what I'm saying? The Yankees are playing against Boston. Jeb and me dig watching in HD. That's why I'm asking.'

There was another moment of hesitation.

'Maybe he has one,' Rochester said.

'That would be groovy. That DLP technology is good too. Anything with high-def, I guess. By the way, do you, like, got a plan or anything?'

'I'm going to wait until he comes back home,' Dominick Rochester said. 'I'll tell him I want to talk to him. We go inside. You go inside.'

'Radical.'

'Where is he going now?'

Orville checked the navigator on the car. 'Hey, like, unless I'm mistaken, we're heading back to Bolitar's crib right now.'

21

Myron was two blocks from home when the cell ráng. Win asked, 'Did I ever tell you about Cingle Shaker?'

'No.'

'She's a private eye. If she were any hotter, your teeth would melt.'

'That's swell, really.'

'I've had her,' Win said.

'Good for you.'

'I went back for seconds. And we still talk.'

'Yikes,' Myron said.

Win still talking to a woman he'd slept with more than once – in human terms, that was like a marriage celebrating its silver anniversary.

'Is there a reason you're sharing this warm moment with me right now?' Then Myron remembered something. 'Wait, a private eye named Cingle. Hester Crimstein called her when I was being interrogated, right?'

'Exactly. Cingle has gathered some new information on the disappearances.'

'You set up a meet?'

'She's waiting for you at Baumgart's.'

Baumgart's, long Myron's favorite restaurant serving both Chinese and American dishes, had recently opened a branch in Livingston.

'How will I recognize her?'

'Hot enough to make your teeth melt,' Win said. 'How many women at Baumgart's fit that description?'

Win hung up. Five minutes later Myron entered the restaurant. Cingle didn't disappoint. She was curvy to the max, built like a Marvel comic drawing come to life. Myron walked up to Peter Chin, the owner, to say hello. Peter frowned at him.

'What?'

'She's not Jessica,' Peter said.

Myron and Jessica used to go to Baumgart's, albeit the original in Englewood, all the time. Peter had never gotten over the breakup. The unspoken rule was that Myron was not allowed to bring other women here. For seven years he had kept that rule, more for himself than Peter.

'It's not a date.'

Peter looked at Cingle, looked at Myron, made a face that said *Who are you kidding?*

'It's not.' Then: 'You realize, of course, I haven't even seen Jessica in years.'

Peter put a finger in the air. 'Years fly by, but the heart stays in the same place.'

'Damn.'

'What?'

'You've been reading fortune cookies again, haven't you?'

'There is much wisdom there.'

'Tell you what. Read Sunday's *New York Times* instead. Styles section.'

'I already did.'

'And?'

Again Peter raised his finger. 'You can't ride two horses with one behind.'

'Hey, I told you that one. It's Yiddish.'

'I know.'

'And it doesn't apply.'

'Just sit down.' Peter dismissed him with a wave. 'And order for yourself. I'm not helping you.'

When Cingle stood to greet him, necks didn't so much turn in her direction as snap. They exchanged hellos and sat down.

'So you're Win's friend,' Cingle said.

'I am.'

She studied him for a moment. 'You don't look psychotic.'

'I like to think of myself as the counterbalance.'

There were no papers in front of her.

'Do you have the police file?' he asked.

'There is none. There isn't even an official investigation yet.'

'So what have you got?'

'Katie Rochester started taking money out at ATMs. Then she ran away. There is no evidence, other than parental protestations, to suggest anything other than that.'

'The investigator who grabbed me at the airport – ' Myron began.

'Loren Muse. She's good, by the way.'

'Right, Muse. She asked me a lot about Katie Rochester. I think they have something solid linking me to her.'

'Yes and no. They have something solid linking Katie to Aimee. I'm not sure it links directly to you.'

'That being?'

'Their last ATM charges.'

'What about them?'

'Both girls used the exact same Citibank in Manhattan.'

Myron stopped, tried to absorb that one.

The waiter came over. New guy. Myron didn't know him. Usually Peter had the waiter bring over a few free appetizers. Not today.

'I'm used to men staring at me,' Cingle said. 'But the owner keeps glaring at me like I urinated on the floor.'

'He misses my old girlfriend.'

'That's sweet.'

'Adorable.'

Cingle met Peter's eye, wiggled her fingers to show a wedding band, and yelled in Peter's direction, 'He's safe. I'm already married.'

Peter turned away.

Cingle shrugged, explained about the ATM charge, about Aimee's face being clear in the security camera. Myron tried to figure it through. Nothing came to him.

'There's one more thing you might want to know about.'

Myron waited.

'There's a woman named Edna Skylar. She's a doctor over at St. Barnabas. The cops are keeping this under heavy wraps because Rochester's father is a nutjob, but apparently, Dr. Skylar spotted Katie Rochester on the street in Chelsea.'

She told him the story, about how Edna Skylar had followed the girl into the subway, that she was with a man, what Katie said about not telling anyone.

'Did the police look into it?'

'Look into what?'

'Did they try to figure out where Katie was, who the guy was, anything?'

'Why? Katie Rochester is eighteen years old. She gathered money before she ran. She's got a connected father who was probably abusive in some fashion. The police have other things to worry about. Real crimes. Muse is handling a double homicide in East Orange. Manpower is short. And what Edna Skylar saw confirmed what they already knew.'

'That Katie Rochester ran away.'

'Right.'

Myron sat back. 'And the fact that they both used the same ATM?'

'Either a startling coincidence . . .'

Myron shook his head. 'No way.'

'I agree. No way. So either that or they both planned to run away. There was a reason they both chose that ATM. I don't know what. But maybe they planned this together. Katie and Aimee went to the same high school, right?'

'Right, but I haven't found any other connection between them.'

'Both eighteen, both graduating high school, both from the same town.' Cingle shrugged. 'There has to be something.'

She was right. He'd need to speak to the Rochesters, see what they knew. He'd have to be careful. He didn't want to open that side of things up. He also wanted to talk to the doctor, Edna Skylar, get a good description of the man Katie Rochester was with, see exactly where she was, what subway she was riding, what direction she was heading in.

'Thing is,' Cingle said, 'if Katie and Aimee are runaways, there might be a reason they ran.'

'I was just thinking the same thing,' Myron said.

'They might not want to be found.'

'True.'

'What are you going to do?'

'Find them anyway.'

'And if they want to stay hidden?'

Myron thought about Aimee Biel. He thought about Erik and he thought about Claire. Good people. Reliable, solid. He wondered what could possibly make Aimee run away from them, what could have been so bad that she'd pull something like this.

'Guess I'll cross that bridge when I get to it,' he said.

Win sat by himself in the corner of the dimly lit strip club. No one bothered him. They knew better. If he wanted someone near him, he'd let them know.

The song on the jukebox was one of the most putrid songs from the eighties, Mr. Mister's 'Broken Wings.' Myron claimed that it was the worst song of the decade. Win countered that 'We Built This City on Rock-n-Roll' by Starship was worse. The argument lasted an hour without resolution. So, as they often did in situations like this, they went to Esperanza to end the tie-breaker, but she sided with 'Too Shy' by Kajagoogoo.

Win liked to sit in this corner booth and look out and think.

There was a major-league baseball team in town. Several of the players had come to the 'gentlemen's club,' a truly inspired euphemism for strip joint, to unwind. The working girls went crazy. Win watched a stripper of questionably legal age hit on one of the team's top pitchers.

'How old did you say you were?' the stripper asked.

'Twenty-nine,' the pitcher said.

'Wow.' She shook her head. 'You don't look *that* old.'

A wistful smile played on Win's lips. Youth.

Windsor Horne Lockwood III was born to great wealth. He did not pretend otherwise. He did not like multibillionaires who bragged about their business acumen when they'd started out with Daddy's billions. Genius is almost irrelevant in the pursuit of enormous riches anyway. In fact, it can be a hindrance. If you are smart enough to see the risks, you might try to avoid them. That type of thinking – safe thinking – never led to great wealth.

Win started life in the lush Main Line of Philadelphia. His family had been on the board of the stock exchange since its inception. He had a direct descendant who'd been this country's first secretary of the treasury. Win was born with not only a silver spoon in his mouth, but an entire silver place setting at his feet.

And he looked the part.

That had been his problem. From his earliest years, with his tow-head blond hair and ruddy complexion and delicate features, with his face naturally set in an expression that looked smug, people detested Win on sight. You looked at Windsor Horne Lockwood III and you saw elitism, undeserved wealth, someone who would always look down his porcelain-sculpted nose at you. All your own failures rose up in a wave of resentment and envy – just by gazing upon this seemingly soft, coddled, privileged boy.

It had led to ugly incidents.

At the age of ten Win had gotten separated from his mother at the Philadelphia Zoo. A group of students from an inner-city school had found him in his little blue blazer with the crest on the pocket and beaten the hell out of him. He'd been hospitalized and nearly lost a kidney. The physical pain was bad. The shame of being a scared little boy was far worse.

Win never wanted to experience that again.

People, Win knew, made snap judgments based on appearances. No great insight there. And yes, there were the obvious prejudices against African-Americans or Jews or what-have-you. But Win was more concerned with the more garden-variety prejudices. If, for example, you see an overweight woman eating a doughnut, you are repulsed. You make snap judgments – she is undisciplined, lazy, sloppy, probably stupid, definitely lacking in self-esteem.

In a strange way, the same thing happened when people saw Win.

He had a choice. Stay behind the hedges, safe in the cocoon of privilege, live a protected albeit fearful life. Or do something about it.

He chose the latter.

Money makes everything easier. Oddly enough, Win always considered Myron to be a real-life Batman, but the Caped Crusader had started off as Win's childhood role model. Bruce Wayne's only superpower was tremendous wealth. He used it to train himself to be a crime fighter. Win did something similar with his money. He hired former squad leaders from both Delta Force and the Green Berets to train him as if he were one of their most elite. Win also found the world's top instructors on firearms, on knives, on hand-to-hand combat. He secured the services of martial artists from a wide variety of countries and either flew them to the family estate in Bryn Mawr or traveled overseas. He spent a full year with a reclusive martial-arts master in Korea, high in the hills in the southern part of the country. He learned about pain, how to inflict it without leaving marks. He learned about intimidation tactics. He learned about electronics, about locks, about the underworld, about security procedures.

It all came together. Win was a sponge when it came to picking up new techniques. He worked hard, ridiculously hard, training at least five hours every day. He had naturally fast hands, the hunger, the desire, the work ethic, the coldness – all the ingredients.

The fear went away.

Once he was sufficiently trained, Win started hanging out in the most drug-infested, crime-ridden corners of the city. He would go there wearing blue blazers with crests or pink polos or loafers without socks. The bad people would see him and lick their lips. There would be hate in their eyes. They would attack. And Win would answer.

There may be better fighters out there, Win assumed, especially now that he was growing older.

But not many.

His cell phone rang. He picked it up and said, 'Articulate.'

'We got a wiretap on a guy named Dominick Rochester.'

The call was from an old colleague Win hadn't heard from in three years. No matter. This was how it worked in their world. The wiretap did not surprise him. Rochester was supposedly connected. 'Go on.'

'Someone leaked to him your friend Bolitar's connection to his daughter.'

Win waited.

'Rochester has a more secure phone. We're not sure. But we think he called the Twins.'

There was silence.

'Do you know them?'

'Just by reputation,' Win said.

'Take what you heard and put it on steroids. One of them has some kind of weird condition. He doesn't feel pain, but man, does he like to inflict it. The other one, his name is Jeb – and yeah, I know how this is going to sound – he likes to bite.'

'Do tell,' Win said.

'We once found some guy the Twins worked over with just Jeb's teeth. The body . . . I mean, it was a red puddle. He bit out the guy's eyes, Win. I still don't sleep when I think about it.'

'Maybe you should buy a night-light.'

'Don't think I haven't thought of it. They scare me,' the voice on the phone said, 'like you scare me.'

Win knew that in this man's world, that was about as big a compliment as he could pay the Twins. 'And you believe that Rochester called them right after he heard about Myron Bolitar?'

'Within minutes, yeah.'

'Thank you for the information.'

'Win, listen to what I'm saying. They're absolutely nuts. We know about this one guy, a big old mafia don from Kansas City. He hired them. Anyway, it didn't work out. The mafia don pisses them off, I don't know how. So the don, no fool, he tries to buy them off, make peace. Nothing doing. The Twins get a hold of his four-year-old grandson. Four years old, Win. They send him back in chewed-up pieces. Then – get this – *after* they're done, then they accept the don's money. The *same* amount of money he'd already offered. They didn't ask for a penny more. Do you understand what I'm telling you?'

Win hung up. There was no need to reply. He understood perfectly.

22

Myron had his cell phone in hand, preparing to call Ali for a much-needed hello, when he noticed a car parked in front of his house. Myron pocketed the cell and pulled into his driveway.

A husky man sat on the curb in front of Myron's yard. He stood when Myron approached. 'Myron Bolitar?'

'Yes.'

'I'd like to talk to you.'

Myron nodded. 'Why don't we go inside?'

'You know who I am?'

'I know who you are.'

It was Dominick Rochester. Myron recognized him from the news reports on TV. He had a ferocious face with pores big enough to get your foot caught in. The smell of cheap musk came off him in squiggly line waves. Myron held his breath. He wondered how Rochester had learned about Myron's connection to the case, but no matter. This would work well, Myron figured. He had wanted to talk to Rochester anyway.

Myron was not sure when the feeling came upon him. It could have been when the other car made the turn. It could have been something in Dominick Rochester's walk. Myron could see right away that Rochester was the real deal – a bad guy you did not want to mess with, as opposed to that poser, Big Jake Wolf.

But again it was a bit like basketball. There were moments when Myron was so in the game, where he would be rising on his jump shot, his fingers finding the exact grooves on the ball, his hand cocked in front of his forehead, his eyes locked on the rim, only the rim, when time would slow down, as if he could stop in midair and readjust and see the rest of the court.

Something was wrong here.

Myron stopped at the door, keys in hand. He turned and looked back at Rochester. Rochester had those black eyes, the kind that view everything with an equal lack of emotion – a human being, a dog, a file cabinet, a mountain range. They never changed no matter what they saw, no matter what horror or delight played out in front of them.

'Why don't we talk out here?' Myron said.

Rochester shrugged. 'If you want.'

The car, a Buick Skylark, slowed.

Myron felt his cell phone vibrate. He looked down at it. Win's SWEET CHEEKS was displayed. He put the phone to his ear.

Win said, 'There are two very bad hombres – '

That was when Myron was jarred by the blow.

Rochester had thrown a punch.

The fist skimmed across the top of Myron's head. The instincts were rusty, but Myron still had his peripheral vision. He'd seen Rochester launch the fist at the last second. He ducked in time to take away the brunt. The blow ended up glancing across the top of Myron's skull. There was pain, but Rochester's knuckles probably felt worse.

The phone fell to the ground.

Myron was down on one knee. He grabbed Rochester's extended arm by the wrist. He curled the fingers of his free hand. Most people hit with fists. That was necessary at times, but in reality you should avoid doing it. You hit something hard with a fist, you'll break your hand.

The palm strike, especially to vulnerable areas, was usually more effective. With a punch, you need to flick or jab. You can't power straight through, because the small bones in the hand can't handle the stress. But if the palm strike is delivered correctly, fingers curled and protected, the wrist tilted back, the blow landing on the meaty bottom of the palm, you put the pressure on the radius, the ulna, the humerus – in short, the larger arm bones.

That was what Myron did. The obvious place to aim right now was the groin, but Myron figured that Rochester had been in plenty of scrapes before. He'd be looking for that.

And he was. Rochester raised a knee for protection.

Myron went for the diaphragm instead. When the shot landed just below the sternum, the air burst out of the big man. Myron pulled on Rochester's arm and threw him in what looked like an awkward judo throw. Truth was, in real fights, all throws look pretty awkward.

The zone. He was in it now. Everything slowed down.

Rochester was still in the air when Myron saw the car stop. Two men came out. Rochester landed like a sack of rocks. Myron stood. The two men were moving toward him now.

They were both smiling.

Rochester rolled through the throw. He'd be up in no time. Then there would be three of them. The two men in the car did not approach slowly. They did not look wary or worried. They charged toward Myron with the abandon of children playing a game.

Two very bad hombres . . .

Another second passed.

The man who'd been on the passenger side wore his hair in a ponytail and looked liked that hip, middle-school art teacher who always smelled like a bong. Myron ran through his options. He did this in tenths of a second. That was how it worked. When you're in danger, time either slows down or the mind races. Hard to say which.

Myron thought about Rochester lying on the ground, about the two men charging, about Win's warning, about what Rochester might be after here, about why he might attack unprovoked, about what Cingle had said about Rochester being a nutjob.

The answer was obvious: Dominick Rochester thought that Myron had something to do with his daughter's disappearance.

Rochester probably knew that Myron had been questioned by the police, and that nothing had come of it. A guy like Rochester wouldn't accept that. So he'd do his best, his damned best, to see if he could shake something loose.

The two men were maybe three steps away now.

Another point: They were willing to attack him right here, on the street, where anyone could see. That suggested a certain level of desperation and recklessness and, yes, confidence – a level Myron wanted no part of.

So Myron made his choice: He ran.

The two men had the advantage. They were already accelerating. Myron was starting from a standing position.

This was where pure athleticism would help.

Myron's knee injury had not really affected his speed much. It was more a question of lateral movement. So Myron faked a step to the right, just to get them to lean. They did. Then he broke left toward his driveway. One of the men – the other one, not the hippy art teacher – lost his footing but only for a split second. He was back up. So was Dominick Rochester.

But it was the hippy art teacher who was causing the most trouble. The man was fast. He was almost close enough to make a diving tackle.

Myron debated taking him on.

But no. Win had called in a warning. If it had reached that level, this was probably indeed a very bad hombre. He wouldn't go down with one blow. And even if he did, the delay would give the other two the chance to catch up. There was no way to eliminate the art teacher and keep moving.

Myron tried to accelerate. He wanted to gain enough distance to get Win on the cell phone and tell him –

The cell phone. Damn, he didn't have it. He'd dropped it when Rochester hit him.

They kept chasing him. Here they were, on a quiet suburban street, four adults running all-out. Was anybody watching? What would they think?

Myron had another advantage: He knew the neighborhood.

He didn't look over his shoulder, but he could hear the art teacher panting behind him. You don't become a professional athlete – and brief as his career was, he did play professional ball – without having a million things go right internally and externally. Myron had grown up in Livingston. His high school class had six hundred people in it. There had been zillions of great athletes going through the doors. None had made the pros. Two or three had played minor league baseball. One, maybe two, had been drafted for one sport or another. That was it. Every kid dreams about it, but the truth is, none make it. None. You think your kid is different. He's not. He won't make it to the NBA or NFL or MLB. Won't happen.

The odds are that long.

The point here, as Myron began to increase his lead, was that, yes, he had worked hard, shot baskets by himself for four to five hours a day, had been frighteningly competitive, had the right mind frame, had and did all those things, but none of that would have helped him reach the level he'd gotten to if he hadn't been blessed with extraordinary physical gifts.

One of those gifts was speed.

The panting was falling behind him.

Someone, maybe Rochester, shouted: 'Shoot him in the leg!'

Myron kept accelerating. He had a destination in mind. His knowledge of the neighborhood would help now. He hit the hill up Coddington Terrace. As he reached the top, he prepared. He knew that if he got there enough ahead of them, there'd be a blind spot on the curve back down.

When he reached that down-curve, he didn't look back. There was a somewhat hidden path between two houses on the left. Myron had used it to go to Burnet Hill Elementary School. All the kids did. It was the strangest thing – a paved walking path between two houses – but he knew it was still there.

The very bad hombres would not.

The paved walk was public enough, but Myron had another idea. The Horowitzes used to live in the house on the left. Myron had built a fort in the woods there with one of them a lifetime ago. Mrs. Horowitz had been furious about it. He veered into that area now. There used to be a crawling path under the bush, one that led from the Horowitzes' backyard on Coddington Terrace to the Seidens' on Ridge Road.

Myron pushed the first bush to the side. It was still there. He got down on his hands and knees and scrambled through the opening. Brown branches whipped his face. It didn't hurt so much as bring him back to a more innocent time.

As he emerged on the other side, in the old Seidens' backyard, he wondered if the Seiden family still lived here. The answer came to him fast.

Mrs. Seiden was in the backyard. She wore a kerchief and gardening gloves.

'Myron?' There was no hesitation or even much surprise in her voice. 'Myron Bolitar, is that you?'

He had gone to school with her son, Doug, although he had not crawled through this path or even been in this backyard since he was maybe ten years old. But that didn't matter in towns like this. If you were friends in elementary school, there was always some kind of link.

Mrs. Seiden blew the strands of hair out of her face. She started toward him. Damn. He hadn't wanted to involve anyone else. She opened her mouth to say something, but Myron silenced her with a finger to his lips.

She saw the look on his face and stopped. He gestured for her to get in the house. She gave a slight nod and moved toward it. She opened the back door.

Someone shouted, 'Where the hell did he go?'

Myron waited for Mrs. Seiden to disappear from view. But she didn't go inside.

Their eyes met. Now it was Mrs. Seiden's turn to gesture. She motioned for him to come inside too. He shook his head. Too dangerous.

Mrs. Seiden stood there, her back rigid.

She would not move.

A sound came from the brush. Myron snapped his head toward it. It stopped. Could have been a squirrel. No way they could have found him already. But Win had called them 'very bad' meaning, of course, very good at what they did. Win was never one for overstatement. If he said these guys were very bad . . .

Myron listened. No sound now. That scared him more than noise.

He did not want to put Mrs. Seiden in further danger. He shook his head one more time. She just stood there, holding the door open.

There was no sense in arguing. There are few creatures more stubborn than Livingston mothers.

Keeping low, he sprinted across the yard and through the open door, dragging her in with him.

She closed the door.

'Stay down.'

'The phone,' Mrs. Seiden said, 'is over there.'

It was a kitchen wall unit. He dialed Win.

'I'm eight miles away from your house,' Win said.

'I'm not there,' Myron said. 'I'm on Ridge Road.' He looked back at Mrs. Seiden for more information.

'Seventy-eight,' she said. 'And it's Ridge Drive, not Road.'

Myron repeated what she'd said. He told Win there were three of them, including Dominick Rochester.

'Are you armed?' Win asked.

'No.'

Win didn't lecture him, but Myron knew that he wanted to. 'The other two are good and sadistic,' Win said. 'Stay hidden until I get there.'

'We're not moving,' Myron said.

And that was when the back door burst open.

Myron turned in time to see Hippy Art Teacher fly through it.

'Run!' Myron shouted at Mrs. Seiden. But he didn't wait to see if she obeyed. Art Teacher was still off balance. Myron leapt toward him.

But Art Teacher was fast.

He sidestepped Myron's lunge. Myron saw that he was going to miss. He stuck out his left arm, clothesline style, hoping to get under Art's chin. The blow touched down on the back of Art's head, cushioned by the ponytail. Art staggered. He turned and hit Myron a short shot to the rib cage.

The man was very fast.

Everything slowed down again. In the distance, Myron could hear footsteps. Mrs. Seiden making a run for it. Art Teacher smiled at Myron, breathing hard. The speed of that punch told Myron that he probably shouldn't stand and trade blows. Myron had the size advantage. And that meant taking him to the floor.

Art Teacher revved up to throw another punch. Myron crowded in. It was tougher to hit someone hard, especially someone bigger, when you crowded in. Myron grabbed Art Teacher's shirt by the shoulders. He twisted to take him down, raising a forearm at the same time.

Myron hoped to put the forearm against the man's nose. Myron weighed two hundred fifteen pounds. That kind of size, you land full force with your forearm resting on someone's nose, the nose is going to snap like a dried-out bird's nest.

But again Art Teacher was good. He saw what Myron intended to do. He tucked down just a little. The forearm was now resting on the rose-tinted glasses. Art Teacher closed his eyes and pulled them both down harder. He also raised a knee up to Myron's midsection. Myron had to curve in his belly to protect himself. That took a good part of the power away from his forearm blow.

When they landed, the wire-framed glasses bent, but there was no serious power behind the shot. Art Teacher had the momentum now. He shifted his weight. His knee hadn't landed with much force either because of the way Myron had rounded his back. But the knee was still there. And the momentum.

He threw Myron over his head. Myron took it with a roll. In less than a second they were both on their feet.

The two men faced each other.

Here was what they don't tell you about fighting: You always feel crippling, paralyzing fear. The first few times, when Myron felt that stress-induced tingle in his legs, the kind that got so bad you wondered if you'd be able to stay on your feet, he felt like the worst sort of coward. Men who only get into a scrape or two, who get that leg tingle when they argue with a drunk lout at a bar, feel awash with shame. They shouldn't. It is not cowardice. It is a natural biological reaction. Everyone feels that way.

The question is, what do you do with that? What you learn with experience is that it can be controlled, harnessed even. You need to breathe. You need to relax. If you get hit when you're tensed up, it'll cause more damage.

The man threw off his bent glasses. He met Myron's eye. This was part of the game. The staring down. The guy was good. Win had said so.

But so was Myron.

Mrs. Seiden screamed.

To both men's credit, neither of them turned away at the sound. But Myron knew that he had to get to her. He faked a charge, just enough so that Art would back up, and then he darted toward the front of the house, where the scream had originated.

The front door was open. Mrs. Seiden was standing there. And next to her, with his fingers digging into her upper arm, was the other man who'd chased him from the car. This guy was a few years older than Art Teacher and wore an ascot. An ascot, for crying out loud. He looked like Roger Healey from the old *I Dream of Jeannie* show.

No time.

Art Teacher was behind him. Myron slid to the side and threw a roundhouse right. Art Teacher ducked it, but Myron was ready. He stopped mid-punch and looped his arm around the man's neck.

Myron had him in a headlock.

But now, with a grotesque rebel yell, Ascot leapt toward Myron.

Tightening his grip on the neck, Myron aimed a mule kick. Ascot let it land on his chest. He made his body soft and rolled with the blow, holding on to Myron's leg.

Myron lost his balance.

Art Teacher managed to free himself then. He threw a knife hand, aiming for Myron's throat. Myron tucked so that the blow hit his chin. It rattled his teeth.

Ascot held on to Myron's leg. Myron tried to kick him off. Art Teacher was laughing now. The front door burst open again. Myron prayed it was Win.

It wasn't.

Dominick Rochester arrived. He was out of breath.

Myron wanted to call out a warning to Mrs. Seiden, but that was when a pain unlike any other he had felt ripped through him. Myron let loose a blood-curdling howl. He looked down at his leg. Ascot had his head lowered.

He was biting Myron's leg.

Myron screamed again, the sound mixing in with the laughter and cheers coming from Art Teacher.

'Go, Jeb! Woo-hoo!'

Myron kept kicking, but Ascot dug in deeper, holding on, growling like a terrier. The pain was excruciating, all-encompassing.

Panic filled Myron. He stamped down with his free leg. Ascot held on with his teeth. Myron kicked harder, finally landing a kick on top of the man's head. He pushed hard. His flesh ripped off as he finally pried himself free. Ascot sat up and spit something out of his mouth. Myron realized with horror that it was a meaty chunk of leg.

Then they were on him. All three. Piled on.

Myron ducked his head and started swinging. He connected with somebody's chin. There was a grunt and a curse. But someone else hit him in the stomach.

He felt the teeth on his leg again, the same spot, opening up the wound.

Win. Where the hell was Win . . . ?

He bucked up in pain, wondering what to do next, when he heard a singsong voice say, 'Oh, Mr. Bolitar . . . ?'

Myron looked. It was Art Teacher. He had a gun in one hand. In the other, he had Mrs. Seiden by the hair.

23

They moved Myron to a large cedar closet on the second floor. Myron was flat on the floor. His hands were duct-taped behind his back, his feet bound together too. Dominick Rochester stood over him, a gun in his hand.

'Did you call your friend Win?'

Myron said, 'Who?'

Rochester frowned. 'You think we're stupid?'

'If you know about Win,' Myron said, meeting his eye, 'about what he can do, then the answer is yes. I think you're very stupid.'

Rochester sneered. 'We'll see about that,' he said.

Myron quickly assessed the situation. No windows, one entrance. That was why they'd brought him up here: no windows. So Win couldn't attack from the outside or at a distance. They had realized that, considered it, been smart enough to bind him and bring him up here.

This was not good.

Dominick Rochester was armed. So was Art Teacher. It would indeed be nearly impossible to get in here. But he knew Win. Myron just needed to give him time.

On the right, Ascot Bite was still smiling. There was blood – Myron's blood – on his teeth. Art Teacher was on the left.

Rochester bent down so his face was close to Myron's. The cologne smell was still on him, worse than ever. 'I'm going to tell you what I want,' he said. 'Then I'm going to leave you alone with Orville and Jeb. See, I know you had something to do with that girl disappearing. And if you had something to do with her, you had something to do with my Katie. Makes sense, doesn't it?'

'Where's Mrs. Seiden?'

'No one is interested in hurting her.'

'I didn't have anything to do with your daughter,' Myron said. 'I just gave Aimee a ride. That's all. The police will tell you.'

'You lawyered up.'

'I didn't lawyer up. My lawyer arrived. I answered every question. I told them that Aimee called me for a ride. I showed them where I dropped her off.'

'And what about my daughter?'

'I don't know her. I've never met her in my life.'

Rochester looked back at Orville and Jeb. Myron didn't know which was which. His leg was throbbing from the bite.

Art Teacher was redoing his ponytail, making it tight and wrapping it with the band. 'I believe him.'

'But,' Ascot Bite added, 'we got to be, got to be certain, *tengo que estar seguro.*'

Art Teacher frowned. 'Who was that?'

'Kylie Minogue.'

'Whoa, pretty obscure, dude.'

Rochester stood upright. 'You guys do your thing. I'll keep watch downstairs.'

'Wait,' Myron said. 'I don't know anything.'

Rochester looked at him for a moment. 'It's my daughter. I can't take that chance. So what's going to happen here is, the Twins are going to work you over. You still telling the same story after that, I know you had nothing to do with it. But if you did, maybe I save my kid. You understand what I'm saying?'

Rochester moved to the door.

The Twins crept closer. Art Teacher pushed Myron back. Then he sat on Myron's legs. Ascot straddled Myron's chest. He looked down and bared his teeth. Myron swallowed. He tried to buck him off, but with his hands taped behind him, it was impossible. His stomach did flips of fear.

'Wait,' Myron said again.

'No,' Rochester said. 'You'll stall. You'll sing, you'll dance, you'll make up stories – '

'No, that's not – '

'Let me finish, okay? It's my daughter. You have to understand that. You need to crack before I'll believe you. The Twins. They're good at making a man crack.'

'Just hear me out, okay? I'm trying to find Aimee Biel – '

'No.'

' – and if I find her, there's an excellent chance I'll find your daughter too. I'm telling you. Look, you checked me out, right? That's how you know about Win.'

Rochester stopped, waited.

'You must have heard this is what I do. I help people when they're in trouble. I dropped that girl off and now she's gone. I owe it to her parents to find her.'

Rochester looked at the Twins. In the distance Myron heard a car radio, the song fading in and then fading out. The song was 'We Built This City on Rock-n-Roll' by Starship.

The *second* worst song in the world, Myron thought.

Ascot Bite started singing along, 'We built *este ciudad*, we built *este ciudad*, we built *este ciudad*. . .' Hippy Art Teacher, still holding Myron's legs, started bobbing his head, clearly digging his colleague's vocals.

'I'm telling the truth,' Myron said.

'Either way,' Rochester said, 'if you're telling the truth or not, the Twins here. They'll find out. See? You can't lie to them. Once they hurt you some, you'll tell us everything we need to know.'

'But by then it's too late,' Myron said.

'They won't take long.' Rochester looked at Art Teacher.

Art Teacher said, 'Half an hour, hour max.'

'That's not what I meant. I'll be too hurt. I won't be able to function.'

'He has a point,' Art Teacher said.

'We leave marks,' Ascot added, flashing his teeth.

Rochester thought about it.

'Orville, where did you say he was before he came home?'

Art Teacher – Orville – gave him Randy Wolf's address and told him about the diner. They'd been tailing him, and Myron hadn't picked up on it. Either they were very good or Myron was awfully rusty – or both. Rochester asked Myron why he visited both places.

'The house is where her boyfriend lives,' Myron said. 'But he wasn't home.'

'You think he has something to do with it?'

Myron knew better to answer in the positive. 'Just talking to Aimee's friends, see what was up with her. Who better than her boyfriend?'

'And the diner?'

'I met a source. I wanted to see what they had on your daughter and Aimee. I'm trying to find a connection between them.'

'So what have you learned so far?'

'I'm just starting.'

Rochester thought some more. Then he shook his head slowly. 'Way I heard it, you picked up the Biel girl at two A.M.'

'That's right.'

'At two A.M.,' he repeated.

'She called me.'

'Why?' His face reddened. 'Is it because you like picking up high school girls?'

'That's not it.'

'Oh, I suppose you gonna tell me it was innocent?'

'It was.'

Myron could see the anger mounting. He was losing him.

'You watch that trial with that perv Michael Jackson?'

The question confused Myron. 'A little, I guess.'

'He sleeps with little boys, right? He admits it. But then he says, "Oh but it's innocent."'

Now Myron saw where this was going.

'And here you are, just like that, telling me you pick up pretty high school girls, late at night. At two A.M. And then you say, "Oh, but it's innocent."'

'Listen to me – '

'Nah, I think I listened enough.'

Rochester nodded for the Twins to go ahead.

Enough time had passed. Win was, Myron hoped, in place. He was probably waiting for one last distraction. Myron couldn't move, so he tried something else.

Without warning, Myron let loose a scream.

He screamed as long and as loud as he could, even after Orville the Art Teacher snapped a fist into his teeth.

But the scream had the desired effect. For a second, everyone looked at him. Just for a second. No more.

But that was enough.

An arm snaked around Rochester's neck as a gun appeared at his forehead. Win's face materialized next to Rochester's.

'Next time,' Win said, crinkling his nose, 'please refrain from buying your cologne at your local Exxon station.'

The Twins were greased lightning. They were off Myron in under a second. Art Teacher took to the far corner. Ascot Bite flipped behind Myron and pulled him up, using Myron as a shield. He had a gun out now too. He put it against the back of Myron's neck.

Stalemate.

Win kept his arm around Rochester's neck. He squeezed the windpipe.

Rochester's face darkened red as the oxygen drained away. His eyes rolled back. A few seconds later, Win did something a little surprising: He released his grip on the throat. Rochester retched and sucked in a deep breath. Using him as a shield, Win's gun stayed near the back of the man's head but now angled toward Art Teacher.

'Cutting off his air supply, what with that awful cologne,' Win said, by way of an explanation. 'It was too merciful.'

The Twins studied Win as though he were something little and cute they'd stumbled across in the forest. They did not appear to be afraid of him. As soon as Win had come upon the scene, they'd coordinated their movements as if they'd done this before.

'Sneaking up like that,' Hippy Art Teacher said, smiling at Win. 'Dude, that was one radical move.'

'Far out,' Win said. 'Like, dig it.'

He frowned. 'Are you mocking me, man?'

'Tripping. Groovy. Flower power.'

Art Teacher looked at Ascot Bite as if to say, *Do you believe this guy?*

'Man oh man, dude, you don't know who you're messing with.'

'Put your weapons down,' Win said, 'or I'll kill you both.'

The Twins smiled some more, enjoying this.

'Dude, you ever do, like, math?'

Win gave Art Teacher the flat eyes. 'Like, yah.'

'See, we got two guns. You got one.'

Ascot Bite rested his head on Myron's shoulder. 'You,' he said to Win, excited, licking his lips. 'You shouldn't threaten us.'

'You're right,' Win said.

All eyes were on the gun pressed near Rochester's temple. That was the mistake. It was like a classic magician's trick. The Twins had not wondered why Win had released his grip on Rochester's throat. But the reason was simple:

It was so that Win – using Rochester's body to block their view – could ready his second gun.

Myron tilted his head a little to the left. The bullet from the second gun, the one that had been hidden behind Rochester's left hip, struck Ascot Bite square in the forehead. He was dead instantly. Myron felt something wet splash on his cheek.

At the same time, Win fired the first gun, the one that had been at Rochester's head. That bullet slammed into Art Teacher's throat. He went down, his hands clawing at what had been his voice box. He may have been dead or at least bleeding to death. Win didn't chance it.

The second bullet hit the man square between the eyes.

Win turned back to Rochester. 'Breathe funny and you end up like them.'

Rochester made himself stay impossibly still. Win bent down next to Myron and started ripping off the duct tape. He looked down at Ascot Bite's dead body.

'Chew on that,' Win said to the corpse. He turned back to Myron. 'Get it? The biting, chew on that?'

'Hilarious. Where's Mrs. Seiden?'

'She's safe, out of the house, but you'll need to make up a cover story for her.'

Myron thought about that.

'Did you call the police?' Myron asked.

'Not yet. In case you wanted to ask some questions.'

Myron looked at Rochester.

'Talk to him downstairs,' Win said, handing Myron a gun. 'I'll pull the car into the garage and start the cleanup.'

24

The cleanup. Myron had some idea of what Win meant, though they wouldn't discuss it directly. Win had holdings all over the place, including a tract of land in a secluded section of Sussex County, New Jersey. The property was eight acres. Most of it was undeveloped woods. If you ever tried to trace down ownership, you'd find a holding company from the Cayman Islands. You would find no names.

There was a time when Myron would have been upset over what Win had done. There was a time when he would have mustered up all his moral outrage. He would give his old friend long, complicated musings about the sanctity of life and the dangers of vigilantism and all that. Win would look at him and utter three words:

Us or them.

Win probably could have given the 'stalemate' another minute or two. He and the Twins might have come to an understanding. You go, we go, no one gets hurt. That sort of thing. But that wasn't meant to be.

The Twins were as good as dead the moment Win entered the scene.

The worst part was that Myron no longer felt bad about it. He would shrug it off. And when he'd started doing that, when he knew that killing them was the prudent thing to do and that their eyes would not haunt his sleep . . . that was when he knew it was time to stop doing this. Rescuing people, playing along that flimsy line between good and bad – it robbed a little sliver of your soul.

Except maybe it didn't.

Maybe playing along that line – seeing the other side of it – just grounded you in awful reality. The fact is this: A million Orville the Art Teachers or Jeb the Ascots aren't worth the life of even one innocent, of one Brenda Slaughter or one Aimee Biel or one Katie Rochester or, as in the case overseas, the life of his soldier son, Jeremy Downing.

It might seem amoral to feel this way. But there it was. He applied this thinking to the war too. In his most honest moments, the ones he dare not speak out loud, Myron didn't care that much about the civilians trying to scrape by in some dump-hole desert. He didn't care if they got democracy or not, if they experienced freedom, if their lives were made better. What he did care about were the boys like Jeremy. Kill a hundred, a thousand, on the other side, if need be. But don't let anyone hurt my boy.

Myron sat across from Rochester. 'I wasn't lying before. I'm trying to find Aimee Biel.'

Rochester just stared.

'You know that both girls used the same ATM?'

Rochester nodded.

'There has to be a reason why. It's not a coincidence. Aimee's parents don't know your daughter. They don't think Aimee knew her either.'

Rochester finally spoke. 'I asked my wife and kids,' he said, his voice soft. 'None of them think Katie knew Aimee.'

'But the two girls went to the same school,' Myron said.

'It's a big school.'

'There's a connection. There has to be. We're just missing it. So what I need you and your family to do is start searching for that connection. Ask Katie's friends. Look through her stuff. Something links your daughter and Aimee. We find it, we'll be that much closer.'

Rochester said, 'You're not going to kill me.'

'No.'

His eyes traveled upstairs. 'Your guy made the right move. Killing the Twins, I mean. You let them go, they'd have tortured your mother until she cursed the day you were born.'

Myron chose not to comment.

'I was stupid to hire them,' Rochester said. 'But I was desperate.'

'If you're looking for forgiveness, go to hell.'

'I'm just trying to make you understand.'

'I don't want to understand,' Myron said. 'I want to find Aimee Biel.'

Myron had to go to the emergency room. The doctor looked at the bite on his leg and shook his head.

'Jesus, you get attacked by a shark?'

'A dog,' Myron lied.

'You should put it down.'

Win took that one: 'Already done.'

The doctor used sutures and then bandaged it up. It hurt like hell. He gave Myron some antibiotics and pills for the pain. When they left, Win made sure Myron still had the gun. He did.

'You want me to stay around?' Win said.

'I'm fine.' The car accelerated down Livingston Avenue. 'Are those two guys taken care of?'

'Gone forever.'

Myron nodded. Win watched his face.

'They're called the Twins,' Win said. 'The older one with the ascot, he would have bitten off your nipples first. That's how they warm up. One nipple, then the other.'

'I understand.'

'No lecture on overreacting?'

Myron's fingers touched down on his chest. 'I really like my nipples.'

It was late by the time Win dropped him off. Near his front door, Myron found his cell phone on the ground where he'd dropped it. He checked the caller ID. There were a bunch of missed calls, mostly business related. With Esperanza in Antigua on her honeymoon, he should have stayed in touch. Too late to worry about that now.

Ali had also called him.

A lifetime ago he had told her that he'd come by tonight. They had joked about him stopping by for a late-night 'nooner.' Man, was that really today?

He debated waiting until morning, but Ali might be worried. Plus, it would be nice, *really* nice, to hear the warmth in her voice. He needed that, in this crazy, exhausting, hurting day. He was sore. His leg throbbed.

Ali answered on the first ring. 'Myron?'

'Hey, hope I didn't wake you.'

'The police were here.'

There was no warmth in her voice.

'When?'

'A few hours ago. They wanted to talk to Erin. About some promise the girls made in your basement.'

Myron closed his eyes. 'Damn. I never meant to involve her.'

'She backed your story, by the way.'

'I'm sorry.'

'I called Claire. She told me about Aimee. But I don't understand. Why would you make the girls promise something like that?'

'To call me, you mean?'

'Yes.'

'I overheard them talking about driving with someone who was drunk. I just didn't want that to happen to them.'

'But why you?'

He opened his mouth but nothing came out.

'I mean, you just met Erin that day. That was the first time you ever talked to her.'

'I didn't plan it, Ali.'

There was a silence. Myron didn't like it.

'We okay?' he asked.

'I need a little time with this,' she said.

He felt his stomach clench.

'Myron?'

'Sooo,' he said, stretching out the word, 'I guess there's no rain check on that nooner?'

'This isn't the time for jokes.'

'I know.'

'Aimee is missing. The police came around and questioned my daughter. This might be routine for you, but this isn't my world. I'm not blaming you, but . . .'

'But?'

'I just . . . I just need time.'

' "Need time," ' Myron repeated. 'That sounds a whole lot like "need space."'

'You're making a joke again.'

'No, Ali, I'm not.'

25

There was a reason Aimee Biel wanted to be dropped off on that cul-de-sac. Myron showered and threw on a pair of sweats. His pants had blood on them. His own. He remembered that old Seinfeld routine about laundry detergent commercials that talk about getting out bloodstains, how if you have bloodstains on your clothes, maybe laundry wasn't your biggest worry.

The house was silent, except for those customary house noises. When he was a kid, alone at night, those noises would scare him. Now they were just there – neither soothing nor alarming. He could hear the slight echo as he walked across the kitchen floor. The echo only happened when you were alone. He thought about that. He thought about what Claire had said, about him bringing violence and destruction, about him still not being married.

He sat alone at the kitchen table of his empty house. This was not the life he'd planned.

Man plans, God laughs.

He shook his head. Truer words.

Enough wallowing, Myron thought. The 'plans' part got his mind back on track. To wit: What had Aimee Biel been planning?

There was a reason she chose that ATM. And there was a reason she chose that cul-de-sac.

It was almost midnight when Myron got back in his car and started north to Ridgewood. He knew the way now. He parked at the end of the cul-de-sac. He turned off the car. The house was dark, just like two nights ago.

Okay, now what?

Myron went through the possibilities. One, Aimee actually went into that house at the end of the cul-de-sac. The woman who'd answered the door before, the slim blonde with the baseball cap, had lied to Loren Muse. Or maybe the woman didn't know. Maybe Aimee was having a fling with her son or was a friend of her daughter's, and this woman didn't know about it.

Doubtful.

Loren Muse was no idiot. She had been at that door a fair amount of time. She would have checked into those angles. If they existed, she would have followed up.

So Myron ruled that out.

That meant that this house had been a diversion.

Myron opened the car door and stepped out. The road was silent. There was a hockey goal at the end of the cul-de-sac. This was probably a neighborhood with kids. There were only eight houses and almost no traffic. The kids probably still played on the street. Myron spotted one of those roll-out basketball hoops in one of the driveways. They probably did that too. The cul-de-sac was a little neighborhood playground.

A car turned down the block, just like when he'd dropped Aimee off.

Myron squinted toward the headlights. It was midnight now. Only eight houses on the street, all with lights out, all tucked in for the evening.

The car pulled up behind his and came to a stop. Myron recognized the silver Benz even before Erik Biel, Aimee's father, got out. The light was dim, but Myron could still see the rage on his face. It made him look like an annoying little boy.

'What the hell are you doing here?' Erik shouted.

'Same thing as you, I guess.'

Erik came closer. 'Claire may buy your story about why you drove Aimee here but . . .'

'But what, Erik?'

He didn't reply right away. He was still in the tailored shirt and trousers, but the look wasn't as crisp. 'I just want to find her,' he said.

Myron said nothing, letting him talk his way down.

'Claire thinks you can help. She says you're good at stuff like this.'

'I am.'

'You're like Claire's knight in shining armor,' he said with more than a trace of bitterness. 'I don't know why you two didn't end up together.'

'I do,' Myron said. 'Because we don't love each other that way. In fact, in all the time I've known Claire, you're the only man she ever really loved.'

Erik shifted his feet, pretending the words didn't matter, not quite pulling it off. 'When I made the turn, you were getting out of your car. What were you going to do?'

'I was going to try to retrace Aimee's footsteps. See if I can figure out where she really went.'

'What do you mean, "really went"?'

'There was a reason she picked this spot. She used this house as a diversion. It wasn't her real destination.'

'You think she ran away, don't you?'

'I don't think it was a random abduction or anything like that,' Myron said. 'She led me to this specific spot. The question is, why?'

Erik nodded. His eyes were wet. 'You mind if I tag along?'

He did, but Myron shrugged and started toward the house. The occupants might wake up and call the police. Myron was willing to risk that. He opened the gate. This was where Aimee had gone in. He made the same turn she made, went behind the house. There was a sliding glass door. Erik stayed silent behind him.

Myron tried the glass door. Locked. He ducked down and ran his fingers along the bottom. Some kind of crud had accumulated. Same with the door frame going up.

The door had not been opened in a while.

Erik whispered, 'What?'

Myron signaled him to keep quiet. The curtains were pulled closed. Myron stayed low and cupped his hands around his eyes. He looked into the room. He couldn't see much, but it looked like a standard family den. It was not a teen's bedroom. He moved toward the back door. That led to a kitchen.

Again no teen bedroom.

Of course Aimee might have misspoken. She might have meant that she went through a back door to get to Stacy's room, not that the bedroom was right there. But heck, Stacy didn't even live here. So either way, Aimee had clearly lied. This other stuff – the fact that the door hadn't been opened and didn't lead to a bedroom. That was just the icing.

So where had she gone?

He got on all fours and took out his penlight. He shined it on the ground. Nothing. He hoped for footprints, but there hadn't been much rain lately. He put his cheek flat on the grass, tried to look not so much for prints as any sort of ground indentation. More nothing.

Erik started looking too. He didn't have a penlight. There was almost no other illumination back here. But he looked anyway and Myron didn't stop him.

A few seconds later Myron stood. He kept the penlight low. The backyard was half an acre, maybe more. There was a pool with a whole other fence surrounding it. This gate was six feet high and kept locked. It would be hard, though not impossible, to scale. But Myron doubted Aimee had come here for a swim.

The backyard disappeared into woods. Myron followed the property line into the trees. The nice wooden picket fence ran around the side property lot, but once you got into the wooded area, the barrier became wire mesh. It was cheaper and less aesthetic, but back here, mixed in with branches and thicket, what did it matter?

Myron was pretty sure what he would find now.

It was not unlike the Horowitz – Seiden border near his own home. He put his hand on top of the fence and kept moving through the brush. Erik followed. Myron wore Nikes. Erik had on tasseled loafers without socks.

Myron's hand dipped down near an overgrown pine bush.

Bingo, this was the spot. The fence had caved in here. He shined the penlight. From the rusted-out look of it, the post had buckled years ago. Myron pulled down on the mesh a little and stepped over. Erik did likewise.

The cut-through was easier to find. It ran no more than five, six yards. It had probably been a longer path years ago, but with the value of land, only the thinnest clump of brush was now used for privacy. If your land could be made usable, you made sure that it was.

He and Erik ended up between two backyards on another cul-de-sac.

'You think Aimee went this way?'

Myron nodded. 'I do.'

'So what now?'

'We find out who lives on this street. We try to see if there's a connection to Aimee.'

'I'll call the police,' Erik said.

'You can try that. They might care, they might not. If someone she knows lives here, it might just further back up the theory that she's a runaway.'

'I'll try anyway.'

Myron nodded. If he were in Erik's shoes, he would do that too. They moved through the yard and stood on the cul-de-sac. Myron studied the homes as if they might give him answers.

'Myron?'

He looked at Erik.

'I think Aimee ran away,' he said. 'And I think it's my fault.'

There were tears on his cheek.

'She's changed. Claire and I, we've both seen that. Something happened with

Randy. I really like that boy. He was so good with her. I tried to talk to her about it. But she wouldn't tell me. I . . . this is going to sound so stupid. I thought maybe Randy had tried to pressure her. You know. Sexually.'

Myron nodded.

'But what decade do I think we're living in? They'd been together two years already.'

'So you don't think that was it?'

'No.'

'Then what?'

'I don't know.' He went silent.

'You said it was your fault.'

Erik nodded.

'When I drove Aimee here,' Myron said, 'she begged me not to say anything to you and Claire. She said that things weren't good with you two.'

'I started spying on her,' Erik said.

That wasn't a direct answer to the question, but Myron let it go. Erik was working up to something. Myron would need to give him room.

'But Aimee . . . she's a teenage girl. Remember those years? You learn how to hide things. So she was careful. I guess that she was more practiced than I was. It's not that I didn't trust her. But it's part of a parent's job to keep tabs on their children. It doesn't do much good because they know it.'

They stood in the dark, staring at the houses.

'But what you don't realize is that even while you're spying on them, maybe every once in a while, they turn the tables on you. Maybe they suspect something's wrong and they want to help. And maybe the child ends up keeping tabs on the parent.'

'Aimee spied on you?'

He nodded.

'What did she find, Erik?'

'That I'm having an affair.'

Erik almost collapsed with relief when he said it. Myron felt blank for a second, totally empty. Then he thought about Claire, about how she was in high school, about the way she'd nervously pluck her bottom lip in the back of Mr. Lampf's English class. A surge of anger coursed through him.

'Does Claire know?'

'I don't know. If she does, she's never said anything.'

'This affair. Is it serious?'

'Yes.'

'How did Aimee find out?'

'I don't know. I don't even know for sure that she did.'

'Aimee never said anything to you?'

'No. But . . . like I said. There were changes. I would go to kiss her cheek and she'd pull back. Almost involuntarily. Like I repulsed her.'

'That might be normal teenage stuff.'

Erik hung his head, shook it.

'So when you were spying on her, trying to check her e-mails, besides wanting to know what she was up to . . .'

'I wanted to see if she knew, yes.'

Again Myron flashed to Claire, this time to her face on her wedding day, starting a new life with this guy, smiling like Esperanza had on Saturday, no doubts about Erik even though Myron had never warmed to him.

As if reading his mind, Erik said, 'You've never been married. You don't know.'

Myron wanted to punch him in the nose. 'You say so.'

'It doesn't just happen all at once,' he said.

'Uh-huh.'

'It just starts to slip away. All of it. It happens to everyone. You grow apart. You care but in a different way. You're about your job, your family, your house. You're about everything but the two of you. And then one day you wake up and you want that feeling back. Forget the sex. That's not really it. You want the passion. And you know you're never going to get it from the woman you love.'

'Erik?'

'What?'

'I really don't want to hear this.'

He nodded. 'You're the only one I've told.'

'Yeah, well, I must live under a lucky star then.'

'I just wanted . . . I mean, I just needed . . .'

Myron held up a hand. 'You and Claire are none of my business. I'm here to find Aimee, not play marriage counselor. But let me just make something clear because I want you to know exactly where I stand: If you hurt Claire, I'll . . . '

He stopped. Stupid to go that far.

'You'll what?'

'Nothing.'

Erik almost smiled. 'Still her knight in shining armor, eh, Myron?'

Man, Myron *really* wanted to punch him in the nose. He turned away instead, turned toward a yellow house with two cars in the driveway. And that was when he saw it.

Myron froze.

'What?' Erik said.

He quickly averted his gaze. 'I need your help.'

Erik was all over that. 'Name it.'

Myron started walking back toward the path, cursing himself. He was still rusty. He should have never let that show. The last thing he needed was Erik going off half-cocked. He needed to hash it out without Erik.

'Are you good with a computer?'

Erik frowned. 'I guess so.'

'I need you to go online. I need you to put all the addresses on this street into a search engine. We need a list of who lives here. I need you to go home right away and do that for me.'

'But shouldn't we do something now?' Erik asked.

'Like what?'

'Knock on doors.'

'And say what? Do what?'

'Maybe someone is holding her hostage right here, right on this very block.'

'Very, very doubtful. And even so, knocking on doors will probably get them to panic. And once we knock on one door at this hour, that person will call the police. The neighbors will be warned. Listen to me, Erik. We need to figure out what's what first. This could all be a dead end. Aimee might not have taken that path.'

'You said you thought she did.'

'Thought. That doesn't mean much. Plus maybe she walked five blocks after that. We can't just stumble around. If you want to help, go home. Look those addresses up. Get me some names.'

They were through the path now. They moved past the gate and walked back to their cars.

'What are you going to do?' Erik asked.

'I have a few other leads I want to follow up on.'

Erik wanted to ask more, but Myron's tone and body language cut him off. 'I'll call you as soon as I've finished the search,' Erik said.

They both got in their cars. Myron watched Erik drive off. Then he picked up the cell phone and hit Win's speed dial.

'Articulate.'

'I need you to break into a house.'

'Goody. Please explain.'

'I found a path where I dropped Aimee off. It leads to another cul-de-sac.'

'Ah. Do we have a thought then about where she ended up?'

'Sixteen Fernlake Court.'

'You sound fairly certain.'

'There's a car in the driveway. On the back windshield is a sticker. It's for teacher parking at Livingston High School.'

'On my way.'

26

Myron and Win met up three blocks away near an elementary school. A parked car here would be less conspicuous. Win was dressed in black, including a black skull cap that hid his blond locks.

'I didn't see an alarm system,' Myron said.

Win nodded. Alarms were minor nuisances anyway, not deal breakers. 'I'll be back in thirty minutes.'

He was. On the dot.

'The girl isn't inside the house. Two teachers live there. His name is Harry Davis. He teaches English at Livingston High School. His wife is Lois. She teaches at a middle school in Glen Rock. They have two daughters, college age, judging by the pictures and the fact that they weren't home.'

'This can't be a coincidence.'

'I put a GPS tracker on both cars. Davis also has a well-worn briefcase, stuffed with term papers and lesson plans. I put one on that too. You go home, get some sleep. I'll let you know when he wakes up and starts to move. I'll follow. And then we'll be on him.'

Myron crawled into bed. He figured sleep would never come to him. But it did. He slept deep until he heard a metallic click coming from downstairs.

His father had been a light sleeper. In his youth, Myron would wake up at night and try to walk past his parents' room without stirring Dad. He had never made it. His father did not wake up slowly either. He woke with a start, like someone had poured ice water down his drawstring bottoms.

So that was how it was when he heard the click. He shot up in the bed. The gun was on the night table. He grabbed it. His cell phone was there too. He hit Win's speed dial, the line that rang for Win to mute and eavesdrop.

Myron sat very still and listened.

The front door opened.

Whoever it was, they were trying to keep quiet. Myron crept to the wall next to his bedroom door. He waited, listened some more. The intruder had gone through the front door. That was odd. The lock was old. It could be picked. But to be that silent about it – just one quick click – it meant whoever it was, or whoever they were, they were good.

He waited.

Footsteps.

They were light. Myron pressed his back against the wall. The gun tightened in his hand. His leg ached from the bite. His head pounded. He tried to swim through it, tried to focus.

He calculated the best place to stand. Pressed against the wall next to the door, where he was now – that was good for listening, but it wouldn't be ideal, despite what you see in the movies, if someone entered his room. In the first place, if the guy was good, he'd be looking for that. In the second place, if there were more than one of them, jumping someone from behind the door would be the worst place to be. You're forced to attack right away and thus expose your location. You might nail the first guy, but the second one would lay you to waste.

Myron padded toward the bathroom door. He stood behind it, kept low, the door almost closed. He had a perfect angle. He could see the intruder enter. He could shoot or call out – and if he did shoot, he'd still be in a good position if someone else either charged in or retreated.

The footsteps stopped outside his bedroom door.

He waited. His breath rang in his ears. Win was good at this, the patience part. That had never been Myron's forte. But he calmed himself. He kept his breathing deep. His eyes stayed on the open doorway.

He saw a shadow.

Myron aimed his gun at the middle of it. Win might go for the head, but Myron zeroed in on the center of the chest, the most forgiving target.

When the intruder stepped through the doorway and into a bit of light, Myron nearly gasped out loud. He stepped out from behind the door, still holding the gun.

'Well, well,' the intruder said. 'After seven years, is that a gun in your hand or are you just happy to see me?'

Myron did not move.

Seven years. After seven years. And within seconds, it was like those seven years had never happened.

Jessica Culver, his former soul mate, was back.

27

They were downstairs in the kitchen. Jessica opened up the refrigerator. 'No Yoo-hoo?'

Myron shook his head. Chocolate Yoo-hoo had been his favorite beverage. When they lived together, he'd always had plenty on hand.

'You don't drink it anymore?'

'Not much.'

'I guess one of us should note that everything changes.'

'How did you get in?' he asked.

'You still keep the key in the gutter. Just like your father did. We used it once. Do you remember?'

He did. They'd sneaked down to the basement, giggling. They'd made love.

Jessica smiled at him. The years showed, he guessed. There were more lines around the eyes. Her hair was shorter and more stylized. But the effect was still the same.

She was knock-you-to-your-knees beautiful.

Jessica said, 'You're staring.'

He said nothing.

'Good to know I still have it.'

'Yeah, that Stone Norman is a lucky man.'

'Right,' she said. 'I figured you'd see that.'

Myron said nothing.

'You'd like him,' she said.

'Oh, I bet.'

'Everyone does. He has lots of friends.'

'Do they call him Stoner?'

'Only his old frat buddies.'

'I should have guessed.'

Jessica studied him for a moment. Her gaze made his face warm. 'You look like hell, by the way.'

'I took something of a beating today.'

'Some things don't change then. How's Win?'

'Speaking of things that don't change.'

'Sorry to hear that.'

'We going to keep this up,' Myron said, 'or are you going to tell me why you're here?'

'Can we keep this up for a few more minutes?'

Myron shrugged a *suit-yourself* at her.

'How are your parents?' she asked.

'Fine.'

'They never liked me.'

'No, I don't suppose they did.'

'And Esperanza? Does she still refer to me as Queen Bitch?'

'She hasn't so much as mentioned your name in seven years.'

That made her smile. 'Like I'm Voldemort. In the Harry Potter books.'

'Yep, you're She-who-must-not-be-named.'

Myron shifted in his chair. He turned away for a few seconds. She was just so damn beautiful. It was like looking into an eclipse. You need to look away every once in a while.

'You know why I'm here,' she said.

'One last fling before you marry Stoner?'

'Would you be willing?'

'No.'

'Liar.'

He wondered if she was right, so he took the mature route. 'Are you aware that "Stoner" rhymes with "boner"?'

'Making fun of someone's name,' Jessica said, 'when yours is Myron.'

'Throwing stones, glass houses, yeah, I know.' Her eyes were red. 'Are you drunk?'

'Tipsy maybe. I had enough to get my courage up.'

'To break into my house?'

'Yes.'

'So what is it, Jessica?'

'You and I,' she said. 'We're not really through.'

He said nothing.

'I pretend we're done, you pretend we're done. But we both know better.' Jessica turned to the side and swallowed. He watched her neck. He saw hurt in her eyes. 'What was the first thing that went through your mind when you read I was getting married?'

'I wished you and Stoner nothing but the best.'

She waited.

'I don't know what I thought,' he said.

'It hurt?'

'What do you want me to say, Jess? We were together a long time. Of course there was a pang.'

'It's like' – she paused, thought about it – ''it's like, despite the fact I haven't talked to you in seven years, it was always just a question of time before we got back together. Like this was all part of the process. Do you know what I mean?'

He said nothing, but he felt something deep inside him start to fray.

'And then today, I saw my announcement in print – the announcement I wrote – and suddenly it was like, "Wait, this is for real. Myron and I don't end up together."' She shook her head. 'I'm not saying this right.'

'Nothing to say, Jessica.'

'Just like that?'

'You being here,' he said. 'It's just prewedding jitters.'

'Don't patronize me.'

'What do you want me to say?'

'I don't know.'

664

They sat there for a while. Myron held out his hand. She took it. He felt something course through him.

'I know why you're here,' Myron said. 'I don't even think I'm surprised.'

'There's still something between us, isn't there?'

'I don't know. . . .'

'I hear a "but."'

'You go through what we went through – the love, the breakups, my injuries, all that pain, all that time together, the fact that I wanted to marry you – '

'Let me address that part, okay?'

'In a second. I'm on a roll here.'

Jessica smiled. 'Sorry.'

'You go through all that, your lives become so entwined with one another. And then one day, you just end it. You just sever it off like with a machete. But you're so entwined, stuff is still there.'

'Our lives are enmeshed,' she said.

'Enmeshed,' he repeated. 'That sounds so precious.'

'But it's somewhat accurate.'

He nodded.

'So what do we do?'

'Nothing. That's just part of life.'

'Do you know why I didn't marry you?'

'It's irrelevant, Jess.'

'I don't think it is. I think we need to play through this.'

Myron let go of her hand and signaled, *fine, go ahead.*

'Most people hate their parents' lives. They rebel. But you wanted to be just like them. You wanted the house, the kids – '

'And you didn't,' he interrupted. 'We know all this.'

'That's not it. I might have wanted that life too.'

'Just not with me.'

'You know that's not it. I just wasn't sure. . . .' She tilted her head. 'You wanted that life. But I didn't know if you wanted that life more than me.'

'That,' Myron said, 'is the biggest load of crap I've ever heard.'

'Maybe, but that's how I felt.'

'Great, I didn't love you enough.'

She looked at him, shook her head. 'No man has ever loved me like you did.'

Silence. Myron held back the 'what-about-Stoner' remark.

'When you blew out your knee – '

'Not that again. Please.'

Jessica pushed ahead. 'When you blew out your knee, you changed. You worked so hard to move past it.'

'You'd have preferred the self-pity route,' Myron said.

'That might have worked better. Because what you did instead, what you ended up doing, was running scared. You grabbed so tight to everything you had that it was suffocating. All of a sudden you were mortal. You didn't want to lose anything else and suddenly – '

'This is all great, Jess. Hey, I forget. At Duke, who taught your Intro to Psychology class? Because he'd be proud as punch right about now.'

Jessica just shook her head at him.

'What?' he said.

'You're still not married, are you, Myron?'

'Neither,' he said, 'are you.'

'Touché. But have you had a lot of serious relationships over the past seven years?'

He shrugged. 'I'm involved right now.'

'Really?'

'What, that's such a surprise?'

'No, but think about it. You, Mr. Commitment, Mr. Long-Term Relationship – why is it taking you so long to find anybody else?'

'Don't tell me.' He held up a hand. 'You spoiled me for all other women?'

'Well, that would be understandable.' Jessica arched an eyebrow. 'But no, I don't think so.'

'Well, I'm all ears. Why? Why aren't I happily married by now?'

Jessica shrugged. 'I'm still working on it.'

'Don't work on it. It doesn't involve you anymore.'

She shrugged again.

They both sat there. It was funny how comfortable he was with all this.

'You remember my friend Claire?' Myron said.

'She married that uptight guy, right? We went to their wedding.'

'Erik.' He didn't want to go into it all, so he started with something else. 'He told me tonight that he and Claire are having troubles. He says it's inevitable, that eventually it all dims and fades and that it becomes something else. He says he misses the passion.'

'Is he messing around?' Jessica asked.

'Why do you ask that?'

'Because it sounds like he's trying to justify his actions.'

'So you don't think there's anything to that dimming passion stuff?'

'Of course there's something to it. Passion can't stay at that fevered pitch.'

Myron thought about that. 'It did for us.'

'Yes,' she said.

'There was no fade.'

'None. But we were young. And maybe that's why, in the end, we blew up.'

He considered that. She took his hand again. There was a charge. Then Jessica gave him a look. *The* look, to be more specific. Myron froze.

Uh-oh.

'You and this new woman,' Jessica said. 'Are you exclusive?'

'You and Stoner-Boner,' he countered. 'Are you exclusive?'

'Low blow. But it's not about Stone. It's not about your new missus. It's about us.'

'And you think, what, a quick boink will help clarify things?'

'Still a wordsmith with the ladies, I see.'

'Here's another word from the wordsmith: no.'

Jessica toyed with the top button of her blouse. Myron felt his mouth go a little dry. But she stopped.

'You're right,' she said.

He wondered if he was disappointed that she hadn't pushed it further. He wondered what he would have done if she had.

They started talking then, just catching up on the years. Myron told her about Jeremy, about his serving overseas. Jessica told him about her books, her family, her time working out on the West Coast. She didn't talk about Stoner. He didn't talk about Ali.

Morning came. They were still in the kitchen. They'd been talking for hours, but it didn't feel like it. It just felt good. At seven A.M., the phone rang. Myron picked it up.

Win said, 'Our favorite schoolteacher is heading to work.'

28

Myron and Jessica hugged good-bye. The hug lasted a long time. Myron could smell Jessica's hair. He didn't remember the name of her shampoo, but it had lilacs and wildflowers and was the same one she'd used when they'd been together.

Myron called Claire. 'I have a quick question,' he said to her.

'Erik said he saw you last night.'

'Yeah.'

'He's been on the computer all night.'

'Good. Look, do you know a teacher named Harry Davis?'

'Sure. Aimee had him for English last year. He's also a guidance counselor now, I think.'

'Did she like him?'

'Very much.' Then: 'Why? Does he have something to do with this?'

'I know you want to help, Claire. And I know Erik wants to help. But you have to trust me on this, okay?'

'I do trust you.'

'Erik told you about the cut-through we found?'

'Yes.'

'Harry Davis lives on the other side of it.'

'Oh my God.'

'Aimee is not in his house or anything. We already checked.'

'What do you mean, you checked? How did you check?'

'Please, Claire, just listen to me. I'm working on this, but I need to do it without interference. You have to keep Erik off my back, okay? Tell him I said to search all the surrounding streets online. Tell him to drive around that area, but not on that cul-de-sac. Or better yet, have him call Dominick Rochester – that's Katie's father – '

'He called us.'

'Dominick Rochester?'

'Yes.'

'When?'

'Last night. He said he met with you.'

Met, Myron thought. Nice euphemism.

'We're getting together this morning – the Rochesters and us. We're going to see if we can find a connection between Katie and Aimee.'

'Good. That'll help. Listen, I have to go.'

'You'll call?'

'As soon as I know something.'

Myron heard her sob.

'Claire?'

'It's been two days, Myron.'

'I know. I'm on it. You might want to try to pressure the police more too. Now that we've crossed the forty-eight-hour mark.'

'Okay.'

He wanted to say something like *Be strong,* but it sounded so stupid in his head that he let it go. He said good-bye and hung up. Then he called Win.

'Articulate,' Win said.

'I can't believe you still answer the phone that way. "Articulate."'

Silence.

'Is Harry Davis still heading to the high school?'

'He is.'

'On my way.'

Livingston High School, his alma mater. Myron started up the car. The total ride would be maybe two miles, but whoever was tailing him either wasn't very good at it or didn't care. Or maybe, after the debacle with the Twins, Myron was being more wary. Either way, a gray Chevy, maybe a Caprice, had been on him since he made the first turn.

He called Win and got the customary 'Articulate.'

'I'm being followed,' Myron said.

'Rochester again?'

'Could be.'

'Make and license plate?'

Myron gave it to him.

Win said, 'We're still on Route 280, so stall a little. Take them down past Mount Pleasant Avenue. I'll get in behind them, meet you back at the circle.'

Myron did as Win suggested. He turned into Harrison School for the U-turn. The Chevy following him kept going straight. Myron started back down the other way on Livingston Avenue. By the time he hit the next traffic light, the gray Chevy was back on his tail.

Myron hit the big circle in front of the high school, parked, and got out of his car. There were no stores here, but this was the nerve center of Livingston – a plethora of identical brick. There was the police station, the courthouse, the town library, and there, the large crown jewel, Livingston High School.

The early morning joggers and walkers were on the circle. Most were on the elderly side and moved slowly. But not all. A group of four hotties, all hard-bodied and maybe twenty-ish, were jogging in his direction.

Myron smiled at them and arched an eyebrow. 'Hello, ladies,' he said as they passed.

Two of them snickered. The other two looked at him as though he'd just announced that he had a poopie in his pants.

Win sidled up next to him. 'Did you give them the full-wattage smile?'

'I'd say a good eighty, ninety watts.'

Win studied the young women before making a declaration: 'Lesbians,' he said.

'Must be.'

'A lot of that going around, isn't there?'

Myron did the math in his head. He probably had fifteen to twenty years on them.

When it comes to young girls, you just never want to feel it.

'The car following you,' Win said, keeping his eyes on the young joggers, 'is an unmarked police vehicle with two uniforms inside. They're parked in the library lot watching us through a telephoto lens.'

'You mean they're taking our picture right now?'

'Probably,' Win said.

'How's my hair?'

Win made an *eh* gesture with his hand.

Myron thought about what it meant. 'They probably still see me as a suspect.'

'I would,' Win said. He had what looked like a Palm Pilot in his hand. It was tracking the car's GPS. 'Our favorite teacher should be arriving now.'

The teachers' lot was on the west side of the school. Myron and Win walked over. They figured that it would be better to confront him here, outside, before class started.

As they headed over, Myron said, 'Guess who stopped by my house at three A.M.?'

'Wink Martindale?'

'No.'

'I love that guy.'

'Who doesn't? Jessica.'

'I know.'

'How . . .' Then he remembered. He'd called Win's cell when he heard the click at the door. He'd hung up as they headed down to the kitchen.

Win said, 'Did you do her?'

'Yes. Many times. But not in the last seven years.'

'Good one. Pray tell, did she stop by to shag for old times' sake?'

'"Shag?"'

'My Anglo ancestry. Well?'

'A gentleman never kisses and tells. But yes.'

'And you refused?'

'I remain chaste.'

'Your chivalry,' Win said. 'Some would call it admirable.'

'But not you.'

'No, I'd call it – and I'm breaking out the big words here so pay attention – really, really moronic.'

'I'm involved with someone else.'

'I see. So you and Miss Six-Point-Eight have promised to shag only one another?'

'It's not like that. It's not like one day you turn to the other and say, "Hey, let's not sleep with anybody else". '

'So you didn't specifically promise?'

'No.'

Win held up both hands, totally lost. 'I don't understand then. Did Jessica have BO or something?'

Win. 'Just forget it.'

'Done.'

'Sleeping with her would only complicate things, okay?'

Win just stared.

'What?'

'You're a very big girl,' Win said.

They walked a little more.

Win said, 'Do you still need me?'

'I don't think so.'

'I'll be in the office then. If there's trouble, hit the cell.'

Myron nodded as Win headed off. Harry Davis got out of his car. There were clusters of cliques in the lot. Myron shook his head. Nothing changed. The Goths wore only black with silver studs. The Brains had heavy backpacks and dressed in short-sleeved button-down shirts of one hundred percent polyester like a bunch of assistant managers at a chain drugstore convention. The Jocks took up the most space, sitting on car hoods and wearing leather-sleeved varsity jackets, even though it was too hot for them.

Harry Davis had the easy walk and carefree smile of the well-liked. His looks landed him smack in the average category, and he dressed like a high school teacher, which was to say poorly. All the cliques greeted him, which said something. First, the Brains shook his hand and called out, 'Hey, Mr. D!'

Mr. D?

Myron stopped. He thought back to Aimee's yearbook, her favorite teachers: Miss Korty . . .

. . . and Mr. D.

Davis kept moving. The Goths were next. They gave him small waves, much too cool to do more than that. When he approached the Jocks, several offered up high-fives and 'Yo, Mr. D!'s.

Harry Davis stopped and started talking to one of the Jocks. The two moved a few feet away from the cluster. The conversation appeared more animated. The jock had a varsity jacket with a football on the back of it and the letters *QB* for *quarterback* on the sleeve. Some of the guys were calling to him. They yelled out, 'Hey, Farm.' But the quarterback was focused on the teacher. Myron moved closer for a better look.

'Well, hello,' Myron said to himself.

The boy talking with Harry Davis – Myron could see him clearly now, the soul patch on his chin, the Rastafarian hair – was none other than Randy Wolf.

671

29

Myron considered his next move – let them keep talking or confront them now? He checked his watch. The bell was about to sound. Both Harry Davis and Randy Wolf would probably head inside then, lost to him for the day.

Showtime.

When Myron was about ten feet away from them, Randy spotted him. The boy's eyes widened with something akin to recognition. Randy stepped away from Harry Davis. Davis turned to see what was going on.

Myron waved. 'Hi, guys.'

Both froze as though caught in headlights.

'My father said I shouldn't talk to you,' Randy said.

'But your father never got to know the real me. I'm actually quite a sweetheart.' Myron waved to the confused teacher. 'Hi, Mr. D.'

He was almost on them when he heard a voice behind him.

'That's far enough.'

Myron turned around. Two cops in full uniform stood in front of them. One was tall and lanky. The other was short with long, dark, curly hair and a bushy mustache. The shorter one looked like he'd just stepped out of a VH1 special on the eighties.

The tall one said, 'Where do you think you're going?'

'This is public property. I'm walking on it.'

'Are you smarting off to me?'

'You think that's smarting off?'

'I'll ask you again, wise guy. Where do you think you're going?'

'To class,' Myron said. 'There's a bitch of an algebra final coming up.'

The tall one looked at the short one. Randy Wolf and Harry Davis stared without saying a word. Some of the students began to point and gather. The bell rang. The taller officer said, 'Okay, nothing to see here. Break it up, get to class now.'

Myron pointed at Wolf and Davis. 'I need to talk to them.'

The taller officer ignored him. 'Get to class.' Then looking at Randy, he added: 'All of you.'

The crowd thinned and then vanished. Randy Wolf and Harry Davis were gone too. Myron was alone with the two officers.

The tall one came up close to Myron. They were about the same height, but Myron had at least twenty or thirty pounds on him. 'You stay away from this school,' he said slowly. 'You don't talk to them. You don't ask questions.'

Myron thought about that. Don't ask questions? That was not the kind of thing you say to a suspect. 'Don't ask who questions?'

'Don't ask anybody anything.'

'That's pretty vague.'

'You think I should be more specific?'

'That would help, yes.'

'Are you being a smart guy again?'

'Just looking for clarification.'

'Hey, asswipe.' It was the shorter cop with the VH1-eighties look. He took out his nightstick and held it up. 'This clarification enough for you?'

Both cops smiled at Myron.

'What's the matter?' The shorter cop with the bushy mustache was slapping the nightstick against his palm. 'Cat got your tongue?'

Myron looked first at the tall cop, then back at the short one with the mustache. Then he said: 'Darryl Hall called. He wants to know if the reunion tour is still on.'

That made the smiles vanish.

The taller officer said, 'Put your hands behind your back.'

'What, are you going to tell me he doesn't look like John Oates?'

'Hands behind your back now!'

'Hall and Oates? "Sarah Smile"? "She's Gone"?'

'Now!'

'It's not an insult. Many chicks dug John Oates, I'm sure.'

'Turn around now!'

'Why?'

'I'm cuffing you. We're taking you in.'

'On what charge?'

'Assault and battery.'

'On whom?'

'Jake Wolf. He told us you trespassed on his residence and attacked him.'

Bingo.

His cop-needling had worked. Now he knew why these guys were on him. It wasn't about him being a suspect in Aimee's disappearance. It was the pressure brought upon them by one Big Jake Wolf.

Of course, the plan hadn't gone perfectly. They were arresting him now.

The John Oates cop snapped on the cuffs, making the obvious move of having them pinch his skin. Myron checked out the taller one. He looked a little nervous now, his eyes darting about. Myron figured that was a good thing.

The shorter one dragged him by the cuffs back to the same gray Chevy that had been tailing him since he'd left his house. He pushed Myron into the backseat, trying to hit his head on the doorframe, but Myron was ready and ducked it. In the front seat, Myron spotted a camera with a telephoto lens, just as Win had said.

Hmm. Two cops taking pictures, following him from his house, stopping him from talking to Randy, cuffing him – Big Jake had some juice.

The taller one stayed outside and paced. This was all going a little too fast for him. Myron decided that he could play that. The short one with the bushy mustache and dark curly hair slid into the seat next to Myron and grinned.

'I really liked "Rich Girl,"' Myron said to him. 'But "Private Eyes" – I mean, what was up with that song? "Private eyes, they're watching you." I mean, don't all eyes watch you? Public, private, whatever?'

The short guy's fuse blew faster than anticipated. He took a swing at Myron's gut. Myron was still ready. One of the lessons Myron had learned over the years was how to take a punch. It was crucial if you were going to get into any physical confrontation. In a real fight, you almost always get hit, no matter how good you are. How you reacted psychologically often decided the outcome. If you don't know what to expect, you shrivel up and cower. You get too defensive. You let the fear conquer you.

If the blow is a headshot, you need to play the angles. Don't let the punch land square, especially on the nose. Even slight head tilts can help. Instead of four knuckles landing, maybe it will only be two or one. That makes a huge difference. You also have to relax your body, let it go. You should turn away from the strike, literally roll with the punch. When a blow is aimed at your abdomen, especially when your hands are cuffed behind your back, you need to clench the stomach muscles, shift, and bend at the waist so it doesn't wallop the bread-basket. That was what Myron did.

The blow didn't hurt much. But Myron, noting the taller guy's nervousness, put on a performance that would have made De Niro take notes.

'Aarrrgggggghhh!'

'Damn, Joe,' the tall one said, 'what the hell are you doing?'

'He was making fun of me!'

Myron stayed bent over and faked loss of breath. He wheezed, he retched, he started coughing uncontrollably.

'You hurt him, Joe!'

'I just knocked the wind out of him. He'll be fine.'

Myron coughed more. He faked like he couldn't breathe. Then he added convulsions. He rolled back his eyes and started bucking like a fish on the dock.

'Calm down, dammit!'

Myron stuck his tongue out, gagged some more. Somewhere, a casting agent was speed-dialing Scorsese.

'He's choking!'

'Medicine!' Myron managed.

'What?'

'Can't breathe!'

'Dammit, get the cuffs off him!'

'Can't breathe!' Myron gasped and made his body wrack. 'Heart medicine! In my car!'

The taller one opened the door. He grabbed the keys from his partner and unlocked the cuffs. Myron kept up with the convulsions and eye rolls.

'Air!'

The tall one was wide-eyed. Myron could see what he was thinking: out of hand. This was getting too out of hand.

'Air!'

The tall one stepped aside. Myron rolled out of the car. He got up and pointed to his car. 'Medicine!'

'Go,' the taller one said.

Myron ran to his car. The two officers, dumbfounded, just watched. Myron had expected that. They were just here to scare him off. They had not expected any back talk. They were town cops. The citizens of this happy suburb obeyed them without question. But this guy hadn't bowed to them. They'd lost their cool and assaulted a man. This could mean huge trouble. They both just wanted it to end. So did Myron. He had learned what he needed to – Big Jake Wolf was scared and trying to hide something.

So when Myron reached his car, he slid into the driver's seat, put the key in the ignition, started it up, and simply drove off. He glanced in his rearview mirror. He figured that the odds were on his side, that the two cops would not chase him.

They didn't. They just stood there.

In fact, they looked relieved to just let him go.

He had to smile. Yep, there was no question about it now.

Myron Bolitar was baaack.

30

Myron was trying to figure out what to do next when his cell phone rang. The caller ID read out of area. He picked it up. Esperanza said, 'Where the hell are you?'

'Hey, how's the honeymoon going?'

'Like crap. Do you want to know why?'

'Is Tom not putting out?'

'Yeah, you men are so tough to seduce. No, my problem is that my business partner is not answering calls from our clients. My business partner is also not in the office to cover my absence.'

'I'm sorry.'

'Oh, well, that covers it.'

'I'll have Big Cyndi transfer all the calls directly to my cell. I'll be in as soon as I can.'

'What's wrong?' Esperanza asked.

Myron didn't want to disrupt her honeymoon any more than he already had, so he said, 'Nothing.'

'You so lie.'

'I'm telling you. It's nothing.'

'Fine, I'll ask Win.'

'Wait, okay.'

He briefly filled her in.

'So,' Esperanza said, 'you feel obligated because you did a good deed?'

'I was the last to see her. I dropped her off and let her go.'

'Let her go? What kind of crap is that? She's eighteen, Myron. That makes her an adult. She asked you for a ride. You gallantly – and stupidly, I might add – gave her one. That's it.'

'That's not it.'

'Look, if you gave, say, Win a ride home, would you make sure he got all the way into the house safely?'

'Good analogy.'

Esperanza snickered. 'Yeah, well. I'm coming home.'

'No, you're not.'

'You're right, I'm not. But you can't handle both on your own. So I'll tell Big Cyndi to transfer the calls down here. I'll take them. You go play superhero.'

'But you're on your honeymoon. What about Tom?'

'He's a man, Myron.'

'Meaning?'

'As long as a man gets some, he's happy.'

'That's such a cruel stereotype.'

'Yeah, I know I'm awful. I could be talking on the phone at the same time or, hell, breast-feeding Hector, Tom wouldn't blink. Plus this will give him more time to play golf. Golf and sex, Myron. It'll pretty much be Tom's dream honeymoon.'

'I'll make it up to you.'

There was a moment of silence.

'Esperanza?'

'I know it's been a while since you've done something like this,' she said. 'And I know I made you promise you wouldn't again. But maybe . . . maybe it's a good thing.'

'How do you figure?'

'Damned if I know. Christ, I got more important things to worry about. Like stretch marks when I wear a bikini. I can't believe I have stretch marks now. The kid's fault, you know.'

They hung up a minute later. Myron drove around, feeling conspicuous in his car. If the police decided to keep an eye on him or if Rochester decided another tail might be in order, this car would be inconvenient. He thought about it and called Claire. She answered on the first ring.

'Did you learn something?'

'Not really, but do you mind if I switch cars with you?'

'Of course not. I was about to call you anyway. The Rochesters just left.'

'And?'

'We talked for a while. Trying to find a connection between Aimee and Katie. But something else came up. Something I need to run by you.'

'I'm two minutes from your house.'

'I'll meet you in the front yard.'

As soon as Myron stepped out of the car, Claire tossed him her car keys. 'I think Katie Rochester ran away.'

'What makes you say that?'

'Have you met that father?'

'Yes.'

'Says it all, doesn't it?'

'Maybe.'

'But more than that, have you met the mother?'

'No.'

'Her name is Joan. She has this wince – like she's waiting for him to smack her.'

'Did you find a connection between the girls?'

'They both liked to hang out at the mall.'

'That's it?'

Claire shrugged. She looked like hell. The skin was pulled even tighter now. She looked like she'd lost ten pounds in the last day. Her body teetered as she walked, as though a strong gust would knock her all the way to the ground. 'They ate lunch at the same time. They had one class together in the past four years – PE with Mr. Valentine. That's it.'

Myron shook his head. 'You said something else came up?'

'The mother. Joan Rochester.'

'What about her?'

677

'You might miss it because like I said, she cowers and looks scared all the time.'

'Miss what?'

'She's scared of him. Her husband.'

'So? I met him. I'm scared of him.'

'Right, okay, but here's the thing. She's scared of him, sure, but she's *not* scared about her daughter. I have no proof, but that's the vibe I'm getting. Look, you remember when my mom got cancer?'

Sophomore year of high school. The poor woman died six months later. 'Of course.'

'I met with other girls going through the same thing. A support group for cancer families. We had this picnic once, where you could bring other friends too. But it was weird – you knew exactly who was really going through the torment and who was just a friend. You'd meet a fellow sufferer and you'd just know. There was a vibe.'

'And Joan Rochester didn't have a vibe?'

'She had a vibe, but not the "my daughter is missing" vibe. I tried to get her alone. I asked her to help me make some coffee. But I didn't get anywhere. I'm telling you, she knows something. The woman is scared, but not like I am.'

Myron thought about that. There were a million explanations, especially the most obvious – people react differently to stress – but he wanted to trust Claire's intuition on this. The question was, what did it mean? And what could he do about it?

'Let me think this through,' he said at last.

'Did you talk to Mr. Davis?'

'Not yet.'

'How about Randy?'

'I'm on it. That's why I need your car. The police ran me off the high school campus this morning.'

'Why?'

He didn't want to get into Randy's father so he said, 'I'm not sure yet. Look, let me get going, okay?'

Claire nodded, closed her eyes.

'She'll be okay,' Myron said, stepping toward her.

'Please.' Claire held up a hand to stop him. 'Don't waste time handing me platitudes, okay?'

He nodded, slipped into her SUV. He wondered about his next destination. Maybe he'd head back to school. Talk to the principal. Maybe the principal could call Randy or Harry Davis into his office. But then what?

The cell phone sounded. Again the caller ID gave him no information. Caller ID technology was fairly useless. The people you wanted to avoid just blocked the service anyway.

'Hello?'

'Hey, handsome, I just got your message.'

It was Gail Berruti, his contact from the phone company. He had forgotten all about the crank calls referring to him as a 'bastard.' It seemed unimportant now, just some sort of childish prank, except that maybe, just maybe, there was a connection. Claire had noted that Myron brought destruction. Maybe someone from his past was out to get him. Maybe somehow Aimee had gotten tangled up in that.

It was the longest of long shots.

678

'I haven't heard from you in forever,' Berruti said.

'Yeah, I've been busy.'

'Or not busy, I guess. How are you?'

'I'm pretty good. Were you able to trace the number?'

'It's not a trace, Myron. You said that in your phone message. "Trace the number." It's not a trace. I just had to look it up.'

'Whatever.'

'Not whatever. You know better. It's like on TV. You ever watch a phone trace on TV? They always say to keep the guy on the line so they can trace the call. That's nonsense, you know. You trace it right away. It's immediate. It doesn't take time. Why do they do that?'

'It's more suspenseful,' Myron said.

'It's dumb. They do everything ass-backward on TV. I'm watching some cop show the other night, and it takes five minutes to do a DNA test. My husband works in the crime lab at John Jay. They're lucky if they get a DNA confirmation in a month. Meanwhile the phone stuff – all of which can be done in minutes with the touch of a computer – that takes them forever. And the bad guy always hangs up just before they get the location. Have you ever seen the trace work? Never. Pisses me off, you know?'

Myron tried to get Berruti back on track. 'So you looked up the number?'

'I got it here. Curious though: Why do you need it?'

'Since when do you care?'

'Good point. Okay, let's get to it then. First off, whoever it was wanted to be anonymous. The call was from a pay phone.'

'Where?'

'The location is near one-ten Livingston Avenue in Livingston, New Jersey.'

The center of town, Myron thought. Near his local Starbucks and his dry cleaner. Myron thought about that. A dead end? Maybe. But he had a thought.

'I need you to do me two more favors, Gail,' Myron said.

'Favor implies nonpayment.'

'Semantics,' Myron said. 'You know I'll take care of you.'

'Yeah, I know. So what do you need?'

Harry Davis taught a lesson on *A Separate Peace* by John Knowles. He tried to concentrate, but the words were coming out as if he were reading off a prompter in a language he didn't quite understand. The students took notes. He wondered if they noticed that he wasn't really there, that he was going through the motions. The sad part was, he suspected that they didn't.

Why did Myron Bolitar want to talk to him?

He did not know Myron Bolitar personally, but you don't walk around the corridors of this school for more than two decades without knowing who he was. The guy was a legend here. He held every basketball record the school ever had.

So why had he wanted to talk to him?

Randy Wolf had known who he was. His father had warned him not to talk to Myron. Why?

'Mr. D? Yo, Mr. D?'

The voice fought through the fog in his head.

'Yes, Sam.'

'Can I, like, go to the bathroom?'

'Go.'

Harry Davis stopped then. He put down the chalk and looked over the faces in front of him. No, they weren't beaming. Most of them were eyes-down in their notebooks. Vladimir Khomenko, a new exchange student, had his head down on his desk, probably asleep. Others looked out the window. Some sat so low in their chairs, with spines seemingly created from Jell-O, Davis was surprised that they didn't slip to the floor.

But he cared about them. Some more than others. But he cared about all of them. They were his life. And for the first time, after all these years, Harry Davis was starting to feel it all slip away.

31

Myron had a headache, and quickly realized why. He hadn't had coffee yet that day. So he headed over to Starbucks with two thoughts in mind – caffeine and pay phone. The caffeine was taken care of by a grunge barista with a soul patch and long frontal hair that looked like a giant eyelash. The pay phone problem would take a little more work.

Myron sat at an outdoor table and eyed the offending pay phone. It was awfully public. He walked over to it. There were stickers on the phone advertising 800 numbers to call for discount calls. The most prominent one was offering 'free night calls' and had a picture of a quarter moon in case you didn't know what night was.

Myron frowned. He wanted to ask the pay phone who had dialed his number and called him a bastard and said that he'd pay for what he'd done. But the phone wouldn't talk to him. It had been that kind of day.

He sat back down and tried to figure out what he needed to do. He still wanted to talk to Randy Wolf and Harry Davis. They probably wouldn't tell him much – they probably wouldn't talk to him at all – but he would figure a way to get a run at them. He also needed to interview that doctor who worked at St. Barnabas, Edna Skylar. She had purportedly seen Katie Rochester in New York. He wanted some details on that.

He called St. Barnabas's switchboard and after two brief explanations, Edna Skylar got on the phone. Myron explained what he wanted.

Edna Skylar sounded annoyed. 'I asked the investigators to keep my name out of this.'

'They have.'

'So how do you know it?'

'I have good contacts.'

She thought about that. 'What's your standing in this, Mr. Bolitar?'

'Another girl has gone missing.'

No response.

'I think there may be a connection between this girl and Katie Rochester.'

'How?'

'Could we meet? I can explain everything then.'

'I really don't know anything.'

'Please.' There was a pause. 'Dr. Skylar?'

'When I saw the Rochester girl, she indicated that she didn't want to be found.'

'I understand that. I just need a few minutes.'

'I have patients for the next hour. I can see you at noon.'

'Thank you,' he said, but Edna Skylar had already hung up.

Lithium Larry Kidwell and the Medicated Five shuffled into Starbucks. Larry headed right for his table.

'Fourteen hundred eighty-eight planets on creation day, Myron. Fourteen hundred eighty-eight. And I haven't seen a penny. You know what I'm saying?'

Larry looked as awful as always. Geographically, they were so close to their old high school, but what had his favorite restaurateur, Peter Chin, said about years flying by but the heart staying the same? Well, only the heart then.

'Good to know,' Myron said. He looked back at the pay phone and a thought struck him hard and fast: 'Wait.'

'Huh?'

'Last time I saw you there were fourteen hundred eighty-seven planets, right?'

Larry looked confused. 'Are you sure?'

'I am.' Myron's mind started racing. 'And if I'm not mistaken, you said the next planet was mine. You said it was out to get me and something about stroking the moon.'

Larry's eyes lit up. 'Stroking the moon sliver. He hates you bad.'

'Where is that moon sliver?'

'In the Aerolis solar system. By Guanchomitis.'

'Are you sure, Larry? Are you sure it's not . . .' Myron rose and walked him to the pay phone. Larry cringed. Myron pointed to the sticker, to the image of the quarter moon on the ad for free night calls. Larry gasped.

'Is this the moon sliver?'

'Oh please, oh my god, oh please . . .'

'Calm down, Larry. Who else wants that planet? Who hates me enough to stroke the moon sliver?'

Twenty minutes later, Myron headed into Chang's Dry Cleaning. Maxine Chang was there, of course. There were three people in line. Myron didn't get behind them. He stood to the side and crossed his arms. Maxine kept sneaking glances at him. Myron waited until the customers were gone. Then he approached.

'Where's Roger?' he asked.

'He has school.'

Myron met her eye. 'Do you know he's been calling me?'

'Why would he call you?'

'You tell me.'

'I don't know what you're talking about.'

'I have a friend at the phone company. Roger called me from that booth over there. I have reliable witnesses who can place him there at the right time.' That was more than an exaggeration, but Myron went with it. 'He threatened me. He called me a bastard.'

'Roger wouldn't do that.'

'I don't want to get him in trouble, Maxine. What's going on?'

Another customer came in. Maxine shouted something out in Chinese. An elderly woman came out of the back and took over. Maxine gestured with her head for Myron to follow her. He did. They walked past the tracks of moving hangers. When he was a kid, the metallic whir of the tracks had always amazed him, like something out of a cool sci-fi movie. Maxine kept walking until they were out in the back alley.

'Roger is a good boy,' she said. 'He works so hard.'

'What's going on, Maxine? When I was in here the other day, you were acting funny.'

'You don't understand how hard it is. To live in a town like this.'

He did – he had lived here his whole life – but he held his tongue.

'Roger worked so hard. He got good grades. Number four in his class. These other kids. They're spoiled. All have private tutors. They don't work a real job. Roger, he works here every day after school. He studies in the back room. He doesn't go to parties. He doesn't have a girlfriend.'

'What does any of this have to do with me?'

'Other parents hire people to write their children's essays. They pay for classes to improve their boards. They donate money to the big schools. They do other things, I don't even know. It's so important, where you go to college. It can decide your whole life. Everyone is so scared, they do anything, *anything* to get their kid in the right school. This town, you see it all the time. Nice people maybe, but you can justify any evil as long as you can say, "It's for my child." You understand?'

'I do, but I don't see what that has to do with me.'

'I need you to understand. That's what we have to compete with. With all that money and power. With people who cheat and steal and will do anything.'

'If you're telling me that college acceptance is competitive in this town, I know that. It was competitive when I graduated.'

'But you had basketball.'

'Yes.'

'Roger is such a good student. He works so hard. And his dream is to go to Duke. He told you that. You probably don't remember.'

'I remember him saying something about applying there. I don't remember him saying it was his dream or anything. He just listed a bunch of schools.'

'It was his first choice,' Maxine Chang said firmly. 'And if Roger makes it, there is a scholarship waiting for him. He'd have his tuition paid for. That was so important to us. But he didn't get in. Even though he was number four in his class. Even though he had very good boards. Better boards – and better grades – than Aimee Biel.'

Maxine Chang looked at Myron with heavy eyes.

'Wait a second. Are you blaming me because Roger didn't get into Duke?'

'I don't know much, Myron. I'm just a dry cleaner. But a school like Duke almost never takes more than one student from a specific high school in New Jersey. Aimee Biel made it. Roger had better grades. He had better board scores. He had great teacher recommendations. Neither of them are athletes. Roger plays the violin, Aimee plays guitar.' Maxine Chang shrugged.

'So you tell me: Why did she get in and not Roger?'

He wanted to protest, but the truth stopped him. He had written a letter. He had even called his friend in admissions. People do stuff like that all the time. It doesn't mean that Roger Chang was denied admission. But simple math: When one person gets a spot, someone else doesn't.

Maxine's voice was a plea. 'Roger was just so angry.'

'That's no excuse.'

'No, it's not. I will talk to him. He will apologize to you, I promise.'

But another thought came to Myron. 'Was Roger just mad at me?'

'I don't understand.'

'Was he mad at Aimee too?'

Maxine Chang frowned. 'Why would you ask that?'

'Because the next call on that pay phone was to Aimee Biel's cell phone. Was Roger angry with her? Resentful maybe?'

'Not Roger, no. He's not like that.'

'Right, he'd only call me and make threats.'

'He didn't mean anything. He was just lashing out.'

'I need to talk to Roger.'

'What? No, I forbid it.'

'Fine, I'll go to the police. I'll tell them about the threatening calls.'

Her eyes widened. 'You wouldn't.'

He would. Maybe he should. But not yet. 'I want to talk to him.'

'He'll be here after school.'

'Then I'll be back at three. If he's not here, I'm going to the police.'

32

Dr. Edna Skylar met Myron in the lobby of St. Barnabas Medical Center. She had all the props – a white coat, a name tag with the hospital logo, a stethoscope dangling across her neck, a clipboard in her hand. She had that impressive doctor bearing too, complete with the enviable posture, the small smile, the firm-but-not-too-firm handshake.

Myron introduced himself. She looked him straight in the eye and said, 'Tell me about the missing girl.'

Her voice left no room for arguments. Myron needed her to trust him, so he launched into the story, keeping Aimee's last name out of it. They both stood in the middle of the lobby. Patients and visitors walked on either side of them, some coming very close.

Myron said, 'Maybe we could go somewhere private.'

Edna Skylar smiled, but there was no joy in it. 'These people are preoccupied with things much more important to them than us.'

Myron nodded. He saw an old man in a wheelchair with an oxygen mask. He saw a pale woman in an ill-fitted wig checking in with a look both resigned and bewildered, as if she was wondering if she'd ever check out and if it even mattered anymore.

Edna Skylar watched him. 'A lot of death in here,' she said.

'How do you do it?' Myron asked.

'You want the standard cliché about being able to detach the personal from the professional?'

'Not really.'

'The truth is, I don't know. My work is interesting. It never gets old. I see death a lot. That never gets old either. It hasn't helped me to accept my own mortality or any of that. Just the opposite. Death is a constant outrage. Life is more valuable than you can ever imagine. I've seen that, the real value of life, not the usual platitudes we hear about it. Death is the enemy. I don't accept it. I fight it.'

'And that never gets tiring?'

'Sure it does. But what else am I going to do? Bake cookies? Work on Wall Street?' She looked around. 'Come on, you're right – it's distracting out here. Walk with me, but I'm on a tight schedule so keep talking.'

Myron told her the rest of the story of Aimee's disappearance. He kept it as short as possible – kept his own name out of it – but he made sure to hit upon the fact that both girls used the same ATM. She asked a few questions, mostly small clarifications. They reached her office and sat down.

'Sounds like she ran away,' Edna Skylar said.

'I'm aware of that.'

'Someone leaked you my name, is that correct?'

'More or less.'

'So you have some idea what I saw?'

'Just the basics. What you said convinced the investigators that Katie was a runaway. I'm just wondering if you saw something that makes you think differently.'

'No. And I've gone over it a hundred times in my head.'

'You're aware,' Myron said, 'that kidnap victims often identify with their abductors.'

'I know all that. The Stockholm syndrome and all its bizarre offshoots. But it just didn't seem that way. Katie didn't look particularly exhausted. The body language was right. There wasn't panic in her eyes or any kind of cult-like zealousness. Her eyes were clear, in fact. I didn't see signs of drugs there, though granted I only got a brief look.'

'Where exactly did you first see her?'

'On Eighth Avenue near Twenty-first Street.'

'And she was heading into the subway?'

'Yes.'

'A couple of trains go through that station.'

'She was taking the C train.'

The C train basically ran north – south through Manhattan. That wouldn't help.

'Tell me about the man she was with.'

'Thirty to thirty-five. Average height. Nice looking. Long, dark hair. Two-day beard.'

'Scars, tattoos, anything like that?'

Edna Skylar shook her head and told him the story, how she'd been walking on the street with her husband, how Katie looked different, older, more sophisticated, different hair, how she wasn't even positive it was Katie until Katie uttered those final words: '*You can't tell anybody you saw me.*'

'And you said she seemed scared?'

'Yes.'

'But not of the man she was with?'

'That's right. May I ask you something?'

'Sure.'

'I know something about you,' she said. 'No, I'm not a basketball fan, but Google works wonders. I use it all the time. With patients too. If I'm seeing someone new, I check them out online.'

'Okay.'

'So my question is, why are you trying to find the girl?'

'I'm a family friend.'

'But why you?'

'It's hard to explain.'

Edna Skylar gave that a second, seemingly unsure if she should accept his vague response. 'How are her parents holding up?'

'Not well.'

'Their daughter is most likely safe. Like Katie.'

'Could be.'

'You should tell them that. Offer them some comfort. Let them know she'll be okay.'

'I don't think it'll do any good.'

She looked off. Something crossed her face.

'Dr. Skylar?'

'One of my children ran away,' Edna Skylar said. 'He was seventeen. You know the nature versus nurture question? Well, I was a crappy mother. I know that. But my son was trouble from day one. He got into fights. He shoplifted. He got arrested when he was sixteen for stealing a car. He was heavily into drugs, though I don't think I knew it at that time. This was in the days before we talked about ADD or put kids on Ritalin or any of that. If that was a serious option, I probably would have done it. I reacted instead by withdrawing and hoping he'd outgrow it. I didn't get involved in his life. I didn't give him direction.'

She said it all matter-of-factly.

'Anyway, when he ran away, I didn't do anything. I almost expected it. A week passed. Two weeks. He didn't call. I didn't know where he was. Children are a blessing. But they also rip your heart out in ways you could never imagine.'

Edna Skylar stopped.

'What happened to him?' Myron asked.

'Nothing overly dramatic. He eventually called. He was out on the West Coast, trying to become a big star. He needed money. He stayed out there for two years. Failed at everything he did. Then he came back. He's still a mess. I try to love him, to care about him, but' – she shrugged – 'doctoring comes natural to me. Mothering does not.'

Edna Skylar looked at Myron. He could see that she wasn't finished, so he waited.

'I wish . . .' Her throat caught. 'It's a horrible cliché, but more than anything, I wish I could start over again. I love my son, I really do, but I don't know what to do for him. He may be beyond hope. I know how cold that sounds, but when you make professional diagnoses all day, you tend to make them in your personal life too. My point is, I've learned that I can't control those I love. So I control those I don't.'

'I'm not following,' Myron said.

'My patients,' she explained. 'They are strangers, but I care a great deal about them. It's not because I'm a generous or wonderful person, but because in my mind, they are still innocent. And I judge them. I know that's wrong. I know that I should treat every patient the same, and in terms of treatment, I think I do. But the fact is, if I Google the person and see that they spent time in jail or seem like a lowlife, I try to get them to go to another doctor.'

'You prefer the innocents,' Myron said.

'Precisely. Those whom – I know how this will sound – those whom I deem pure. Or at least, purer.'

Myron thought about his own recent reasoning, how the life of the Twins held no value to him, about how many civilians he'd sacrifice to save his own son. Was this reasoning that much different?

'So what I'm trying to say is, I think about this girl's parents, the ones you said aren't doing well, and I worry about them. I want to help.'

Before Myron could respond, there was a light rap on the door. It opened, and a head of gray hair popped through. Myron rose. The gray-haired man stepped all the way in and said, 'I'm sorry, I didn't know you were with someone.'

'It's okay, honey,' Edna Skylar said, 'but maybe you could come back later?'

'Of course.'

The gray-haired man wore a white coat too. He spotted Myron and smiled. Myron recognized the smile. Edna Skylar wasn't a basketball fan, but this guy was. Myron stuck out his hand. 'Myron Bolitar.'

'Oh, I know who you are. I'm Stanley Rickenback. Better known as Mr. Dr. Edna Skylar.'

They shook hands.

'I saw you play at Duke,' Stanley Rickenback said. 'You were something else.'

'Thank you.'

'I didn't mean to interrupt. I just wanted to see if my blushing bride wanted to join me for the lunchtime culinary delight that is our hospital cafeteria.'

'I was just leaving,' Myron said. Then: 'You were with your wife when she saw Katie Rochester, weren't you?'

'Is that why you're here?'

'Yes.'

'Are you a police officer?'

'No.'

Edna Skylar was already up. She kissed her husband's cheek. 'Let's hurry. I have patients in twenty minutes.'

'Yes, I was there,' Stanley Rickenback said to Myron. 'Why, what's your interest?'

'I'm looking into the disappearance of another girl.'

'Wait, another girl ran away?'

'Could be. I'd like to hear your impressions, Dr. Rickenback.'

'Of what?'

'Did Katie Rochester seem like a runaway to you too?'

'Yes.'

'You seem pretty sure,' Myron said.

'She was with a man. She made no move to escape. She asked Edna not to tell anybody and – ' Rickenback turned to his wife. 'Did you tell him?'

Edna made a face. 'Let's just go.'

'Tell me what?'

'My darling Stanley is getting old and senile,' Edna said. 'He imagines things.'

'Ha, ha, very funny. You have your expertise. I have mine.'

'Your expertise?' Myron said.

'It's nothing,' Edna said.

'It's not nothing,' Stanley insisted.

'Fine,' Edna said. 'Tell him what you think you saw.'

Stanley turned to Myron. 'My wife told you about how she studies faces. That was how she recognized the girl. She looks at people and tries to make a diagnosis. Just for fun. I don't do that. I leave my work at the office.'

'What is your specialty, Dr. Rickenback?'

He smiled. 'That's the thing.'

'What is?'

'I'm an ob-gyn. I didn't really think about it then. But when we got home, I looked up pictures of Katie Rochester on the Web. You know, the ones released to the media. I wanted to see if it was the same girl we saw in the subway. And that was why I'm fairly certain of what I saw.'

'Which is?'

Stanley suddenly seemed unsure of himself.

'See?' Edna shook her head. 'This is such total nonsense.'

'It might be,' Stanley Rickenback agreed.

Myron said, 'But?'

'But either Katie Rochester put on some weight,' Stanley Rickenback said, 'or maybe, just maybe, she's pregnant.'

33

Harry Davis gave his class a phony-baloney read-this-chapter-now assignment and headed out. His students were surprised. Other teachers played that card all the time, the do-busy-silent-work-so-I-can-catch-a-smoke card. But Mr. D, Teacher of the Year four years running, never did that.

The corridors at Livingston High were ridiculously long. When he was alone in one, like right now, looking down to the end made him dizzy. But that was Harry Davis. He didn't like it quiet. He liked it lively, when this artery was loaded with noise and kids and backpacks and adolescent angst.

He found the classroom, gave the door a quick knock, and stuck his head in. Drew Van Dyne taught mostly malfeasants. The room reflected that. Half the kids had iPods in their ears. Some sat on top of their desks. Others leaned against the window. A beefy guy was making out with a girl in the back corner, their mouths open wide. You could see the saliva.

Drew Van Dyne had his feet on the desk, his hands folded on his lap. He turned toward Harry Davis.

'Mr. Van Dyne? May I speak with you a moment?'

Drew Van Dyne gave him the cocky grin. Van Dyne was probably thirty-five, ten years younger than Davis. He'd come in as a music teacher eight years ago. He looked the part, the former rock 'n' roller who woulda-shoulda made it to the top except the stupid record companies could never understand his true genius. So now he gave guitar lessons and worked in a music store where he scoffed at your pedestrian taste in CDs.

Recent cutbacks in the music department had forced Van Dyne into whatever class was closest to babysitting.

'Why of course, Mr. D.'

The two teachers stepped into the hallway. The doors were thick. When it closed, the corridor was silent again.

Van Dyne still had the cocky grin. 'I'm just about to start my lesson, Mr. D. What can I do for you?'

Davis whispered because every sound echoed out here. 'Did you hear about Aimee Biel?'

'Who?'

'Aimee Biel. A student here.'

'I don't think she's one of mine.'

'She's missing, Drew.'

Van Dyne said nothing.

'Did you hear me?'

'I just said I don't know her.'

'Drew – '

'And,' Van Dyne interrupted, 'I think we'd be notified if a student had gone missing, don't you?'

'The police think she's a runaway.'

'And you don't?' Van Dyne held on to the grin, maybe even spread it a bit. 'The police will want to know why you feel that way, Mr. D. Maybe you should go to them. Tell them all you know.'

'I might just do that.'

'Good.' Van Dyne leaned closer and whispered. 'I think the police would definitely want to know when you last saw Aimee, don't you?'

Van Dyne leaned back and waited for Davis's reaction.

'You see, Mr. D,' Van Dyne went on, 'they'll need to know everything. They'll need to know where she went, who she talked to, what they talked about. They'll probably look into all that, don't you think? Maybe open up a full investigation into the wonderful works of our Teacher of the Year.'

'How do you . . . ?' Davis felt the quake start in his legs. 'You have more to lose than I do.'

'Really?' Drew Van Dyne was so close now that Davis could feel the spittle in his face. 'Tell me, Mr. D. What exactly do I have to lose? My lovely house in scenic Ridgewood? My sterling reputation as a beloved teacher? My perky wife who shares my passion for educating the young? Or maybe my lovely daughters who look up to me so?'

They stood there for a moment, still in each other's face. Davis couldn't speak. Somewhere in the distance, another world maybe, he heard a bell ring. Doors flew open. Students poured out. The arteries filled with their laughter and angst. It all grabbed hold of Harry Davis. He closed his eyes and let it, let it sweep him away to someplace far away from Drew Van Dyne, someplace he'd much rather be.

The Livingston Mall was aging and trying hard not to show it, but the improvements came across more like a bad face-lift than true youth.

Bedroom Rendezvous was located on the lower level. To some, the lingerie store was like Victoria's Secret's trailer-park cousin, but the truth was, the cousins were really a lot alike. It was all about presentation. The sexy models on the big posters were closer to porno stars, with wagging tongues and suggestive hand placement. The Bedroom Rendezvous slogan, which was centered across the buxom models' cleavage, read: *what kind of woman do you want to take to bed?*

'A hot one,' Myron said out loud. It was again not that different from Victoria's Secret commercials, the one where Tyra and Frederique are all oiled up and ask, 'What is sexy?' Answer: Really hot women. The clothing seems beside the point.

The saleswoman wore a tight tiger print. She had big hair and chewed gum, but there was a confidence there that somehow made it work. Her tag read SALLY ANN.

'Looking to make a purchase?' Sally Ann asked.

'I doubt you have anything in my size,' Myron said.

'You'd be surprised. So what's the deal?' She motioned toward the poster. 'You just like staring at the cleavage?'

'Well, yes. But that's not why I'm here.' Myron pulled out a photograph of Aimee. 'Do you recognize this girl?'

'Are you a cop?'

'I might be.'

'Nah.'

'What makes you say that?'

Sally Ann shrugged. 'So what are you after?'

'This girl is missing. I'm trying to find her.'

'Let me take a look.'

Myron handed her the photograph. Sally Ann studied it. 'She looks familiar.'

'A customer maybe?'

'No. I remember customers.'

Myron reached into a plastic bag and pulled out the white outfit he'd found in Aimee's drawer. 'This look familiar?'

'Sure. It's from our Naughty-pout line.'

'Did you sell this one?'

'It could be. I've sold a few.'

'The tag is still on it. Do you think you could trace down who purchased it?'

Sally Ann frowned and pointed at the picture of Aimee. 'You think your missing girl bought it?'

'I found it in her drawer.'

'Yeah, but still.'

'Still what?'

'It's too slutty and uncomfortable.'

'And, what, she looks classy?'

'No, not that. Women rarely buy this one. Men do. The material is itchy. It rides up the crotch. This is a man's fantasy, not a woman's. It's a bit like porno videos.' Sally Ann cocked her head and worked the gum. 'Have you ever watched a porno flick?'

Myron kept his face blank. 'Never, ever, never,' he said.

Sally Ann laughed. 'Right. Anyway, when a woman picks out the film, it's totally different. It usually has a story or maybe a title with the word "sensuous" or "loving" in it. It might be raunchy or whatever, but it usually isn't called something like *Dirty Whore 5*. You know what I mean?'

'Let's assume I do. And this outfit?'

'It's the equivalent.'

'Of *Dirty Whore Whatever*?'

'Right. No woman would pick it out.'

'So how do I find out who bought it for her?'

'We don't keep records or anything like that. I could ask some of the other girls, but . . .' Sally Ann shrugged.

Myron thanked her and headed out. As a young boy, Myron had come here with his dad. They had frequented Herman's Sporting Goods back then. The store was now out of business. But as he exited Bedroom Rendezvous, he still looked down the corridor, to where Herman's used to be. And two doors down, he spotted a store with a familiar name.

PLANET MUSIC.

Myron flashed back to Aimee's room. Planet Music. The guitars had been from Planet Music. There had been receipts in Aimee's drawer from there. And here it was, her favorite music shop, located two stores down from Bedroom Rendezvous.

Another coincidence?

In Myron's youth, the store in this spot had sold pianos and organs. Myron had always wondered about that. Piano-organ stores at malls. You go to the mall to buy clothes, a CD, a toy, maybe a stereo. Who goes to the mall to buy a piano?

Clearly not many people.

The pianos and organs were gone. Planet Music sold CDs and smaller instruments. They had signs for rentals. Trumpets, clarinets, violins – probably did a big business with the schools.

The kid behind the counter was maybe twenty-three, wore a hemp poncho, and looked like a seedier version of the average Starbucks barista. He had a dusty knit hat atop a shaved head. He sported the now seemingly prerequisite soul patch.

Myron gave him the stern eye and slapped the picture down on the counter. 'You know her?'

The kid hesitated a second too long. Myron jumped in.

'You answer my questions, you don't get busted.'

'Busted for what?'

'Do you know her?'

He nodded. 'That's Aimee.'

'She shops here?'

'Sure, all the time,' he said, his eyes darting everywhere but on Myron. 'And she understands music too. Most people come in here, they ask for boy bands.' He said *boy bands* the way most people say *bestiality*. 'But Aimee, she rocks.'

'How well do you know her?'

'Not very. I mean, she doesn't come here for me.'

The poncho kid stopped then.

'Who does she come here for?'

'Why do you want to know?'

'Because I don't want to make you empty your pockets.'

He raised his hands. 'Hey, I'm totally clean.'

'Then I'll plant something on you.'

'What the . . . You serious?'

'Cancer serious.' Myron worked the stern eye again. He wasn't great at the stern eye. The strain was giving him a headache. 'Who does she come here to see?'

'My assistant manager.'

'He have a name?'

'Drew. Drew Van Dyne.'

'Is he here?'

'No. He comes in this afternoon.'

'You got an address for him? A phone number?'

'Hey,' the kid said, suddenly wise. 'Let me see your badge.'

'Bye now.'

Myron headed out of the store. He found Sally Ann again.

She clacked the gum. 'Back so soon?'

'Couldn't stay away,' Myron said. 'Do you know a guy who works at Planet Music named Drew Van Dyne?'

'Oh,' she said, nodding as though it all made sense now. 'Oh yes.'

34

Claire jumped at the sound of the phone. She had not slept since Aimee had gone missing. In the past two days Claire had imbibed enough coffee, and thus the caffeine, to be wired for sound. She kept going back to the Rochesters' visit, the father's anger, the mother's meekness. The mother. Joan Rochester. Something was definitely up with that woman.

Claire spent the morning going through Aimee's room while wondering about how to get Joan Rochester to talk. A mother-to-mother approach, maybe. Aimee's room held no new surprises. Claire started going through old boxes, stuff she'd saved from what seemed like two weeks ago. The pencil holder Aimee made Erik in preschool. Her first-grade report card – all As, plus Mrs. Rohrbach's comment that Aimee was a gifted student, fun to have in class, and had a bright future. She stared at the words *bright future*, letting them mock her.

The phone jangled a nerve. She dove for it, hoping once again that it was Aimee, that this was all some silly misunderstanding, that there was a perfectly reasonable explanation for where she was.

'Hello?'

'She's fine.'

The voice was robotic. Neither male nor female. Like an edgier version of the one who tells you that your call is valued and to hold for the next available representative.

'Who is this?'

'She's fine. Just let it be. You have my word.'

'Who is this? Let me speak to Aimee.'

But the only response was a dial tone.

Joan Rochester said, 'Dominick isn't home right now.'

'I know,' Myron said. 'I want to talk to you.'

'Me?' As if the very idea of someone wanting to talk to her was a shock on par with a Mars landing. 'But why?'

'Please, Mrs. Rochester, it's very important.'

'I think we should wait for Dominick.'

Myron pushed past her. 'I don't.'

The house was neat and orderly. It was all straight lines and right angles. No curves, no surprising splashes of color, everything standing upright, as if the very room didn't want to draw attention to itself.

'Can I fix you some coffee?'

'Where is your daughter, Mrs. Rochester?'

She blinked maybe a dozen times in rapid succession. Myron knew men who blinked like that. They were always the guys who were bullied in school as kids and never got over it. She managed to stammer out the word, 'What?'

'Where is Katie?'

'I . . . I don't know.'

'That's a lie.'

More blinking. Myron did not let himself feel sorry for her. 'Why . . . I'm not lying.'

'You know where Katie is. I assume you have a reason for keeping quiet about it. I assume it involves your husband. That isn't my concern.'

Joan Rochester tried to straighten her back. 'I'd like you to leave this house.'

'No.'

'Then I'm going to call my husband.'

'I have phone records,' Myron said.

More blinking. She put up her hand like she was warding off a blow.

'For your mobile. Your husband wouldn't check that. And even if he did, an incoming call from a pay phone in New York City probably wouldn't mean much. But I know about a woman named Edna Skylar.'

Confusion replaced the fear. 'Who?'

'She's a doctor at St. Barnabas. She spotted your daughter in Manhattan. More specifically, near Twenty-third Street. You've received several phone calls at seven P.M. from a phone booth four blocks away, which is close enough.'

'Those calls weren't from my daughter.'

'No?'

'They were from a friend.'

'Uh-huh.'

'My friend shops in the city. She likes to call when she finds something interesting. To get my opinion.'

'On a pay phone?'

'Yes.'

'Her name?'

'I'm not going to tell you that. And I insist you leave this very instant.'

Myron shrugged, threw up his hands. 'I guess this is a dead end for me then.'

Joan Rochester was blinking again. She was about to start blinking some more. 'But maybe your husband will have more luck.'

All color drained from her face.

'I might as well tell him what I know. You can explain about your friend who likes to shop. He'll believe you, don't you think?'

Terror widened her eyes. 'You have no idea what he's like.'

'I think I do. He had two goons try to torture me.'

'That's because he thought you knew what happened to Katie.'

'And you let him, Mrs. Rochester. You'd have let him torture and maybe kill me, and you knew that I had nothing to do with it.'

She stopped blinking. 'You can't tell my husband. Please.'

'I have no interest in harming your daughter. I'm only interested in finding Aimee Biel.'

'I don't know anything about that girl.'

'But your daughter might.'

Joan Rochester shook her head. 'You don't understand.'

'Don't understand what?'

Joan Rochester walked away, just leaving him there. She crossed the room. When she turned back to him, her eyes were filled with tears. 'If he finds out. If he finds her . . .'

'He won't.'

She shook her head again.

'I promise,' he said.

His words – yet another seemingly empty promise – echoed in the still room.

'Where is she, Mrs. Rochester? I just need to talk to her.'

Her eyes started moving around the room as if she suspected her breakfront might overhear them. She stepped toward the back door and opened it. She signaled for him to go outside.

'Where is Katie?' Myron asked.

'I don't know. That's the truth.'

'Mrs. Rochester, I really don't have time – '

'The calls.'

'What about them?'

'You said they came from New York?'

'Yes.'

She looked off.

'What?'

'Maybe that's where she is.'

'You really don't know?'

'Katie wouldn't tell me. I didn't ask either.'

'Why not?'

Joan Rochester's eyes were perfect circles. 'If I don't know,' she said, finally meeting his eye, 'then he can't make me tell.'

Next door a lawn mower started up, shattering the silence. Myron waited a moment. 'But you've heard from Katie?'

'Yes.'

'And you know she's safe.'

'Not from him.'

'But in general, I mean. She wasn't kidnapped or anything like that.'

She nodded slowly.

'Edna Skylar spotted her with a dark-haired man. Who is he?'

'You're underestimating Dominick. Please don't do that. Just let us be. You're trying to find another girl. Katie has nothing to do with her.'

'They both used the same ATM machine.'

'That's a coincidence.'

Myron did not bother arguing. 'When is Katie calling again?'

'I don't know.'

'Then you're not much use to me.'

'What's that supposed to mean?'

'I need to talk to your daughter. If you can't help me, I'll have to take the chance that your husband can.'

She just shook her head.

'I know she's pregnant,' Myron said.

Joan Rochester groaned.

'You don't understand,' she said again.

'Then tell me.'

'The dark-haired man . . . His name is Rufus. If Dom finds out, he'll kill him. It is that simple. And I don't know what he'll do to Katie.'

'So what's their plan? Hide forever?'

'I doubt they have a plan.'

'And Dominick doesn't know about any of this?'

'He's not stupid. He thinks Katie probably ran away.'

Myron thought about it. 'Then I don't get something. If he suspects Katie ran away, why did he go to the press?'

Joan Rochester smiled then, but it was the saddest smile Myron had ever seen. 'Don't you see?'

'No.'

'He likes to win. No matter what the cost.'

'I still don't – '

'He did it to put pressure on them. He wants to find Katie. He doesn't care about anything else. That's his strength. He doesn't mind taking hits. Big hits. Dom doesn't embarrass. He never feels shame. He's willing to lose or suffer to make you hurt and suffer more. That's the kind of man he is.'

They fell quiet. Myron wanted to ask why she stayed married to him, but that wasn't his business. There were so many cases of abused women in this country. He'd like to help, but Joan Rochester wouldn't accept it – and he had more pressing matters on his mind. He thought back to the Twins, about not being bothered by their deaths, about Edna Skylar and the way she handled what she thought of as her purer patients.

Joan Rochester had made her choice. Or maybe she was just a little less innocent than the others.

'You should tell the police,' Myron said.

'Tell them what?'

'That your daughter is a runaway.'

She snorted. 'You don't get it, do you? Dom would find out. He has sources in the department. How do you think he found out about you so fast?'

But, Myron realized, he hadn't learned about Edna Skylar. Yet. So his sources weren't infallible. Myron wondered if he could use that, but he didn't see how. He moved closer now. He took Joan Rochester's hands in his and made her look him in the eye.

'Your daughter will be safe. I guarantee it. But I need to talk to her. That's all. Just talk. Do you understand?'

She swallowed. 'I don't have much choice, do I?'

Myron said nothing.

'If I don't cooperate, you'll go to Dom.'

'Yes,' Myron said.

'Katie is supposed to call me tonight at seven,' she said. 'I'll let you talk to her then.'

35

Win called Myron on the cell phone. 'Drew Van Dyne, your assistant Planet Music manager, is also a teacher at Livingston High.'

'Well, well,' Myron said.

'Indeed.'

Myron was on his way to pick up Claire. She had told him about the 'she's fine' phone call. Myron had immediately reached out for Berruti, who was, as the voice mail informed him, 'away from her desk.' He told her what he needed in the message.

Now Myron and Claire were going to Livingston High to check out Aimee's locker. Myron also hoped to catch up with her ex, Randy Wolf. And Harry 'Mr. D' Davis. And now, most of all, Drew 'Music Teacher – Lingerie Buyer' Van Dyne.

'You have anything else on him?'

'Van Dyne is married, no kids. He's had two DUIs in the past four years and one drug arrest. He has a juvie record but it's sealed. That's all I have so far.'

'So what is he doing buying lingerie for a student like Aimee Biel?'

'Pretty obvious, I would say.'

'I just talked to Mrs. Rochester. Katie got pregnant and ran away with her boyfriend.'

'A not-uncommon story.'

'No. But what – do we think Aimee did the same?'

'Ran away with her boyfriend? Not likely. No one has reported Van Dyne missing.'

'He doesn't have to go missing. Katie's boyfriend is probably afraid of Dominick Rochester. That's why he's with her. But if no one knew about Aimee and Van Dyne . . .'

'Mr. Van Dyne would have little to fear.'

'Exactly.'

'So pray tell, why would Aimee run away?'

'Because she's pregnant.'

'Bah,' Win said.

'Bah what?'

'What precisely would Aimee Biel be afraid of?' Win asked. 'Erik is hardly a Dominick Rochester type.'

Win had a point. 'Maybe Aimee didn't run away. Maybe she got pregnant and wanted to have it. Maybe she told her boyfriend, Drew Van Dyne . . .'

'Who,' Win picked up the thread, 'as a schoolteacher, would be ruined if word got out.'

'Yes.'

It made awful sense. 'There's still one big hole,' Myron said.

'That being?'

'Both girls used the same ATM machine. Look, the rest doesn't even rise to the level of coincidence. Two girls getting pregnant in a school with almost a thousand girls? It is statistically insignificant. Even if you add two girls running away because of it, okay, the odds that there is a connection rise, but it's still more than plausible that they aren't related, wouldn't you say?'

'I would,' Win agreed.

'But then you add in both using the same ATM machine. How do we explain that?'

Win said, 'Your little statistical diagnosis goes through the roof.'

'So we're missing something.'

'We're missing everything. At this stage, this whole matter is too flimsy to label supposition.'

Another point for Win. They might be theorizing too early, but they were getting close. There were other factors too, like Roger Chang's threatening 'bastard' phone calls. That might be connected, might not be. He also didn't know how Harry Davis fit in. Maybe he was a liaison between Van Dyne and Aimee, but that seemed a stretch. And what should Myron make of Claire's 'she's fine' phone call? Myron wondered about the timing and the motive – to comfort or terrorize; and either way, why? – but so far, nothing had come to him.

'Okay,' Myron said to Win, 'are we all set for tonight?'

'We are indeed.'

'I'll talk to you later then.'

Win hung up as Myron pulled into Claire and Erik's driveway. Claire was out the front door before Myron came to a complete stop.

'You okay?' he asked.

Claire didn't bother answering the obvious. 'Did you hear from your phone contact?'

'Not yet. Do you know a teacher at Livingston High named Drew Van Dyne?'

'No.'

'The name doesn't ring a bell?'

'I don't think so. Why?'

'You remember the lingerie I found in her room? I think he might have bought it for her.'

Her face reddened. 'A teacher?'

'He worked at that music store at the mall.'

'Planet Music.'

'Yes.'

Claire shook her head. 'I don't understand any of this.'

Myron put a hand on her arm. 'You have to stay with me, Claire, okay? I need you to be calm and focus.'

'Don't patronize me, Myron.'

'I don't mean to, but look, if you go off half-cocked when we get to the school –'

'We'll lose him. I know that. What else is going on?'

'You were dead-on about Joan Rochester.' Myron filled her in. Claire sat there and stared at the window. She nodded every once in a while, but the nod didn't seem to be connected to anything he said.

'So you think Aimee might be pregnant?'

Her voice was indeed calm now, too matter-of-fact. She was trying to disengage. That might be a good thing.

'Yes.'

Claire put her hand to her lip and started plucking. Like in high school. This was all so weird, driving this route they'd gone on a thousand times in their youth, Claire plucking her lip like the algebra final was coming up. 'Okay, let's try to look at this rationally for a moment,' she said.

'Right.'

'Aimee broke up with her high school boyfriend. She didn't tell us. She was very secretive. She was erasing e-mails. She wasn't herself. She had lingerie in her drawer that was probably bought by a teacher who worked in a music store she used to frequent.'

The words hung heavy in the air.

'I have another thought,' Claire said.

'Go on.'

'If Aimee was pregnant – God, I can't believe I'm talking like this – she would have gone to a clinic of some sort.'

'Could be. Maybe she'd just buy a home pregnancy test though.'

'No.' Claire's voice was firm. 'Not in the end. We talked about stuff like this. One of her friends got a false positive on one of those once. Aimee would get it checked. She'd probably find a doctor too.'

'Okay.'

'And around here, the only clinic is at St. Barnabas. I mean, that's the one everyone uses. So she might have gone there. We should call and see if someone could check the records. I'm the mother. That should count for something, right?'

'I don't know what the laws on that stuff are now.'

'They keep changing.'

'Wait.' Myron picked up his mobile phone. He dialed the hospital's switchboard. He asked for Dr. Stanley Rickenback. Myron gave his name to the secretary. He pulled onto the circle in front of the high school and parked. Rickenback picked up the phone, sounding somewhat excited by the call. Myron explained what he wanted. The excitement vanished.

'I can't do that,' Rickenback said.

'I have her mother right here.'

'You just told me she's eighteen years old. It's against the rules.'

'Listen, you were right about Katie Rochester. She was pregnant. We're trying to find out if Aimee was too.'

'I understand that, but I can't help you. Her medical records are confidential. With all the new HIPAA rules, the computer system keeps track of everything, even who opens a patient's file and when. Even if I didn't think it was unethical, it would be too big a personal risk, I'm sorry.'

He hung up. Myron stared out the window. Then he called the switchboard back.

'Dr. Edna Skylar, please.'

Two minutes later, Edna said, 'Myron?'

'You can access patient files from your computer, can't you?'

'Yes.'

'All the patients in the hospital?'

'What are you asking?'

'Remember our talk about innocents?'

'Yes.'

'I want you to help an innocent, Dr. Skylar.' Then, thinking about it, he said, 'In this case, maybe two innocents.'

'Two?'

'An eighteen-year-old girl named Aimee Biel,' Myron said, 'and if we're correct, the baby she's carrying.'

'My God. Are you telling me Stanley was right?'

'Please, Dr. Skylar.'

'It's unethical.'

He just let the silence wear on her. He had made his argument. Adding more would be superfluous. Better to let her think it through on her own.

It didn't take long. Two minutes later, he heard the computer keys clacking.

'Myron?' Edna Skylar said.

'Yes.'

'Aimee Biel is three months pregnant.'

36

Livingston High School principal Amory Reid was dressed in Haggar slacks, an off-white short-sleeve dress shirt made of material flimsy enough to highlight the wife-beater tee beneath it, and thick-soled black shoes that might have been vinyl. Even when his tie was loosened, it looked as though it were strangling him.

'The school is, of course, very concerned.'

Reid's hands were folded on his desk. On one hand he wore a college ring with a football insignia on it. He had uttered the line as though he'd been rehearsing in front of a mirror.

Myron sat on the right, Claire on the left. She was still dazed from the confirmation that her daughter, the one she knew and loved and trusted, had been pregnant for the past three months. At the same time there was a feeling akin to relief. It made sense. It explained recent behavior. It might provide an explanation for what had been, so far, inexplicable.

'You can, of course, check her locker,' the principal informed them. 'I have a master key to all the locks.'

'We also want to talk to two of your teachers,' Claire said, 'and a student.'

His eyes narrowed. He looked toward Myron, then back to Claire. 'Which teachers?'

'Harry Davis and Drew Van Dyne,' Myron said.

'Mr. Van Dyne is already gone for the day. He leaves on Tuesdays at two P.M.'

'And Mr. Davis?'

Reid checked a schedule. 'He's in room B-202.'

Myron knew exactly where that was. After all these years. The halls were still lettered from A to E. Rooms beginning with 1 were on the first floor, 2 on the second floor. He remembered one exasperated teacher telling a tardy student that he wouldn't know his E hall from his – get this – his A hall.

'I can see if I can pull Mr. D out of class. May I ask why you want to talk to these teachers?'

Claire and Myron exchanged a glance. Claire said, 'We'd rather not say at this time.'

He accepted that. His job was political. If he knew something, he'd have to report it. Ignorance, for a little while, might just be bliss. Myron had nothing big on either teacher yet, just innuendo. Until he had more, there was no reason to inform the school principal.

'We'd also like to talk to Randy Wolf,' Claire said.

'I'm afraid I can't let you do that.'

'Why not?'

'Off school grounds, you can do whatever you want. But here, I would need to get parental permission.'

'Why?'

'That's the rules.'

'If a kid is caught cutting class, you can talk to them.'

'I can, yes. But you can't. And this isn't a case of cutting class.' Reid shifted his gaze. 'Furthermore, I'm a little confused why you, Mr. Bolitar, are here.'

'He's my representative,' Claire said.

'I understand that. But that doesn't give him much standing in terms of talking to a student – or, for that matter, a teacher. I can't make Mr. Davis talk to you either, but I can at least bring him into this office. He's an adult. I can't do that with Randy Wolf.'

They started down the corridor to Aimee's locker.

'There is one more thing,' Amory Reid said.

'What's that?'

'I'm not sure it relates, but Aimee got into a bit of trouble recently.'

They stopped. Claire said, 'How?'

'She was caught in the guidance office, using a computer.'

'I don't understand.'

'Neither did we. One of the guidance counselors found her in there. She was printing out a transcript. Turns out it was just her own.'

Myron thought about that. 'Aren't those computers password-protected?'

'They are.'

'So how did she get in?'

Reid spoke a little too carefully. 'We're not sure. But the theory is, someone in the administration made an error.'

'An error how?'

'Someone may have forgotten to sign out.'

'In other words, they were still logged on so she could gain access?'

'It's a theory, yes.'

Pretty dumb one, Myron thought.

'Why wasn't I informed?' Claire asked.

'It wasn't really that big a deal.'

'Breaking into school transcripts isn't a big deal?'

'She was printing out her own. Aimee, as you know, was an excellent student. She has never gotten in trouble before. We decided to let her go with a stern warning.'

And save yourself some embarrassment, Myron thought. It wouldn't pay to let it out that a student had managed to break into the school computer system. More sweeping under the rug.

They arrived at the locker. Amory Reid used his master key to unlock it. When he opened the door, they all stood back for a moment. Myron was the first to step forward. Aimee's locker was frighteningly personal. Photographs similar to the ones he'd seen in her room adorned the metallic surface. Again no Randy. There were images of her favorite guitar players. On one hanger was a black Green Day American Idiot tour T-shirt; on the other, a New York Liberty sweatshirt. Aimee's textbooks were piled on the bottom, covered in protective sleeves. There were hair ties on the top shelf, a brush, a mirror. Claire touched them tenderly.

But there was nothing in here that seemed to help. No smoking gun, no giant sign reading THIS WAY TO FINDING AIMEE.

Myron felt lost and empty, and staring into the locker, at something so Aimee

– it just made her absence that much more obscene.

The mood was broken when Reid's mobile phone buzzed. He picked it up, listened for a moment, and then he hung up.

'I found someone to cover Mr. Davis's class. He's waiting for you in the office.'

37

Drew Van Dyne was thinking about Aimee and trying to figure out his next step when he arrived at Planet Music. Whenever he did that, whenever he got too confused by life and the poor choices he'd often made, Van Dyne either self-medicated or, as he was doing now, he turned to music.

The iPod ear buds were jammed deep into the canals. He was listening to Alejandro Escovedo's 'Gravity,' enjoying the sound, trying to put together how Escovedo had written the song. That was what Van Dyne liked to do. He'd tear a song down in the best way possible. He'd come up with a theory about the origin, how the idea had come, the first bit of inspiration. Was that first seed a guitar riff, the chorus, a specific stanza or lyric? Had the writer been heartbroken or sad or filled with joy – and why specifically had he been feeling that way? And where, after that first step, did he go with the song? Van Dyne could see the songwriter at the piano or strumming the guitar, taking notes, altering it, tweaking it, whatever.

Bliss, man. Pure, simple bliss. Figuring out a song. Even if. Even if there was always a small voice, deep in the background, saying, 'It should have been you, Drew.'

You forget about the wife who looks at you like you're a dog turd and now wants a divorce. You forget about your father, who abandoned you when you were still a kid. You forget about your mother, who tries now to make up for the fact that she didn't give a rat's ass for too many years. You forget the mind-numbing, regular-Joe teaching job you hate. You forget that the job is no longer something you're doing while waiting for your big break. You forget that your big break, when you're honest with yourself, will never come. You forget that you're thirty-six years old and that no matter how hard you try to kill it, your damn dream will not die – no, that would be too easy. Instead the dream stays and taunts and lets you know that it will never, ever, come true.

You escape into the music.

What the hell should he do now?

That was what Drew Van Dyne was thinking as he walked past the Bedroom Rendezvous. He saw one of the salesgirls whisper to another. Maybe they were talking about him, but he didn't much care. He entered Planet Music, a place he both loved and loathed. He loved being surrounded by music. He loathed being reminded that none of it was his.

Jordy Deck, a younger, less talented version of himself, was behind the counter. Van Dyne could see from the young kid's face that something was wrong.

'What?'

'A big dude,' the kid said. 'He came in here looking for you.'

'What was his name?'

The kid shrugged.

'What did he want?'

'He was asking about Aimee.'

A lump of fear hardened in his chest. 'What did you tell him?'

'That she comes in here a lot, but I think he already knew that. No big deal.'

Drew Van Dyne stepped closer. 'Describe this guy.'

He did. Van Dyne thought about the warning call he'd received earlier today. It sounded like Myron Bolitar.

'Oh, one other thing,' the kid said.

'What?'

'When he left, I think he went to Bedroom Rendezvous.'

Claire and Myron decided to let Myron talk to Mr. Davis alone.

'Aimee Biel was one of my most gifted students,' Harry Davis said.

Davis was pale and shaking and didn't have the same confident stride Myron had seen just that morning.

'Was?' Myron said.

'Pardon me?'

'You said "was." "Was one of my most gifted students."'

His eyes went wide. 'She isn't in my class anymore.'

'I see.'

'That's all I meant.'

'Right,' Myron said, trying to keep him on the defensive. 'When exactly was she your student?'

'Last year.'

'Great.' Enough with the prelims. Straight for the knockout punch: 'So if Aimee wasn't your student anymore, what was she doing at your house Saturday night?'

Beads of sweat popped up on his forehead like plastic gophers in one of those arcade games. 'What makes you think she was?'

'I dropped her off there.'

'That's not possible.'

Myron sighed and crossed his legs. 'There are two ways to play this, Mr. D. I can get the principal in here or you can tell me what you know.'

Silence.

'Why were you talking to Randy Wolf this morning?'

'He's also a student of mine.'

'Is or was?'

'Is. I teach sophomores, juniors, and seniors.'

'I understand that the students here have voted you Teacher of the Year the past four years.'

He said nothing.

Myron said, 'I went here.'

'Yes, I know.' There was a small smile on his lips. 'It would be hard to miss the lingering presence of the legendary Myron Bolitar.'

'My point is, I know what an accomplishment winning Teacher of the Year is. To be that popular with your students.'

Davis liked the compliment. 'Did you have a favorite teacher?' he asked.

'Mrs. Friedman. Modern European History.'

'She was here when I started.' He smiled. 'I really liked her.'

'That's sweet, Mr. D, really, but there's a girl missing.'

'I don't know anything about it.'

'Yeah, you do.'

Harry Davis looked down.

'Mr. D?'

He didn't look up.

'I don't know what's going on, but it's all coming apart now. All of it. You know that, I think. Your life was one thing before we had this chat. It's another thing now. I don't want to sound melodramatic, but I won't let go until I find out everything. No matter how bad it is. No matter how many people are hurt.'

'I don't know anything,' he said. 'Aimee has never been to my house.'

If asked right then, Myron would have said that he wasn't all that mad. In hindsight, that was the problem: a lack of warning. He had been talking in a measured voice. The threat had been there, sure, but it wasn't even worth checking. If he had felt it coming, he would have been able to prepare himself. But the fury just flooded in, snapping him into action.

Myron moved fast. He grabbed Davis from behind the neck, squeezed the pressure points near the base of the shoulders, and pulled him toward the window. Davis let out a little cry as Myron pushed his face hard against the one-way glass.

'Look out there, Mr. D.'

In the waiting area Claire sat upright. Her eyes were closed. She thought that no one was watching. Tears ran down her cheeks.

Myron pushed harder.

'Ow!'

'You see that, Mr. D?'

'Let go of me!'

Damn. The fury spread, diffused. Reason bled back in. As with Jake Wolf, Myron scolded his loss of temper and released his grip. Davis stood back and rubbed the back of his neck. His face was scarlet now.

'You come anywhere near me,' Davis said, 'and I'll sue you. Do you understand?'

Myron shook his head.

'What?'

'You're done, Mr. D. You just don't know it yet.'

38

Drew Van Dyne headed back to Livingston High School. How the hell had Myron Bolitar connected him to this mess?

He was in full panic mode now. He had assumed that Harry Davis, Mr. Friggin' Dedicated Teacher, wouldn't say anything. That would have been better, would have left Van Dyne to handle whatever arose. But now, somehow, Bolitar had ended up at Planet Music. He had been asking about Aimee.

Someone had talked.

As he pulled up to the school, he saw Harry Davis burst out the door. Drew Van Dyne was no student of body language, but man, Davis did not look like himself. His fists were clenched, his shoulders slumped, his feet in a fast shuffle mode. Usually he walked with a smile and a wave, sometimes even whistling. Not today.

Van Dyne drove through the lot, pulling the car into Davis's path. Davis saw him and veered to the right.

'Mr. D?'

'Leave me alone.'

'You and me, we need to have a little chat.'

Van Dyne was out of the car. Davis kept moving.

'You know what will happen if you talk to Bolitar, don't you?'

'I haven't talked,' Davis said, teeth clenched.

'Will you?'

'Get in your car, Drew. Leave me the hell alone.'

Drew Van Dyne shook his head. 'Remember, Mr. D. You got a lot to lose here.'

'As you keep pointing out.'

'More than any of us.'

'No.' Davis had reached his car. He slid into the front seat and before he closed his door he said, 'Aimee has the most to lose, wouldn't you say?'

That made Van Dyne pause. He tilted his head. 'What do you mean by that?'

'Think about it,' Davis said.

He closed the door and drove off. Drew Van Dyne took a deep breath and moved back to his car. Aimee had the most to lose. . . . It got him thinking. He started up the engine and began to pull out when he noticed the school's side door open again.

Aimee's mother came out the very same door that beloved educator Harry Davis had stormed out just minutes ago. And behind her was Myron Bolitar.

The voice on the phone, the one that had warned him earlier: *Don't do anything stupid. It's under control.*

It didn't feel under control. It didn't feel that way at all.

Drew Van Dyne reached for the car radio as though he were underwater and it held oxygen. The CD feature was on, the latest from Coldplay. He drove away, letting Chris Martin's gentle voice work on him.

The panic would not leave.

This, he knew, was where he usually made the wrong decision. This is where he usually messed up big-time. He knew that. He knew that he should just back up, think it through. But that was how he lived his life. It was like a car wreck in slow motion. You see what you're heading for. You know there is going to be an ugly collision. You can't stop or get out of the way.

You're powerless.

In the end, Drew Van Dyne made the phone call.

'Hello?'

'We may have a problem,' Van Dyne said.

On the other end of the phone, Drew Van Dyne heard Big Jake Wolf sigh.

'Tell me,' Big Jake said.

Myron dropped Claire off before heading to the Livingston Mall. He hoped to find Drew Van Dyne at Planet Music. No luck. The poncho kid wouldn't talk this time, but Sally Ann said that she'd seen Drew Van Dyne arrive, talk briefly to the poncho kid, and then sprint out. Myron had Van Dyne's home number. He tried it, but there was no answer.

He called Win. 'We need to find this guy.'

'We're spread a little thin right now.'

'Who can we get to watch Van Dyne's house?'

Win said, 'How about Zorra?'

Zorra was a former Mossad spy, an assassin for the Israelis, and a transvestite who wore stiletto heels – literally. Many transvestites are lovely. Zorra was not one of them.

'I'm not sure she'll blend into the suburbs, are you?'

'Zorra knows how to blend.'

'Fine, whatever you think.'

'Where are you headed?'

'Chang's Dry Cleaning. I need to talk to Roger.'

'I'll call Zorra.'

Business was brisk at Chang's. Maxine saw Myron enter and gestured with her head for him to come forward. Myron moved ahead of the line and followed her into the back. The smell of chemicals and lint was cloying. It felt like dust particles were clinging to his lungs. He was relieved when she opened the back door.

Roger sat on a crate in the alley. His head was down. Maxine folded her arms and said, 'Roger, do you have something to say to Mr. Bolitar?'

Roger was a skinny kid. His arms were reeds with absolutely no definition. He did not look up as she spoke.

'I'm sorry I made those phone calls,' he said.

It was like he was a kid who'd broken a neighbor's window with an errant baseball and his mother had dragged him across the street to apologize. Myron did not need this. He turned to Maxine. 'I want to talk to him alone.'

'I can't let you do that.'

'Then I go to the police.'

First Joan Rochester, now Maxine Chang – Myron was getting damn good at threatening terrified mothers. Maybe he'd start slapping them around too, really feel like a big man.

But Myron did not blink. Maxine Chang did. 'I will be right inside.'

'Thank you.'

The alley reeked, as all alleys do, of past garbage and dried urine. Myron waited for Roger to look up at him. Roger didn't.

'You didn't just call me,' Myron said. 'You called Aimee Biel, right?'

He nodded, still not looking up.

'Why?'

'I was calling her back.'

Myron made a skeptical face. Since the kid's head was still down, the effort was a bit of a waste. 'Look at me, Roger.'

He slowly raised his eyes.

'Are you telling me that Aimee Biel called you first?'

'I saw her in school. She said we needed to talk.'

'About what?'

He shrugged. 'She just said we needed to talk.'

'So why didn't you?'

'Why didn't we what?'

'Talk. Right then and there.'

'We were in the hall. There were people all around. She wanted to talk privately.'

'I see. So you called her?'

'Yes.'

'And what did she say?'

'It was weird. She wanted to know about my grades and extra-curricular activities. It was more like she wanted to confirm them. I mean, we know each other a little. And everyone talks. So she already knew most of that stuff.'

'That's it?'

'We only talked for, like, two minutes. She said she had to go. But she also said she was sorry.'

'About?'

'About my not making Duke.' He put his head down again.

'You got a lot of anger stored up, Roger.'

'You don't understand.'

'Tell me then.'

'Forget it.'

'I wish I could, but see, you called me.'

Roger Chang studied the alley as though he'd never really seen it before. His nose twitched, and his face twisted in disgust. Finally he found Myron's face. 'I'm always the Asian geek, you know? I was born in this country. I'm not an immigrant. When I talk, half the time people expect me to sound like an old Charlie Chan movie. And in this town, if you don't have money or you're not good at sports . . . I see my mother sacrifice. I see how hard she works. And I think to myself: If I can just stick it out. If I can just work hard in high school, not worry about all that stuff I'm missing, just work hard, make the sacrifice, it will all be okay. I'll be able to move out of here. I don't know why I focused on Duke. But I did. It was, like, my one goal. Once I made it, I could relax a little. I'd be away from this store. . . .'

His voice drifted off.

'I wish you'd have said something to me,' Myron said.

'I'm not good at asking for help.'

Myron wanted to tell him he should do more than that, maybe get some therapy to deal with the anger, but he hadn't walked a mile in the kid's shoes. He didn't have the time either.

'Are you going to report me?' Roger asked.

'No.' Then: 'You could still get in on wait-list.'

'They've already cleared it.'

'Oh,' Myron said. 'Look, I know it seems like life and death now, but what school you make isn't that important. I bet you'll love Rutgers.'

'Yeah, sure.'

He didn't sound convinced. Part of Myron was angry, but another part – a growing part – remembered Maxine's accusation. There was a chance, a decent chance, that by helping Aimee, Myron had destroyed this young man's dream. He couldn't just walk away from that, could he?

'If you want to transfer after a year,' Myron said, 'I'll write a letter.'

He waited for Roger to react. He didn't. So Myron left him alone in the stench of the alley behind his mother's dry cleaning store.

39

Myron was on his way to meet up with Joan Rochester – she was afraid to be home when her daughter called in case her husband was around – when his mobile phone rang. He checked the caller ID and his heart skipped a beat when he saw the name ali wilder pop up.

'Hey,' he said.

'Hey.'

Silence.

'I'm sorry about before,' Ali said.

'Don't apologize.'

'No, I sounded hysterical. I know what you were trying to do with the girls.'

'I didn't want to get Erin involved.'

'It's all right. Maybe I should be concerned or whatever, but I just really want to see you.'

'Me too.'

'Come over?'

'I can't right now.'

'Oh.'

'And I'll probably be working on this until late.'

'Myron?'

'Yes.'

'I don't care how late.'

He smiled.

'Whatever the time, come by,' Ali said. 'I'll be waiting. And if I fall asleep, throw pebbles at my window and wake me up. Okay?'

'Okay.'

'Be careful.'

'Ali?'

'Yes?'

'I love you.'

There was a little intake of air. Then, with a little song in the voice: 'I love you too, Myron.'

And suddenly, it was as if Jessica were a wisp of smoke.

Dominick Rochester's office was a depot for school buses.

Outside his window was a plethora of yellow. This place was his cover. School buses could do wonders. If you transport kids in the seats, you could pretty much transport anything else in the undercarriage. Cops might stop and search a truck.

712

They never do that with a school bus.

The phone rang. Rochester picked it up and said, 'Hello?'

'You wanted me to watch your house?'

He did. Joan was drinking more than ever. It could have been from Katie's disappearance, but Dominick was no longer so sure. So he had one of his guys keep an eye. Just in case.

'Yeah, so?'

'Earlier today some guy stopped by to talk to your wife.'

'Earlier today?'

'Right.'

'How much earlier?'

'Couple of hours maybe.'

'Why didn't you call then?'

'Didn't think much about it, I guess. I mean, I wrote it down. But I thought you only wanted me to call you if it was important.'

'What does he look like?'

'His name is Myron Bolitar. I recognized him. He used to play ball.'

Dominick pulled the receiver closer, pushing it against his ear as though he could travel through it. 'How long did he stay?'

'Fifteen minutes.'

'Just the two of them?'

'Yeah. Oh, don't worry, Mr. Rochester. I watched them. They stayed downstairs, if that's what you're wondering. There was no . . .' He stopped, not sure how to put it.

Dominick almost laughed. This dopey guy thought he was having his wife watched in case she was sleeping around. Man, that was rich. But now he wondered: Why had Bolitar come by and stayed so long?

And what had Joan told him?

'Anything else?'

'Well, that's the thing, Mr. Rochester.'

'What's the thing?'

'There is something else. See, I wrote down about Bolitar's visit, but since I could see where he was, I didn't worry much, you know?'

'And now?'

'Well, I'm following Mrs. Rochester. She just drove to some park in town here. Riker Hill. You know it?'

'My kids went to elementary school there.'

'Good, okay. She's sitting on a bench. But she's not alone. See, your wife is sitting there with that same guy. With Myron Bolitar.'

Silence.

'Mr. Rochester?'

'Get a man on Bolitar too. I want him followed. I want them both followed.'

During the Cold War, the Riker Hill Art Park, located right smack in the bosom of suburbia, had been a military control base for air-defense missiles. The army called it Nike Battery Missile Site NY-80. For real. From 1954 until the end of the Nike air defense system in 1974, the site was operational for both Hercules and Ajax missiles. Many of the U.S. Army's original buildings and barracks now serve as studios where painting, sculpture, and crafts flourish in a communal setting.

Years ago, Myron had found this all somewhat poignant and oddly comforting – the war relic now housing artists – but the world was different now. In the eighties and nineties, it had all been cute and quaint. Now this 'progress' felt like phony symbolism.

Near the old military radar tower, Myron sat on the bench with Joan Rochester. They hadn't done more than nod at each other. They were waiting. Joan Rochester cradled her mobile phone as if it were an injured animal. Myron checked his watch. Any minute now, Katie Rochester was supposed to call her mother.

Joan Rochester looked off. 'You're wondering why I stay with him.'

In truth, he wasn't. First off, awful as this situation was, he was still feeling a little giddy from his phone call with Ali. He knew that was selfish, but this was the first time in seven years he had told a woman that he loved her. He was trying to push all that from his mind, trying to focus on the task at hand, but he couldn't help feeling a little high from her response.

Second – and maybe more relevant – Myron had long ago stopped trying to figure out relationships. He had read about battered woman syndrome and perhaps that was at play here and this was a cry for help. But for some reason, in this particular case, he didn't care enough to reach out and answer that call.

'I've been with Dom a long time. A very long time.'

Joan Rochester went quiet. After a few more seconds, she opened her mouth to say more, but the phone in her hand vibrated. She looked down at it as though it had suddenly materialized in her hand. It vibrated again and then it rang.

'Answer it,' Myron said.

Joan Rochester nodded and hit the green button. She brought the phone to her ear and said, 'Hello?'

Myron leaned close to her. He could hear a voice on the other end of the line – sounded young, sounded female – but he couldn't make out any of the words.

'Oh, honey,' Joan Rochester said, her face easing from the sound of her daughter's voice. 'I'm glad you're safe. Yes. Yes, right. Listen to me a second, okay? This is very important.'

More talking from the other end.

'I have someone here with me – '

Animated talk from the other end.

'Please, Katie, just listen. His name is Myron Bolitar. He's from Livingston. He means you no harm. How did he find . . . it's complicated. . . . No, of course I didn't say anything. He got phone records or something, I'm not really sure, but he said he would tell Daddy – '

Very animated talk now.

'No, no, he hasn't done that yet. He just needs to talk to you for a minute. I think you should listen. He says it's about the other missing girl, Aimee Biel. He's looking for her. . . . I know, I know, I told him that. Just . . . hold on, okay? Here he is.'

Joan Rochester began to hand him the phone. Myron reached out and snatched it from her, afraid of losing this tenuous connection. He strapped on his calmest voice and said, 'Hello, Katie. My name is Myron.'

He sounded like a night host on NPR.

Katie, however, was a tad more hysterical. 'What do you want with me?'

'I just have a few questions.'

'I don't know anything about Aimee Biel.'

'If you could just tell me – '

'You're tracing this, aren't you?' Her voice was cracking with hysteria. 'For my dad. You're keeping me on the line so you can trace the call!'

Myron was about to launch into a Berruti-type explanation of how traces didn't really work that way, but Katie never gave him the chance.

'Just leave us alone!'

And then she hung up.

Like another dopey TV cliché, Myron said, 'Hello? Hello?' when he knew that Katie Rochester had hung up and was gone.

They sat in silence for a minute or two. Then Myron slowly handed her back the phone.

'I'm sorry,' Joan Rochester said.

Myron nodded.

'I tried.'

'I know.'

She stood. 'Are you going to tell Dom?'

'No,' Myron said.

'Thank you.'

He nodded again. She walked away. Myron stood and headed in the opposite direction. He took out his cell phone and hit the speed-dial number one slot. Win answered it.

'Articulate.'

'Was it Katie Rochester?'

He had expected something like this – Katie not cooperating. So Myron had prepared. Win was on the scene in Manhattan, ready to follow. It was, in fact, better. She would head back to wherever she was hiding. Win would tag along and learn all.

'Looked like her,' Win said. 'She was with a dark-haired paramour.'

'And now?'

'After hanging up, she and said paramour began heading downtown by foot. By the way, the paramour is carrying a firearm in a shoulder holster.'

That wasn't good. 'You're on them?'

'I'll pretend you didn't ask me that.'

'I'm on my way.'

40

Joan Rochester took a pull from the flask she kept under the car seat. She was in her driveway now. She could have waited until she got inside. But she didn't. She was in a daze, had been in a daze for so long that she no longer remembered a time when she really felt truly clear-headed. Didn't matter. You get used to it. You get so used to it that it becomes normal, this daze, and it would be the clear head that would throw her out of whack.

She stayed in her car and stared at her house. She looked at it as though for the first time. This was where she lived. It sounded so simple, but there it was. This is where she was spending her life. It was unremarkable. It felt impersonal. She lived here. She had helped choose it. And now, as she looked at it, she wondered why.

Joan closed her eyes and tried to imagine something different. How had she gotten here? You don't just slip, she realized. Change was never dramatic. It was small shifts, so gradual that it becomes imperceptible to the human eye. That was how it had happened to Joan Delnuto Rochester, the prettiest girl at Bloomfield High.

You fall in love with a man because he is everything your father isn't. He is strong and tough and you like that. He sweeps you off your feet. You don't even realize how much he takes over your life, how you start to become merely an extension of him, rather than a separate entity or, as you dream, one grander entity, two becoming one in love, like out of a romance novel. You acquiesce on small things, then large things, then everything. Your laugh starts to quiet before disappearing altogether. Your smile dims until it is only a facsimile of joy, something you apply like mascara.

But when had it turned the dark corner?

She couldn't find a spot on the time line. She thought back, but she couldn't locate a moment when she could have changed things. It was inevitable, she supposed, from the day they met. There wasn't a time when she could have stood up to him. There wasn't a battle she could have waged and won that would have altered anything.

If she could go back in time, would she walk away the first time he asked her out? Would she have said no then? Taken up with another boyfriend, like that nice Mike Braun, who lived in Parsippany now? The answer would probably be no. Her children wouldn't have been born. Children, of course, change everything. You can't wish it all never happened, because that would be the ultimate betrayal: How could you live with yourself if you wished your children never existed?

She took another swig.

The truth was, Joan Rochester wished her husband dead. She dreamed about it. Because it was her only escape. Forget that nonsense about abused women standing up to their man. It would be suicide. She could never leave him. He would find her and beat her and lock her up. He would do lord-knows-what to their children. He would make her pay.

Joan sometimes fantasized about packing up the children and finding one of those battered-women shelters in the city. But then what? She dreamed about turning state's evidence against Dom – she certainly had the knowledge – but even Witness Protection wouldn't do the trick. He'd find them. Somehow.

He was that kind of man.

She slipped out of her car. There was a wobble in her step, but again that had become almost the norm. Joan Rochester headed to her front door. She slipped the key in and stepped inside. She turned around to close it behind her. When she turned back around, Dominick stood in front of her.

Joan Rochester put her hand to her heart. 'You startled me.'

He stepped toward her. For a moment she thought that he wanted to embrace her. But that wasn't it. He bent low at the knees. His right hand turned into a fist. He swiveled into the roundhouse blow, using his hips for power. The knuckles slammed into her kidney.

Joan's mouth opened in a silent scream. Her knees gave way. She fell to the floor. Dominick grabbed her by the hair. He lifted her back up and readied the fist. He smashed it into her back again, harder this time.

She slid to the ground like a slit bag of sand.

'You're going to tell me where Katie is,' Dominick said.

And then he hit her again.

Myron was in his car, talking on the phone to Wheat Manson, his former Duke teammate who now worked in the admissions office as assistant dean, when he realized yet again that he was being followed.

Wheat Manson had been a speedy point guard from the nasty streets of Atlanta. He had loved his years in Durham, North Carolina, and had never gone back. The two old friends started off exchanging quick pleasantries before Myron got to the point.

'I need to ask you something a little weird,' Myron said.

'Go ahead.'

'Don't get offended.'

'Then don't ask me anything offensive,' Wheat said.

'Did Aimee Biel get in because of me?'

Wheat groaned. 'Oh no, you did *not* just ask me that.'

'I need to know.'

'Oh no, you did *not* just ask me that.'

'Look, forget that for a second. I need you to fax me two transcripts. One for Aimee Biel. And one for Roger Chang.'

'Who?'

'He's another student from Livingston High.'

'Let me guess. Roger didn't get accepted.'

'He had a better ranking, better SAT scores – '

'Myron?'

'What?'

717

'We are not going there. Do you understand me? It's confidential. I will not send you transcripts. I will not discuss candidates. I will remind you that acceptance is not a matter of scores or tests, that there are intangibles. As two guys who got in based much more on our ability to put a sphere through a metallic ring than rankings and test scores, we should understand that better than anyone. And now, only slightly offended, I will say good-bye.'

'Wait, hold up a second.'

'I'm not faxing you transcripts.'

'You don't have to. I'm going to tell you something about both candidates. I just want you to look it up on the computer and make sure what I'm saying is true.'

'What the hell are you talking about?'

'Just trust me here, Wheat. I'm not asking for information. I'm asking you to confirm something.'

Wheat sighed. 'I'm not in the office right now.'

'Do it when you can.'

'Tell me what you want me to confirm.'

Myron told him. And as he did, he realized that the same car had been with him since he left Riker Hill. 'Will you do it?'

'You're a pain in the ass, you know that?'

'Always was,' Myron said.

'Yeah, but you used to have a sweet jumper from the top of the key. Now what do you got?'

'Raw animal magnetism and supernatural charisma?'

'I'm going to hang up now.'

He did. Myron pulled the hands-free from his ear. The car was still behind him, maybe two hundred feet back.

What was up with all the car tails today? In the old days, a suitor would send flowers or candy. Myron pined for a brief moment, but now was hardly the time. The car had been on him since he left Riker Hill. That meant it was probably one of Dominick Rochester's goons again. He thought about that. If Rochester had sent a man to follow Myron, he'd probably at the very least known or seen that Myron was with his wife. Myron debated calling Joan Rochester, letting her know, but decided against it. As Joan had pointed out, she'd been with him a long time. She'd know how to handle it.

He was on Northfield Avenue heading to New York City. He didn't have time for this, but he needed to get rid of this tail as quickly as possible. In the movies, this would call for a car chase or a swift U-turn of some sort. That didn't really play in real life, especially when you need to get to a place in a hurry and don't want to attract the cops.

Still, there were ways.

The music store teacher, Drew Van Dyne, lived in West Orange, not far from here. Zorra should be in place now. Myron picked up his cell phone and called. Zorra picked up on the first ring.

'Hello, dreamboat,' Zorra said.

'I assume there's been no activity at the Van Dyne house.'

'You assume correctly, dreamboat. Zorra just sits and sits. So boring this, for Zorra.'

Zorra always referred to herself in the third person. She had a deep voice, a thick accent, and lots of mouth phlegm. It was not a pleasant sound.

'I have a car following me,' Myron said.

'And Zorra can help?'

'Oh yes,' Myron said. 'Zorra can definitely help.'

Myron explained his plan – his frighteningly simple plan. Zorra laughed and started coughing.

'So Zorra like?' Myron asked, falling, as he often did when speaking to her, into Zorra-talk.

'Zorra like. Zorra like very much.'

Since it would take a few minutes to set up, Myron took some unnecessary turns. Two minutes later, Myron took the right on Pleasant Valley Way. Up ahead, he saw Zorra standing by the pizzeria. She wore her '30s blond wig and smoked a cigarette in a holder and looked just like Veronica Lake after a real bad bender, if Veronica Lake was six feet tall and had a Homer Simpson five o'clock shadow and was really, really ugly.

Zorra winked as Myron passed and raised her foot just a little bit. Myron knew what was in that heel. The first time they met, she had sliced his chest with the hidden 'stiletto' blade. In the end, Win had spared Zorra's life – something that surprised the heck out of Myron. Now they were all buddies. Esperanza compared it to her days in the ring when a famed bad-guy wrestler would all of a sudden turn good.

Myron used the left-turn signal and pulled to the side of the road, two blocks ahead of Zorra. He rolled down his window so he could hear. Zorra stood near an open parking spot. It was natural. The car following Myron's pulled into the spot to see where Myron was headed. Of course, he could have stopped anywhere on the street. Zorra had been ready for that.

The rest was, as already noted, frighteningly simple. Zorra strolled over to the back of the car. She had been wearing high heels for the past fifteen years, but she still walked like a newborn colt on bad acid.

Myron watched the scene in his rearview mirror.

Zorra unsheathed the dagger in her stiletto heel. She raised her leg and stomped on the tire. Myron heard the whoosh of air. She quickly circled to the other back tire and did the same thing. Then Zorra did something that was not part of the plan.

She waited to see if the driver would get out and accost her.

'No,' Myron whispered to himself. 'Just go.'

He had been clear. Stomp the tires and run. Don't get into a fight. Zorra was deadly. If the guy got out of his car – probably some macho goon who was used to breaking heads – Zorra would slice him into pizza topping. Forget the morals for a moment. They didn't need that kind of police attention.

The goon driving the car yelled, 'Hey! What the – ?' and started getting out of the car.

Myron turned around and stuck his head out the window. Zorra had the smile. She bent her knees a little. Myron called out. Zorra looked up and met Myron's eye. Myron could see the anticipation, the itch to strike. He shook his head as firmly as he knew how.

Another second passed. The goon slammed his car door shut. 'You dumb bitch!'

Myron kept shaking his head, more urgently now. The goon took a step. Myron held Zorra's gaze. Zorra reluctantly nodded.

And then she ran away.

'Hey!' The goon gave chase. 'Stop!'

Myron started up his car. The goon looked back now, unsure what to do, and then he made a decision that probably saved his life.

He ran back to his car.

But with slashed back tires, he wouldn't go anywhere.

Myron pulled back onto the road, on his way to his encounter with the missing Katie Rochester.

41

Drew Van Dyne sat in Big Jake Wolf's family room and tried to plan his next move. Jake had given him a Corona Light. Drew frowned. A real Corona, okay, but light Mexican beer? Why not just pass out piss water? Drew sipped it anyway.

This room reeked of Big Jake. There was a deer head hanging above the fireplace. Golf and tennis trophies lined the mantel. The rug was some sort of bear skin. The TV was huge, at least seventy inches. There were tiny expensive speakers everywhere. Something classical drifted out from the digital player. A carnival popcorn machine with flashing lights sat in the corner. There were ugly gold statues and ferns. Everything had been selected not based on fashion or function, but by what would appear most ostentatious and overpriced.

On the side table was a picture of Jake Wolf's hot wife. Drew picked it up and shook his head. In the photograph, Lorraine Wolf wore a bikini. Another of Jake's trophies, he guessed. A picture of your own wife in a bikini on a side table in the family room – who the hell does that?

'I spoke to Harry Davis,' Wolf said. He had a Corona Light too. There was a wedge of lime jammed into the top. Van Dyne rule of alcohol consumption: If a beer needs a fruit topping, choose another beer. 'He's not going to talk.'

Drew said nothing.

'You don't believe it?'

Drew shrugged, drank his beer.

'He has the most to lose here.'

'You think?'

'You don't?'

'I reminded Harry of that. You know what he said?'

Jake shrugged.

'He told me that maybe Aimee Biel had the most to lose.' Drew put down his beer, intentionally missing the coaster. 'What do you think?'

Big Jake pointed his beefy finger at Drew. 'Who the hell's fault would that be?'

Silence.

Jake walked over to the window. He gestured with his chin at the house next door. 'You see that place over there?'

'What about it?'

'It's a friggin' castle.'

'You're not doing too badly here, Jake.'

A small smile played on his lip. 'Not like that.'

Drew would point out that it's all relative, that he, Drew Van Dyne, lived alone in a crap-hole that was smaller than Wolf's garage, but why bother? Drew could also point out that he didn't have a tennis court or three cars or gold statues or a theater room or even really a wife since the separation, much less one with a hot enough body to model in bikinis.

'He's a big-time lawyer,' Jake droned on. 'Went to Yale and never lets anyone forget it. He has a Yale decal on his car window. He wears Yale T-shirts when he takes his daily jog. He hosts Yale parties. He interviews Yale applicants in his big castle. His son is a dope, but guess what school still accepted him?'

Drew Van Dyne shifted in the chair.

'The world is not a level playing field, Drew. You need an in. Or you have to make one. You, for example, wanted to be a big rock star. The guys who make it – who sell a zillion CDs and fill up outdoor arenas – do you think they're more talented than you? No. The big difference, maybe the only difference, is that they were willing to take advantage of some situation. They exploited something. And you didn't. Do you know what the world's greatest truism is?'

Drew could see that there was no stopping him. But that was okay. The man was talking. He was revealing things in his own way. Drew was getting the picture now. He had a pretty good idea of where this was heading. 'No, what?'

'Behind every great fortune is a great crime.'

Jake stopped and let that sink in. Drew felt his breathing go a little funny.

'You see someone with beaucoup bucks,' Jake Wolf went on, 'a Rockefeller or Carnegie or someone. Do you want to know the difference between them and us? One of their great-grandpas cheated or stole or killed. He had balls, sure. But he understood that the playing field is never level. You want a break, you make it yourself. Then you peddle that hard-work, nose-to-the-grindstone fiction to the masses.'

Drew Van Dyne remembered the warning call: *Don't do anything stupid. It's under control.*

'This Bolitar guy,' Drew said. 'You already had your cop friends lay into him. He didn't budge.'

'Don't worry about him.'

'That's not much of a comfort, Jake.'

'Well,' Jake said, 'let's just remember whose fault this is.'

'Your son's.'

'Hey!' Again Jake pointed with the beefy finger. 'Keep Randy out of it.'

Drew Van Dyne shrugged. 'You're the one who wanted to place blame.'

'He's going to Dartmouth. That's a done deal. No one, especially not some dumb slut, is going to ruin that.'

Drew took a long deep breath. 'Still. The question is, if Bolitar keeps digging, what is he going to find?'

Jake Wolf looked at him. 'Nothing,' he said.

Drew Van Dyne felt a twinge start in the base of his spine.

'How can you be so sure?'

Wolf said nothing.

'Jake?'

'Don't worry about it. Like I said, my son is on his way to college. He's done with all this.'

'You also said that behind every great fortune is a great crime.'

'So?'

'She means nothing to you, does she, Jake?'

722

'It's not about her. It's about Randy. It's about his future.'

Jake Wolf turned back to the window, to his Ivy League neighbor's castle. Drew gathered his thoughts, reined in his emotions. He looked at this man. He thought about what he had said, what it all meant. He thought again about the warning call.

'Jake?'

'What?'

'Did you know that Aimee Biel was pregnant?'

The room went quiet. The background music was between songs now. When it started up again, the beat had picked up a step, an old ditty from Supertramp. Jake Wolf slowly turned his head and looked back over his shoulder. Drew Van Dyne could see that the news was a surprise.

'That doesn't change anything,' Jake said.

'I think maybe it does.'

'How?'

Drew Van Dyne reached into his shoulder holster. He removed the gun and aimed it at Jake Wolf. 'Take a wild guess.'

42

The storefront was a nail salon called Nail-R-Us in a not-yet-redeveloped section of Queens. The building had that decrepit thing going on, as if leaning against it would cause a wall to collapse. The rust on the fire escape was so thick that tetanus seemed a far greater threat than smoke inhalation. Every window was blocked by either a heavy shade or a plank of wood. The structure was four levels and ran almost the entire length of the block.

Myron said to Win, 'The R on the sign is crossed out.'

'That's intentional.'

'Why?'

Win looked at him, waited. Myron did it in his head. Nail-R-Us had become Nail Us.

'Oh,' Myron said. 'Cute.'

'They have two armed guards stationed at windows,' Win said.

'They must do a mean manicure.'

Win frowned. 'Moreover, the two guards didn't take up position until your Ms. Rochester and her beau returned.'

'They're worried about her father,' Myron said.

'That would be a logical deduction.'

'You know anything about the place?'

'The clientele is below my level of expertise.' Win nodded behind Myron. 'But not hers.'

Myron turned. The setting sun was blocked now as though by an eclipse. Big Cyndi was ambling toward them. She was dressed entirely in white spandex. Very tight white spandex. No undergarments. Tragically, you could tell. On a seventeen-year-old runway model, the spandex jumpsuit would be a fashion risk. On a woman of forty who weighed more than three hundred pounds . . . well, it took guts, lots of them, all of which were on full display, thank you very much. Everything jiggled as she trundled toward them; various body parts seemed to have lives of their own, moving of their own accord, as if dozens of animals were trapped in a white balloon and trying to squirm their way out.

Big Cyndi kissed Win on the cheek. Then she turned and said, 'Hello, Mr. Bolitar.' She hugged him, wrapping her arms around him, a feeling not unlike being wrapped in wet attic insulation.

'Hey, Big Cyndi,' Myron said when she put him down. 'Thanks for getting down here so quick.'

'When you call, Mr. Bolitar, I run.'

Her face remained placid. Myron never knew if Big Cyndi was putting him on or not.

'Do you know this place?' he asked.

'Oh yes.'

She sighed. Elk within a forty-mile radius began to mate. Big Cyndi wore white lipstick like something out of an Elvis documentary. Her makeup had sparkles. Her fingernails were in a color she'd once told him was called Pinot Noir. Back in the day, Big Cyndi had been the bad-guy professional wrestler. She fit the bill. For those who have never watched professional wrestling, it is merely a morality play with good pitted against evil. For years, Big Cyndi had been the evil 'warlordess' named Human Volcano. Then one night, after a particularly grueling match where Big Cyndi had 'injured' the lovely and lithe Esperanza 'Little Pocahontas' Diaz with a chair – 'injured' her so badly that the fake ambulance came in and strapped on the neck brace and all that – an angry mob of fans waited outside the venue.

When Big Cyndi left for the night, the mob attacked.

They might have killed her. The crowd was drunk and fired up and not really into the reality-versus-fiction equation at work here. Big Cyndi tried to run, but there was no escape. She fought hard and well, but there were dozens wanting her blood. Someone hit her with a camera, a cane, a boot. They moved in. Big Cyndi went down. People started stomping her.

Seeing the mayhem, Esperanza tried to intervene. The crowd would have none of it. Even their favorite wrestler could not halt their bloodlust. And then Esperanza did something truly inspired.

She jumped on a car and 'revealed' that Big Cyndi had only been pretending to be a bad guy to gather information. The crowd almost paused. Furthermore, Esperanza announced, Big Cyndi was really Little Pocahontas's long lost sister, Big Chief Mama, a rather lame moniker but hey, she was making this stuff up on the fly. Little Pocahontas and her sister were now reuniting and would become tag-team partners.

The crowd cheered. Then they helped Big Cyndi to her feet.

Big Chief Mama and Little Pocahontas quickly became wrestling's most popular team. The same scenario played out weekly: Esperanza would start every match winning on skill, their opponents would do something illegal like throw sand in her eye or use the dreaded foreign object, the two baddies would team up on poor, helpless Pocahontas while someone distracted Big Chief Mama, they'd beat the sensuous beauty until the strap on Pocahontas's suede bikini ripped, and then Big Chief Mama would give out a war cry and ride in to the rescue.

Massively entertaining.

When she left the ring, Big Cyndi became a bouncer and sometimes stage performer for several lowlife sex clubs. She knew the seedier side of the streets. And that was what they were counting on now.

'So what is this place?' Myron asked.

Big Cyndi put on her totem-pole frown. 'They do a lot of things, Mr. Bolitar. Some drugs, some Internet scamming, but mostly, these are sex clubs.'

'Clubs,' Myron repeated. 'As in the plural?'

Big Cyndi nodded. 'Six or seven different ones probably. Remember a few years ago when Forty-second Street was loaded with sleaze?'

'Yes.'

'Well, when they forced them all out, where do you think the sleaze went?'

Myron looked at the nail salon. 'Here?'

'Here, there, everywhere. You don't kill sleaze, Mr. Bolitar. It just moves to a new host.'

'And this is the new host?'

'One of them. Here, in this very building, they offer specialty clubs catering to an international variety of tastes.'

'When you say "specialty clubs" – ?'

'Let's see. If you care for flaxen-haired women, you go to On Golden Blonde. That's on the second floor, far right. If you're into African-American men, you head up to the third floor and visit a place called – you might like this, Mr. Bolitar – Malcolm Sex.'

Myron looked at Win. Win shrugged.

Big Cyndi continued in her tour guide voice: 'Those with an Asian fetish will enjoy the Joy Suck Club – '

'Yeah,' Myron said, 'I think I get the picture. So how do I get in and find Katie Rochester?'

Big Cyndi thought about that for a moment. 'I can pose as a job applicant.'

'Excuse me?'

Big Cyndi put her enormous fists on her hips. This meant that they were about two yards apart. 'Not all men, Mr. Bolitar, have petite fetishes.'

Myron closed his eyes and rubbed the bridge of his nose. 'Right, okay, maybe. Any other thoughts?'

Win waited patiently. Myron had always thought that Win would be intolerant of Big Cyndi, but years ago, Win surprised him by pointing out what should have been obvious: 'One of our worst and most accepted prejudices is against large women. We never, ever, see past it.' And it was true. Myron had been deeply ashamed when Win pointed that out. So he started treating Big Cyndi as he should – like everyone else. That pissed Big Cyndi off. Once, when Myron smiled at her, she hit him hard on the shoulder – so hard he couldn't lift his arm for two days – and shouted, 'Cut that out!'

'Perhaps you should try a more direct route,' Win said. 'I will stay out here. Keep your cell phone on. You and Big Cyndi try and talk your way in.'

Big Cyndi nodded. 'We can pretend we're a couple looking to try a threesome.'

Myron was about to say something when Big Cyndi said, 'Kidding.'

'I knew that.'

She arched a shiny eyebrow and leaned toward him. The mountain coming to Muhammad. 'But now that I planted that most erotic seed, Mr. Bolitar, you may find performing with a petite difficult.'

'I'll muddle through. Come on.'

Myron stepped through the door first. A black man at the door sporting designer sunglasses told him to halt. He wore an earplug like someone in the Secret Service. He patted Myron down.

'Man,' Myron said, 'all this for a manicure?'

The man took away Myron's cell phone. 'We don't allow pictures,' he said.

'It's not a camera phone.'

The black man grinned. 'You'll get it back on the way out.'

He held the grin until Big Cyndi filled the doorway. Then the grin fled, replaced with something akin to terror. Big Cyndi ducked inside like a giant

726

entering a kid's clubhouse. She stood upright, stretched her arms over her head, and spread her legs apart. The white spandex cried out in agony. Big Cyndi winked at the black man.

'Frisk me, big boy,' she said. 'I'm packing.'

The outfit was tight enough to double as skin. If Big Cyndi was indeed packing, the man didn't want to know where.

'You're okay, miss. Step through.'

Myron thought again about what Win had said, about accepted prejudice. There was something personal in the words, but when Myron had tried to follow up, Win closed down on the subject. Still, about four years ago, Esperanza had wanted Big Cyndi to take on some clients. Outside of Myron and Esperanza, she had been with MB Reps the longest. It sort of made sense. But Myron knew it would be a disaster. And it was. No one felt comfortable with Big Cyndi repping them. They blamed her outlandish clothes, her makeup, her manner of speech (she liked to growl), but even if she got rid of all that, would it have changed anything?

The black man cupped his ear. Someone was talking to him through the earpiece. He suddenly put an arm on Myron's shoulder.

'What can I do for you, sir?'

Myron decided to stick with the direct route. 'I'm looking for a woman named Katie Rochester.'

'There's no one here by that name.'

'No, she's here,' Myron said. 'She walked in that very door twenty minutes ago.'

The black man took a step closer to Myron. 'Are you calling me a liar?'

Myron was tempted to snap his knee into the man's groin, but that wouldn't help. 'Look, we can go through all the macho posturing, but really, what's the point? I know she came in. I know why she's hiding. I mean her no harm. We can play this one of two ways. One, she can talk to me quickly and that's the end of it. I say nothing about her whereabouts. Two, well, I have several men positioned outside. You throw me out the door and I call her father. He brings several more. It all gets ugly. None of us need that. I just want to talk.'

The black man kept still.

'Another thing,' Myron said. 'If she's afraid I work for her father, ask her this: If her father knew she was here, would he be this subtle?'

More hesitation.

Myron spread his arms. 'I'm in your place. I'm unarmed. What damage could I do?'

The man waited another second. Then he said, 'You finished?'

'We might also be interested in a threesome,' Big Cyndi said.

Myron hushed her with a look. She shrugged and kept quiet.

'Wait here.'

The man headed to a steel door. It buzzed. The man opened it and went inside. It took about five minutes. A bald guy with spectacles entered the room. He was nervous. Big Cyndi started giving him the eye. She licked her lips. She cupped what might have been her breasts. Myron shook his head, afraid she'd drop to her knees and pantomime lord-knew-what when the door mercifully opened. The man with the sunglasses poked his head out.

'Come with me,' he said, pointing to Myron. He turned toward Big Cyndi. 'Alone.'

Big Cyndi didn't like it. Myron calmed her with a look and stepped into the other room. The steel door closed behind him. Myron looked around and said, 'Uh-oh.'

There were four of them. Various sizes. Lots of tattoos. Some grinned. Some grimaced. All wore jeans and black T-shirts. None were clean-shaven. Myron tried to figure out who the leader was. In a group fight, most people mistakenly believe you look for the weakest link. Always the wrong move. Besides, if the guys were any good, it didn't matter what you did.

Four against one in a tight space. You were done.

Myron found a man who stood a little in front of the others. He had dark hair and more or less fit the description of Katie Rochester's beau given to him by both Win and Edna Skylar. Myron met his eye and held it.

Then Myron said, 'Are you stupid?'

The dark-haired man frowned, surprised and insulted. "You talking to me?"

'If I say, "Yeah, I'm talking to you," will that be the end of it or will you come back with "You talking to me" again or "You better not be talking to me"? Because, really, neither one of us has the time.'

The dark-haired man smiled. 'You left one option off when you talked to my friend here.'

'What's that?'

'Option three.' He held up three fingers in case Myron didn't know what the word *three* meant. 'We make sure you *can't* tell her father.'

He grinned. The other men grinned.

Myron spread his arms and said, 'How?'

That made the man frown again. 'Huh?'

'How are you going to make sure of that?' Myron looked around. 'You guys are going to jump me – that's the plan? So then what? The only way to shut me up would be to kill me. You willing to go that far? And what about my lovely associate out in the front room? Are you going to kill her too? And what about my other associates' – might as well exaggerate with the plural – 'who are outside? Are you going to kill them too? Or is your plan, what, to beat me up and teach me a lesson? If so, one, I'm not a good learner. Not that way at least. And two, I'm looking at all of you and memorizing your faces, and if you do attack me, you better make sure I'm dead because if not, I'll come after you, at night, when you're sleeping, and I'll tie you down and pour kerosene on your crotch and set it on fire.'

Myron Bolitar, Master of Melodrama. But he kept his eyes steady and looked at their faces carefully, one at a time.

'So,' Myron said, 'is that your option-three plan?'

One of the men shuffled his feet. A good sign. Another sneaked a glance at the third. The dark-haired man had something close to a smile on his face. Someone knocked on the door on the far side of the room. The dark-haired man opened it a crack, talked to someone, closed it, turned back to Myron.

'You're good,' he said to Myron.

Myron kept his mouth shut.

'Come this way.'

He opened the door and swept his hand for Myron to go ahead. Myron stepped through it into a room with red walls. The walls were covered with

728

pornographic pictures and XXX-rated movie posters. There was a black leather couch and two folding chairs and a lamp. And sitting on the couch, looking terrified but unharmed, was none other than Katie Rochester.

43

Edna Skylar had been right, Myron thought. Katie Rochester looked older, more mature somehow. She twiddled a cigarette in her hand, but it remained unlit.

The dark-haired man stuck out his hand. 'I'm Rufus.'

'Myron.'

They shook hands. Rufus sat down on the couch next to Katie. He took the cigarette from her hand.

'Can't smoke in your condition, honey,' Rufus said. Then he put the cigarette between his lips, lit it up, threw his feet up on the coffee table, and let loose a long plume of smoke.

Myron stayed standing.

'How did you find me?' Katie Rochester asked.

'It's not important.'

'That woman who spotted me in the subway. She said something, right?'

Myron did not reply.

'Damn.' Katie shook her head and put a hand on Rufus's thigh. 'We're going to have to find a new place now.'

'What,' Myron said, pointing to a poster of a naked woman with her legs spread, 'and leave all this behind?'

'That's not funny,' Rufus said. 'This is your fault, man.'

'I need to know where Aimee Biel is.'

'I told you on the phone,' she said. 'I don't know.'

'Are you aware that she disappeared too?'

'I didn't disappear. I ran away. My choice.'

'You're pregnant.'

'That's right.'

'So is Aimee Biel.'

'So?'

'So you're both pregnant, both from the same school, both ran away or disappeared – '

'A million pregnant girls run away every year.'

'Do they all use the same ATM machine?'

Katie Rochester sat up. 'What?'

'Before you ran, you went to an ATM machine – '

'I went to a bunch of ATM machines,' she said. 'I needed money to run away.'

'What, Rufus here couldn't spot you?'

Rufus said, 'Go to hell, man.'

'It was my money,' Katie said.

'How far along are you anyhow?'

730

'That's none of your business. None of this is your business.'

'The last ATM machine you visited was at a Citibank on Fifty-second Street.'

'So?'

Katie Rochester sounded younger and more petulant with every response.

'So the last ATM machine Aimee Biel visited before she disappeared was at the same Citibank on Fifty-second Street.'

Now Katie looked genuinely puzzled. It wasn't faked. She hadn't known. She slowly swiveled her head toward Rufus. Her eyes narrowed.

'Hey,' Rufus said. 'Don't look at me.'

'Rufus, did you . . . ?'

'Did I what?' Rufus threw the cigarette to the ground and jumped to his feet. He raised his hand as if about to slap her backhand. Myron slid between them. Rufus stopped, smiled, raised his palms in mock surrender.

'It's okay, baby.'

'What was she talking about?' Myron asked.

'Nothing, it's over.' Rufus looked at her. 'I'm sorry, baby. You know I'd never hit you, right?'

Katie said nothing. Myron tried to read her face. She wasn't cowering, but there was something there, something he'd seen in her mother. Myron lowered himself to her level.

'Do you want me to get you out of here?' he asked.

'What?' Katie's head shot up. 'No, of course not. We love each other.'

Myron looked at her, again trying to read distress. He didn't see any.

'We're having a baby,' she said.

'Why did you look at Rufus like that? When I mentioned the ATM?'

'It was stupid. Forget it.'

'Tell me anyway.'

'I thought . . . but I was wrong.'

'You thought what?'

Rufus put his feet back on the coffee table, crossing them. 'It's okay, baby. Tell him.'

Katie Rochester kept her eyes down. 'It was just, like, a reaction, you know?'

'Reaction to what?'

'Rufus was with me. That's all. It was his idea to use that last ATM. He thought it being midtown and all, it would be hard to trace to any spot, especially down here.'

Rufus arched an eyebrow, proud of his ingenuity.

'But see, Rufus has lots of girls working for him. And if they have money I figure he takes them to an ATM and gets them to clear out the cash. He has one of the clubs in here. A place called Barely Legal. It's for men who want girls that are — '

'I think I can put together what they want. Go on.'

'Legal,' Rufus said, raising a finger. 'The name is Barely *Legal*. The key word is *legal*. All the girls are over eighteen.'

'I'm sure your mother must be the envy of her book group, Rufus.' Myron turned back to Katie. 'So you thought . . . ?'

'I didn't think. Like I said, I just reacted.'

Rufus put his feet down and sat forward. 'She thought maybe this Aimee was one of my girls. She's not. Look, that's the lie I sell. People think these girls run

731

away from their farms or their homes in the burbs and come to the big city to become, I don't know, actresses or dancers or whatever and when they fail, they end up turning tricks. I sell that fantasy. I want the guys to think they're getting some farmer's daughter, if that gets his rocks off. But the fact is, these are just street junkies. The luckier ones work the flicks' – he pointed to a movie poster – 'and the uglier ones work the rooms. That simple.'

'So you don't recruit at high schools?'

Rufus laughed. 'I wish. You want to know where I recruit?'

Myron waited.

'At AA meetings. Or rehab centers. Those places are like casting couches, you know what I'm saying? I sit in the back and drink that badass coffee and listen. Then I talk them up during the breaks and give them a card and wait until they fall off the wagon. They always do. And there I am, ready to scoop them up.'

Myron looked at Katie. 'Wow, he's terrific.'

'You don't know the real him,' she said.

'Yeah, I'm sure he's deep.' Myron felt the itch in his fingers again, but he swallowed it down. 'So how did you two meet?'

Rufus shook his head. 'It ain't like that.'

'We're in love,' Katie said. 'He knows my dad through business. He came to the house and once we saw each other . . .' She smiled and looked pretty and young and happy and dumb.

'Love at first sight,' Rufus said.

Myron just looked at him.

'What,' he said, 'you don't think it's possible?'

'No, Rufus, you seem like quite the catch.'

Rufus shook his head. 'This here, this is just a job for me. That's all. Katie and that baby, they're my life. You understand?'

Myron still said nothing. He reached into his pocket and pulled out the picture of Aimee Biel. 'Take a look at this, Rufus.'

He did.

'Is she here?'

'Dude, I swear on my unborn child I've never seen this chick before and I don't know where she is.'

'If you're lying – '

'Enough with the threats, okay? What you got there is a missing girl, right? The police want her. Her parents want her. You think I want that trouble?'

'You have a missing girl right here,' Myron said. 'Her father will move heaven and earth to find her. And the police are interested too.'

'But that's different,' Rufus said, and his tone turned into a plea. 'I love her. I'd walk through fire for Katie. Don't you see? But this girl . . . she'd never be worth it. If I had her here, I'd give her back. I don't need that kind of hassle.'

It made sad, pathetic sense.

'Aimee Biel used the same ATM,' Myron said again. 'Do you have any explanation for that?'

They both shook their heads.

'Did you tell anyone?'

Katie said, 'About the ATM machine?'

'Yes.'

'I don't think so.'

Myron kneeled down again. 'Listen to me, Katie. I don't believe in coincidences. There has to be a reason why Aimee Biel went to that ATM. There has to be a connection between you two.'

'I barely knew Aimee. I mean, yeah, we went to the same school, but we never hung out or anything. I'd see her at the mall sometimes, but we wouldn't even say hello. At school she was always with her boyfriend.'

'Randy Wolf.'

'Yeah.'

'Do you know him?'

'Sure. The school's Golden Boy. Rich daddy who always got him out of trouble. Do you know Randy's nickname?'

Myron remembered something from the school parking lot. 'Farmboy, something like that?'

'Pharm, not Farm Boy. It's with a *PH*, not *F*. You know how he got it?'

'No.'

'It's short for *Pharmacist*. Randy is the biggest dealer at Livingston High.' Katie smiled then. 'Wait, you want to know my connection to Aimee Biel? Here's the only one I can come up with: Her boyfriend sold me nickel bags.'

'Hold up.' Myron felt the room begin to spin ever so slowly. 'You said something about his father?'

'Big Jake Wolf. Town hotshot.'

Myron nodded, almost afraid to move now. 'You said something about him getting Randy out of trouble.' His own voice suddenly sounded very far away.

'Just a rumor.'

'Tell me.'

'What do you think? A teacher caught Randy dealing on campus. Reported him to the cops. His dad paid them off, the teacher too, I think. They all chuckled about not wanting to ruin the star quarterback's bright future.'

Myron kept nodding. 'Who was the teacher?'

'Don't know.'

'Heard any rumors?'

'No.'

But Myron thought that maybe he had an idea who it was.

He asked a few more questions. But there was nothing else here. Randy and Big Jake Wolf. It came back to them again. It came back to the teacher/guidance counselor Harry Davis and the musician/teacher/lingerie buyer Drew Van Dyne. It came back to that town, Livingston, and how the young rebelled, and how much pressure there was on all those kids to succeed.

At the end, Myron looked at Rufus. 'Leave us alone for a minute.'

'No way.'

But Katie had some of her poise back. 'It's okay, Rufus.'

He stood. 'I'll be right behind the door,' Rufus said to Myron, 'with my associates. You got me?'

Myron bit back the rejoinder and waited until they were alone. He thought about Dominick Rochester, how he was trying to find his daughter, how maybe he knew that Katie was in a place like this with a man like Rufus and how maybe his overreaction – his desire to find his daughter – was suddenly understandable.

Myron bent close to her ear and whispered, 'I can get you out of here.'

She leaned away and made a face. 'What are you talking about?'

'I know you want to escape your father, but this guy isn't the answer.'

'How do you know what the answer is for me?'

'He runs a brothel, for crying out loud. He almost hit you.'

'Rufus loves me.'

'I can get you out of here.'

'I wouldn't go,' she said. 'I'd rather die than live without Rufus. Is that clear enough for you?'

'Katie . . .'

'Get out.'

Myron rose.

'You know something,' she said. 'Maybe Aimee is more like me than you think.'

'How's that?'

'Maybe she doesn't need rescuing either.'

Or, Myron thought, maybe you both do.

44

Big Cyndi stayed behind and flashed Aimee's photograph around the neighborhood, just in case. Those employed in these illicit fields wouldn't talk to cops or Myron, but they'd talk to Big Cyndi. She had her gifts.

Myron and Win headed back to their cars.

'Are you coming back to the apartment?' Win asked.

Myron shook his head. 'I got more to do.'

'I'll relieve Zorra.'

'Thanks.' Then looking back at the warehouse, Myron added: 'I don't like leaving her here.'

'Katie Rochester is an adult.'

'She's eighteen.'

'Exactly.'

'So what are you saying? You turn eighteen, you're on your own? We only rescue adults?'

'No,' Win said. 'We rescue those we can. We rescue those in trouble. We rescue those who ask and need our help. We do not – repeat, not – rescue those who make choices we don't agree with. Bad choices are a part of life.'

They kept walking. Myron said, 'You know how I like to read the paper at Starbucks, right?'

Win nodded.

'Every teenager who hangs out there smokes. All of them. I sit there and watch them and when they light up, not even thinking about it, just as casual as you please, I think to myself, "Myron, you should say something." I think I should go up to them and excuse myself for interrupting and then beg them to stop smoking now because it'll only get harder. I want to shake them and make them understand how stupid they're being. I want to tell them about all the people I know, people who were living wonderful, happy lives like, say, Peter Jennings, a great guy from all I've heard, and how he was living this amazing life and how he lost it because he started smoking young. I want to shout at them the full litany of health problems they will inevitably face because of what they're so casually doing right now.'

Win said nothing. He looked ahead and kept pace.

'But then I think I should mind my own business. They don't want to hear it. And who am I anyway? Just some guy. I'm not important enough to make them stop. They'd probably tell me to take a hike. So of course, I keep quiet. I look the other way and go back to my paper and coffee and meanwhile these kids are sitting near me, slowly killing themselves. And I let them.'

'We pick and choose our battles,' Win said. 'That one would be a loser.'

'I know, but here's the thing: If I said something to every kid, every time I saw them, maybe I'd perfect my antismoking pitch. And maybe I'd reach one. Maybe one would stop smoking. Maybe my prying would save just one life. And then I wonder if staying quiet is the right thing – or the easy thing.'

'And then what?' Win asked.

'What do you mean?'

'Are you going to hang out at McDonald's and scold the people eating Big Macs? When you see a mother encouraging her overweight son to snarf down his second supersized order of fries, are you going to warn her about what the boy's horrible future will be like?'

'No.'

Win shrugged.

'But okay, forget all that,' Myron said. 'In this specific case, right now, a few yards away from us, there is a pregnant girl sitting in that whorehouse – '

' – who has made up her own, adult mind,' Win finished for him.

They kept walking.

'It's like what that Dr. Skylar told me.'

'Who?' Win asked.

'The woman who spotted Katie near the subway. Edna Skylar. She talked about preferring the innocent patients. I mean, she took the Hippocratic oath and all and she follows it, but when push comes to shove, she'd rather work with someone more deserving.'

'Human nature,' Win said. 'I assume you weren't comfortable with that?'

'I'm not comfortable with any of it.'

'But it's not just Dr. Skylar. You do it too, Myron. Put aside Claire's guilt trip on you for a moment. Right now, you're choosing to help Aimee because you perceive her as an innocent. If she were a teenage boy who had a history of drug problems, would you be so apt to find her? Of course not. We all pick and choose, like it or not.'

'It goes beyond that.'

'How so?'

'How important is what college you make?'

'What does that have to do with anything?'

'We were lucky,' Myron said. 'We went to Duke.'

'And your point is?'

'I got Aimee in. I wrote a letter, I made a phone call. I doubt she would have been accepted if it wasn't for me.'

'So?'

'So where do I get off? As Maxine Chang pointed out to me, when one kid makes it, another is denied.'

Win made a face. 'Way of the world.'

'Doesn't make it right.'

'Someone makes the choice based on a fairly subjective set of criteria.' Win shrugged. 'Why shouldn't it be you?'

Myron shook his head. 'I can't help but think that it's connected to Aimee's disappearance.'

'Her college acceptance?'

Myron nodded.

'How?'

'I don't know yet.'

They separated. Myron got into his car and checked his cell phone. One new message. He listened to it.

'Myron? Gail Berruti here. That call you asked about, the one that came to the residence of Erik Biel.' There was noise behind her. 'What? Damn, hold on a second.'

Myron did. This was the call Claire had received from the robotic voice telling her that Aimee 'is fine.' A few seconds later, Berruti was back.

'Sorry about that. Where was I? Right, okay, here it is. The call was placed from a pay phone in New York City. More specifically, from a bank of pay phones in the Twenty-third Street subways. Hope that helps.'

Click.

Myron thought about that. Right where Katie Rochester had been spotted. It made sense, he guessed. Or maybe, with what he'd just learned, it made no sense at all.

His cell phone buzzed again. It was Wheat Manson, calling back from Duke. He did not sound happy.

'What the hell is going on?' Wheat asked.

'What?'

'The ranking you gave me for that Chang kid. It matched.'

'Fourth in the class, and he didn't get in?'

'Are we going there, Myron?'

'No, Wheat. We're not. What about Aimee's ranking?'

'There's the problem.'

Myron asked a few follow-up questions before hanging up.

It was starting to fit.

Half an hour later Myron arrived at the home of Ali Wilder, the first woman in seven years he'd told that he loved. He parked and sat in the car for a moment. He looked out at the house. Too many thoughts ricocheted through his head. He wondered about her late husband, Kevin. This was the house they'd bought. Myron saw that day, Kevin and Ali coming here with a Realtor, both young, both choosing this vessel as the one where they would live their lives and raise their kids. Did they hold hands as they toured their future abode? What appealed to Kevin, or was it maybe his beloved's enthusiasm that won him over? And why the hell was Myron thinking about such things?

He had told Ali that he loved her.

Would he have done so – said 'I love you' like that – if Jessica hadn't visited him last night?

Yes.

Are you sure about that, Myron?

His cell phone rang. 'Hello?'

'Do you plan on sitting out in the car all night?'

He felt his heart soar at the sound of Ali's voice. 'Sorry, just thinking.'

'About me?'

'Yes.'

'About what you'd like to do to me?'

'Well, not exactly,' he said. 'But I can start now, if you want.'

'Don't bother. I got it all planned out already. You'll only interfere with what I've come up with.'

'Do tell.'

'I'd rather show. Come to the door. Don't knock. Don't talk. Jack is asleep and Erin is upstairs on her computer.'

Myron hung up. He caught his reflection – the goofy smile – in the car's rearview mirror. He tried not to sprint to the door, but he couldn't help but do one of those run-walks. The front door opened as he approached. Ali had her hair down. Her blouse was clingy and red and shiny. It stretched at the top, just asking to be unbuttoned.

Ali put a finger to her lips. 'Shh.'

She kissed him. She kissed him hard and deep. He felt it in his fingertips. His body sang. She whispered in his ear, 'The kids are upstairs.'

'So you said.'

'I'm usually not much of a risk-taker,' she said. Then Ali licked his ear. Myron's entire body jerked in pleasure. 'But I really, really want you.'

Myron held back the quip. They kissed again. She took his hand, quickly leading him down the hall. She closed the kitchen door. They went through the family room. She closed another door.

'How's the couch work for you?' she said.

'I don't care if we do it on a bed of nails at half court at Madison Square Garden.'

They dropped to the couch. 'Two closed doors,' Ali said, her breathing heavy. They kissed again. Their hands began to wander. 'No one can sneak up on us.'

'My, haven't we been planning,' Myron said.

'Pretty much all day.'

'Worth it,' he said.

She wiggled her eyebrows. 'Oh, just you wait and see.'

They kept their clothes on. That was the most amazing thing. Sure, buttons were undone and zippers were lowered. But they'd kept their clothes on. And now, as they panted in each other's arms, fully spent, Myron said the same thing that he said every time they finished.

'Wow.'

'You've got quite the vocabulary.'

'Never use a big word when a small one will suffice.'

'I could make a crack here, but I won't.'

'Thank you,' he said. Then: 'Can I ask you something?'

Ali snuggled closer. 'Anything.'

'Are we exclusive?'

She looked at him. 'For real?'

'I guess.'

'It sounds like you're asking me to go steady.'

'What would you say if I did?'

'Asked me to go steady?'

'Sure, why not?'

'I'd exclaim, "Oh yes!" Then I'd ask if I can doodle your name on my notebook and wear your varsity jacket.'

He smiled.

Ali said, 'Does your asking have anything to do with our earlier exchange of I-love-yous?'

'I don't think so.'

Silence.

'We're adults, Myron. You can sleep with whom-ever you wish.'

'I don't want to sleep with anyone else.'

'So why are you asking me this right now?'

'Because, well, before? I don't, uh, think very clearly when I'm in a state of, you know . . .' He sort of gestured. Ali rolled her eyes.

'Men. No, I mean, why tonight. Why did you ask about exclusivity tonight?'

He debated what to say. He was all for honesty, but did he really want to get into Jessica's visit? 'Just clarifying where we stand.'

Footsteps suddenly began to pound down the stairs.

'Mom!'

It was Erin. A door – that first of two doors – banged open.

Myron and Ali moved with a speed that would intimidate NASCAR. Their clothes were on, but like a couple of teenagers, they made sure everything was fastened and tucked in by the time the second doorknob began to turn. Myron jumped to the other side of the couch as Erin threw open the door. They both tried to wipe the look of guilt off their faces with mixed results.

Erin burst into the room. She looked at Myron. 'I'm glad you're here.'

Ali finished adjusting her shirt. 'What's wrong, honey?'

'You better come quick,' Erin said.

'Why, what's up?'

'I was on the computer, instant messaging with my friends. And just now – I mean, like thirty seconds ago – Aimee Biel signed on and said hello to me.'

45

They all hurried up to Erin's room. Myron took the stairs three at a time. The house shook. He didn't much care. The first thing that struck him when he entered the bedroom was how much it reminded him of Aimee's. The guitars, the photographs in the mirror, the computer on the desk. The colors were different, there were more pillows and stuffed animals, but you would have no doubt that both rooms belonged to high school girls with much in common.

Myron headed to the computer. Erin came in behind him, Ali after her. Erin sat at the computer and pointed to a word:

GuitarlovurCHC.

'CHC stands for Crazy Hat Care,' Erin said, 'the name of the band we were forming.'

Myron said, 'Ask Aimee where she is.'

Erin typed: **WHERE ARE YOU?** Then she hit the return button.

Ten seconds passed. Myron noticed the icon on Aimee's profile. The band Green Day. Her wallpaper was for the New York Rangers. When she typed back a sliver of her 'buddy sound,' a song from Usher, came through the speakers:

I can't say. But I'm fine. Don't worry.

Myron said, 'Tell her that her parents are upset. That she should call them.'

Erin typed: **YOUR PARENTS ARE FREAKING OUT. YOU NEED TO CALL THEM.**

I know. But I'll be home soon. I'll explain everything then.

Myron thought how to approach this. 'Tell her I'm here.'

Erin typed: **MYRON IS HERE.**

Long pause. The cursor blinked.

I thought you were alone.

SORRY. HE'S HERE. NEXT TO ME.

I know I got Myron in trouble. Tell him I'm sorry, but I'm fine.

Myron thought about it. 'Erin, ask her something only she would know.'

'Like what?'

'You guys have private talks, right? Share secrets?'

'Sure.'

'I'm not convinced it's Aimee. Ask her something only you and she would know.'

Erin thought a moment. Then she typed: **WHAT IS THE NAME OF THE BOY I HAVE A CRUSH ON?**

The cursor blinked. She wasn't going to answer. Myron was pretty sure about that. Then GuitarLovur CHC typed:

Did he finally ask you out?!?!

Myron said, 'Insist on a name.'

'Already on it,' Erin said. She typed: **WHAT'S HIS NAME?**

I have to go.

Erin did not need prompting: **YOU'RE NOT AIMEE. AIMEE WOULD KNOW THE NAME.**

Long pause. The longest yet. Myron looked back at Ali. Her eyes were on the screen. Myron could hear his own breathing in his ears, as if he'd stuck seashells on them. Then finally an answer came:

Mark Cooper.

The screen name vanished. GuitarLovurCHC was gone.

For a moment, no one moved. Myron and Ali had their eyes on Erin. She stiffened. 'Erin?'

Something happened to her face. A quiet quake in the corner of her lip. It spread. 'Oh God,' Erin said.

'What is it?'

'Who the hell is Mark Cooper?'

'Was it Aimee or not?'

Erin nodded. 'It was Aimee. But . . .'

Her tone made the room drop ten degrees.

'But what?' Myron said.

'Mark Cooper is not the boy I have a crush on.'

Myron and Ali both looked confused.

Ali said, 'Then who is he?'

Erin swallowed. She looked back, first at Myron, then her mother. 'Mark Cooper was this creepy guy who went to my summer camp. I told Aimee about him. He used to follow some of us around with this awful leer, you know. Whenever he'd walk by, we would laugh and whisper to one another. . . .' Her voice dropped off, came back, but lower now. 'We'd whisper, "Trouble."'

They all watched the monitor now, all hoping that screen name would pop up again. But nothing happened. Aimee did not reappear. She had delivered her message. And now, once again, she was gone.

46

Claire was on the phone in seconds. She dialed Myron's cell. When he answered, she said, 'Aimee was just online! Two of her friends called!'

Erik Biel sat at the table and listened. His hands were folded. He had spent the past day or so online, searching per Myron's instructions for people who lived in the area of that cul-de-sac. Now, of course, he knew that he'd been wasting his time. Myron had spotted a car with a Livingston High School decal right away. He had traced it back to one of Aimee's teachers, a man named Harry Davis, that very night.

He had simply wanted to keep Erik out of the way.

So he gave him busywork.

Claire listened and then let out a little cry. 'Oh no, oh my God. . . .'

'What?' Erik said.

She shushed him with her hand.

Erik felt the rage once more. Not at Myron. Not even at Claire. At himself. He stared down at the monogram on his French cuff. His clothes were tailor-made, a custom fit. Big deal. Who did he think he was impressing? He looked up at his wife. He had lied to Myron about the passion. He still longed for her. More than anything he wanted Claire to look at him the way she used to. Maybe Myron had been right. Maybe Claire had indeed loved him. But she had never respected him. She didn't need him.

She didn't believe in him.

When their family was in crisis, Claire had run to Myron. She had shut Erik out. And of course, he had taken it.

Erik Biel had done that his whole life. Taken it. His mistress, a mousy thing from his office, was pitiful and needy and treated him like royalty. That made him feel like a man. Claire didn't. It was that simple. And that pitiful.

'What?' Erik asked again.

She ignored him. He waited. Finally Claire asked Myron to hold on a second. 'Myron says he saw her online too. He had Erin ask her a question. She answered in a way . . . it was her, but she's in trouble.'

'What did she say?'

'I don't have time to go into details right now.' Claire put the phone back to her ear and said to Myron – to Myron! – 'We need to do something.'

Do something.

The truth was, Erik Biel was not much of a man. He knew that early on. When he was fourteen, he backed out of a fight. The entire school was there. The bully was ready to pounce. Erik had walked away. His mother called him prudent. In the media, walking away is the 'brave' thing to do. What a load of crap.

No beating, no hospital stay, no concussion or broken bones could have hurt Erik Biel more than not standing up had. He had never forgotten it, never gotten over it. He had chickened out of a fight. The pattern continued. He abandoned his buddies when they got jumped at a fraternity party. At a Jets game, he let someone spill beer on his girlfriend. If a man looked at him wrong, Erik Biel always averted his gaze first.

You can couch it in all the psychological vernacular of modern civilization – all that garbage about strength coming from within and that violence never solved anything – but it was all a bunch of self-rationalization. You can live with fooling yourself like that, for a while anyway. And then a crisis hits, a crisis like this, and you realize what you really are, that nice suits and fancy cars and pressed pants make you nothing.

You're not a man.

But still, even with wimps like Erik, there was one line you don't cross. You cross it, you never come back. It had to do with your children. A man protects his family at all costs. No matter what the sacrifice. You will take any hit. You will go to the ends of the earth and risk everything to keep them from harm. You don't back away. Never. Not until your dying breath.

Someone had taken away his little girl.

You don't sit that fight out.

Erik Biel took out the gun.

It had been his father's. A Ruger .22. It was an old gun. Probably hadn't been fired in three decades. Erik had brought it to a gun shop this morning. He purchased ammunition and other sundries he might need. The man behind the counter had cleaned the Ruger for him, tested it out, smirking in disgust at the little man in front of him, so pitiful that he didn't even know how to load and use his own damn gun.

But the gun was loaded now.

Erik Biel was listening to his wife talk to Myron. They were trying to figure out what to do next. Drew Van Dyne, he heard them say, wasn't home. They wondered about Harry Davis. Erik smiled. He was ahead of them on that count. He had used Call Block and dialed the teacher's number. He pretended to be a mortgage broker. Davis had answered and said he wasn't interested.

That was half an hour ago.

Erik started toward his car. The gun was tucked into his pants.

'Erik? Where are you going?'

He didn't answer. Myron Bolitar had confronted Harry Davis at the school. The teacher hadn't talked to Myron. But one way or the other, he sure as hell was going to talk to Erik Biel.

Myron heard Claire say, 'Erik? Where are you going?'

His phone clicked.

'Claire, I have someone on the other line. I'll call you back.' Myron clicked over to the other line.

'Is this Myron Bolitar?'

The voice was familiar. 'Yes.'

'This is Detective Lance Banner from the Livingston Police Department.

We met yesterday.'

Was it only yesterday? 'Sure, Detective, what can I do for you?'

'How far are you from St. Barnabas Hospital?'

'Fifteen, twenty minutes, why?'

'Joan Rochester has just been rushed into surgery.'

47

Myron sped and made it to the hospital in ten minutes. Lance Banner was waiting for him. 'Joan Rochester is still in surgery.'

'What happened?'

'You want his story or hers?'

'Both.'

'Dominick Rochester said she fell down the stairs. They've been here before. She falls down the stairs a lot, if you get my drift.'

'I do. But you said there were his and her stories?'

'Right. She's always backed up his before.'

'And this time?'

'She said he beat her up,' Banner said. 'And that she wants to press charges.'

'That must have surprised him. How bad is it?'

'Pretty bad,' Banner said. 'Several broken ribs. A broken arm. He must have pounded the hell out of her kidneys, because the doctor is speculating about removing one.'

'Jesus.'

'And, of course, not a mark on her face. The guy's good.'

'Comes with practice,' Myron said. 'Is he here?'

'The husband? Yeah. But we've got him in custody.'

'For how long?'

Lance Banner shrugged. 'You know the answer to that.'

In short: not very.

'Why did you call me?' Myron asked.

'Joan Rochester was awake when she came in. She wanted to warn you. She said to be careful.'

'What else?'

'That was it. It's a miracle she got that out.'

Rage and guilt consumed him in equal measure. Joan Rochester could handle her husband, Myron had thought. She lived with him. She made her choices. Gee, what would be his next justification for not helping her – she'd been asking for it?

'Do you want to tell me how you're involved in the lives of the Rochesters?' Banner asked.

'Aimee Biel isn't a runaway. She's in trouble.'

He filled him in as quickly as possible. When he finished, Lance Banner said, 'We'll get an APB out on Drew Van Dyne.'

'What about Jake Wolf?'

'I'm not sure how he fits in.'

'Do you know his son?'

'You mean Randy?' Lance Banner shrugged a little too casually. 'He's the high school quarterback.'

'Has Randy ever gotten into any trouble?'

'Why are you asking?'

'Because I heard his father bribed you guys to get him off a drug charge,' Myron said. 'Care to comment?'

Banner's eyes turned black. 'Who the hell do you think you are?'

'Save the indignation, Lance. Two of your fellow finest braced me on Jake Wolf's orders. They stopped me from talking to Randy. One punched me in the gut when I was cuffed.'

'That's a load of crap.'

Myron just looked at him.

'Which officers?' Banner demanded. 'I want names, dammit.'

'One was about my height, skinny. The other had a thick mustache and looked like John Oates from Hall and Oates.'

The shadow hit Lance's face. He tried to cover it.

'You know who I'm talking about.'

Banner tried to hold it back. He spoke through gritted teeth. 'Tell me exactly what happened.'

'We don't have the time. Just tell me what the deal with the Wolf kid is.'

'No one got bribed.'

Myron waited. A woman in a wheelchair headed toward them. Banner stepped aside and let her pass. He rubbed his face with his hand.

'Six months ago a teacher claimed that he caught Randy Wolf selling pot. He searched the kid and found two nickel bags on him. I mean, penny-ante stuff.'

'This teacher,' Myron said. 'Who was he?'

'He asked us to keep his name out of it.'

'Was it Harry Davis?'

Lance Banner didn't nod, but he might as well have.

'So what happened?'

'The teacher called us. I had two guys go in. Hildebrand and Peterson. They, uh, fit your description. Randy Wolf claimed that he was framed.'

Myron frowned. 'And your guys bought that?'

'No. But the case was weak. The constitutionality of the search was questionable. The amounts were small. And Randy Wolf. He was a good kid. No past record or anything.'

'You didn't want to get him in trouble,' Myron said.

'None of us did.'

'Tell me, Lance. If he'd been a black kid from Newark caught selling at Livingston High, would you have felt the same way?'

'Don't start that hypothetical crap with me. We had a weak case to begin with and then, the next day, Harry Davis tells my officers he won't testify. Just like that. He backs out. So now it's over. My officers had no choice.'

'My, how convenient,' Myron said. 'Tell me: Did the football team have a good season?'

'It was a nothing of a case. The kid had a bright future. He's going to Dartmouth.'

'I keep hearing that,' Myron said. 'But I'm beginning to wonder if it'll happen.'

Then a voice shouted, 'Bolitar!'

Myron turned. Dominick Rochester stood at the end of the corridor. His hands were cuffed. His face was red. Two officers were on either side of him. Myron started toward him. Lance Banner jogged behind, calling out a soft warning.

'Myron . . . ?'

'I won't do anything, Lance. I just want to talk to him.'

Myron stopped two feet in front of him. Dominick Rochester's black eyes burned. 'Where is my daughter?'

'Proud of yourself, Dominick?'

'You,' Rochester said. 'You know something about Katie.'

'Did your wife tell you that?'

'No.' He grinned. It was one of the most frightening sights Myron had ever seen. 'Just the opposite, in fact.'

'What are you talking about?'

Dominick leaned in closer and whispered. 'No matter what I did to her, no matter how much she suffered, my dearest wife wouldn't talk. See, that's why I'm sure you know something. Not because she talked – but because no matter how much hell I put her through, she wouldn't.'

Myron was back in his car when Erin Wilder called him.

'I know where Randy Wolf is.'

'Where?'

'There's a senior party at Sam Harlow's house.'

'They're having a party? Aren't any of Aimee's friends concerned?'

'Everyone thinks she ran away,' Erin said. 'Some of them saw her online tonight, so they're even more sure.'

'Wait, if they're at a party, how did they see her online?'

'They have BlackBerrys. They can IM from their phones.'

Technology, he thought. Keeping people together by allowing them to be apart. Erin gave him the address. Myron knew the area. He hung up and started on his way. The ride did not take long.

There were a bunch of cars parked out on the Harlows' street. Someone had set up a big tent in the backyard. This was a real party, an invite party, as opposed to a few kids hanging out and sneaking beers. Myron threw the car into park and entered the yard.

There were parents here – chaperones, he guessed. That would make this more difficult. But he didn't have time to worry about it. The police might be mobilizing, but they weren't anxious to look at the big picture. Myron was getting it now. It was coming into focus. Randy Wolf, he knew, was one of the keys.

The festivities were nicely partitioned. The parents hung out in the house's screened-in porch. Myron could see the adults in the dim light. They were laughing and had a keg. The men wore long shorts and loafers and smoked cigars. The women sported bright Lilly Pulitzer skirts and flip-flops.

The seniors gathered at the far end of the tent, as far away from adult supervision as possible. The dance floor was empty. The DJ played a song by the Killers, something about having a girlfriend who looked like a boyfriend that somebody had in February. Myron headed straight for Randy and put his hand on the boy's shoulder.

Randy shrugged Myron's hand away. 'Get off me.'

'We need to talk.'

'My father said – '

'I know all about what your father said. We're talking anyway.'

Randy Wolf was surrounded by about six guys. Some were huge. The quarter-back and his offensive line, Myron figured.

'This butt-face bothering you, Pharm?'

The one who said that was huge. He grinned at Myron. The guy had spiky blond hair, but what you first noticed, what you couldn't help but notice, was that he wasn't wearing a shirt. Here they were at a party. There were girls and punch and music and dancing and even parents. And this guy wasn't wearing a shirt.

Randy didn't say anything.

Shirtless had barbed-wire tattoos around his bloated biceps. Myron frowned. The tattoos couldn't have been more wannabe without the word *wannabe* actually being stenciled in. The guy was slabs and slabs of beef. His chest was so smooth it looked like someone had taken a sander to it. He rippled. His forehead was sloped. His eyes were red, indicating that at least some of the beer had found its way to the under-aged. He wore calf-length pants that might have been capris, though Myron didn't know if guys wore those or not.

'What are you looking at, Butt-face?'

Myron said, 'Absolutely – and I mean this sincerely – absolutely nothing.'

There were several gasps from the crowd. One of them said, 'Oh man, is this old dude gonna get a beating or what!'

Another said, 'Bring it on, Crush!'

Shirtless aka Crush made his best tough-guy face. 'Pharm ain't talking to you, you got me, Butt-face?'

That got a laugh from his friends.

'Butt-face,' Myron repeated. 'It's even funnier the third time you say it.' He took a step toward the kid. Crush didn't budge. 'This isn't your business.'

'I'm making it my business.'

Myron waited. Then he said, 'Don't you mean, "I'm making it my business, Butt-face"?'

There was another gasp. One of the other guys said, 'Oh, mister, run and hide. Nobody wises off to Crush like that.'

Myron looked at Randy. 'We need to talk now. Before this gets out of hand.'

Crush smiled, flexed his pecs, stepped forward. 'It's already out of hand.'

Myron didn't want to take out a kid, not with the parents around. It would cause too many problems.

'I don't want trouble,' Myron said.

'You already got it, Butt-face.'

Some of the guys oooed at that one. Crush folded his massive arms across his chest. A stupid move. Myron needed to get this out of the way fast, before the parents started noticing. But Crush's friends were watching. Crush was the resident tough guy. He couldn't afford to back down.

Arms folded across the chest. How macho. How dumb.

Myron made the move. When you need to take out somebody with a mini-mum of fuss or mess, this technique was one of the most effective. Myron's hand started at his side. The natural resting spot. That was the key. You don't cock the wrist. You don't pull the arm back. You don't wind up or make a fist. The smallest distance between two points is a straight line. That's what you remember. Using his natural hand speed and the element of surprise, Myron shot the hand in that straight line, from the resting point near his hip to Crush's throat.

He didn't hit him hard. Myron used the knife edge below the pinky and found the neck's sweet spot. Few points on the human body are more vulnerable. If you hit someone in the throat, it hurts. It makes them gasp and cough and freeze. But you have to know what you're doing. You hit it too hard, you could do some serious damage. Myron's hand darted in and struck cobra-like.

Crush's eyes bulged. A choking sound got locked in his throat. With almost casual ease, Myron swept out Crush's legs with his instep. Crush went down. Myron did not wait. He grabbed Randy by the scruff of the neck and started dragging him away. If any kid so much as moved, Myron froze them with a stare-down, all the while hustling Randy into the neighbor's backyard.

Randy said, 'Ow, let me go!'

Screw that. Randy was eighteen, an adult, right? No reason to go soft on him because he was a kid. He took him behind the garage two houses down. When Myron released him, Randy rubbed the back of his neck.

'What the hell is your problem, man?'

'Aimee is in trouble, Randy.'

'She ran away. Everyone said so. People talked to her online tonight.'

'Why did you two break up?'

'What?'

'I said – '

'I heard you.' Randy thought about it, then shrugged. 'We outgrew each other, that's all. We're both going to college. It was time to move on.'

'Last week you went to the prom together.'

'Yeah, so? We'd been planning for it all year. The tux, the dress, we rented a stretch Hummer with a bunch of friends. The whole group of us. We didn't want to ruin everyone's time. So we went together.'

'Why did you two break up, Randy?'

'I just told you.'

'Did Aimee find out you were dealing drugs?'

Randy smiled then. He was a handsome kid and he had a damn good smile. 'You make it sound like I'm hanging in Harlem hooking kids on heroin.'

'I'd get into a moral debate with you, Randy, but I'm a little pressed for time.'

'Of course Aimee knew about it. She even partook on more than one occasion. No big deal. I was only providing for a few friends.'

'One of those friends Katie Rochester?'

He shrugged. 'She asked a few times. I helped her out.'

'So again, Randy: Why did you and Aimee break up?'

He shrugged again and his tone quieted just enough. 'You'd have to ask Aimee.'

'She broke up with you?'

'Aimee changed.'

'Changed how?'

'Why don't you ask her old man?'

That made Myron pull up. 'Erik?' He frowned. 'What does he have to do with it?'

He didn't reply.

'Randy?'

'Aimee found out her father was screwing around.' He shrugged. 'It made her change.'

'Change how?'

'I don't know. It's like she wanted to do anything to piss him off. Her dad liked me. So all of a sudden' – another shrug – 'she didn't.'

Myron thought about it. He remembered what Erik had said last night, on the end of that cul-de-sac. It added up.

'I cared about her, man,' Randy went on. 'You have no idea how much. I tried to win her back, but it just backfired in my face. I'm over her now. Aimee's not a part of my life anymore.'

Myron could hear the crowd gather. He reached to grab Randy again by the neck, drag him farther away, but Randy pulled back. 'I'm fine!' Randy yelled out to his approaching friends. 'We're just talking here.'

Randy turned back to Myron. His eyes were suddenly clear. 'Go ahead. What else do you want to know?'

'Your father called Aimee a slut.'

'Right.'

'Why?'

'Why do you think?'

'Aimee started seeing somebody else?'

Randy nodded.

'Was it Drew Van Dyne?'

'Doesn't matter anymore.'

'Yeah, it does.'

'Nah, not really. With all due respect, none of this does. Look, high school is over. I'm going to Dartmouth. Aimee is going to Duke. My mom, she told me something. She said that high school isn't important. The people who are happiest in high school end up being the most miserable adults. I'm lucky. I know that. And I know it won't last unless I take the next step. I thought . . . we talked about it. I thought Aimee understood that too. How important the next step was. And in the end, we both got what we wanted. We got accepted to our first choices.'

'She's in danger, Randy.'

'I can't help you.'

'And she's pregnant.'

He closed his eyes.

'Randy?'

'I don't know where she is.'

'You said you did something to try to win her back, but it backfired. What did you do, Randy?'

He shook his head. He wouldn't say. But Myron thought that maybe he had an idea. Myron gave him his card. 'If you think of anything . . .'

'Yeah.'

Randy turned away then. He headed back to the party. The music still played. The parents kept laughing. And Aimee was still in trouble.

48

When Myron got back to his car, Claire was there. 'It's Erik,' she said.

'What about him?'

'He ran out of the house. With his father's old gun.'

'Did you call his cell?'

'No answer,' Claire said.

'Any idea where he went?'

'A few years ago I represented a company called KnowWhere,' Claire said. 'You heard of it?'

'No.'

'They're like OnStar or LoJack. They put a GPS in your car for emergencies, that kind of thing. Anyway, we got one installed in both cars. I just called the owner at home and begged him to get me the location.'

'And?'

'Erik is parked in front of Harry Davis's house.'

'Jesus.'

Myron jumped into his car. Claire slipped into the passenger seat. He wanted to argue, but there was no time.

'Call Harry Davis's home,' he said.

'I tried,' Claire said. 'There was no answer.'

Erik's car was indeed parked directly in front of the Davis residence. If he'd wanted to hide his approach, he hadn't done a very good job.

Myron stopped the car. He took out his own gun.

Claire said, 'What the hell is that for?'

'Just stay here.'

'I asked you – '

'Not now, Claire. Stay here. I'll call if I need you.'

His voice left no room for argument and, for once, Claire just obeyed. He started up the path, keeping a low crouch. The front door was slightly ajar. Myron didn't like that. He ducked low and listened.

There were noises, but he couldn't make out what they were.

Using the barrel of the gun, he pushed the door open. There was no one in the foyer. The sounds were coming from the left. Myron crawled in. He turned the corner and there, lying on the floor, was a woman he assumed was Mrs. Davis.

She was gagged. Her hands were tied behind her back. Her eyes were wide with fear. Myron put a finger to his lips. She looked to her right, then back at Myron, then back to her right again.

He heard more noises.

There were other people in the room. On her right.

Myron debated his next move. He considered backing out and calling the police. They could surround the house, he guessed, start talking Erik down. But that might be too late.

He heard a slap. Someone cried out. Mrs. Davis squeezed her eyes shut.

There was no choice. Not really. Myron had the gun at the ready. He was about to leap, preparing to turn and aim in the direction where Mrs. Davis had been looking. He bent his legs. And then he stopped.

Jumping in with a gun. Would that be the prudent move here?

Erik was armed. He might, of course, react by surrendering. He might also react by firing in a panic.

Fifty-fifty.

Myron tried something else.

'Erik?'

Silence.

Myron said, 'Erik, it's me. Myron.'

'Come on in, Myron.'

The voice was calm. There was almost a lilt in it. Myron moved into the center of the room. Erik stood with a gun in his hand. He had on a dress shirt with no tie. There were splatters of blood across the chest.

Erik smiled when he saw Myron. 'Mr. Davis is ready to talk now.'

'Put the gun down, Erik.'

'I don't think so.'

'I said – '

'What? Are you going to shoot me?'

'Nobody is shooting anybody. Just put the gun down.'

Erik shook his head. The smile remained. 'Come all the way in. Please.'

Myron stepped into the room, his gun still up. Now he could see Harry Davis in a chair. His back was to Myron. Nylon cuffs were around his wrists. Davis's head lolled on the neck, chin down.

Myron came around the front and took a look.

'Oh, man.'

Davis had been beaten. There was blood on his face. A tooth was out and on the floor. Myron turned to Erik. Erik's posture was different. He wasn't as ramrod as usual. He didn't look nervous or agitated. In fact, Myron had never seen him look more relaxed in his life.

'He needs a doctor,' Myron said.

'He's fine.'

Myron looked at Erik's eyes. They were placid pools.

'This isn't the way, Erik.'

'Sure it is.'

'Listen to me – '

'I don't think so. You're good at this stuff, Myron, no question. But you have to follow rules. A certain code. When your child is in danger, those niceties go out the window.'

Myron thought about Dominick Rochester, how he had said something so very similar in the Seidens' house. You couldn't start off with two guys more different than Erik Biel and Dominick Rochester. Desperation and fear had rendered them near identical.

Harry Davis raised his bloodied face. 'I don't know where Aimee is, I swear.'

Before Myron could do much of anything, Erik aimed his gun at the ground and fired. The sound was loud in the small room. Harry Davis screamed. A groan came from behind Mrs. Davis's gag.

Myron's own eyes widened as he looked down at Davis's shoe.

There was a hole in it.

It was near the edge of the big toe. Blood began to run. Myron raised his gun and pointed it at Erik's head. 'Put it down now!'

'No.'

He said it simply. Erik looked at Harry Davis. The man was in pain, but his head was up now, his eyes more focused. 'Did you sleep with my daughter?'

'Never!'

'He's telling the truth, Erik.'

Erik turned to Myron. 'How do you know?'

'It was another teacher. A guy named Drew Van Dyne. He works at the music store where she hung out.'

Erik looked confused. 'But when you dropped Aimee off, she came here, right?'

'Yes.'

'Why?'

They both looked at Harry Davis. There was blood on his shoe now. It oozed out slowly. Myron wondered if the neighbors had heard the gunfire, if they'd call the police. Myron doubted it. People out here assume the sound is a car backfiring or fireworks, something explainable and safe.

'It's not what you think,' Harry Davis said.

'What's not?'

And then Harry Davis's eyes darted toward his wife. Myron understood. He pulled Erik to the side. 'You cracked him,' Myron said. 'He's ready to talk.'

'So?'

'So he's not going to talk in front of his wife. And if he did something to Aimee, he's not going to talk in front of you.'

Erik still had the small smile on his face. 'You want to take over.'

'It's not about taking over,' Myron said. 'It's about getting the information.'

Erik surprised Myron then. He nodded. 'You're right.'

Myron just looked at him as if waiting for the punch line.

'You think this is about me,' Erik said. 'But it's not. It's about my daughter. It's about what I'd do to save her. I'd kill that man in a second. I'd kill his wife. Hell, Myron, I'd kill you too. But none of that will do any good. You're right. I cracked him. But if we want him to talk freely, his wife and I should leave the room.'

Erik walked over to Mrs. Davis. She cowered.

Harry Davis shouted, 'Leave her alone!'

Erik ignored him. He reached down and helped Mrs. Davis to her feet. Then Erik looked back at Harry. 'Your wife and I will wait in the other room.'

They moved into the kitchen and closed the door behind them. Myron wanted to untie Davis, but those nylon cuffs were tough to do by hand. He grabbed a blanket and stemmed the blood flow from the foot.

'It doesn't hurt much,' Davis said.

His voice was far away. Strangely enough, he too looked more relaxed. Myron had seen that before. Confession is indeed good for the soul. The man was carrying a heavy load of secrets. It was going to feel good, at least temporarily, to unburden himself.

'I've been teaching high school for twenty-two years,' Davis began without being prompted. 'I love it. I know the pay isn't great. I know it's not prestigious. But I adore the students. I love to teach. I love to help them on their way. I love when they come back and visit me.'

Davis stopped.

'Why did Aimee come here the other night?' Myron asked.

He didn't seem to hear. 'Think about it, Mr. Bolitar. Twenty-plus years. With high-schoolers. I don't say high school kids. Because many of them aren't kids. They're sixteen, seventeen, and even eighteen. Old enough to serve in the military and vote. And unless you're blind, you know that those are women, not girls. You ever check out the *Sports Illustrated* swimsuit issue? You ever look on the runway at top fashion shows? Those models are the same age as the beautiful, fresh-faced ones that I'm with five days a week, ten months a year. Women, Mr. Bolitar. Not girls. This isn't about some sick attraction or pedophilia.'

Myron said, 'I hope you're not trying to justify sexual affairs with students.'

Davis shook his head. 'I just want to put what I'm about to say in context.'

'I don't need context, Harry.'

He almost laughed at that. 'You understand what I'm saying more than you want to admit, I think. The thing is, I am a normal man – by that I mean, a normal heterosexual male with normal urges and desires. I'm surrounded year after year with mind-bogglingly beautiful women wearing tight clothes and low-cut jeans and plunging necklines and bare midriffs. Every day, Mr. Bolitar. They smile at me. They flirt with me. And we teachers are supposed to be strong and resist it every day.'

'Let me guess,' Myron said. 'You stopped resisting?'

'I'm not trying to make you sympathize. What I'm telling you is, the position we're in is unnatural. If you see a sexy seventeen-year-old walking down the street, you look. You desire. You might even fantasize.'

'But,' Myron said, 'you don't act.'

'But why don't you? Because it's wrong – or because you don't really have a chance? Now imagine seeing hundreds of girls like that every day, for years on end. From the earliest times, man has striven to be powerful and wealthy. Why? Most anthropologists will tell you that we do it to attract more and better females. That's nature. Not looking, not desiring, not being attracted – that would make you a freak, wouldn't you say?'

'I don't have time for this, Harry. You know it's wrong.'

'I do,' he said. 'And for twenty years I fought back those impulses. I stuck with the looking, the imagining, the fantasizing.'

'And then?'

'Two years ago I had a wonderful, gifted, beautiful student. No, it wasn't Aimee. I won't tell you her name. There's no reason for you to know. She sat in the front of the class, this amazing bounty. She stared at me like I was a deity. She kept the top two buttons of her blouse undone. . . .'

Davis closed his eyes.

'You gave in to your natural urgings,' Myron said.

'I don't know many men who could have resisted.'

'And this has what to do with Aimee Biel?'

'Nothing. I mean, not directly. This young woman and I started an affair. I won't go into details.'

'Thank you.'

'But eventually we got found out. It was, as you might imagine, a disaster. Her parents went crazy. They told my wife. She still hasn't forgiven me. Not really. But Donna has family money. We paid them off. They wanted to keep it quiet too. They were worried about their daughter's reputation. So we all agreed to not say anything. She went on to college. And I went back to teaching. I'd learned my lesson.'

'So?'

'So I put it behind me. I know you want to make me out a monster. But I'm not. I've had a lot of time to think about it. I know you think I'm just trying to rationalize, but there's more to it. I'm a good teacher. You pointed out how impressive winning Teacher of the Year was – and that I'd won it more than any other teacher in that school's history. That's because I care about the kids. It's not a contradiction – having these urges and caring about my students. And you know how perceptive teens are. They can spot a phony a mile away. They vote for me, they come to me when they have a problem, because they know I truly care.'

Myron wanted to vomit, and yet the arguments, he knew, were not without some perverse merit. 'So you went back to teaching,' he said, trying to get him back on track. 'You put it behind you and . . . ?'

'And then I made a second mistake,' he said. He smiled again. There was blood on his teeth. 'No, it's not what you think. I didn't have another affair.'

'What then?'

'I caught a student selling pot. And I turned him in to both the principal and the police.'

'Randy Wolf,' Myron said.

Davis nodded.

'What happened?'

'His father. Do you know the man?'

'We've met.'

'He did some digging. There were a few scant rumors about my liaison with the student. He hired a private eye. He also got another teacher, a man named Drew Van Dyne, to help him. Van Dyne, you see, was Randy's drug supplier.'

'So if Randy was prosecuted,' Myron said, 'Van Dyne had a lot to lose too.'

'Yes.'

'So let me guess. Jake Wolf found out about your affair.'

Davis nodded.

'And he blackmailed you into keeping quiet.'

'Oh, he did more than that.'

Myron looked down at the man's foot. The blood had let up. Myron should get him to a hospital, he knew that, but he didn't want to lose this momentum either. The odd thing was, Davis did not seem in pain. He wanted to talk. He had probably been thinking about these crazy justifications for years, rattling along in his brain, and now finally he was being given the chance to express them.

'Jake Wolf had me now,' Davis went on. 'Once you start down the blackmail road, you never really get off it. Yes, he offered to pay me. And yes, I took the money.'

Myron thought about what Wheat Manson had told him on the phone. 'You were not just a teacher. You were a guidance counselor.'

'Yes.'

'You had access to student transcripts. I've seen how far parents in this town will go to get their kids into the right college.'

'You have no idea,' Davis said.

'Yeah, I do. It wasn't that different when I was a kid. So Jake Wolf had you change his son's grades.'

'Something like that. I just switched the academic part of his transcript. Randy wanted to go to Dartmouth. Dartmouth wanted Randy because of his football. But they needed him to be in the top ten percent. There are four hundred kids in his class. Randy was ranked fifty-third – not bad, but not top ten percent. There is another student, a bright kid named Ray Clarke. He's ranked fifth in the class. Clarke got into Georgetown early decision. So I knew he wouldn't be applying anywhere else. . . .'

'So you switched Randy's transcript with this Clarke kid's?'

'Yes.'

Now Myron remembered something else, something Randy had said about trying to win Aimee back, about that backfiring, about having the same goal. 'And you did the same thing for Aimee Biel. To make sure she got into Duke. Randy asked you to do that, didn't he?'

'Yes.'

'And when Randy told Aimee what he'd done, he figured that she'd be grateful. Except she wasn't. She started investigating. She tried to break into the school computer and see what happened. She called Roger Chang, the number-four kid in the class, to see what his grades and extracurricular activities were. She was trying to put together what you guys had done.'

'That I don't know,' Davis said. He was losing the adrenaline flow. He was wincing in pain now. 'I never talked to Aimee about it. I don't know what Randy said to her – that's what I was asking him about when you saw us in the school parking lot. He said he hadn't used my name, that he'd just told her he was going to help her get into Duke.'

'But Aimee put it together. Or at least she was trying to.'

'That could be.'

He winced again. Myron didn't care.

'So now we're up to the big night, Harry. Why did Aimee have me drop her off here?'

The kitchen door swung open. Erik stuck his head into the room. 'How are we doing?'

'We're doing okay,' Myron said.

Myron expected an argument, but Erik just disappeared back into the kitchen.

'He's crazy,' Davis said.

'You have daughters, don't you?'

'Yes.' Then he nodded as if he suddenly understood.

'You're stalling, Harry. Your foot is bleeding. You need medical attention.'

'I don't care about that.'

'You've come this far. Let's get it done. Where is Aimee?'

'I don't know.'

'Why did she stop by?'

He closed his eyes.

'Harry?'

His voice was soft. 'God forgive me, but I don't know.'

'You want to explain?'

'She knocked on the door. It was ridiculously late. Two, three in the morning. I don't know. Donna and I were asleep. She scared the hell out of us. We went to the window. We both saw her. I turned to my wife. You should have seen the look on her face. There was so much hurt. All the distrust, all that I'd been fighting to mend, it all ripped apart. She started to cry.'

'So what did you do?'

'I sent Aimee away.'

Silence.

'I opened the window. I said it was late. I told her we could talk Monday.'

'What did Aimee do?'

'She just looked up at me. She didn't say a word. She was disappointed, I could tell that.' Davis squeezed his eyes shut. 'But I was also afraid that maybe she was angry.'

'She just walked away?'

'Yes.'

'And now she's missing,' Myron said. 'Before she could reveal what she knew. Before she could destroy you. And if the cheating scandal came out, well, it was like I said when we first talked. It's over for you. It would all come out.'

'I know. I thought of that.'

He stopped. Tears started running down his cheeks.

'What?' Myron said.

'My third big mistake,' he said, his voice soft.

Myron felt a chill run down his spine. 'What did you do?'

'I wouldn't hurt her. Not ever. I cared about her.'

'What did you do, Harry?'

'I was confused. I didn't know what the situation was. So I got scared when she showed up. I knew what it could mean – like you said. Everything could come out. All of it. And I panicked.'

'What did you do?' Myron asked again.

'I called someone. As soon as she left. I called someone I thought could help figure out what to do next.'

'Who did you call, Harry?'

'Jake Wolf,' he said. 'I called Jake Wolf and told him that Aimee Biel was right outside my door.'

49

Claire met them as they ran out. 'What the hell happened in there?' Erik did not break stride. 'Go home, Claire. In case she calls.'

Claire glanced at Myron, as though looking for help. Myron did not offer any. Erik was already in the driver's seat, figuratively and literally. Myron quickly slid to the passenger side before Erik zoomed off.

'You know the way to the Wolfs' house?' Myron asked.

'I dropped my daughter off there plenty of times,' he said.

He hit the gas. Myron studied his face. Normally Erik's expression landed somewhere in the vicinity of disdainful. There'd be furrowed brows and deep lines of disapproval. None of that was there now. His face was smooth, untroubled. Myron half expected him to snap on the radio and start whistling along.

'You're going to get arrested,' Myron said.

'Doubtful.'

'You think they'll keep quiet?'

'Probably.'

'The hospital will have to report the bullet wound.'

Erik shrugged. 'Even if they do talk, what would they say? I'm entitled to a jury of my peers. That would mean some parents with teenagers. I take the stand. I talk about how my daughter was missing and how the victim is a teacher who seduced a student and took bribes to change academic records. . . .'

He let his voice trail off as if the verdict was too obvious to mention. Myron was not sure what to say. So he sat back.

'Myron?'

'What?'

'I'm to blame, aren't I? My affair was the catalyst.'

'I don't think it's that simple,' Myron said. 'Aimee is pretty strong willed. It may have contributed, but in a weird way, it sort of adds up. Van Dyne is a music teacher and works in her favorite music store. There would be some appeal there. She had probably outgrown Randy. Aimee has always been a good kid, right?'

'The best,' he said softly.

'So maybe she just needed to rebel. That would be normal, right? And there was Van Dyne, at the ready. I mean, I don't know if that's how it worked. But I wouldn't put all of it on you.'

He nodded, but he didn't seem to be buying it. Then again, Myron wasn't selling that hard either. Myron considered calling the police, but what exactly would he tell them? And what would they do? The local police could be in Jake Wolf's pocket. They might warn him. Either way, they'd have to respect his rights. He and Erik need not worry about that.

'So how do you figure this all played out?' Erik asked.

'We have two suspects left,' Myron said. 'Drew Van Dyne and Jake Wolf.'

Erik shook his head. 'It's Wolf.'

'What makes you so sure?'

He cocked his head. 'You still don't get the parental bond, do you, Myron?'

'I have a son, Erik.'

'He's over in Iraq, right?'

Myron said nothing.

'And what would you give to save him?'

'You know the answer.'

'I do. The same as me. And the same as Jake Wolf. He's already shown how far he'll go.'

'There's a big difference between paying off a teacher to switch transcripts and . . .'

'Murder?' Erik finished for him. 'It probably doesn't start that way. You start by talking to her, trying to make her see things your way. You explain how she could get in trouble too, what with her acceptance to Duke and all. But she won't back down. And suddenly you understand: It's a classic us-or-them scenario. She holds your son's future in her hands. It's either her future or your son's. Which are you going to choose?'

'You're speculating,' Myron said.

'Perhaps.'

'You have to keep your hopes up.'

'Why?'

Myron turned toward him.

'She's dead, Myron. We both know that.'

'No, we don't.'

'Last night, when we were on that cul-de-sac, do you remember what you said?'

'I said a lot of things.'

'You said you didn't think she'd been randomly abducted by a psycho.'

'I still don't. So?'

'So think about it. If it was someone she knew – Wolf, Davis, Van Dyne, take your pick – why would they abduct her?'

Myron said nothing.

'They all had reasons to keep her quiet. But think it through. You said it could be either Van Dyne or Wolf. My money is on Wolf. But either way, they were all afraid of what Aimee could reveal, right?'

'Right.'

'You don't simply abduct someone if that's what you're after. You kill them.'

He said it all so calmly, his hands at ten and two o'clock on the steering wheel. Myron was not sure what to say. Erik had spelled it out in pretty convincing fashion. You don't kidnap if the goal is to silence. That doesn't work. That fear had been gnawing around in Myron too. He had tried to smother it, not let it free, but now here it was, excavated by the one man who'd want to paint the rosiest picture of what could have happened.

'And right now,' Erik went on, 'I'm fine. You see? I'm fighting. I'm battling to find out what happened. When we find her, if she's dead, it's over. Me, I mean. I'm done. I'll put on a façade. I'll move on for the sake of my other children. That's the only reason I won't just shrivel up and die. Because of my other kids. But trust me on this: My life will be over. You might as well bury me with Aimee. That's what this is about. I'm dead, Myron. But I'm not going out a coward.'

'Hang on,' Myron said. 'We don't know anything yet.'

Then Myron remembered something else. Aimee had been online tonight. He was going to remind Erik of this, give him some hope, but he wanted to play it through in his head first. It wasn't adding up. Erik had raised an interesting point. From what they had learned, there'd be no reason to abduct Aimee – only reason to kill her.

Had it really been Aimee online? Had she sent Erin a warning?

Something wasn't adding up.

They veered off Route 280 at a speed that put the car on two tires. Erik braked as they hit the Wolfs' street. The car crawled up the hill, stopping two houses away from the Wolfs'.

'What's our next move?' Erik asked.

'We knock on the door. We see if he's home.'

They both got out of the car and started up the drive. Myron took the lead. Erik let him. He rang Wolf's doorbell. The sound was trilling and pretentious and droned on too long. Erik stood a few steps back, in the dark. Myron knew that Erik had the gun. He wondered how to play that. Erik had already shot one man tonight. He didn't seem disinclined to doing it again.

Lorraine Wolf's voice came over a speaker. 'Who is it?'

'It's Myron Bolitar, Mrs. Wolf.'

'It's very late. What do you want?'

Myron remembered the short white tennis dress and double-entendre tone. There was no double entendre now. The voice was drum-tight.

'I need to talk to your husband.'

'He's not here.'

'Mrs. Wolf, could you please open the door?'

'I'd like you to leave.'

Myron wondered how to play this. 'I spoke to Randy tonight.'

Silence.

'He was at a party. We talked about Aimee. Then I talked to Harry Davis. I know everything, Mrs. Wolf.'

'I don't know what you're talking about.'

'You either open this door or I go to the police.'

More silence. Myron turned and looked at Erik. He was still at ease. Myron didn't like that.

'Mrs. Wolf?'

'My husband will be back in an hour. Come back then.'

Erik Biel took that one. 'I don't think so.'

He took out the gun, put it against the lock, and fired. The door flew open. Erik rushed in, gun drawn. So did Myron.

Lorraine Wolf screamed.

Erik and Myron veered toward the sound. When they arrived in the family room, they both pulled up.

Lorraine Wolf was alone.

For a moment, no one moved. Myron just studied the situation. Lorraine Wolf stood in the center of the room. She wore rubber gloves. That was the first thing he noticed. Bright yellow rubber gloves. Then he looked at those hands more closely. In one of them, her right hand, she held a sponge. In the other – the left, obviously – she carried a yellow bucket that matched the gloves.

There was a wet spot on the carpet where she had just been cleaning.

Erik and Myron both took a step forward. Now they could see that there was water in the bucket. The water had an awful pink tinge.

Erik said, 'Oh no . . .'

Myron turned to grab him, but he was too late. Something behind Erik's eyes exploded. He let out a howl and leapt toward the woman. Lorraine Wolf screamed. The bucket dropped to the carpet. The pink liquid poured out.

Erik tackled her. They both went over the back of the couch. Myron was right behind, not sure how to play it. If he made too aggressive a move, Erik might just pull the trigger. But if he did nothing . . .

Erik had Lorraine Wolf now. He pressed the gun against her temple. She cried out, gripping his hand with her own. Erik did not move.

'What did you do to my daughter?'

'Nothing!'

Myron said, 'Erik, don't.'

But Erik wasn't listening. Myron raised his own gun. He pointed it at Erik. Erik saw it, but it was obvious he didn't care.

'If you kill her . . .' Myron began.

'What?' Erik shouted. 'What do we lose, Myron? Look at this place. Aimee is already dead.'

Lorraine Wolf shouted, 'No!'

'Where is she then, Lorraine?' Myron asked.

She pressed her lips shut.

'Lorraine, where is Aimee?'

'I don't know.'

Erik raised the gun. He was going to hit her with the butt end.

'Erik, don't.'

He hesitated. Lorraine looked up, meeting Erik's eye. She was scared, but Myron could see that she was bracing herself, ready to take the blow.

'Don't,' Myron said again. He took a step closer.

'She knows something.'

'And we'll find out what, okay?'

Erik looked at him. 'What would you do? If it was somebody you love?'

Myron inched closer. 'I do love Aimee.'

'Not like a father.'

'No, not like that. But I've been there. I've pushed too hard. It doesn't work.'

'It worked with Harry Davis.'

'I know, but – '

'She's a woman. That's the only difference. I shot him in the foot and you asked him questions and let him bleed. Now we're face-to-face with someone who is cleaning up blood and all of a sudden you're squeamish?'

Even in this haze, even in this craziness, Myron could actually see his point. It was the guy – gal thing again. If Aimee was a boy. If Harry Davis had been a pretty, flirty woman.

Erik put the gun back against her temple. 'Where is my daughter?'

'I don't know,' she said.

'Whose blood are you cleaning up?'

Erik aimed the gun at her foot. But the control was gone. Myron could see that. Tears started streaming down Erik's face. His hand shook.

'If you shoot her,' Myron said, 'it contaminates the evidence. The blood will be mixed up. They'll never put together what happened here. The only one who will go to jail is you.'

The argument didn't make full sense, but it was enough to slow Erik down. His entire face collapsed now. He was crying. But he held on to the gun. He kept it pointed at her foot.

'Just take a breath,' Myron said.

Erik shook his head. 'No!'

The air was still. Everything had stopped. Erik looked down at Lorraine Wolf. She looked up without a flinch. Myron could see Erik's finger on the trigger.

No choice now.

Myron had to make a move.

And then Myron's cell phone chirped.

It made everyone stop. Erik took his finger off the trigger and wiped his face with his sleeve. 'Check it,' he said.

Myron took a quick glance at the caller ID. It was Win. He hit the answer button and put it to his ear.

'What?'

'Drew Van Dyne's car just pulled into his driveway,' Win said.

50

County homicide inspector Loren Muse was working on her new case, the one involving the two murders in East Orange, when her line rang. It was late, but Muse wasn't surprised. She often worked late. Her colleagues knew that.

'Muse.'

The voice was muffled but sounded female. 'I have some information for you.'

'Who is this?'

'It's about that missing girl.'

'Which missing girl?'

'Aimee Biel.'

Erik was still holding the gun on Lorraine Wolf. 'What is it?' he asked Myron.

'Drew Van Dyne. He's home.'

'What does that mean?'

'It means we should talk to him.'

Erik gestured at Lorraine Wolf with his gun. 'We can't just leave her here.'

'Agreed.'

The smartest move, Myron realized, would be to get Erik to stay here and keep an eye on Lorraine Wolf, not let her warn anybody or clean up or whatever. But he didn't want to leave her alone with Erik. Not like this. Not in the state he was in.

'We should bring her with us,' Myron said.

Erik pressed the gun against her head. 'Get up,' he said to her. She obeyed. They led her outside. Myron called Detective Lance Banner as they headed for the car.

'Banner.'

'Get your best crime lab guys over to Jake Wolf's house,' Myron said. 'I don't have time to explain.'

He hung up. In other circumstances, he might have asked for backup. But Win was at Drew Van Dyne's home. There would be no need.

Myron drove. Erik sat in the back with Lorraine Wolf. He kept the gun pointed at her. Myron glanced into the rearview mirror and met her eye.

'Where's your husband?' Myron asked, making a right turn.

'Out.'

'Where?'

She did not reply.

'Two nights ago, you got a call,' Myron said. 'At three in the morning.'

Her eyes found his in the mirror again. She didn't nod, but he thought that he could see agreement.

'The call came from Harry Davis. Did you answer it or did your husband?'

Her voice was soft. 'Jake did.'

'Davis told him that Aimee had been there, that he was worried. And then Jake ran to his car.'

'No.'

Myron paused, considered the answer. 'What did he do then?'

Lorraine shifted in her seat again, looking straight at Erik. 'We liked Aimee very much. For God's sake, Erik, she dated Randy for the past two years.'

'But then she dumped him,' Myron said.

'Yes.'

'How did Randy react to that?'

'It broke his heart. He cared about her. But you can't think . . .' Her voice died off.

'I'll ask you again, Mrs. Wolf. After Harry Davis called your house, what did your husband do?'

She shrugged her shoulders. 'What could he do?'

Myron paused.

'What, you think Jake drove up there and grabbed her? Come on. Even with no traffic it's half an hour from Livingston to Ridgewood. Do you think Aimee would just wait on the street for Jake to come along?'

Myron opened his mouth, closed it. He tried to picture it now. Harry Davis had just rejected her. Would she just stand there, on that dark street, for half an hour or more? Did that make sense?

'So what happened?' Myron asked.

She said nothing.

'You get this call from Harry Davis. He's in a panic about Aimee. What did you and Jake do?'

Myron made a left. They were on Northfield Avenue now, one of Livingston's bigger roads. He hit the accelerator harder.

'What would you have done?' she asked.

No one replied. Lorraine locked eyes on Myron's via the rearview.

'It's your son,' she went on. 'His entire future is on the line. He had this girl-friend. This wonderful sweet girlfriend. Something happened to her. She changed. I don't know why.'

Erik squirmed, but he kept the gun on her.

'All of a sudden she wants no part of him. She has an affair with a teacher. She goes knocking on doors at three in the morning. She's erratic and if she talks, she could bring your whole world down. So what would you have done, Mr. Bolitar?' She turned to look at Erik. 'If the situation was reversed – if Randy had dumped Aimee and started acting like this, threatening to destroy her future – what would you have done, Erik?'

'I wouldn't have killed him,' Erik said.

'We didn't kill her. All we did . . . We worried. Jake and I sat up and talked. We wondered how to handle it. We tried to plan it out. First, we'd have Harry Davis change the computer records. Put them back the way they were, if he could. Make it look like there'd been a computer glitch or something. People might suspect the truth, but if they couldn't prove it, maybe we'd be safe. We tried to think up other scenarios. I know you want to call Randy a drug dealer, but he was just a contact. Every school has a few. I won't defend it. I remember when I went to Middlebury, I won't mention his name, but a man who is a leading politician now, he was the supplier. You graduate, it's over and done with. But now we needed to make sure that it didn't come out. And mostly we wanted to figure out a way to reach Aimee. We were going to call you, Erik. We thought maybe you could reason with her. Because it wasn't just Randy's future. It was hers too.'

They were getting close to Drew Van Dyne's house now.

'That's a nice story, Mrs. Wolf,' Myron said. 'But you left out one part.'

She closed her eyes.

'Whose blood is on your carpet?'

No answer.

'You heard me call the police. They're on their way there now. There are tests. DNA and whatever. They'll find out.'

Lorraine Wolf still said nothing. They were on Drew Van Dyne's street now. The homes were smaller and older. The lawns weren't quite as green. The shrubbery dipped and teetered. Win had told Myron exactly where he'd be standing, otherwise Myron would have never spotted him. He pulled to a stop and looked back at Erik.

'Stay here a second.'

Myron put the car in park and moved behind the tree. Win was there.

Myron said, 'I don't see Van Dyne's car.'

'It's in the garage.'

'How long has he been here?'

'How long ago did I call?'

'Ten minutes ago.'

Win nodded. 'There you go then.'

Myron looked at the house. It was dark. 'No lights on.'

'I noticed that too.'

'He backed into his garage ten minutes ago and he hasn't gone into the house yet?'

Win shrugged.

There was a grinding noise. The garage door opened. Headlights shone in their faces. The car zoomed out. Win took out his gun, preparing to shoot. Myron put his hand on his friend's arm.

'Aimee could be in there.'

Win nodded.

The car flew down the drive and squealed right. It drove past the parked car, the one with Erik Biel and Lorraine Wolf in the back. Van Dyne's Toyota Corolla hesitated and then accelerated.

Myron and Win sprinted back to the car. Myron got in the driver's side, Win the passenger's. In the backseat, Erik Biel still had the gun pointed at Lorraine Wolf.

Win turned and smiled at Erik. 'Hi,' he said.

Win reached back as though to shake Erik's hand. Instead, he quickly grabbed Erik's gun and pulled it away from him. Just like that. One second Erik Biel was holding a gun. The next he wasn't.

Myron threw the car into drive as Van Dyne's vehicle disappeared around the corner. Win looked at the gun, frowned, emptied it out.

The chase was on. But it wouldn't last long.

51

It was not Drew Van Dyne driving the car. It was Jake Wolf. Jake drove fast. He made a few quick turns, but he only drove about a mile. He had a big enough lead. He hit the old Roosevelt Mall, sped around back, shifted into park. He walked across the dark soccer fields in the general direction of Livingston High School. He figured that Myron Bolitar was following him. But he also figured that he had enough of a head start.

He heard the party noises. After a few more steps, he could start to see the glow of lights. The night air felt good in his lungs. Jake tried to look at the trees, the houses, the cars in the driveways. He loved this town. He loved his life here.

As he came closer, he could hear the laughter. He thought about what he was doing here. He swallowed and moved behind a row of pine trees on the neighboring property. He found a spot between two of them and looked out at the tent.

Jake Wolf spotted his son right away.

It had always been like that with Randy. You never missed him. He stood out, no matter what the circumstance. Jake remembered going to Randy's first soccer program when the boy was in first grade. There must have been three, four hundred kids, all there, all running and bouncing around like molecules in heat. Jake had arrived late, but it took mere seconds to find his radiant boy in the waves of look-alike children. Like there was a spotlight coming down from above, illumin-ating his every step.

Jake Wolf just watched. His son was talking to a bunch of his pals. They were all laughing at something Randy said. Jake stared and felt his eyes well up. There was plenty of blame to go around, he guessed. He tried to think where it all started. With Dr. Crowley maybe. Damn history teacher calls himself *doctor*. What kind of pretentious crap was that anyhow?

Crowley was a small, meaningless man with a bad comb-over and slumped shoulders. He hated athletes. You could smell the envy a mile away. Crowley looked at someone like Randy, someone so good-looking and athletic and special, and he saw all his own adolescent failures.

That was how it all began.

Randy had written a wonderful essay on the Tet Offensive for Crowley's history class. Crowley had given him a C-minus. A goddamn C-minus. A friend of Randy's, a guy named Joel Fisher, had gotten an A. Jake read both essays. Randy's was better. It wasn't just Jake Wolf who thought so. He tried them both out on various people. He didn't let them know which essay was his son's and which was Joel's.

'Which is better?' he'd asked.

And almost all agreed. Randy's paper – the C-minus paper – was superior.

It might have seemed like a small thing, but it wasn't. That paper was three-quarters of the grade. Dr. Crowley gave Randy a C. It kept Randy off the honor roll for that semester, but more than that, more than anything else, it knocked him out of the class's top ten percent. Dartmouth had been clear. With Randy's SATs, he needed to be in the top ten percent. If that C had been a B, Randy would have been accepted.

That was the difference.

Jake and Lorraine had gone in to talk to Dr. Crowley. They had explained the situation. Crowley wouldn't budge. He had been dismissive, enjoying his power play, and it took all Jake's willpower not to put the man through a plate-glass window. But Jake was not about to give up that easy. He'd hired a private eye to dig into the man's past, but Crowley's life had been so pathetic, so nothing, so obviously unremarkable, especially next to the bright beacon that was Jake's son . . . There was nothing he could use against the man.

So if Jake Wolf had played by the rules, that would have been it. That would have kept his son out of an Ivy League education – the whim of a nothing like Crowley.

Uh-uh. No way.

And so it began.

Jake swallowed and stared. His son stood in the middle of the party, the sun with dozens of orbiting planets. He had a cup in his hand. Randy had such natural ease. Such poise in everything he did. Jake Wolf stood there, in the shadows, and wondered if there was any way to save it all. He didn't think so. It was like holding water in your hand. He had tried to sound confident for Lorraine. He thought that maybe he could dump the body in Drew Van Dyne's house. Lorraine would clean up the stain. It could have still worked.

But Myron Bolitar had showed up. Jake had spotted him from the garage. He was trapped. Jake hoped to speed away, lose them, dump the body somewhere else. But when he made that first turn and saw that Lorraine was in the backseat, he knew that it was over.

He'd hire a good attorney. The best. He knew a guy in town, Lenny Marcus. Great defense lawyer. He'd call him, see what they could work out. But in his heart, Jake Wolf knew that it was over. For him, at least.

That was why he was here now. In the shadows. Watching his beautiful, perfect son. Randy was the only thing he had ever gotten right. His boy. His precious boy. But that was enough. From the first time he had laid eyes on the baby in the hospital, Jake Wolf was mesmerized. He went to every practice he could. He went to every game. It wasn't just to show support – often, during practices, Jake would stand behind a tree, almost hide, as he was doing now. He just liked to watch his son. That was all. He liked getting lost in this very simple bliss. And sometimes, when he did, he couldn't believe how lucky he was, how someone like Jake Wolf, also a nothing when you thought about it, could have been part of creating something so miraculous. The world was cruel and awful and you had to do all you could to get that edge, but then every once in a while, he'd look at Randy and realize that there was something other than the dog-eat-dog horror, that there had to be something better out there, some higher being, because here, in front of him, there was indeed perfection and beauty.

'Hey, Jake.'

He turned at the sound of the voice. 'Hi, Jacques.'

It was Jacques Harlow, the father of one of Randy's closest friends and the party host. Jacques came up next to him. They both looked out at the party, at their sons, soaking it in for almost a full minute without speaking.

'Can you believe how fast it went by?' Harlow said.

Jake just shook his head, afraid to speak. His eyes never left his son.

'Hey, how about coming in for a drink?'

'I can't. I just had to drop something off for Randy. Thanks though.'

Harlow slapped his back. 'Sure.' He headed back toward the porch.

It took another five minutes. Jake enjoyed every second. Then he heard the footsteps. He turned and saw Myron Bolitar. Myron had a gun in his hand. Jake Wolf smiled and turned back to his son.

'What are you doing here, Jake?'

'What's it look like?'

Jake Wolf did not want to move, but he knew that it was time. He soaked up one last look at his son. That was what this felt like. The last time he would see him like this. He wanted to say something to his son, offer some words of wisdom, but Jake wasn't good with words.

So instead he turned and raised his hands.

'In the trunk,' Jake Wolf said. 'The body is in the trunk.'

52

Win stood a few feet behind Myron. Just in case. But he could see right away that Jake Wolf was not about to make a move. He was surrendering. For now. There might be something else, something later. Win had dealt with men like Jake Wolf. They never really believe that it's over. They look for an out, an escape hatch, a loophole, a legal maneuver, something.

A few minutes earlier, they'd spotted Van Dyne's car in the Roosevelt Mall lot. Myron and Win had run ahead, leaving Lorraine Wolf and Erik Biel in the car. Erik still had a few nylon cuffs he'd bought at the same store where he'd picked up the ammunition. So they cuffed Lorraine's hands behind her back and hoped like hell that Erik wouldn't do something stupid.

Not long after Myron and Win disappeared into the dark, Erik got out of the backseat. He moved toward Van Dyne's car. He opened the front door. He didn't know what he was doing exactly. He just knew he had to do something. He slid into the driver's seat. There were guitar picks on the floor. He remembered his own daughter's collection, how much she loved them, how her eyes would close when she strummed the strings. He remembered Aimee's first guitar, a crappy thing he'd bought at a toy store for ten bucks. She'd been only four years old. She banged on it and did a wonderful rendition of 'Santa Claus Is Coming to Town.' More like Bruce Springsteen than something you'd see from a preschooler. He and Claire had clapped like mad when she finished.

'Aimee rocks,' Claire had declared.

They had all been smiling. They had all been so happy.

Erik looked out the windshield, back toward his car, back toward Lorraine Wolf. Their eyes met. He had known Lorraine for two years now, since Aimee had first started dating her son. He liked her. Truth be told, he had even semi-fantasized about her. Not that he would have ever done anything about it. Not like that. Just a harmless fantasy for an attractive woman. Normal stuff.

He looked in the backseat now. There was sheet music, handwritten. He froze. His hand moved slowly. He saw the handwriting and realized that it was Aimee's. He picked it up, brought it closer, holding it as if it were porcelain.

Aimee had written this.

Something caught in his throat. His fingertips touched down on the words, the notes. His daughter had held this paper. She had scrunched up her face the way she always did and delved into her life experiences and produced this. It was a simple thought, really, but suddenly it meant the world to him. His anger was gone. It would be back. He knew that. But at that moment, his heart just felt heavy. There was no anger. Just pain.

That was when Erik decided to pop the trunk.

He looked back over at Lorraine Wolf. Something crossed her face. He didn't know what. He opened the car door and stepped back into the night. He moved toward the trunk, took hold of the hatch with one hand, began to lift it. He heard rustling from the field. He turned and saw Myron come flying into view.

'Erik, wait. . . .'

Erik opened the trunk then.

The black tarp. That was what he saw first. Something wrapped in black tarp. His knees buckled, but he held on. Myron started toward him, but Erik held up a hand as if telling him to stay back. He tried to rip the tarp. It wouldn't give. He pulled and tugged. The tarp held in place. Erik started to panic now. His chest heaved. His breath caught.

He took out his key chain and dug the end of a key into the plastic. It made a hole. There was blood. He slit the tarp and reached his hands in. They grew wet and sticky. Erik desperately pulled at the tarp, ripping at it as if he were trapped inside, running out of air.

He saw the dead face and fell back.

Myron was next to him now.

'Oh my God,' Erik said. He collapsed. 'Oh thank you. . . .'

It wasn't his daughter in the trunk. It was Drew Van Dyne.

53

Lorraine Wolf said, 'I shot him in self-defense.' In the distance Myron could hear the police sirens. Myron stood next to the trunk with Erik Biel and Lorraine Wolf. He had called the police. They'd be here soon. He looked across the field. He could see distant silhouettes of Win and Jake Wolf. Myron had run ahead. Win had taken care of securing their suspect.

'Drew Van Dyne was in the house,' she went on. 'He pulled a gun on Jake. I saw it. He was yelling all kinds of crazy stuff about Aimee – '

'What stuff?'

'He said that Jake didn't care about her. That she was just some dumb slut to him. That she was pregnant. He was ranting.'

'So what did you do?'

'We keep guns in the house. Jake likes to hunt. So I got a rifle. I pointed it at Drew Van Dyne. I told him to put down the gun. He wouldn't. I could see that. So . . .'

'No!' It was Wolf who had said that. They were close enough to hear. 'I shot Van Dyne!'

Everyone stared at him. The police sirens sounded.

'I shot him in self-defense,' Jake Wolf insisted. 'He pulled a gun on me.'

'So why did you stick the body in the trunk?' Myron asked.

'I was afraid no one would believe that. I was going to bring him home, dump him in his own house. Then I realized that would be stupid.'

'When did you realize that?' Myron said. 'When you saw us?'

'I want a lawyer,' Jake Wolf said. 'Lorraine, don't say anything else.'

Erik Biel stepped forward. 'I don't care about any of this. My daughter. Where the hell is my daughter?'

No one moved. No one spoke. The night stayed silent except for the scream of sirens.

Lance Banner was the first cop out of his car, but dozens of squad cars descended on the Roosevelt Mall parking lot. They kept the flashing lights on. Everyone's face went from blue to red. The effect was dizzying.

'Aimee,' Erik said softly. 'Where is she?'

Myron tried to keep calm, tried to concentrate. He stepped to the side with Win. Win's face, as ever, remained unruffled.

'So,' Win said, 'where are we?'

'It's not Davis,' Myron said. 'We checked him out. It doesn't look like it was Van Dyne. He pulled a gun on Jake Wolf because he thought that he'd done it. And the Wolfs claim, somewhat convincingly, that it wasn't them.'

'Any other suspects?'

'Not that I can think of.'

Win said, 'Then we need to look at them again.'

'Erik thinks she's dead.'

Win nodded. 'That's what I mean,' he said. 'When I say we need to look at them again.'

'You think one of them killed her and got rid of the body?'

Win did not bother replying.

'My God,' Myron said. He looked back over at Erik. 'Have we been looking at this wrong from the beginning?'

'I can't see how.'

Myron's cell phone chirped. He looked down at the caller ID and saw the number was blocked.

'Hello?'

'It's Investigator Loren Muse. Do you remember me?'

'Of course.'

'I just got an anonymous call,' she said. 'Someone claimed they spotted Aimee Biel yesterday.'

'Where?'

'On Livingston Avenue. Aimee was in the passenger seat of a Toyota Corolla. The driver pretty much fits the description of Drew Van Dyne.'

Myron frowned. 'Are you sure?'

'That's what she said.'

'He's dead, Muse.'

'Who?'

'Drew Van Dyne.'

Erik came over and stood next to Myron.

And that was when it happened.

Erik's cell phone rang.

He brought the phone up. When he saw the number on the caller ID, Erik nearly screamed.

'Oh my God. . . .'

Erik snapped the phone to his ear. His eyes were wet. His hand shook so badly he hit the wrong button to answer. He tried again and brought the phone back up. His voice was a panicked scream. 'Hello?'

Myron leaned in close enough to hear. There was a moment of static. And then a voice, a teary voice, a familiar voice said, 'Daddy?'

Myron's heart stopped.

Erik's face collapsed, but his voice was all father. 'Where are you, honey? Are you all right?'

'I don't . . . I'm fine, I think. Daddy?'

'It's okay, honey. I'm here. Just tell me where you are.'

And she did.

54

Myron drove. Erik stayed in the passenger seat. The ride was not a long one. Aimee had said that she was behind the Little Park near the high school – that same park that Claire had taken her to when she was only three. Erik would not let her off the line. 'It's okay,' he kept saying. 'Daddy's on his way.'

Myron cut time by taking the circle in the wrong direction. He drove over two curbs. He didn't care. Neither did Erik. Speed was the thing here. The lot was empty. The headlights danced through the night and then, as they made the final turn, the lights landed on a solitary figure.

Myron hit the brake.

Erik said, 'Oh my God, oh my sweet dear God. . . .'

He was out of the car. Myron was out fast too. They both started sprinting. But somewhere along the way, Myron let up. Erik took the lead. That was how it should be. Erik swept his daughter into his arms. He took careful hold of her face, as though fearing it was only a dream, a puff of smoke, and that she might vanish again.

Myron stopped and watched. Then he picked up his own cell phone and called Claire.

'Myron? What the hell is going on?'

'She's okay,' he said.

'What?'

'She's safe. We're bringing her home to you now.'

In the car, Aimee was groggy.

'What happened?' Myron asked.

'I think,' Aimee began. Her eyes went wide. Her pupils were dilated. 'I think they drugged me.'

'Who?'

'I don't know.'

'You don't know who kidnapped you?'

She shook her head.

Erik sat in the back with Aimee. He held her. He stroked her hair. He told her over and over again that it was okay now, everything was okay.

Myron said, 'Maybe we should take her to a doctor.'

'No,' Erik said. 'She needs to go home first.'

'Aimee, what happened?'

'She's been through hell, Myron,' Erik said. 'Give her a chance to catch her breath.'

'It's okay, Daddy.'

'Why were you in New York?'

'I was supposed to meet someone.'

'Who?'

'About . . .' Her voice faded. Then she said, 'This is tough to talk about.'

'We know about Drew Van Dyne,' Myron said. 'We know you're pregnant.'

She closed her eyes.

'Aimee, what happened?'

'I was going to get rid of it.'

'The baby?'

She nodded. 'I went to the corner of Fifty-second Street and Sixth. That's what they told me to do. They were going to help me out. They pulled up in a black car. They told me to get money from the ATM.'

'Who?'

'I never saw them,' Aimee said. 'The windows were tinted. They were always in disguise.'

'Disguise?'

'Yes.'

'They. There was more than one?'

'I don't know. I know I heard a woman's voice. That much I'm sure.'

'Why didn't you just go to St. Barnabas?'

Aimee hesitated. 'I'm so tired.'

'Aimee?'

'I don't know,' she said. 'Someone from St. Barnabas called. A woman. If I went there, my parents would find out. Something about shield laws. I just . . . I'd made so many mistakes. I just wanted to . . . But then I wasn't so sure. I got the money. I was going to get in the car. But then I panicked. That's when I called you, Myron. I wanted to talk to someone. It was going to be you, but, I don't know, I know you were trying, but I thought maybe it would be better to talk to someone else.'

'Harry Davis?'

Aimee nodded. 'I know this other girl,' she said. 'Her boyfriend got her pregnant. She said Mr. D was really helpful.'

'That's enough,' Erik said.

They were almost at Aimee's house. Myron did not want to let this go. Not yet.

'So what happened then?'

'The rest is fuzzy,' Aimee said.

'Fuzzy?'

'I know I got into a car.'

'Whose?'

'The same one that was waiting for me in New York, I think. I felt so deflated after Mr. D sent me away. So I thought I might as well go with them. Get it over with. But . . .'

'But what?'

'It's all fuzzy.'

Myron frowned. 'I don't understand.'

'I don't know,' she said. 'I was drugged almost the whole time. I only remember waking up for a few minutes at a time. Whoever it was, they held me in some kind of log cabin. That's all I remember. It had this fireplace with white and brown stone. And then suddenly I was in that field behind the playground.

I called you, Daddy. I don't even know . . . how long was I gone?'

She started crying then. Erik put his arms around her.

'It's okay,' Erik said. 'Whatever happened, it's over now. You're safe.'

Claire was in the yard. She sprinted up to the car. Aimee managed to get out, but she could barely stand. Claire let out a primordial cry and grabbed for her daughter.

They hugged, they cried, they kissed, the three of them. Myron felt like an intruder. They started toward the door then. Myron waited. Claire looked back. She caught Myron's eyes. She ran back to him.

Claire kissed him. 'Thank you.'

'The police are still going to need to talk to her.'

'You kept your promise.'

He said nothing.

'You brought her home.'

Then she ran back to the house.

Myron stood there and watched them disappear inside. He wanted to celebrate. Aimee was home. She was healthy.

But he didn't feel in the mood.

He drove again to the cemetery that overlooked a schoolyard. The gate was open. He found Brenda's grave and sat next to it. The night closed in. He could hear the swishing of highway traffic. He thought about what had just happened. He thought about what Aimee had just said. He thought about her being home, safe and with her family, while Brenda lay in the ground.

Myron sat there until another car pulled up. He almost smiled as Win stepped into view. Win kept his distance for a moment. Then he approached the headstone. He looked down at it.

'Nice to have one in the win column, no?' Win said.

'I'm not so sure.'

'Why not?'

'I still don't know what happened.'

'She's alive. She's home.'

'I'm not sure that's enough.'

Win gestured toward the stone. 'If you could go back in time, would you need to know everything that happened? Or would it be enough if she were alive and home?'

Myron closed his eyes, tried to imagine that bliss. 'It would be enough if she were alive and home.'

Win smiled. 'There you go then. What else is there?'

He stood. He didn't know the answer. He only knew that he had spent enough time with ghosts, with the dead.

55

The police took Myron's statement. They asked questions. They told him nothing. Myron slept in the house in Livingston that night. Win stayed with him. Win rarely did that. They both woke up early. They watched SportsDesk on TV and ate cold cereal.

It felt normal and right and rather wonderful.

Win said, 'I've been thinking about your relationship with Ms. Wilder.'

'Don't.'

'No, no, I think I owe you an apology,' Win continued. 'I may have misjudged her. Her looks do grow on you. I'm thinking that perhaps her derriere is of a finer quality than I originally thought.'

'Win?'

'What?'

'I don't much care what you think.'

'Yes, my friend, you do.'

At eight in the morning Myron walked over to the Biel house. He figured that they were awake by now. He knocked gently on the door. Claire answered it. She wore a bathrobe. Her hair was disheveled. She stepped outside and closed the door behind her.

'Aimee is still sleeping,' Claire said. 'Whatever drugs the kidnappers gave her, they really knocked her out.'

'Maybe you should take her to the hospital.'

'Our friend David Gold – do you know him? He's a doctor. He came by last night and checked her out. He said she'd be fine once the drugs wear off.'

'What drugs did they give her?'

Claire shrugged. 'Who knows?' They both stood there a moment. Claire took a deep breath and looked up and down the street. Then she said, 'Myron?'

'Yes.'

'I want you to let the police handle it from here.'

He did not reply.

'I don't want you to ask Aimee about what happened.'

There was just enough steel in her voice. Myron waited to see if she'd say more. She did. 'Erik and I, we just want it to end. We hired an attorney last night.'

'Why?'

'We're her parents. We know how to protect our daughter.'

The implication being: Myron didn't. She hadn't needed to mention again that first night, how Myron had dropped Aimee off and hadn't looked out for her. But that was what she was saying here.

'I know how you are, Myron.'

'How am I?'

'You want answers.'

'You don't?'

'I want my daughter to be happy and healthy. That's more important than answers.'

'You don't want whoever did this to pay?'

'It was probably Drew Van Dyne. And he's dead. So what's the point? We just want Aimee to be able to put this behind her. She's going to college in a few months.'

'Everyone keeps talking about college like it's a great big do-over card,' Myron said. 'Like the first eighteen years of your life don't count.'

'In a way, they don't.'

'That's crap, Claire. What about her baby?'

Claire moved back to the door. 'With all due deference – and no matter what you want to think about our decisions – that's not your concern.'

Myron nodded to himself. She had him on that one.

'Your part in this is over,' she said, and again he heard the steel. 'Thank you for what you've done. I have to get back to my daughter now.'

And then Claire closed the door on him.

56

A week later, Myron sat at Baumgart's Restaurant with Livingston police detective Lance Banner and Essex County investigator Loren Muse. Myron had ordered the Kung Pao Chicken. Banner had ordered a Chinese fish special. Muse was having a grilled cheese sandwich.

'Grilled cheese at a Chinese restaurant?' Myron said.

Loren Muse shrugged mid-bite.

Banner used chopsticks. 'Jake Wolf is pleading self-defense,' he said. 'He claims that Drew Van Dyne pulled a gun on him. Said that he made wild threats.'

'What kind of threats?'

'Van Dyne was ranting that Wolf hurt Aimee Biel. Something like that. They're both a little vague on the specifics.'

'Both?'

'Jake Wolf's star witness. His wife, Lorraine.'

'That night,' Myron said, 'Lorraine told us she pulled the trigger.'

'My guess is, she did. We did a powder residue check on Jake Wolf's hand. He was clean.'

'Did you check his wife?'

'She refused,' Banner said. 'Jake Wolf forbade it.'

'So he's taking the hit for his wife?'

Banner looked at Loren Muse. He nodded slowly.

'What?' Myron asked.

'We'll get to that.'

'Get to what?'

'Look, Myron, I think you're right,' Banner said. 'Jake Wolf is trying to take the hit for the whole family. On the one hand, he's claiming self-defense. There is some evidence to back it up. Van Dyne had a bit of a history. He also had a gun on him – it's registered in his name. On the other hand, Jake Wolf is willing to do some time in exchange for giving his wife and kid a pass.'

'His kid?'

'He wants a guarantee that his son still goes to Dartmouth. And that Randy will be cleared of all subsequent allegations, including anything related to the shooting, the cheating scandal, and his possible relationship with Van Dyne and drugs.'

'Well,' Myron said. But it added up. Jake Wolf was an ass, but Myron had seen the way he looked at his son at that graduation party. 'He's still trying to salvage Randy's future.'

'Yep.'

'Will he be able to?'

'I don't know,' Banner said. 'The prosecutor has no jurisdiction over Dartmouth.

If they want to rescind their acceptance, they can and probably will.'

'What Jake is doing,' Myron said. 'It's almost admirable.'

'If not twisted,' Banner added.

Myron looked at Loren Muse. 'You're awfully quiet.'

'Because I think Banner has it wrong.'

Banner frowned. 'I don't have it wrong.'

Loren put down the sandwich and brushed the crumbs off her hands. 'For starters, you're going to put the wrong person in jail. The powder residue test proves that Jake Wolf didn't shoot Drew Van Dyne.'

'He said he wore gloves.'

Now Loren Muse frowned.

Myron said, 'She has a point.'

'Gee, Myron, thanks.'

'Hey, I'm on your side here. Lorraine Wolf told me she shot Drew Van Dyne. Shouldn't she be the one on trial?'

Loren Muse turned to him. 'I never said I thought it was Lorraine Wolf.'

'Excuse me?'

'Sometimes the most obvious answer is the right one.'

Myron shook his head. 'I'm not following you.'

'Go back a second,' Loren Muse said.

'How far back?'

'All the way to Edna Skylar on the streets of New York City.'

'Right.'

'Maybe we had it right all along. From the moment she called us.'

'I'm still not following.'

'Edna Skylar confirmed what we already knew: that Katie Rochester was a runaway. And at first, that's what we all thought about Aimee Biel too, right?'

'So?'

Loren Muse said nothing.

'Wait a minute. Are you saying you think Aimee Biel ran away?'

'There are a lot of unanswered questions,' Loren said.

'So ask them.'

'Ask who?'

'What do you mean, who? Ask Aimee Biel.'

'We tried.' Loren Muse smiled. 'Aimee's lawyer won't let us talk to her.'

Myron sat back.

'Don't you find that odd?'

'Her parents want her to put it behind her.'

'Why?'

'Because it was a traumatic experience for her,' Myron said.

Loren Muse just looked at him. So did Lance Banner.

'That story she told you,' Loren said. 'About being drugged and held in some log cabin.'

'What about it?'

'There are holes.'

A cold pinprick started at the base of Myron's neck and slid south down his spine. 'What holes?'

'First off, we have the anonymous source who called me. The one who saw her tooling around with Drew Van Dyne. If Aimee were kidnapped, how could that be exactly?'

'Your witness was wrong.'

'Right. She happened to pick out the make of the car and described Drew Van Dyne to a tee. But hey, she's probably wrong.'

'You can't trust anonymous sources,' Myron tried.

'Fine, then let's move on to hole two. This late-night abortion story. We checked at St. Barnabas. Nobody told her anything about parental notification. More than that, it's not true. The laws might change on that subject, but either way, in her case – '

'She's eighteen,' Myron interrupted. Eighteen. An adult. That age again.

'Exactly. And there's more.'

Myron waited.

'Hole three: We found Aimee's fingerprints at Drew Van Dyne's house.'

'They had an affair. Of course her prints were there. They could be weeks old.'

'We found prints on a soda can. The can was still on the kitchen counter.'

Myron said nothing, but he felt something deep inside of him start to give way.

'All your suspects – Harry Davis, Jake Wolf, Drew Van Dyne. We checked them all out thoroughly. None of them could have pulled off a purported kidnapping.' Loren Muse spread her hands. 'So it's like that old axiom in reverse. When you've eliminated all the other possibilities, you have to go back to your first, most obvious solution.'

'You think Aimee ran away.'

Loren Muse shrugged, shifted in her chair. 'Here she is, a confused young woman. Pregnant with a teacher's child. Her dad is having an affair. She's caught up in this cheating scandal. She must have felt trapped, don't you think?'

Myron found himself almost nodding.

'There is no physical evidence – none at all – that Aimee was abducted. And think about it. Why would someone kidnap her anyway? What would be the motive in a case like this? The normal motives are, what, sexual assault, for one. We know that didn't happen. Her doctor told us that much. There was no physical or sexual trauma. Why else are people kidnapped? For ransom. Well, we know that didn't happen either.'

Myron kept very still. It was almost exactly what Erik had said. If you wanted to keep Aimee quiet, you didn't kidnap her. You killed her. But now she was alive. Ergo . . .

Loren Muse kept pounding at him. 'Do you have a motive for a kidnapping, Myron?'

'No,' he said. 'But what about the ATM machine? How do you figure that in?'

'You mean both girls using the same one?'

'Yes.'

'I don't know,' she said. 'Maybe it was a coincidence after all.'

'Come on, Muse.'

'Okay, fine, then let's turn it around.' She pointed at him. 'How does that ATM transaction fit into a kidnapping scenario? Would Wolf know about it? Davis, Van Dyne?'

Myron saw her point. 'But there are other things too,' he countered. 'Like that phone call from a pay phone in the subway. Or the fact that she was online.'

'All of which fit into her being a runaway,' Loren said. 'If someone did abduct her like she claims, why would they risk a call from a pay phone? Why would you put her on the Internet?'

Myron shook his head. He knew that she was making sense. He just refused to accept it. 'So that's how this ends? It's not Davis. It's not Wolf or Van Dyne or anyone. Aimee Biel just ran away?'

Loren Muse and Lance Banner exchanged another glance.

Then Lance Banner said, 'Yes, that's the working theory. And remember: There's no law against what she did. In the end a lot of people got hurt or even killed. But running away is not against the law.'

Loren Muse kept quiet again. Myron didn't like it. 'What?' he snapped at her.

'Nothing. What Banner said – the evidence all points that way. It might even explain why Aimee's parents don't want us talking to her. They don't want all that coming out – her affair, her pregnancy, heck, like it or not, she was helped in the cheating scandal too. So keeping it all quiet. Making her look like a victim instead of a runaway. It's the right move.'

'But?'

She looked at Banner. He sighed and shook his head. Loren Muse started fiddling with her fork. 'But both Jake and Lorraine Wolf wanted to take the blame for shooting Drew Van Dyne.'

'So?'

'You don't find that odd?'

'No. We just explained why. Lorraine killed him. Jake wants to take the fall to protect her.'

'And the fact that they were cleaning up the evidence and moving the body?'

Myron shrugged. 'That would be the natural reaction.'

'Even if you killed in self-defense?'

'In their case, yes. They were trying to protect it all. If Van Dyne is found dead in their house, even if they shot him in self-defense, all the stuff about Randy would come out. The drugs, the cheating, all of it.'

She nodded. 'That's the theory. That's what Lance here believes. And that's probably what happened.'

Myron tried not to sound too impatient. 'But?'

'But maybe that's not how it happened. Maybe Jake and Lorraine came home and found the body there.'

Myron stopped breathing. There is something inside of you. It can bend. It can stretch. But then, every once in a while, you can feel it pulling too far. If you let it go there, you will break inside. You will snap in two. You know that. Myron had known Aimee his whole life. And right now, if he was right about where Loren Muse was going, he was close to breaking. 'What the hell are you talking about?'

'Maybe the Wolfs came home and saw a body. And maybe they assumed that Randy had done it.' She leaned closer. 'Van Dyne was Randy's drug supplier. He had also stolen Randy's girlfriend. So maybe Mom and Dad saw the body and figured that Randy shot him. Maybe they panicked and loaded the body in his car.'

'What, you think Randy killed Drew Van Dyne?'

'No. I said that's what they thought. Randy has an alibi.'

'So what's your point?'

'If Aimee Biel hadn't been kidnapped,' Muse said, 'if she ran away and stayed with Drew Van Dyne, maybe she was with him in the house. And maybe, just maybe, Aimee, our scared little girl, really did want to put it all behind her. Maybe she was ready for college, ready to move on and cut off all ties, except this guy, this Drew Van Dyne, wouldn't let go. . . .'

Myron closed his eyes. That little thing inside of him – it was being pulled hard. He stopped it, shook his head. 'You're wrong.'

She shrugged. 'Probably.'

'I've known this girl all my life.'

'I know, Myron. She's a young, sweet girl, right? Young sweet girls can't be killers, can they?'

He thought about Aimee Biel, the way she laughed at him in his basement, the way she climbed up the jungle gym when she was three. He remembered her blowing out candles at her birthday party. He remembered watching her in a school play when she was in eighth grade. He remembered it all and he felt the anger starting to mount.

'You're wrong,' Myron said again.

He waited on the sidewalk across the street from their house.

Erik came out first. His face was tight, grim. Aimee and Claire followed. Myron stood there and watched. Aimee spotted him first. She smiled at him and waved. Myron studied that smile. It looked the same to him. The same smile he'd seen on the playground when she was three. The same one he'd seen in the basement a few weeks ago.

There was nothing different.

Except now the smile gave him a chill.

He looked at Erik and then at Claire. Their eyes were hard, protective, but there was something else there, something beyond exhaustion and surrender, something primitive and instinctive. Erik and Claire walked with their daughter. But they did not touch her. That was what Myron noticed. They were not touching their own daughter.

'Hi, Myron!' Aimee shouted.

'Hi.'

Aimee ran across the street. Her parents did not move. Neither did Myron. Aimee threw her arms around him, almost knocking him over. Myron tried to hug her back. But he couldn't quite do it. Aimee gripped him harder.

'Thank you,' she whispered.

He didn't say anything. Her embrace, it felt the same. It felt warm and strong. No different than before.

And yet he wanted it to end.

Myron felt his heart drop and shatter. God help him, he just wanted her to let go, to get her away from him. He wanted this girl he'd loved for so long to be gone. He took hold of her shoulders and gently pushed her off.

Claire was behind her now. She said to Myron, 'We're in a rush. We'll get together soon.'

He nodded. The two women walked away. Erik waited by the car. Myron watched them. Claire was next to her daughter, but she still wouldn't touch her. Aimee got in the car. Erik and Claire glanced at each other. They did not speak. Aimee was in the back. They both sat in the front. Natural enough, Myron supposed, but it still seemed to him as if they were trying to keep their distance from Aimee, as if they wondered – or perhaps knew – about the stranger who now lived with them. Claire looked back at him.

They know, Myron thought.

Myron watched the car pull away. As it disappeared down the street, he realized something:

He hadn't kept his promise.

He hadn't brought home their baby.

Their baby was gone.

57

Four Days Later

Jessica Culver did indeed marry Stone Norman at Tavern on the Green. Myron was in his office when he read about it in the paper. Esperanza and Win were both there too. Win was standing near a full-length mirror, checking out his golf swing. Win did that a lot. Esperanza watched Myron carefully.

'You okay?' she asked him.

'I am.'

'You realize that her getting hitched is the greatest thing that's ever happened to you?'

'I do.' Myron put the paper down. 'I came to a realization that I wanted to share with both of you.'

Win stopped his air swing midway. 'My arm isn't straight enough.'

Esperanza waved him quiet. 'What?'

'I've always tried to run away from what I now see are my natural instincts,' Myron said. 'You know. Playing the hero. You both warn me against it. And I've listened. But I've figured something out. I'm supposed to do it. I'll have my defeats, sure, but I'll have more victories. I'm not going to run away from it anymore. I don't want to end up being cynical. I want to help people. And that's what I'm going to do.'

Win turned toward him. 'Are you done?'

'I am.'

Win looked at Esperanza. 'Should we applaud?'

'I think we should.'

Esperanza stood and applauded wildly. Win put down his air club and offered up a polite golf clap.

Myron bowed and said, 'Thank you so very much, you're a beautiful audience, don't forget your waitress on the way out, hey, try the veal.'

Big Cyndi popped her head through the doorway. She'd gone heavy on the rouge this morning and looked like a traffic light.

'Line two, Mr. Bolitar.' Big Cyndi batted her eyes. Picture two scorpions trapped on their backs. Then she added, 'It's your new sweetie pie.'

Myron picked up the phone. 'Hey!'

Ali Wilder said, 'What time are you coming over?'

'I should be there about seven.'

'How about pizza and a DVD with the kids?'

Myron smiled. 'Sounds great.'

He hung up. He was smiling. Esperanza and Win exchanged a glance.

'What?' Myron said.

'You're so doofy when you're in love,' Esperanza said.

Myron looked at his watch. 'It's time.'

'Good luck,' Esperanza said.

Myron turned to Win. 'You want to come along?'

'No, my friend. This one is all yours.'

Myron stood. He kissed Esperanza on the cheek. He hugged Win. Win was surprised by the gesture, but he took it. Myron drove back to New Jersey. It was a glorious day. The sun shone like it'd just been created. Myron fiddled with the radio dial. He kept hitting all his favorite songs.

It was that kind of day.

He did not bother stopping at Brenda's grave. He thought that she'd understand. Actions speak louder and all that.

Myron parked at St. Barnabas Medical Center. He headed up to Joan Rochester's room. She was sitting up when he got there, ready to leave.

'How are you feeling?' he asked.

'Fine,' Joan Rochester said.

'I'm sorry about what happened to you.'

'Don't be.'

'Are you going home?'

'Yes.'

'And you're not going to press charges?'

'That's right.'

Myron figured as much. 'Your daughter can't run forever.'

'I know that.'

'What are you going to do?'

'Katie came home last night.'

So much for the happy ending, Myron thought. He closed his eyes. This was not what he'd wanted to hear.

'She and Rufus had a fight. So Katie came home. Dominick forgave her. It's all going to be okay.'

They looked at each other. It wouldn't be okay. He knew that. She knew that.

'I want to help you,' Myron said.

'You can't.'

And maybe she was right.

You help those you can. That was what Win had said. And you always, *always* keep a promise. That was why he had come today. To keep his promise.

He met up with Dr. Edna Skylar in the corridor outside the cancer ward. He had hoped to see her in her office, but this would be okay.

Edna Skylar smiled when she saw him. She wore very little makeup. The white coat was wrinkled. No stethoscope hung around her neck this time.

'Hello, Myron,' she said.

'Hi, Dr. Skylar.'

'Call me Edna.'

'Okay.'

'I was just on my way out.' She pointed with her thumb toward the elevator. 'What brings you here?'

'You, actually.'

Edna Skylar had a pen tucked behind her ear. She took it out, made a note on a chart, put it back. 'Really?'

'You taught me something when I was here last time,' Myron said.

'What's that?'

'We talked about the virtuous patient, remember? We talked about the pure versus the sullied. You were so honest with me – about how you'd rather work with people who seemed more deserving.'

'A lot of talk, yes,' she said. 'But at the end of the day, I took an oath. I treat those I don't like too.'

'Oh I know. But you see, you got me thinking. Because I agreed with you. I wanted to help Aimee Biel because I thought she was . . . I don't know.'

'Innocent?' Skylar said.

'I guess.'

'But you learned that she's not.'

'More than that,' Myron said. 'What I learned was, you were wrong.'

'About?'

'We can't prejudge people like that. We become cynical. We assume the worst. And when we do that, we start to see only the shadows. You know that Aimee Biel is back home?'

'I heard that, yes.'

'Everyone thinks she ran away.'

'I heard that too.'

'So nobody listened to her story. I mean, really listened. Once that assumption came about, Aimee Biel was no longer an innocent. You see? Even her parents. They had her best interests at heart. They wanted so much to protect her that even they couldn't see the truth.'

'Which is?'

'Innocent until proven guilty. It's not just for the courtroom.'

Edna Skylar made a production of checking her watch. 'I'm not sure I see what you're getting at.'

'I believed in that girl her whole life. Was I wrong? Was it a lie? But at the end of the day, it's like her parents said – it's their job to protect her, not mine. So I was able to be more dispassionate. I was willing to risk learning the truth. So I waited. When I finally got Aimee alone, I asked her to tell me the whole story. Because there were too many holes in the other one – the one where she ran away and maybe killed her lover. That ATM machine, for one. That call from the pay phone, for another. Stuff like that. I didn't want to just shove it all aside and help her get on with her life. So I talked to her. I remembered how much I loved and cared for her. And I did something truly strange.'

'What?'

'I assumed that Aimee was telling the truth. If she was, then I knew two things. The kidnapper was a woman. And the kidnapper knew that Katie Rochester used the ATM machine on Fifty-second Street. The only people who fit that bill? Katie Rochester. Well, she didn't do it. Loren Muse. No way. And you.'

'Me?' Edna Skylar began to blink. 'Are you serious?'

'Do you remember when I called and asked you to look up Aimee's medical file?' Myron asked. 'To see if she was pregnant?'

Again Edna Skylar checked her watch. 'I really don't have time for this.'

'I said it wasn't just about one innocent, it was about two.'

'So?'

'Before I called you, I asked your husband to do the same thing. He worked in that department. I thought he'd have an easier time. But he refused.'

'Stanley is a stickler for the rules,' Edna Skylar said.

'I know. But you see, he told me something interesting. He told me that with all the new HIP laws nowadays, the computer date-stamps a patient's file every time you look into it. You can see the name of the doctor who viewed the file. And you get the time he or she viewed it.'

'Right.'

'So I checked Aimee's file. Guess what it shows?'

Her smile began to falter.

'You, Dr. Skylar, looked at that file two weeks *before* I asked you to. Why would you do that?'

She folded her arms across her chest. 'I didn't.'

'The computer is wrong?'

'Sometimes Stanley forgets his code. He probably used mine.'

'I see. He forgets his own code but remembers yours.' Myron tilted his head and edged closer. 'You think he'll say that under oath?'

Edna Skylar did not reply.

'Do you know where you were really clever?' he went on. 'Telling me about your son. The one who was trouble from day one and ran away to make it big. You said that he was still a mess, do you remember?'

A small, pain-filled sound escaped her lips. Her eyes filled with tears.

'But you never mentioned your son's name. No reason you should, of course. And there's no reason why anybody would know. Even now. It wasn't part of the investigation. I don't know the name of Jake Wolf's mother. Or Harry Davis's. But once I saw that you'd been in Aimee's medical file, I did a little checking. Your first husband, Dr. Skylar, was named Andrew Van Dyne, am I right? Your son's name was Drew Van Dyne.'

She closed her eyes and took several deep breaths. When she opened them again, she shrugged, aiming for nonchalance but not even coming close. 'So?'

'Odd, don't you think? When I asked you about Aimee Biel, you never mentioned that your son knew her.'

'I told you that I was estranged from my son. I didn't know anything about him and Aimee Biel.'

Myron grinned. 'You have all the answers, don't you, Edna?'

'I'm just telling the truth.'

'No, you're not. It was yet another coincidence. So many damn coincidences, don't you think? That's what I couldn't shake from the beginning. Two pregnant girls at the same high school? Okay, that one was no big deal. But all the rest – both girls running away, both using the same ATM, all that. Again, let's assume Aimee was telling the truth. Let's assume that someone – a woman – did indeed tell Aimee to wait on that corner. Let's say that this mystery woman did tell Aimee to take money out of that ATM. Why? Why would someone do that?'

'I don't know.'

'Sure you do, Edna. Because they weren't coincidences. None of them. You arranged them all. The two girls using the same ATM? Only one reason for that.

The kidnapper – you, Edna – wanted to hook Aimee's disappearance with Katie Rochester's.'

'And why would I want to do that?'

'Because the police were sure that Katie Rochester had run away – in part because of what you saw in the city. But Aimee Biel was different. She didn't have a Mob-connected, abusive daddy, for example. Her disappearance would cause commotion. The best way – the only way – to keep that heat from coming down was to make Aimee look like a runaway too.'

For a moment they both just stood there. Then Edna Skylar shifted to the right as if preparing to pass him. Myron shifted with her, blocking the path. She looked up at him.

'Are you wearing a wire, Myron?'

He raised his arms. 'Frisk me.'

'No need. This is all nonsense anyway.'

'Let's go back to that day on the street. You and Stanley are walking in Manhattan. Fate lends a hand here. You see Katie Rochester, just like you told the police. You realize that she's not missing or in serious trouble. She's a runaway. Katie begs you not to tell. And you listen. For three weeks, you say nothing. You go back to your regular life.' Myron studied her face. 'You with me so far?'

'I'm with you.'

'So why the change? Why after three weeks do you suddenly call your old buddy Ed Steinberg?'

She folded her arms. 'Why don't you tell me?'

'Because your situation changed, not Katie's.'

'How?'

'You talked about your son being trouble from day one. That you'd given up on him.'

'That's right.'

'Maybe you did, I don't know. But you were in touch with Drew. At least some-what. You knew that Drew fell in love with Aimee Biel. He told you about it. He probably told you that she was pregnant.'

She crossed her arms. 'You can prove that?'

'No. That part is speculation. The rest isn't. You looked up Aimee's medical files on the computer. That we know. You saw that yes, she was indeed pregnant. But more than that, you saw that she was going to terminate it. Drew didn't know about that. He thought that they were in love and going to get married. But Aimee just wanted out. Drew Van Dyne had been nothing but a foolish, albeit not uncommon, high school mistake. Aimee was on her way to college now.'

'Sounds like motive for Drew to kidnap her,' Edna Skylar said.

'It does, doesn't it? If that had been all. But again I kept wondering about all the coincidences. The ATM machine again. Who knew about it? You called your old buddy Ed Steinberg and pumped him for info on the case. He talked. Why not? Nothing was confidential. There wasn't really even a case. When he mentioned the Citibank ATM, you realized that would be the clincher. Everyone would assume Aimee was a runaway too. And that's exactly what happened. Then you called Aimee. You said you were from the hospital, which was true enough. You told her what she had to do to terminate the pregnancy in secret. You set up that meeting in New York. She's waiting at the corner. You drive by. You tell her to pick up some cash at the machine. Your clincher. Aimee does as she's told. And then she panics. She wants to think it through now. There you are, waiting to grab her, a syringe in your hand, and all of a sudden she runs off. She calls me. I get there. I drive her to Ridgewood. You follow – it was your car I saw that night follow us into the cul-de-sac. When she gets rejected by Harry Davis, you're waiting. Aimee doesn't remember much after that. She claims she was drugged. That fits –

her memory would be fuzzy. Propofol would cause a lot of the symptoms. You're familiar with that drug, aren't you, Edna?'

'Of course I am. I'm a doctor. It's an anesthetic.'

'You've used it in your practice?'

She hesitated. 'I have.'

'And that will be your downfall.'

'Really? How's that.'

'I have other evidence, but it's mostly circumstantial. Those medical records, for one. They show you not only viewed Aimee's medical records earlier than you indicated, but you didn't even bring them up again when I called. Why would you? You already knew she was pregnant. I'll also have phone records. Your son called you, you called your son.'

'So?'

'Right, so. And I can even show how you called the school and spoke to your son right after I left you the first time. Harry Davis wondered how Drew knew something was up before he confronted him. That's how. You called and warned him. And you remember the call you made to Claire, the one from that pay phone near Twenty-third Street . . . first off, that was overkill. It was nice of you, trying to comfort the parents a little. But see, why would Aimee call from there – right where Katie Rochester had been spotted? She wouldn't know about that. Only you would. And we already checked your E-ZPass records. You went into Manhattan. Took the Lincoln Tunnel twenty minutes before the call was made.'

'Hardly rock-solid,' Edna said.

'No, probably not. But here's where you're going down. The Propofol. You can write prescriptions, sure, but you also had to order it. The police at my behest already checked with your office. You did purchase plenty of Propofol, but no one can explain where it went. Aimee was given a blood test. The stuff was still in her bloodstream. You see?'

Edna Skylar took a deep breath, held it, let it loose. 'Do you have a motive for this purported kidnapping, Myron?'

'Are we really going to play this game?'

She shrugged. 'We've played it this far.'

'Fine, okay. The motive. That was the problem for everyone. Why would anyone kidnap Aimee? We all thought that someone wanted to keep her quiet. Your son could lose his job. Jake Wolf's son could lose everything. Harry Davis, well, he had a ton to lose too. But abducting her wouldn't help. There was also no ransom demand, no sexual assault, nothing like that. So I kept asking myself. Why would someone kidnap a young woman?'

'And?'

'You talked about the innocent.'

'Right.' There was resignation in her smile now. Edna Skylar knew what was coming next, Myron thought, but she won't move out of the way.

'Who was more innocent,' Myron said, 'than your unborn grandchild?'

She may have nodded. It was hard to tell. 'Go on.'

'You said it yourself when we talked about choosing patients. It's about prioritizing. It's about saving the innocents. Your motives were almost pure, Edna. You were trying to save your own grandchild.'

Edna Skylar turned and looked down the corridor. When she faced Myron again, the sad smile was gone. Her face was oddly blank. 'Aimee was already almost three months pregnant,' she began. Her tone had changed. There was something gentle in it, something distant too. 'If I could have held that girl for another month or two, it would have been too late to terminate. If I could just put off Aimee's decision for a little while longer, I would save my grandchild. Is that so wrong?'

Myron said nothing.

'And you're right. I wanted Aimee's disappearance to parallel Katie Rochester's. Part of it was already there for me, of course. They both went to the same school and both were pregnant. So I added the ATM. I did all I could to make it look like Aimee was a runaway. But not for the reasons you said – not because she was a nice girl with a nice family. Pretty much the opposite, in fact.'

Myron nodded, seeing it now. 'If the police started investigating,' he said, 'they may have found out about her affair with your son.'

'Yes.'

'None of the suspects owned a log cabin. But you do, Edna. It even has the brown and white fireplace like Aimee said.'

'You've been a busy boy.'

'Yes, I have.'

'I had it pretty well planned out. I would treat her well. I would monitor the baby. I made that call to the parents hoping to offer some comfort. I would keep doing stuff like that – leaving hints that Aimee was a runaway and was okay.'

'Like going online?'

'Yes.'

'How did you get her password and screen name?'

'She gave it to me in a drug stupor.'

'You wore a disguise when you were with her?'

'I kept my face covered, yes.'

'And the name of Erin's boyfriend. Mark Cooper. How did you get that?'

Edna shrugged. 'She gave me that too.'

'It was the wrong answer. Mark Cooper was a boy nicknamed Trouble. That was another thing that bothered me.'

'Clever of her,' Edna Skylar said. 'Still. I would have held her a few months. I would have kept leaving hints that she ran away. Then I would let her go. She would have told the same story about being abducted.'

'And no one would have believed her.'

'She would have the baby, Myron. That was all I was concerned with. The plan would have worked. Once that ATM charge came in, the police were certain that she was a runaway. So they were out of it. Her parents, well, they're parents. Their concerns were dismissed just like the Rochesters'.' She met his eye. 'Only one thing messed me up.'

Myron spread his hands. 'Modesty prevents me from saying it.'

'Then I will. You, Myron. You messed me up.'

'You're not going to call me a meddlesome kid, are you? Like on *Scooby-Doo*?'

'You think this is funny?'

'No, Edna. I don't think it's funny at all.'

'I never wanted to hurt anyone. Yes, it would inconvenience Aimee. It might even be somewhat traumatic for her, though I'm pretty good at administering drugs. I could have kept her comfortable and the baby safe. And her parents, of course they'd go through hell. I thought if I could convince them that she was a runaway – that she was all right – it might make it easier on them. But add up the pros and cons. Even if they all had to suffer a little, don't you see? I was saving a life. It was like I told you. I messed up with Drew. I didn't look out for him. I didn't protect him.'

'And you weren't going to make those same mistakes with your grandchild,' Myron said.

'That's right.'

There were patients and visitors, doctor and nurses, all sorts of people moving to and fro. There were *ding*ing noises from above. Someone walked by with a huge bouquet of flowers. Myron and Edna saw none of that.

'You said it to me on the phone,' Edna went on. 'When you asked me to look up Aimee's records. Protect the innocent. That's all I was trying to do. But when she vanished, you blamed yourself. You felt obligated to find her. You started digging.'

'And when I got too close, you had to cut your losses.'

'Yes.'

'So you let her go.'

'I had no choice. Everything went to hell. Once you got involved, people started dying.'

'You're not blaming me for that, are you?'

'No, and I'm not blaming me either,' she said, head high. 'I never killed anyone. I never asked Harry Davis to switch transcripts. I never asked Jake Wolf to pay anybody off. I never asked Randy Wolf to sell drugs. I never told my son to sleep with a student. And I didn't tell Aimee Biel to get pregnant with his baby.'

Myron said nothing.

'You want to take it another step?' Her voice edged up a notch. 'I didn't tell Drew to pull a gun on Jake Wolf. Just the opposite. I tried to keep my son calm, but I couldn't tell him the truth. Maybe I should have. But Drew had always been such a screw-up. So I just told him to relax. That Aimee would be okay. But he didn't listen. He thought Jake Wolf must have done something to her. So he went after him. My guess is, the wife was telling the truth. She shot him in self-defense. That's how my son ended up dead. But I didn't do any of that.'

Myron waited. Her lips were trembling, but Edna fought through it. She would not collapse. She would not show weakness, not even now when it was all unraveling, when her actions not only failed to produce the desired results but had ended the life of her own son.

'All I wanted to do was save my grandchild's life,' she said. 'How else could I have done it?'

Myron still didn't reply.

'Well?'

'I don't know.'

'Please.' Edna Skylar clutched his arm as if it were a life preserver. 'What is she going to do about the baby?'

'I don't know that either.'

'You'll never be able to prove any of this.'

'That's up to the police. I just wanted to keep my promise.'

'What promise?'

Myron looked down the corridor and called out, 'It's okay now.'

When Aimee Biel stepped into view, Edna Skylar gasped and put her hand to her mouth. Erik was there too, on one side of Aimee. Claire stood on the other. They both had their arms around their daughter.

Myron walked away then, smiling. His step felt light. Outside the sun would still be shining. He knew that. The radio would play his favorite songs. He had the whole conversation on tape – yes, he'd lied to her about that – and he'd give it to Muse and Banner. They might make a case. They might not.

You do what you can.

Erik nodded at Myron as he passed. Claire reached out to him. There were tears of gratitude in her eyes. Myron touched her hand but he kept moving. Their eyes met. He saw her as a teen again, in high school, in the study hall. But none of that mattered anymore.

He had made a promise to Claire. He had promised to bring back her baby.

And now, at long last, he had.

Acknowledgments

Over the past six years, the one question I always get on the road is, 'How tall are you?' The answer: Six-four. But the second most common question is, 'When are you going to bring Myron and the gang back?' The answer: Now. I've always said that I wouldn't force his return, that I'd wait for the right idea. Well, the right idea came, but your encouragement and enthusiasm inspired and touched me. So first acknowledgment – to those who missed Myron, Win, Esperanza, Big Cyndi, El-Al and the rest of this motley crew. Hope you had fun. And for those of you who don't know what I'm talking about, there are seven other novels featuring Myron Bolitar. Go to HarlanCoben.com for more information.

This is my fourth book working with Mitch Hoffman as my editor and Lisa Johnson as my everything else. They both rock. Brian Tart, Susan Petersen Kennedy, Erika Kahn, Hector DeJean, Robert Kempe, and everyone at Dutton rock too. Lots of rocking. Thanks also to Jon Wood, Susan Lamb, Malcolm Edwards, Aaron Priest, and Lisa Erbach Vance.

David Gold, M.D., had helped me with medical research on a lot of books. This time he even gets his name mentioned as a character. You're a good friend, David.

Christopher J. Christie, the U.S. Attorney for the state of New Jersey, provides great and wonderfully twisted legal insights. I've known Chris since we played Little League together when we were ten. For some reason, he does not put that on his resume.

I'm grateful to the Clarke family – Ray, Maureen, Andrew, Devin, Jeff, and Garrett – for inspiring the idea. The boys have always been open with me about what it's like to be a kid, a teenager, and now young men. I thank them for it.

Lastly, thanks to Linda Fairstein, Dyan Machan, and, of course, Anne Armstrong-Coben, M.D. Too much brains and beauty – that's the problem with all three of you.